Zarathustra's Journey

Zarathustra's Journey

NANETTE V. HUCKNALL

Inner Journey Publishing

Published by Inner Journey Publishing,
a division of
Higher Self Yoga, Inc.

ISBN: 978-1-7370162-2-9

Library of Congress Control Number: 2022938549

PROLOGUE

"No! My God, this can't be! This can't have happened!" Anton's startled cry pierced the silence. Looking at the surreal scene, Anton felt shock waves of fear. I must be dreaming! This can't be real! he thought. But there was no denying what was before his eyes—a vast wall of fallen boulders blocked the very path he needed to take.

He suddenly felt a faucet had opened up inside him and poured out all of his energy, making him feel powerless.

His greatest dread had materialized. From his campsite in the beautiful Swiss valley he had known since childhood, the night before he had heard what he thought was thunder. Instead, it had been an avalanche.

Now, in the morning, having climbed up the trail from the valley to this path, he found that insurmountable boulders barricaded his only way out. He had scaled these mountains for years, but these boulders were too large and too high to traverse without proper gear. Some of them stood straight up, like the enormous pillars in ancient Greek temples. Climbing to a vantage point, he saw that miles of huge rocks surrounded him. It would be impossible for anyone, even experienced rescuers, to get through.

But people in the nearby village must have heard the avalanche's roar, he consoled himself. And he had told his friend, Stefan, where he would be.

Then he realized, Oh, God! He'll think I'm dead, crushed under falling stones.

Anton knew that there was no way out. Trapped and panicked, he started screaming for help "I'm going to die!" The menacing rocks enveloped his cries, first muffling them, then sending back echoes that surrounded him in waves of terror.

"Why did I listen to Jacques? Why did I return here?"

Unexpectedly Anton heard a voice, coming from nowhere, say, "Don't be frightened, you will be rescued. You will live. Go back to your valley and make a sign."

"A sign? What does that mean ?" Then a thought occurred to him. Yes! He would need to make a sign that could be seen from the air. Stefan wouldn't just assume that he was dead. He would at least try to see if Anton was visible from the air.

With hope in his heart, Anton returned to the valley. He quickly gathered tree branches from the ground and in a clearing made a sign: spelling the word HELP. Then he pitched his tent again and unpacked his backpack.

He had very little in the way of food, and the vegetation that grew in the valley wasn't edible. He just had to wait and pray. To keep himself from feeling distressed, he started to recall the events that had brought him to this valley again.

PART ONE

Anton's Journey

CHAPTER 1

It had all started on an uncommonly sunny day in March. Stopped in traffic, Anton Bauer glanced out the open window and saw an elderly, white-haired man on the sidewalk next to his car. Abruptly, the man reached in and handed Anton a calling card.

"Someday you will want to see me," the man said. "Put this card away for now and remember it when the time comes."

A moment later, he disappeared into the crowd.

How strange, Anton thought. But he believed in unusual occurrences, so he put the card in his pocket and, when traffic began moving again, drove as fast as possible toward downtown Zürich.

Looking at his watch, he saw that he was already late for his lunch date with Beatrice. She would be furious, and he didn't blame her. It had been his fault for losing track of the time that morning. He thought about Beatrice, her black hair flowing, a wild waterfall down her back, and her olive skin, tanned from days of sun worshiping. His whole body felt a surge of energy when he pictured her long, sensuous legs and her soft skin that smelled like morning dew on lilacs.

But that's over, he told himself—definitely over. The meeting was just to finalize some of the finances and say goodbye, for the last time, to their life as a couple.

Anton could tell Beatrice had already drunk some wine when he arrived at the restaurant. Her dark eyes expressed her irritation, but she didn't comment when he bent down to kiss her lightly on the lips.

"Sorry, traffic. Have you ordered?"

"Yes, your favorite appetizer and wine." She pointed to the half-full bottle, raised her glass, and said, "Thought this called for a celebration, so I ordered Chateauneuf du Pape."

Anton shrugged and didn't respond to her sarcasm. In a lighter mood, he poured some wine and lifted his own glass, saying, "To our years together. May we always be friends."

This made her smile.

"But of course, Darling. How could we not be friends? It's the thing to do these days. Besides, you have been very generous."

It was his turn to smile, knowing the voraciousness of her requests and the relentlessness of her notorious lawyer. He looked at her beautiful elegance and knew that none of the demands mattered. Behind them were five years of great sex, socializing in the top circles, and no real love. A grand illusion while it lasted, worn thin with time. Underneath, there was nothing to hold them together. The previous year, she had started to cheat on him. And he didn't care.

"How are your parents?" she asked.

It was a loaded question. Both their sets of parents were furious at their decision to split. The older couples had been friends for years. They had always felt that the union of their respective children would make the best of all marriages and presumed Anton and Beatrice would produce the best of all children. Fortunately, that last part hadn't happened. Both Anton and Beatrice knew on some level that their passion would dissolve into non-nourishing water, and before it became too muddy, it was best to end the flow.

To others, they appeared to be the handsome, glamorous couple. Beatrice was always so classy with her tall slim body, clothed in the latest fashions. She moved gracefully—a gazelle with an edge of defiance that challenged and provoked the men she encountered. Anton also dressed stylishly, with an attitude of erudition that sometimes put people off. Gray-blue eyes, inherited from his father, were his best feature. Beatrice always knew what he was truly feeling because his eyes reflected his emotions—even when he tried to conceal them, which he often attempted to do.

The rest of the lunch was filled with chitchat about their friends and plans—all the nonsense that had surrounded their lives since they had been childhood playmates.

When lunch ended, Anton handed Beatrice a final, signed document stating the agreed-upon alimony. They embraced as they said farewell.

"You know, it was good. A fling once in a while could still be fun." Beatrice tugged his shirtfront.

"Maybe," he replied, knowing he never wanted to take her up on it. In fact, something in him recoiled at the suggestion. Too much had happened, too much had been lost. No matter how attracted he still was to her, the desire evaporated when he looked into her dead eyes. She was now in the drug scene that was so prevalent in their crowd. Drugs and sex made love disappear, and even kindness no longer existed. He felt relieved to be free of that world. More and more it had become her scene, and he had retreated into solitude: a better place than the mania of Zürich nightlife.

In the morning, he received a phone call from his sister, Kristina. "You need to relax and have some fun," she said. "Beatrice has already started. I saw her last night with a new man, and obviously she doesn't have any regrets. My Dear, I know you're just as happy; but the whole town is gossiping about the divorce, spreading rumors about how terrible it must have been for you."

"But that's not true," Anton responded.

"Yes, I know, but it is true that no one believes you can be happy about it. Everyone thinks you were taken for a ride and really burned because of the settlement."

"Money never has been important to me."

"Yes, but my God, you paid her for half the condo—something you owned long before you were married—and you're paying her all that alimony when she's young and can get a job. Why did you give her so much?" Kristina's voice became critical.

"You know I don't like dealing with conflict. That's why I chose to just give her the money. I knew exactly what I was doing, and it wasn't out of love."

"Well, that's not what everyone is saying, and since there's no reason for some of what you've done, I can understand why people feel you are still madly in love with her."

Kristina became the caring, big sister again. "Anyway, let me give you some good advice: get out of Zürich for a while until this thing blows over. Don't you have an Easter break from the university soon?"

"Yes, but I think I will stay here to catch up on some writing I need to do. Also, I need to redecorate my place and get Beatrice's vibes out."

"Anton, you'll have time this summer to do that, and until then you can always do your work at home. Go home to Grindelwald; it's quiet there now. Mom and Dad, as you know, are in Italy again."

Home! It would be good, he thought, to get away from city crowds and once again experience the majestic mountains and how sometimes they mystically reached through high clouds to embrace the heavens.

"Let me think about it. Maybe I'll take your advice."

"Please do. By the time you return to Zürich, everyone will be into other things. No more gossip, if you know what I mean."

Yes, indeed, Anton knew about the gossip. Most of Beatrice's crowd invented all sorts of stories about him, some of which were not only false but made him even angrier with Beatrice, as she went along with them. Once, one of her "buddies" had asked him why he couldn't get it up with such a sexy wife: was there something wrong with him? He had felt so angry he wanted to punch the guy, but instead he had just walked away. Later, he wondered why he had reacted so strongly.

This incident had happened at the beginning of their separation. It surprised and hurt Anton since sex had never been their problem. He could only believe it was something Beatrice had made up to excuse herself for being unfaithful.

Anton told Kristina he would get back to her, but even as he spoke, he knew she was right. He should go home to the mountains and away from the stench of this world.

Anton taught philosophy and Eastern studies at the University of Zürich. When Easter break began, he drove home. The family always referred to their house in the Alps as "home," even though they lived, most of the time, in other houses and condos, near their jobs and friends.

It was large for a mountain house, designed in a typical Bernese Oberland style (or what was called a "Swiss chalet"). Its low-pitched roof was steep, the eaves wide—a design that helped shed snow in the winter months. Anton loved the wood that had been used to construct the house. It was old timber, with a deep, reddish-brown color that gave the house a welcoming warmth. In the summertime, his mother filled window boxes with an array of colorful flowers that she hung from small balconies on each level.

The village of Grindelwald, where the house was located, was nestled in a valley. The house itself was set above the town against the side of the mountain, which somewhat protected it from the winds that arose from nowhere and tore across the valley floor. Sometimes the family retreated to the cellar to feel safe when the winds were particularly strong and relentless. As a child, Anton had loved to hear the whistle of the wind as it swept up from the town below, making its way through the narrow passageways between buildings. It sounded as if it came from another world. Some claimed it was the groan of the mountain spirit feeling irritated because its timber was slowly being cut down for commercial use.

When the household descended into the cellar on those occasions, Anton's father would open a bottle of brandy and let them all drink to keep warm, as the stones below ground were many degrees colder than the house above. It was one of Anton's favorite memories of childhood, imbued with simple living and a time for closeness. His older brothers, Erick and Jonas, played cards and sometimes let him join in. Kristina would always get a little drunk and make up plays for them to perform to pass the time, since the winds could last for days, making it too dangerous to return upstairs. There had always been enough food and bedding kept in dry bins for use when necessary.

It was late afternoon when Anton arrived in Grindelwald, one of the few mountain villages that could be reached by car. Many towns could only be reached by cable car or by mountain train. On this day the sky was clear, and the mountain views were unencumbered by the low-lying clouds that often cloaked the landscape. He stopped several times on the road just to experience the scene.

Strange how the mountains called him; even stranger, the call seemed to be different every time he returned. This time, it was a call that made his heart expand as if the mountain spirit was gently reaching into his chest and lovingly pulling it outward. The sense of it was elusive, so elusive that when he stopped at a clearing and looked out over the mountains, it felt more like a breath not breathed, or a sigh not sounded. Later, he would remember that moment and understand.

It was close to dusk when he arrived at the house. Later that night, after dinner, Anton sat by the stone fireplace enjoying the fire, sipping brandy. Suddenly, he began to feel a strange dread that something would occur to sweep away this comfort — sweep it away with a force almost like the mountain winds.

The phone rang. He looked at his watch and saw it was after midnight.

"Hello, who is this?" He answered in a stern voice.

"Anton, it's me. I need your help".

"Kristina, what is it? What's wrong?"

"I can't tell you. Please come. I'm in Interlaken. I wanted to surprise you and come up for the weekend. But something has happened. Come right away."

"What happened?"

"I'm at the Goldey Hotel in Interlaken. Come now." The phone clicked off.

The drive down to Interlaken was dark and difficult. The mountain roads were never lit, and there was no moonlight to illuminate the sharp turns. Anton drove carefully, even though he wanted to speed along as fast as possible. On the way, he made up stories about what could be wrong. Kristina was practical. Kristina was not frivolous. She was a doctor by profession and the most responsible of all the siblings in the family. Anything that needed to be done was assigned to her, and they all knew she would do it with great care and thoroughness.

By the time Anton arrived at the Goldey Hotel, it was around two a.m. He rang the bell and banged on the door, feeling extremely anxious. After a long pause, some-one cracked it open.

"What do you want at this hour? We are full."

"I need to see my sister, Kristina von Himsen. It's an emergency."

"Who? Wait a minute." The man backed away from the door, went to the desk, picked up the guest book, and looked through it.

"There is no one here with that name."

"But there must be, she called me from here two hours ago and told me to come right away. Try Kristina Bauer, that's her maiden name."

Again, he looked at the book and said she wasn't registered.

Feeling desperate, Anton phoned his sister's home. When her husband, Felix, answered, Anton asked if he knew where Kristina was. He told Felix about the phone call.

"That's impossible, Kristina is here asleep. She went to bed early with a headache and took a sleeping pill. Are you drunk?"

"No, no, I don't understand it. It was Kristina's voice on the phone. Tell her I'll talk to her in the morning."

By now it was close to 3 a.m. On the drive home, Anton found a café in a small town that opened early for construction workers and had a hot cup of coffee,   he felt so tired that he decided not to drive the mountain roads. Instead, he parked on a street there and took a nap. When he awoke, dawn was breaking. He drove to the mountain road in Grindelwald that led to his family home to find it barricaded with a couple of police cars. He pulled over and asked one of the men what the problem was.

"One of the big houses caught fire last night. Fortunately, a neighbor woke up when he heard an explosion and called the fire department, but there still was some damage."

"What house?"

"Don't know, but it was a big one."

When Anton explained that he lived up there, they let him through.

As he ascended the road, he thought about the sense of doom he had felt the previous night when he had been sitting by the fireplace, sipping brandy. Immediately, he knew that the home that had caught fire must be his own.

CHAPTER 2

The right wing of the house was damaged beyond repair, but the rest of it seemed to be fine. For a few minutes, Anton could only gaze at the damage in stunned disbelief. The right wing was where his room was. It was where he had slept and studied. And in the basement below it, he had played many hours of ping pong in the wintertime with his local friends.

This was his home. He had lived here full time as a child and had spent many weekends here during his teen years and adulthood.

Finally noticing the fire warden who stood nearby, Anton introduced himself, "I'm Anton Bauer, and I live here. Can you determine what caused the fire?"

He feared that, somehow, the fire that he had left unattended the night before had started it, even though he had been very careful to put the screen up and cover the last remaining embers with a coat of ashes.

"It looks as if your water tank in the basement blew up. Maybe the relief pressure valve needed to be replaced," said the warden. "I'm sorry."

Anton's stomach recoiled: the living room and his bedroom were above the basement furnace room where the water tank was positioned. "Thank you, and thank your men, for all the help."

In his shock, Anton realized that the phone call was a miracle that had saved his life. He had read many stories from India that talked about miracles such as this one, but he never thought that such a thing would happen to him.

He called his parents in Italy and called his siblings who lived in various places in Zürich. They all said they would be there as soon as possible.

Later, when they were all in Grindelwald, he told everyone the story of the call he had received from someone sounding like Kristina, insisting he go to Interlaken. They were all astonished and relieved that he was alive. Gretchen, his mother, hugged him as tears—in a cascade of joy—ran down her face. Kristina said, "It wasn't me, that's for sure. Whoever impersonated me must love you very much."

Erick, his father, was very positive and said, "Thank God you were saved! That is the main thing. It shouldn't be a problem rebuilding that section. At least most of the house is intact and can be refinished. No problem, this is our home. By the end of the summer, we should have it back in good condition."

Anton's siblings left as soon as they could, but he and his parents stayed to start plans for clearing and rebuilding. The summer lay ahead of him; there would be ample time to help them when the spring semester ended.

In the meantime, they rented a furnished apartment in town, adequate accommodations for the time being.

For the next few weeks, with Anton coming up on weekends, they worked with an architect to reconstruct the design of the old house. It would look the same but be newer, and that aspect was positive.

At last the design was finished and approved. Construction was to begin on the first of June.

One Saturday in late May, Anton asked his mother to go on a picnic in the hills above their home. Their relationship was more like that of friends than of mother and son. He could always persuade her to go on excursions when no one else wanted to go, and she was more likely to follow his suggestions than those of his brothers or sister.

It was a beautiful day, sunny and pleasantly warm, even though the evenings were still chilly and the early mornings were cool.

The first stretch of the walk was through the woods. When Anton and his mother came out of the thick overgrowth, they found themselves in a meadow filled with wildflowers — all in bloom. Awed, they stopped to look across the field of colors.

"Oh, my God, how beautiful!" his mother whispered.

It looked as if a rainbow had fallen from the sky and blended itself into the grasses. There were tall alpine columbines in deep-violet colors, yellow bear's ears, rust-leaved alpenrose, vivid orange lilies, and white anemones everywhere. Pale blue edelweiss grew and snuggled between the rocks as though demanding, "Let me through, I need the sun."

Anton loved the sight of the alpine aster with its purple petals surrounding brilliant yellow buds. The green leaves and grasses only served to enhance the purity of the colors.

They walked in silence, a standard ritual that his mother had begun when Anton and his siblings were kids. They had made so much noise scrambling here and there that one day their mother had sat them down on the hillside and said, "We are in nature, and the noise disturbs the nature spirits and other creatures. It's important to honor their world by being silent," she'd explained. "Only then will we be able to really look at them and feel their beauty."

His mother had gone over to a bank of flowers, picked a yellow one, and brought it to the children. "Now just breathe deeply and concentrate on looking at this flower. Notice everything."

When they had done so, Anton felt the flower's energy. It was a warm sensation.

"It has energy and I feel it," he'd said aloud.

"Yes, where do you feel it?" his mother had asked.

"Here in my heart." He'd pointed to his chest.

The other children had giggled.

"He's right, you all should be able to feel it," his mother had chided. "And if you don't, it's because you talk too much and don't take the time. From now on, all of you need to be quiet and try to feel what Anton feels."

That was when he and his mother had created a certain bond that had never changed. He knew she felt it, and he was grateful to her for what she had given him at such a young age. He had only been five years old at the time, and from then on he had felt he had a special connection with nature.

Anton suddenly longed to be, once again, the little boy who looked up to his mother. It was hard to imagine that now. He towered over her. She was only five feet five and very small-boned, with small delicate features, and he was 6 feet tall. She always looked so attractive to him — even now, with silver streaks shining through her black hair and fine lines around her eyes and mouth. Her hair was short and curly with wandering wisps that wanted to divert themselves from the rest and fall into her dark eyes. His dark hair resembled hers. It also was wavy, and no matter how much he wet it down there was a curl that wanted to escape and be on its own — a metaphor of who he was. He wanted everything in his life to be orderly, which made him feel secure, but sometimes a part of him wanted to take off and do something differently.

On the picnic, as they sat and ate lunch, they talked about the renovation of the house. Then his mother said, "Anton, how are you feeling about your divorce?"

"Fine, really. We both realized that the marriage wasn't going to last. Our likes and dislikes were very different, as was our social life."

He had rarely talked about his relationship with Beatrice with his parents and brothers, and had never expressed what those differences were. Only Kristina was privy to some of the happenings.

"That's good, but I do worry about you."

"Why? Because of what happened with Beatrice?"

"No, I could see a year ago that it wasn't working, but you have always been my most sensitive child, and you have changed so much that it worries me."

"What do you mean?"

"You *have* become an academic. Maybe it's the Ph.D. or the job, but you had a softer quality when you were younger, and now that is gone. You've become very serious and a little austere."

"I think that's a good thing. When I was younger I was much too sensitive and impulsive and governed by my emotions. I'm very happy now that I no longer am that way."

How sad, she thought as she looked at him. Aloud, she said, "The mind is very important, especially in your work, but the heart is also important and should be used."

Anton considered what she said and thought, she wants me to be her little boy. He wondered if she really understood him. That thought disturbed him.

"Mother, you have a warm heart, and maybe that's because you are a woman, but my heart has never been much help to me. I'm fortunate to have a good mind that I can trust."

"Men have warm hearts, too, and your heart is beautiful, but maybe you are afraid to use it."

He looked at her and didn't know how to reply to that, so he simply said, "I do use it when it comes to feeling the beauty of nature. You taught me that, and you're the one person I do use my heart with." He smiled at her. "Let that suffice."

Anton took his mother's hand. "We need to get back now. It's getting late, and I think Father may be waiting for us to have cocktails."

CHAPTER 3

June came, and Anton was now on summer vacation. His parents had to go on a business trip, so he took over supervising the construction work on the house. It went well and quickly.

One day, taking a break, he went on a four-day camping trip into the mountains, checking first to be certain that the weather would be good. He hiked for several miles until he came to where the mountains became more rugged. Always a good climber, Anton had never been afraid of heights.

Climbing for a full day, he came to an old camp, one he had used before, and decided to spend the night there. The air cooled as the sun went down, and he could feel the winds taking control of their domain at this higher altitude. Anton was glad he had brought a warm sleeping bag and some good outer clothing. After eating, he cuddled down in the brisk night air to enjoy the array of stars that spread across the sky as the final light fell behind the mountaintops.

Meditating with open eyes, he focused on the brilliance of the stars and felt their vitality and light fill his being. This image was still inside him when he finally slept.

During the night, something happened that Anton couldn't explain. He dreamed that he sat where he was, on the ridge of the mountain, and a woman stood in front of him, dressed in a blue gown with long veils that covered her body and face. Her diaphanous body seemed to blend into the stars in the background, and it seemed as if their radiance had given birth to her to represent their glorious domain. His first impulse was to embrace her as a lover would upon seeing his beloved after a long period of time; but he saw that, like the stars, she was also beyond his reach.

"Who are you?" he asked.

She didn't answer him at first but just sent him a wave of energy. It felt cold when it hit him.

"You have a special mission," she said. "Look for it in the mountains. Find it in the mountains. Bring it down from the mountains."

"What do you mean?"

Without replying, she disappeared into an empty blue mist. The feeling in his heart was as if he had just lost everyone and everything of importance and was left totally alone.

The next day, it was difficult for Anton to leave the ridge. He wanted to stay, hoping that the woman would return. He even tried to sleep some more, wishing the dream would recur, but that night he had a very different dream. Again, in front of him on the ridge was a figure, but this figure was clothed in a black robe. It was a man with a face hidden under a black beard, with his collar turned up as if to keep the winds away. The moon shone through dark, dense clouds that hid the stars. This time Anton had no desire to reach out to the figure before him. In fact, he wanted to turn away and run down the mountain. Mustering courage, he demanded, "Who are you?"

"I am you. Don't you recognize me?"

"That is a lie. You are not me."

"Feel me." The dark figure sent a wave of energy to him that felt like a heavy blanket of pollution entering his body and poisoning all his organs.

"Stop!" Though he wanted to fight the ominous figure, all he could do was shout in protest.

"You can never stop me." The figure laughed and turned around, dropping his robe. Anton saw that he was nude and his bare back had a red scar that ran down it like a river of blood, from the top of his head to his feet.

"The scar is you," said the figure. "It represents who you truly are. Do you know how very evil you have been? You can never escape me. If you listen to her it will destroy you, and my scar will get bigger."

Anton awoke with dread in his heart. It was all he could do to stop himself from turning back. When he had studied Eastern philosophy, he had learned to meditate, and now he decided to meditate about what had happened. Afterward, his feeling was — if I have been evil, I have been so only in a past lifetime, not this one. He needed to let go of the man in the dream and continue onward.

Planning to spend one more night on the mountain, Anton intended to find a cave where he could sleep, a place that would help him feel closer to the stones and not so vulnerable. He didn't want to climb higher, as he wanted to arrive home the next day before sunset.

He remembered there were some caves a few miles away on a different ridge. Anton traveled in that direction, using his compass to guide himself. The trail crossed some level areas of enormous flat rocks, carved on the mountainside as if a giant had placed them there as stepping-stones for his travels. He sat and meditated on one of them and breathed in the wondrous air of the high altitude, scented with a flowery fragrance that only the mountains could emit. It felt gentle, like a loved one kissing his cheek.

That night, Anton found a small cave and was bedded down inside it. He wanted only to sleep, with no more dreams, but again he dreamed. This time the dream was even stranger, feeling as if it weren't a dream at all. In it, he seemed to awaken and sit up. Before him shone a brilliant light, so strong that it illuminated the cave, and he could see the whole surface as if it were floodlit. An older man stood in front of him, and Anton recognized him as the white-haired man who had given him his calling card when he'd stopped for a traffic light earlier in the year.

"What are you doing here?" Anton asked.

"I am here to warn you. Be careful tomorrow. Go down another way. There is a trail close by this cave on the right. Take that trail instead of the one you planned to take. There will be a mountain slide. Remember, the trail to take is to the right of this cave, and starts a few yards away. Be careful there, also." And he disappeared.

The brilliant light stayed for several minutes and then slowly dimmed back into the darkness. Anton touched the walls to see if he truly was awake. He couldn't sleep again but just sat and wondered what had happened.

As soon as dawn broke, he found the trail the man had indicated. Anton didn't know this trail and wouldn't have found it had it not been for the directions the man had given him. It was very narrow and looked seldom used. The trail he had planned to take was a few miles farther on the left and was the main trail that all the mountain climbers used.

Even though the forecast called for sunshine, Anton could tell that a storm was brewing. He walked quickly and even ran in flat places, as storms on the mountain can be treacherous. It would be best to be farther down, closer to where the grasses were. The ground was easier to walk on there, with fewer rocks that could become slippery in the rains. He had brought cleats in his backpack for rougher terrain; and, when the rain started, he slipped them on to have a better grip.

The rain started quietly at first, just a soft mist that caught the edge of his clothing and face. Fortunately, it stayed that way for several hours; but, as Anton entered the meadows, the downpour began in full force. He wanted to find shelter until it passed, but an inner urging said, *go faster,* and he followed that voice without question.

Running toward the tall grasses, he heard the mountain open and the loud, rolling crash of rocks, sounding like the angry roars of ancient gods going into battle. He ran toward a tree and huddled close to it with his arms around its trunk, feeling the roughness of its bark as he tightened his hold.

As he clung to the tree, the mountain's anger suddenly became *his* anger; all the negative, repressed feelings toward his family, Beatrice, and friends who had been hurtful spilled out of him. With uncontrolled emotion, he cried in unison with the mountain. Rocks rolled past him. The ground shook in protest. When it all ended, he lay spent on the ground. If he had taken his usual route instead of the one the white-haired man suggested, he could have been seriously injured.

Something happened to Anton in this unnerving process. He slept a short time and had no dreams. But he awoke soon to a stillness that felt as if the mountain had spit up all its feelings and now was calm and content again — and he was totally at one with it. For the first time in his life, he felt he had a mission. The feeling sprang from deep within him, and he had no idea what it was. But he knew his journey had begun.

CHAPTER 4

The house in Grindelwald was rebuilt and was again home and back to normal. The family spent the rest of the summer enjoying the mountains and doing family things on weekends.

Anton returned to Zürich and resumed teaching. One Saturday as he walked downtown, he saw a group of people in conversation with someone. Coming closer, he realized that it was the older man of his dream who had warned him about the landslide. He had wanted to call the man afterward to thank him but then realized he'd put the man's card in the pocket of a jacket that burned in the fire. Anton remembered that the man's first name was Jacques, but he couldn't think of his last name.

He hurried to join the group just in time to hear the man say, "Come to my house this evening. I plan to have a small party and you are all welcome."

Then he got into a car parked next to him and left before Anton could reach him. Anton asked one of the bystanders, "Can you tell me the name of the man who just left?"

"You don't know him?"

"No, but he saved my life, and if you can give me his number, that would be great. I want to thank him."

"You must come then. The party's at eight." And the bystander gave him Jacques' name and address.

Looking at the address, Anton recognized the location — it was in the town of Greifensee, one of the oldest historical towns in Switzerland. He and his friends liked to bicycle around the eleven-and-a-half miles perimeter of Lake Greifensee, stopping to view the abundant flora, fauna, and nature reserves, which were breeding grounds for a myriad of migrating bird species. The lake was under the protection of UNESCO, so there were no houses allowed on its shores.

Anton arrived early at Jacques' address in the hope that he could have a private moment with him. The house was on the outskirts of town in a countryside location with a view of the Alps in the distance. It was an unusual, modern house with two slanted white walls on either side of a tall chimney in the middle that went from the ground to above the house. A steep, black-tiled roof angled down from the third story to the second. The top floor-to-ceiling windows embraced the roof on either side of the chimney, eyes watching anyone coming to enter. Other windows lined up with the top ones coming straight down the side. It was not a large house— in fact, it looked small because tall evergreen trees snuggled and surrounded it.

He parked his car in a large lot by the side of the house and walked a stone path to the front entryway.

The door opened after the second ring.

"Come in. I was expecting you," Jacques greeted him.

"But how? You don't know me."

"Of course, I know you."

Jacques led Anton to a sitting room on the left. Anton could not have said what the furnishings were. He saw only Jacques — taller than he remembered, around six feet, dressed in a royal-blue, velvet lounge jacket, with gray trousers and a white shirt with an open collar. Full-bodied, white hair framed a face that was wrinkled with age, yet still very handsome, with sharp features and bottomless blue eyes that when Anton turned and looked at him were like candles with flames that heated his heart. Jacques' body was lean and straight, and Anton gathered Jacques had been athletic or maybe still was, as he walked in strong strides, with none of the carefulness of most people his age.

Maybe he's not as old as I assumed, Anton thought.

"Yes, I am old, but I don't think about myself that way. I just turned seventy-two. But I'm still in good shape. I ski, play tennis, and walk a lot," said Jacques.

Jacques had just answered Anton's thoughts, although Anton didn't realize it at the time.

"Sit down." Jacques pointed to a couch.

"I want to thank you." Anton found himself stammering — something he had never done before. "Thank you for saving my life."

"You are welcome."

Anton didn't need to say more; he knew Jacques understood what he was referring to.

Jacques looked at Anton with grave eyes and thought, "Is he ready? All our work has been on the subtle plane, but is he ready? His spirit is the color of purple that swirls around him; his soul is old and full of wisdom; but now, is he ready?"

Finally, Jacques said, "When you go home, you need to find your private valley. Take a leave from your work and stay there for at least a year."

His "private" valley! How did Jacques know about it? Anton had discovered the valley when he was a boy and had never mentioned it to anyone.

"But I don't know where it is. The map to it was burned in the fire," he replied.

"No, it wasn't." And Jacques reached into his pocket, pulled out a carefully drawn map, and handed it to him.

Again, Anton didn't question this.

"What should I do there?"

"You will know."

Jacques rose from his chair. "My guests are now arriving. I think it best that you do not stay. Your journey is laid out for you. Just follow the path."

With those words, he left the room.

When Anton left the house and was going to his car, he saw a woman walk up the driveway. She was quite lovely — tall and elegant, with long, blond hair spreading across the shoulders of her black dress like the feathers in the wings of a golden eagle. But what he also noticed was the way she walked. It resembled Jacques' walk, but her long legs made it look more graceful. She seemed very familiar, so he stopped and asked, "Have we met before?"

Her deep blue eyes thoughtfully looked into his.

"Not recently."

Before he could reply, she passed him without a backward glance. This is a strange bunch of people, Anton thought. He quickly got into his car and left.

CHAPTER 5

Besides his love of mountains, Anton had a deep affinity for water. His condo in Zürich was on the top floor of a new building, and from the balcony he could see the Limmat River, with mountains in the distance. The building was on the east bank that faced west, and a clear view of the sunset gave birth and beauty to the evening. During the day, he had a view of the city with its towering buildings and high-steepled churches. There was St. Peter's Church, the oldest church in Zürich, dating before AD 900, with its beautiful clock tower, the largest one in Europe. But Anton's favorite clock tower was the one belonging to Fraumunster Church, with its long, blue-green, copper spire, a unique sight in the city skyline. At night, he sat on his balcony and looked at the skyline illuminated in glowing blue and golden lights that cast reflected swirls in the dark water, reminding him of Monet's paintings.

Anton's condo was located close enough to the university for him to walk there. One day, as he worked at his desk, he came across the map of his private valley that Jacques had given him. He had put it in a drawer after their meeting and then forgotten about it.

Looking at the map, he realized it was well done. Years ago, when he was twelve, he had found the narrow path that led to that valley by chance. He had been on the main trail and needed to pee. As always, to do so he went way off the trail to avoid other hikers. Urine had a strong stench on hot days.

He had come upon a small clearing that led through some trees into a meadow. When he had finished peeing, Anton saw at the other end of the meadow some pretty flowers and went to get a closer look; then he noticed that behind the flowers was a narrow path that led through the woods. Since he was at an exploring age and welcomed adventure, he eagerly went down the path. It wove through trees and boulders and even climbed upward in places. After an hour or more of some difficult walking, he arrived at the top of a steep hill. Looking down, he felt overwhelmed by what he saw below at the bottom of deep crevices of stones. It was as if an angel passing by had seen the desolation of the terrain and dropped a tear that flowed down the side of the mountain, enriching and forming a small valley full of trees, grass, and flowers. Then the tear came to rest and became a crystal blue lake, in the middle.

Anton had followed the trail that wove slowly downward through the stone formations that formed the sides of the ridges: they were blue gray, with veins of purple and deep red running through them. When the stones reached the valley floor, they branched out into fingers leading through a forest of pine trees and ending at the lake.

When he had reached the bottom, Anton again felt excited by the awe-inspiring view of the mountains now cradling him. The valley itself couldn't have spanned more than a few acres. The lake comprised most of it, and the rest of the land was flat, with small woods toward the far side.

On his way back, he'd marked the entry near the main trail by putting together three stones; then he had timed how long it took him to reach home. The next day, he had returned with paper and pen and drawn a map to the little valley in great detail.

During the next couple of summers, Anton spent a lot of time there. When it was warm enough, he would go swimming in the lake and sunbathe on its banks. It was the perfect getaway, and he chose not to tell anyone — friends or family — about it. It was his private oasis. In his late teens, he became more involved in the world around him and slowly forgot about it.

Now, as Anton looked at the map, he was in a quandary about what Jacques wanted him to do. "When you go home, find your valley," Jacques had said when he had returned the map to Anton.

How did Jacques get the map? When he and Anton were talking, Anton had never thought to question him. And Jacques wanted Anton to live there for a year? That was madness. How could he survive in such wilderness? He couldn't stockpile food for an entire year. It would be too difficult to carry such an amount of supplies into the valley. And what was he to do there, anyway? At least he had asked Jacques that question, but all the man had answered was that Anton "would know," with no further explanation. The whole idea now seemed absurd.

Before he went back to Grindelwald, Anton needed to know more.

When he called Jacques' home, there was no answer. He left his number and waited a couple of days and tried again with no answer. Since Jacques traveled a lot, he had given Anton the number of his cleaning lady, Lina, whom he explained had his schedule and could tell him if he was out of town. When Anton called Lina, she told him that Jacques was away and wasn't expected back for several months.

"Where is he? How can I get in touch with him?"

Lina didn't know or wouldn't tell him. All she said was, "Jacques frequently takes long trips and phones a couple of weeks before he returns, notifying me to have the house ready."

Anton gave Lina his number and asked her to let him know when Jacques was to return, saying that it was very important.

Why hadn't he called Jacques earlier? Now his questions would have to wait until he returned — whenever that would be.

CHAPTER 6

Anton was able to schedule his classes and lectures so that he usually had a three-day and sometimes a four-day weekend, during which he often went home to Grindelwald when the weather was good.

In late August, after the family had left the house, he rescheduled a lecture to extend his trip to the mountains to five days. He needed that much time to locate the valley and stay there a couple of days.

Since he knew the valley would be difficult to rediscover, he decided to try to find it first and then return with the proper camping gear. He found that the main trail was still there, but some of the markers were worn down and others had disappeared. The locals knew these trails so well they hadn't replaced them. Thankfully, Anton had brought a small jar of red paint and a brush to make certain he wouldn't get lost on the smaller path on the way back from the valley, but this time he used it even on the main trail.

The day was warm and sunny, with a slight breeze coming from the hills. When Anton first started the hike, he felt as if someone were with him and even stopped to look around, thinking that other hikers must be on the trail, but everything was quiet. When he again started to walk, he heard footsteps behind him. Turning, he saw no one. This happened at least three times, until Anton finally said out loud, "If you follow me, don't make any noise, as it's freaking me out!"

After that, the noise ceased, but he felt the presence all the way to the valley, and then it left him for a while. Anton surmised that it was a guide of some kind who wanted to be certain he found his way. When at one point he went down a wrong path, in about a hundred yards he felt the presence in front of him, not letting him pass. Anton turned back and found the right way again. This made him very nervous, even though he felt the presence was benign. He even thought about returning home. But would the presence — whoever it was — let him? It was strange that whenever these phenomena happened to Anton, he never questioned them. Somehow, they seemed natural and right, even though they were disturbing.

It took him the better part of the morning to recognize the area where he had turned off the main trail years ago. The three stones he had arranged were still there but barely visible, hidden now in the tall grass. Finding the trail on the other side was a problem as well because it was so overgrown, but it was still a path. Using his knife to trim branches, Anton cleared the entry so that it would be more visible. He even put some red paint on the grasses.

The path itself was yet more difficult to follow — if the map hadn't been so good,

Anton certainly would have become lost. As he walked, he marked the trees with paint to find his way back. That being uppermost in his mind, he paid little attention to the topography around him, which is why he didn't notice the extreme changes in the mountain slopes that bordered the path. Large boulders hung over it, with little terrain for support, but Anton was oblivious to them. Only on his return did he realize that the mountain had undergone major alterations.

When Anton arrived at the top of the ridge and looked down, the scene below was also greatly changed. Trees that he remembered as young had grown, and new ones had invaded some of the flat land. The lake was still there, but it seemed smaller because of the new growth that now overran its boundaries.

He descended into the valley. When he arrived at the lake, he stopped to rest and eat. His rest turned into a meditation, during which he asked why he was there. Nothing came. After what he thought was an hour, he opened his eyes, but when he looked at his watch, he realized that he was mistaken. He must have fallen asleep. The one hour was really three hours, and it was now too late to go back and reach home before dark.

Anton had brought a strong flashlight, so he decided to risk it anyway. The paint markers were very bright, and the difficult part could be walked before nightfall. But as he started back, Anton felt the presence blocking him, and each time he tried to walk ahead, the block became stronger.

Why didn't the presence want him to go back? Was it too dangerous? He had a strong feeling that it wanted him to stay. But he couldn't camp in the valley, since he had no sleeping bag or woolens to protect him from the cold night. It seemed he really didn't have a choice, and Anton demanded that the guide let him pass. He even began to believe the presence was malignant and wanted to harm him.

Finally, he pushed through the block and managed to get to the top ridge, where again the presence tried to stop him. As Anton evaded it and walked down the path, he looked up and, for the first time, noticed the boulders hovering above him—perched stone ogres—waiting for a breeze to start them rolling. Walking under them, he listened for the slightest noise, wondering if the threat they posed was why he shouldn't leave.

Where was his intuition now? It had deserted him, and Anton felt wrapped in a blanket of fear. He began to run, but that only caused small rocks to fall. Catching his breath, he looked upward again, now feeling that the presence was forming a shield over him. This calmed him down, but he realized that the boulders were more precarious than he had previously realized. Some of them even looked loose, as if they had already fallen and were only temporarily at rest before their next descent.

Don't look up, he told himself, just keep going and watch the markers.

Relief came when Anton finally reached the meadow. The boulders were behind him. He imagined that he heard them rumbling, taunting him that they would wait for his return to frighten him again. They became torturers on his journey, and even though there might be more obstacles ahead of him, they somehow became symbolic of anything negative he would encounter.

Anton arrived home late and collapsed on the sofa, too tired to do anything. Darkness surrounded him, broken only by moonlight shining through the large, glass windows, softly soothing his aching body.

The next day, he stayed at home and found countless tasks that needed to be done. He sensed he should have returned to the valley that day, but he still felt shaken by the prospect of having to walk under the boulders again. And if there were a landslide, how would he get out? Many a trail had been closed permanently by the mountain's capricious need for a new look. Anton had no desire to fulfill a quest a stranger had given him. In retrospect, he realized that if he had stayed the night in the valley, as the presence had wanted him to do, perhaps the answer would have come to him in a dream and he would not have to return.

Back and forth Anton chided himself for being a coward and admonished himself for taking undue risks. Finally, he decided to brave the trip again, but this time he drew a duplicate map and gave it to his friend Stefan, so that someone else would know where he was going.

He carried a backpack and provisions and relied on the good weather to continue. It was a difficult hike, as he hadn't carried weight for a long time. City living had softened him, and even though he worked out, he still wasn't up to handling full mountain-hiking gear. But persist he did and finally reached the valley in the afternoon. It took him until dusk to set up a tent and find wood for a fire. Exhausted, he ate; then he decided to meditate to try to find some answers about why he needed to be there.

During meditation, Anton saw an extraordinary creature in front of him. It had a woman's face and body and was completely covered with small white feathers. Even her ears were shaped in feathers. She was exotically beautiful.

"Do you know why you are here?" she asked.

"You tell me!" he demanded.

"You need to find out for yourself."

"How should I do that?"

"Ask your Higher Self — it knows."

"Higher Self? That's part of the Eastern yogic tradition. What does that have to do with me?"

"You are a philosopher. You should know."

"But I don't know. Please tell me."

"When you know, I will return."

And with those words, she disappeared.

What a strange, fascinating vision, Anton thought. What did Feathers (as he named her) mean? When will I know, and how do I ask my Higher Self?

The whole experience with her made him edgy. But at this point, with all that had transpired, he wanted to be open to anything. And at least something had happened. That meant more would take place, and maybe then he would gain some insight about when he had asked Jacques, "What should I do there," and Jacques had said, "You will know."

Anton meditated some more, but it brought him no answers. Instead, he only felt frustrated.

He called out to the surroundings, "You are supposed to tell me something." And his voice disappeared into silence.

He had brought a book to read, but somehow he felt that reading was forbidden.

Patience, he needed patience.

The wait began.

The next morning, though Anton walked every mile of the valley, he found very little in the way of wildlife: a few rabbits and squirrels, but no tracks of bobcats or even deer. Of course, it would be too difficult for a deer to get down there; but bobcats would have found it a good haven, although there wasn't enough food around to make them want to stay.

Thick areas of majestic, green pine and spruce trees were clustered near the cliffs. Ash trees grew closer to the valley's center, and some lined the lake. Here and there, older ash trees dominated the others, with bark a sculpture of diamond patterns so very different from the younger trees, whose bark remained smooth as a snake's skin.

Midday, Anton returned from his walk, ate lunch, and again meditated. The evening proved clear and warm, so he lay on a blanket and star gazed in a reverie of thoughts. Soon, he fell asleep, unaware of the night sounds surrounding him. Later, he awoke and heard them. The valley was so sharply cut into the cliffs that, when the winds whistled over the top, it made unearthly sounds — a chorus of ghosts rather than the singing currents of air. It took a while for Anton to get used to this concert, which seemed to gain in intensity as the night wore on.

When morning broke, misty fog covered the lake. He watched it roll over the water into the woods and obscure the mountains; it surrounded and penetrated his bones. It wasn't as damp as most mists—it was more like a spray of perfume that evaporated into the skin without leaving any surface moisture. Anton sniffed his bare arm, expecting to smell a strong fragrance, but instead the scent was like fresh morning air when taking a brisk walk.

Since he planned to leave the next day, he spent most of his time meditating and asking for guidance as to why he needed to be there. Disappointingly, nothing came.

Night arrived, and Anton slept in his tent. When he awoke and went outside, he found himself encircled by fog so thick he couldn't see in front of him. Sitting in the fog became very strange after a while. It felt as if thick cotton candy surrounded him, and, when he reached through it, the candy moved, quickly closing over his hands until he couldn't see them. That's how thick it was. The novelty soon wore off, and, as the fog started to make him feel claustrophobic, Anton decided to go into his tent. The fog felt like a prison, and he knew it was there for a reason. It lasted most of the day, making it impossible to leave as planned.

He was awakened that night by the distant rumbling of what he thought was thunder, but he went back to sleep when it became quiet again. The next morning dawned clear; but when he left the valley and reached the path, he saw huge boulders piled in a distorted tower, blocking his way, and understood that the rumbling he had heard the night before had been a landslide. He was trapped.

CHAPTER 7

When Anton recalled all the events that had led him to being trapped here in the valley, he realized for the first time that the macabre fog of the previous day had been a deterrent to stop him from leaving. This frightened him even more. But then, when surveying the landslide, he heard the voice saying, "Don't be frightened, you will be rescued. You will live. Go back to your valley and make a sign." Using sticks and branches, he created the sign, HELP, and looking at it now gave him a feeling of reassurance.

But until someone saw his sign from the air, he would be a prisoner of the surrounding boulders. Aware that he could die before rescue came, he realized that his desire to believe those words, "*You will live,*" might be an inner delusion, a self-protecting need to hold on to life. Anton started to pray.

Every day, Anton searched the skies for the sight of a plane. He heard several above the valley, but, evidently, they didn't see the sign; being made of brown branches, it was probably invisible from the air. Now in need of food, he hunted inside and outside the valley but found nothing. If there had been any wildlife, it had disappeared. Hope left him and, with it, the feeling that he would survive.

When his food ran out, he ate the grasses, which tasted like dirt even though he washed them thoroughly, and he knew that grass would not keep him alive for long.

On the third day, he awoke to find a huge, burlap bag next to his tent. Inside it were food staples: rice, cheese, vegetable seeds to plant, and even a cooked chicken that was warm and smelled of charcoal. It was then that Anton realized his confinement was planned. Maybe even the landslide had been arranged by otherworldly beings. This thought made him very angry and more frightened than before, but after he calmed down, he thanked those beings — whoever or whatever they were — for the food. This was the first of many supplies of food that would constantly be left. His invisible benefactors always knew when he ran out.

Days passed, and he realized that now his family and friends must believe him to be dead. Everything he loved—his condo, his job—would be gone when, or if, he returned.

As more weird things occurred, he truly worried that he was losing his mind. He kept thinking, what is happening to me? I'm thirty-two years old and have a Ph.D; my first book is on European philosophy, and I am writing my second book on Eastern philosophy. And here I am, going crazy in a place where reality has become elusive. I'm beginning to believe things that my rational mind says are impossible.

Suddenly, the exotic creature, Feathers, appeared, but this time while he was awake, not in a meditation. She said, "Let go of your mind. Be in your heart; then you will understand."

Anton looked at her and had to laugh. It was laughter of sheer relief. He didn't know how or why, but he knew that what she said was true. Maybe it was part of being crazy and scared, but laughing made him feel a lot better.

She said, "Anton, try to believe you will be all right. You have a special mission, and there are many forces who will take care of you."

Somehow, in his delirium, he felt his only choice was to follow Feather's advice. If he was truly mad, then it was a good madness, and in a strange way it made sense to him.

Anton looked at Feathers for the first time as a friend, "Thank you, I'm glad you came."

She smiled, causing her feathers to curl upward around her mouth, and he felt her love.

"But can you tell me what my mission is?"

"What are you good at?"

"I think I am a good teacher."

"And what else?"

"I'm a good writer."

"Yes, you are a good writer, and you need to write here in the valley."

"I'm now writing a book on Eastern philosophy. Should I work on that?"

"No, that's not it."

"But what, then, should I write?"

"Let your heart guide you. The answer will be given to you."

Anton slept soundly that night, but the next day he regressed into his fear of becoming insane. Was the whole scene with Feathers real, or was it an illusion prompted by his situation?

When he meditated, he linked with the invisible beings — whoever they were — and asked what it was they wanted from him and how long he would have to stay there. This time he saw something in his mind's eye. It appeared like a long ticker tape with words that said, "Your stay is as long as you need to be here to prepare you for your journey. When you are ready, the journey will begin, and you will be taken back home, as that is the starting place. Remember who you are, and you will understand."

That was all; the words on the ticker tape ended then. What did they mean—his journey? Where was he to travel? How could he prepare when he didn't understand where he was supposed to go? What did they mean about remembering who he was? All these questions and more streamed through his mind.

Anton found a book of blank paper in the sack and wrote down his questions. He decided to meditate on each one in the hope of discovering more. It was difficult work, but in the process more clues appeared to him. Always, the clues were words of some kind that either flashed across his vision or ran across an inner screen. They were always precise but never explanatory. Here was an example:

When you go back, you will no longer be you.
The return will bring you to a new place to live.
Your friends will no longer want you as a friend.
Your family will be disturbed by your presence.
You will find yourself alone and forsaken.
No one you know will want to follow you.

The message went on and on; the words spoke about the future when he would have returned home, not about how long he would be here in the valley, or what he would do that would cause such a reaction from his loved ones.

Anton meditated every day, but nothing new happened other than the occasional message. When he grew tired, he slept and had no dreams. He walked as much as possible and investigated any new areas he stumbled on. The valley, even though it was high on the mountain, must be sheltered because the trees were full — not stunted by the winds that made the rest of the mountainside so barren and bleak.

Day after day, much was the same. His surroundings kept him a total prisoner. He felt like Robinson Crusoe, except that Crusoe had the advantage of a whole island to explore and good weather all year round. During this time, Anton trusted that someone or something would finally rescue him.

One morning he rose early, and, since it was an unusually sunny, warm day, he swam in the lake. The water was cold, making his skin feel wonderfully refreshed. Afterward, he lay naked on the beach, breathing in the fresh air, absorbing the sun, abandoning himself to its warm rays as he would to the warmth of a lover's hands massaging his skin. He had closed his eyes and was napping when he was startled by a sound. Jumping to his feet, he saw an animal disappear into the woods.

It looked like a dog at first, but later, when it returned, he saw that it was a hybrid. It had a body resembling a dog's but with the black fur, head, and claws of a bear. When standing on all four legs, it was about three feet high, but later he discovered that the animal could stand on its two hind feet, which made it almost his own height. Anton found it fascinating.

He also discovered that the dog-bear could talk to him through telepathic messages. The creature didn't give a name, so Anton called him Merlin, after the magician who was King Arthur's teacher.

After Anton first glimpsed him, Merlin did not come back for three days. When he did return, he sat at the edge of the forest and watched Anton quietly. Anton put his knife in his belt and waited, not knowing if Merlin was friendly or not.

Finally, one evening as the light began to dim, Merlin slowly approached him and said, "When are you going to begin your work?"

"What do you mean? What work?"

Merlin pointed to Anton's pad and said, "Write." Then he walked away.

Anton picked up a pen and pad and started to write. He had no memory of what he wrote. The words simply flowed from his hand, and he wrote for at least two hours until it was almost dark.

Only the next day, in the afternoon, did he pick up the pad to read what he had written. But then he realized he didn't want to read it — or maybe he didn't have the courage — and decided he wouldn't review any of it until it was finished. He wrote some more that day, and the next, and he kept writing until the pad was full. When that happened, another pad appeared with the delivery of food.

His days were long now. He swam and sunbathed when there was a warm day, went for long walks exploring the woods and greenery, gathered wood for a fire, and tended a small garden of fall vegetables. But mainly, he wrote for two or three hours at a time and never read what he had written. In the process, the little he picked up was that this writing was a spiritual, esoteric teaching that would be given to everyone. How he would make this happen, he didn't know. All he knew was that the writing was a flowing stream that had no beginning or end. He was concerned only with the stream moving onward and not stopping along the way. His heart knew that this teaching would challenge him and cause him anguish, and somehow, he felt it didn't matter. What mattered was the work.

There were many days when nothing came, and he didn't write. On those days, feelings of loneliness would invade him, loneliness he hadn't felt since childhood. Except for his early years, he had always been very social, his life full of friends and parties and outings. He had never even lived alone for very long.

One day, as he sat by the lake, he was suddenly overwhelmed with fear. It felt as if someone had forced him into a black hole where he was trapped.

A part of him knew he would survive, otherwise, the gifts of food wouldn't be coming. But it was as if he were disconnected from that reality. The fear he felt was not only of dying — he could have handled that. It was more a fear of being controlled by an unseen force.

The more he felt this fear, the more it overpowered him, becoming a sickness that speared his soul.

Thoughts flooded his mind: Why did I follow Jacques and do what he told me without questioning it? I can't believe I did that! Why?

Jacques saved my life. He has magical abilities, which exist in my teaching of Eastern philosophy. He's older—like my father—so maybe I projected my father onto him.

Anton had a sinking feeling in his stomach. That's it, he thought. I followed what Jacques wanted because he reminded me of my father, and that's why I'm here. That's sick! I'm a grown man and still doing what my father, or someone like my father, tells me to do. It's true. As a child, when did I ever rebel against my father? None of us did. He ran the family and controlled all of us, including my mother.

He remembered his father saying to him, "Anton, you are very smart and will do well as a professor, but you need to make money. Since you never wanted to be a banker and follow me and your brothers in this vocation, it would be important for you to write a book that is well received."

Anton followed his suggestion and wrote his first philosophy book, which became part of the courses at his university and many other colleges and was still giving him a good income.

And now, just as his father had always controlled him, he felt even more controlled by his circumstances. He was here in this valley to write a book again. But this was not a book of his own choosing; rather, it was being given to him. And only when it was finished would he be rescued. This control was even worse than his father's!

As Anton was feeling the full force of his helplessness, Merlin came through the trees and sat down next to him. "Anton, you are feeling as if you are a prisoner here, and that's not true. If you really want to leave, just ask and you will be rescued. But first please read what you are writing and then decide, because, if you go now, someone other than you will finish the book."

"All right, I will read some chapters, even though I don't want to."

When Merlin left, Anton picked up the first pad and started to read. What he had written was about a journey—the journey of a spiritual teacher named Zarathustra, who came down from the mountain to teach people about the Higher Self, a part that exists in everyone.

When he read the first few chapters, Anton knew the writing was true, and that this was a book he *wanted* to write—a book he wanted to study and learn from.

When he saw Merlin the next day, Anton thanked him.

Merlin smiled and said, "You can always leave any time you want. No one wants to hurt you, and the others and I want you to write this book, but it has to be a book that you want to write. "

"Why can't I go home and do this book? Why do I have to be here?"

"If you were home, you would be working and seeing people, and you wouldn't be able to experience who you really are. You would be back in your superficial life. It's important if you are to do this work that you start to understand who you are."

"I know who I am."

"No, you don't, Anton. You haven't looked at who you truly are and what you feel. You live in your mind, which governs your life, and the mind isn't who you are. Your real knowledge comes from your heart."

"My mother told me the same thing."

Later, when he was thinking about the book, Anton asked himself: Why was I the one chosen to write this book? This is a teaching I know nothing about. Was it because I am a philosophy teacher at the university?

He asked these questions in meditation but got no reply. Obviously, he, and not anyone else, was meant to write this book, for some reason unknown to him.

Another time when he asked "Why me?" he felt a strong warmth fill his heart and knew his heart had accepted his writing the book. Even though he didn't understand it, that helped him to continue the work.

To say that Anton was unhappy would not be telling the whole truth. The work fulfilled him, but as the days and weeks passed, he felt more and more lonely.

During those difficult times, sometimes Merlin would keep him company. There was something strong and courageous about his friend, yet gentle and caring. Merlin would lie by Anton's feet, and they would talk about nature, which Merlin knew more about than anyone Anton had ever encountered. Merlin told him about the seasons and the cycles of life, and about how he had evolved in another place where he usually lived.

Merlin loved to swim, even in the cold, and his fur was almost dry five minutes afterward. When Anton asked him why, Merlin laughed. "It's not fur at all. Feel it."

When he touched it, the texture was like silk, smooth and wispy. It shimmered with sunlight and held the rays in its depth. Anton had to move away quickly. He felt a longing to rest his head in Merlin's shining locks but knew that, if he did, it would be an invasion of Merlin's privacy.

Merlin explained, "My home uses sunlight differently than yours. It's our food."

"How can it be food?"

"We don't need to eat. We just need the energy that food provides, and the sun is our food, the best energy there is."

"So, you never get hungry?"

"Only hungry for the sun, and it is very strong where I live."

Weeks turned into months. Fall ended, and then the snows came and made the valley an even more supernatural place. Anton heard the winds blow relentlessly down from the mountaintops; but, when they came his way, they simply passed straight over the valley, leaving only a warm breeze to flow down and protect him from the harsh winters of this terrain. The snows, always so severe and unremitting throughout the winter, fell as soft down that never was deep or dangerous.

When it first became cold, Anton found warm clothing and blankets had been left for him, and his tent was lined with sheepskins that made him cozy and warm. By then he had realized he would be protected through any storm. So many miraculous things occurred that were beyond human comprehension.

With the winter came a more intense feeling of isolation, mainly because he could no longer go for walks or sit by the lake, which was frozen over. He had a lot of time to think about life and about himself, and the more he thought, the more he started to dislike who he had become. This disturbed him, as he'd always felt he was a good worker, a good professor, and someone people liked and respected. Now he wondered, Was that true?

He taught philosophy, but was he a philosopher? Had he ever taken the great philosophic concepts and really explored them? Or did he only teach the textbooks?

He thought he brought analysis into his courses with his students and helped them study concepts. But did he ever have his students examine them for a deeper understanding?

He realized that he lacked the desire to look at the inner truth, as opposed to the outer experience of hypotheses. What did he really believe? He honestly didn't know.

Anton's self-examination now also brought up feelings about his childhood, which made his heart, once again, tighten in terror; but this time, it was a new fear that carried all the emotions he had repressed during his late teens and twenties.

He cried inwardly, Why do I have such strong sensitivities, as my mother said? This trait has bothered me my whole life, and I thought I had changed it completely, but it's still here. I feel it all again, and it makes me more afraid than when I was a child. Being here alone has brought back all the strange things from my childhood— talking to the trees, the plants, and all the nature companions I played with and loved. Feathers and Merlin are the new illusions.

Oh, my God! I really am going crazy here. I know I will be rescued, but what will my mental state be then? I must remember—I am a scholar; I am a professor. All these other things are imaginations I had as a child.

Anton continued to have such thoughts, which expanded into areas he had long forgotten about.

One day, the delivered sack of food included a note: "In the spring, you will start your journey. The real work is ahead of you."

Anton didn't see Feathers again, but he knew she was there. Sometimes he found a feather or two, and once he saw her run away after she had left him a sack of food. Someday, he knew, they would talk some more. But when Anton asked Merlin about her, Merlin just smiled and said that at a later time Anton would know her better.

The snow takes a long time to melt in the mountains, but in the valley it melted away after only a week of sunshine. Almost immediately, Anton saw the first sprouts of the perennial vegetables — asparagus and artichokes — that he had planted the previous fall.

When he tried hiking to the top of the ridge, he found that the snow was still too deep. He could only return to the valley and await his departure.

It was May before he finally had a clear path to the boulders. They were still there. He had half expected to find that they were not real. He had hoped that when he was ready to leave, they would have disappeared. This was not the case. When he discovered a large, red paint can in his sack one day, he realized that was a signal for him to make another sign.

This time, Anton made the sign even bigger than before. To form the word HELP, he cut several branches and tied them together, painting the bark bright red. He displayed the sign so that it covered about thirty feet flat on the land bordering the lake. Then he waited.

After reading only a few chapters of his writing, he had reverted to his practice of not reading what he had written, so when his last pad was full, and no more pads were sent to him, he knew his work there was finished. He carefully put all the pads together in a sack and spent his days meditating. He walked and even tried to swim a little, but the water was very cold. Merlin would often join him, and they had some interesting discussions about life.

During this time, Anton thought a lot about his family and friends: They all think I am dead. What will I say to them? How can I explain the fact that I lived here for almost a year and survived?

I miss my friends very much and want to see them right away, especially Stefan, but Stefan knows these mountains and won't believe my story, so how can I explain what happened to me? Stefan doesn't believe in phenomena of any kind. How will he react when I tell him the truth?

Mainly, though, I know something has happened to me, Anton continued musing. I am not the same. All that has occurred here has awakened deep feelings in me—feelings that I don't know how to handle, feelings that I don't understand. I was told that my journey was beginning right now, and I know this to be true. But, on this journey, I am like a child learning to walk for the first time—a child who has so many things to explore and examine.

A week passed. One day as Anton sat meditating, he opened his eyes to see Feathers there. She pointed to the sky; and, as he watched, he saw a small plane fly overhead. The plane then circled the valley. Obviously, the pilots could read his sign, and Anton waved his arms, hoping they would see him. The valley was very narrow, so he couldn't be positive.

Several hours passed. Then he heard it—the roar of a helicopter slowly descending. He was rescued.

CHAPTER 8

Anton asked to go home, to his home in the mountains, and when his rescuers saw that he was in good condition they complied. There were two of them: the pilot and a police officer, who kept asking him questions. "How long have you been there? How did you survive?"

His answers were vague. He basically lied, telling them that there was a lot of wildlife around he had killed for food and that he had packed warm gear, etc. It was a story he had composed carefully.

They remembered that he had been missing and asked, "Why didn't you make the sign right away? We were looking for you after the avalanche."

Anton explained, "I did make the sign, but I didn't have the red paint, so no one saw it from the air. When I was out hunting recently, I found a can of paint under some grasses. Someone marking a trail must have left it there or dropped it from the cliff."

"Boy, are you ever lucky!"

"Yes, I know."

Anton begged them not to alert the press, saying he needed time to readjust and contact his family. They seemed to understand.

When he arrived home, he felt enormous relief finally to be there again. It was a Monday and, fortunately, no one was there. He had become so used to solitude that talking to his rescuers had made him feel as jittery as a schoolboy trying to cover up a bad mistake. He needed to be alone again now, even for a day or two, to prepare for future meetings with people.

Even though Anton felt happy, at the same time he felt sad, knowing he would never try to return to the valley and so would never see Merlin again. Adjusting was difficult, so for the first few days, he didn't call anyone. He mainly took baths and made himself some good food. Then, on the third day, he called his parents. His mother answered the phone.

"Mom, this is Anton." He heard a gasp.

"Who is this?" Her voice was quivering.

"It's me, Anton. I'm at home. I was just rescued from my place in the mountains."

"You're not dead?? Oh my God, you're alive!" And she cried and called to his father while she sobbed Anton his name.

It took some time for them to calm down. Even his father wept, which surprised him. His father was always so unemotional that his reaction made Anton feel warm

34

and loved. Anton also cried with the joy of being reunited with those he loved.

His siblings had similar reactions, especially his sister. It took a while to convince her that he wasn't a ghost.

Anton then called Jacques' house and then Lina when there was no answer. Lina told him, "When Jacques returned from his last trip, I gave him your previous message, and he smiled and said something about 'later.' And when he left a couple of weeks ago, he told me to tell you, when you called, that he will see you when he returns. He also said, 'Welcome back.'"

"How long will he be gone this time?"

"I never know; he visits a lot of people. But I think he will contact you."

"Thank you." Anton felt a wave of disappointment. He really needed to talk to Jacques about everything that had happened.

The next couple of weeks were full of family and friends who came to see him, amazed by the miracle of his being alive. Anton forced himself to be social, but it was very awkward. Yet a part of him wanted to do it, to become the man he had been before his sojourn in the valley.

Everyone believed his story except Kristina. She looked at him and said, "No way you could have survived the winter there." She was a mountain person and she knew.

He looked at her and said, "I did get help. Someday I will tell you."

She smiled, "Tell me soon. I'm anxious to know."

When Anton told his fabricated story of survival to Stefan, his friend immediately said he didn't believe him. So, Anton told him what really happened, wondering how he would react.

Stefan looked astonished and perplexed. "I don't believe this story, either." He looked a bit angry. "Anton, we've been friends since childhood, close friends; why can't you tell me the truth?"

"I know you don't believe in miraculous things, Stefan, but I'm telling you the truth. I swear I'm not lying! I wouldn't do that, as I cherish our friendship. I don't know how to make you believe me."

"I'll have to think about it."

As they said goodbye, for the first time in their friendship Anton felt Stefan's coldness. Then he remembered what one of the writings had said: *Your friends will no longer want you as a friend.*

Fortunately, his family hadn't sold his condo yet but had rented it out. The shock of his death had been so great that none of his belongings had been properly taken care of. Everything from his condo had been stored in the building's basement to await the time when Anton's mother could get up the courage to go through it.

The only true loss he had was his job at the university. It had been filled; but, when Anton called and surprised his department head, Bruno Brander, Bruno said that it had been very difficult to replace him. The man who took Anton's position didn't have the proper background, but they had hired him anyway, hoping that he would work out. Unfortunately, that wasn't the case, and they had decided to search for someone else when his contract was up.

Bruno was delighted that Anton was alive and could come back. He wanted him to start again either in the fall or in January because they had to give his replacement adequate notice.

Anton's mind said Yes, but his intuition said, Wait a little longer. He had other work to do now, so he told Bruno, "Don't let my replacement go yet. I want to come back, but first I have to write a book that I started when I was lost, and that will require my full time for now. Hopefully, next year?"

Bruno accepted this answer with disappointment in his voice. "Can you at least commit to several lectures in the meantime?"

Anton agreed as he was anxious to see his colleagues and the students to whom he felt close.

His Zürich friends threw him a party, which he reluctantly attended; being around a lot of people was still problematic for him. He wanted to tell them the truth about what had happened in the valley, but he knew they would never understand. These were his closest friends, but when he saw them, he felt alienated and uncomfortable. He realized how superficial they were and knew that he also had been the same way. They had always done things together — doubled dated, discussed politics, attended art openings and concerts, and traveled — but now he was aware that he knew very little about their feelings and who they really were.

Anton felt his friends' joy in seeing him, knowing he was alive, but he also felt he had changed and couldn't go back to that kind of social group. But was he being fair? Was his evaluation of things off because of what had happened to him? Don't reject your friends, he told himself.

Anton found himself caught between two conditions: an animal that is free but also has a safe cage to go to. His past—all his friends, his beliefs, his former identity— had been his security. Now he had a new identity; but there was no security in it. He had no friends, and his new beliefs still felt foreign to him. He *needed* friends and a cultural life, or did he? He suddenly felt very lonely, even lonelier than when he had been in the valley.

As he was ruminating about his relationships one day at home alone, Feathers appeared. Anton was surprised. "You are here! You are not my sick illusion in the valley. You are still around me."

"Of course, Anton. I am your friend and want to help you. You have forgotten what I told you about using your heart. Use your heart; then you will know how to relate to all kinds of people. You are in between the old you and the new you."

"But what is the new me?"

"A man who uses his heart and can connect to others in a way you have.

"The new you is who you really are; and, believe me, everyone will feel your warmth and genuinely like you."

"But people like me now. I have a lot of friends."

"Those friends like your mind, but your heart will attract new friends who will be much closer because they will love you."

"But don't my friends love me?"

"What do you think?"

Anton thought about that but didn't reply. Instead, he asked, "You keep telling me to use my heart. How do I do that?"

"It's very easy. Simply connect with the heart center, which is in the middle of your chest. Concentrate on it and try to feel its warmth. When you feel it, listen to its wisdom. It can help you not only in your relationships but in your work and in your daily life."

That sounded difficult and he thought, That's nonsense.

The family chose to spend the summer with Anton in Grindelwald. Somehow, his resurrection bonded them all together in a way that never had happened before. Even his brothers, Erick and Jonas, who had always been distant, were solicitous and spent more of their time with him rather than with each other, which had been their habit in the past. Anton was the focal point, but the new comradeship caused them all to learn more about one another. Astonishingly, friendships formed, and any old sibling rivalries seem to dissolve like mist falling into dark water.

Erick was the oldest, nine years Anton's senior, serious and remote, disappearing even when he was there. They resembled each other the most in their angular features, except that Erick's black hair was straight and sharpened his face more. Being the oldest, he had followed in his father's footsteps and was now a vice president at his father's bank.

Jonas, seven years older than Anton, was much smaller in height and resembled their mother, with smaller features and bluer eyes. He was the jokester of the family. Unfortunately, Anton used to be the focus of his jokes. Once, when Anton was five years old and in bed, someone had called his name. When he got up, he suddenly felt hands from under the bed grab his legs. "I have you now!" cried a voice. When Anton screamed, someone laughed, and Anton knew it was his brother. Jonas had also gone into banking, but he was more in the investment end of the business.

Neither of his brothers had married, which bothered their parents. Jonas was more of a playboy, dating a lot, whereas Erick was a loner. He kept his love life very private.

Kristina, his sister, was five years older than Anton and didn't resemble any of them. She even went through a period of feeling she might be adopted, but actually, she looked very much like their paternal grandmother—tall, slender, and regal, with reddish-brown hair and blue-green eyes.

Some would call Kristina beautiful and even exotic looking. As she matured, she became more intellectual and reserved, like Erick, and her seriousness and lack of expression often made her beauty lifeless, like a porcelain doll.

It felt so strange to be in the world again that there were times when Anton had to get away and be alone. Also, all this unexpected, new family love sometimes felt over-whelming and, in some ways, artificial. Everyone acted as if everything was normal, but he felt there were a lot of unexpressed feelings concerning him.

Anton tried to be in his heart but found himself questioning everything. Did they all really love one another? he wondered. How could that be? For years, they had only seen one another a few times a year; and, while the meetings had been cordial, they weren't meaningful. His mother and Kristina were the only ones he ever saw on more occasions or even called.

The old Anton would have basked in the attention he was getting, but now he looked at it with new eyes that saw deeper into what was real. In some ways, he felt about his family the same as he had about his friends at the party in Zürich. Did he truly know any of them, and did they truly know him? But then, even he didn't know who he was anymore.

Eventually, Anton became tired of telling lies when his family asked him why he hadn't lost weight in the valley and what had really happened. Finally, one night he told them the whole story, except that he didn't say anything about the book, other than that a philosophical book had been given to him and he now had to work on it. He also didn't mention his strange friends, Feathers and Merlin, but he did say, "I meditated every day and was sent messages to help me."

He told them, "When I needed food, sacks of food were delivered by an unseen hand while I slept, and I was given seeds to plant."

"But how did you survive the cold winter?" his father asked.

"The valley was protected from the winter winds, which I heard howling above me. Sheepskin clothing and blankets appeared, and warm air was blown into my tent." He looked at their astonished faces and added, "Believe me, that happened, and I was very comfortable."

They listened in silence, a silence that became a descent into a tomb that had never been opened.

Erick said, "Anton, I know you believe how you survived, but could something else have happened that you don't remember?"

"I assure you, what I remember is true. I survived because of this help."

Anton realized then that they would never believe his story. He saw waves of doubt in his father's and brothers' eyes, yet they still listened with an open heart. When he was done, no one spoke.

Finally, his mother said, "Whoever these benefactors are, I thank them."

And the others agreed.

Erick said, "If I didn't know you so well, I would say that was one of the biggest yarns I've ever heard. But Anton, I accept your story. It's hard to accept, but I will try."

Obviously taken aback, Jonas nodded his head but said nothing.

Addressing Anton, his father added, "I've never known you to be a liar. Why would you make up such a story? There are stranger things on this planet than we know about. The main thing is you are here — thank God!" And, again, tears came to his eyes.

His sister just looked hard at him and said, "I knew it was something like that. There are no animals or even birds to eat in the wintertime on those mountains. They move down to warmer terrain. The town's people have mentioned this to me, also. They know something more happened on the mountain. They believe in such miracles, and I do, too."

Anton smiled at her, knowing that Kristina and his mother both believed in the supernatural, and it felt good to share his experience with them. His brothers and father were trying, and that was fine. In time, they would discover the magic for themselves.

When the summer was over, the family left, and everything calmed down. Once more, Anton was alone. His writings were still in the sack in his room. He needed to put them into his computer and study them. His recall was vague, as he'd written them in a semitrance state and had never had the time even to question the material he was given.

The manuscript held many ideas that were foreign to Anton, so it wasn't just about reading it and typing it. He also had to learn and understand it.

One day Feathers appeared and said, "Anton, try to be open to changing some of this writing. This is your book."

"My book? Not really. It was given to me."

"Don't you realize the language is in your style?"

"Well, yes, I guess it is; but there is a lot that is new to me. How could I have written it?"

"Long before you were in the valley, you were guided to write this book while you slept. On a certain level, you understand all of it."

"If that's true, then why do I have to study it now?"

"Because you need to bring the unconscious into your conscious mind, and realize that it isn't difficult to do. If you link with your heart and don't just stay in your mind, then the concepts will be much easier to comprehend."

"Yes, you keep telling me that, but instead I keep reverting to my usual academic mode. Thank you for reminding me about the heart."

The days became weeks, and still, there was so much more Anton needed to comprehend. But it was easier when he put the information in his heart. Anton also found that when he studied something, additional thoughts would flow into his head from somewhere beyond his reasoning that would further explain a given passage. He wrote down the thoughts and later added them to the manuscript.

He called Stefan and they had dinner, but he felt the change. They talked about mundane things but not the problem between them. He wanted to approach the subject of their relationship and his stay in the valley, but he felt Stefan wouldn't hear him. Anton wanted to ask him what his theories were concerning his survival, but he couldn't. It was one of the most difficult times Anton had ever experienced, and afterward, he felt he had truly failed by not confronting Stefan. He resolved to do so in the future.

CHAPTER 9

In late October, Jacques called and invited Anton for lunch the following week. On the drive there, Anton started again to feel angry about having been controlled. So, when he arrived and Jacques greeted him warmly, he responded with barely a hello. They went directly into his study and sat down.

Anton almost shouted, "Why did you do this to me? What power do you have to control me this way?"

Jacques thought for a minute and responded, "The power of the heart."

"What the hell do you mean?"

"You and I have been together many times, and I care about you."

"That's crazy. If you care about me, why did you do this to me? Why did I have to be lost in the valley for almost a year?"

"Anton, what did you learn in that experience? Who are you now?"

"Oh yes, it's changed me! I'm not who I was. I feel alienated from my family and friends. I feel constantly lonely, unsure of myself, and definitely unhappy."

"Well, maybe you are starting to feel your true feelings, feelings you had as a child. Your parents — did they abandon you in any way when you were young?"

"What do you mean? I saw them."

"You just saw them? You didn't live with them?"

"No, but I saw them on weekends once in a while. I went to school in the mountains."

"Who raised you?"

"I had a wonderful couple who took care of me." Anton was starting to feel very uncomfortable.

"Yes, but they weren't your parents. Have you ever asked your mother and father why they left you in the mountains to go to school?"

"No, but I think it was because they traveled a lot."

"And your siblings? Where were they?"

"They were in boarding schools."

"Did this also happen to you when you got older? Did they put you in a boarding school?"

"Yes, but I loved it, and I learned a lot. All of us spent our vacations together. I love my family."

Jacques smiled and said, "Of course you do."

Anton suddenly felt a question arise: Is Jacques implying that I don't love them? Immediately, he discarded that thought. "Why are you bringing this up?"

"Because you asked me why you needed to be in the valley for almost a year."

"But you didn't answer me."

"Yes, I did." And Jacques looked at him with such love in his eyes that Anton couldn't say another word.

Christmas came and went, and the days were full of family and friends. But when they all left, Anton felt relieved so that he could resume his work.

In late January, he went to Zürich to start his lecture courses. At first, he was worried about teaching again, but then he realized that his intellect was still a strong part of his identity. He hadn't lost that. The rest of his identity, though, was an arrow shot into the sky that could land nearby or in an unforeseen place full of unresolved mysteries. Somewhere in that landing, he needed to find himself, to make the landing true to who he needed to be.

One day in early April, when he was nearly finished with the first revision of the book, Anton heard a woman's voice speaking to him indistinctly. Turning, he expected to see Feathers behind him, but there was no one there. He thought it was his imagination and returned to his work; but again, he heard the woman's voice, this time in distinct words.

"You need to take a break," she said.

He turned and still saw no one, but he realized that the voice wasn't Feathers'.

"Who are you? Please let me see you," he demanded.

"No, you can't see me. But know I am your friend and have come here to warn you that you are overdoing it; you will collapse if you don't take a break and eat properly."

"If you are a friend, at least tell me your name."

"My name is Lea Heroch, and now I must go. Please take my advice right away."

Anton was tired and quite thin by this time. He ate dinners in the evening but not much in the morning or at lunch. Kristina had arranged for a woman from town to cook and freeze food for him, but he often forgot to eat. He also used to take walks every day, but he gave those up when the weather became colder. Now, his normally muscular body was soft and lacked strength.

This new friend of his, Lea, was right. He needed to go to a sunny place where he could swim, exercise, and regain some of his vitality.

Anton chose the South Seas. He had never been to that part of the world, and he had heard from friends that some of the islands, such as Tahiti, were lovely.

He planned to fly out of Zürich in May and went a day early to be with his parents. After dinner, his mother retired and left him alone with his father to talk.

His father was very kind but firm when he said, "I know you have gone through a lot, and I feel grateful, as you know, that you are all right. But I have to tell you that both your mother and I are worried about you. People have noticed your appearance and that you seem very remote, which makes it difficult to have a conversation with you. You never say very much, whereas before you used to be talkative and interested in everything."

He added, "Now you don't seem to even care about what's going on in the world. It's clear that you're not reading the newspapers or listening to the news. This is not like you, Anton."

"That's true. I'm no longer interested in those things."

"But when you first returned, you were the old Anton. Now you've become a hermit again, as you were in the valley. The last thing I would expect is for you to continue the lifestyle you had when you were lost to us."

"Dad, the experience did change me. I'm not the same. Maybe I'll become more social when the book is finished and I'm back here at work, but I have to be honest. I will never be as I was before. My values are different."

"What do you mean, your values are different? You're one of the finest people I know. Why would you change your values?"

"I'm not changing all my values; mainly, I have added to them. I don't care about the things I used to care about. I look at this world we are in from a different view-point. I can't explain it to you now, but when my book is published, you'll understand more about what I mean."

His father shook his head. "All I know is that you are very distant, as if you're somewhere else all the time. If I didn't know better, I would say you were a stranger in my son's body."

Anton smiled, "Well, that can happen, but not to me. I assure you I am your son, but not the son you've always known. You, and Mom, and the others just have to learn to accept the new me."

"The new you, we feel, has problems."

Anton's father reached into his pocket and pulled out a business card. "We want you to think about going to someone for help."

He raised his hand to stop Anton's protest. "Please hear me out. You may feel that you're okay, but your behavior and your appearance indicate the opposite. Anton, you went through a life-and-death experience, as well as the other—God knows what! — weird phenomenon. Of course, it has changed you, but not for the better. We all love you and respect you, but I have to be honest. We all feel you need help."

Anton shook his head. "I know I've been very intense, but I'm going on vacation tomorrow. That's all the help I need."

"Maybe a rest will help. I hope so, but please promise me that, if it doesn't, you will at least go for an evaluation with a therapist," his father persisted. He handed Anton the card.

"This woman comes highly recommended. She is away now, but when you return, I'm begging you to go and see her and just tell her your experience. Please, for all our sakes, do this."

Anton looked at the card. The name on it was Lea Heroch, psychotherapist. Trying not to show the shock he felt, Anton quickly asked, "Where did you hear about her?"

"Several of our friends, who also are concerned, mentioned her to me. Even though she is young, she has worked with some of the top people here and is highly respected. Allan's daughter went to her. She was falling apart from a broken love affair and was even suicidal, but now she's fine."

His father added, "I don't mean to imply that you're falling apart. It's just that it might help you to talk with her."

Anton nodded seriously. "I will be glad to see her as soon as I come back. In fact, please set up an appointment for me the day after my return."

His father's eyes revealed how surprised and happy he was that Anton had suddenly responded so positively. Dad will never know why, Anton thought. He was amazed at the way people are connected.

CHAPTER 10

Tahiti was crowded and full of tourists. Anton canceled his reservation at a luxurious resort on the waterfront outside of Papeete and rented a car to find a less congested place. It was a small island, so it didn't take long for him to arrive to the south coast. He settled on a place near the village of Afaahiti that seemed less touristy. There he rented a small, thatched-roof bungalow on the beach for an exorbitant amount of money. The old days when Gauguin had painted there were certainly gone. But it didn't matter; it was still perfect. The setting was lovely, with tall palm trees that separated his place from the other bungalows and sheltered him from the sweltering afternoon sun.

Every night the sound of the breaking waves lulled him to sleep, and his eyes opened to the sun as it rose over the glistening water. For most of the two weeks, Anton swam, walked the beach, read, and lay in the sun until he was almost as golden-brown-skinned as the native people. In the mornings, he went to the market and bought *firi firi*—long, sweet donuts, made with flour and coconut milk and coated in sugar. Sometimes he dipped them in passion-fruit jam. In the evenings, he ate at a small, out-of-the-way restaurant that served huge plates of fresh, exotic seafood, which helped to restore his lost appetite. And he drank Tahiti rum punch, strong and deeply satisfying, that finally relaxed his fatigued body. He began to fill out, and the swimming and walking helped him regain some of his muscle tone.

Local women tried to catch his eye. Their striking beauty—long black hair with flowers nuzzled in their locks and smoldering black eyes—tempted him, but his desire to be alone and to rest won out.

Every time Anton thought about the manuscript, he stopped himself and focused on a seashell; and, when he thought about Lea, he did the same. She came up the most in his mind, mainly because she piqued his curiosity, and it took a lot for him to focus on something else.

His airplane reservation was for a two-week stay, but he changed it to three and informed everyone at the last minute. He didn't know why he added the week, as he was ready to return, but something held him back.

Anton decided to spend the last week exploring the island in the mornings and resting on the beach in the afternoons when the heat made it impossible to travel. His routine was to leave early, in the cool of the morning, and drive to a small village. There he would have breakfast and walk around, conversing with those natives who spoke French, or just listening to Tahitian—an interesting language influenced by the many foreigners who had settled into the population. French, English, Greek, Latin, and even Hebrew words had merged into the language.

Then, Anton would drive on to another village and end up back at his bungalow in the early afternoon. Because Tahiti is a small island, he had plenty of time to see all the attractions and still wander around in places where tourists didn't go.

It happened on his last day of touring. He came to a village that was nestled at the foot of a mountain—or what the Swiss would call a hill. The village was tiny, with only about twenty huts surrounding a lake that had tall palm trees clustered with lush, tropical flowerbeds around them.

Anton was going to pass it by, but he saw something that made him stop. It was a tall sculpture, around eight feet high, standing in the middle of a courtyard. The sculpture looked like something Gauguin might have done. It had two intertwined figures, made of wood, and colored in deep sienna tones. The figures held something that he couldn't distinguish at first. When he got out of the car and walked close to them, he could see they were two women trying to transport a large jug full of what was probably water. He then noticed that there was a well in the courtyard, just for the same purpose.

He wondered who the artist was and asked a woman who was filling her jug at the well. She shook her head and pointed to a small shop that stood close by. The shop, when he entered it, was primarily a mishmash offering everything from old bicycle wheels to jars of honey and other produce. Behind the counter was a young woman with long, raven-black hair and bronze skin, dressed in a red-patterned sarong with a red flower in her hair. When she smiled at him, her face was full of sunlight, and her dark eyes glowed with luminosity. Anton felt spellbound at her natural beauty and found it difficult to speak. His heart beat fast with the inner excitement of being swept up in her radiance.

"Can I help you?" Her English was perfect.

"Yes, can you tell me who the sculptor is that created the sculpture outside?"

"Do you like it?"

"Yes, very much. It's quite beautiful."

"Thank you. It's my work. I made it for my mother. She is one of the figures."

Anton was flabbergasted. "*Your* sculpture? It's wonderful! But what are you doing here in this small village? You should be in Papeete, with your work in a gallery."

She smiled. "Why do you assume I'm not?"

Anton mumbled a small apology.

"I'm in a gallery, and I live and work in Papeete; but this was my home, and I'm here now on vacation to help my grandfather in the shop." She extended her hand. "My name is Orama Remoin."

"You're French?" Another surprise.

"My father. I take after my mother, who is a native, as you can see from my sculpture."

"Yes, which reminds me: I would really like to buy one—obviously, much smaller. Do you have any pieces here?"

"Yes, but they are not for sale. They belong to my family. I do have more in my studio and in my gallery in the city. If you would like, I could meet you there in the morning. But what are your plans? Would that be convenient for you?" As she talked, she put her hand on her hair and caressed it downward.

"Yes." His heart felt uncontrollable. "I'm flying out in the evening, but I can meet you in the morning, and, if you have time, I would like to take you to lunch afterward."

The arrangements were made, and Anton reluctantly left to continue his sightseeing. After that encounter, nothing interested him. His full attention was focused on Orama. He hadn't felt such an attraction for a woman since his teenage crush on a local rock singer. He'd gone to every one of her concerts and felt very depressed when she left on a tour and didn't come back.

The next morning, Anton met Orama at her gallery in the Vaima Center, the largest shopping complex in Papeete, located on the waterfront. It was a big tourist attraction, so he had avoided shopping there, even though he had heard about her gallery and been tempted to visit it. The gallery was known for its fine collection of South Pacific carvings.

Orama was dressed this time in white slacks and a blue silk shirt, but she still had a flower in her hair, this time a white one. She greeted Anton warmly and took him to one of the main rooms, where she had a display of wooden sculptures. Exceptionally beautiful, they were mainly figures of women and children. Some were made from a dark wood that looked like mahogany, and others were painted in pastel colors on bleached wood. All were skillfully carved and full of expression. She had managed to capture the sadness of a woman with a dead child in her arms and the happiness of a woman who played with a young boy. Anton walked around them, loving them, but felt upset that they were all too large for him to carry home.

Orama read his disappointment. "Don't worry, I have many smaller ones in my studio."

Her studio was on the other side of the town, in a warehouse that obviously had been converted into artist studios. As they walked through the studio door, the morning light flowed through large windows, causing the bigger sculptures to cast shadows on the polished wooden floor. It made the wood sculptures look like flesh, and Anton half expected them to stir from their positions and greet him. At first glance, he saw that Orama was working on three large pieces that stood in the center of the room, and there was also a table with several half-finished, smaller ones.

"Looks as if you're very busy," he commented.

"Yes, I like to work on several pieces at the same time. It keeps me from getting bored with the same one and gives me a new perspective when I return. But here is what you may be interested in." She walked over to a shelving unit that held many small, finished pieces and began putting them onto a large table under the skylight so they could be seen from all angles.

Anton took his time to look at each piece as he walked around the table and tried to feel the energy while asking questions about the subject. In this grouping were figures but also some very modern work—shapes that blended into other shapes. They, too, were made of wood, but in the modern work Orama had polished and finished the wood to a glossy finish, using the grain to enhance the curves in the sculpture.

"This is my newer work. As you can see, I'm moving away from representation more into abstract form. I haven't shown these yet, as I need to finish some larger ones for a show."

"Nice, really nice. I like both styles. It makes it difficult for me to choose. I may have to buy two."

In the end, he did just that. He bought a small modern one, which resembled two mountains that folded into each other. The peaks embraced and separated at the very top, and the bottom spread into a base of petals. The grain was dark on one side and much lighter on the other, resulting in a blend of dark to light. Strangely, he felt that in some way it represented him and his conflict. The other sculpture he bought looked like a small version of the one he had seen in the village, and it turned out that it was one of the models she'd made for the larger piece.

After the transaction, they walked down the street to a small, outdoor café to have lunch. Anton was again fully spellbound by Orama's loveliness and wanted just to sit and look into her dark, dazzling eyes — potent pools of mystery that made him long to hold her close. The feeling was so intense that he consciously had to stop himself from grabbing her. For a short time after they had ordered, Anton was shy and couldn't speak, an old childhood condition that he thought he had left behind with adulthood. But nothing was the same. He had no knowledge of what spell she had cast over him. He only knew that he was mesmerized by her.

Finally, he was able to talk to her about the island and her work, trying to keep the conversation impersonal. Just before lunch she surprised him by asking, "Maybe I can see you in the fall? I've planned a trip to Zürich, as I have some business contacts there."

This made him extremely happy. "Wonderful! I will be back in town at that time. Have you ever been to Zürich?"

"No, this will be my first trip."

"Then you must let me give you the grand tour."

"That would be very nice, but I will have a lot of business there. I have a couple of galleries interested in my work, and I hope to convince one of them to give me a show. Since I have no idea what that will entail, I can't make promises about seeing you, but yes, I do hope we can spend some time together." She smiled at him in what he thought, or maybe hoped, was a seductive manner.

After they parted, Anton did some more last-minute shopping. When he returned to his hotel room to pick up his luggage, he found a note that said, "When we meet again, you may not recognize me. Remember me."

He thought this odd.

CHAPTER 11

When Anton returned to Zürich, there was a message from Bruno Brander at the university, to contact him. They met the next day, and Bruno explained that the man who had replaced him refused to resign because his contract was for another year. They even offered him a generous sum to step down but to no avail. This meant that Anton couldn't start in August as planned but would have to wait until August of the following year. In the meantime, the university would gladly use him for special lectures and perhaps even an evening course that was non-matriculating. He would receive the same salary, so there would be no financial loss. Bruno assured Anton that the university would make good use of his services since he was very much esteemed by the faculty, and he hoped this news would not cause him to look elsewhere.

Anton was dumbfounded by this turn of events, but, after his initial disappointment of not going back to work, he was quite happy about it. Now he would have more time to work on the new manuscript and also on the manuscript on Indian philosophy, which he hadn't finished.

Also, on his return he discovered his friend was still in his apartment, even though he was supposed to be gone. The friend apologized and explained that it was impossible to find something suitable. He needed more time. Since his job wasn't pressing, Anton extended the lease until the end of the year, even though it meant he would have to continue to stay with his parents now and then when he was in Zürich. He actually felt relieved, as this gave him a genuine excuse to return home to the mountains to work.

With all this happening, and because Orama still overpowered his thoughts, Anton forgot about his appointment with Lea Heroch. Fortunately, his father reminded him. He tried to find an excuse to cancel, but his father became so upset that he agreed to go through with it. He had almost forgotten about the mystery that surrounded her.

When he walked into her office, Lea was sitting at her desk, but she immediately stood up and came toward him to shake hands. Standing, she was almost his height. For him to describe her was difficult. Her face was a mysterious mixture of Asian, Caucasian and maybe Black—a phoenix with slanted hazel eyes that sometimes flashed green and light brown skin with angular facial features. She was slim and wore a navy-blue suit that was straight and masculine in detail but somehow made her look even more feminine. Anton assessing her quickly realized that was it. She was one hundred percent feminine — in the way she moved her body, in her eyes, in her high voice, and in the way she tossed her short, straight, dark brown hair.

She must have picked up his staring thoughts because she said, "My mother was Japanese, my father Jewish, and my mother's father black. Sit down." She smiled with her eyes. "How was your trip?"

"Very relaxing but uneventful."

"Oh, really." Her look questioned him.

"Who are you, and how could you talk to me in the mountains?" The words sprang from his mouth.

Lea smiled and said, "Don't you know?"

"No, I don't. So much has happened to me that I don't know anything. Can you explain what is going on?"

"If I tell you, will you promise never to repeat it to anyone, and I mean anyone?"

"I promise." Even as he said the words, he knew it was a promise that would be difficult to keep.

"There are people on this planet who have special knowledge, knowledge that takes the form of clairvoyance or clairaudience, so that things that are foreseen can be helped to materialize. Some of us have developed abilities that facilitate this evolution. I am one of those people, and I think you encountered others in the valley. You also have this ability but have not yet developed it. The time has come for you to own who you are, and not only to accept it but to celebrate it."

"I have no idea what you are talking about."

"Oh, but you do! How do you think you survived in the valley? Why do you think you can write a book with no previous knowledge about the subject? How did you hear me? And what about your mysterious encounters? How can you explain it all?"

"I can't explain any of it. I can only think all the things that happened to me were phenomena, and, as a philosopher, I believe phenomena come from unknown sources. I accept that, but I certainly won't try to clarify it."

"Can you accept that the unknown sources can be known?"

"Yes."

"Let me show you something." Lea got up from her desk and went to a cupboard on the side of the room. Taking out a key, she unlocked the door, removed what looked like a manuscript, and handed it to him. He opened to the title page and saw the title, *Zarathustra's Journey*, by Anton Bauer. Shocked, he turned to the first page of writing and read his own opening to the book. Flipping through the typed pages, he saw there were more chapters he had yet to transcribe from his notes and some that looked like new material. Lea took the book from his hands before he could read any of it and locked it back in the cupboard.

"But that's impossible!"

"Nothing is impossible."

"Give me back my manuscript, please. It's mine! I don't know how you got it, but it's mine and I want it back."

"No. You need to complete it, not copy it. And it isn't yours. Nothing belongs to anyone."

"When did you steal this from me? I left it at home. You must have broken into my house and taken it." His voice grew loud with anger.

"Calm down, Anton. When you go home you will find it exactly where you left it. I never touched it."

"Of course, you did! That's why it's here. You must have copied it, and you even gave it a title and added chapters to it while I was away."

"Never. What you see is the image of a completed book. It looks real, but it's not made of gross matter."

"But I held it. Of course, it is matter."

"Yes, but it is densified matter and not gross matter. In other words, you can hold it because its subtle body has been materialized."

"I don't understand what you are saying." Anton was feeling more and more frustrated.

"Let me show you." Lea walked to her bookshelf and handed him a book.

"Feel the book. It is very material."

"Yes." He punched the book to make certain.

She took the book from him and put it on her desk and stared at it. Suddenly, the book completely disappeared from where it was lying.

"What did you do with it?" Anton was surprised and curious.

"Watch." Just as she spoke, the book appeared on a small table at the far end of the room. She went over, picked it up, and handed it to him.

It felt the same but maybe a little lighter. He wasn't certain.

"Is this the same book?" he asked.

"Yes, it's the same book; but it is not the exact same one you held before." Lea pointed to the desk again, and suddenly the book appeared there, even though he was still holding it.

"I don't understand."

"You are holding a copy of the book, which was first put into its subtle form and then copied, and the copy was densified so you could hold it and even read it. The original was then brought back into its true material form. This is how I have your manuscript. When I talked to you in your house, I was in my subtle body. I again went to your home after you left and retrieved the portion that you had already copied. The rest has been written previously in the subtle form, so I simply carried it over and added it to what you have already transcribed. You still need to finish it in its material form. What you just saw was your book in its densified form. That will stay here until the material one is finished."

"How extraordinary! It's hard even to imagine. I think you must be tricking me in some way. Why should I believe you?"

"You believed Jacques, why not me?"

"You know Jacques?"

"Of course."

"So, all of this was planned—my captivity for a year on the mountain in order to receive all the information for the book? All of this was planned by him and you?"

"And you! It was planned by all three of us on the subtle plane. You did not do this unwillingly. Just the opposite; it was and is a passion for you."

"I did this on the subtle plane? No, I would have realized it. That's a lie."

"Is it?"

Lea's words stopped Anton for a minute. He thought back to all that had happened the previous year, and part of him knew that what she said could possibly be true. Writing the book had never made him feel like a victim of some psychic experiment. Maybe she was right. It felt very normal to him.

"If this is true, why not just copy the manuscript you have? Why do I have to spend any time writing it?"

"Because it needs to be in the material world, and it must be brought in by you in your physical body. In so doing, you will make changes. What you saw is a rough copy. When it is finished, it will have your intellect and your thinking added to it. It is yours, inspired on the subtle plane but written by you in your style."

That's what Feathers had told him. He thought about it, and it made sense. Subtle forms and bodies he knew about already, though he didn't necessarily believe in them. These hidden worlds were very much a part of Eastern philosophies and religions. He had touched on them briefly in his courses, but he certainly had never personally experienced them. His logical mind would need time to absorb all this. He couldn't even focus on questions to ask, it was too overwhelming. All he could think about was the title he had been given.

"*Zarathustra's Journey*" — who gave it that title?"

"You did, when you were working on the book in the subtle world. You based the title on Nietzsche's book, *Thus Spake Zarathustra*. We all thought it was appropriate."

Anton nodded. Indeed, it was appropriate. Nietzsche had always been one of his favorite philosophers. He taught his philosophy in one of his university courses.

Nietzsche had died long before Hitler had corrupted Nietzsche's beautiful theory that all people had a higher perfect being within them and this higher being was the true Self. The "Superman" was this true Self, not an example of the Aryan race that Hitler wanted to create, superior in the egoistic and mundane sense to all others. Nietzsche's "Superman" or "Overman" was the inner, Wise Being or Higher Self that everyone contained and needed to discover and strive to become. Hitler, who dealt in black magic, knew what he was doing; his distortion gave Nietzsche a bad reputation, and some people even felt Nietzsche was part of Hitler's regime. Nietzsche's sister was the one who had been a friend of Hitler. Nietzsche himself had never met him or known about him.

Anton was lost in these thoughts when Lea said, "I have a client coming now, so I will have to say goodbye." She smiled and added, "Let's have lunch sometime."

Yes, that would be very good." Anton smiled back.

CHAPTER 12

Anton spent the summer months mainly with his family, who came for weekends and vacations. He tried to be more social, and some work got done, but not too much. He regretted giving his friend an extension on his condo, as he would have liked to get away on some weekends. Sometimes he found himself wishing the family wouldn't come.

Finally, everyone left, and September arrived. Early in the month it became chilly, which usually predicted a cold winter.

He was determined to finish the manuscript that winter, so he would still have time to edit and make changes. He wanted it to be ready to read by the late spring. He also needed to prepare for the university's assignment of eight lectures, which were to occur at the end of September and in October, before the heavy snows. He declined the night course, as it would mean he'd have to live in Zürich full time when he would rather be in the mountains away from the pull of city life.

It came as a surprise when Anton received an email from Orama, saying she would be in Zürich and could meet him the third week in September. In fact, he had completely forgotten about her. His first reaction was no, he couldn't do that, as he would be back at work and couldn't take the time. Then her exotic face came to mind, and he felt such a longing to see her that he couldn't resist. Besides, his first lecture was the last week in September, so he would only have to go into the city a week earlier than planned.

The night Orama arrived, Anton met her at her hotel. They planned to have dinner together but make it an early evening, as she always suffered from jet lag. When she came into the lobby, the note she had left him came true: he didn't recognize her at first. Orama no longer looked like an islander— instead, she looked like she had just stepped out of *Vogue*. She was dressed in a black pants outfit that fit her body in a way that left no room for excess pounds. The pants sat low on her hips, and her top emphasized the roundness of her breasts. She wore no jewelry except for single dia-mond drop earrings. Her long hair was swept up in a French twist, which made her look even more elegant and mysterious. Anton had forgotten how beautiful she was and seeing her again now was a warm caress that made his whole body vibrate.

He kissed her lightly in welcome and found his arm naturally encircling her waist as they walked out of the hotel.

The evening was like a long breath that never ended. He remembered very little of it — what was said, the restaurant, the food, the hotel room — all that had happened to transform the breath into deep desire. His need to possess her overwhelmed him with a fiery energy in the most primitive part of his being. He needed to own her, to have her surrender herself completely to him, to feel her part of him. When she let go and gave in, he felt the vibrations pulsing through them both, climaxing in a passion that kept moving, expanding into waves of ecstasy. Their orgasms rolled into a sea of desires, only to rise again. Desire — what is desire? It became lost in the breakers of fulfilled longing. What is longing? It is part of destiny. Orama was his destiny. They were now together; that's all he knew.

The rest of her stay there was a blur to him. She had business during the day. Anton taught his lectures with ease and then wandered the streets, thinking about her. The nights called to them, seeking their rapture. He never wanted them to end. Each evening gave them a new chance of discovery. The romantic settings were backdrops to their passion: the food, the wine, served as ambrosia to prepare their bodies.

Everything flowed in perfect harmony. Someone might ask, "What did you talk about?"

"Everything and nothing," was all he could have answered.

Someone might ask, "What do you have in common?"

"Everything and nothing," was all he could have answered. "She loves the warmth of the South Seas, and I love the cold of the mountains. She loves to lie in the sun and swim in blue waters, and I love the sun sparkling on the snow and snowshoeing across winter meadows. She loves indigenous music, and I love listening to Mahler or Wagner."

Even her tastes in art were nothing like his. If Anton thought about what they had in common, it came down to the way their bodies claimed each other in the fervor of heightened senses as they sought fulfillment. Mainly, they shared a deep knowing that they belonged together. When he tried to analyze it, he couldn't. Maybe he was consumed with this passion because he hadn't had sex for a couple of years, but that didn't feel true, either. And there was much more that he couldn't comprehend. Finally, he just had to give in to the feelings and let go of trying to understand them.

He thought that most people would say this sounded like a great sexual experience and not to read more into it. Yes, he would reply, that's true; the sex was fabulous. But it was more than sex, and that "more" couldn't be expressed. Most would say it was a great fling. He would say, yes, it was a great fling, but it would continue and become more than a fling. Most would say it will never work, you come from different worlds. Yes, he would say, that's true. We come from different worlds, but they are now becoming one. There was nothing rational about his relationship with Orama. How could there be? How could one be rational when convinced that it was destiny?

The day she had to leave to return home came faster than he had anticipated. To say goodbye felt excruciating, even knowing he would follow her soon to Tahiti. Anton planned to go as soon as his lectures were finished. He said as much the night before she left and felt shocked when she said, "No, you can't visit me yet. I need time. There are things I need to do first."

"What things?"

She didn't answer but instead tried to comfort him, saying, "Darling, I assure you everything will be okay. I'll let you know when to come, and I will be returning here, also."

He had never thought for a moment that she could be with someone else, yet the way she spoke he knew for the first time that there must be another man. He felt betrayed, and heartbroken, and lost, and even her loving arms couldn't relieve him of the feeling that she would never be with him again.

That feeling became even stronger when Anton saw Orama board the plane. Just before, he begged her to tell him about the man at home; all she said was that there was someone else, but it was over. She held his head in her hands and told him not to be afraid, that she loved him now. He waited until the plane was a speck on the horizon. As it grew smaller, he felt that he would never see her again, that his fears were based on truth, and that her life and her surroundings would make her passion fade. He would be forgotten.

CHAPTER 13

After Orama left, Anton marveled at what had happened. I was lost in a wilderness and was lonely, he thought. I was saved to discover that my life was best when I am alone; then I meet someone who makes me long for eternal companionship. I have to know more about her. I need to go to her home. I need to not let this relationship in any way lessen. Otherwise, I will be lost again.

As soon as Anton's lectures were finished, he flew to Tahiti. This plane ride seemed much longer than the first one. He sat through most of it thinking about Orama and trying to decide what he would say to her. How could he explain his impulse, when she had made it clear that he was not to come? Would she understand? He prayed harder than he had ever prayed in his life. He prayed to the God of love, of mercy, of hope. He prayed to be helped to convince her that it was right for him to come. He thought of the tale of Orpheus, in which the musician had looked back at his love and lost her because he hadn't listened.

Halfway to Tahiti, Anton became calm again and decided to take the next plane home. He couldn't decide whether to even call Orama or simply to go back without any exchange; but then the thought of not seeing her became overwhelming. He had to see her again, if only for 5 minutes. To come this distance and not see her felt too difficult.

The day was beautiful and sunny when he arrived. He called his former hotel and was pleased to find a room available. Perfect, everything seemed perfect. When Anton entered his room, his thoughts were on when and how to call her, so his surprise could not have been greater when he saw a flower arrangement on the table with a card in it.

The card read, "Days and nights are but a dream in the reality of all the worlds. Do not call me. I will call you." It was signed, "Orama."

Overpowering terror engulfed him, as if black liquid was poured through the top of his head to the soles of his feet. He could weather the experience of the mountains and a book given to him by unseen beings. He could accept the supernatural happenings, question them, be amazed by them, but Orama's note took him over the edge. She now became part of this strange world that kept unfolding; and, because Anton felt she was destined, he also knew it all might be a dream, never to continue. She became no longer real, and in her short message lay the ashes of what could have been. He felt victimized and frightened. Suddenly, he realized that others were controlling even his feeling of falling in love. The wonder that all the previous experiences had given him was gone. All that remained was dread of the unknown.

Anton took a taxi back to the airport and boarded the next plane to Zürich. His decision was final. Certain people were ruling his life, and he had to put a stop to that immediately. His destiny belonged to him. He would no longer allow strangers to take charge of it.

When he arrived in Zürich, he called Jacques' number and found he had returned.

"I need to talk to you right away."

"All right, you know where I live. I will be here."

Anton was tired, very tired. He'd dozed very little on the plane rides, and in the taxi to Jacques' home he felt a need just to sleep. His body and mind felt exhausted. He almost told the driver to take him to his parents' place instead, so he could rest before he talked to Jacques. But part of him was insistent on seeing Jacques now. I'm here, he thought. See him *now*, and don't wait.

Jacques led him into the same drawing room. A fire burned in the fireplace, and even though it wasn't cold enough outside to warrant it, the flames felt warm and friendly and increased his need to curl up and sleep. Jacques excused himself and left, returning with a tray of steaming coffee and sandwiches.

"Please join me." Jacques poured Anton coffee and piled a plate with food.

They didn't speak as they ate. It was a silent ritual. As Anton drank the strong coffee and ate, he felt some life return to him. It was welcome, as he had been so tired he couldn't focus on all that he needed to say.

"I can no longer do this work. My life has been torn apart; my real work interrupted. My heart has been broken, and I feel used by you and this group of yours, as if I'm a pawn you've played with. Writing this book has been a joy, I must admit, but what's happened to my life makes even that no longer feasible. I will give you the manuscript as is. Find someone else to finish it."

As Anton spoke, he fought back sadness. He felt much more attached to the book than he'd imagined. To give it back felt like giving a child away, but he fought the feeling with a relentless determination.

Jacques didn't answer at once. First Anton saw surprise in his eyes, then thoughtfulness. "Tell me why you feel this way now," Jacques eventually said. "Before, you accepted the work unquestioningly, because the work gave you the answers. What has happened to you?"

"You know what has happened. I thought Orama was part of my private life, but now I know she was a gift, and a hold over me to keep me going, to keep me from questioning. If that is what happens to Zarathustra, if that is what happens to me, it's wrong and controlling and I don't want it."

"Orama? Who is Orama?"

He laughed, "Don't lie to me. You planted her in my life. She works for you. I know that now. It was all a set-up."

"Anton, I do not know Orama. Tell me what happened." He looked at him with such sincerity that Anton momentarily believed him.

"She knows everything about me. Just like you do and like Lea does. Are you going to tell me you don't know Lea, either?"

"No, of course, I know Lea, and I asked her to work with you. Orama is not part of our group, but I'm beginning to understand who she is. Tell me about her; tell me everything."

And Anton did. He told Jacques about their passion, their love, about his need for her, and about her note. He told him about feeling betrayed, lost, and disillusioned.

Jacques thought carefully before he spoke. "That is how she wants you to feel, Anton. Your journey is into spiritual realms, realms that have always existed but are unseen by most people. Within that journey comes the realization that many types of beings inhabit these realms." Anton felt Jacques' compassion toward him.

"These beings are not all benevolent. There is an entire order of them that wants to stop the evolution of this planet, and of you and any other person who is on the journey to find the true Self. They want to stop the enlightened ones and impede those who are seeking the spirit within. These beings, which we call 'negative forces,' use every means to accomplish their goal. I'm sorry to tell you, but it sounds as if Orama is one of them."

"That can't be true," Anton protested. "She's beautiful and kindhearted. Her nature is spiritual. I know that."

"They are great deceivers. She will appear to be that way in order to capture your love, and, in doing that, destroy your faith. You have come a long way, Anton. You have found many answers, and in your heart you know truth. I knew that someday soon you would be a target of theirs. Their power is great, but it can never equal ours. Good always conquers evil."

Jacques paused and then said, "I want to show you something."

He stood up and went to a cabinet. Taking out a key, he unlocked the drawer. What he took out was small and delicate. He brought it back and put it in Anton's hands.

Anton looked down at a small cameo painting of an extraordinary, beautiful woman. She was as dark haired as Orama, but her eyes were a deep blue. Her face was animated and seemed alive and full of laughter.

"She's beautiful. Who is she?"

"She was my wife. I loved her very much, but she became enamored with the negative forces. They promised her power over love, and she wanted desperately to have that. Her father had victimized her, and, even though I was very different, she saw every man as wanting to control her, so she chose the power they offered her. Now, she works closely with them and is my worst enemy. She uses her beauty and intellect to work against us. She moves in high political circles in America and is married to a very powerful man who is also in that order."

Jacques sighed, and Anton saw sadness shadow his eyes.

"I have no photos of her, just this small painting" Jacques said. "Photos would give her access to my house."

"How is that possible?"

"They can focus on the photo and make a line of energy that will penetrate any energy protection I have put here. It gives them easy access."

"You have protection around your house?"

"Spiritual teachers do that, as they are constantly under attack."

Jacques looked at the portrait again. "I showed you this to tell you how they operate. Orama wants you to believe in her, and, I assure you, she will show up again in your life. I warn you, the negative forces are very strong."

During this whole conversation, Anton felt like he was in a fog. Jacques' words made his heart ache. He wanted desperately not to believe him, but he did. Jacques was his teacher. Anton had always known this, and, in that knowing, had faith in him and in the work.

Anton put his head in his hands. "But I love her so very much. It is difficult to believe that she follows a negative teaching and is evil."

"I know." Jacques put his hand on Anton's back. "My wife was also very receptive, and seemed loving, and kindhearted. It took me many years to accept that she belonged to them. Then, of course, I tried to save her, but I couldn't."

Anton felt the energy from Jacques' hand going through him, and it comforted him. "But why did she write me that note? Why not just wait until I called her? If she hadn't written the note, I would still be under her spell."

"Remember, they will cast doubt. Her note made you doubt your work and me. She will have a reason for it. My advice is never to see or talk to her again. I know it will be difficult for you, but try; and, if you do talk to her or see her, imagine a suit of armor around your body that will shield you from her energy."

Never to see her again! The finality of that statement upset Anton. How would that be possible? he thought.

"I will try," he said, and then added, "How did you let go of the feeling of loss?"

"I never did. I chose to keep her in my heart and pray for her each day. But you are young; there will be love in your life again, love that will be shared and based on positive values. The old saying is right: 'Time heals all wounds.' In my case, my wife and I had many wonderful years together before this happened."

"Can't I have the same, or even a couple years?"

"What do you think?"

Anton sighed. "I guess not. I would be living with evil, and I would never finish the book."

"Exactly. Remember, that is what they want, to block your mission."

"On the subject of missions. Can you tell me what that is? The book is nearly done. What is next?"

Jacques stared at him. "Don't you know?"

He could see by Anton's expression that he didn't know.

"The book is a teaching that you can use in your classroom."

CHAPTER 14

Later, when Anton returned home, Orama called, just as Jacques had predicted, and explained the note. She sounded a bit agitated.

"I knew you would take it wrongly. I had the feeling that you followed me, so I called the hotels and your hotel verified you had booked a room there. I was in a hurry, so I quickly wrote the note and left it for you. Darling, I had no idea you would be offended by it. Please forgive my investigating you. But why did you follow me when I asked you not to?"

"I needed to see you, to be with you." Anton's words felt hollow. Talking to her brought up the pain again, the pain in knowing that she was negative and had tried to bind him to her, along with the pain that he had to lose her.

"I want to be with you too, Darling. Soon, I promise, soon."

How can I reply to her? he thought. Jacques said not to see her again, but how can I explain that to her? He also said not to reveal my knowledge of who she is, because then I would be attacked in a major way.

So, all Anton said was, "Yes, that will be nice, but not for a while. Winter is setting in here, and I am very busy with my book. Maybe in the spring."

"But that's too long," she protested, with a hint of coolness in her voice.

He tried to sound warmer. "Yes, I know, but when I'm with you I really want to be with you completely. The book hangs over my head. Let me finish it and then I'll be free."

"This book sounds very important. I look forward to reading it. Tell me, what is it about?" In Zürich, Anton had briefly mentioned the book to her but never went into any details. She herself had been the center of his attention.

"I can't. There is an old superstition that you should never talk about a creative work in progress until it's finished. Something about not dispersing the energy."

"But surely you can tell me. I promise not to mention it to anyone."

"Sorry, can't do it. I won't even tell my mother, and we're very close."

As they talked, Anton could feel Orama's energy come at him, almost as if she were in the room. It was very powerful. He tried to step back and consider it objectively, noticing the way it tried to persuade him to do things. Now that he knew the truth, he was vigilant; but if he hadn't known, he would have told her everything and begged to see her right away. It took all his will to withstand her. If he talked to her any longer, he would give in; so, he told her he had to leave for an appointment and would be in touch soon.

As soon as Anton hung up, he grabbed some sage and burned it to purify the room. Orama's energy was still there and hung over him, an invisible cloud circling his face to take away his sight. It was only then that he remembered Jacques' advice about putting a shield around himself when he talked to her. Too late for this time, but Anton wrote himself a note and put it on his desk so when she called again, he would see it.

This was difficult. How to break it off completely? In a month or two, he could tell her that he had met someone else with whom he was falling in love. In the meantime, he would not answer the phone if he saw her ID on it, but then how could he avoid calling her back? She would know he was lying.

He called Jacques for more advice, but Jacques had left on another trip and wouldn't return for a month. Anton had his emergency number but decided not to use it. This wasn't an emergency. He could handle it, or so he thought.

A month passed, and Anton realized that he hadn't heard from Orama. It was a relief and a sorrow at the same time. It would take time for him to let her go fully.

Winter came on the scene in a snowfall in early November, blanketing the mountains like a mother caringly covering a cold child.

Early one evening, Anton sat by the fire reading a book when he heard a knock at the door. Opening it, he was shocked to see Orama there.

"Darling, let me in! It's freezing out here." And she came inside with a rush of mixed aromas, wrapped in white furs and smelling of Tahiti sunshine and flowers. She flung her arms around his neck, and soon he was smothered with her kisses.

Her body, an octopus, enfolded his. There was no time to resist. How could he? She was incredible, and all his longing for her returned. While he was tearing off her clothes, Anton picked her up in his arms, so that by the time he put her down on the rug in front of the fire, she was fully naked, her body glowing in the firelight. If this was hell, he wanted it forever, and he made love to her again and again.

Sometime in the night Anton woke and heard a whisper. It was close to him, so close, yet there was no one there. He was in bed, but the whisper came and went, in the voice of Jacques. It said, "Vigilance, Vigilance," over and over again. Anton sat up immediately and realized that the bed was empty beside him. He then heard the water run in the bathroom.

When Orama returned to bed, he closed his eyes. She touched him gently, but he didn't respond and hoped she would think he was asleep. It was quiet, very quiet, and as he felt her body snuggle into his, he kept thinking the word *vigilance*. She moved her body against his thighs and up into his groin, slowing moving against him until he could no longer control his desire. Vigilance! he thought, as he grabbed her closer and moved into her; vigilance disappeared into her soft mouth; vigilance dissolved and was forgotten.

The days and weeks that followed were a haze. When did Anton give in to her energy? When did he begin to believe her? When did he finally succumb? All he knew was that she was real and everything else took on a spell of illusion. He remembered Jacques and his warnings; he remembered but no longer believed. His book suddenly looked amateurish and uninteresting. Anton lost all concern for anything. Orama was his only reality and only desire. He had to have her with him every moment of the day. If she left his side to go food shopping, he paced the room in fear that she wouldn't return. He wanted to possess her to the extreme, as if his life's breath depended on her being with him.

Such was his passion and love. Some would wonder at the use of the word 'love' and even he thought that what he felt could be a momentary passion that would cease or lessen as time moved on. A part of him hoped this would happen, as his will was completely bound to hers; but as the days progressed, his heart began to love her. It wasn't just the sex but something deeper, like an old forgotten promise brought to life into a world of unrequited dreams that now, for the first time, were being fulfilled. When did he first know that she had waited for him for so long? Maybe it was the day he looked at her in passing and saw her turn into a small, full bodied, blond woman, or was it the time when she turned her back and he saw a lean, young boy who held his hand and called him Father?

When Orama left to go to Zürich, Anton wanted to go with her. She said no, and he knew she really meant it. If he followed her again, it would be very destructive. He recognized this even as he protested.

"Why can't I come with you?" he asked.

"I have business to accomplish, and you will be distracting. Besides," and she smiled sensuously, "when I return you will have missed me, and then it will be divine."

"It's always divine." He didn't realize how mistaken that word could be. "All right, then, but promise you will work quickly and return to me."

"I promise."

The day she drove away was a beautiful day; low, blue clouds banked the sky and the mountains, and the crisp, cold air felt like ice refreshing a drink. It was a day in early December, and, even though it had snowed, the major storms hadn't arrived yet. Orama's car was a small one not really suited for the mountains. Anton begged her to drive carefully, as the roads were difficult for the best of drivers. She waved, and laughed, and blew him a kiss.

That was the last time he saw her. Three days later the phone rang. It was Orama's gallery in Zürich calling to inform him that she had been in an automobile accident and had died instantly. They said her body had been cremated and the ashes flown back to Tahiti. She had given them his phone number when she was staying with him; that's why they called.

Anton asked for her family number in Tahiti, as he wanted to attend the funeral. The number he was given was supposedly her brother's number. A man answered. After expressing his condolences, Anton said, "I loved Orama, and I plan to fly there tomorrow to attend her funeral. Can you give me the details as to where and when it will be?"

"I'm sorry, you'll be too late. We are planning to throw her ashes into the ocean tomorrow morning."

"Please, can't you wait a day? It's very important to me to say goodbye."

"No, I'm sorry. Besides, only the family is attending the ceremony."

Anton felt as if he'd been slapped in the face and again thought about her ex-lover. Maybe the man he had talked to hadn't been the brother but her lover instead, and their relationship had never ended, after all.

It was evening. Anton put on his coat and walked out into the night, seeing nothing but blackness all around him. It was bitter cold, but he felt nothing. Silently he walked on, not caring where he walked. He knew there was a ravine ahead of him, but he didn't stop. He didn't care. An inner part of him wailed at life and didn't want it anymore. He walked until he put one foot out and felt no ground beneath it. He stepped backward, stood there in a place of indecision, and then felt the need to go forward. He started to put his foot forward but again stopped and drew his foot back. When he did this once more, he felt himself being pulled back a few feet; and he stood shaking, for what seemed like an eternity, until he fell on the ground sobbing.

CHAPTER 15

Pain — had he known it before? Anton remembered when his grandmother had died. He loved her very much, and he still missed her laugh and when she smiled at him with such love, but that pain was not like this. When he had fallen while skiing and had broken his leg, it hurt badly until they got him down from the mountain, but that pain was not like this. This was different. It was as if he had lost a limb: the feel of it remained, but it was completely gone.

When the pain became numbness, he cursed Jacques, and in his craziness believed that Jacques had caused this to happen. If he didn't want me to be with Orama, couldn't he have done something to prevent it? Anton blamed Jacques, and, when he cursed him, burned the printed pages of the book; but when he went to erase it from his computer, he couldn't do it. The creative instinct was so strong in him that he could never destroy what he had written, just as he could never destroy a painting or any inspired object. The book came from his soul, so he couldn't destroy it, and, even in his anguish, he carefully made another copy of his transcribed notes just in case he might go insane and erase them from his computer.

Anton put the copy in a box and mailed it and a computer disk to his post-office box in Zürich. Then he could rant and rage at Jacques without worry.

He wanted to kill him, and, if there hadn't been a snowstorm that prevented him from leaving home, would have acted on his desire. He would have found him no matter where he was and would have murdered him. That was how strong his rage was.

As the snow fell on the mountains, Anton's anger subsided into cold resolve. He would never see Jacques or anyone connected with him again. Whether Jacques had purposely killed Orama or not, he had been wrong about her. And he would have caused Anton to lose her, even if she hadn't come. But to lose her this way was much worse. He blamed himself for luring her to Grindelwald. If he hadn't listened to Jacques, he would have gotten in touch with her and gone back to Tahiti or met her in Zürich. She would still be alive if he hadn't listened to him. And if he had insisted on going back with her to Zürich, he would have driven. Anton knew these roads. There would have been no accident. Guilt consumed him for days on end.

Soon it would be Christmas, and the family, as always, planned to spend it at their home in the mountains. He could not see them, he couldn't see anyone. He thought about telling them about Orama, but he couldn't do that either. Anton had never talked about anyone he was dating, except Beatrice, because they knew her.

When he called his father to tell him he had to go to America on business—something to do with a publisher about the book—there was a long silence. Then his father protested and said, "Except for the time you were in the valley, you have never missed Christmas with the family. Why can't you go to New York after the holidays?"

"That's the only time the publisher can see me. Sorry, Dad, this has to come first."

His father hung up with a sad, soft farewell. It was Anton's first withdrawal from the family.

He decided that rather than lie completely he would do what he had said and go to America. He hadn't been to New York City for a while, and maybe seeing an opera and some shows would help lift his mood.

Anton never knew how lonely Christmas could feel. He walked the city streets of New York, looked at all the decorations in the shop windows of Fifth Avenue, sipped hot chocolate at a café, and thought about Orama. He saw the beautiful clothes in Saks and thought about how they would look on Orama. He stood at the rail at Rockefeller Center, looked down at the skaters below, and imagined skating with Orama. Everywhere he went he saw her. She ran for a bus when he reached out to her. She sat down on a park bench and patted a dog. Every dark-skinned woman became Orama until Anton couldn't stand it anymore and just stayed in his hotel room watching Christmas festivities on TV.

He planned to stay for a week to make certain that all the family were gone when he returned. On Christmas Eve he called to wish them happy holidays and spoke to his mother. He could tell she was worried about him. Her voice was so loving that he felt tempted to tell her everything; but instead, he said he would see them soon and hung up.

Later, he watched an old film on TV: *It's a Wonderful Life*, the one with James Stewart, who lost his business and nearly killed himself but was saved at the end. He turned it off in the middle, as being saved on Christmas Eve made his feelings erupt. Instead, he went downstairs to the bar for a drink. Anton felt like drinking away the evening, drinking away Christmas and all the good memories.

The bar was practically deserted. It was dark inside with red carpeting and black leather bar chairs—a warm and cozy ambiance for the up-scale customers. Tonight, it felt right.

At other times, he loathed places catering to wealthy clientele, with prices for only those who could afford the luxury of such settings. But now, he welcomed the soft elegance of the leather chair and sat back in it with a sigh, enjoying the dark surroundings and the mellow atmosphere.

As Anton sipped his drink, a tall woman entered the room and came directly in his direction, sitting in the bar chair next to him. Since the bar was empty, he thought this odd, but he just swiveled his chair in another direction to make it clear he didn't want to talk. He felt a tap on his arm. As he turned around, he looked at the woman who sat next to him.

"What do you want?" he indignantly asked, expecting some trite answer.

"I need to talk to you," she quietly replied.

Anton could see her clearly now and was startled. She reminded him of someone, but he couldn't place her. She was very attractive, tall, with blond hair that gently flowed around her oval face and rested on her shoulders before moving down her back. Her eyes were a deep blue, with some green reflected from her simple green dress.

"Do I know you?" His voice was calmer.

"We know of each other. I am Jacques' daughter, Samantha. I think we bumped into each other in his driveway."

"Jacques' daughter. Yes, I remember. But what are you doing here? Don't tell me I'm being followed?" He could feel his fury rising.

"Yes, and it's important that we speak."

She looked around the bar. "But not here, it's too open, and there are spies who also know where you are. Here is my card. Stay after I leave and then come to my room. It's in this hotel. Be careful." She touched his hand and he felt her card come into it.

He turned away and heard her put down a glass and ask for the bill. After she left, Anton ordered a third drink, and really took time to drink it. He looked around the room and noticed that the only other people there were a couple holding hands at a table in the corner. But he still waited. Somehow, he felt the need to wait, watching everything through half-closed eyes. A man came in and sat at the bar. Even he was a threat now. The longer Anton waited the more paranoid he became, until he finally said to himself, The hell with it! He needed to find out why he was being followed, what new scheme was on the burner. He paid his bill and hurried out onto the street.

After walking a couple of blocks in the wrong direction, he turned quickly and doubled back to see if the man or the couple were following him. It was already late, and he was the only one on the street. When he entered the hotel, he took the elevator to the woman's room and quietly knocked. There was no answer, so Anton knocked a little louder. He could hear someone stir and finally call, "Who's there?"

"Is Samantha there?"

He could hear footsteps now and the door opened. The man starring at him was a stranger. Anton looked at his card and saw that he wasn't mistaken. This was the number she'd given him.

"Come in, Anton. My name is Martin. I must have fallen asleep while I waited for you."

He opened the door wider, and Anton walked into a large room with a sitting area and a bed on the other side of the room.

"I thought Samantha wanted to see me. Where is she?"

"Gone to spend Christmas with her father, I expect. It seemed more likely that you would follow Sam than me. You know, a man doesn't question a beautiful woman. She was to find you and I was to talk to you. Sit down, have a drink." And he walked over to the bar and poured two straight scotches.

Earlier Anton had had three drinks, but suddenly he was very clear-headed and focused. Still, he was cautious drinking this one and put it on the table to sit for a while.

"Okay, I'm here. What does Jacques want?"

Martin smiled, "Jacques never wants anything, but he asked me to help you remember a past life."

"But why does he want me to do this now, at this time, when he knows how I am feeling about him?"

"He believes it will help you understand your feelings more."

"But how can you help me remember a past life?"

"I'm a psychotherapist, and I do past life regression."

Anton believed in reincarnation, but this felt bizarre. "If he wants me to know about a past life, why couldn't he just email me the information?"

"It's important for you to experience it. Otherwise, it's just a story. Have you ever seen a past life before?"

"Not really. Once in meditation, I saw a scene that looked Egyptian, but it lasted only for a minute, and recently I had a glimpse of two lifetimes with a woman I knew."

"Well, are you willing to try now?"

Anton wanted to say no, but somehow his reply was, "Yes, I'll try."

Martin took him through an induction that was somewhat hypnotic. Anton was asked to visualize himself walking over a bridge, and when he stepped down on the other side, he saw himself in a scene.

He was standing by the railing of a small balcony several stories up with a lovely view of gardens and rolling hills. Behind him were open French doors that led into a small sitting room. He knew himself as "Robert," and he was trying to decide whether to jump. His reasoning was cold and calculating, without emotion, and his thoughts were clear: "If I jump, I will end the turmoil. No one will have to choose between us. My brother Richard will inherit it all — the title, the manor — and Harriet won't have to decide about marrying me. Ending my life would be so easy, but it would devastate Richard, as he would know I did it because I loved him. He would be the heir then, and the family would stop fighting."

He heard Martin's voice say, "Go to an earlier scene with him."

"I see myself playing with another boy. I think he is my twin brother."

Martin said, "How old are you?"

"Around eight years old."

"Can you see his face? If you can, look into his eyes and notice if he is someone you know in this life."

"I don't know. I can't see him clearly."

Martin said, "All right. Go forward in time to the next important thing that happens to you."

"I think we are older, maybe in our twenties, and we are sitting in the living room with our parents. They are arguing. Since we are twins, the question is who should inherit the estate and title. In English law there could only be one heir. My father is adamant that, since I, Robert, was the first child to emerge from the womb, I am legally the heir. My mother, though, insists that my brother, Richard, is more responsible and would do a better job, so he should be the heir. He is her favorite, and I think she feels he would take better care of her. The more they argue, the more I feel Richard detach himself from me. He desires the inheritance so very much." Anton paused, still in the scene, listening to his parents.

"I want to tell my father to give it to him. I don't want the money or the title. But then there is Harriet."

Martin said, "Who is Harriet? Go to a scene with Harriet."

"I see a young woman around my age, blond hair, really beautiful and charming."

"Can you see her face?"

"No, not really, but I fell desperately in love with her."

"Does she love you?"

"I don't know. I know she loves my status."

Martin said, "Go forward in time to the next important thing that happens."

"I'm back on the balcony. My hands are on the rail, and I start to push myself up. I feel someone grab me from behind. He says, 'No you don't. That is never the answer!'

"'Let me go!' I shout. 'You have no right to stop me.'

"'I have every right,' my brother shouts back. 'Damn them, damn the law! This is about us. Let us decide what's fair.'

"And then I turn to look into my brother's eyes—and see that they are not Richard's but Jacques' eyes. 'It's not fair that I get everything.' I say. 'Mother's right: what's fair is that you have the title and the estate. But if that happens, I may lose Harriet.'

"'We can run the estate together,' my brother answers. 'I don't need the title of Earl. I need you and we need each other; we always have. Does Harriet only want you for your title?'

"'I don't know, I think it's important to her.'

"'If that is the case and she doesn't love you for yourself, it's going to end up a loveless marriage. I suggest you tell her that you gave everything to me and then see if she still loves you enough to marry you.'"

Martin interjected, "If you do decide to do as Richard suggests, go forward to that scene with Harriet."

"We are seated outside on a bench in the garden. I tell her that I gave my inheritance to Richard. She looks shocked."

"'Why did you do that?'"

"'He will do a better job than I would.'"

"'I can't believe you would give everything up.'"

"'But I'm not giving everything up. We can still be together. I will have enough money for a family and us. Richard and I plan to do the work together, so we can still live here in the manor.'"

"Harriet's beautiful face becomes distorted with anger, and she says, 'No way would I be second to Richard and his family. That was stupid of you, really stupid!' As she gets up to leave and turns to me to say farewell, I see her face clearly and am startled to recognize Orama. When I recognize who she is, I again feel my loss and know that, if I hadn't listened to Richard/Jacques, I wouldn't have lost either woman."

The shock woke Anton out of the past life, and he opened his eyes and told Martin, "It's Orama! I can't believe it's her!"

Martin took a sip of his drink. "I think that's enough for now. How do you feel?"

"I don't know. I think I feel upset."

"Anything else?"

"My feelings are mixed. A part of me feels angry that I listened to him because I lost her." He thought for a minute. "Jacques saved me from her in that life, and he wanted to save me from her in this life, but I didn't listen."

"That's a good understanding."

"Martin, thank you. Why did you do this? It's Christmas Eve! Do you have a family?"

"Yes, close by in Westchester." Martin looked at his watch. "I think I can still get the last train home."

"But why do you follow Jacques' request and leave your family to come here to help me?"

Martin thought a minute. "Both my wife and I are his disciples. Of course, I would help you."

"He's your teacher? He's a spiritual teacher, like a guru?"

"Yes, don't you know that?"

"Yes and no. I knew he was my teacher, and I felt he had certain powers, but I never thought about him being a spiritual teacher, a guru in the Eastern tradition with disciples."

Though, in retrospect, of course it made sense that Jacques was a guru, thought

Anton. That would explain everything that had happened to him. He suddenly remembered how he'd cursed Jacques and felt ashamed. He also realized that Jacques had saved him from committing suicide, not only in his past life but also in this one. Both times, the hand that had pulled him back from the brink had been Jacques'.

CHAPTER 16

When Anton awoke the next day, he meditated on his past life. He then stayed in his room all morning and thought about his relationship with Jacques. The distrust he felt toward him in this life had been caused by what had happened with Orama. Before that, he had questioned but then eventually accepted everything Jacques had said to him. Now, understanding what happened in the other lifetime, he realized that his anger toward Jacques in this life had hidden roots in what had happened before. How could he blame him for Orama's death? But he did, which was also odd.

Before lunch, Anton felt tired and took a nap. He dreamed he saw Jacques dressed in the clothing of that past life. In a very kindly way, Jacques said, "I think we need to talk."

"No, I never want to talk to you again!" Anton responded in the dream. And then he woke up, surprised at his reaction. Was it because of the feelings he still had about Orama's death, or was it because of his shame?

Anton flew home the first week in January, feeling less sad and with seeds of hope again in his heart. The past was the past. He could never bring Orama back, so why not move on? He couldn't resolve his feelings around Jacques, so he put those aside, also.

His condo was vacant, and he moved back in. Going home to the mountains would only bring up memories, and part of starting over was to be in Zürich with family and friends and lots of activities.

Soon, he settled down into a good routine of writing during the day and spending his evenings socializing. After a couple of weeks, he decided to go to Orama's gallery to see if some of her work was still there. He liked what he had bought from her and thought about buying another piece. It was good to have her sculptures in his home; strangely enough, it made him feel not sad but happy. He still couldn't believe she had followed a negative teaching, as he felt her art was full of positive energy. It didn't occur to him that it could be otherwise.

Anton visited the gallery one afternoon and introduced himself to the manager, an American named Harvey Green. Mr. Green was a small man in his fifties, with dark hair splattered with gray and bold, brown eyes that looked at him with business-like intent. He was the man to whom Anton had spoken when Orama had had her accident. When Anton told him his name, he could tell Mr. Green was taken aback, but he quickly recovered and said, "It's so good to meet you, Anton." His eyes looked downward. "Such a tragic accident. We all miss her terribly."

Anton agreed and asked, "I would like to get another one of her statues. Do you have any for sale?"

"No, I'm afraid not. They have all been sold."

Just then, Anton noticed a statue in the corner that looked very much like her work, and he immediately went to look at it. Mr. Green followed, saying, "That one has already been sold. As I said, they have all been sold."

Indeed, it was her work, but the style was different from the ones Anton had seen.

"This is lovely. When did she do it? It's unlike her other work."

"I think it's an early one." He grabbed a sheet with names and prices, glanced down at it, and said, "Yes, it was done five years ago. We had it in the backroom and brought it out recently."

For some reason, Anton felt he was lying. But why would he lie? It didn't make sense.

"Are you certain there are no more back there?"

"Yes, but if we receive any more from Tahiti, I will call you."

They exchanged cards, and then Mr. Green's assistants called him to the phone.

Anton took one final look at the sculpture and turned to go. By the door, he saw another sheet with prices on it and looked at the selling price of the sculpture. To his astonishment, the date the sculpture had been created was listed as this year, not five years earlier.

This explained Mr. Green's strange behavior: he had lied to Anton about the date and put a false date on the piece.

Anton waited for him to finish his phone call, and then he asked him, "Why did you put a false date on her piece?"

Even more taken aback, Mr. Green hesitated and said, "I am so sorry. Yes, it's true; I lied about the date because her collectors don't know about her death. Many times, when an artist dies and the artist hasn't developed a large enough reputation, the remaining works are not bought up. If the collector thinks an artist is still producing, that's another story. We will announce her death later this year after we have sold her remaining pieces."

"But that's fraud and you're a reputable gallery!" Anton felt very indignant.

"What can I say? It's a common practice of the best of galleries, not just us. Now I must prepare for an appointment." He turned and walked back to his office.

By the end of February, Anton longed to return to the mountains. But before he left Zürich he made a date with Lea Heroch. They had not spoken for a long time, and he looked forward to telling her all the things that had happened. They met at a new Italian restaurant in town.

Seated across from her in the soft candlelight, he realized how very attractive she was. He was beginning to miss the companionship of women and could feel a tinge of renewed interest rising in him. Almost in response, she said, "I heard that you lost someone you loved deeply."

He wasn't surprised that she knew. "Yes, it was sudden, in a car accident, and I guess I blame myself because I hadn't insisted on driving her. The mountain roads can be treacherous if you don't know them."

"Don't blame yourself, Anton. People's death dates are predestined. It is obvious that she was meant to go. Sad, but that is fate."

They talked for a while, and then Anton asked, "How is Jacques?"

"He's fine and at home for a while. Why don't you call him? I know he would love to see you."

"Maybe I will." He didn't mean those words. He wasn't ready to see Jacques yet.

Lea read him so well. "It shouldn't be that difficult. You know he loves you."

"Yes." Anton changed the subject. "I would like your advice about something. I've been thinking about teaching some of the material that is in the book, particularly about the subtle world. Is it crazy for me to consider this, and, if I should try, where would I start? Probably not Switzerland; it's just too conservative here."

Lea took up her knife, and, holding it vertically, spun it on its base until it fell onto the tablecloth. "You see what happened to the knife. It cannot spin by itself without falling."

Then she spun it again and, this time when it started getting off balance, grabbed it to spin it anew. "Just like the knife, you cannot teach by yourself. You need help, the unseen hand to keep you focused in the work. The knife knows its job is to cut through food, just as your job is to cut through old ways of thinking. Believe in that, and believe in the help, and it will happen. Just know you are not alone."

Her words comforted Anton and soothed his fears. She was right. He knew intuitively that, if he were meant to teach this material, everything would fall into place.

Lea laughed, placed the knife down, and then became very serious. "That doesn't mean that the knife doesn't crash once in a while, spinning too fast to be held. But that is also about learning. Even the knife has to learn when to cut or let a sharper knife do the job."

Looking into her eyes, he felt her compassion. "It's never easy, Anton. It's never easy to walk the path. I'm on it, too, you know, and even when there are others who share the same knowledge, it's still a lonely path because it's up to each individual to set the pace."

"I know. I'm still on the road, but I know, when it turns into a path, it will be like my paths in the mountains. Sometimes they are straight and easy to walk, and then some turn into rocky terrain and need great skill and climbing ability to maneuver. I've always known that no one's path is the same. When I take the difficult paths on the mountain, I rarely meet another person, even though I know that others before and after me travel the same path. Telling me that I will be alone makes sense."

"Alone, but not really. We can share some things, and help is always there."

When they parted, Anton kissed Lea lightly on the lips and resisted pressing for more. Something had happened during their time together. Their relationship had changed; how was still to be discovered.

CHAPTER 17

At home in the mountains, Anton became the recluse again. The family called often, but no one came up. Even his brothers found another place to ski closer to their own homes. They all somehow sensed his wanting to be alone, and, even though no one spoke about it, he could feel an underlying worry about him when he talked to them, especially his mother. In the daytime, he wrote and edited the book, but at night he relaxed by the fire and read.

One day he decided to change his routine, going into town to buy a paper and have some Swiss hot chocolate. The café he went to was a very popular one. It had an arrangement of good pastries and loaves of homemade bread beside the yummy chocolate. Since it was still skiing season, many skiers were around who had finished their early morning run and were having a break before resuming. Anton arrived before most of them came in and so was able to find a small table in the corner.

Today, he didn't look at anyone but was bent over immersed in reading the news as he sipped his chocolate. When he felt a tap on his shoulder it startled him. He looked up to see Hedy Brunner, an old university friend.

Jumping up, he embraced her and then offered her a seat. Anton looked at her and saw how much she had changed. In school, she had been pretty, with a girlish quality that made her face shine with energy.

She was short and a little stocky, which before wasn't noticeable because she moved quickly, with enthusiasm; but now, somehow, she had lost that quality and looked heavier, tired, and reserved. Her long brown hair currently was cut in a short bob, but her hazel eyes still had life in them.

Hedy smiled at him, "Darling Anton, how wonderful to see you! I'd forgotten that you lived in this part of the world."

"Yes, but I'm never normally here at this time. I've taken a sabbatical to work on a book I am writing. But how are you? How is Graf? And your children?"

"Fine, all of us are fine. He is still on the mountain, and Erik and Jeanne are both with their grandparents nursing colds. But tell me about your book."

"Oh, it's just another book about my work: not a textbook but a teaching book, nevertheless. But you're the writer. Whatever happened to your novel?"

"Marriage and children are what happened. It's on the shelf waiting for the time when I'm freer to complete it. I'm teaching also now, so I'm just too busy."

"What a shame, it sounded like a good story. You must promise to finish it and not wait too long. Where are you teaching?"

"At my local gymnasium. Teaching English and really enjoying it. Quite a departure from teaching university courses, but it's fun and keeps me in the field."

She ordered a hot chocolate, and he ordered another one. The talk turned to the usual, about people they knew and what had happened to them. Hedy and Graf lived in Rapperswil, a small town on the north shore of Lake Zürich, just far enough away for Anton to have lost contact with them over the years, so it was wonderful to see her and schmooze about the past.

When she got up to leave to meet Graf on the slope, he suddenly felt lonely and didn't want her to go. "Can the two of you have dinner at my place this evening? I'm not a great cook, but if you don't mind simple fare, I would love to have you come."

"That would be great. I'm sure Graf would be delighted to see you again."

That evening was crystal clear. It had snowed earlier, but the night sky was cloudless, and the stars were supreme in their radiance, taking over the blackness of the sky.

When the Brunners arrived, Anton had a big fire blazing in the fireplace and hors d'oeuvres and wine on the table in front of it.

Anton liked Graf even though he had only seen him a few times. Graf had met Hedy after university when she returned to Basel, her hometown. He was Black, six feet tall, with curly black hair that playfully spiraled and swirled around his square face. His intelligent, warm dark eyes made Anton feel he was a friend right away.

Anton expected this to be a casual, social evening, but tonight was different. Maybe it was the warmth of the fire or the wine, but before long they were no longer chit-chatting but talking about more serious subjects.

Graf started it. "Anton, a strange thing happened to me today when I was skiing. It concerns you, so maybe you can explain it."

"I'll try. What happened?"

He looked at Hedy, "I haven't told Hedy, but I took a nasty fall. I thought I might have broken my leg, as it hurt terribly and immediately started to swell. I was sitting on the snow, feeling the leg to see if there were any bones sticking out, when another skier stopped and asked me what the matter was. I told him, and he said the strangest thing. I will try to repeat it as I heard it." Graf paused for a moment, looking very intense.

"The man said, 'Graf, your leg is fine. It isn't broken, and you will be able to stand on it in about five minutes. Tell Anton this evening that I hope he is well and working on the book. Tell him also that there is a section of the book that still needs to be received. It will be given to him next week when he meditates. And he then skied away. Of course, I didn't know what he was talking about until I met Hedy, and she said we were invited to your house for dinner."

"He knew your name and that you were going to see Anton?" Hedy was shocked.

"Yes, but I didn't realize that was odd at the time; otherwise, I would have asked him how he knew my name. I assure you, I've never met him before that I know of. And by the way, my leg suddenly felt fine, when before I had been in a great deal of pain."

"What did he look like?" I asked.

"It was difficult to tell because he had on a ski mask. His eyes were blue, and that's about all I can tell you. He was a good skier, tall and slim."

"Did he look old?" It had to be Jacques, as he'd told Anton he was a good skier.

"Well, you know, I did have a sense that he was older. Something in the manner of his speech, and he did have wrinkles around his eyes—beautiful eyes, kindly, and even fatherly."

"Thank you for delivering the message."

"He must know you and know you are here. Why didn't he just come and tell you himself?" Hedy made a good point.

"Yes, he knows me, and I know him, but right now we aren't speaking." Anton could see that his words had a negative effect and added, "It's not about us having a disagreement. It's something much different, which I can't explain."

They looked at each other, and he realized what they were thinking.

"No, we're not lovers. I'm very heterosexual, as you should know, Hedy. He's my spiritual teacher, and he chooses to let me do my work without any interference." He spoke the words almost casually and then instantly regretted it.

"Your spiritual teacher! Please tell us about it," Graf said, truly looking interested.

Anton found himself telling them the whole story of how he had met Jacques and of his stay in the mountains and writing the teaching book. The words spilled out of his mouth and, even when he felt he should stop, more came. Finally, he ended by saying, "I'm sorry for going on and not letting you talk. I didn't realize how much I needed to talk about all this. I've been pretty isolated here."

"No, please," Graf replied, "I find your story fascinating, and this teacher of yours is extraordinary. How does one get to meet him other than on a ski slope?"

Anton hesitated, "I don't really know. I think if you really truly want that you can simply send the desire to him, and he will respond. I somehow think that is the proper way. Otherwise, I can give you the name of a close disciple of his who I'm sure would convey your message. But why are you interested in meeting him?" he added.

Graf thought for a minute. "I can still see his eyes and feel his energy, and something in me has a strong desire to speak to him again. I don't know anything about spiritual things. I've never been religious, but this is different, and I want to know more about it."

Anton noticed that Hedy was staying too quiet. She looked at Graf with bewilderment and disbelief in her eyes.

Graf also noticed and took her hand. "Darling, it's okay. I'm not going to do anything crazy."

"But getting involved in a cult? That's crazy!"

"It's not a cult," Anton protested. "There is nothing cultist about it."

Hedy turned to him with anger in her eyes, "It's not a cult? How can you say that? It sounds as if you are completely controlled by him and that you have to do as he says. Your whole life is wrapped up in this. That speaks of cultism to me. And now you are influencing Graf."

"Wait a minute, Hedy. That's not true," Graf responded. "Anton has done nothing to influence me. How I feel comes from meeting Jacques this afternoon. If you had been there, you would understand."

"Well, I wasn't there, and I assure you no stranger would control my life. Look at Anton here. He is totally controlled by him. I listened to his story, also, and I'll be honest, Anton." She looked at me. "It scared me. You're a brilliant man; don't let this happen to you."

Anton again protested, but something in his heart felt her fear.

He quietly said to Graf, when Hedy went to the bathroom, "Put it all in your heart. Let your heart direct you as to what you need to do. There is nothing to fear that way. Don't listen to Hedy."

He nodded. But Anton could see that Graf had become uncertain.

After they left, he sat by the fire and tried not to feel the fear in his heart. Jacques was his teacher, and he was very powerful. What if he *were* the leader of a cult—a different kind of cult, but essentially a cult, anyway? The people around Jacques were different types from most, but would any of them question anything Jacques said? He remembered his questions in the past and how they always fell apart when he saw Jacques. Didn't that come under the definition of cultism? The leader controlled everything and everyone.

The manuscript of his book was on the table next to his chair. He picked it up and read the first page. He needed to read it for reassurance:

PROLOGUE

In the beginning, all was energy, and what came out of this energy was form, and that form had life. Throughout the ages, the form changed and became new forms, but the energy within them stayed the same. Whether these forms were rocks, or trees, or animals, or men and women, the energy within them came from the original Source, which was given many names by many religions. Whether it was called God, or Brahman, or Zoroaster, or the sun, or any of the ancient names long forgotten, the Divine Source was within all forms of matter.

We, as individuals, feel this energy in what we term the soul; we feel it in our hearts, we feel it when we experience beauty, and we feel it most of all when we love. Men and women, no matter what their ethnic or religious background, feel this energy the same way.

Zarathustra guides others to recognize this energy within. His mission is to help them use this energy in their daily lives. Men and women at this time hide the energy by pursuing life in a fatalistic way rather than as a journey to return to the Source.

> *Zarathustra's journey begins with love and ends with love.*
> *Zarathustra's journey comes at a time when all need to understand the difference between life in the physical and life in the subtle.*
> *Zarathustra's journey acknowledges all forms of the Divine, whether it be man and woman, animal, plant, or even the water that surrounds the planet.*
> *Zarathustra's journey encounters all kinds of prejudice, deceit, hatred, malice, and fanaticism.*
> *If you want to make this journey, you need to open your heart, your mind, and your desire for learning more about the different planes of existence.*
> *If you want to make this journey, you need to be willing to face change, obstacles, and being alone.*
> *If you want to make this journey, you must become strong and courageous, loving, and caring, disciplined, and unafraid of any challenge.*
> *Most of all, you must be willing to give up old concepts and open your heart to new ways of seeing.*
> *Zarathustra has come again to teach about the divine energy.*

Anton laid down the manuscript and thought about some of the concepts taught in it. He himself experienced this divine energy and knew it to be true. He felt his heart respond in joy when it was filled with this energy, and he found bliss that he could never explain to anyone. This came from his inner being, not from Jacques. All Jacques did, like Zarathustra in the book, was to guide him to that Source within himself. He thought:

A true teacher does this. A teacher in a cult is false and doesn't give but only takes.

A true teacher guides. A false teacher controls.

A true teacher protects. A false teacher only protects those that are submissive to him/her.

A true teacher leads students forward on the path, letting them face their own obstacles. A false teacher keeps students in the same place, not letting them face anything for themselves, knowing that, if the students become strong, then they may see the teacher's false nature.

A true teacher is training all the students to become teachers. A false teacher would never train any student to that level. The false teacher has to be the only teacher.

The fear left Anton's heart. His teacher was true. He was not in a cult but in an esoteric teaching that would guide him on the path to God—what he called the Divine Source within himself—and help him realize new knowledge about the levels of existence. It was an exciting adventure from which he could never turn back.

He also knew that if Graf's heart felt strong enough, he would not listen to Hedy. Jacques would find him again. If it was destined, it would happen.

He fell asleep by the fire, feeling happy and thankful.

CHAPTER 18

It was late April. Anton had just returned from Zürich after doing a couple of lectures and visiting friends. The weather became brisk, and spring descended on the mountains so that he now could take long invigorating walks. The days were longer and the nights clearer. He always liked being alone; it was too early for the hikers, and the skiers were still on the slopes.

The book was almost finished. The additional notes were given to him in meditation. He didn't see Hedy or Graf again, but he heard from Jacques. It was a short note that arrived in the mail. It simply said that Graf had contacted him, and they met. This delighted Anton for some reason. Maybe what he said had been instrumental. He knew somehow that the meeting went well, and Graf was now on the path with or without Hedy's approval. "Bravo Graf," he cried out in excitement, and the sound echoed throughout the house.

He had just finished his coffee when a voice behind him said, "Who's Graf and what has he done?"

Anton jumped up and saw his sister there, full of bundles and with a big grin on her face.

"Kristina, what are you doing here?"

"I thought I would surprise you, and I guess I have."

"Yes, it's a wonderful surprise!" And he hugged her.

"Watch out for the eggs. Let me put these down." And she dumped all the packages into a chair nearby.

"Are you alone, or is Felix with you?"

"All alone, Brother dear. I'll be the only one pestering you for a week. Unless, of course, you can't stand me. Then I will leave sooner."

"That never would happen. I'm so happy to see you."

"When I saw the good weather forecast, I decided on the spur of the moment to take time off and come home. Did try to phone you but never got through, so I came anyway. But tell me about Graf."

"Oh, he's just a friend. You don't know him. He did something that was brave, and it made me happy. It's nothing important. But tell me, how is everyone? I've heard very little in the past few months."

"Everyone's fine. But let me put these groceries away and then we can talk. I figured you haven't had a good meal for a long time."

"You're right. I'll get your luggage."

After everything was settled, they sat down with fresh coffee, and she told him the news. "As you know, Mom and Dad are traveling again, this time to America, but they're not too happy about it." And she told him some new gossip about their friends there.

"And Erick and Jonas are both doing well." She took a breath. "They are still the confirmed bachelors, but there is a new love interest for Jonas. Who knows, maybe he will finally settle down." And she talked a little bit about Jonas's girlfriend, and about Felix and the boys.

They ended the day in quiet companionship by the fire.

The next day they went on a picnic, and when they returned, they sat on the closed-in porch enjoying the afternoon sun. Anton told Kristina a little bit about the book, still not wanting to have the family inquire too deeply. He knew that when it was published most of his family would be astonished by its content. Kristina took after their mother, open and receptive, so he explained the general contents without going into any details. She asked to read some of it while she was there, and he said no, that he wanted to give it to everyone at the same time. She promised not to tell anyone, and finally, after a lot of cajoling on her part, he said he would let her read the first few chapters. Later he regretted it, but at the time he wanted to please her.

That evening he gave her the chapters, and they sat quietly in front of the fire reading. Once in a while, he glanced up to see her expression. She looked calm enough, but there was a tension in the way her mouth set that made him feel she wasn't understanding the book or thought it was totally off. If his sister reacted this way, he could imagine what the rest of the family would do. Maybe his mother would be more open. That was his only hope at this point.

When Kristina finished her reading, she put it down and said nothing. Finally, she looked at him and said, "Anton, this is very strange; it's really hard for me to believe or understand. Is the rest of the book the same as these chapters?"

"Yes, of course. This is the essence of what the book is about."

"How do you expect anyone to accept this?"

"I have no expectations at all."

"But surely you must see how it will be taken by your profession and your colleagues. They will think you mad."

"I don't care what they think. What I wrote is true."

"And the family. My God! Dad will be very upset."

He could feel her negative energy filling the room. "I made a mistake in letting you read it, Kristina. I hold you to your promise not to say anything to the family."

He looked at his watch. It was only 10 p.m., but he said, "It's getting late and I feel tired, and you also must be fatigued from the long hike today. Let's call it a day." He stood up and added, "I don't want to discuss my book again."

"But—" Before she could finish the sentence, he was on his way to his room. He remembered to pick up the manuscript on the way out.

When Anton awoke the next morning, he found the manuscript on his bedside table where he had put it the previous night. But picking it up, he saw that it had been opened to a particular page by some hand other than his. At the top of the page was a red mark next to the line where Zarathustra mentions his teacher. The mark hadn't been there before, and he sat in wonderment about phenomena such as this one that constantly happened to him. It was a shame he couldn't share some of it with Kristina. He felt the loneliness suddenly of what it was like never to be able to talk to anyone in his family or friends about the most important things that happened in his life. Kristina was right. They would all consider him deranged because of living in the valley.

It was late. Anton had slept longer than he usually did, so he quickly dressed and went downstairs to find Kristina busy making breakfast.

"Good, you're up. I was just about to call you."

He poured himself a cup of coffee. "Whatever you are making smells wonderful."

"Just an omelet. Hope you like a lot of cheese."

They ate in silence for a while until the phone rang.

"It's your office," and he handed her the phone.

"Oh, that's terrible. All right, I'll leave right away."

After she hung up, he asked, "What happened?"

"A five-year-old patient of mine has suddenly taken a turn for the worse, so I need to get back to take care of him. He's been recovering from meningitis and doing really well." She shook her head. "Such a sweet kid. It would be terrible if he doesn't make it."

Kristina quickly gathered her things and drove away. A part of him felt relieved. She hadn't mentioned the book again, but the tension around it remained.

The day was sunny and crisp, so he put on his jacket and hiking boots and set off on a trail that passed through meadows and around some of the scattered forests of arolla pines, their branches curved upward like a many-armed candelabrum. He picked a couple of nuts from a tree and ate them. They tasted like pine nuts, which Anton knew came from stone pine or Swiss pine.

The trail also went through spruce trees with bark adorned with many shades of gray. Anton stayed low on the terrain to avoid trails that were still icy. Walking at a leisurely pace, he enjoyed being alone in the mountain's nobility.

After a couple hours of hiking, he found a big tree to rest against comfortably for what he thought would be a short time. But as soon as he sat down and leaned against the trunk, he fell into a deep meditation in which he saw the following:

He was climbing the mountain again, but the mountain was different from any of the mountains in Switzerland. The path was black dirt, and the mountainside was bare, with only patches of red-clay dirt and stunning boulders of crimson-colored rock. He felt as if he were floating upward, even though he could see his feet firmly on the path. Looking up, he saw at the top of the mountain a Tibetan temple. It had a series of square-shaped sections that looked like descending blocks all attached to one another. The sides were white-washed and had dark-brown beams cutting through them horizontally. At the top of each unit was a dark-brown tile roof that tilted upward at the corners. A tall, white wall surrounded the temple and sat on top of a sheer cliff that dropped down the mountain. The full sun highlighted the building in its serene surroundings, making it an abode of the gods.

The temple seemed far away, but in just a short time he stood in front of the gate-way. No one was around. He expected to see monks there, but none were in sight, and he had a sense that this temple was too problematic to be lived in. Not only was it at the top of the mountain, which was very steep, but it also felt remote; there were no roads that came close to the path he was on.

Whoever lived in it ages ago had had to grow their own food and carry other supplies on mules from the nearest town, which he knew was many miles away. It seemed very familiar to him, and he instantly felt he had been a monk there during the early days.

The wooden door looked closed and bolted with big locks, but he simply walked through it in his subtle body. The feel of the wood molecules passed through him, creating a strange sensation. For a moment he believed that he couldn't do it and would end up trapped inside the door. The interior of the temple was dark, but he walked forward toward the central shrine as if he had done so hundreds of times. A little light flowed through a row of small, high windows. These monasteries were built with very thick walls and very small openings to keep out the cold.

The shrine stood in the rear with a gold-leaf Buddha around six feet high seated in the middle. As Anton knelt in front of it, his heart filled with a deep sadness. Looking up, he saw a different scene. The room was lit with candles, and the temple was full of monks all sitting and chanting. Small statues, candles, incense, and food offerings covered the shrine. In front of it stood a chair on a platform, and in the chair was an elderly monk who led the chanting. On the walls hung huge wall hangings, called *thangkas*, depicting the different Tibetan deities and Buddha's life. The whole interior seemed very rich with elaborate furnishings and statues that were finely carved.

Anton sat quietly listening to the chanting, noticing everything. When he looked down, he saw that he also was dressed in a yellow lama's robe and that he seemed to sit apart from most of the monks. There was a narrow mantle over the robe that had embroidered symbols on it, and he felt that a large, pointed hat was on his head. The old monk gestured to him to rise, and Anton came forward and prostrated himself before him. The elderly monk took the hat off Anton's head and placed his hands there, saying words that Anton couldn't understand but which he intuitively knew referred to his achieving some special honor. The old monk placed the hat back on Anton's head, rose, and gestured for Anton to take his seat, which he did. Then all the monks came one at a time and bowed down in front of him. The sense was that the old monk would now return home to the main seat of the order and Anton would replace him.

As this happened in his vision, Anton felt a change in himself. He was no longer Anton but had become the monk in the scene, and he felt him in his own body. How to describe it? If he were to toss a coin straight up in the air, and the coin were to flip around and around in its descent, that would be an image of himself today, striving for something but always flipping back and forth in achieving it, wasting time and energy. In contrast, in the monk's toss the coin was an arrow finding its target — straight, pure energy directed by him for a specific purpose. Anton felt the monk's energy as being strongly focused and 100 percent dedicated. The energy felt awesome, and he enjoyed it completely.

How could he take it back with him when he returned to his body; how could it be recaptured so he could have it again? In the meditation, these were Anton's thoughts as he experienced this energy, and he suddenly knew that the cause of his previous sadness had to do with his having lost the energy along the way, lost the purity of the spirit, and lost who he really was. He sat and looked at all the monks bowing and singing and felt the sadness turn into joy.

At the end of the meditation, when Anton returned to his body and opened his eyes, the joy was still there. He felt it flow through him. It wasn't a happy, elated kind of joy, but a joy of profound inner peace: "The peace that passes all understanding." He now understood Jesus's words for the first time.

The joy stayed with him for two days. He sat and meditated and felt it. He walked and observed nature and felt it. He looked at people from afar with love and felt it. He ate his food, enjoying the flavors, and felt it. He watched cats play in the grass and felt it. And most of all, he felt it within every fiber of his being, making him whole for the first time.

When it left him, he felt the loss, and with it came the longing to have it again. Over and over, he thanked the one who sent him this gift. He knew it was a gift.

CHAPTER 19

Afterr the meditation, Anton felt it was time to reconnect with Jacques. He called him, and Jacques invited him to lunch the next day at his home. When he arrived, Samantha was there and joined them. He hadn't seen her since New York and found himself happy to meet her again. She was very welcoming in her greeting and said she was pleased to see him.

Because of her presence, Jacques and Anton couldn't talk confidentially but instead spoke in general about world news.

Jacques needed to speak to someone privately after lunch, so Samantha and Anton had coffee in the living room. "Well, you are looking much better than the last time I saw you." When she spoke, he felt her warmth.

"Yes, I am better and glad to be here."

"I'm glad you're here, too. Dad said you're spending the night. That will give us more time to get to know each other. New York was very frantic." She smiled.

He had thought he would be returning home or would stay at his apartment that night, but nothing surprised him these days.

"Yes, that will be nice."

Jacques came in and invited Anton to join him in his study. They talked about all that had happened to him, and Anton looked into Jacques' blue eyes and felt a surge of love. "I have fought you, and resisted you, and denied you, but I'm over that. You are my teacher, and I trust you completely now."

"Then I think it's time for the real work to begin. You are now ready to become my disciple if you are willing to strive on the path and let go of inner desires that divert you from it."

"What do you mean by 'inner desires'?" Anton immediately thought of his sexual urges.

"No, sex is part of normal existence. I'm not asking you to become celibate, but I am asking you to let go of your attachments, such as your attachment to perfectionism and your need for others also to be perfect; your attachment to negative thoughts; your attachment to seeing things too critically; and, most of all, your attachment to wanting others to accept you. You also need to work on your emotions. These are some of the things that will keep you from expanding your horizons and facing the obstacles that can help you grow spiritually."

"That sounds like a lot to work on."

"Yes, it is, and since all these attachments mainly come from your childhood, I think it best that you do some therapy with someone who can work with the inner child. Your inner child has some deep wounds around abandonment, and it reflects in your personal relationships with women, which is why you had an obsession about Orama."

"Yes, her death was devastating for me, and her family wouldn't allow me to attend her funeral."

"Tell me what happened."

Anton explained the situation with her family and how the man, who said he was her brother, refused to let him come for the services.

Jacques thought for a minute. "How strange that they wouldn't let you go to the funeral."

"Maybe they didn't know about us."

"But she was with you for a couple of weeks, and they knew that."

"You're right, and now I do recall her saying that she had told all her close friends about me. I also told her brother that I loved her, and he said they all did, but it would be best for me not to come. I guess I felt so brokenhearted and in shock that I didn't think any more about it."

"Yes, of course, but how do you know she really died? You nearly killed yourself because of it."

Anton felt stunned and then remembered what had happened at the gallery. He told Jacques about the sculpture and the date on it.

"But why would she fake her own death? I felt she loved me."

"If she's in a negative order, which I suspect is true, she has to follow orders. She has no choice. They certainly wanted you to kill yourself."

"But why? I'm not even a disciple yet."

"They see your potential and want to stop you from achieving it."

This led to a discussion about the book, and then Jacques reached into his pocket, pulled out a box, and opened it. "I would like you to look at this. I gave it to my wife as a wedding present."

Anton saw a platinum pendant set with diamonds and emeralds. "It's very beautiful, but why are you showing it to me?"

"Look at it closely."

Anton observed that the jewels were set in a pattern of what looked like two interlocking triangles, one pointed upward and the other pointing downward. The diamonds were pointing up and the emeralds down. The final shape looked like a six-pointed star.

"It's the Jewish star."

"Yes, but it's more than that. It existed long before the Jews adopted it; in fact, it goes back to the Sumerians, but most historians believe its origin was Egyptian. It is an esoteric symbol that represents many things."

"He gave it to Anton, who held it in his hand for a minute, then returned it. "I feel the energy, but it feels positive. That's strange: Since your wife wore it, doesn't it hold her energy? You said she is now negative."

"Yes, it has some of her energy, but when she wore it, she was still positive. Before that, it was charged with a special energy to protect the wearer. She tried to keep it, but I managed to retrieve it before she left. The energy is very special as my Mahatma charged it."

"I've heard about the Mahatmas in my Eastern studies. Can you tell me more about them?"

"The Mahatmas are enlightened beings who are in charge of the evolution of the planet. In the esoteric tradition, when a disciple receives the seventh initiation, he or she becomes a Mahatma or a Tara — the name of a feminine Mahatma — and continues to help humanity and work with nature." Jacques held up the pendant. "The energy is too difficult for a normal person to handle. It can burn a person. Here, I want you to put the pendant on and feel it."

Anton put the long chain around his neck. The pendant lay directly over his heart, and he immediately felt a pulse there. The feeling was extremely powerful, and he closed his eyes to experience it. Right away he saw purples, blues, and yellows — brilliant colors flowed in front of his inner vision. It was wonderful, and he could have stayed with it a long time, but he heard, "That's enough," as Jacques reached over to take the pendant back.

"Wow! How is that possible?"

"It is very sacred, and even my wife, who was a high initiate, could only wear it for short periods of time."

Jacques paused while he put the pendant on the table next to him.

"This pendant symbolizes the highest attainments, but to achieve them you must be willing to face your lower nature and transmute your negative energies into the positive. As you progress on the path, you will encounter many obstacles — or what I like to call 'challenges' — as well as influences from negative forces. Each of those challenges will cause you to search deeper within to find who you truly are. The search is full of sorrow and full of joy. This path is not easy, and each one's journey is unique. Yours has only begun, and you have already encountered emotions you never knew existed before."

"That's true. I know it will become more difficult. Can you tell me about that?"

"Difficult but never unsurpassable. I am your teacher and friend. My job is to protect you and guide you on the path, but you must do the work. Are you willing to strive to achieve the highest?"

"What do you mean by the highest?"

"It can be called God Consciousness, or Wisdom, or full assimilation of the Higher Self. Any of these terms are correct. You have walked this path before in past lives, and therefore you will know the twists and turns. Each life is different, but the challenges are the same, as you will reawaken many characteristics from before. In the past, you achieved some very high initiations; but, of course, you must achieve those again, and they will still be difficult." Jacques took the pendant and put it in Anton's hand.

"Put this in your pocket for the next couple of hours. Do not wear it over your heart, but feel it in your hand. Feel its energy and know that this is the type of energy you must strive to assimilate fully. Tomorrow, you can tell me if you are willing to do the work needed."

Anton knew then and started to say yes, but Jacques put his finger to Anton's lips.

"No, take time; this is a very serious decision. You have two choices. Concerning the book, you need to finish it and have it published. The book is your dharma, meaning part of your destiny in this life. This teaching is your spiritual path, which you can do in this life or the next or next. Take time to think about it, and ask me or Samantha any questions you have."

Jacques got up from his chair. "It's a beautiful day. I need to run some errands. I suggest you take a walk alone and think about this."

Anton took Jacques' suggestion, and he drove to the lake and for the next couple of hours walked on the path around it. The weather was brisk and exhilarating. The shining sun was a positive omen concerning his decision. There was nobody around. He rapidly felt very alone and, in that realization, knew that Jacques was helping him experience an important part of this path: You had to walk it alone. Jacques and others would be there along the way, but from now on his life would be similar to his year in the valley. The difference was that there he had been physically alone, but now he would be experiencing a different kind of loneliness.

A part of him knew it would be difficult because there would be no one who would understand his personal journey, except for his teacher—and even he could only guide him. Anton had to do the work himself.

Anton sat down on a bench by the water. His heart felt full and heavy at the same time. He held the pendant in his hand, and its energy filled him with longing. Yes, it was a lonely path, but to achieve God Consciousness would keep him focused as long as he didn't forget it. He had a sudden desire to run away with the pendant and laughed aloud, realizing how quickly his lower nature came in to tempt him.

In the future, he thought to himself, I will look back on this day as a pivotal time in my life. If he said yes to Jacques there would be no turning back; and, if he said no, his life would never be the same. He again laughed out loud. What choice did he really have?

He sat quietly for a long time in deep meditation.

It was four o'clock when he returned to the house. Everything was still. He walked into the library and found Samantha there reading a book.

She looked up. "How was your walk?"

"Good, very good, I went down to the lake and meditated."

"I do that sometimes. Water soothes me."

"What are you reading?"

"Hesse, I love his work. This is one of my favorites: *Journey to the East.*"

"Yes, I remember it. Isn't it all about his meeting his teacher? I read it years ago."

"You might want to reread it because you are on a journey, also. I find it more interesting now that I am older."

"But you were raised in a spiritual family. It must be easy for you."

"Not necessarily. I was raised Protestant. Both my parents felt I needed to study traditional religion, and all my friends were Protestant. Even though I knew my parents were into something else, I didn't start asking questions until I was twelve. Then they never pushed anything on me; they just answered my questions and raised my curiosity. Both mother and father always honored my individuality and encouraged me to make my own decisions." She smiled at him. "The teaching is never given out, even to children, unless they truly want it and are ready for it."

Anton was surprised. "That really is remarkable."

"I feel fortunate that I did want it; it certainly has been my good karma."

"May I ask, are you Jacques' disciple?"

"Yes, I am. He didn't want me as a disciple at first because he is my father. He felt it might be too difficult for me to see him as my teacher. But I insisted as I knew he had been my teacher many times. We set up some strict boundaries concerning our talks. If I go to him as my father, it is different from when I speak to him as my teacher."

"That must be complex, but you both are extraordinary people. I look forward to joining this spiritual group or 'family'—isn't that what it's called?"

"Yes, 'spiritual family.' So, you've decided?"

"I know I have to wait until tomorrow, but yes, I've decided."

"I'm happy for you; Jacques is a wonderful teacher, a true teacher, and that is so important."

"This is an unsettling question for me, but would you mind telling me about your mother? I find it difficult to believe that she could be a high initiate and turn away."

Anton saw a wave of sadness come over Samantha's face. "I'm sorry, I shouldn't have asked."

"No, that's all right. The path is a difficult one, and there are many temptations. My mother was very young when she married my father. He was thirty-nine and she was only twenty-one, so there was a big difference in their ages. He adored her.

Mother was very beautiful and very spiritual. She was an American doing a college exchange program here in Zürich when she met him on vacation in the mountains. Later, she went to meet Jacques' teacher in India and became her disciple right away. Their teacher was very encouraging about their relationship. She said they were destined to be teachers together and carry on the teaching." Samantha looked deep in thought and became silent.

"What happened?"

She looked at Anton intensely. "It's a long story. What happened took many years and many challenges they both faced. I was born when my mother was twenty-six, so she was busy the first few years taking care of me, but as soon as I was in school, she went back to working on her spiritual practice. Their teacher had died a couple of years after their marriage, and Jacques was the one destined to continue the work. By the time my mother met him, he had progressed to being a teacher and already had students. Mom became his right-hand person and helped him, learning from him and growing spiritually as a result. Unfortunately, she hadn't spent much time with her teacher, but her connection was good, and she saw and heard her on the subtle plane."

"But if she was dead, why didn't her teacher move on?"

"She did go on to be reborn, but one of her bodies remained in the subtle world to work with her disciples, and she will stay there until the last one has died. Then that body will connect to the body in her new life."

Anton felt how wonderful that was. "But what happened then?"

Samantha sighed. "Mother was very charming. Everyone loved her, and, regrettably, some of the adoration went to her head. Even though she didn't have the advanced initiation to be a teacher, students were coming to her. My father saw what was happening and warned her that she shouldn't accept students until she was ready. She thought he was jealous of her, and they started to have small fights around this issue. I was fifteen at the time, and I remember coming home one evening and finding my father alone in the living room. He was crying."

Anton could see that Samantha also had tears in her eyes, and he wanted to hold her but knew it wouldn't be right to do so. Instead, he handed her his handkerchief from his pocket.

She smiled a thank you and continued, "My mother left us. She met a man her age with whom she became totally enthralled. He was evil and powerful. In her infatuation, he convinced her that she was in the wrong teaching, that her talents were wasted in our group, and that she needed to claim her power by working with him. He made her a teacher in his negative sect. They were people who had broken from the spiritual path and instead sought power and domination over others. She broke her discipleship with her Indian teacher and became that man's wife."

"How awful for you."

"Yes, it was awful. I had just learned about the teaching but knew enough to realize what a horrible decision my mother made. Of course, we never saw her again. My father received divorce papers, which he signed, and that ended it."

"She never said goodbye to you?" Anton asked.

"No, not physically, but she called me and begged me to go with her. She paused in thought, "I did think about it, but I couldn't leave my father. My mother gave me a certain kind of love that was caring and motherly, but my father gave me love that was all encompassing. It's hard to describe. It had no boundaries, no expectations, just unconditional; whereas, my mother made me feel there were conditions connected to her love. Sometimes I felt she covered me with an invisible veil that would not let me explore who I was.

"It still must have been difficult to have to make that decision. Did you ever hear from her again?

"Yes, recently she has tried to talk to me in meditation and dreams. She naturally wants me to leave my father and work with her. It makes me very angry, and I tell her to leave me alone, which she does for a while; then she returns."

Samantha looked at Anton intensely. "Please don't mention this to anyone. I told my father, but I didn't tell him how persistent she is. If I remember to call on him, he comes immediately to my rescue and she leaves, but my anger toward her sometimes makes me forget to call him. My test, I guess."

"What a test! I'm so sorry; it must be very distressing for you," Anton replied.

"It's worse for my father. I always felt closer to him than her, but he cherished her. I think he felt responsible for having put her on a pedestal and for not seeing how strong her ego was becoming. It was a lesson for all of us who knew her. Some of her students who lacked discernment went with her; others stayed with my father. It's nearly fifteen years, and no one will speak her name. Others, too, have seen her in dreams calling them, and we have lost one or two in recent years. She tempts them with power."

Samantha shuddered involuntarily. "You're fortunate to have never met her."

He couldn't reply. His emotions danced all over the place. They sat in silence for a few minutes. Then Anton got up and went over to her. Sitting next to her, he pulled her into his arms and held her. He needed to do it. She trembled at first and then relaxed into his embrace. It lasted for what seemed a long time. He wanted to take her pain away. Finally, when he knew it had left, he released her.

"I would love a cup of tea, how about you?" He got up to walk toward the kitchen.

"Yes, but let me make it." She grabbed his hand and pulled him after her.

They sat on stools at a counter and looked through the wide window at the landscape. It was a soothing view of the lawn and gardens with the mountains beyond.

They sipped their tea and ate some scones; their bodies bathed in the sunlight, which was strong at this time of day. Neither one of them spoke or needed to.

Beyond the fence, a young couple was strolling on the street holding hands and affectionately smiling at each other. Anton took it to be a sign of something good. He reached into his pocket and felt the pendant. Its warmth shot through him.

He looked at Samantha, and she returned his look, and he knew they both were feeling a strong heart connection.

That evening after supper, the two of them and Jacques played cards, something Anton had always enjoyed, having grown up in a card-loving family. It was fun, and they talked about world news, life, and all those things not related to anything spiritual. He felt relieved, as it made him more at ease with them both. Later, Jacques went to bed, leaving Samantha and Anton alone to talk.

The next morning, Anton told Jacques his decision. It was easy. His heart felt full, and he knew it was the best decision he had ever made in his life, one that would have difficulties but also give him great joy.

Later that day, Jacques initiated Anton in a ceremony, and Anton became his disciple. It was the beginning of his journey.

CHAPTER 20

Anton returned home to Grindelwald right away, not stopping even to see his family. He wanted to continue working on the book. The days grew brighter, the sun lasted longer, and the last snows melted. Spring was fully here — his favorite time of the year.

He spoke with Jacques and Samantha often by phone. In his conversations with Sam, he found out more about her. She was thirty-one, rented an apartment in Zürich across the river from him, had an MBA in business. She worked as a consultant in corporations, doing team building, and her occupation required that she travel a lot. Intuitively Anton knew Sam had a brilliant mind and had to be successful. He was really curious to know further details about her work; yet when Anton asked her about her consulting jobs, she said very little, except that she had partners with whom she worked.

Then Jacques left for one of his trips, and Samantha stayed behind for a while. She was also planning a trip, but neither she nor Jacques would tell Anton where. He felt this mystery was a secret he wasn't ready to learn yet. He asked her to come for a visit, and she accepted but wouldn't give him a time; she just said she would call him when she expected to be free and to find out if he was still alone. His family visits weren't set yet but would be soon.

Kristina called, and the reality of his family came back to him in full force.

"Anton, we need to talk, and I don't want to do it on the phone. May I come up tomorrow?" There was urgency in her voice.

"Is something wrong?"

"No, everything is fine. I just need to see you. I'll tell you then."

He felt disturbed and really wanted to get back to work, but he told her to come. She arrived with an attitude of determination, signaling at once that she had planned this trip for a while. She kissed him and tried to be friendly, but he knew she was steaming underneath, and that was bad news. He had prepared a nice lunch with wine and set it up on the porch, as it was another beautiful spring day. She said she wasn't hungry, even though it was one o'clock and she hadn't eaten. Finally, she sat down with him, picking at her food, and they talked about their parents, who were planning another trip to the Far East in June. She told him the latest news about their brothers, all light chitchat, and then they had coffee and the hammer hit.

"I have to talk to you about your book. I've been thinking about it a lot, and I can't stop imagining how it will affect your career. First, the title is similar to Nietzsche's book, *Thus Spake Zarathustra*. And it touches on his philosophy, a philosophy that Hitler used to design his Super Race and justify genocide."

"Yes, that's true. Hitler took Nietzsche's philosophy, but he distorted it," Anton answered reasonably. "Besides, I used the name *Zarathustra* because he was an ancient teacher. Nietzsche's book has Zarathustra coming down from the mountain to teach, and my book also has him coming down the mountain to teach. The only other connection to Nietzsche's work is his theory that everyone has a super being within them, and my book teaches about the Higher Self, which is a similar concept to his."

"That's right, it's a radical religious book; don't tell me it's not."

Anton opened his mouth to protest. "Kristina, I teach philosophy, and a lot of the concepts in my book come from Eastern philosophy. The Higher Self comes from the yogic tradition; it is not in any way radical."

"It's one thing to teach about what has been established for centuries, but it sounds as if you are developing your own religion, a new one."

"It's not new. It's just been put in a new form."

"What I read sounds very new to me."

"That's your opinion."

"You have no idea how this could ruin your career and your standing in the intellectual community. You are a well-known scholar. People will believe you have gone off. I am so worried about you."

"Kristina, do you honestly think I'm crazy?"

"Yes, in some ways you are, and that's why I'm here. Dad said you had been to a good therapist, and I think you need to return to Zürich and do the therapy full time. One or two sessions can't help you."

Anton wanted to laugh, but he did his best to refrain. If only she knew the truth about Lea!

She must have seen him start to smile. "It's not funny; it's your whole life; and you have to think about your family, and how this book is going to affect all of us."

"So, this is about you, not me?" He began to feel angry.

"No, I said it's about you, but it does affect everyone. If you won't think about us, what about your friends, your colleagues? Do you honestly think they will accept this book?"

"If they don't, that's their problem. Kristina, I'm not giving up on the book. I will finish it and publish it. And if you, or my family, or my friends, think I'm crazy, so be it."

"So, you're telling me that none of us matter to you?"

"I didn't say that. I love all of you, and if the feeling is the same, you wouldn't want me to give up writing what I believe in."

"I knew the valley changed you, but I didn't know how much."

"I learned a lot there, and the main thing that kept me alive was the ability to connect with my Higher Self. The book was given to me to write for that reason. I'm sorry, Kristina, that it upsets you so much."

"I want you to be happy, and you know I love you; you're my kid brother." Her face softened now. "But I also know how this will affect your life and the world you live in."

"Yes, I am fully aware of that, but I need to write this book more than I need the world you are talking about. I love you, also, Kristina, and my whole family and my friends; but this mission of mine is something I have to do. I am happy, really happy."

"If you publish this book, it will cause a split between you and most of us. I know Father, Erick, and Jonas will agree with me. Only Mother will be on your side."

"Somehow, I always felt you and Mother would understand. It saddens me that you don't and that appearances are more important to you than our close relationship."

"It saddens me, too, that you care so little for us that you won't at least change the title. Our family name goes back generations as being conservative Catholics. We are highly respected in the community and church. This teaching of yours is very radical."

Anton thought about it for a minute and said, "I can't change the title, but I will consider using a pseudonym."

Immediately he felt wrong in pacifying her, but before he could recant, Kristina said, "That may help, but word would eventually get out among our friends that you are the author."

"That's true, and besides, I plan to do lectures about the book, so a pseudonym won't work."

"What! You plan to do *what*?" Kristina's voice rose an octave.

"I plan to do lectures. You heard me."

"You mean publicity talks?"

"No, the book is a teaching book, and even though I haven't thought about it yet, I plan to teach the material in it." He added, "Kristina, the book hasn't even been brought out yet — that's all up in the air — so maybe your worries are for nothing." Again, he felt that he was pacifying her and that he wasn't speaking the truth.

"You've already written a very successful book. Your publisher loves you, so you know he will probably take this one. It will get published. I know that, and now you're talking about *teaching* this material. Where do you think you will do that? At your university? Do you honestly think they would accept a book like this?"

"How can you condemn my book when you've only read a few chapters?"

"That was enough to see where it's going."

"Well, I'm sorry, Kristina, but my book is meant to help many people; it's not about appeasing a few. And you're right: I plan to publish it even if I have to do so myself, and I plan to teach it to as many people as I can. If the university won't let me do that, then I will do it on my own. Now, how about more coffee?" He stood up, making it obvious that the conversation was ended.

But she wouldn't stop. "You leave me no choice but to talk to the family about this."

"I wish you would wait until the book is finished, and then I will give everyone a copy of it, so they can make up their own minds."

"Then it would be too late. I will talk to them now." She got up and added, "I'm leaving." And she left the room and the house.

Anton sat for a long time and thought about their relationship...all the years of good conversation and deep, insightful probing of worldly subjects—and, for the first time, he realized that it had all been simply intellectual. There had never been deep discussions about the meaning of life or any thinking about nature and how it related to them. Only Anton and his mother had those kinds of talks. His mother was the spiritual one who gave balance to the others; the rest of them were all intellectuals.

He decided he needed to talk to her now before Kristina told everyone he was nuts, so he called her and fortunately found her in.

"Mom, I need to see you right away, just you. If I drive in now, can you have dinner with me?"

"Anton, is something wrong?" Her voice sounded worried.

"Yes and no, but I do have to talk to you right away. I've had a quarrel with Kristina, and before she starts spreading false accusations about me, I need to tell you about it."

"All right. I can't make dinner, we have plans; but can you come in now, or better still, can I meet you halfway? Let's meet at the Zugersee Inn, where we can have tea. That's not too far for me, and it's a beautiful day to sit by the lake."

"Are you sure? That will be nearly an hour's drive. And what about your dinner plans?"

"It's a late dinner, eight o'clock, so I'll be back in plenty of time."

The Zugersee Inn was a lovely place on the outskirts of Zug, on a lake not too far from Luzern. Anton stopped there often on his way back to Zürich to enjoy the beauty of the water. He arrived before his mother and sat in the outside café. It was after lunchtime, so the café wasn't crowded.

As he drank a cup of coffee and waited, he thought about what he would say to her.

His mom arrived a half hour later.

"Sorry, it took me longer to get out. Your father wanted to talk about the couple we are meeting tonight, bigwigs in the Canton. He had to brief me about them."

Anton got up and hugged and kissed her. It felt good and soothing.

She settled down in the chair, and they ordered some more coffee, and Anton ordered a sandwich.

"So, tell me, Anton, what is this all about?"

He briefly told her the whole story about Kristina and explained in more detail about his mission, saying that it wasn't entirely clear yet, but he knew he had to teach the material in his book.

His mother listened with startled eyes. Her expression made him want to explain more, to tell her about Jacques, but an inner voice said to be quiet.

She sat in silence for a while, and he began to worry that he may have been wrong about her. But then she spoke. "I'm sure you understand what a surprise this is to me. I've always known that you felt deeply about spiritual matters, but to this extent, I had no idea."

She paused in thought. "Do you remember, when you were a child, you told me that you saw fairies in the garden? And I told you that was wonderful but not to tell anyone else except me because the others wouldn't accept what you were saying?"

"Yes, I remember very well, and I knew then that you would always understand me."

"Well, I did understand, and I even envied you, as I wasn't able to see the fairies myself. I believe in nature spirits because I feel that nature is alive — not with its outer clothing of greenery but with an inner life that unfortunately I can't see."

"I thought you saw them, too."

"No, never. When I heard your story about living in the valley, it was clear to me that you still had a special connection to this hidden world of nature and that it not only saved your life but also changed you completely. But, my dear, I never dreamed that it would take you out of our world, take you away from us." Her eyes filled with tears.

"Mother, please, it will never take me away from you."

"It already has. I understand Kristina's anger. It's not about Nietzsche and the Zarathustra name. That's her excuse. It's about her fear that you have truly left us; that the you we loved is gone, and that this new you, even though it looks like you, is a stranger."

"But that's not true," Anton protested.

"We have all felt it. Your father and brothers have talked to me about it. They have even asked me to talk to you because we are alike, you and I."

"Yes, I know. Mother, you are the one that told me, a couple of years ago, that I had become an intellectual and had forgotten to use my heart. Using my heart is what I'm trying to do now. That's why I have changed. I'm telling you all this *because* we are alike, as I felt you would understand."

"Understand and approve. Is that what you want?"

"Yes, I guess so."

"When I encouraged you as a child, encouraged your connection with nature, I never dreamed that the thing I loved the most, nature, would take you away from me. I was only happy for you that you had those abilities."

"But it hasn't taken me away from you. It could never do that."

"Oh, but it has. You aren't aware of it yet. You have distanced yourself, and when you finally fulfill your mission to teach, then you really will be gone. My heart tells me that. You want me to approve of what you are doing, but how can I when I know the end result?"

"Can you at least understand how important this is to me?"

"Yes, and if you asked me whether you should do this work or not, I would have to say to follow your dream, even knowing it would take you away from me and the others; but I can't approve. I can understand, but I can't approve."

"But that's contradictory. If you want me to follow my dream, how can you not approve?"

"I'm sorry, I can accept your need to fulfill this mission, and maybe I can even accept the material you will teach, but my heart is too heavy right now to approve of your doing it. I know the others — your father, your brothers — will agree with Kristina and not accept what you're doing, and that makes me very sad, as it will change everyone."

Anton knew his mother was right. Pursuing his mission would break the bonds they all had together. For the first time, he realized there might never be the same family gatherings anymore. He was the splinter that would crack the connection that made it so perfect. He thought about the days after his return; the joy of being with them again and the love they all felt for one another.

"But it needn't be like that." He could hear the urgency in his voice. "Why can't they accept who I am—why can't it be the same? I have never judged any of you. Why now do I have to be so judged? I don't understand why."

She smiled, albeit weakly, for the first time. "This family was built around right thinking and strong minds. We educated you well, not only in the schools but also at home. But in so doing, the concentration has been on the development of the mind, not the heart, in decision-making. It's my fault as well as your father's. I knew better, but I followed his strong will. It was only with you that I had any impact, and now that is the wedge that will cause the change. You will go on and achieve what you need to do, and I am proud of that; but the others will never understand, because using the heart was never taught to them."

"You know that's not completely true. They all came in with what they had accumulated. If they had been spiritual, they would have discovered it and talked to you about it, just as I did. We all went to church, but do any of them follow Christ's teachings? I always have, as they touched my heart. Mother, it can't be any different, you know that."

"Maybe you're right. This had to happen someday, but I wish I could have taught them more. I simply gave up." And her eyes again filled with tears.

After she left, Anton sat in the inn for another hour and thought about the family. He planned to be in Zürich in a week, and he wondered if he should try to phone his brothers to see them at that time. A part of him said no, that it wouldn't matter. They were pretty limited in their beliefs, and he doubted if they would be open to his book, especially if his father and Kristina were against it. Nevertheless, it might be worth a try. Erick sometimes surprised him.

CHAPTER 21

Within a week, Kristina had spoken to the whole family, and Anton received calls from his father and brothers politely asking what was happening: was it true that he had become some kind of religious fanatic? Both his brothers were very flippant about the whole thing and treated him like the erring younger sibling; but his father, as Anton expected, was the most irate about what his father called his "postulating."

They calmed down a bit when he explained that Kristina had overreacted and not been fair, that she had read only a few chapters. They agreed that it was better to form their own opinions after reading the whole book. His father asked for a copy anyway, and Anton explained that he hadn't finished it yet but would give him a copy when it was done. His father wanted Anton not to give it to his publisher until he had read it, but Anton ignored this request and made no promises.

A couple of days after Jacques' return, he invited Anton to dinner. It was wonderful to see him again. Jacques had been to a spa in Mexico and was tanned, rested, and looked healthy. Anton asked about Sam, but she was still away, although she was expected home soon. It had been a while since Anton had heard from her.

After dinner, they went into Jacques' study, and Anton told him the entire story about what had happened with his family. "I know you mentioned I might have difficulties with my family someday, but I never anticipated this!"

"Family relationships are always karma. In your case, it's a mix between good and bad. When you give them the book to read, I'm afraid it will make things worse. Eventually, your brothers will come around, but at this point, I don't know about the others."

"My father is more stubborn than my sister. It makes me sad, as I love them both."

"I know. Try not to be hurt by them. That keeps the karma moving back and forth. It's best to let them go. You can still love them but let them go."

"That's hard to do. I've had trouble with my father in the past. In fact, all of us have at one time or another. But Kristina! We were so close, or so I thought."

"If that closeness is truly there, she will come around, not now but in time."

"I hope so." Jacques' words made him feel a little better.

When they said goodbye, Anton told him that he was going home to the mountains, but he would come back to see him after Jacques returned from his next trip. Jacques was leaving in a couple of days to go to America.

After he got back to Grindelwald, Anton realized that he had no idea what the future might hold. Maybe he would no longer be welcomed at his home and would be unable to stay there.

One day he chanced upon some land for sale on the other side of town and seriously thought about purchasing it to build his own house. The land was quite nice and the price fairly reasonable, probably, he thought, because the road to it was narrow with sharp curves that might discourage most city buyers, who were the ones now buying property there. Grindelwald had become a popular resort.

The land consisted of twenty acres and abutted the mountains, with an expanse of thick, evergreen woods. But what he fell in love with was the encompassing view it had of the Bernese Oberland mountain range across the valley. A secondary road passed it, which meant it would be cleared by the town in the winter. On the property, close to the road, was a small cabin and a goat shed big enough for a car. The more he looked at it and walked the land, the more it felt right to him. He bought it, thinking that even if things were resolved with the family, he might still want to build his own place someday. Then, too, he knew in his heart that the hope of their accepting his new lifestyle was in vain.

Each of the children in the family had a large trust fund left to them by their grandparents, so there was plenty of money to have separate houses in Grindelwald; but, surprisingly enough, none of them had ever thought to do that. The family home had been big enough for all of them, but now Anton knew that would change. He even thought of going to another location and buying property in the mountains, but he couldn't bear the thought of leaving Grindelwald and all the memories it held for him. If he was no longer welcomed in his home, he would at least stay in his town, walk his trails, see his friends, and spend time with his mother when she was there.

He tried to shake off his pessimism and tell himself that he had exaggerated the whole thing on the sole basis of Kristina's reaction. But when he looked at the land for sale, one of the reasons he decided so quickly to buy it came from a feeling of foreboding.

Just at that time, Samantha called, and Anton told her the whole story. He expected her to make light of it, but instead, she responded in a very serious way.

"I'm sorry that this has happened. The spiritual path is always a difficult one, especially when a person has to deal with family."

Then she added, "I have a few days off, and Dad is still away. May I come and spend the time with you, or are you busy?"

"Yes, absolutely!" His heart felt good for the first time in days. "It will be wonderful to have you here and show you my mountains."

She arrived in a rainstorm. He was watching for her car and ran out with a large umbrella to fetch her.

"How gallant," she exclaimed as she reached up to give him a resounding kiss on the lips. He wanted to grab her for more, but she locked her arm in his and they ran to the front porch for shelter.

Anton said, "The weather isn't favoring us today." The rain was falling as if all the gods were crying in unison.

She protested, "Oh, I love the rain, especially in the spring. It smells good."

When she was finally in the house and was reasonably dried off, with a caftan wrapped around her, Anton reached for her and drew her into his arms.

"Anton, no!" She pushed him away and laughed.

"Why not?" He pulled her back to his chest and kissed her passionately. She started to push away again, but slowly he felt her body give in, and her arms went around his neck, pulling him even closer. The kiss didn't end. They were still kissing as he picked her up and carried her. They were still kissing as he laid her on his bed. They were still kissing as they pulled each other's clothes off, and they were still kissing as their lovemaking came together in a climax of ecstasy. Only then did their lips part for the first time, and they looked into each other's eyes in wonderment.

In the days that followed, they came to know each other, not just by their love-making, or their ventures into the mountains, or their talks in the evening, but in a way he had never known another human being. They were so much a part of each other that he knew her thoughts and she, his. Their bond was a rope that held them so tightly that one could not move without the other one yielding.

When they made love, it was very different from his experience with Orama. That had been pure animal passion, but with Samantha, it was a kind of love that joined them on a higher level: emotional, psychological, and spiritual. Everything in their bodies seemed to fit, not only making them one but also making every part more complete, like two intersecting gears that caused one movement. There wasn't a need to possess her. They simply belonged together. Maybe it was because of their spiritual connection. The orgasms were different, also. They both felt the essence of what the yogis might call *samadhi*—a pure state of bliss. One time he felt himself going out into the subtle world, only to have Sam pull him back, whispering, "No, we need to do it together." Those words were profound.

Both being extremely private people, they experienced a vulnerability that some-how helped to develop trust in their newly formed relationship.

She extended her stay by two days. When it was her morning to leave, he told her he felt they were meant to be together, and she said she felt the same way. They hugged their hearts close for a long time.

"I don't want to leave you," she whispered.

"I know. Stay longer, don't leave," he begged.

"I have to, but this is only the beginning. There's time, lots of time." She tried to be cheerful.

"When will you come back?" he asked.

"My work is planned until July. I had no idea this would happen. I never knew I could feel this way." And she kissed him again and again.

"I can't wait until July. I will come with you, and we can at least spend the evenings together."

"That's not possible." Samantha's voice was low and sad.

"But why not? Why can't I travel with you? I have a laptop and can write while you do your work."

"The work I am doing is not just business. I have spiritual work also to do, and being with you would be a distraction. I would only think about you and want to be with you. I can't have you with me, even though I would love to." Her words were final, and Anton knew he couldn't ask to know more. He also knew he shouldn't become possessive, as he had with Orama.

"Then promise me you will not make more plans until we can be together for at least the rest of the summer. We can be here in July and, when my family comes in August, we will go away—anywhere you want."

"I will try. I will try my best to make that happen. Dad will understand that I have to be with you, now that we need this time together."

With that resolved, they parted.

The next day, Anton sat at home thinking over every minute they had spent together. It was almost surreal, a euphoric dream that he still experienced, a dream that was embedded in his heart. He thought about the women he'd loved: Beatrice, so young, wanting so very much to make life exciting and using her love as a camouflage for her needs. Now it didn't seem possible that he had actually loved her. She was his youth's illusion, an illusion from a world he soon grew out of.

Then he thought a long time about Orama and the psychic hold she'd held on him. Had he really loved her? It seemed now more like a consuming lust that was a blanket smothering him. He remembered his deep sense of loss when she died and how it almost made him insane and suicidal. He wondered what would have happened if she had lived. He probably would have married her and lost his chance to be with Samantha. That thought made his heart contract, and he was almost happy that Orama was dead, or pretending to be dead. How awful to love so much that he would have even a fleeting thought like that!

Even if he had married Orama, he would have left her when he saw Samantha — or would he have? It didn't matter now. Samantha was his destiny. They were meant to be together. Somewhere in their past they had loved each other, and that love was a magnet that had pulled them back together.

The next morning, he awoke with a strong feeling that Lea was there. He heard her voice say, "Anton, remember that your mission comes before anything else."

"Of course, it does!" he replied, knowing that he lied, that Samantha now came first.

"You need to understand more. You need to know yourself better." Then she left before he had a chance to ask her what she meant. Anton had a strong sense that Jacques was with her and had told her what to say.

On the third day, Samantha phoned. She sounded a long way away. "I can only talk for a minute; I just wanted to say I love you." Then he lost the connection, which was obviously via a cell phone.

On the fourth day, he went to the local tavern and got drunk, something he hadn't done for a long time. He just wanted to drink and drink and drink so that he would stop thinking about her. He needed to get on with his work.

The fifth day, he had a hangover, so he slept a lot.

Then on the sixth day, he went back to work, and at night, held her in his arms in his dreams.

The next time he heard from Sam, the connection was better, and she could talk for a while. When he thought about the conversation later, he couldn't remember all they said. Mainly they had talked about missing each other and about wanting to be together always. But he totally remembered the last sentence.

Samantha said, "Anton, I hope you will want to be with me after I tell you about my work. When I see you next, I promise to explain what I mean."

He started to protest. She interjected, "Shhh, Darling, don't ask now, I just want you to love me forever. I can take a couple of days off next week. I'll come to you, if that's okay."

"Of course." It was a nice surprise. July seemed an endless way off.

He spent the week trying to put the place into order. The flowers on the hills were blooming, so he cut masses of them and had vases in every room. They filled the house with their scent and color. Usually, he enjoyed the flowers the most when they were outside; but somehow now, even cut and in the house, they held the glory of the sunshine and the freshness of the mountain air.

Samantha arrived in the early evening looking very tired. Anton settled her on the couch with plates of prosciutto and melon and a glass of white wine. When he first embraced her, her body was stiff and somewhat unyielding. After she seemed settled, he asked her, "Is something wrong?"

"Yes, wrong and right, bad and good." She sighed deeply and thought: How is he going to receive this news? Will it end our relationship? But then she quickly told herself, No, it can't happen. Our karma to be together is preordained. Our love is too strong.

Anton felt her anxiety in his heart and waited in anticipation of the worst.

"I spoke to Dad and he said I could tell you, that it would be best for you to know."

Sam looked into Anton's eyes and was a Samurai, speaking direct, clear, calm, and strong words. "Around four years ago, I was approached by the *Bundesamt für Polize* or what is called "fedpol," our government's secret service, to do some specialized work. As you know, I have done corporate consulting, but the job they asked me to do was astounding. They basically asked me to work undercover for them."

"Undercover? You mean you're a spy?" Anton was shocked.

"Yes, more or less. I am asked on occasion to investigate some of the corporations here in Switzerland. There have been some underhanded dealings with outside financial institutions that have made our government concerned about maintaining the ethical code that's been established for centuries.

"For example, unmarked bank accounts have always been part of our financial institutions and were originally set up for privacy reasons. This type of banking has caused international controversy, especially with outside governments, who claim they are used for tax evasion, money laundering, and other clandestine activities. International deals are being made in which monies are passed to and through here without government knowledge."

"You mean our government wants to stop this practice? How is that possible without destroying confidentiality?"

"We want to stop the criminal interests and the practice of tax evasion, and yes, to do that will require a loss of confidentiality."

Samantha thoughtfully continued. "It would be easy just to close it all down, but the financial institutions, which are our main economic support, won't allow this to happen. But they are willing to look at some of the underhanded activity that is taking place and not allow criminals to leave their money in hidden bank accounts. Tax evasion is important but not as important as fighting the mafia or corrupt corporations that use their monies to make illegal arms deals or machinery for war. These are the areas that concern us the most."

"But what do *you* do? How are you involved in this?"

"I am given names of people who are executives in some of the corporations under suspicion. I approach them with the idea of developing more branches in other countries and can prove professionally how financially beneficial this would be."

"Do you do this yourself?"

"I am given some of the best experts and advisers who know each company's specialty to help me work up the plans. But I'm also pretty skilled myself at this type of work."

"Do they usually hire you?"

"My proposal is unique, and if it doesn't interest them, I have another one, which is a detailed plan on how to train their employees in team building to enhance performance and productivity. This is an area in which everyone is interested, and, as I said, my research advisers are the best. Both proposals are very comprehensive, so it's rare that I'm not hired."

She paused and looked at Anton intensely. "My background is excellent, as is my resume, and I have great recommendations from some of the top corporations here. This was why our government chose me in the first place. Since the targeted corporations have to maintain a good exterior face to the auditors, they usually hire my services."

"But once you are inside, how do you spy on them?"

Usually, I can find out a lot about the inner workings of the company, and if I can't, I can intuitively feel if something is going on. I'm really good at spotting discrepancies. A lot of these companies only have branches here. That's where the front comes in, so I try to arrange some work at their corporate headquarters, wherever that is."

"But how can you get classified information? I would assume it is classified?"

"I don't have to. I become friends with the upper management and can usually persuade them to tell me more, just enough to start an investigation."

"When you say, 'friends with the upper management,' what do you mean?"

"No, no, I don't sleep with them if that's what you mean. I'm not a Mata Hari. I make a professional relationship that becomes a little personal. But I keep it in the friendship realm. People still drink a lot, so I learn a lot over cocktails."

"All right, but what happens after you report them?"

"That's easy. First of all, some suspicious corporations come out clean according to my feedback, so we are only talking about a few. Usually they do an audit long after I have left, so there is no connection. They can also do one while I'm there so that I also am investigated.

Remember, the branches here are small, and most of my work is done in the headquarters, which aren't under Swiss jurisdiction. Only the branches can be closed down and the bank accounts closed. Of course, the information is then given to the governments who have asked for it in the first place."

"But you could be caught!"

"Yes, that's true; that's the chance I take."

"But it's dangerous. If you're caught, you could be killed."

"Yes, but I'm protected by Jacques."

"But I. . . "

She leaned over and kissed him. "Darling, it's okay. I've been thinking of stopping now for a while, as it takes a lot of my time. And now—"

Her kisses became stronger, and Anton forgot his fears in her embrace.

The weekend passed quickly, and all too soon they were saying their goodbyes. Anton asked her at the end, "Why did you think I would ever want to give you up because of your work?"

"I didn't know how you would react. Some men would find my lifestyle too difficult to relate to, and others would feel that they also could be targeted if something happened."

This surprised him, and he realized that Samantha didn't really know him. All he said was, "I would never leave you, no matter what you did. I love you."

She nodded, and her eyes became teary as she said she loved him, too.

CHAPTER 22

Anton's father called and said that the whole family was coming up the first weekend in June. Anton knew they planned to confront him about the book and immediately felt anxious, as he knew they would gang up on him like coyotes surrounding a marmot.

He hid his manuscript just in time before their arrival. Soon they would ask to see it, and he planned to tell them that it wasn't ready to read. His brothers never took no for an answer, and he knew they would look around and try to find the manuscript. His hiding place was a metal box that he buried on his new land with a stone marker to tell him where it was. He changed his private password on his computer at home so that no one could get through, and his backup disk was a flash drive that he carried in his pocket at all times. It felt strange to have to hide everything, something he had never done before.

The family members arrived at different times on Friday evening. Everyone seemed cordial except Kristina, who was distant and didn't hug him as she usually did. The next day started out very pleasantly at breakfast. Everyone was catching up with news of one another and of family friends. In fact, this took most of the morning. Lunch was to be a picnic, and they all pitched in to make the food and prepare the baskets. Nothing was said. Only one or two quick glib remarks were made by his brothers, such as, "How is the preacher?" and, "If the spirit moves you, please do this for me."

The picnic went well with help from the weather, which was warm and sunny, but by late afternoon tensions were rising, and, as they sat down on the porch for cocktails, his father finally brought the subject up.

"Anton, all of us have questions to ask you about your book. Is it ready for us to read, since that would give us a better perspective about its content?"

"Dad, the manuscript isn't ready, and even if it were, I don't want anyone to read it until it's published."

"But you said I could read it."

"Yes, that was a mistake; I've changed my mind."

"Then how can we critique it?"

"That's the point. I don't want any of you critiquing it."

"But . . ." Everyone started talking at once.

"Calm down. Please!" his mother exclaimed. Then, turning to Anton, she asked, "If we can't read it, how can we discuss it with you?"

"I will be happy to give you a brief outline of the story, and then I am willing to answer your questions."

Kristina blurted out, "I can tell you what I read and why he doesn't want any of you to read it."

"Kristina, please be quiet," his mother admonished. "Let's give Anton a chance to tell us his story."

So, he began. He talked for well over half an hour, even going into some detail about the journey. Halfway through he could tell they all seemed surprised. Even his mother looked taken aback at Zarathustra's story.

There was a long silence when Anton was finished, but it was a silence filled with emotion and therefore, not truly silent. It felt as if cold reality was a stone figure ready to find life but still had to wait. In time, when he looked back at this scene, what he remembered the most was the wait.

Finally, his father spoke first, "Anton, except for your mother, we are not a spiritual family. For us to comment on this spiritual journey would be very difficult. How can we? But I for one can comment on how this book will affect all of us."

His brother Erick spoke up. "Comment for yourself, Dad, not for me or the others."

"You're right, though I would think you all would agree with me." His father continued. "In this country, our family has a fine reputation that goes back several generations, not only for our contributions, but also for our intellectual and leadership abilities. This so-called spiritual book will shake the foundation of that. If you insist on publishing it, and I know you will, at least change your name. Take a pseudonym, so no one will know it comes from someone in this family."

"I planned to do that, but now I can't."

"Why not?" Kristina asked.

"Because I will be teaching this material, and maybe I will have to do that in the same way as Zarathustra, by going from town to town and school to school."

This made them all cry out, "Oh, no!" He even heard his mother's voice among them.

"Preaching? You'll be preaching!" Erick exclaimed.

"No, *teaching*, just teaching."

"How can you say *'just teaching'*? It's about religion."

"No, it's not about religion. It's about individuals finding who they are."

"Nonsense." Now his father raised his voice.

"Please." His mother put her hand on his dad's arm to calm him down.

Jonas finally spoke up, "Can I know how you plan to do this teaching? Who is going to hire you?"

"I don't know yet. All I know is that I will be teaching the material in my book."

"Well, if you need to do that, okay, but at least promise us that you will be teaching abroad, in America or France, but not here. Dad's right, it could cause a real schism with our friends, not to mention our coworkers. Remember, this is a conservative country."

"I can't promise that. If I'm meant to teach here, I will. In fact, I'm hoping to make it a course at the university."

This brought a groan from Erick. "Will you listen to us at all?"

"I will listen, and I will do my best to keep from offending you, but I have to follow my heart and fulfill my mission."

"I fear you suffered some brain disorder because of your long stay in the mountains." His father's face looked ashen and grim.

"Thank you for your concern." Anton's tone was sarcastic. "But I assure you my brain is fully functioning. And it upsets me" — his voice wavered a minute — "that none of you will give me any support. It's not been easy."

"How can you expect support when your preaching will make this family look ridiculous?" Kristina quickly retorted.

Anton looked at her. "Especially you, Kristina! I thought you would understand."

"I understand all right, but not in the way you want me to." Her cold eyes glared, and suddenly he felt truly alone. He looked around the room at each one there and knew that what he dreaded had come true. Only his mother looked soft, as if she, at least, knew how he felt.

He stood up and excused himself. As he left and closed the door, he could hear them starting to talk about what they needed to do to stop him. For the first time in his life, he became afraid of his family: it was a feeling he would want no one else to have to experience. Anton suddenly felt paranoid about his computer—not that they could break the code, but that they would destroy it. He found it in his room, put it in his briefcase, and left the house. When he knocked on Stefan's door, he was there, and was surprised to see Anton.

"Anything wrong, Anton?"

"Yes and no. I can't tell you, but I would appreciate a favor. Keep this for me until I ask for it back." And he handed him the briefcase.

"Sure, no problem. Are you afraid it will be stolen?"

"Yes, but not by a thief — my family wants to destroy something on it."

Stefan looked concerned. "But why?"

"I'll tell you another time. It's a long story."

When Anton returned to the house, he heard them still talking in the living room. He didn't know whether to confront them again or just go quietly to his room, but before he could decide, his father called out, "Is that you Anton?"

He answered yes and started toward his room at the end of the house.

"We want to speak to you now." His tone left no room for argument. It sounded like the same tone he'd used when Anton had done something wrong as a child.

Walking into the living room, he felt like an innocent man just sentenced for a hideous crime. "Yes, what is it?" His voice sounded too mild.

His father was now standing, his mother was crying, and his sister and brothers looked very tired and strained.

"Sit down; we have something to say to you. Except for your mother, we have decided that if you go through with publishing this book under your name and conducting classes around the material, then we have no recourse but officially to disown you, and to inform all our friends and family that we have done so. Of course, that means you will no longer be welcomed here or at any of our homes in Zürich."

His father paused and tried to give him a small smile. "But honestly, Anton, we all love you and want you to be happy. We only hope that you will want the same for us. If you must publish this book, just promise you will do it under a pseudonym; and, if you must teach it, just promise us you will do so abroad and not in Switzerland. That's not much to ask, is it?"

"Yes, it is. My teaching reputation is here in Switzerland, not abroad."

"After you teach this, you will no longer have a reputation," Kristina said.

"Do you think it's fair to ask anything of me when you haven't read the book?"

"We don't need to read it. What you said about it is enough," Erick said.

"What I said were a few facts. You need to read how those facts are translated into some interesting theories. If you love me, read the book first; then you can pass judgment."

"We'll read it if you give us a copy, but you say you won't do that," his father remarked.

"That's correct. I will give you a copy when I am done, not now."

"Will that copy be printed, or will it be a manuscript?"

"I am willing to concede and make it the manuscript."

"Fine, when will you have it?"

"I think by the end of the year."

"Will you accept our suggestions?"

"It depends on what they are. I guess I haven't made myself clear that I have no intention of making major changes."

"Then what's the use of reading it when you won't listen to our feedback?" His father sounded angry now.

"Well, if you read it, you might even like it."

The room fell silent. "Please, let's wait. Give Anton a chance," his mother said.

"All right," his father responded, "But on one condition. You are not to send it out until all of us have read it."

"As I said before, I can't promise that."

"But why not, Anton?" his mother asked.

"It will take too long. I have a deadline."

"Screw the deadline." Kristina was belligerent

"I can't, and besides, like I said, I'm not changing the manuscript for anyone."

"Then there's no need to continue this discussion. You are to pack and be out of this house by the end of the weekend." His father turned and walked out of the room.

Anton looked at the others. "You follow everything he says. Don't you know how he controls all of you?" Then he said to his mother, "Are you, too, going to disown me?"

"No, no, he'll change his mind, I'm sure." His mother got up and hugged him and then ran after his father.

But his father didn't change his mind. The next morning, Anton booked a room at the inn and began to pack his things. There was a lot to pack. Besides the clothes, he had almost an entire bookcase of books and lots of hiking gear. He asked his mother if he could leave some of the things in the garage until he could get a bigger van to move them out. She agreed and said it was only temporary, that his father wouldn't disown him—that was ridiculous. Anton knew better but didn't argue.

He told her that he'd bought some land with a cabin on it that he could stay in temporarily until he had built a more permanent house. That would have to wait until next year, after the book was finished. He made her promise not to mention it to anyone.

"Your father is very proud; having control over the family's conservative, Catholic image is paramount to him; and you have been the first to oppose him. He has told me I am not to speak to you anymore, but I can't do that. I will always be your mother. You know how much you mean to me." And she cried again.

This made Anton feel sad and angry. The reality of it all hadn't hit him so far, but now it was beginning to.

The next morning, Anton put everything he didn't immediately need into the garage and then went to the inn for the evening. The next day, he drove to his new place. The cabin was small, just a one-room living area and kitchen with a small bedroom and bath. He hadn't spent much time thinking about what he would need there, but he had a new stove and refrigerator put in, just in case he had problems with the family. He spent the day scrubbing everything down and then thought about how he was going to paint the interior.

The family had planned to stay most of that week, but they usually didn't go into town at all, and, since Anton was busy with the cabin, fortunately he didn't bump into them. On Wednesday, he hired a van in Interlaken and picked up all his things. He called ahead to the house to say he was coming, so he wasn't surprised that they all were gone. It felt odd to walk through the rooms and say goodbye to his home. He had spent a lot of time there and loved the place very much. Maybe when the book was published, they would change their minds, but somehow he knew that wasn't true. Anton also wondered how his friends and relatives would take this turn of events. Hopefully, some of them would remain loyal to him. It would be interesting to see what happened.

In the following days, he bought furniture and had it delivered. By the end of the second week, he was settled in with his computer back and a fine wooden desk under a window, ready to start work. He called Zürich during the day, knowing his father was at the office, and his mother answered. They talked briefly. He gave her his address and phone number and invited her to come see him. She said she would soon but sounded a little anxious. He asked her what was wrong. She hesitated; "Your father told me that if I saw you again, he would leave me. I'm going to have to wait a while until he's not so angry. Then I'll call you."

Anton was stunned. The certainty of her words made him feel the full, fierce impact of what was happening. He couldn't fathom not seeing his mother: it was an unthinkable reality, too harsh for him to imagine. He would miss the others, but not seeing Mother was devastating. When he put the receiver down, he wanted to throw out the book and all that it had done to him.

"Stay calm." He felt a reassuring hand on his shoulder, and love poured over him and cleansed his grief. Jacques was with him.

July passed quickly. He knew the family was up in July, so he chose to stay inside, working. Some days he walked his property, which had some hills that rose to the big cliffs. He found a perfect place low on the mountain with a large, flat stone that he could climb to. He loved to meditate there, as it was a secluded spot sheltered from the winds and sun, and it seemed to be full of energy from the rocky cliffs. When he felt tired and lonely, he would go there to become energized. Also, a silvery stream surged in the back part of his land, where he could strip down and swim naked, knowing no one could see him. The hiking trails were a distance from his place, none close enough to disturb the quiet of his surroundings.

One day he called some old friends in town and invited them out for a barbecue—just a couple of guys and their wives, including Stefan. The weather was a perfect present that boosted the small gathering, filling his place with fun and laughter. He needed that energy there, as it had become too much like a hermit's dwelling. His friend Frederick told him that his family had just left, but he thought maybe Anton's mother was remaining for a couple more weeks. That gave him hope. The next day the phone rang, and it was she. "I can now come to see you; may I?"

She arrived with her arms full of packages.

"Knowing you, I figured you would have only the basics here. No linens or curtains or good pots." His mother looked around. "Yes, I guessed right." Then she looked at him and ran into his arms, hugging and hugging him so tightly that he gasped for breath.

"But it's charming, and it's you." She walked around observing everything. "And the view! It is wonderful, even better than ours."

"That's why I bought it. This cabin is okay for now, and I'll be going back in September to my apartment. Next summer I will build a good house."

"Maybe you'll marry again. It would be nice for you to have someone to share this with."

"Yes, there is someone I have in mind." And he told her about Samantha.

"Oh, she sounds lovely. I can't wait to meet her." Then her face saddened. "But it's so difficult. Your father hasn't changed his mind. I have never seen him like this. It's Kristina, you know—she has made it a huge issue. The boys don't really care, but they don't want to be banished with you, and that is the threat if anyone of us sees you."

"I always thought Kristina would understand; that's why I showed her the chapters. Her reaction came as a shock."

"She used to be more liberal and even an existentialist when she was in her twenties, but being married to Felix had changed her, more than even I thought." His mother sighed.

"I agree. I certainly supposed Kristina, of all people, would never take on her husband's conservative views. They used to argue about politics when they were first married, but the years must have changed that, perhaps along with the need for security." Anton added, "She always came crying to me when the fights were really bad, and I would try to help her."

"That's what I mean, Anton. You and she have always been so close, yet she is so nasty about this! It's beyond my understanding."

"Mine, also."

His mother stayed for lunch, and they talked the whole afternoon until she left. He wanted her to have dinner with him, but she felt his father would be wondering where she was: she figured she could explain an afternoon but not longer than that.

Anton watched her drive away with feelings of great love for her. He would miss her the most—not seeing her on a regular basis. He could only pray that when the book was out, his father would change his mind, particularly if some of his friends accepted it.

CHAPTER 23

Anton continued to talk to Samantha on a regular basis, but no longer asked about her work. He wanted to do that when he saw her in person. Already he felt the need to tell her to stop, that it was too dangerous. The thought of losing her made him feel sick with apprehension, so he tried to be positive and not go in that direction.

One day, he had a telephone call from Jacques.

"Where are you?" Anton immediately inquired.

"Back home. How are you?"

"Fine, just fine. Can I come see you?" He felt eager to reconnect.

"No, I'm coming to see you instead, if you'll have me."

Anton was thrilled. "If you don't mind an old cabin and some plain living."

"I look forward to it. One must always be so neat when one lives in a large house. It will be nice just to hang out for a change and rusticate."

Jacques arrived the following week. When Anton embraced him, he felt happy for the first time since his family had deserted him.

They sat and talked for a while, and then Jacques said, "I'm sorry about your family. It may take time, but I'm certain they will come around."

"I hope so. I really miss them, especially my mother. She is on my side but has only been able to sneak in one visit since this all happened. She does call weekly when my father isn't around, and that helps a little. I've never been close to my brothers, but, you know, I'm finding that I really miss them more than I thought."

"And your sister?" Jacques inquired.

"She's totally off and is the one who has influenced my father the most. I don't understand it. We were so close."

"Your sister is going through some changes, and much of her attitude concerns the way people perceive her. Her husband will leave her for another woman, and when he does, it will end the marriage. She will need you then, and of course you will forgive her and be there for her."

"I'm sorry to hear that, and I'm not surprised about Felix, but I really feel disappointed that she can't be here for me."

"Yes, often the ones we love the most end up hurting us the most."

Jacques' eyes looked at Anton for a few minutes. They expressed an intensity that Anton hadn't felt before. Then Jacques said, "I'm here to talk to you about something very important to me. I need your help in a venture that could be dangerous. It concerns Samantha."

"Is she in danger?" Anton reacted immediately.

"Possibly. She told me she explained her work to you. It's a job I have long been concerned about, but she really wanted to help our government, so I've tried to accept it. But now, she has a new client who I believe could be the most dangerous of them all."

"Why doesn't she refuse the job?"

"Her secret service boss informed her that this was the biggest illegal trafficking company on the books and could potentially do the most harm. The company makes and supplies weapons to the Far East, and for the Taliban and Al-Qaeda, and now they think for Isis. When Samantha was hired, this company told her that they were building new machines for the tobacco industry, machines that will take out more of the nicotine and make cigarettes safer to smoke. They said they want her to do some team building and training, and work in some of the branches that will be producing these 'tobacco machines.' In actuality, they are using her as a go-between to transfer secret information to their employees making the weapons. They give her a program to teach the employees that is full of hidden codes, codes they dare not send through the Internet or telephone. They are unaware, of course, that Sam knows what they are doing. She copies the codes for our secret service and hands them over to them to be deciphered. The company is bound to find out sooner or later that she is betraying them and, when they do, they will kill her."

"She has to quit now before it's too late." Anton felt his heart become a tight binding in his chest.

"I know, but she won't. She has a contract, and it's too late to quit without a very good reason. That's where you come in."

"Me? How me?"

"First, you need to help me convince her to stop, and secondly, you need to be her good reason. She will tell them she is getting married and that her husband has taken a job as a professor at Harvard University, and he insists she go with him and start a family. She will also recommend someone else to replace her, and, of course, that person will also be a spy."

"Well, I will be happy to do that, but won't they check to see if it is true or not?"

"But it will be true."

"What?" Anton stammered. "Yes, I'm happy to marry Samantha. I want that anyway. But I certainly don't have a job at Harvard."

"Now you do. I have some very good friends there, and they are looking forward to your being with them and teaching some regular philosophy courses and even a course in Eastern religion in the Divinity School. You can incorporate some of the things from your book in it."

"My book? At Harvard? Surely that's not true!"

"It is true. The job is for the spring semester, which starts at the end of January."

"But I have a commitment to go back to work this September in Zürich."

"You can do that and then take a leave for the Harvard job. It will be for one semester, and then you can return here. By then your book will be published. Harvard will be a way of testing it out."

Anton felt speechless. Then he thought of Samantha, "Have you said anything to Sam about this?"

"No, I feel that's up to you. All I've told her is to quit the contract and get a replacement. Catching small tax-evasion companies is very different from catching those engaged in arms dealing. I know she loves you, too." Jacques smiled for the first time. "So, the marriage isn't something that will be a sacrifice to either one of you."

"I guess not. I was planning to ask her the next time I saw her." He added, "I'm happy you approve."

"Who said I approved?" Jacques laughed when he saw Anton's look. "I'm only joking. Of course, I approve, I love you both and feel you will be happy together."

"Getting back to dangerous: at the beginning, you said it would be dangerous for me."

"Of course. If they find out she is a spy, they will kill you both; but I will do everything to protect you so that doesn't happen."

"It would be like living each day as if it were the last one."

"More or less, for a time."

"That's not bad, particularly if it's with Sam. I would rather live like that than never be with her."

"The other danger is that they may insist she finish out the year. Since you're not going to Harvard until January, they may want her to stay until you have to move. If need be, she may have to do that. Her contract is for two years, so at least she wouldn't have to fulfill the full contract."

"They wouldn't do anything to me so that she couldn't go, would they?" The thought flashed into his head.

"They might; that's why she has to have a good replacement to fill in."

"I guess so."

"I assure you that you will be safe, otherwise I wouldn't suggest it. In fact, I have looked into the future and have seen you back here teaching at the university; and your teaching will be based on a lot of the material from the book."

"That's wonderful! And it's exciting to know that they will accept such a course."

"It will have to be modified some to fit into the subject of Eastern philosophy, but that can be done. The concept of the Higher Self appears in many of the yogic traditions, so you'll have to include some of those, also; it won't be strictly Zarathustra's journey. And, of course, the presentation has to be more academic."

"That makes sense. In the Eastern religion classes, the instructor teaches the Bhagavad Gita, which is about the Higher Self. But my courses have been mainly about European philosophy, although I do teach a course in Indian philosophy, which just touches on the yogic tradition. I can expand that course."

"That's good, and you also teach about Nietzsche, don't you?"

"Yes, I do."

"That subject will make it easy to bring in your book. Eventually, I see you doing a course on the book's content alone, but maybe at first you will just make small additions to your existing courses. In any case, I bring this up to emphasize that you will be safe when you marry Sam."

"And will she be safe?"

"That I can't say. I'm too close to her to get an accurate reading, but I can assure you she is very intelligent and has excellent instincts and intuition. She's also very careful and wouldn't do anything foolish. Her boss promised that the replacement would be a good one, and that is all that is needed to free her."

Jacques then suggested that they have a meditation together. It was a long one, and Anton went into a very deep place where he saw brilliant colors. Toward the end of it, he thought he saw an image of Sam. It was very hazy, but he saw her eyes just for a minute, clearly. They looked sad, and that disturbed him. When he told Jacques about this, Jacques said it could be coming from Anton's fears that things will go badly for them.

Jacques stayed another day, and they spent it talking, and walking, and simply being together. It was wonderful for Anton to have that time with him. It was beginning to dawn on him slowly that, when he married Sam, Jacques would be his father-in-law. He would be part not only of Anton's spiritual family but also of his personal family. Since Anton had just lost his own family, to become a part of Jacques' felt like a delightful replacement.

Jacques' personality was the opposite of his father's. He never expressed himself in a judgmental way, but always seemed open and willing to explore any subject. Intelligent and widely read, Jacques had a fullness of information and knowledge that made it very interesting to talk to him. In all fairness, Anton's father was also very literary and well informed, but not very receptive. He came to conclusions and could obviously be very opinionated. Jacques, on the other hand, was far more flexible. He saw life as a flow of energy that could take you in any direction, which makes for change and personal growth. His acceptance brought out the best in Anton. Only Anton's mother made him feel that way in his family.

After Jacques left, Anton felt his energy still with him.

CHAPTER 24

The end of July finally came, and Samantha arrived for her week's visit. Anton filled the house with flowers again and placed candles everywhere, lighting them around the time she was driving up the mountain road. She looked tired standing at the door, but she smiled all the tiredness away when she saw him, and he picked her up in his arms and carried her over the threshold.

"Put me down!"

But he could tell she liked it, and he danced around the living room with her laughing in his ear.

Later, as they sat on the small-screened porch, he took her hand and asked her to marry him.

She sat silently looking into his eyes, and for a moment he almost believed she was going to say no. But instead, she replied, "Except for my father, I have never loved anyone the way I love you. The intensity frightens me at times, but that probably will lessen in thirty years." She got up and jumped onto his lap and kissed him.

When he came up for breath he gasped, "I guess that means yes."

He told her about Jacques' recent visit and his concern as well as his own about her safety. She agreed that she felt apprehensive concerning this new contract and was thrilled to hear about the Harvard plan.

"Jacques is brilliant. But I don't think they'll let me go until you need to leave," she said. A look of concern crossed her face. "That isn't the reason you're asking me to marry you, is it?"

He laughed. "What do you think?" Then he added, "Thirty years with you wouldn't begin to be enough."

The week went quickly, most of it spent making plans for their wedding. Since none of Anton's family would come, it would be a small wedding, with just a few of their close friends. He wanted it there in the mountains, but that would be awkward, as Grindelwald was a small town and people would wonder why the family wasn't attending. Jacques' gardens were the second-best choice, and they both wanted him to write the ceremony.

Samantha thought she could get away the last week in August when most of the companies in Europe took their vacations. But the big question was where to go for a honeymoon. Booking a place at this late date would prove difficult anywhere in Europe, but it might be easier in another country. They both had traveled a lot, so they wanted a place where neither of them had ever been.

"Let's ask Jacques," Samantha suggested. "He's traveled everywhere. He might have some ideas."

Anton ignored this thought, wanting the decision to be their own. He had an old atlas, and they examined it carefully, ending up with three countries neither of them had been to but that interested them. Then they spent a day looking at pictures of those on the Internet.

They finally agreed on renting a villa on the island of Martinique in the Caribbean. There was one available the last week in August. It would be hot then, but the beaches were lovely, and they would have their own private pool secluded enough to go skinny dipping. Also, the place was modern and had air conditioning. The photos were appealing: open interiors with gardens, and porches, and a good distance from the next place.

The week was over much too fast, and as soon as Samantha was out of sight, Anton's heart started aching to be with her again.

He knew the family's schedule, so on those days when they were at home, he stayed at his place and didn't go to town, stocking up on things beforehand. Only his mother knew where he was living, and since she had sworn to not tell any of them, he felt safe in his quiet domain. Let them think he was no longer in the vicinity. Except for a few friends, all the locals still believed he was living at home.

Mother came twice, surprising him. She looked worn out and even ill, which concerned him. She claimed to be just tired and wouldn't talk about what was going on, but he knew it was about him.

He couldn't decide whether to tell her about his marriage. It would grieve her, as it did him, that she wouldn't know his wife and couldn't be at their wedding. But some mutual friends would be coming, and in no time the news would be out, which would hurt her even more. So, he told her about Samantha, and about their spiritual connection with Jacques. Mainly, he told her about their love and about how important it was to have someone who would understand him and encourage him to fulfill his mission. He even showed her a picture he had of Samantha and himself.

He talked for a long time, and she listened and said nothing; she just listened with serious and loving eyes. When he finally had no more words to express his heart, she smiled. It wasn't a happy smile, but one that spoke of years of caring.

"My dear Anton. You have chosen your path, the one that is right for you, and because it is right, you have met the people with whom you need to be. I will meet Samantha and get to know her. She will be the daughter I have always wanted, a daughter who senses, and knows, and searches, someone like you, and who is sensitive and courageous. I know her already, here." And she pressed her hand against her heart. "She will be my child. I know it."

And then his mother hugged him, and he knew she was right, that Sam would be as dear to her as she was to him.

"I will come to your wedding. He needn't know. You will tell me where to come."

"But what if he finds out? People you know will be there. He said he would leave you." Anton protested.

"That's my concern. I will not miss my son's wedding." He felt her sudden wrath, which was an incoming tide of water striking stone cliffs, and he knew it had been truly difficult at home. His mother was a constant surprise. In light of the family criticism, he had never imagined that she would consider coming to his wedding. He felt delighted.

Suddenly it meant that the future would be all right, that maybe even his brothers and sister would come back. His father he knew wouldn't, but now Anton could hope about the others. Maybe someday after the book was out and there was less negative energy around it, maybe then things would change.

They talked about the wedding and who to invite. It would be perhaps thirty or forty people at the most, just friends, as Sam had no relatives except for Jacques. Just before his mother left, she sat down with him on the porch and told him something that she had never talked about before.

"Anton, when I was a child, around eight years old, I had many out-of-body experiences. And I saw into the other worlds. I remember telling my mother about it, and she thought I had a mental disorder and took me to a psychiatrist. He terrified me to the extent that I never told anyone ever again about my experiences. You are the first person. I stopped having those experiences because he made me believe they were wrong. But your valley story reminded me of them, and I have felt such anguish for not having continued to develop and work with those energies and images."

"But Mother, you can still develop it. It's never too late."

She shook her head. "I love your father, and he is just like that psychiatrist. He would never approve. I'm too old now, but you and Samantha can give that gift to your children, just as I tried to give a little of it to you."

"Thank you for that. When you read my book, I think you will at least want to meditate and learn more. Father needn't know. At least don't shut the door on your gifts. If you do, they may be lost to you in your next life, and that would be a shame."

She smiled. "All right, I promise to leave the door open until I read your book, and then we can talk more. Now I must leave. I'm so happy for you."

Everything was falling into place. The appointment at Harvard went through as planned. Anton had been so busy with everything that he hadn't really thought about what it meant to teach at Harvard. The prospect now made him very excited. It was such a prestigious university, with high-level academics who should prove interesting to work with. Mainly, to experiment with some of the material in his book would be not only challenging but also helpful in the future, when he would try to incorporate it into his courses in Zürich.

His biggest problem was telling his department director, Bruno Bauer, that he needed an additional leave in January—a leave for the spring semester. He hadn't signed a contract yet, but it would still be breaking the promise he had given him. Anton felt blocked about telling him the truth. He ended up calling Jacques and asking him how to renege without making difficult karma.

Jacques thought for a minute and said, "You said you were returning in September, but did you say how long you would be teaching?"

"No, it was understood, as it's a permanent post."

"But you didn't say that?"

"No."

"Then you are free of any karma around this issue. You also never signed a contract. If you had, you would be bound by it. As it is, you will simply be teaching in the fall as you promised."

"But what if he says no to the leave?"

"Then you have to resign."

Anton felt very unhappy at those words. He loved teaching, and his years at the university were full of joy for him. To lose that job felt devastating. It was the best university in Zürich, and since Zürich was to remain his and Samantha's home, not teaching there seemed inconceivable.

Jacques must have picked up his thought, as he interjected, "Anton, even if you have to resign, I assure you they will want you back when you return. They will hire someone else who will fall short of your abilities. Don't worry."

Reassured, Anton went to Zürich and met with Bruno. He explained that because of personal matters, he had no choice but to go to America for next year's spring semester. Bruno was visibly upset. He told him, "Anton, you know that I am going to have to replace you. And, in all fairness, if your replacement is a good teacher, I will keep that person."

"I realize that."

Then Bruno did add, "Even though I am disappointed, I still believe you are the best teacher for the post, and your Harvard background will be valuable. Will you still be able to teach the fall semester?"

"Yes, I don't need to leave until after the holidays."

The meeting ended congenially, with their promising to keep in touch with each other, and Bruno adding that he hoped to see Anton when he returned from the States.

While he was in Zürich, Anton went to see Jacques. Samantha was doing some last minute traveling. She had already given the company her notice and promised to train someone new after her honeymoon. The interview process had begun, and several agents were already grooming themselves for the job application. Anton was nervous that someone would get wise to their plan, and when he talked about it to Jacques, he could feel butterflies in his stomach.

"Surely someone is going to get suspicious and wonder why the sudden move, especially during the semester change. Teachers leave jobs after a year is up, not during the year."

"But you're dealing with criminals, not teachers. You can always point out exceptions to the rule. Let it go, Anton. Worrying about Sam will direct negative energy to her, and I don't think you want that."

"No, of course not, but it's difficult not to worry. In retrospect, wouldn't it have been better if Sam were pregnant, making it difficult to travel? Then we could stay in Zürich."

Jacques looked at him with serious eyes. "Pregnancy doesn't assure her safety. The company wouldn't take that as an excuse until she gives birth, and nine months more on this job could prove fatal, particularly when the government starts clamping down on them. The people interviewing for the job now are hardcore police officers who know how to protect themselves. They have promised to wait long enough so that the clampdown is in no way associated with Samantha."

Jacques then changed the focus. "There is a possibility that they will investigate you to make certain you are on the up and up. I'm certain they also have connections in the States and can look into your appointment."

"Could there be a problem?"

"I don't think so, but you never know. I think it's important that you make some phone calls from your home to the department deans at Harvard; that way if the company has a way of checking your call numbers, it will look like you are communicating with the university directly."

"That's fine. I want to do that anyway to talk about my curriculum."

The courses had been set. He was teaching two courses in the Philosophy Department on European Philosophers and a new course called, "Who Am I? Exploring Philosophical Questions." And in the Divinity School, he was teaching a course on the Bhagavad Gita. In these two courses he would be able to introduce some of the material from his book.

He had the directors' names: Richard Evans, the head of the Philosophy Department, and John Watts, the dean of the Divinity School. "When would be a good time to make those calls?" Anton asked.

"I think right away, even if just to make the connections, but any follow-up correspondence could have been by mail, and now a phone call and a couple of emails is enough to be appropriate. Besides Sam's company doesn't know what connections you had with the university before you marry her, and if they do any checking, you were in New York in January and could have gone to Boston to make those contacts."

They talked some more about all the arrangements. Sam was to precede Anton to Boston to look for a place to live. This gave her a reason to leave the company at the end of November. While they were talking, Anton felt some anxiety returning. This entire affair was on the edge of bizarre for him. He had never lived like this and never would want to, and yet the last two years had been filled with such disturbing things happening.

Anton thought about the book. "The book is finished, and of course, I would like you to be the first to read it."

"Not Samantha?" Jacques asked.

"No, she's second on the list."

"Thank you. I look forward to it."

"I still don't know about the title. It sounds pompous somehow to name it after Nietzsche's book. The Zarathustra in my book is very different from his. The only similarity is that, in both books, Zarathustra comes down from the mountain to teach, but what he teaches in mine is very different."

"Do you think changing the title will make your father feel differently about it?"

"Probably not, particularly after he reads it. No, I honestly am bothered by it myself."

"Nietzsche wrote his book in the nineteenth century. This is the twenty-first century, and a lot has changed, so of course if Zarathustra comes down from the mountain in this age his teachings will be very different.

"It is the concept that everyone has the ability to develop his or her highest potential and open to the inner Self that contains wisdom. This self is the Higher Self and belongs to every human being on the planet. Your words are very different, but the intent is the same: it is to awaken in humanity the desire to find the Higher Self and, in so doing, to be able to discover the real meaning of our existence."

Jacques' words felt right in Anton's consciousness. "Yes. I understand that, but still, why not give this man or this adept another name? Other writers have written similarly, Hermann Hess, for example. His books are full of these concepts, not to mention the writings of Eastern teachers such as Ramana Maharshi, whose teaching is about the Higher Self, or the other yoga disciplines that teach about the Self. Even the Gita is about the Higher Self and the conflict between the ego and the Self. It's in all the Eastern teachings. Even in America, the Higher Self has become well known now."

"For select people, that is true. But your book is going further. It is uncovering esoteric information that hasn't been written about. You describe the subtle worlds. How many books do that? This is information that has always been secret, but now is the time for it to be revealed to everyone. Some will read it and understand, and others won't. Your time in the valley was to prove to you that these other worlds do exist, giving you the ability to write about them from first-hand experience."

"But why me? Why not a teacher, like you?" Anton asked.

"Because you are very spiritual, highly educated, a Ph.D, and a teacher of philosophy. People listen and respect university teachers, and your resume will have the Harvard credentials as well as those from Zürich University. You have also published a very successful book. People may not believe you, but they will listen and be interested. And those who are ready will want to know more. That's why you were the best person to do this. It is your destiny,"

CHAPTER 25

By August, the book was completed. It was a relief for Anton and, at the same time, a loss. It felt like losing a child when he or she becomes an adult. When the book was his "child," it had inspired his life, giving it stimulation and adventure. Now, that was ended. His creativity no longer had an outlet, a way to express his innermost feelings. And especially, writing this book had been a learning process, making it different from his other writing on subjects about which he was knowledgeable. For the first time, he was the student as well as the author, which was an odd combination but one that he had thoroughly enjoyed.

Anton made several copies of the manuscript and sent one to Jacques; another one he held for Sam, who was returning in a week.

The mountains were cool that summer, and August almost seemed like autumn. Leaves were already starting to turn color and fall off the trees. The prediction was that it would be a very cold winter. It made Anton feel a little better about their being in America.

Things were going well with Sam's departure from her job. A male agent was hired to replace her, and she was in the process of training him. Plans for their wedding were complete, as well as for their honeymoon in Martinique.

Anton returned to Zürich and started to clean out space in his apartment for Sam to move in. Since she had her own apartment in Zürich, there were a few things she wanted to keep. Her apartment was small, so it was mainly a couple of pieces of furniture, some personal possessions, books, and her clothing. They made the move the week before the wedding, and she settled in with ease.

That week together, just feeling how their life would be, was one of the happiest weeks Anton had ever experienced. Sam worked full days, but since he was now free, he cooked their dinners and loved doing it, looking through recipe books to find exotic cuisine. Even though Sam was tired when she came home, she was a refreshing light that filled the apartment, making it her home as much as his.

Fortunately, they had the same taste in art and decor. Beatrice's taste had been more decorative than his, with fancy, colorful designs on the upholstery. After she'd moved her things out, he replaced them with modern Scandinavian pieces mixed with a few antique tables and cabinets. He was willing to change everything for Sam, but she loved it all and only added the furniture she brought and three or four of her paintings.

Their wedding day bathed itself in sunlight. Jacques' gardens were in full bloom, an intermingling of colors that formed a lovely background for the ceremony. Around forty people attended, mainly friends of Sam's and Jacques' and Anton's and those disciples of Jacques' who lived nearby, some of whom Anton had met. Anton's mother arrived early, before the other guests. She and Samantha had both wanted to have a few minutes alone just to talk and get to know each other. They went for a walk, and when they came back Anton could tell they had made a good connection.

Sam wore an off-white dress that was elegant, long, and classic in its lines, with lace around the V-neckline and on the sleeves. Her jewelry was a pearl necklace and matching earrings that Jacques had given her. The open pattern of her veil allowed her blond hair to glimpse through and shimmer in the sunlight. Her bouquet was made of small white orchids that had a touch of purple in their centers. They hung down gracefully in long trails against the straight lines of her gown. Always breathtaking, on this day Samantha seemed more regal, and Anton wondered if she had been a queen in some distant land and time.

Anton wore a gray morning tuxedo, as did Jacques. He and Samantha had one close friend stand up with them. He thought about his brothers regretfully but dropped the thought as best he could.

The wedding was simple but full of depth. The minister was a disciple of Jacques' and close to Samantha. Jacques wrote the ceremony, and when Anton spoke his lines to Samantha, a deep emotion filled his heart with timeless light. Her words to him blended with his own, and he knew her heart felt the same. Halfway through, many were sniffling, and Anton felt that he and Sam were surrounded by love. He realized the sanctity of marriage when he looked into her eyes and put a ring on her finger and when she put a ring on his.

The reception was also held in the garden. The tables were arranged under some big oak trees that provided a green canopy, sheltering the people from the sun.

Anton's mother sat next to Jacques, and they spoke quietly for a long time. Anton's curiosity tempted him to eavesdrop, but the chatter of the guests dissuaded him. When he finally took a walk with her alone later in the day, she said, "Anton, I am so happy for you, to have such a good man as your father-in-law, and I love Samantha. She is perfect for you. I regret that your father can't know her." Unhappiness filled her eyes. "But they will be your family now—your real family."

"Mother, I still have you. Just know my love for you is always there."

"I know, and I plan to see more of you both. I've decided not to be intimidated any more by your father. If he finds out and leaves me, so be it."

This surprised him. "I don't want that to happen. It would ruin your life."

"Not seeing you ruins my life, and if he is going to be so stubborn, I don't want to be with him, and I mean that." By the intensity of her gaze, he could see that what she said was genuine.

Later, when his mother said goodbye, she gave them a present. It was a small package, and Anton gave it to Samantha to unwrap. There was lots of paper around it, and when it all came off there was a key, and he could tell it was a Swiss bank-account key. He looked questioningly at his mother. She smiled, "The account is in your name. It belonged to my mother and was kept private, even from your father. I have had it a long time and knew that someday it would be for you, but when and why I didn't know. It will build your house on the mountain."

"But Mother. I don't need this. I have my trust from your father, and that is plenty."

"I know that. It's not about the money. Building your house in the mountains means so much to me. They took away your home, Anton, and even if someday all is reconciled, it will never be the same for you. Please let me do this for you both."

Anton looked at Sam and she nodded. They both put their arms around his mother and held her. He said, "Only if you know you will always be welcome there."

"Yes, there will be a room for you to come and stay any time," Samantha added.

"Maybe I'll take you up on that," his mother laughed. "Now I must leave."

When all the guests had left, Jacques, Samantha, and Anton sat outside, sipping mugs of black coffee. They sat in silence and enjoyed feeling the oneness of their love for one another.

When Jacques spoke, it finished off the day, giving them something to remember in the years ahead. He said, "I know you both will be happy, and I also know that in that happiness you will embrace those around you. There will be many people in your lives who will find you and love you. Remember that love is the gift of God that makes your spirit soar. When you meet challenges, hold tightly to that gift. When you need to be apart, keep that gift always in your hearts; and, most of all, use it with all those you meet, even when you meet your enemies. Use the gift, as it will conquer them. May your hearts be united forever." And he rose and embraced them both, then left them alone, standing in a gentle embrace.

CHAPTER 26

Anton and Samantha spent a perfect honeymoon on the island of Martinique, basking in the sun, holding hands running down the beach, and dining under starry skies. They both felt this time together solidified their bond that was an unending road paved in love.

Just after they returned to Zürich, they talked about their relationship and the best way to handle any disagreements that arose. Samantha suggested, "Confronting is probably the most difficult thing for people to do. Even married couples have trouble doing it, which brings up something I want to suggest. Once a week, maybe at breakfast on Sundays, let's discuss the previous week. If I've done something that bothers you, you tell me, and vice versa. And the opposite, too: let's compliment each other in terms of what we've liked about each other."

"There's nothing about you I don't like. So that will be easy."

Sam looked serious. "Sweetie, that's why they call what we've just had a honeymoon; but honeymoons do end, and things will come up. I, for one, like for them to be resolved right away instead of building up."

"You're right." He thought about Beatrice. "If I had done that with Beatrice, maybe things wouldn't have changed so much. But then I wouldn't be here now with you, and it would have been terrible to have lost you."

"Oh, I think we still would have found each other. You're my destiny." She leaned over and kissed him lightly on the lips.

Beyond the deep love they had for each other was the sexual passion that ripened as they explored erogenous places on their bodies. Often, they turned off the air-conditioning and walked around the condo naked, touching and rubbing against each other until the sweat of their bodies pulled them into a new place to consummate their love.

They were spent with love and desire that was never ending. When she fell asleep in his arms, he loved just to look at her. She sometimes seemed beatified. Often, she smiled in her sleep, a child's smile, innocent, as if she were playing in some imaginary, magical land. He'd seen her smile like that when they took walks by the river or when he bought her an ice cream cone. It was a different smile from when she smiled at him with coquettishness and longing or when she smiled with love from the heart.

Their friendship also matured. They were avid readers and spent many evenings discussing books they had read or wanted to read, and even though their ideas were different on certain subjects, they found themselves in agreement on many issues.

Most of all, it was wonderful to share their spiritual practice. They honored that in each other. One of the joys of being together was to meditate and share beliefs around the teaching. Samantha was very knowledgeable about yoga philosophy, having read most of the Eastern teachings. Anton learned a great deal from her, and she in turn liked his scholarly perspective and viewpoint that came from teaching philosophy. He was more creative in his thinking and wanted to explore every concept, whereas she was more practical and down to earth and saw how concepts worked together. It was a good combination. They were enough alike to enjoy the same things together and different enough to make their conversations interesting. Was it the perfect marriage? Well, nothing's perfect, but they were certainly off to a good start.

His university added a course for him to teach in the fall, and it felt great to be back in front of a lecture hall and classroom. Anton hadn't realized how much he missed the students and the challenge of teaching. He also needed to refresh his skills to be qualified to teach at Harvard. The course he taught was on Greek myths and how they affected the social and economic systems of ancient Greece. It was a new course for him, but one that he was interested in and had done extensive research on.

In the meantime, Sam and Jacques were reading Anton's book, and, after their comments and corrections, he planned to send it to his agent.

During one of Sam's trips, something happened that was disturbing. The man who was to replace her at the company suddenly became ill and had to be rushed to a hospital. It was his appendix, and, thankfully, he survived. It would take at least three weeks for him to recover, which meant he wouldn't be able to work again until December. This caused a real problem for Samantha, as she hadn't finished his train-ing. Her boss insisted that she stay until the man was better and the training was done. If she didn't do this, they might hire someone else outside the agency. She had no choice but to agree. This meant she wouldn't be able to go to Boston to look for an apartment.

Anton had an old girlfriend in Boston, Ginny, who'd attended the university with him, and they had kept in contact with each other. He decided to ask her to help him find a place for Samantha and him to live. Ginny had good taste, and he could trust her judgment. He intended to go during the Christmas break to help. She agreed and even invited him to stay in her place, as she had two bedrooms. He accepted without asking Sam, and when he told her, she became very upset. This was their first real fight.

"How could you even consider staying in a single woman's apartment?"

"Why not? Ginny's an old friend. I told you about her." He looked at Sam, "You don't trust me? My God, how can you not trust me?" He felt angry and hurt.

"It's not about trust. Of course, I trust you, but what will everyone think?"

"What do you mean?"

"Besides Ginny's friends, Jacques has a class in Boston, and he plans to introduce you to those people when you're there."

"Let them think what they want to think. There's nothing wrong with staying at a friend's apartment. If it were reversed, and it were you staying at a man's apartment, it wouldn't bother me."

"But did you at all question how I might feel? How people might talk about this behind our backs?"

"You're paranoid. Do you think people care enough to talk about us?"

"I'm not paranoid. I'm realistic. I would like to be Ginny's friend. But how do you think I'm going to feel if her friends or Jacques' disciples even speculate about the two of you being together, particularly since you were a couple before?"

"Sam, that's nuts. You've made this into a big deal, and—"

"And" she interrupted, "they all know you're wealthy. Don't you think they may wonder why you wouldn't simply go to a hotel, just as I'm wondering?"

"If we're looking at apartments together, it's a hell of a lot easier to start from the same place instead of having to meet up somewhere. It's about convenience."

It went on and on, battling like two bulls unrelentingly locking horns. Finally, Anton left to go for a walk; otherwise, he would have started to shout at her, and he didn't want to do that.

After he left, Samantha sat in stony silence and thought, I know Anton has been spoiled, but I never realized until now how selfish he can be! He doesn't have the least sense of how hurtful this is to me.

She tried to connect with her Higher Self and feel its calm, but her heart felt too agitated and heavy. She thought, I'm leaving tomorrow on my most dangerous assignment, and I can't go with the solace of knowing Anton is here waiting for me with love and understanding.

Sam suddenly decided that it would be better for her to leave for her trip then and not spend an evening in nervous tension, as she had to carefully prepare mentally for the trip. She wanted to stay and try to work it out when Anton returned, but she already felt overloaded. She hadn't really explained to him how dangerous this work was and how very focused and alert she had to be at all times. It would have worried him too much, and now Sam realized that course of action had been correct.

In some ways, Anton lacked a depth of comprehending, which, for the first time, she unhappily realized.

Samantha then remembered a recent conversation with her father. He had said, "I know you love Anton very deeply, and he loves you, but understand that you are much more advanced than he is spiritually. You need to use discernment about what you say to him, mainly because he hasn't achieved that deeper understanding of himself yet."

"Dad, I know that. I also know he needs to do therapy around his childhood," she said. "Not doing it will not only affect him spiritually, but it will also influence our relationship. I'm waiting to mention it to him. Now it's difficult."

"Yes, I have already asked him to do therapy, but I felt his reluctance, and he hasn't followed through, even though Lea has also mentioned it to him."

"It's a man thing, you know," she laughed sarcastically. "Why do men feel therapy is unmanly?"

"It's part of our culture. A man feels it's weak to do therapy. You know, even I did some therapy only because my teacher requested it, and it really was helpful."

"Yes, it was for me, too, particularly after Mother left us."

And Sam remembered him sadly smiling at her at that time.

When Anton got back, Samantha was gone, leaving a note that said she had left early for her trip, which made him even angrier. What about all that talk about confronting problems? he thought. Going a day sooner also makes her more vulnerable. Damn! He had decided to change his arrangements with Ginny, but now he felt obstinate again.

He made himself supper and was watching a movie on TV, trying not to think about it, when the doorbell rang. Eagerly, he ran to the door, hoping to see Samantha, only to be surprised to find Jacques standing there.

"Anton, we need to talk."

"What did she do, go running to you?"

"Who do you mean?"

"Samantha; we had a fight."

"No, in fact I wanted to talk to her, also. She's not here?"

"No, she left a note saying that she was leaving a day early for her trip. I hoped you were she just now and that she'd changed her mind."

Jacques' face blanched. "I came to stop her from going. We fear a leak has happened. We have to stop her."

Anton ran to the phone. "Let's try Alitalia. Her flight is to Milan. Maybe she hasn't left yet."

He got through right away, but it was too late. Her flight had left a half-hour earlier. It was on time.

"What do we do?"

"What hotel does she stay at?" Jacques asked.

"Different ones." Anton ran to her desk and found her day planner. "Thank God, she left it."

He called the hotel and was told she had booked a room for this evening but hadn't arrived yet. He looked at Jacques. "If I give my name she might not call me back."

Jacques took the receiver and told the desk clerk that it was an emergency, that

Samantha needed to call her father as soon as she arrived.

"We'll have to go to my house immediately. She'll call me there."

"What if she thinks it's still from me and doesn't call?"

"Remember, I'm also her teacher. She will call."

And she did. An hour later Jacques' phone rang.

"Samantha, we have a problem. You need to leave immediately and take the next plane home. There's been a leak and they know something's up. Come to my house. It's safer here. And fedpol will send guards." There was a pause as he listened. "Yes, he's here with me now." And he handed Anton the phone.

"Darling, I'm so sorry, please forgive me," Sam said. "If I hadn't run off, I would be there with you now."

"I'm sorry, too. Forgive me. Call us from the airport so we can meet your plane — and hurry!"

The two men sat quietly for a few minutes, and then Anton asked, "What happens now? We're not safe anywhere."

"Right now, fedpol is trying to find out what the leak is about. It still may not involve Sam, but they don't know. They should know before tomorrow; so, if she's not been exposed, she can go back to Milan as planned."

"Over my dead body! I'm not letting her return. It's too risky."

"It's too risky for her not to. I pray she'll be cleared; otherwise, it may be very dangerous for you both."

A half hour later the phone rang. "I missed the last flight home. I'll stay in the hotel here and take a 6 a.m. plane in the morning. It arrives at 6:45."

"Be careful, and get room service," Jacques said. "Don't talk to anyone. We'll meet you in the morning."

Jacques made some calls to try to find out more about the leak. Anton poured himself a drink and sat on the porch in the dark. He felt frightened, helpless, and guilty. He was eight years old again, lost on a forbidden trail in the mountains. Fortunately, a hiker had saved him.

In the morning, a police car took them to the airport to meet her plane. It was on time, but Samantha was not on it. They checked the airline. She had never shown up. They called the hotel with the hope that she had simply overslept. She hadn't checked out, but there was no answer in the room. They tried her cell phone. No answer. A government official was able to persuade the hotel manager to check her room. Her bag was gone, and the bed hadn't been slept in.

CHAPTER 27

When fedpol went to raid the company's office in Zürich to arrest its main officers, they found that it had been vacated. The company had moved all its records and taken off. The few workers remaining there didn't know what had happened. When they had come to work that morning, they were shocked to find none of the managers there and all their files vanished. The managers had successfully gotten away to another country. Even though the Swiss bank that had their account was on alert to inform fedpol if anything strange took place, the officers had managed to withdraw their money the evening before.

Anton and Jacques went to fedpol's headquarters and sat in meetings. They were doing an interdepartmental search for the informer and had a suspect but no proof. Hermann Levitt, head of fedpol, said they would do everything in their power to find out where Samantha had been taken. Herman was a tall, middle-aged, dignified looking man, with gray hair and gray-blue eyes, resembling a reserved banker more than a secret-service executive. He still wasn't certain if Sam's company knew she was an agent. Only one or two top people in the fedpol agency had that information.

"Why would they take her if she weren't under suspicion?" Anton asked him.

Hermann's reply was, "That is something that still needs to be found out."

When Jacques and Anton finally arrived home in the afternoon, they were faced with what to do next. Anton made some coffee while Jacques went to his office to check his phone messages. Anton heard him cry out, "It's Samantha!" He ran to the office as her recorded voice was saying, "Dad, Anton, I'm okay. I can't talk now. Don't try to find me." And she had hung up.

They called Hermann, who had the call traced to a phone booth on a main avenue in Milan. Either her captors had let her call from there, or she had made the call on her own. There was no way of knowing, except that, if they were holding her captive, it was more likely they would call themselves, particularly if they wanted something. Regardless, the good news was she was still alive, so there was hope.

"I'm going to Milan," Anton announced to Jacques.

"You can't do that. If she's in danger you will make it worse, and besides, they could take you also."

"Then let them—at least I will be with her. If they kill her, there's no way I want to live anyway."

"Don't be stupid. Remember she said not to try to find her. If she's running from them, you would only make it harder for her to escape."

"But I feel so powerless here." Anton put his head in his hands and felt extremely frustrated.

"I know, I feel the same way." Jacques put his arms around him, and they held each other for a few minutes. Anton felt Jacques' sorrow, which in some way lessened his own.

"Here I am a teacher, and I can't get a read on it because it's too close to me! But I'm going to try." Jacques left to go to his meditation room, and Anton knew he would send Samantha energy and help.

Anton tried to meditate too, but had no success. Instead, he blamed himself for the fight. His stubbornness had made it all happen, but how was he to know? What good was it to be in a spiritual teaching if you couldn't protect your loved ones? Negative thoughts invaded him, and he finally consciously erased them, as he knew they were foreign. But the fear kept assaulting him. Oh, God, he prayed, what if I lose her? His mind went over all the things about their relationship. He kept seeing her so clearly, as if her face were burned into his inner vision. It was an image he would never lose, but he didn't want the *image*, he wanted *her* there with him.

The phone rang. Anton picked it up and heard Hermann's voice. "We think she's being held in an office building in downtown Milan. We're working with the authorities there, and they received an anonymous phone call from a man who said he saw a young blond woman being taken into a building, and she looked as if she were being forced to enter it. They're investigating the lead right now. We also have extradition papers to arrest them in Italy. We think that is where they all went. The informant disappeared. We were right about whom we believed it to be. We'll find him. He can't leave the country."

Hermann said he'd call as soon as he found out anything more. Anton thanked him, but he still felt that finding Samantha wouldn't be that easy. Later, Hermann called back to say that the blonde woman had turned out to be someone else's wife who had run away.

In the meantime, Jacques returned from his meditation room.

"Could you see anything?" Anton anxiously asked.

"No, nothing is clear. I keep hitting resistance when I try to reach her and find out where she is, and even though I used a lot of energy to dispel it, the block came up again. If I didn't know better, I would say it was coming from a positive outside force and not from negative ones. The energy is different."

"Why would that happen?"

"I'm not sure. Something strange is happening. I'm going to try again to go through it in about an hour. Right now, I need to rest."

He patted Anton's shoulder and went upstairs. For the first time, Anton was aware of Jacques' age and realized that his energy was very low. He must have used up a lot of it in his meditation and was now going to recoup. He anxiously realized that if Jacques, who was so powerful, could become depleted like this, then how in the world could they save Sam? At this stage in Anton's development, he personally didn't know how to focus and use energy. He was of no help and he felt that way, totally useless. Neither of them had had any sleep the previous night, so maybe that was why Jacques was so tired. Anton decided to lie down also. In a few minutes he was in a deep sleep, and he had a dream, an incredible dream.

The dream began with Samantha seated at a table with him in their living room playing cards. Anton was the observer, watching Sam and him play. The deck was made up of all jokers, and the images were animated: they smiled, winked, and even had scowling expressions. Anton and Sam were playing for high stakes, as there was a pile of money on Sam's side of the table. Obviously, she was winning.

What kind of game was this? The negative jokers wore red and black costumes, and the positive ones wore purple and white. It seemed as if the scowling jokers could win when either Sam or he were leading. When one of them wasn't leading, that person could easily use the positive jokers and maneuver them anywhere the person wanted to. There was a board where the cards were placed. The purpose of the game was to defeat the negative jokers by placing them in positions where the positive ones could surround them. The more negative jokers that were defeated, the more money was made. Sam smiled at him and said, "You see who's winning." Then she disappeared, and he was left with his scowling jokers laughing maliciously at him.

Anton woke up with a start and felt surrounded by full-size jokers. Then they disappeared one at a time, but not without first saying, "You have lost! You have lost!" But Sam had been winning, so he reassured himself that the dream had been a positive one, indicating that she was okay, that she was in control of the situation.

Later, when he told Jacques the dream, Jacques mused for a minute and said, "Yes, that sounds right, but the last part—where the jokers say you have lost—bothers me. But that could just be your fear," he reassured Anton.

They went to bed early and woke up the next morning to a clear, sunny sky. Anton went out on the porch and felt the sunshine comfort and ease his thoughts about Samantha. Before breakfast, he took a walk down the garden path in Jacques' yard and even meditated on one of the benches there. He was beginning to feel the loss. They had always spoken on the phone every day when she was away. Her absence already felt like forever, and yet it had only been three days since she left.

Anton's thoughts became philosophical: What, after all, is the nature of love? Once ego-centered or selfish love has found its source, it is unyielding in wanting sustenance. It is a disease that enters the vessels and nerves and opens the heart, leaving no room for anything else. When the target of its need is no longer there, it can shift in form, crying like a lost kitten trying to find its mother to be fed. While love in its selfless fullness is the Divine: in its emptiness, it is the void, a void not of peace but of utter aloneness.

His meditation was mainly a prayer, an ongoing chant to the higher beings to save Samantha. He would do anything and everything to save her. He prayed and prayed until he felt Jacques' hand on his shoulder.

"Anton, it will be all right, I know it will be all right."

"You're certain?"

"Yes, I'm certain. How or when I don't know. I can't receive the information, but I feel certain she is alive and that she will be saved."

Anton wanted so much to believe him, but an inner voice said, He's so close to her. Is he right, or is that just his desires talking? Nevertheless, he hugged Jacques and said, "That makes me feel better. Thank you."

But as if in answer to his thoughts, Jacques said, "It's true, Anton. Believe me, it's true. Someday she will return."

In the days and weeks that followed, those words echoed in Anton's mind. He returned home and went to work and tried not to think about Sam. But at night he would finger her clothes in the closet and see her in them. Everywhere in the apartment were memories of their nakedness and spontaneous lovemaking. He would wait for her to telephone. Every night when he arrived, he would open the door and call her name, hoping to hear her run across the room into his arms. But Samantha did not return, and no one could find out anything about her. Her disappearance was complete, and there were no leads. Fedpol also wasn't able to locate any of the corporate heads. Obviously, they had left Italy and had taken on new names and passports.

Jacques had nothing more to add about it except that he didn't know when she would come back, and when Anton questioned him Jacques would kindly say, "Have faith." This answer made Anton want to scream. "How can I have faith at this time?" Everything in his world was falling apart, and he could not relate to faith.

CHAPTER 28

Anton was due to start classes at Harvard on January 29. Ginny had found him an apartment near Harvard Square, so he wired her a check to take it for him. It no longer mattered to him what it looked like since a place without Samantha would never be home for him. He tried to be released from his contract with Harvard. He didn't want to go so far away in case Sam was found, but the dean could not replace him at such a late date. Besides, Jacques felt it would be better for Anton to be away, as being in his apartment in Zürich just reminded him daily of his loss. This was true. He was over-socializing, going out to dinner and parties with friends, in order not to be home in the evenings alone.

By now his mother knew about Samantha's disappearance, and she called him almost daily to see if he was all right. Anton tried to be positive when he talked about it, which was seldom. People honored his feelings by not asking questions; and, as the weeks passed, there was a heavy silence around anything connected to her. Even Jacques never spoke about her and kept a stoic manner if Anton happened to bring the subject up. Jacques remained strong in his belief that Samantha was alive. But if she were alive, where was she? Was she a prisoner? That thought also filled Anton with anguish. Even though he maintained an outward calm with friends, his inner being kept crying. Sometimes he felt her presence, but that scared him even more, as then he truly believed she was dead and was visiting him on the subtle plane. What was true? His sense of reality took on dimensions that seemed to end up nowhere.

On weekends, he went back to bed after having breakfast and slept most of the day away. Sleep blanketed his feelings and kept him from thinking about her and about the underlying cause that was destroying him.

Jacques read Anton's book and made a few changes. It was now in the hands of the agent, and so now Anton had an additional worry as to what the agent would think of it. In his stressed state, he wasn't prepared to defend or fight for anything.

He and Samantha had planned to rent out the apartment in Zürich while they were in Boston, but now he decided just to close it up. It needed to be free in case Sam suddenly returned. He was not ready yet to pack up her clothes and put them into storage.

Anton planned to spend Christmas with Jacques. The family was home in the mountains for the holidays, so his mother arranged to have dinner with him after New Year's, before he left for Boston.

Christmas Eve morning he was packing an overnight bag for his stay with Jacques later that evening when the phone rang. It was Samantha.

"Darling, I can't talk. I am well; that's all I can say. Believe me, I am all right."

And before he could say anything she hung up. He was stunned. What was happening? Her voice sounded calm and reassuring, not in any way scared. A part of him felt very happy that she was alive, and another part was furious at not knowing more. What was going on? If she was really all right then could she be in collusion with her bosses? That thought had never crossed his mind before, and now it overpowered his thinking until he finally rejected it. But what else could it be? If she was a prisoner, how did she get to the phone? And why keep her a prisoner?

He called Jacques, and before he could finish Jacques interrupted, "Yes, she just called me and said the same thing."

"Did you talk to her?"

"No, she hung up, just as she did with you."

"I don't understand it, Jacques. Is she working with them? Is she a prisoner? I just don't understand." And he stopped talking as he felt his emotions began to overwhelm him.

"Anton, I think this is very difficult because we don't know. She never confided even in me—and remember, I'm her teacher, not just her father. All I know is that she is telling the truth, that she is fine and is doing something she can't explain to either of us. You must have faith in her ability to make sound judgments. Whatever is happening, I know she has the wisdom to handle it correctly."

Anton felt an edge of uncertainty in Jacques' last sentence but didn't say so. "What's next?"

"I'll call Hermann, but I don't think he's there today. In any case, I don't believe he knows either, or if he does, he's not going to tell us."

"Could she be in contact with him?"

"Anything's possible. This operation may be much more complicated than either of us knows."

"But surely, he would tell us that she was okay if that were the case?"

"Fedpol doesn't reveal very much, and if it were in their best interest to keep us in the dark, he would do so."

It never dawned on Anton that this could be the case, that she was still working for Hermann, and that he wouldn't at least tell them she wasn't dead. He was furious.

"I want to call him."

"No, but come over right away, and we'll call him from here."

When he arrived, Jacques was meditating in the living room. He phoned fedpol and found it was closed for the holidays, but then he went to a notebook that was open. "I remember that he gave me his home number."

Anton picked up the other phone to listen in.

Hermann answered right away. Jacques politely told him what had happened but added, "We need to talk about this. What's really going on?"

"I can't tell you, but I'm happy for you that she's still alive. Really, it's a miracle that they haven't done away with her."

"There's got to be a reason for that."

"Yes, I agree. I hate to say this, but maybe she's working for them now."

"That's a lie and you know it." Jacques' voice was calm but icy.

"It's the only conclusion I can come to. I wouldn't think she could phone if she were a prisoner; and, if she's free, why hasn't she come home?"

"Maybe she's there because of a special assignment from you?"

"I have no idea what you are talking about, but I am very happy that she's alive. That's a nice Christmas gift! We'll look into it more next week. Now I must go. Have a good holiday." And he hung up.

"He's lying," Jacques said. "I could feel it. She must be on a special mission for them. I told her not to continue that work anymore, that it's too dangerous, but sometimes Samantha can be very stubborn."

"Yes, I know. But how could she do this to me? Doesn't she care enough not to take such risks?" Not only did Anton suddenly feel abandoned, but also for the first time he questioned their relationship.

Jacques looked at him kindly, "You're a yogi, she's a yogi. The difference is that she has been one for most of her life and you have only recently become one. A yogi has no fear and does what she or he feels can help humanity the most. If her job is in that service, then it will come first, before her marriage."

"A dead yogi can't help anyone," Anton bitterly replied.

"You're right. I agree with you, but neither one of us is Samantha." Jacques paused and then added, "Do you honestly think she would want this? Don't just look at your needs; look at what she must be going through."

Later, when he was alone, Anton thought a lot about what Jacques said. He still felt that her abandoning him was wrong; but then, in retrospect, he considered that they'd had a bad fight, and who knew what had happened after he left the house? Maybe they'd called her then and given her this assignment, and she took it while feeling angry with him. That was a lot of maybes; but at this point, who cared? The most important thing was that she was alive.

Before retiring, he and Jacques had a final talk. Jacques asked, "Is there anything you need from me before you leave for America?"

Anton thought for a minute. "I think I just need to know that I can reach you at any time. You travel so much I am concerned that if something happens to Sam, I won't know about it."

"Of course, you will know about it. When we meet with Hermann on Monday, we will give him all the details on how to contact both of us."

"But you don't trust him."

"Yes, but if anything happens to Samantha, he won't withhold that."

"But Sam will no longer be able to call me when I'm in Boston because my European cell phone won't work there. I will have to buy a new one for the States."

"Believe me, she will get your phone number; just make certain it's listed."

"True, she's very resourceful." He thought about their meeting in New York.

Christmas was a small gathering of Jacques' disciples, some of whom Anton had met in the class that Sam and he had attended even when Jacques was away. Most of the people had been studying with Jacques for several years, and he learned a lot just by listening to them.

Lea was also there, and they sat together and spoke quietly about Samantha. Her insight was quite profound. "Sam and I have been friends, besides being spiritual sisters, for a long time. When she feels strongly about anything, nothing will stop her from pursuing it. Jacques is right in feeling she doesn't think about the danger involved. If she had, she wouldn't have taken this job in the first place. Because of that, she will never be easy to live with — but neither will you. The good thing is that both of you truly have a strong inner drive for happiness, and love, and have found it in each other."

"I find that difficult to believe at this point. If it were true, she wouldn't have gone to Milan. She wouldn't have completely abandoned me without telling me anything. The longer she's gone, leaving me with this mystery, the more I feel she really doesn't love me."

"I can understand why you feel that way, but I know that's not true. I assure you, she is deeply in love with you."

Anton didn't want to argue with Lea; and besides, what good would it do when in fact Sam was gone? But he added, "What I can't understand is how she could do this to Jacques. I know he's been affected by it. Look how he's aged in the past couple of months."

"Yes, I know, and it worries me. His wife left in a similar manner — just disappeared, and then called to say she wasn't coming back. It was only later that he found out she had turned negative and had joined the other order."

Anton had a sudden thought he hadn't even considered before. "Could Sam be doing the same thing? She told me her mother is always trying to see her."

"I don't think so. Sam has very deep integrity and morals about right and wrong. But, Anton, I don't really know."

They both sat in silence for a while, thinking about it, and Anton wondered if Jacques had thought about it, too.

CHAPTER 29

The next day, Anton went up to his cabin on the mountain. He planned to stay there through New Year's and return the following week for last-minute errands before leaving for the States. He checked to make certain the weather would be good, with no forecast of major snows that could possibly keep him stranded.

When he arrived, it was clear, with a chill that penetrated the warmth of his jacket. There was a note under the door from his mother. She was there and wanted him to contact her by leaving a note at the post office. She would pick up the mail personally.

He knew the whole family was there, so he hadn't expected to see her until he returned to Zürich, where they had already made a date for after the holidays. That he could see her now was a nice surprise. He wrote a note saying he would always be home in the mornings and evenings but planned some outings in the afternoons. There was a deep blanket of snow, and he intended to go snowshoeing across the meadows on the lower slopes, a sport he had always enjoyed.

The next morning his mother arrived. He told her that he had heard from Sam. She expressed her happiness that Samantha was still alive, but of course she was as perplexed as Anton about what was happening.

His mother then told him why she was there. "I need to tell you some difficult news. There's been a lot happening lately. First, on a personal level, I have decided to leave your father, not just because of what happened with you, Anton, but also because he has been having an affair with another woman. I've known about it for a while, but he claimed he was no longer seeing her. A friend saw them in an out-of-the-way restaurant and felt she needed to tell me because I had confided in her in the first place."

Anton wasn't shocked. He recalled seeing his father with a younger woman, and when he had confronted him about it, his father had lightly brushed it off and said it was none of his business. But now he still said to his mother, "That's hard for me to believe! Dad's always been so much in love with you. We all felt it amazing all these years that you've been close and seemed very happy together."

"Well, I thought so, too, but I found out a couple of years ago that he had been having an affair with this woman for some time. I've been naïve all these years. My friends who knew about it finally felt I should know, as he was beginning to act brazenly about her. He appeared with her at an event and introduced her to them as a close friend of the family. They asked me about her, and, of course, I knew nothing."

"You're saying it's been going on a long time?"

"Yes, several years. When I confronted him, he readily admitted it. He said that, after all, this sort of thing is to be expected in any upper-class family in Zürich. All his friends had mistresses, and he was glad that it was now out in the open and he didn't have to hide her anymore."

"He actually said that?" Anton's mind was whirling. A brief affair is different from having a mistress for years. His puritanical father always preached a moral code that had to be followed.

"That and a lot more. Naturally, I asked for a divorce, and that really shocked him. He couldn't understand why I would be so upset. Can you believe that? He thought I would accept it. Next, he would be asking me to invite her over for tea."

"Why didn't you tell me?"

"I didn't want to tell anyone. Why upset all of you until I filed for divorce? Before I could have a family meeting, he begged me not to go through with it; he loved me far more than this woman and swore he would end it permanently. If I felt that upset, he would never have an affair again. He wanted always to be with me and never to lose me. On and on he went, beseeching me, and he even broke down and cried."

"He cried?" The idea of his hardhearted father crying was beyond Anton.

"Oh yes, real tears, and of course that melted my heart, and I forgave him. That was two years ago, and now he is back with her. This time I'm not even talking to him about it. I've been to a lawyer, and your father will be served papers at the end of this month."

"Mother, I can't believe this. What a bastard! But is he with you now? And what about the others?"

"We're all here, the whole family. Everything is the same as usual. No one knows but you, Anton. Unfortunately, I can't leave the house until a separation agreement is signed, and that is what will be served to him. After that, I will see the others and tell them. Our wonderful family — our wonderful marriage — is no more." And she started to cry.

Anton held her close and felt her sorrow. It flowed from her heart into his, a river overflowing in a sudden downpour. It awakened in him his own loss, and in that moment they were one in spirit.

She stayed with him until the afternoon and called home to say she had met a friend with whom she was having lunch. They spent the rest of the time talking on a very deep level. It was a conversation that covered many levels of pain. It was about life, and love, and relationships, and his father, as well as about her and her needs and desires. She told him, "I've always been a follower, giving in to your father, mainly because when I was a child, my mother taught me that a woman's role is to follow her husband in all things."

She paused in thought. "When Mother taught me this, I felt it was wrong, but I guess I was too weak willed to protest."

"Don't be hard on yourself. That was true of your generation."

"I know. My brothers were always given the attention and the encouragement. All my mother told me was that I needed to marry well. It was never about *my* needs or what I could accomplish. I hated them all, and most of all I hated being a girl. They made me feel that being feminine was inferior."

"I hope you don't feel inferior now."

"No, I got over that; but at the time I had fantasies, daydreams, in which I was a man and went out in the world and did wonderful, adventurous things."

Hearing all this made Anton feel strange, and disturbed, and loving at the same time. He knew she was saying these things because she was very upset, but it was changing their relationship. They were no longer speaking as mother and son, but as a confidant and confidant, friend to friend. It was wonderful and terrible at the same time. A part of him felt another loss, yet another part felt so honored that she chose him to confide in. Why did heartache tie people together who should be able to be together without having to go through pain?

When everything had been said, like threads unraveling to the last strand, they changed the subject and discussed the ideas for his new house. He offered her the money back since Sam was gone, but she refused, saying that even if Sam didn't return, he would still need a good house. It was too cold to go for a picnic, so they spread one on his living room floor and even celebrated the New Year with a bottle of champagne he had in his fridge. In the afternoon, they went for a short walk on some plowed roads and found the air brisk and energizing. The mountains in their armor of snow felt more silent than usual. It seemed as if the stillness knew what their thoughts were and in that knowing gave them solace.

The time went quickly and, when she finally left, he felt sad again. He wanted to be there for his mother in her ordeal. She said she would be in touch often now that she no longer needed to hide that they were seeing each other.

That evening Anton felt very alone, more alone than he had felt since he'd been in the valley. Everything in his life seemed to be falling apart. All the realities that had been stable, like his parents' marriage, had become an illusion. What was real? One day something was made of concrete, the next it could be smashed as easily as if it were a piece of glass. Jacques' teaching talked about the ability to be in the moment, to welcome change because change promoted movement and growth. That sounded good, but when change actually occurred, it could jar a person's whole world, throwing one into a whirlwind of uncertainty. How could change be beneficial when it brought so much pain? All these questions bombarded Anton's mind as he sat there.

Would this change for his mother make her happy? he wondered. What would happen to her life, which had centered for so many years on his father? All their friends—would they choose to stay close to her or go with his father? In his own case, it hadn't been a problem, because Beatrice and he each had their own set of friends, but his parents' world consisted of years of shared, close relationships. And their houses — would there be a fight over who got what house? The thought of his mother losing the mountain house made him sick. Like Anton, she'd spent her childhood in the mountains. At least he would have a large house for her to come to. Recently, he'd thought about making the house a small one, just for himself, but now he would go back to the original plans he had made with Samantha and make it larger. Samantha, Samantha, where are you? He fell asleep with that question in his heart.

That night he dreamed of her. She was wearing a long black gown that was torn at the hem, and she looked frightened. He tried to reach her, but she kept turning away from him and said repeatedly, "Don't look for me. Please don't look for me. You will ruin everything. Don't look for me."

He cried, "What do you mean, I will ruin everything? What do you mean?" This made her run faster away from him.

He woke up in a sweat of anguish. It was a nightmare — not just a dream — but also his life, at this point. He wanted to go for a walk, but it was still dark and too cold. So instead, he got up and lit a fire in the fireplace and huddled close to it.

CHAPTER 30

W hen he got back to Zürich, Anton telephoned Jacques and they made dinner plans for a couple of nights before he was to leave for the States.

They met in a small restaurant in his neighborhood. Jacques looked at him quietly for a few minutes and said, "Anton, I know it's difficult for you to go now, but it still remains the best place to be at this time. Harvard is a great university, and you will make some lifelong friends there."

They sat in silence for a while. Then Jacques said, "When you get settled in Boston, I want you to spend some time with another disciple of mine. His name is Charles Hansford, and he serves as the chairman of the board of an old law firm in Boston. He is retired from the firm, but keeps that post to be active. He has a house on the ocean, and I visit him every spring, so I will be seeing you soon in Boston."

They talked some more about the teaching, and about Harvard, and Jacques' other disciples in Boston, and attending their class there. They tried not to mention Samantha or what was happening to her. As they got up to leave, Jacques said, "Remember to have faith, Anton. She will be back, I see that clearly, but when I can't say."

The next morning, Anton took a long walk around his favorite streets of Zürich. He didn't expect to return until the spring break, so he wanted just to absorb all the places he loved. His favorite outdoor café was now a cozy indoor one with wonderful coffee and pastries. He lingered there and even ordered another cup of cappuccino. A few people came and went, but he knew none of them, and he was thankful about that. He wanted to be alone. Being alone was a relief from having to tell people there still was no word of Sam. Only Jacques and his mother understood this. His friends all wanted to be of help and didn't realize that their help wasn't needed. Good intentions fall flat when they can't make any difference.

Looking up from his thoughts, he saw something move just outside the window where he was seated. It was a woman running, and for a moment he thought it was Samantha. She turned to look back, and he jumped up. It was Sam! He was sure it was Sam. Grabbing his coat, he ran out of the café, calling that he would be back to pay.

The woman was quite a distance ahead, but Anton had long legs and was a good runner, and he ran as if he were still on the track team in high school. She turned the corner, and when he got there and looked down the street, there was no sign of her. The street was lined with shops and a department store. She must have gone into the larger store, as it was nearest to the corner. He entered the store and suddenly felt hopeless. It was crowded with people coming for the after-Christmas sales, and there were many floors and many exits. He spent some time checking a couple of the floors with no luck and then went back to the café.

As he sat down at the table, he saw a note on it. He had left his hat and gloves, so no one had been at the table. Then he saw that the note had his name on it. He opened it and read:

Darling,

I'm so sorry. I wanted to say goodbye to you before you leave, but I can't do it in person. Someday you will understand. For now, suffice it to say, I am well. Have a good semester at Harvard. I want very much to be with you there — maybe someday.

You are in my heart always. I love you.

Samantha

Anton wanted to scream out loud, but he could see the waitress looking at him with concern. She came over and said, "Anton, is everything all right? I saw a woman run in here and put that on your table, but she was so fast I didn't see her well enough, as I was serving another customer."

"It's okay, I'll be okay. May I have the check, please?"

At home, he telephoned Jacques and told him what had happened. There was a long silence, and then Jacques said, "Let's talk about it later, not on the phone. I have an early dinner date, but I should be home around eight. Come over then."

After he hung up, he felt somehow that Jacques knew that Samantha was in Zürich — he must have seen her. Anton became very angry. "I'm her husband, God damn it. Why am I being told nothing?" He shouted the words at his walls.

The rest of the day was anquishingly long. There was nothing to do. His bags were packed, and the apartment was in order.

He spoke briefly to his mother on the phone. She was hoping the papers would come through soon. He had offered her his apartment while he was away, and she gladly accepted, since she still hadn't really looked for a place of her own. When he suggested that his father leave instead, she explained, "He likes to entertain more than I do, and, you know, he loves the house here, whereas I'll be fine with a nice condo like yours."

"Have you talked yet about our home?"

"Not really. It's going to take time to figure out all the legal details, but I feel in the end that I will have the house in the mountains, and he will have the house here. He's never loved nature and the mountains the way I do, so probably that's the way it will work out."

That was encouraging news; they planned to have breakfast in the morning before his plane left.

CHAPTER 31

Thinking about what he would tell Anton when he arrived, Jacques sat in his living room. Samantha had been here to see him, and he had to tell Anton the truth about that. She had only stayed for a few minutes, but it relieved Jacques' heart to see that she was well, focused, and strong. She couldn't tell him about what was happening, but it was clear to him that she must be working for the government still.

When he asked if she was going to see Anton, she replied, "I want to, but I don't think I can. You know he will insist that I stay and not go back, or he will become impetuous and insist that he go with me. When I refuse and leave, he will again be terribly hurt."

"But if he knows you saw me — and I will have to tell him — he will be even more upset."

"Yes, I know, but at least I won't see him and feel his hurt and have misgivings. Knowing him, I'm sure he is beginning to distrust me." Her voice cracked a little. "I should never have married him until this job had ended. In fact, I think it best that we get an annulment. Hopefully, after this is all over, we can be together again. Maybe you could suggest that to him?"

"But Samantha, why do that? It will make him think you don't love him."

"Yes, I know, but I am really afraid for his safety; and, if our marriage is ended, they may not keep checking on him. I'm sure they are doing that now."

"Be honest with me. Is there some way you can quit? I also worry about how much danger you are in."

Her look was focused and serious. "I wish I could, but it is impossible now. I need to stay until the end."

Jacques greeted Anton warmly at the door; and, when they hugged, he held him close much longer than usual.

"Come in, come in! I have a good fire going and some hot cider to warm you on this very cold evening."

Settled on the sofa, sipping the fragrant brew, Anton looked at Jacques and said, "You saw her, didn't you?"

"Yes, I did."

"How could she do this to me? I'm her husband. She sees you and runs from me."

"I know how you must be feeling." He paused, and Anton could tell he was thinking about what to say. "It's very complicated. She only saw me for a couple of minutes to tell me something privately. It's dangerous for her even to do that."

"So, she is a spy, and all of this was in the plan from the beginning?"

"I don't know, Anton. She works for our government; she won't even tell me that, but I'm certain of it. Was it all planned? I don't know that either, all I know is that it's dangerous work, so neither one of us can say a word to anyone."

Anton felt exasperated. "If you love someone, you don't hurt him like this."

"She definitely loves you, without question."

"I'm sorry, I question it, and after this last episode, I'm beginning to feel exasperated. In fact, maybe I should file for an annulment. It's just so hard for me to think about doing that."

"Maybe that would be a good idea."

Anton was shocked at Jacques' response.

"If you get an annulment now, then they may believe she doesn't care about you anymore. You are a question in these people's minds. They may wonder why, as a newlywed, she would be so willing to leave you to continue her work with them."

"You seem to know more now than you did before. Did she tell you this?"

"Yes, and it's easy to surmise. You would be much more of a problem to explain than I would be. A father can be written off as someone you see only occasionally, but a new husband—that's a different story."

Well, maybe I should be accommodating. Let me think about it. I can always call my lawyer from America." He was trying not to direct his feelings toward Jacques, but they welled up in him, wanting to burst at anyone and anything.

"Don't feel this way. She really does love you and wants to be with you."

"I can't believe that anymore. I really can't. If risking her life for the government is more important to her than marriage and a family, then that's her choice. I'm going to America because that was going to save her from risk. Now all those plans are useless, and I'm stuck there, away from my home, for at least six months. It's not your fault, Jacques, but couldn't you have stopped her from doing this?"

"No, I couldn't, and neither could she. I think she got herself into it and didn't know how to get out, particularly when her replacement got sick. I think that she had no choice and still doesn't. Don't be so hard on her. It will work out in the end."

"From the very beginning, she knew this work was dangerous; even you were against it, and she didn't listen. This proves she has a reckless spirit; and, if it weren't this, it would have been something else that appeals to that part of her. If I get an annulment, that will be it. You know I love her very much, but now I'm starting to realize that I don't know if I want to be married to someone who has those proclivities. I've lost my family. I don't want always to be wondering when I will lose my wife for good. I want some security to fall back on."

"There is no security in life," Jacques replied. "There is only make-believe that always gets foiled at some time or other. If Samantha lives through this, I think it will be her last adventure. It is more than she expected."

"I don't know if I can trust that, or her, anymore."

Jacques shook his head sadly and thought, Anton, you are acting like a hurt child again and not really considering what Samantha is going through. Then he said, "That's between the two of you, but real love is rare, very rare. I hope you will give it a chance."

Anton didn't answer. He couldn't. He was leaving tomorrow and wanted to have a final conversation with his teacher that wasn't full of anger and indignation. He took some deep breaths and changed the topic. "Jacques, do you have any advice for me before I leave? Is there anything else I need to know about Harvard or Boston?"

"My main advice is to be careful when you talk about Samantha. Say she hasn't contacted you, and you have decided she must have disappeared for some negative reason. Tell them that her company was dishonest, and you had no idea she was involved in anything like that. It's been disappointing for you, but now you need to move on. Say you are filing for an annulment since you had only been married a couple of months when she disappeared under scandalous circumstances. You can probably get an annulment without her consent because of what happened. Stress that you haven't heard a word from her."

"Why say anything?"

"They have spies, and I would think you could meet someone connected to this group, someone who can report back to them. If they feel you don't know anything, it will be better for her as well as for you. The annulment will make that clear."

"All right."

"Also, I really think you need to do some therapy, especially now, around your abandonment issues. Ask around for a good therapist there."

"I guess you're right. I'll look into it."

"My other advice is to go out on some dates. Make it look as if you are a free man and no longer interested in your ex-wife."

"Would that be fair to the woman?"

"It's fair as long as you keep it platonic. But an outsider needn't know what the relationship is."

"Well, if the woman is attractive and stable, I can't promise I will keep it platonic."

"So be it." Jacques looked sad, and Anton knew it would bother him if he were unfaithful to Sam, but what could he or she expect? He suddenly felt very tired. All his emotion had drained him, and he didn't want to think anymore.

They talked some more, and both tried to end the evening on a high note, but the note hit a blank wall and fell silently down.

Anton made an excuse and left at nine. At the door, Jacques gave him another long embrace and said, "Take care, my son. I will miss you. If I hear anything, I will see that the information gets to you. I love you."

And Anton felt that love warm his heart. This was no longer about Samantha. It was about Jacques and him, and it felt good.

That night he had a dream. It started out well and ended badly. He was with Sam, and they were on a tall sailing ship. There were several other passengers along, none of whom he recognized. The boat was taking on a lot of speed, due to some sudden high winds that were blowing against the sails. It was exhilarating and scary at the same time. Sam especially was excited and refused to sit down. Instead, she stood against the wind, letting it blow hard against her body. He urged her to be careful, and she looked at him and said, "I'm always careful. Don't be mistaken about that."

As soon as she spoke those words, the winds became a gale and blew her overboard. He tried to rescue her, but the boat was moving so fast it was impossible. He grabbed a life jacket and jumped overboard to go after her. She had vanished into the sea, and even though he dove and dove he could not see her. Anton then realized that the boat had disappeared, and he was drifting on the choppy waves moving toward nothing. He was totally alone.

He awoke with a start in the middle of the night and thought about the dream. Its meaning was pretty obvious, but somehow there was something missing that he couldn't remember. It was something about the other passengers. He remembered a woman there, a very attractive woman, and then he realized that the woman was Samantha's mother. She was on their boat. Then he became frightened.

CHAPTER 32

The next day was Anton's departure. In the morning, as planned, he had breakfast with his mother. It was a difficult breakfast. Mother looked sad and lost. He knew the divorce was taking a huge toll on her. She was dressed almost too casually, as if she had thrown on a pair of pants without checking to see if they were pressed. Usually, she was immaculate, so he was surprised to see the change; but what could he expect?

The first thing she said was, "The separation papers have come through. I can now leave."

"Have you finally told him?"

"Yes, I gave them to him last night and told him I would be moving out as soon as everything of mine was packed. Unfortunately, I could do very little without him noticing."

"How did he take it?"

She looked even sadder. "I don't know. At first, he was angry and screamed a lot; but when I didn't answer him, he calmed down into a pouting child. I don't think the reality of it all has sunk in."

"I'm so sorry I won't be here to help you with all this. Have you told the others yet?"

"No, I think I will do that after I move out. Whether he says something is another story. It doesn't matter. I think Kristina will understand, but she has always been closer to your father. Erick and Jonas have their own lives; I don't think it will affect them either way. Neither one of us hear from them very often, as you know. Jonas, by the way, may be getting married."

"Really? I thought he was the confirmed bachelor, like Erick."

"Well, I did, too, but he seems very much in love. Her name is Lillian Panmer, and she's only twenty-four, but just lovely. You would like her."

"I'm glad for him. For some reason, I've always seen him with a bunch of kids. But what's that going to do to Erick? They're inseparable."

"Well, maybe it will be good for them both. I always felt their closeness kept them from forming other relationships. If Erick doesn't have Jonas to run around with, he might have to settle down himself."

"No, that'll never happen. He's never been attracted to women."

"Do you think he's gay?"

"I don't know, but I wouldn't be surprised."

"Neither would I, but your father would never accept it."

"Well, maybe that's why, if he is gay, he won't ever tell the family. What a pity."

Anton didn't think it was up to him to tell his mother that he had on several occasions seen Erick in the company of an obviously gay group, and one man in particular seemed to be a very close friend. Jonas had also alluded to it, and he wondered now whether Jonas were nervous about being associated with the gay community. Perhaps part of the reason he was getting married was to disprove any rumors about that. It didn't matter to Anton. They were both great guys and had called him a couple of times since the split, more sympathetic than he thought they would be.

"Mom, are you going to be okay? I really am worried about how you look."

"How can I be okay? This is the hardest decision of my life, and I keep praying that he will let me go without a huge fuss. I won't be persuaded to change my mind, but I also don't relish being hassled by him before I can get out of there."

"My plane doesn't leave until nine tonight, and I'm all packed. Can I come home with you and help?"

"Heavens no! He could come home at any time, and that would make matters worse."

They talked some more, and she went back to his apartment so he could show her where everything was. He had cleaned out all his closets and put things in his storage room, so she could bring as many things as she wanted. He was very happy that it worked out for her to stay there. The hardest job had been packing up Sam's clothes. It seemed so final.

When she saw the framed picture of Samantha and Anton on his desk, she asked, "Aren't you going to take this?"

"No, I'd rather not look at it. I can put that in storage." He went to take it, but she said, "Let it stay. I would like to see it there and pray that you will be together again someday."

Anton didn't want to say that he felt it was over.

He decided to phone Jonas at his office to say goodbye and congratulate him. Jonas sounded pleased that he had called and said that, when Anton returned in the spring, he would like for him to meet Lillian. That made Anton happy. He had always been closer to Jonas than to Erick, and of the two he missed Jonas the most.

CHAPTER 33

Boston was dark and dreary. Anton arrived just after a snowstorm, and all the streets were white with snow and still being plowed. The sky appeared overcast and looked as if it were preparing to let loose another storm. The taxi he took at the airport sat stalled in late afternoon traffic. Looking at the lines of cars, he felt more and more miserable. What was meant to be a fun six months with Samantha now was a time he wasn't looking forward to at all.

Boston was a nice city, but it wasn't Zürich, nor were there surrounding villages full of Swiss architecture and lighthearted people. Sitting in the taxi, already home-sick, he had to fight an inclination to tell the cabbie to go back to the airport.

His apartment was in the old section of Cambridge. Ginny phoned the night before to say something had come up, so she couldn't meet him earlier but told him where he could find a hidden key to his place. It was a walk-up. Tired, he dragged his bags up three flights and entered the apartment with very little expectations.

He was pleasantly surprised. It looked small, much smaller than any place he had ever lived in, but it breathed charm. The furniture was old antiques, mostly of the French period rather than English, but all the pieces were in good condition and very well designed. It had a small office with a huge, flat desk that would fit all his needs; and even the bedroom contained a high, four-poster bed that looked so inviting that after Anton put down his bags, he flopped right into it. When he awoke, it was dark outside, and the streetlamps shined a soft light through the thin curtains. He wanted just to lie there and never get up, but when he looked at his watch, he realized that it was almost time for Ginny to arrive. They were to have dinner together.

He'd just finished shaving when the doorbell rang.

Ginny looked fresh and beautiful in a long, black wool coat and a gray fur hat and scarf.

They embraced warmly. "It's very good to see you again," he murmured in her ear.

"You, too. How was your flight?"

"Boring and tiring. But Ginny, this place is lovely. Thank you so much."

When he took her coat off, he couldn't help but observe how her small body fit her brown pantsuit as if it were tailor-made for her, and the light touch of a flowing red scarf embraced the red in her hair and showed off the highlights.

Trying to stop looking at her, he looked around and noticed new things he hadn't seen before. There were flowers everywhere; and, on the table, champagne glasses waited to be filled.

"And thank you for the lovely flowers. Really, you've done too much."

"Oh, that's nothing. It's a dark place with the old windows, so I felt you needed some color."

The windows were old casement windows with small panes and dark trim. "But they're wonderful." He looked around some more. "These high ceilings and moldings denote the 1920s, and I love that period. How did you ever find this place?"

His condo at home was very modern, but Anton meant it when he said he loved that period, too.

"A friend told me about it, and the timing was just right. The owner is going abroad on a sabbatical and only wanted to rent it to someone who was referred to him."

"I can understand why." He saw a glass case with some antique statues in it. "Some of these things are valuable."

She went into the kitchen and came out with the champagne and a tray of cheeses.

Some of his doldrums started to melt away, and they sat, and chatted, and ate, and drank, and chatted some more until it was time to leave for dinner.

Later that evening, after Ginny had gone home, he turned on a gas fire in the old, converted fireplace, and, for the first time that evening, remembered he was alone.

The following day, he walked the streets of Cambridge and familiarized himself with Harvard and the surrounding area. It was a sunny but cold day, and even though he was used to the cold, he found a dampness here that seemed to penetrate his bones. It wasn't the dry cold of the mountains or the nippy cold of Zürich. Anton changed into some heavier sweaters and finally felt better. He spent a quiet evening eating in a local restaurant that Ginny had recommended and enjoyed the absence of the students, who were still on break. It would be different in a week or two when school officially recommenced.

Anton telephoned Charles Hansford, the retired lawyer who was another disciple of Jacques', and arranged to visit him the following weekend. He looked forward to meeting him and talking with him about the teaching. Before Anton had left Zürich, Jacques told him that he had given Charles the news about Samantha, whom Charles genuinely cared about.

Charles's house was on the coast, north of Boston. It rested on land above tall, gray cliffs that fell steeply down into the water, a malevolent torrent beating and pushing at the rocks as if it wanted to tear them away, only to be pushed back by the tow to return for another assault.

Anton parked the car and stood in silence for a few minutes and watched the upheaval of the tide, sensing the drama of the moment.

As he looked at the waves, he felt their energy fill his body. Never having spent time at the ocean except for a vacation or two, he found this scene exhilarating. Once in a while, the waves hit the rocks so hard that the spray flew up and hit his face, but instead of moving back, he walked closer to the edge, almost hypnotized by the pounding of the water.

After a few minutes, he returned to the parking lot and noticed that there were several cars there. His heart sank. Other people must be there; Anton wanted private time to get to know Charles.

Charles answered the door and greeted him warmly, kissing both cheeks. "Welcome, Brother! I called some other members of our group to be here to greet you. Come in, come in!"

He was notable looking with a full head of thick, gray hair, alive blue eyes, and a tall, thin body that made the gray suit he wore seem even more stylish.

His home was lovely, an old English, Tudor-style mansion with white stucco walls, a pitched roof, and dark wood trim, majestic yet charming. There were two living rooms, one on either side of the hall. Roaring flames in the fireplaces competed with each other to entice a visitor to come in. One of the rooms led to a glorious ceiling-to-floor library, one of the finest Anton had ever seen.

Four men and two women awaited him with open arms. The warmth that emanated from them made him feel very welcomed. Their ages and ethnic backgrounds were mixed, yet everyone seemed to be on an equal footing, and even though it felt strange at first, Anton soon settled into an open conversation about the teaching in this part of the world.

It was a wonderful day, a wonderful evening. After they all left, Charles and Anton sat by the fire and talked some more. Anton told him about the book and about the valley, about the loss of his family, and about Samantha. By this time, he sensed he could talk to Charles about everything he was feeling. He felt Charles was the first person who would understand, even from the spiritual point of view. Anton mainly told him about Sam and how betrayed and hurt he felt concerning her actions. What he said to Charles he couldn't have said to Jacques, because Jacques was her father.

Charles listened quietly, and then he said something Anton would never forget. "Anton, I am an old man who has lived through many hardships and many cherished times of happiness. Someday, when you are my age, you will look back on your life the same way. There will be times when the path can be walked without diversion, straight and focused; and there will be times, such as the one you are going through now, when the path branches into twists and turns, going in directions where there is no knowing where it will end up. When those times happen, you need to be even stronger in your heart and in your love, for only that will take you back to the main path where you can walk again."

"When you say be 'strong in your heart,' how can I do that when my heart feels broken?"

"A broken heart can still be strong. The breaks are just scars that heal; the strength is always there. It never leaves you from lifetime to lifetime. Know that no hurt can penetrate to the core of your heart. That core is who you truly are. Find it and hold it sacred."

"How do I find it?"

"By believing in yourself."

"But I do believe in myself."

"Do you really, Anton? Can you honestly say you believe in yourself?"

"I thought I did."

Charles smiled. "Sometimes what we believe is based on superficial things. It's the core that I'm talking about. If you believe in that core, then no one can ever hurt you, disturb you, or make you feel upset."

"So, what you are saying is that, if I find my core, no one — no woman or man — can ever hurt me?"

"Yes, finding the core is finding freedom. How can anyone hurt you when you have found freedom? Hurts dissolve in the energy of love that has no personal needs. Love Samantha that way and she can never hurt you."

"But that state you're describing is of being one with my Higher Self. That's a long way off for me."

"It's as long as you make it. Believe in yourself and know that you can achieve it."

Anton looked at Charles and suddenly saw him as an old Tibetan lama. He knew that he had been with him then and that Charles had been one of his teachers.

Charles looked at his watch. "It's past midnight; time for bed."

The rest of the weekend was wonderful and relaxing. The weather was cold but sunny, so they took walks together and spent long hours in front of the fireplace. They even played cards and watched a couple of good TV shows.

Charles was so knowledgeable and wise! Anton felt a great bond of love toward him.

CHAPTER 34

Boston proved to be an exhilarating city. Now that he was living there, Anton had the opportunity to discover the thought-provoking history of the original founders and to see the old architecture that still stood there. In contrast, the new sections of downtown Boston were beautifully designed, and he found the waterfront with its stores and restaurants enjoyable places to wander through. His classes were beginning in a couple of weeks, so he had time to explore the museums and even go to some concerts of the Boston Symphony Orchestra.

Ginny was free from school to accompany him on many of his excursions and showed him some of the areas that she really loved. She had returned to Harvard to get an advanced degree in sociology. They renewed their friendship; even though he speculated about having an affair with her, he felt it too soon and too complicated. They talked about it once, and she also felt it better, at this time, just to remain friends when he was going through his marriage breakup.

Something about the way she expressed herself made him laugh a lot. Her sense of humor was very dry and somehow touched his own, so they often acted like kids together, which is what Anton needed.

When school started for them both, they regrettably realized that most of their time could no longer be spent together, as they both had a full schedule. Anton was teaching three undergraduate courses and one graduate course. It was a full load, but the material was mainly the same as he taught in Zürich, so he didn't have to prepare too much. The one course in the Divinity School on Eastern religion had to be revised to include the material from his book, but he had done most of that in Zürich before he came.

Two were lecture courses, and two were smaller classroom courses. He liked the smaller courses best as he could then develop a personal connection with the students. The graduate class in philosophy was very advanced, and he looked forward to that one the most because the students were serious, dedicated, and well informed, which were prerequisites for challenging debates.

At first, it was a little difficult because he was new and didn't know any of the professors. This soon changed, as he found his colleagues open and welcoming, very different from the more reserved professors at the university in Zürich. Anton had lunch a few times with Richard Evans, the department head, and found him to be very intelligent with a sound sense of practicality.

The students were also very approachable and interesting to talk to. Some of the graduate ones were older, returning for an advanced degree, and were his contemporaries. New friendships began, and Anton no longer felt lonely and disconnected. Samantha wasn't on his mind as much, and he found there were days at a time when he didn't even think about her.

Anton remembered what Jacques had advised him to do and contacted a therapist whom one of his new friends recommended. Her name was Karen Courtney. She was married, in her late fifties, plain looking; but her warm heart, which he felt right away, made her seem beautiful, like an ordinary black bird whose wings, when they opened, were full of colorful feathers.

One of the first things they talked about was his relationship with women. For a start, he had never known women as friends. Only recently did he feel a bond of friendship with Lea. Kristina had been his friend as a child, but then she became the big-sister advisor.

Mostly, when he thought about his life with women, he realized that it was guided by sex. Beatrice had been sex and the social life until it became too extreme for him. Orama had also been fabulous sex, which enticed him, but had they ever talked? Maybe a little about art, but his obsession with her was about the sex.

Even Samantha at the beginning was about sex, but Anton also realized that, with her, he felt something different for the first time. He had a respect for who she was, and he wanted to know her not only with his body but also with his mind and, yes, with his heart — not just loving her with his heart but also understanding her with his heart.

He told Karen what his mother said to him about being afraid to use his heart. Why? Was it the abandonment in his childhood or more than that?

When he had been eight, Anton remembered, he had a crush on a girl in school named Eva. They were inseparable, doing everything together. It was heartbreaking for him to leave her to go away to boarding school when he was twelve. They wrote frequently and planned their summer together. Then he got a letter from her saying that she had a new boyfriend and couldn't see him that summer as planned. Not only was he deeply hurt, but he felt anger toward his parents because they had sent him to boarding school, where it was all boys and no girls.

Then when he had started dating, the questions became who to have sex with, how to experiment, and what the best condoms were. Later, many girls took care of their own contraception, which made it much better sexually for him.

He had had several affairs and some one-night stands before he married Beatrice. It was great fun. But, again, when he thought about each and every woman, had they really been friends? Not enough to be more than quick affairs.

Was he afraid of women, afraid to use his heart, afraid to discover how shallow he really was? The more he worked with Karen, the more he realized he didn't have a good understanding of women. He felt lost in illusions of what he thought they were.

Anton heard from Jacques on a regular basis and often felt his presence when he meditated or in dreams. They usually telephoned and emailed every week. He had no news to report, so they kept their conversations around the work, the teaching, and sometimes his therapy.

Charles came to visit during a couple of weekends when Anton was free of school-work. He introduced him to Janet Sommers and Gregory Levy, both disciples of Jacques, and Anton liked them right away. In her forties, Janet was Black, married, and worked as a French teacher at a local high school. Gregory was around the same age, single, and a businessman working for a computer company. They invited him to join their class, which was held every other week in Gregory's apartment.

It was an interesting class. There were a couple of other students: Vivian Gary, a student at Emerson College, and Huan Liu, who attended MIT. They were not disciples and were new to the teaching. Anton learned a lot in just a few weeks and looked forward to every time they met. One day in late March when he arrived for class, he found a note on the door that read, "Sorry, class is canceled, Janet and I had to go somewhere unexpectedly. Anton, I will call you when we return, which should be around ten this evening."

Disappointed, Anton returned home and was watching TV when Gregory called.

"I have some disturbing news. Janet and I have been to see Jacques. He arrived this afternoon and was at his hotel. He felt very ill and asked us to come and do some healing on him."

"What's wrong?" Anton cried.

"I'm not certain, but we think it's pneumonia. We took him to my doctor who admitted him into the hospital right away."

"What hospital?"

"Mass General."

"Why didn't you ask me to come with you?" Anton felt upset.

"Jacques was too sick even to talk. He wanted us there just for healing purposes. But when we realized how serious it was, we persuaded him to see my doctor. You can see him tomorrow."

"But I just talked to him earlier this week, and he never told me he was coming!"

"He didn't tell us, either. He wanted to surprise us. The plane ride was a long and difficult one. They stopped for hours in Newfoundland, and it was very cold there. He wasn't dressed warmly enough, even for here. I gather Zürich has been having a warm spell. He can barely talk, but he told us to tell you that he'll see you soon and he loves you."

When Anton hung up, he called Mass General. Gregory had given him Jacques' room number, but he didn't want to disturb him; he finally got through to the nursing station. When Anton asked about Jacques' condition, the nurse said he had just been moved to the intensive care unit. They wouldn't tell him what Jacques' illness was, even when he said he was his son-in-law. Anton asked if he could come and see him, even for a minute, and they said no—maybe in the morning. But they gave him the doctor's name. Anton phoned his service, left his name and number, explained who he was, and asked to be called at any time—even in the middle of the night.

Feeling desperate, Anton then called Charles, even though it was almost eleven at night by now. Charles was just going to bed and was shocked at the news.

"Anton, I knew Jacques was coming. It was all arranged; that's why I invited you all down next weekend. He wanted to surprise you by being here."

"It's a surprise, all right — a very bad one!"

"I'll come up first thing in the morning."

Anton then phoned Gregory to tell him the latest news and finally collapsed on his couch. He woke up when the phone rang. It was one in the morning. It was Doctor Ward. He said that Jacques was in serious condition. It was pneumonia, and he couldn't say whether he would pull through. It was very deep in his lungs. No one was allowed to see him, but since Anton was a relative, he could visit him in the morning, just for five minutes. The doctor asked if Jacques had any other close family; and, when Anton said he had a daughter, the doctor advised that she be informed about his condition. The next day or two were the most critical.

When Anton went to bed, he prayed to his Mahatma for help. He prayed and prayed the same prayer over and over again. The words kept repeating in his mind, "Please save Jacques. Don't take him from us at this time." He prayed until he felt his heart would break, and then he thought about Sam. She had to come. If Jacques died, and she wasn't here, she would never forgive herself. But it was impossible. There was no way to get in touch with her. So, he prayed again. This time he linked with his Higher Self and asked it to link with her Higher Self and give her the message that her father could be dying. She needed to phone Charles; she needed to phone him. Anton had a listed number. He kept sending the message until he fell asleep in exhaustion.

In the middle of the night, the phone rang. It was Samantha.

"What's wrong?" Her voice sounded frightened.

Anton told her about Jacques. There was silence.

"I will come as soon as I can." And she hung up.

The next day Anton was at the hospital at six in the morning. He waited a long time, and during that time Gregory and Janet arrived. They all waited in silence. Finally, at nine, a nurse said Anton could see Jacques for five minutes, and she made him put a mask on. When he saw Jacques in bed, Anton thought he had already died. His skin was white, and he looked frail and childlike. He was awake and tried to smile. Anton took Jacques' thin hand and forced himself to smile back. He told

Jacques that he had contacted Sam, that she was coming, and that he had to hang in there for all of them. It was an effort for Jacques to speak, so Anton told him not to try. Anton just kept talking about how much he loved him, and how they all loved him and needed him until the nurse came and took him away. She said the doctor would talk to him later in the morning.

Anton went for breakfast with Janet and Gregory and made some phone calls to arrange for covering his classes. Janet and Gregory left, saying they would be back in the afternoon. Anton told them he would call if anything happened.

Charles arrived around eleven, just as the doctor came into the waiting room to talk to Anton. He said there was little change. They were trying to keep Jacques' lungs from filling up and were hoping the antibiotics would kick in. It would be touch and go for at least another day or so.

Anton said Jacques' daughter was coming and that Charles was his brother-in-law—could he see him? The doctor nodded and said he would tell the nurse to let Charles in. But only Jacques' daughter would be allowed in thereafter; even Anton wouldn't be allowed to see Jacques again until he was through this crisis.

Charles came back ashen. When he sat down, Anton could tell he carried an overwhelming burden. He was one of Jacques' oldest disciples, so Anton could imagine what he must be feeling.

"Do you think there's hope?" he asked Charles.

"There's always hope, but whether he makes it or not is up to his teacher and Mahatma at this point. Let's go to the chapel here and meditate."

The chapel was small, with just a simple cross on the altar. They were the only ones there, and they sat in meditation and prayer for over an hour. During that time, Anton had a flickering image of Jacques, and he wanted to believe that Jacques was reassuring him.

He and Charles had a long, silent lunch in the cafeteria and then returned to the waiting room. The nurse said that Jacques' condition was the same.

Samantha arrived around five. The air in the room changed when she walked in. Its heaviness lifted and became refreshed, like mud flowing and dissipating into a clear, flowing river.

Anton was reading his book but looked up immediately, knowing it had to be her. She wore a tan, tailored pants suit with her hair rolled in a French twist on top of her head; and even though her face was drawn and tired, she radiated an inner vitality. He stood up, and she threw her arms around him and kissed him lightly on the lips.

"How is he?"

"The same."

Charles stood and greeted her somberly.

"I must see him."

"The nurse will arrange it." Anton took her hand and led her to the nurse's desk.

They said nothing while she waited to be admitted to her father's room. When she got up to go, he told her, "Be prepared, he looks very bad."

Her eyes glistened with tears that came and went. "I'll try."

When she returned, her hollow cheeks were more sunken, and her eyes had a lost look. Anton put his arms around her and held her close, feeling her sadness penetrating his heart.

"He's going to make it; I know he will," she whispered in his ear.

"I hope so! Oh God, I hope you're right!"

"I said goodbye to him, just in case. He couldn't speak, but his eyes were strong, and they smiled at me with affection and love."

She buried her head into his chest and cried silent sobs, wetting his shirt with her tears. He patted her head and felt strands of her hair fall out of the twist and curl around his fingers.

She looked up at him and pulled away. "I can't stay. My flight leaves at nine. If Father doesn't make it, would you please do all the arrangements? Have him cremated and hold the ashes for me. He wanted them thrown on the mountain, not here, at home, in the Alps."

"How can you leave now? At least stay another day. By then we should know whether he will live or die."

She looked at him and thought, What can I say to him? He's never going to understand, and I can't explain anything to him now.

"I can't, Anton. To come here just for a day was risky, and don't ask me what I am doing because I'm not able to tell you."

"But—"

"No buts." And she put her hand over his mouth.

He felt a cold wave cross his body and said, "The annulment papers are ready. How do I get them to you?"

She wrote down a post-office box number in Rome.

"Don't look for me there. My mail is forwarded to me. Write me about Father."

She smiled at him weakly, hugged Charles goodbye, and left as suddenly as she had come.

They sat deep in thought, and Anton tried not to break down. Charles put his hand over Anton's, and he could feel Charles's loving energy go through him.

Anton didn't know what had happened. What he and Sam felt for each other had been so strong, so vital, and so wonderful. How could it vanish and become a wistful smile? How could something that was so right suddenly be so wrong? He believed they were destined to be together; but when they followed their destiny, something so erroneous, so in opposition, pulled their destiny into shreds. When she walked out of the waiting room, he experienced the final separation. If Jacques died, Anton would have lost them both, and he wasn't certain he could handle that. So, he began to concentrate on Jacques.

Charles and Anton went back to the chapel and meditated some more.

In the afternoon, Janet and Gregory returned, and they all had dinner together at a nearby restaurant. The doctor spoke to them just as they were leaving. He said that Jacques was stronger. He didn't want to give them hope, but he was holding on.

And Jacques kept hanging on. After two more days of touch and go, he made a turn for the better. In a week, he was out of intensive care and into a regular room.

When Jacques was able to leave, Anton helped Charles take him to his home. It was a cold spring day, but the sun was shining, and they were very happy.

Only once did they speak about Samantha. Jacques remembered her being there and saying goodbye. "The goodbye was for me," he said, "but I also felt she was saying goodbye in case she herself didn't make it. She truly is in a dangerous position. Even I never realized how much."

"But I still don't understand why she is doing this. Why take on this work or assignment?" By now Anton realized that she was still an agent for their government.

"I think it's about her mother turning negative. There has always been in Samantha a very strong need to fight evil, and I know that whatever she is doing, she feels it is a just cause."

Anton told Jacques how he felt when he saw her—about their destiny being torn apart—and Jacques explained, "Destiny is controlled by the people involved. If one person follows free will and goes in a different direction, it will cause the other person's destiny to change. Be patient, Anton. If Samantha comes through this, there is still hope for the two of you."

Anton didn't answer him; nor did he tell him that, even if Sam did come back, he didn't want to be with her again. The fact that she couldn't stay another day with her father and teacher bothered him a lot. Her work was more important than the two of them. He could never trust that she wouldn't run off on another mission—and he knew he couldn't handle that again.

CHAPTER 35

In April, Anton's agent called him. The book was going to be published by his first publisher, even though it wasn't the type of book they normally took. Because his first book had been so successful, they were willing to take the risk. They believed he had a good following and thought those people would be buying the new one. Of course, the other book did so well because it was used as a textbook in several colleges and universities; but, even with that consideration, his publisher felt the students would want to read this next one. They expected to release it in the early fall.

This news really made Anton happy.

He called Jacques at Charles's, where he was still recovering.

Jacques responded, "Good! It's right on time."

"What do you mean by that?"

"Well, your time here is up soon, so you will be starting at the university in Zürich with your book in hand."

Anton hadn't thought about that. "You know, Richard wants to extend my contract for a full year here, starting in the fall."

"You can't extend your leave at home. Besides, why stay?"

Anton thought for a minute. "I don't know. I really like it here, and now I have some good friends and a wonderful therapist. At home, I have friends, and my mother, and of course, you when you are there; but somehow being here makes me feel happier."

"Anton, you are going to have to face being without her some time, you know. And your dharma is to be in Zürich, not here. You'll lose your job there if you extend your contract at Harvard. And your therapist can continue working with you via Zoom."

"You're right, and I do miss the mountains. I also need to find an architect and start building my home there, so I can invite my new friends here to come and visit."

May came and the semester ended. The following week, Anton flew back home. His mother and Jacques were both away when he arrived, so, after visiting with some close friends for a week, he decided to go to his cabin in the mountains to be alone. Before he left, he spent a couple of days taking all the boxes of Sam's belongings to Jacques' house. Having them out of the apartment made him feel better and gave him back a sense of this being just his home.

The cabin seemed small and remote. The grasses were growing tall around it, and it looked as if it had gone through a bad winter. Some of the wood shingles had fallen off, and the paint on the door was peeling. The first few days Anton was busy clearing the yard, mowing the grass to the edge of the meadow, which was beginning to bloom with wildflowers. The inside of the cabin also needed a lot of cleaning. He had left the keys with a woman who was going to take care of it, but it didn't look as if she had done so. Later he found out that it had been too difficult for her to go through the snow, which was deep. He hadn't thought about arranging to get the driveway plowed.

It took two weeks of hard work to get the place to look even halfway decent, but it kept him busy, with little time to think about his life and future. In the past, he'd always been with somebody, whether it was Beatrice, or the family, or close friends. He had never experienced being alone until his stay in the valley. Then, he had known the worst of loneliness; and now, after the housework was done, he began to experience what it was like to again be lonely.

He knew he could take a trip back to Zürich and see people or even go into town and meet the locals at the pub, but loneliness in some ways seemed welcome. In part he hated it, yet he also felt it was just what he needed at this time. It was a battle of opposites: One part of him, which had been the main one in his past, was social — seeing friends, loving to entertain, going out to happenings. That's how he had been for the past five months in Boston. That part wanted to close the cabin and go back to the busy life of Zürich; it kept him from delving into his pain and released him from his frequent feelings of despair.

But another part of him wanted to be isolated. He needed to experience the feelings, needed to go through the pain and accept the despair, needed to search even deeper for his true self—the reality of who he truly was that was still so remote to him. He had touched it in the valley, and he had felt it even for a short time in the cabin, but now he needed to face it fully, realistically, and explore where it would take him. He wanted to talk to Karen, but he couldn't Zoom with her from his cabin, and he didn't want to do it in town where some places had wireless connections. It wouldn't be private enough.

Torn between these two parts of himself, Anton tried to find balance, but it never came. He went to the village and had dinner with some of his old friends, but socializing with them was difficult, as he had so little in common with them now. It was strictly an evening out. He had long phone conversations with friends in Zürich but felt empty when he hung up. And when he meditated and let himself drift into the deeper places in his psyche, he felt lost and longed to reach out to someone, anyone. An inner voice would then say, "Who are you?" This would make him feel even more confused. He longed to speak to Jacques, but he would not be back for another three weeks.

He called Lea and told her what was happening; all she could say was that it was a necessary passage, to hang in there, and it would resolve itself. That was encouraging, but since he couldn't feel any resolution, he sank deeper into feelings of being lost.

One time, when he was meditating, Jacques appeared in his inner vision and said, "Be brave and look deeper." But this seemed no help at all. When he tried to look deeper, it only became darker.

He had no dreams, which was unusual for him, as dreams were his main source of spiritual knowledge. Even that had left him.

Anton climbed the hills, sauntered through the meadows, and even camped out on some of the warmer nights. Again, nothing came, other than the usual feelings of being one with nature and knowing that those feelings would never change. He was the one who needed to change. He read his book and felt that Zarathustra must have gone through a similar turmoil. Somehow that gave him hope, except that Zarathustra had lived for years in the mountains before starting his journey. Anton couldn't live for years like this, that he knew.

His mother returned to Zürich and called him. They talked for a long time. He knew she had found a lovely apartment very near his. Now she described it in more detail, and, of course, there was the divorce, which was still being processed. It would take time because of the vast amount of property. She was holding out for the mountain house, but his father selfishly wanted both houses and was willing to pay her a lot more because of it. It would be a fight till the end.

"And the others, what about them?" Anton asked.

"Kristina, as you may guess, is siding with your father. Erick and Jonas are trying to be neutral, but Erick is agreeing more with me. It's hard on all of them to be torn between us. You at least don't have to go through this."

"I guess that is a relief," Anton replied, though he didn't mean it. He would rather have had that problem and be with his brothers and even Kristina. He knew he would have been with Erick siding with his mother, but he still felt sorrow about his father; and, somehow, he didn't want it to be black and white.

"When can you come for a visit?" he asked her.

"Not for a while. I just got back, and I must begin my redecorating. There's a lot to do here, but why don't you come in for a couple of days? I would love to see you."

"I may do that. I'm working on some ideas for the new house and a friend recommended an architect with whom I would like to talk. I'll let you know."

But even as he spoke, Anton knew he wouldn't leave his inner search at least until Jacques returned. Lina said Jacques had changed the date again adding a couple more weeks to his trip. Anton longed to talk to Jacques, but something within him said that even if he could call, he shouldn't. This process had to be done alone, with no external help.

To explain his search to anyone would be difficult. The inner voice said to him,

"Who are you? What is your purpose?" and Anton went through all his character-istics. He even listed them: one column with good, positive qualities and another column with bad, negative ones. He explored every possibility, trying to leave nothing out, so the lists became long and tiring to look at. He looked at everything he had done or wanted to do, feeling very frustrated. Sometimes, he felt rebellious about the process and cried that he wasn't perfect—he didn't want to be perfect—and his heart knew this to be true. But there still needed to be a change or transformation of some of his darkest qualities. And no matter what he did, the voice kept saying, "Who are you? What is your purpose?"

He read yoga books that talked about the lower nature and how it reveals itself when you strive toward the highest; when you have the knowledge of its content, you can slowly transform the negative into the positive. This seemed right to him, but he wasn't convinced that doing it would clarify who he was or what he needed to do.

Anton became exasperated and irrational. And the voice kept saying, "Who are you? What is your purpose?" He looked at everything he could about himself, and yet the voice never stopped saying, "Who are you? What is your purpose?" He ate and drank too much when he was in those moods and always felt worse the next day.

His despair worsened until one evening, as he sat on the couch, the inner voice once more said, "Who are you? What is your purpose?" A deep moan in him came out, and he screamed, "Damn it! I'm one with you. My purpose is totally to become that!" And, suddenly, he felt a burst of joy in his heart and knew for the first time who he truly was.

He was one with Jacques, with his Mahatma, with all those higher beings who had found God. That part in him was one with them all, and that was his true Self. His purpose or path was to achieve that completely, to grow spiritually so that he could become a coworker. He would struggle to fulfill this purpose, but the ability to do it was within him to be found. It wasn't about the characteristics he needed to change; it wasn't about his history of past lives or his vocation. Rather, it was about his pure spirit. Yes, he had to go through changes, love, and loss, but the true part of him was one with them. This was the core that Charles had talked about.

Anton now felt an inner calmness for the first time in weeks. Yes, he could be social, and yes, he could spend time in isolation. Both were part of his reality, but nei-ther had an effect on his true nature. There would be times when he would be in the world, when he would forget who he was, and times when he would remember, but nothing that happened to him could change his knowledge of who he was.

CHAPTER 36

Anton spent the next couple of weeks working on some layout designs of where he wanted the rooms of the new house. He hoped it would be built by winter but didn't think it possible. After interviewing architects in Zürich, he decided to hire Hans Burkhalter, who was a modern designer, which is what he was looking for.

He worried about the fact that a modern house in his town would be completely different from the Alpine architecture that was prevalent there and throughout the Alps. This was one reason why he had moved the location of the house farther back from the road and closer to the mountain, where it wouldn't be seen. Even though it would need more snow plowing, he preferred the privacy the new location would give him. This way, he could keep the old alpine cabin he was in now for an overflow of guests or for a visiting family that needed more privacy.

The house's new location would have a more beautiful view of the Jungfrau, and the sunset could be seen clearly with nothing blocking it. Anton spent a lot of time on the spot, walking it and looking at all the viewpoints at different times of the day. It almost became an obsession for him that the house be positioned so that light would be correct and that the different angles of the sun would always be casting the most beautiful shadows on the rocks of the mountains that stood as a backdrop. He also decided what rooms would be in what location.

When he was finished, he took his crude drawings to the architect. Hans had walked the property several times with him, and Anton had explained his obsession with the light. Anton anxiously waited. Hans said he would have preliminary sketches in three weeks. During that period, he made a couple more trips to spend time at the location.

Three weeks later, Hans called to say the design was ready. When he came with the rolls of paper, they laid them out on the table and Anton looked at them with trepidation. Would the plans work; were they him? The questions crowded his head, but as he began to sift through the sheets of paper, a great sense of relief and exhilaration came over him. The architect had captured Anton's needs perfectly. Except for keeping the views Anton wanted, Hans had changed the plan of Anton's sketches completely into an ultra-modern home with glass curves and arches and floor-to-ceiling windows that would bring the whole outside, inside. It was the most beautiful design Anton had ever seen. He felt overwhelmed. Then Anton looked at him and said, "This is your dream house, isn't it?"

"Yes, how did you know?"

"I could feel the love coming from the drawings."

"Do you like it?"

"It's incredible. How can I not love it? But don't you want to build this for your-self?"

"Not now. When that time comes, I will do a new design that will fit my land as this one fits yours."

It was a large house, about three-thousand-five hundred square feet, and the main rooms in the plan had a view. There were screened-in porches on either side. One was private and small and connected to Anton's bedroom; the other, off the kitchen, was large, for entertaining and dining. Everywhere, there would be decks and patios and even a swimming pool that would open up in summer and be glass enclosed in the winter. It would be wonderful to swim under the winter stars, to see the glow of the moon on the snow-topped mountains as he sat in the hot tub just outside on the deck. For the first time in his life, Anton appreciated the fact that his family had a great deal of money, from which he was now benefiting. Before, he had just taken it for granted. Because of his mother's gift, he could have this house, and he wanted to call immediately to tell her about it and thank her again.

When he had last seen her in Zürich, she was planning a short trip to Italy to see friends; he wasn't certain she had returned yet, but fortunately she had. Anton told her about the house—all the details—and she said, "Anton, it sounds wonderful!"

"Wait till you see it; in fact, can you come up for a visit?"

There was a long pause, too long. "Is something wrong, Mom?"

Finally, she said, "Anton, I don't know how to tell you this. I'm moving back home."

"What? You're doing what?"

"I know, it sounds weak of me, but your father has been after me for months now to return to him, and finally I broke down. Besides, I really feel lonely and miss him."

"But Mother, what about his mistress?"

"He claims it's over, that he wants only me. Besides, the boys and Kristina have also been after me to go home. I'm afraid I capitulated."

Anton fell silent. Then he said, "So we are back to you not being able to see me?"

"Not now, Anton. I'm moving back this weekend. Then we are going on vacation to France for two weeks. We will be in the mountains in August, and I will certainly visit you then."

"But it's going to be in secret again, isn't it?"

"No, one of the conditions of my returning was that I could see you as much as I wanted. He said it would be all right."

"But you know you will limit visits because it will bother him."

"Maybe, maybe not. I don't know yet, but be certain I love you and will never desert you. Besides, I want to see the house going up. When will it be started?"

"I'm hoping to break ground in July and that enough of it will be up so the interior can be worked on in the winter."

They talked some more; when they hung up, he felt sorry that he had called in the first place. It put a damper on his happiness.

He started a fire in the fireplace as the evening was chilly, and then he sat down with a glass of wine and thought about the day and his new home. He thought about how Sam and he had planned the house and how he had kept the house the size they had decided on. Then something in him said no. Don't go in that direction. Don't listen. This house is yours, and someday there will be another woman — maybe not like Sam, but maybe even nicer — who will laugh with you on the patio, and whom you will make love with on the porch under the stars. Life is not over because Samantha is not here to share this with you. His mind went back to his meeting with Hans, and he could envision the house again with happiness in his heart.

Whenever he thought about the house thereafter, he kept the excitement and the feeling of anticipation in his heart. The final plans were finished in another two weeks, and he and Hans sat down with the contractor and went over everything. Anton could tell right away that building a house would be quite an adventure. Everything had to be his decision in this house, from the type of wood on the floors to the cabinets in the kitchen and the counter tops and appliances. Some of it required tough decisions that as a man he had never thought about.

Hans gave Anton some names of decorators who could help him, and he agreed he certainly needed help in that area. Besides, he had no furnishings, so he would need a decorator who could plan most of them. But he knew that, even with a decorator, he needed to make important choices; and he wanted to make those choices with the idea that a woman would be living there with him. That's why he preferred a woman decorator who would be able to look at things from a feminine viewpoint.

Since the building was to be started in the beginning of July, and school started in August, Anton had to make many decisions in a short time. He would have to do a lot in Zürich and on weekends here.

At this time, he started receiving proofs of the book, which needed a final edit. His life became full of details.

Anton researched decorators and found one he liked in Interlaken who worked both in his area and in Zürich. Her name was Ottilia Brode, and her portfolio showed a mix of modern and antiques similar to his own taste. He gave her the list of the essentials needed first and left it up to her to bring him samples and ideas to choose from.

Construction started in early July. A week later, Anton received a phone call from his mother. He was feeling a little upset that it was the middle of July and she hadn't even tried to call him.

At once she apologized. "I'm so sorry not to have been in touch, but we just got here three days ago. We extended our trip in France, as the hotel we were in was so lovely we didn't want to leave."

She talked some more, a little too quickly, and when he asked to see her, she made a date for early the following week.

"Why can't it be sooner? I have a lot to show you."

"Kristina and the kids are coming tomorrow and maybe the boys for the weekend, and I have to do a lot of shopping to get ready. Next week is really the soonest I can make it, but we'll spend the entire day together. I'll come early, around nine if that's okay?"

Anton hung up, still feeling disappointed. He guessed that in the last six months he had become used to her being there for him. Now that he wasn't number one, it made him wish she hadn't gone back to his father.

The day his mother arrived turned out to be very gloomy and overcast with dark clouds. Even though it wasn't supposed to rain, it felt as if there would be a downpour any minute. As Anton hugged her, he felt how thin she had become; and she looked tired and older.

"Mom, are you all right? You've lost a lot of weight."

Anton could tell she was hesitating. "Yes, but I needed to lose weight, and all the anxiety I've been through has made a difference."

"Well, I hope you've made the right decision."

"Yes, I know I have. But let's talk about you and the new house."

They walked out to the site. Most of the excavations for the basement were done, so Anton could show her the position of the house and what area would face which view. The contractor had the plans, so Anton borrowed them, and they went back to the house where he spread them out for her to look at. Her reaction wasn't what he expected. He could see she looked a bit confused.

Anton asked, "Do you like it?"

She paused. "I don't know. I can't say it's my taste, because it's so modern. I didn't know you were into that extreme style."

"Yes, I've always loved contemporary design. I'm sorry you don't like the house, but it's my dream and I will be living here. Maybe when it's finished you will change your mind."

"I'm sure I will, and I am very happy for you. It's a big house for a single man, but you do like to entertain."

"I have no intention of remaining single, as I really do want a family someday. That's why I'm building it larger, so it will be a home for a family."

"I'm glad to hear that. Does that mean you and Samantha are over?"

"No, I will never be over Samantha, but I am over wanting her to be with me."

Her eyes filled with tears. "I so want you to be happy." And she came to him and gave him a hug.

After lunch, she talked about her travels and a new charity she was involved with. Anton told her about Harvard and his new friends there, but he said nothing about the book, and she didn't ask him about it.

It was still early, but Anton noticed her checking her watch several times. Finally, he said, "I thought you could stay the afternoon, but you're looking like you need to leave soon."

"Anton, I'm sorry. It's the first time I've been out for a reasonable period of time, and I am feeling tired from all the family being here."

"I had hoped the weather would have been nicer, so we could have gone on a hike. I've found a couple of new trails that I thought you might enjoy."

"Let's plan it for next week, and we'll check the weather report to be certain which day will be the best."

"Okay, that would be great. I've really missed you."

"And I've missed you." That was the first time today her voice sounded sincere.

After she left, Anton took a walk down into town. It was a long way, but the decline was gradual, and he found the exercise stimulating. His body was in very good shape, not just from the hiking but also from swimming and tennis. He had a local friend with whom he played tennis twice a week.

Today, he took long strides, trying to make his muscles work harder, and tried not to think about his disappointment in his mother's visit. He naturally expected her always to agree with him, so it was a new experience for him to hear otherwise. He thought about her in general: how agreeable she was to all of them. She was a real pleaser. But now he wondered whether, in fact, she had been truthful all those times she had agreed with him. The only thing he could be certain about was her interest in and love of nature and nature spirits.

Anton thought about his parents and realized that his mother did placate his father and follow what he wanted. But she always made it seem as if she wanted the same herself. Now, he wondered about that. In the renovation of their family home, for instance, he had heard his father ask her several times to contribute to the plans. But in recalling the process they went through, it did seem as if all the men—his father and the three sons—had made the final decisions. Even Kristina didn't take much part in the planning stages.

The more Anton thought about his mother, the more he started to realize that maybe his image of her was false. He had talked about her in therapy, but mainly in terms of his abandonment issues. Did he really know her? Her caring charm and graciousness made the rest of them feel good about themselves. Because she never expressed her own needs, it was natural for them never to consider or question why. Probably the first time she ever strongly took a stand was when she left his father, and even that she couldn't maintain.

Anton was beginning to wonder who she was and whether he would ever know her true feelings. This realization felt like such a loss that he sat down for a minute on a rock and closed his eyes in contemplation. An image appeared immediately. It was a figure of a woman, and when he looked closely, he realized it was Lea.

She said, "The way you see your mother is the way you view the women you love." Then she disappeared.

Anton always had viewed the women he loved as being wonderful until, of course, they disappointed him. Did he ever let them express their feelings and really hear them? He knew now that, no, he just kept the women up on pedestals until they fell off, but he had never included his mother in his analysis.

He thought about Samantha and remembered that last day in Zürich when she said that he didn't really know her. Anton had wondered what she meant by that at the time. He believed he knew her, but he didn't. Sam, more than any of them, he looked on as being faultless, and ideal, and genuine, just as he had always viewed his mother.

Karen had bought up the subject of his mother, but he hadn't been ready to talk about her. Damn! She and Lea are right, he thought. It's all about Mother. He looked for women like his mother, attributing to them qualities that didn't exist and wanting them to be perfect—more perfect than was possible. Once they were on the pedestal, he never found out who they really were.

With his mother, he had always felt he was her special child. He'd never asked his brothers and sister if they felt the same way. For the first time, he questioned his relationship with her. He thought about how he and his mother had never spent much time together except in the summers. He spent his childhood in Grindelwald while his siblings were in boarding school and his parents were traveling or in Zürich. His mother had come maybe once or twice a month to see him, and when he was older it was even less because he also was in boarding school. Maybe he had always seen her as being perfect because he didn't really know her.

At least she had turned to him when she left Father and needed someone to talk to, he thought. But maybe he was wrong. Maybe she confided in the others in the same way; and, now that she was back with Father, she was back to being the pleasing wife and mother, making her husband first and foremost. But his father always came first, before any of them. Christmas was their special holiday; yet, one year, Father had had to go abroad during that time, and Mother had chosen to go with him. They arranged for the children to go home with caretakers to watch and care for them. It was a bleak Christmas, one none of them would ever forget. Scenes of other times when his parents weren't around started to pop into his head like a ticker tape of lost hurts, deepening the wound.

Anton tried to think more positively. At least today she had expressed her true feelings about his house. That was a first. Maybe the separation had changed her a little. She was being assertive about her own beliefs.

Anton sat on the rock for a long time, thinking back on how he had accepted and taken part in a grand illusion about his mother, and how that had affected his truly understanding the women in his life. The thought seemed overwhelming, and he wondered if he could ever change this way of perceiving. He felt his inner child wanting help, which he couldn't give him. When he went back to Zürich, he would call Karen and continue his work with her.

In town, he went into a small bar for a drink. He chose a bar that he knew his father never went to, just in case; but he was mistaken. Halfway through his beer, his father came in with Poli, a local fireman friend. Anton turned his back, hoping his father wouldn't see him, and reached into his pocket to pay for the drink. His father walked by and sat at a table in the back. Anton turned to look and found his father staring at him. It felt very disconcerting, particularly at this time when his mind was ruminating about his mother.

Anton swallowed a gulp and, instead of paying the bill, he waved Hello, and stared back. He noticed his father looked tired. His hair was almost gray, and his face had some new wrinkles. Even so, he was still a striking man. He had always projected an air of dignity that came from his social standing and from being the president of a prominent Swiss bank.

Anton ordered another drink. He was here first, and he wasn't going to let his father intimidate him into leaving. He would just ignore him. He drank his drink slowly and talked to the barman, someone he knew casually. He tried not to think about his father being there, but it seemed impossible, like trying to avoid a speeding storm blowing in his direction. After all, he hadn't seen him for over a year.

It was a little early for dinner, but he still ordered a sandwich, as the second beer was starting to go to his head. He was concentrating on eating it when he heard chairs move as the two men got up and started to walk past him.

Suddenly, Anton felt a hand on his shoulder. "Anton, is that you?" It was Poli's voice. "Look, Erick, it's Anton! We didn't even see him!"

"Yes, it is," his father replied.

Anton had to turn and greet them both. "Poli, it's good to see you. Hello, Dad, fancy meeting you here." Anton tried to keep his voice composed.

"Yes, this is my first time here. As you know, I prefer the Spinne."

"And I prefer this one." Making a point.

Poli said, "I hear you're building a fancy home up on this side of the mountain. Rumor is that it's a beauty."

"Yes, I think it will be. You must come and see it."

"Oh, I will, I need to do a fire inspection on it."

"Poli, I have to go. Talk to you later, Anton." And his father walked out, pretending that everything was fine so that the town wouldn't find out otherwise. How long he expected that to last was a big question.

After eating, Anton ordered a brandy, not thinking about the long walk up the hill. When he left the bar, it was getting toward sunset. The stores were already closed, so he couldn't pick up a flashlight in case he didn't make it back before dark. And the clouds now seemed as if they were finally going to spill their innards downward in full force. He ran with ease at first, then slowed to a jog. The movement cleared his brain of the drinks, and when the rain started it felt refreshing; the bar had been hot and sticky, even though the air-conditioning had been on.

Anton followed the road rather than take a shortcut he knew through the fields. This way, if a car passed by, he could try to get a ride. If he didn't make it before dark, he could at least feel the pavement under his feet to head him the right way. He had an automatic house light that went on about now; that would help when he got closer.

He slowed to a walk when he heard a car behind him. The driver saw him in its headlights and stopped. It was his father.

"Get in."

"No, thank you, I am soaking wet."

"Wet doesn't hurt leather; get in."

They drove in silence to his cabin. Anton pointed it out to him and his father stopped the car. He thanked his father, opened the door, and got out, hoping that would be the end of it. But it wasn't. Father also got out and said, "We need to talk."

"All right, come in."

Inside, Anton pointed to the bar in the kitchen and said, "Help yourself while I change."

Anton took his time in the bedroom and tried to compose himself by linking with his Higher Self, asking to be overshadowed so that he would remain calm.

When he went back to the living room, his father was sipping a scotch, looking around the room. Anton poured himself a brandy and turned to him. "Please sit down. What do you want to say?"

They sat down across from each other.

"Small but nice, very nice. But you always had good taste."

Anton made no comment.

"I need to talk to you about your mother."

"What about her?"

"I know she came to see you today, but I imagine she didn't tell you about herself?"

"Didn't tell me about what? She told me about your vacation and that you're back together. What more was there to say?"

"There was only one reason she came back to me. The divorce was almost final when she told me she was ill."

"What? What do you mean, ill?"

"She couldn't tell you, could she? It's hard for her to tell the truth." He paused and took a breath. "Anton, your mother has cancer, a very serious case of uterine cancer."

His words hung in the air between them that formed giant pillows of charred ash. Anton felt smothered by them into a place of little comprehension.

"Cancer," he whispered. "Oh God, no."

"Yes, I'm afraid it's true."

"What are her chances?"

"Not very good. The doctor gives her only six months at the most."

Anton didn't recall what he said next or what his father said. His mind became numb. All he remembered of the scene later was that, at the end, they put their arms around each other and held each other for a long time. The tears came later, after his father left, when Anton could finally accept what he had told him.

CHAPTER 37

When Anton recovered and could think more clearly, he phoned the house and asked to speak to Mother. Kristina answered and said, "Anton, yes. She's resting, but I'll get her."

"No, please don't disturb her, just tell her to call me when she gets up."

"I'll do that." He could hear her voice crack a little. "I'm sorry, Anton; I'm so sorry."

He didn't know if she meant she was sorry about Mother or sorry about them, so he simply said, "Yes, I'm sorry too." And he said goodbye.

An hour later the phone rang. It was Mother.

"Anton, now you know."

"Why couldn't you tell me?"

"I meant to, and I was still going to try to, but it was just too difficult for me. You know I love you very much, and I hate what's happening to me. I'd rather not talk about it or think about it."

"Are you in any pain?"

"Sometimes, but I have medicine that really helps."

"But you need to fight this, Mom. You need to be strong and not give up."

"I've never been very much of a warrior. You know that."

"But you've changed in the last few months: you *have* become a warrior."

"Only a little, but this is a different kind of battle. One that there is little hope in winning."

"There's always hope."

"Just a minute." He could hear someone talking to her.

"Your father asked me to invite you to dinner tomorrow night."

"Yes, I'll be there, but if it's a nice day can I take you on a picnic?"

"I would love that."

The next day favored him by being warm and sunny. She came at eleven and he chose an old trail that they both knew. It was one of the trails she had taken them all on when they were children. It passed through meadows of flowers and a small waterfall and was an easy climb. They spoke very little, and he could see that even this small hike didn't seem easy for her. She quickly became out of breath, so he suggested many small rests along the way. A stream was their final destination. As kids, when it was hot, he and his siblings had gone skinny dipping there, sunbathing afterward on the flat rocks—so many years ago, so many memories.

The hike normally took one hour, but today it took Anton and his mother two, so when they finally arrived, they were very hungry. Anton had made thick sausage sandwiches and had cold beer in a small cooler. These were Mom's favorites, and he always thought it amazing that she was so small and petite, as she ate more like a man. Her hair was shoulder length, longer than she usually had it, and it blew in the breeze, making her look much younger. She wore jeans and a tight yellow cotton top. Today she looked relaxed and happier, very different from yesterday.

They ate in silence, savoring every bite. Then she said, "I always wanted to spend my last years here in the mountains. I envied you taking advantage of every spare moment to be here. I would have done the same, but your father always loved to travel. Mind you, I've enjoyed it, too, but now I regret not having insisted on being here more."

"Can't you do that now? At least now, stay."

"They are going to try some chemotherapy treatments on me, so I have to be in Zürich for those; but yes, after that I plan to return here."

"Have you thought about working with a healer? I'm certain Jacques can give you the name of one."

"Yes, I would like to talk to him about it. Is he in Zürich now?"

"No, but he will be returning soon. I'll let you know."

"I'm glad I didn't tell you myself yesterday. If I had, then you wouldn't have seen your father. It makes me happy that you are reunited."

"This isn't the way I would have wanted that to happen."

"I know, but it did, and I'm so grateful for that. Kristina also is happy you are coming to dinner."

"Is she here with Felix?"

"No, they're having problems."

"I'm sorry to hear that. And my brothers?"

"They're coming up this weekend. We just told them a couple of days ago."

"Mom, I need to talk to you about something that's been bothering me. It came up for me yesterday. I know it's not a good time to do this, but if I don't say something it will bother me and fester, and I want to clear it out."

"What is it?"

"I've been thinking about our relationship and how I project some of my feelings about you onto the women in my life. I realized that, because you were never around for me as a child, I always put you on a pedestal.

"When I saw you, mainly in the summers, you were very special to me, and I thought I was special for you. I never truly got in touch with how much I felt abandoned by you and Dad, especially when I lived here and went to school as a child with only Gretchen and Johann to take care of me. I know you came on weekends sometimes; but they were visits, not everyday living. When I hurt myself skiing, it was Gretchen and Johann who took me to the hospital. You came later, but they were the ones who held me when I was in pain and comforted me."

Anton could see she was looking concerned.

"I'm not saying you weren't a good mother. I'm only saying that you weren't there a lot of the time, and I realize now that the women I married haven't been there, either. Beatrice was always running around with her friends, and now Samantha has left me for her work."

"But, Anton, you know it was your father's position that caused us to be traveling so much. A lot of the trips were for business; that's why we felt it best for you to go to the first few grades of school here, out of the city and in a beautiful environment."

"But, the other kids lived with you in Zürich and went to school there. Why was I different?"

"In the years when they were in the first grades, your father hadn't needed to travel for his work. That only came later, just after you were born. Rather than leave you with the servants in Zürich, we felt it better for you to be with Gretchen and Johann. They were warm, caring people, and I know they really loved you."

"Yes, that's true, but why did you always have to go with Dad? Why couldn't you have stayed home with me?"

He felt the hurt welling up in him.

She leaned over and put her hand on his arm. "I needed to be with your father. A lot of business is conducted over dinner or in the homes of the executives. The spouses were always there. Your father couldn't do that alone. The social part was just as important, in a way, as the business negotiations. If the spouses liked me, and I liked them, it made it a lot easier to make deals. That's the way that world was. I'm sorry it has affected you so much. It pains me that you feel this way. I always thought I made it up to you in the summers, and now I realize I didn't. And you were special. You've always been special to me. I've told you that many times."

"It's not that you didn't give me a lot during the summers, it's just that not having had you all the time has affected the way I relate to women," said Anton. "I don't trust that the woman I'm with will be there for me, and that makes me feel needy. The needy inner child in me comes out in my relationships. I want to be with the woman I love, every minute, every day. Of course, that can't always happen, and it certainly hasn't happened for me—just the opposite. I've chosen women who have abandoned me as you did."

"I'm sorry that I hurt you. I never wanted to do that."

CHAPTER 38

The next day Anton called Jacques' house and discovered that he had just arrived. Anton told him about his mother and the truce for the time being. Jacques expressed his sympathy and said he would pray for her. He was a good healer, so maybe he could cure her. He said he hoped it was her karma to be healed, but if she was meant to go, the healing would not work. It would, though, at least relieve her of any pain. Anton invited Jacques to come for a visit; happily, he said yes, and they chose a date in August.

His father called early the next morning to confirm that Anton's brothers had arrived; Anton was to come for brunch and stay the day.

His brothers greeted him fondly. They hugged for a long time, their hearts touching with the need to share hidden feelings. Their differences seemed to dissolve, becoming dust falling back to earth, and he felt genuine brotherly love from them and for them. Kristina was also open and loving, and Anton felt their hearts had truly reconnected.

Mother joined them as they sat down to eat. She looked paler and more drawn. They greeted her presence in whispers, as if their voices would be too loud and startle her. Finally, she said to Erick, "I can't hear you, and I'm not deaf, so please talk louder."

Then they talked in a more normal tone of voice. They ate and talked about what was happening in their lives and tried to sound as if everything were okay. They knew about Anton's marriage and annulment but politely didn't mention it. Jonas asked him about the book, and Anton said it was in the galley stage and would come out in September or October. That was greeted with silence, and Anton quickly changed the subject.

They talked about doing a hike and Mother declined, saying she wanted to rest; but she encouraged the rest of them to go, as the weather was perfect. They protested but she insisted, so after brunch was finished they all retired to put on hiking gear. Anton had brought his own with him, just in case.

The trail they chose was one the family used a lot. It was off the beaten track, so there weren't many tourists. The five of them walked in silence for some time. Each was deep in thought, and it was clear that the thoughts were around Mother. Finally, they found a cool place to rest for a while and Father said, "We need to talk about Mother. I'm glad she didn't come; it's been very hard for her to discuss her illness with anyone. There's a fatality in her that she holds onto. She's given up, and I think she does the treatments mainly because of all of you."

"I know you said she has six months to live, but won't that change if the treatments are working?" Anton asked.

"No, with treatment it will be six months; without treatment, she would go sooner."

Erick said, "But if the treatments are going to make her sick all the time, maybe she shouldn't have them, particularly if they can't cure her."

Father responded, "I told her that and she wouldn't hear of it. She wants all the time she can have with all of you, which brings me to what we need to talk about."

His voice quivered a bit. "She wants to die here in the mountains, and she's asked me to let her stay here and go back and forth to Zürich just for the treatments."

"How long are the treatments?" Kristina asked.

"For another three months it's every two weeks, and after that once a month."

"But we're talking about her being here in the winter. Six months from now is December."

"Yes, I know, and of course, we all have to work, so there is no one to stay with her during the week. Even Anton — you're back teaching soon?"

"Yes, and I can't change that now. I wish I could."

"My concern is the winter. If there is a lot of snow, we can't even make it up here on weekends and she could miss treatments because of that," Father said.

"Hopefully, the weather reports will give enough warning so that she can get down to Zürich in advance; but still, for her to be alone here is crazy," Kristina said.

"That's why we need to talk. If we gang up on her she won't back down, but if each one of us talks to her separately, maybe she'll be more open. Especially you, Anton; you've always had the most influence on her."

"I'll certainly try, but I understand how she feels. These mountains are what she loves the most."

"More than she loves us?" Kristina asked.

"It's not about comparing us to them. The beauty of the mountains touches her soul, and her soul is what she's listening to now."

Everyone was silent at his words.

"Then what are we to do? Just let her be alone here and die alone?" Father bowed his head in silent despair.

"I have a long winter break at Christmas, so I can be here at that time," Anton offered.

"We all can take time off at Christmas, but what about September, October, November, and December? Dad, can't you get some time off?" Kristina asked.

"I can take long weekends, but you know my job is such that I can't take off big chunks of time; and I still have to travel, even though now your mother won't be going with me. I'll do my best, but I'll still have to be in Zürich every week."

"I have the same problem. I just can't leave my practice," Kristina added.

Anton's brothers had similar difficulties. No one could just take off stretches of time from work. They talked some more about how to change her mind, how to reach her. What they didn't talk about was the reality of the situation: that she was dying.

She would need help here, but Father had already looked into hiring a local couple, Lydia and Theodor Beutler, to live in the house and take care of her. Mother had already met them and liked them very much, so that would not be a problem. Lydia had done some caregiving, so she would be able to handle Mother's sickness. But most of the time, none of us would be here. When they resumed their hike, nothing seemed resolved, and again the silence was poignant with feelings of fatality.

Later, after their return, they sat on the porch and Mother joined them.

"So, has your father told you that I'm staying here except when I have to go for treatments, that I'm staying permanently?"

"Yes, we know," Kristina replied. And they all were silent.

"Well, no protests?" She was challenging them.

Erick answered, "Mom, you must know how we feel. We want to be with you as much as we can. If you stay here, that won't be possible. What do you want us to say?"

"I guess I would want you to understand how much I need to be here."

"We understand, but that doesn't make it easy for us. We love you and want to be close to you. None of us can quit our jobs to be here with you," Kristina added.

"I wouldn't want you to — in fact, that's the last thing I want."

Again, there was silence. They were trying to follow Dad's wishes of not ganging up on her, but finally, Anton said, "Maybe you could change your mind a little bit. When you come for treatments, instead of returning the next day, stay longer for a day or two so we can all be with you."

"I'll think about that, but not after the treatments, as they make me sick. Maybe the day before would work, but you must all promise you will spend that evening with me."

"That's easy to promise," Jonas said, and since he was the one never available for family dinners, it was good that he spoke.

Later, Anton did have a chance to speak to her alone.

"Mother, I understand why you need to be here but, except for Lydia and Theodor, you will be alone, and that thought makes all of us unhappy. Please consider spending more than just a couple of days at a time in Zürich. Make it at least three days so each of us can even see you alone. I, for one, would like that. Just some one-to-one time with you."

"I will think about it, Anton, but right now I just want to be here. It's very joyful to watch the sunrise and sunset over these mountains. I feel the energy here is healing, and my fatigue isn't as great as it is in the city. But mainly I need to be alone. You, of all people, should understand that. I need to prepare to die. It's important to go in peace, to have resolved those things that haven't been resolved, and to feel tranquil. That's why I need to be here."

He acquiesced, knowing she was speaking from the heart. He also told her about Jacques' sending her healing and that at least it would take away her pain. She was grateful and asked Anton when he had spoken to Jacques. When he told her, she said, "That makes sense. I've been feeling different for the last couple of days. Usually, I do have some pain when I wake up, but the pain is no longer there. I must call and thank him."

Dinner was quiet. They talked of pleasant things, but the conversation had long pauses in it, and Anton was glad to say goodnight finally and go home.

He invited everyone to lunch the next day to see the house plans. It was Sunday, so the construction crew wouldn't be there.

Again, it was a beautiful day, and when they walked the site the views were clear and breathtaking. He brought the plans and spread them out, so they could see the position of the rooms and the angles. Everyone loved them and complimented him on his basic design ideas. Father praised it the most, and Erick made a shy remark that being an outcast was the best thing that could have happened to him. All in all, it was a good experience.

Lunch was good, and they all got back into the old familiarities of conversation. It made him realize how much he had missed them all. Anton thought about the book and wondered what was going to happen when it came out. Would he still be part of the family after Mother died?

The house was progressing faster than Anton had anticipated. It was enjoyable to be part of it; the more that could be accomplished before he had to leave, the better.

Jacques was coming during Anton's last week there, which was the second week in August. It would work out well because his brothers and father would be back at work, and he and Jacques would have time alone with his mother.

After Jacques' visit, Anton planned to drive him back to Zürich and stay there himself. From then on, it would only be weekends in the mountains until the Christmas break.

The book proofs were corrected and sent back to the publisher. Except for working on the house, he had some free time, which he arranged to spend with Mother in the mornings.

She wanted him to tell her about the death process, which he found too difficult to explain. Instead, he suggested she ask Jacques when he came. She had telephoned Jacques and thanked him for the healing, and since then she had phoned him several times just to talk. Anton felt at this point that Jacques' visit was really to see her more than to see him, which was okay with him. If Jacques could help her at this time, it would make Anton very happy.

Some last-minute details with the house came up the day Jacques was due to arrive. Anton returned home later than anticipated and found him and Mother sitting outside on the porch. Anton apologized, and Jacques smiled and said, "That's fine; when I found you weren't here, I called your mother, thinking you might be over there. She said you probably were doing something with the house and came right over to keep me company."

"That's good, and of course she was right. It's almost lunchtime, so, Mother, please stay for lunch."

That was the beginning of Jacques' stay, and it typified the rest of it. If Anton didn't invite her to be with them, Jacques would make the offer, and she also invited them for dinner on several occasions. Sometimes Anton had a strong feeling that she wanted to be alone with Jacques, so he would make an excuse concerning the house and take his leave.

The house was completely framed by then, and he could now experience more of the design. When he saw it, Jacques said nothing for a long time. He just walked around slowly, feeling the energy, Anton could tell he really loved it.

When they sat down later, Jacques said, "Your house is wonderful. You will spend many happy hours there. When it's finished, I will come and bless it and set up your shrine room for you."

"Thank you; I was going to ask you to do that for me."

"With your permission, I would like to use your shrine room to initiate your mother. She has asked me to be her teacher."

Anton was shocked and thrilled at the same time. "That's wonderful! I'm so happy for her."

"She will still die, Anton. It's her time, but I will be there for her and help her on the other side. We have talked a lot about it, and I will tell you also what needs to happen at the end. She needs to be lying in a room where she can see the mountains. The beauty will help her pass calmly. There should be no sorrow in the room, no crying to hold her back. If the family is with her, you must tell them that. Surround her with flowers and classical music. She knows to direct her thoughts to the Mahatmas. She feels close to Jesus, so I suggested she have a picture of him in front of her and keep his image in her mind as she begins to leave her body. Holding that thought will take her to him."

"I hope I will be there."

"You will be. I think it will happen right after New Year's."

"Not to cry will be very difficult."

"You can cry later, just not during the death process. She needs to be cremated, but wait three days. It takes three days for the subtle body to separate, so make them wait three days. In the spring, she wants her ashes to be scattered on the mountain and in the fields of spring flowers, but she will tell you that."

Anton nodded.

"It's a great loss for you, I know. But in another life, you will be together again."

"Yes, our love is very special. But another life doesn't mean anything to me at this time. Losing her now, in this one, makes me feel I will never be happy again. It's selfish, I know, but that's how I feel."

"You've had some difficult losses." And Anton knew he was referring to Samantha.

"But Anton, you will be happy again, in your home, with love in your life and a family of your own."

When Anton saw his mother again, he hugged her and told her how happy he was that she was going to be a disciple. She said, "I'm so glad to be able to do this before I die. You know, the first time I met Jacques, I felt he was my teacher; but I didn't follow through with it. Thank you for introducing him to me."

CHAPTER 39

The next morning, Anton and Jacques drove to Zürich. It was a lovely day, and Anton hated to leave his home and Mother, but he had no choice.

During the next few weeks, he was busy with the house, his new courses, and running back and forth on the weekends to the mountains. When his mother came for treatments, she came early as promised, and the whole family had dinner together. She was losing more weight, and they could see her slowly losing the battle. Everyone tried to be in good spirits to make those dinners happy ones, and she, of course, was very joyful. She always had tea with Jacques, and sometimes Anton was free to join them. He was a little worried that she wouldn't live long enough to make her initiation, that his house wouldn't be ready in time. Anton mentioned this to Jacques and asked him why he couldn't initiate her in his shrine room.

Jacques explained, "Your shrine room is in the mountains, and the energy there is important for her. It will help her to pass in an easier manner. Don't worry, it will happen. If I see the time is getting too close, I will do the initiation here."

On October 30, Anton's book came out and was featured in the bookstores. The reviews were mixed. Some felt it was an inspirational book that would help readers look more closely at their inner spirit. Others felt it was too religious, though where they got that idea, he didn't know—spiritual, yes, but not religious by any means. Overall, the reviews were good and interesting. His publisher was pleased, and he booked Anton to do a book signing at one of the larger bookstores in Zürich.

Anton gave a copy to his mother but to no one else in the family. He didn't even want to mention it had been released in case the news would start a new series of arguments. Of course, they all found out. Jonas was the first to call and congratulate him. He said he was just starting to read it and found it interesting. Erick was a little more direct. He said he always knew Anton was a bit crazy, and crazy was okay, but this was definitely not his stuff, as he'd always been a borderline atheist. Kristina never mentioned it, but her energy felt colder. Dad, much to his credit said, "For a religious book, it's not bad."

Mom, of course, loved it and wanted to do all the exercises. Anton said he would be glad to do them with her when he saw her on the weekends.

Anton was worried about what his colleagues at the university would think, but surprisingly, his closest friends felt his book had a lot of depth and wanted to have some discussions with him about it. Bruno Brander was one of those who wanted to find out more. Bruno couldn't understand the reference to Nietzsche's Zarathustra, as Anton's concept was very different except for the explanation of the superman theory in terms of the Higher Self. Overall, the reception to his book was better than he thought it would be.

His biggest surprise came from his students. Most of them bought the book or borrowed it and came into class with some profound questions. Instead of teaching European philosophy, he found himself mainly teaching some of the material from the book. He finally had to stop in order to cover the course material, but he asked the students if they would be interested in a course on Zarathustra's teachings, and, if so, if they would write the chairman and suggest it. Anton thought the chairman received close to fifty letters; as a result, he asked Anton if he would add a course the next semester. Even though Anton was already teaching four courses, he agreed. The name he chose for the course was Higher Self: Theosophical Studies. The main text-book was his own, *Zarathustra's Journey*, but he would also be using the Bhagavad Gita, the Hindu epic which was also about the Higher Self, and some other books from India that were yoga based. Since the course was in a university, he had to bring in more academics, and adding those books would do that. Anton had a long break over the holidays and would use that time to design the new course.

It was very exciting to him and, when Jacques was told, he also was delighted that Anton could begin to do this work. Jacques invited him to dinner shortly thereafter. Anton was surprised to find many of Jacques' disciples there and his mother, as well, who had made a trip to town for the event. It was a great celebration for the book and for Anton.

Mother stayed at his apartment that night and the next day went to be with Father, pretending to have come in for a couple of days of shopping. Her treatments were only every month now, and even those weren't scheduled in advance, as her condition was worsening. The whole family had dinner together and talked about the holidays, which were coming up soon. It would be a full house in the mountains. Everyone was coming, including Felix and the boys; and Jonas had asked Lillian, his fiancée, to come. Anton had just met her recently and liked her very much. He invited them to stay in his small cabin if they wanted more privacy, and they accepted.

Anton himself would be staying in his new house, which was almost finished. The entire exterior was done, and they were now finishing the interior rooms. He had picked out some furnishings already, but not all of them. The rest would have to wait until spring. The main bedroom was finished, as was a guest room. The kitchen would be completely finished, and the living room mainly done, just enough for him to start to live there. The shrine room would be ready, and Jacques planned to come a couple of days before Christmas to do the initiation and bless the house. Anton had invited him to stay for the holidays, but he declined, saying that he needed to entertain all the students in Zürich, as he traditionally did. Anton would have joined them, but since this was his mother's last Christmas, he wanted to stay with her.

His class on Fridays was in the morning, so he was able to take off before lunch for the weekend. He picked up Mother from his father's house and they headed home. It was almost dark when they arrived, and she insisted that he stay with her that night. Since there was an unexpected snowfall, Anton agreed. Mother took a brief nap, and Anton went out to the glass-enclosed porch to look out at the snow. Even though the clouds were thick, the sunset shimmered pink through them, turning the white flakes into luminous gossamers gamboling to the ground. He sat with eyes opened, filled with the beauty of the scene, and fell into a semi-meditation. Suddenly, Samantha was there, watching the scene with him. His impulse was to ask her to leave; but, somehow, he couldn't disturb the splendor of what was happening, so, he let her stay, and again he became lost in the sun's descent. When darkness took away the pink light, Sam left, and Anton went inside.

Lydia prepared a substantial meal for them, and they had a leisurely dinner full of conversation around the teaching.

Mother went to bed right after dinner, but Anton wasn't sleepy, so he poured himself a brandy and curled up on the sofa in front of a fire that was still burning. For a moment, he turned on the outside lights to see if it was still snowing. The wind had picked up, and now there was a blizzard with swirling snow that looked like dancing whirling dervishes.

CHAPTER 40

As planned, Jacques and Anton drove up to Grindelwald a week before Christmas. Fortunately, the weather was favorable, with no snow forecasted. What furniture Anton had already bought looked good, even though it was sparse.

Jacques had said he would decorate the shrine room. Previously, following his direction, Anton had had the walls painted a pale blue and bought some big, Indian-patterned cushions to sit on. Natural wood shelves had been built at one end of the room to hold sacred objects.

Jacques waited for the morning to go to work. Anton wanted to help him, but Jacques said no, this was his job. When he was finished, he came out and invited Anton to meditate with him. Upon entering the room, Anton was completely surprised. The first thing he saw was the shrine. Jacques had placed a very large, seated bronze Buddha on the top shelf. It was one of the Buddhas from his own shrine room—the one that Anton had always admired. On either side of the Buddha were fu dogs, the guardians, also made of bronze. Then there were two vases of roses. The shelves below contained pictures of all the Mahatmas and Taras and a wonderful picture of Jacques.

There were candles lit on all the shelves, flickering light on the photos. Above the Buddha on the wall was a beautiful painting of the Himalayan Mountains by Nicholas Roerich, a painting that Jacques had had in his study and one that Anton loved.

Jacques had arranged the cushions in a semicircle, and next to the main pillow was a large Tibetan gong. Anton must have stood there for a long time with his mouth open, until Jacques said, "Well, do you like it?"

"Like it? It's incredibly beautiful. But Jacques, your Buddha, the painting — they're so precious, surely you're not giving me those?"

"Yes, they are my gifts to you and your new home. The energy coming from them will fill this room and help your meditations, and they will make your home here safe from any harm."

Anton was flabbergasted. "But—"

"No buts, I insist. You are my son, and I want you to have them."

Anton embraced Jacques and felt his heart open with love for him.

They meditated for a long time, and the energy was wonderful. In the meditation, Jacques took him to a mountain that was made of blue ice. It was a clear, sky-blue color and looked very cold but wasn't. He said it was a very special place, and he took Anton to a recessed area cut into the ice and asked him to lie down in it. When Anton did, he felt his body tingle with energy from top to bottom. It was as if he were being given a bolt of electricity, but it felt glorious and not harmful in any way. It lasted for just a couple of minutes, and then Jacques pulled him up and said that was enough. Anton next found himself back in the room feeling a shift in his subtle body, as if in some ways it had become more refined.

Jacques said, "That is another gift to you."

They had lunch with Anton's mother later that day and arranged for her to come the next morning for her initiation. She looked pale and shrunken, and both realized that it was difficult for her to be out of bed for very long. Anton hadn't seen her for a couple of weeks and recognized how much she had faded during that time. He wondered if she would even make it through Christmas, but Jacques said she would probably leave her body a week afterward.

The next morning, they picked Mother up. It was cold, so they wrapped her in blankets in the car, and, as soon as they arrived at Anton's house, sat her down in front of a fire with a hot cup of tea. But she hadn't seen the house finished and wanted to look around.

After slowly moving through all the rooms, she looked at him and said, "It's you. Now I see how much it is you. And it's a side of you that I didn't know about. I'm so glad I've lived to see it finished and to know how wrong I was about the design."

When she came out of the initiation room with Jacques, she looked radiant. Jacques had given her some prayer beads, which she clutched in her hands as she sat down and said, "Thank you. That was what I needed to finish my life correctly."

Jacques stayed for a couple more days, spending them with Mother at her place. Anton came for part of the time, but mainly he left them alone to talk about her next journey.

Mother always retired early, so Anton and Jacques spent their evenings together. It was during one of these times that Jacques said he had heard from Samantha. "I think it's good news. She said the mission is almost over and that she even hoped to be free to spend Christmas with me."

Anton was shocked. "You mean she can leave now and not be harmed?"

"There's always a plan for an agent such as her to get out without being discovered. I expect that's what she means."

"I would think the truth has to come out sooner or later. She's got to be found out."

"Not necessarily. She wouldn't tell me on the phone. All she said was that it's just about over. But, of course, I'll let you know if she does come home."

Anton felt enormous relief. "That's wonderful if it's true. I never thought she could survive this."

"I know you didn't, but I did. You don't know Samantha very well. She's always been very resourceful. Her intuition is marvelous, and I've seen her talk her way out of tough situations that some of the finest strategists would have difficulty managing."

"When she said it's over, do you mean she will be home for good?"

"Yes, it was definite."

"But she'll still be an agent awaiting her next job."

"I don't know about that. I think this last job may have convinced her to leave the agency, but I don't know."

"Well, it doesn't matter either way to me." Anton's voice sounded harsh.

"I know she's hurt you a lot, but maybe you can forgive her. So much of what happened wasn't her fault."

"It doesn't matter to me anymore. I'm embarking on a new life, which is not going to include anyone whom I can't trust."

"I understand that, but I know she will want to see you. In fact, she asked if you would be at my house for Christmas, and I told her about your mother. She was very sad about that. She loves your mother. If she comes home, she will call you, I know."

"Thank you for telling me." I need to be prepared, Anton thought.

Anton drove Jacques to Interlocken the next morning to catch a train back to Zürich. He made it out just in time. There was a big snowstorm in the evening, which wiped out all the roads. The whole family was due to arrive the next day but now had to wait. The conditions made it impossible for Anton to visit Mother. Instead, they talked on the phone.

When he asked how she was, she gently answered, "Soon to go, but I'm okay now that I have Jacques to help me on the other side. But I will miss you and all the others. He told me I could do some work if I wanted to. I could help people, and of course, I agreed. Isn't it wonderful that I can be of service, and not just sit around waiting to be reborn?"

"That's incredible, Mom! Knowing you, you'll be very busy. Just don't forget to come back to us."

She laughed. "Well, you would make a good father. I'll have to ask about that."

"What a great idea. Who knows, stranger things have happened."

Anton felt a sudden wave of sadness, "I'm so sorry I can't be with you now. If the weather isn't better tomorrow, I will put on my snowshoes and walk there."

"Don't be silly. That would take you hours. It will stop; it always does."

She was right about that, but it still turned out to be a huge blizzard that lasted for three days. When it finally was over, they had several feet of snow and a mess to clean up.

Christmas was two days away, and it would be a miracle if everyone could make it up the mountain or even if he could get over to his mother's. He would definitely have to snowshoe over, as he wouldn't think of leaving her alone on her last Christmas with them. But he didn't have to do that. All the men in town took turns around the clock, clearing the snow. Anton also helped, and it felt good to be part of such a caring community.

He was able to drive his car, loaded with food and gifts, to his mother's house the morning of Christmas Eve. As soon as he got there, he ran to her bedroom. She looked as if she wouldn't make it through the day, but he remembered what Jacques had said. As soon as Anton arrived, Lydia and Theodor left to go home for Christmas with their family. Before the storm, they had stocked the freezer and pantry with enough supplies to feed everyone during the holidays. Anton helped his mother into her wheelchair and took her into the kitchen to make some lunch. She sat there quietly watching him heat up some homemade soup and toast some wheat bread.

Finally, she said, "Anton, I want you to know that I am so proud of you."

He turned to look at her. "Thank you. I know that, but why are you saying it now?"

"Just in case I didn't say it enough when you were growing up. There is something else I need to tell you. Samantha called me this morning, and we had a long talk. She wanted to tell me she loves me and was deeply sorrowful that I would be leaving soon. It was really good to talk to her. I love her, too, you know."

"Yes, I know you do."

"She said that if I was still here after Christmas, she would try to come in person to say goodbye."

Anton didn't respond. He couldn't.

"Then she is at Jacques' for Christmas?"

"Yes. She's home."

He turned his back and poured the soup into big earthenware dishes.

"Anton, I know she's done some strange things, but I also know it isn't because she doesn't love you. I think she does, and I hope you will see her when she comes."

"I would prefer not to, so I am asking you to promise me that you will let me know if she does come to see you."

"That's silly. You know that if you're not here she will go find you at your house. She does know where it is."

"Yes, I guess you're right."

"It would make me so happy to know you are back together again."

"It wouldn't make me happy. Please don't expect that. I will marry again, Mother, and I'm sorry you won't meet the woman I will end up with; but maybe you will see her from the other side."

"Oh, I assure you I will definitely try to do that, but won't you reconsider?"

"No, I won't," he interrupted her. "If I go back with Sam, the same things will happen. Her work is more important than any marriage or family is to her. I can't live with someone like that, someone whose priority isn't her family."

"And what about you, Anton? Was your priority the family when it came to publishing and teaching your book?"

"That was different. That was a mission from my teacher—and, yes, the teaching is my priority over any family."

"You're like all the men in this family. Their work comes first, but a woman's work doesn't. I had hoped you wouldn't be like your father in this respect, and it's a shame that you are. Samantha's mission had to mean a lot to her for her to give you up for a time. But you don't see that; you simply expect, as all men do, that their women should think of them first. I hope to God when I return that I will be a woman, a woman who is more like Samantha, someone who knows her values and follows them without needing permission from any man."

"But I'm not like Father! How can you say that?" Anton was upset.

"Oh no? If I had left him to spend Christmas with my children instead of going on that business trip with him, he wouldn't have talked to me for months. I went away with friends for a weekend one time when we were first married, and he was so angry that he didn't talk to me for days. Who does that sound like?"

"But she left me for over a year! How can you compare that to a weekend?"

"She must have had a good reason, and you won't even see her to find out what it was. I don't know the whole story, nor do you. It's always been a big secret, but I do know that the mission Samantha had to carry out must have been very important for her to have disappeared the way she did. She also left Jacques, and he still loves her and accepts her. He doesn't say he never wants to see her again because she went off like that."

"But he's her father and teacher!" Anton was yelling now.

"And you are her husband."

"Not anymore, thank you. I don't want to argue with you, Mother. Sam and I are no longer married, and that's how I want it to remain."

They both fell silent and ate their soup. When they were finished, she asked him to take her back to her room.

Anton felt terrible. "Mom, I'm sorry to distress you. Please forgive me."

"I'm sorry to have brought up the subject and then given my advice. You didn't ask for it. So, forgive me. I just want you to be happy."

"I am happy. Believe that."

She smiled a sweet smile and squeezed his hand. No answer, just the smile.

The family arrived late afternoon. It was a blast of warm air that changed the serious overtones of their conversations. Everyone was there. Anton hadn't seen Kristina's children, Leon and Uli, for a while. He barely recognized them, as they had grown so tall. They were already planning to ski with their father, and, of course, Erick and Jonas would probably join them.

But the next day was Christmas. They would all disappear after that, or so he thought. Mom stayed up in her wheelchair until the tree was decorated and then had to go to bed. The boys took off to carol with some local friends of theirs, leaving the adults quietly to talk about Mom. Anton said he didn't think she had much longer to live. He would remain there until the next semester started, and he added he felt she would be gone by then. Dad said he was staying, also. He might have to go back for a day or two, but he planned to stay with her until the end.

Anton thought, How selfish I am! Somehow, he had believed it would be Mother and him at the end, and he had talked to Jacques about how he could help her in the death process.

The others also said they were going to take some vacation time to remain there. When the doctor had seen her a month earlier, he'd told Father that he wasn't certain she would even make it through the holidays. So, they all were staying, even his brothers. It was time for Anton to let go of his being the special, only one who would care enough to stay with her. They all loved her, probably as much as he did, and of course, she would want them all to be there.

They tried to make the holidays as happy as they used to be. The couch was set up near the fireplace, and they wrapped Mother in afghans and brought many pillows, and that's where she spent most of the time.

They gathered around her, telling stories of some of their past adventures together. She mainly listened and laughed, occasionally telling one of her own remembrances. Sometimes she fell asleep, and then they quietly left to go into the kitchen or take a walk.

When her condition worsened, they moved her back to the bedroom. Lydia and Theodor returned, and Lydia took on the full care of Mother.

One morning the phone rang, and Father answered it. Anton heard him say, "Yes, she wants to see you, but come quickly; there isn't much time left."

When he hung up he said to Anton, "That was Samantha, and she is coming in the afternoon."

"I don't want to see her, so I am going home. Please let me know when she leaves so I can return."

His father didn't question him, so Anton gathered Mother must have told him their story.

He left after lunch. His house seemed strangely isolating. He had been spending all his time at the family home and was even sleeping there, now that Mother was worse.

He guessed he was now used to having his full family back, and his home seemed to lack the love energy that only people could give it.

Only the shrine room was full of warmth, and he went and meditated there for several hours. Back in the living room, he was watching the sunset when the phone rang. It was Father.

"Samantha has left but is planning to stay the night in town. I think she is on her way to see you."

"Thank you for letting me know. How is Mother doing?"

"A little better. She was very happy to see Samantha. By the way, all of us like her very much."

"I'll be there soon."

Anton poured himself a glass of wine and sat down again. If he left now, he wouldn't be there when Sam arrived. What to do? Was he such a coward that he couldn't even see her? He owed it to himself to tell her how he felt.

When Jacques had called Anton to tell him Samantha was there and wanted to see him, he said it was up to Anton, but he hoped he would at least hear her story. But did Anton want to, really? Did he want to hear it? He felt his nerves getting jittery. He needed to calm down and release the anger and hurt that he was feeling. He tried walking up and down the living room, but it didn't seem to help, as his hands were clenched into tight fists.

Linking with his Higher Self, he gave his feelings to it and tried to experience its peaceful energy. In a short time, he was feeling more normal. Then the doorbell rang. It was Sam.

When he opened the door and saw her standing there, he did not feel what he expected to. Instead of the old rush of emotion that vacillated between love and pain, he felt nothing, absolutely nothing. She was thinner, more dazzling, with a tan, and so very elegant in her fur coat. And he felt totally nothing.

"Come in," and he opened the door wide.

Anton thought she knew what he was feeling because she made no attempt to hug or kiss him but simply walked past him into the hall.

He silently took her coat and walked her into the living room. The sunset was in its full glory, and she sat down looking only at it.

"How lovely."

He poured some more wine and silently handed her a glass.

She set it on the table and turned to look into his eyes.

"I'm so sorry, Anton, about your mother."

"Yes, losing her is a great loss for all of us."

"Especially you. I know how close you were, and Jacques told me about her discipleship, which is a real blessing. I also will miss her. Even in the short time I knew her, she was like a real mother to me." Her voice broke a little.

"She really loved you, too, and was so happy to be able to say goodbye."

"Yes." She bowed her head for a moment. "She will die tomorrow, so you must return soon."

"I think she was waiting to see you, so now she can go."

She looked around the room. "Do you mind if I see it?"

"No, just look around." Anton sat where he was as she walked throughout the house. So much of it was her design, her ideas. Even though Anton thought he had changed a lot, in the end, it still had much of her in it. At first it had bothered him, but now he was used to it.

When she returned her only comment was, "You've made it your dream. I hope you will be very happy here."

He wanted to say it had been her dream, too, but he only said thank you.

She picked up her wine, sat down in a chair across from him, and again looked into his face. "What I did to you was horrific. I need to apologize and ask your forgiveness."

Anton started to speak, but she held up her hand and said, "No, let me tell you everything. I needed to make you hate me; otherwise, you wouldn't have done the annulment. I had to do that to keep you from being in danger. I even made up lies about you to the company, explaining that I wanted out of the marriage because I found out you had been cheating on me for a long time. They were watching you for a while, and fortunately, you went out with Lea several times and even stayed late at her place one night."

"But—" he tried to interrupt.

"I know, I know it's just friendship, and I'm so glad it happened. I had a feeling they might be checking up on my story. That was why I couldn't be in touch with you, of course, as the top guys spied on everybody.

"But let me start from the beginning, when I left overnight.

"As you know, Edwin was supposed to replace me; and, unfortunately, when he had the operation and recovery, there wasn't time to train anyone else. It happened so quickly. When the company folded up the office, they asked me if I would go with them. They explained the fast move was because of some government restrictions that made it impossible to stay in Switzerland. They knew you were going to be teaching in Boston but said if I could stay until they could replace me, they would make it worthwhile for both of us. Naturally, they offered me a lot of money and a permanent executive job; and, since there was no undercover replacement, I had to accept. I couldn't say no, as it would have ruined the agency's operation. That's when I told them it wasn't a problem, they wouldn't have to find a replacement — I had found out you were cheating on me all along — and I was getting an annulment.

"We were in Italy and then moved to Alexandria, Egypt. They wanted me to help build the new company there as the main headquarters, which was quite an operation, and also to continue my traveling to their branches. By then they had started to confide in me that some of their work was illegal, and they wanted to know if that bothered me. I said that I had already had my suspicions, and it didn't trouble me; my main interest was in making money, and I wanted a lot of it. I asked them what they were doing that was illegal, but they wouldn't tell me, so I dropped the subject."

"Did you ever find out what it was they were doing illegally?"

"Buying arms from France, Russia, even the United States, and selling them to Al Qaeda and Isis and any other terrorist group that wanted them. When they employed me, they were still claiming to be making industrial machines for manufacturing. But then England found out the truth and told the Swiss authorities because it was the Swiss branch that was hiding the money and shipping the arms. When I found out the extent of the operation, I felt it was too dangerous and wanted out, but I got stuck."

"So how did you get out?"

"That was tricky. The agency's bust didn't happen in Switzerland because of an informant, so it was important to make the next raid work. In Egypt, the company had to hire a lot of new staff. I was part of the hiring process. I told my Swiss boss at fedpol this."

"But how were you getting information back to him?"

"I always carried a secret mic that was hooked up to an outside recorder locally, which was then relayed back home. That's how every place we went we were being tracked."

"But then why didn't the agency arrest everyone when you first were in Italy?"

"They needed to get clearance from the Italian authorities, and the criminals moved too fast for that to happen."

"There was plenty of time in Egypt?"

"There was time, but the government there has a lot of corruption, so we wanted to do the bust without having it involved. Besides, the operation was getting bigger, and we needed more information so that the bust would be a big one."

"But it was just you?"

"No, not just me. By then, America and England were in charge of the operation, so when they heard I was hiring, they sent some agents to apply for the jobs. The applicants knew I was fedpol's agent. When I interviewed them, they silently showed me their credentials so I would hire them."

"How many were there?"

"Six — one woman and five men."

"What nationality?"

"The woman was Italian, married to an Egyptian, and the rest were Egyptian, or claimed to be Egyptian. Two were actually from the States."

"How did you work together?"

"Since they were all Egyptian citizens, new employees, and in similar positions, it would be natural for them to become friends. With me, it was more difficult, since I held a higher position, and, in a couple of instances, I was their boss, so it wouldn't look the same if I suddenly became their friend. Also, I was a different nationality, which set me apart. But the Americans are smart. They chose a man to apply as my assistant in staff training. Sometimes we worked late, so it was natural for us to take a break and have dinner together or even go out to lunch together."

"You couldn't talk privately in your office?"

She laughed. "Are you kidding? In such an operation every office is bugged. Even the ladies' room is bugged! I checked, just for the fun of it."

"Did anyone think your relationship with your assistant was more than work related?"

"One of the directors did ask me if I was dating him. I said no, it was strictly business, and besides, he was married. He also asked me why I didn't find myself a boyfriend, and I said I was still feeling hurt about you and that it wasn't time yet."

She added, "They even tried to fix me up with an Egyptian businessman who was single, but I told them I wasn't interested."

"Why didn't you go out with him?"

"For a lot of reasons, one being that my apartment was bugged, but mainly I was being faithful to you."

"But we were no longer married."

"I know."

"Go on."

"The bust took place at the end of November. They had to work quickly as one of the agents was caught. He was checking out the warehouse and a guard saw him."

"Did he get away?"

"No, they caught him."

"So, they got the mic?"

"He managed to call in to disconnect him, and he swallowed the mike before they grabbed him."

"What happened to him?"

"That's why we did the bust immediately. They were torturing him to death."

"You know, I remember hearing about it in the news, but I didn't know that it was about your company, so I never connected it to you. The agency got everything, yes?"

"Yes, all the records, everything, and they are all awaiting trial."

"But November . . . why didn't you come back right away?"

"I was locked up, too. And believe me, Egyptian prisons are horrible!"

He was shocked, "But why you?"

"The agency had to make it look as if I were in on it. I was an executive, and we were all arrested. The company director immediately got us lawyers, and my lawyer proved to the court that I wasn't part of anything illegal, which was true. Before I left to come home, I spoke to the director and thanked him for his help. I told him I would be glad to testify on his behalf if he needed me. He thanked me and said that probably wouldn't be necessary, as there was so much evidence against him."

"Are they being tried in Egypt?"

"Oh, no. Fortunately, they hadn't completely disbanded the American headquarters, so they will go to the States. They don't have a chance of getting out of that free.

"The director asked me what my plans were. I said I missed my father, and I was going home to see him. I also said you must be back from the States, and I had never stopped loving you, so maybe there was still hope that we could work it out."

She paused and looked at him. "I meant that. Can we?"

Anton couldn't answer right away. Instead, he got up and opened another bottle of wine and filled their glasses.

Finally, he cleared his head enough to say, "Sam, you must understand that what you did hurt me deeply, so deeply that I fell out of love with you. You didn't trust me enough to realize that I still would have been safe; they wouldn't have come after me if they hadn't suspected you. Besides, you could have left after a couple of months, just as they suggested. Why didn't you do that?"

"I couldn't leave my mission like that. There was no one to replace me."

"But that wasn't true. They sent in the other agents. They still would have done the work."

"But I didn't know that when I told them I was leaving you."

"It doesn't matter anymore, Sam. This is about trust. How can I ever trust you again? Why couldn't you trust me enough to support you in the work? Why couldn't you trust me to help you? That's what I lost — my trust in you, and I can never be with someone whom I can't trust or who can't trust me."

"Please don't decide that so quickly. Give me a chance. I've never stopped loving you."

"This is not a quick decision. I thought about it for months. I thought about you when I built this house and how we did the plans together, and all the time I knew that you would never live here with me because your work, your life, would always come before us. I need someone who wouldn't take risks or leave whenever a job came up, who would put a family and me first. I need a wife, and you could never be that with me or anyone."

"That's not true! I quit the agency. If I work, it will be locally. Anton, I love you. I want to be your wife. Please forgive me."

"I can't, and I don't love you anymore." Those words shot from his mouth in a vomit of painful emotions.

She got from her chair and came toward him. "I don't believe you. We had so much. I don't believe you." And she tried to put her arms around him.

He gently pushed her away. "I'm sorry. I need to go to my mother."

And he went to the closet and got her coat out.

She put it on and looked at him one more time. "I'll be waiting for you when you change your mind."

She turned to go, and Anton said, "When I thought about you this last year, I realized that I didn't know you, but most of all that you didn't know me."

Samantha stopped and looked back at him, pausing to collect her thoughts. "I felt you were more open hearted. I believed in our relationship, but now I realize that you never did. You believe in what is right for you. You say you didn't know me and I didn't know you. You are wrong. I knew your potential, and that is what I felt and loved you for. But now I see you are right: I only saw that. I didn't see this part of you that is self-centered and controlling."

She quickly left before he could respond.

When she drove her car down the driveway, he stood at the window and watched her go.

Mother died the next day. She was too weak to talk, and as they one by one kissed her goodbye, she looked at each one of them with so much love in her eyes that it was a gift never to be forgotten. Anton was the youngest and the last, and he held her hand a little longer. She tried to raise her hand to his face. It fell short with her weakness, but the attempted gesture made him realize his spiritual connection to her, that, indeed, he was special, not because he was the child most like her—but because he was part of her spiritual family. Anton was her son and also her spiritual brother, and that connection was extraordinary.

She then closed her eyes and died peacefully. Anton knew that Jacques was with her, and she was free, finally free.

What more could Anton say about his mother? There were no words to express a relationship with someone who meant so much to him. You could be with a person for many years, or maybe only a short time, but the effect is the same. It's about being with someone who can truly see and hear you. Whether it is for a minute or for a lifetime, to have someone who understands you—even more than you understand yourself—is the quality of love that is rare.

His mother knew him, and he knew her; and in that knowing, they were more than mother and son, more than friends. They had gone past that into a place beyond needs, into a place of acceptance. When Anton finally lost her, he understood how much she had simply accepted and believed in him; and that belief had given him a sense of purpose and the ability to do what he needed to do. He was grateful to her for giving him this kind of love.

They had her cremated and placed the ashes in an urn on a shelf in the basement to wait for spring, when they would scatter them on the mountain.

The memorial service was in Zürich for the many friends and family members. It was held at St. Anton's—the Catholic church the family had attended for years—where Anton had been christened with the saint's name. Jacques and Samantha came and sat quietly in the back. It was a snowy day with the sun breaking through every so often, the kind of day his mother had loved.

CHAPTER 41

Anton stayed in Zürich after his mother's service. The city was bleak and cold. There were clouds every day blocking any sunlight, and on occasion there was snow. He never minded the snow on the mountains, but in the city, it quickly turned to dirty slush that left muddy mush on boots and sometimes trousers.

His gloomy mood was enhanced when he walked by the cold, gray buildings of the university. They looked formidable and uninviting, waiting to swath enthusiasm from students as they entered. Even in the spring and summer, when there were blooming trees and flowers in the gardens, they still felt forbidding. When Anton arrived early to his classroom, he had to take a few minutes to shake off his negativity and reconnect with his Higher Self in order to be in a positive place to teach.

In the evenings, he went to beer halls to drink and listen to music with the hope of picking up a tourist for a quick, one-night stand. He wanted sex with no attachments or expectations, just momentary release. He certainly wasn't ready for anything more stable.

Anton sometimes still meditated and studied the teaching, but Zürich was full of activities that kept him distracted. He missed the New York class and the one here, but he found out from one of his spiritual brothers that Samantha was going on a regular basis and that Jacques had gone away again. If Jacques had been there, Anton would have attended anyway. His fellow students understood why he wasn't attending, but they hoped that Anton could resolve his feelings and at least remain friends with Samantha, which would allow him to return. Anton didn't know if that would ever happen. He couldn't see just being friends with her, since the friendship, which had formed a solid base in their marriage, had been broken. It would take time.

He saw Lea the most. She even offered to have a separate class with him, but Anton declined, feeling it was unfair, as she often had to see clients in the evening. He wanted their time together to be just fun and relaxing. His old attraction to her came up occasionally, but he felt it better not to act on it. They had such a good friendship he didn't in any way want to spoil it.

One morning, he got up early and started to meditate before going to school. He was finding it difficult to focus, and then the phone rang, interrupting the effort. It was very early, so he picked up the receiver in apprehension. It was Sam.

"Anton, sorry if I woke you, but something has happened. I've been staying at Jacques' house until I find another job and an apartment. Jacques is in America visiting a student and needs me to go there for at least a week. This student needs some business training, which he felt I could do."

"Yes?" Still wondering why she was calling him.

"Lina is on vacation this week. As you know, she usually takes care of the place when he is away. Jacques likes to have someone here now, not only to water his many plants but because he has accumulated some rare oriental pieces, and there have been robberies in the area. Jacques asked me to call you to see if you could house sit for him."

Anton was thinking Why me? when she added, "I think he particularly asked for you because you are single, whereas most of his other students here are married, and you know the ins and outs of the place because you've stayed here a few times. Besides, you still have a set of keys, don't you?"

That made sense to him. The only other possibility would be Lea, but Anton knew she had a heavy evening schedule. "Yes, I kept the keys. I'll be glad to house sit. When do you want me to come?"

"I was able to book a flight tomorrow afternoon. If that's not okay, I can change it."

"No, that's fine. My plans this week are pretty loose, so I could change them to be there." Then he added, "But why didn't Jacques call me directly?"

"He would have, but he said he could hear thunder in the distance and didn't want to be on the phone again when a storm rolled in."

"Yes, I know; Mom always used to tell me that when I was young. The phone wires can transmit electricity from lightning."

They talked a little longer and made the final arrangements.

After school, late in the afternoon, Anton arrived at Jacques' house. It was very quiet, but the stillness felt full of energy. He felt that Jacques was there, so he closed his eyes and meditated, hoping to see him, but all he saw were colors changing from one into another. Yet he could swear Jacques was there. And his presence made Anton feel good, as he missed him.

Later, he wandered through the house to make certain everything was locked before retiring to the guest room. He made the mistake of going into Samantha's room. She had some clothes thrown over a chair, and her makeup was laid out in the bathroom. It brought back memories of when they had lived together, and he felt a cloak of sadness come over him — not just for what they'd had and lost but what their future might have been.

Tired, Anton fell into bed and dreamed restless dreams. Suddenly, he woke up to the sound of a noise downstairs. Looking around, he saw a cane leaning against the wall and grabbed it. Again, he heard a sound; it seemed to be coming from the living room. Anton quietly walked down the stairs and peeked through the open door. Someone was standing next to the window, and the moonlight was shining on his head. Anton flipped the light switch on — and no one was there. The figure was gone. He felt chills run down his body. He flipped the switch off again and the figure returned.

"Who are you?" Anton asked.

"I am your Mahatma."

Anton felt scared and excited at the same time. He knew about the Mahatmas, the high adepts who took care of the evolution of humankind and the planet, and he knew he had a Mahatma who guided him, but he didn't know who he was.

"If you really are my Mahatma, I need to see light," Anton bravely stated, voicing a lesson Jacques had taught him. Jacques had said that if you see anyone in the subtle world, always ask to see light; otherwise, you could be speaking to an impostor from the lower realms.

Like lightning, a brilliant light struck in front of him, and he saw that the man was young with blond hair and blue eyes. Then he became a dark figure again.

Anton bowed his head and started to kneel.

"No, please remain standing. I have come to warn you to be careful. You are a very spiritual man who needs guidance. Your passions can lead you elsewhere and hold you back from your destiny. Be vigilant and remember to focus on your goal of achieving God Consciousness. Your heart is full. Let it open to others. You are meant to become a spiritual teacher. Become Zarathustra."

He suddenly disappeared! Anton felt the loss immediately, because, when his Mahatma spoke, he experienced waves of love surround and encompass him.

Anton sat on the couch and closed his eyes. The Mahatma said to become Zarathustra! How could he? Even though Jacques had always said the same thing, he had always thought of his role as being a student of Zarathustra learning some of the lessons and never as being the teacher himself. Yet his Mahatma had just told him to be Zarathustra, which is the name of a teacher. He had only had one initiation, so Anton knew that becoming the teacher was impossible at this time. A person needed four initiations to reach that level, and to achieve the next three was very difficult and could take many years. With his lifestyle and all the work he needed to do in the world, he had never considered having more initiations or becoming a teacher.

Anton felt overwhelmed by what his Mahatma had told him — overwhelmed and confused. A part of him started to rebel, saying, "No! I don't want to be a teacher. I want a normal life, a wife and family, not a flock of students. I could never do that."

Then another part said, "But your Mahatma just told you it was your destiny. He didn't say when. You still have a lot of work to do to achieve that destiny, and when you reach those higher levels it won't be a problem. You don't have to become a teacher until you are much older, after your children have grown up. You can have it all."

Anton breathed a sigh. "Yes, that's true."

Then the other part said, "Jacques became a teacher when he was a little older than you, and he had Samantha later. Why do you think you will have to wait that long? If they need you to teach, you will have to do so, according to what they want. It's never your choice."

"Of course, it's always my choice. If I don't do the work, I won't receive the initiations, and therefore I can't teach."

"You're teaching some of it in your university classes right now," the voice responded.

"That's just rudimentary. I don't teach the esoteric material, and besides, I'm not connected to the students in the way a teacher is to a disciple. I have no personal responsibility with my college students."

The voice answered, "True, but that will change. Some of those students will want to learn more, and they will end up as your spiritual students. That's the Mahatma's plan, and it is meant to happen much sooner than you know about."

Anton suddenly felt overpoweringly depressed. It was as if a bat had opened its wings and closed them over his whole body. He knew this feeling came from his lower nature, but he couldn't stop it.

CHAPTER 42

Samantha called Anton at school and left a message on his office machine. She was home and hoped they could have dinner that night in appreciation for his having house sat for her.

He questioned it: Why didn't she let me know ahead of time when she was returning? he thought. But of course, had I known, I would have moved my stuff out of the house this morning. It's sneaky of her to do this. Since I must collect my things, I may as well have dinner, but then, I could say no, move my stuff out, and that would be the end of it.

Anton mulled this over during the next classes and then finally called Sam late in the afternoon to say yes to dinner. It might be a mistake, but he still had the option of leaving at any time if it felt too awkward. They were adults, so it was important to be amicable.

Anton let himself in with the key and found her in the kitchen fixing entrées. He could see they were all the ones she knew he liked. She was dressed in a plain, black dress and pearls, simple and sophisticated, always elegant, with her blond hair pulled back in a French chignon.

"Hi, Anton." She made a move to kiss him on the cheek, but he stepped back.

"Hi Sam. While you're doing that, I'll get my things together."

"Can't it wait until after dinner?" Her voice sounded a little uptight.

"No. I'd rather do it now before having a glass of wine." A poor excuse, but he couldn't think of any other.

On his way to his bedroom, Anton went into the living room to collect a couple of books he had left there. He noticed she had made a fire and placed wine glasses on the coffee table in front of the couch. This meant sitting next to her, so he moved one of the glasses to an end table next to a chair opposite the couch. Maybe she would get the message when she saw it. An inner voice said, I'm out of here the first time she makes a move toward me.

It was sinister and short. If it was his lower nature, fine, he was listening to it.

He quickly packed up his things, which somehow had accumulated. Every time he had gone home, he had picked up a few more things to bring back. His car was next to the entrance, so he ran out and threw everything in the trunk. It was very cold, and he hadn't bothered to put his coat on.

Samantha found him standing in front of the fire warming up when she came in with a tray of hors d'oeuvres. She saw the glass right away and simply said, "I put

211

those together because I thought it would be easier to pour the wine that way, but I guess you got nervous, so let's call a truce. This is just a thank-you dinner, no more than that."

She placed the tray on a side table where there were plates and a bottle of red wine breathing.

Anton felt relieved. "Good, I'm glad you clarified that."

She turned to look at him with eyes that were direct and distant, but they softened when she spoke. "Anton, this is a difficult time for us both. Let's at least keep our relationship on cordial terms for the teaching's sake. I know you haven't been attending class because of me, and I don't want that to happen anymore. It's not fair to you or to me. Surely, we can come to some kind of understanding that will change that."

"Is this what the dinner is about?"

"Partially, and Jacques asked me to talk to you about something more serious."

"More serious than coming to class?"

"Yes, but let's keep that for dinner." Pouring some wine, she handed Anton a glass and then went to fill small plates with cheese and crackers.

They sat and ate, and drank the wine, and made light conversation. She asked him how the book was selling, and he told her that it was attracting a lot of attention, with some good and some bad reviews from the critics. Anton had done some book signings and had even been interviewed on the local TV station.

"In fact, I heard from my publisher just today that bookstores in England, America, and Germany are requesting copies. So yes, it's doing much better than I thought it would."

"Jacques wanted me to tell you it was reviewed last week in the *New York Times*. Let me get the review. He saved it for you." She went over to another table and picked up a newspaper.

"That's wonderful! I guess my publisher hadn't heard about that yet."

She handed Anton the article with the heading, "Zarathustra Revisited." He glanced at it briefly and saw that it was indeed a very good review, and his Harvard credentials were played up. Having taught there must have been important, he thought.

Samantha in the meantime retreated to the kitchen to check on dinner.

She returned to open the doors to the dining room rather than the porch where they normally had casual dining. This was to be a more formal dinner, Anton surmised; and, indeed, it was. The table was laid with the best china and silver. The flames of the lit candles made reflecting, glittering lights on the crystal glasses. It was a long table, but, rather than have them sit at opposite ends, she had put the placemats across from each other in the middle.

"What's the occasion?" he asked, knowing there had to be something happening for her to do all this.

She didn't answer him at first, busy placing covered dishes from the cart onto the table. "It is a special occasion. Sit down."

They sat down and filled their plates with an array of her finest cuisine. For a while they ate in silence; then she said, "Jacques has asked me to tell you this news. It concerns you and me, and he felt it would be better for you to hear it from me."

This surprised Anton, but he said nothing.

"When we were married, he saw that there would be difficulties between us, mainly paying off some old karma. He also saw that it would eventually be worked out and we would someday be friends."

She didn't say lovers, which was good. "If that was the case, why did we have to get married?"

"I guess that was the only way we could pay it off. Just having an affair wouldn't have done it. The main thing was that someday we had to be partners in the teaching, whether or not we were married. Marriage wasn't necessarily our main mission together."

"Mission? What mission?" A feeling of annoyance came up in him.

"Our mission is to carry on this teaching after Jacques dies. We are his successors, the future teachers to carry on the work."

Anton was stunned. Certainly, he could see that as Samantha's mission, but not his. Then he remembered what his Mahatma had said to him, just this week.

She waited for him to answer. When he didn't, she said, "Jacques knows about your Mahatma's visit, and he also knows some of your feelings about it."

"I'm sure he does, but he had no right to tell you about it."

"His Mahatma — who is the same as yours and mine — told Jacques to tell me, since my karma is so intertwined with yours. If you refuse this mission, it will affect me directly. That's why I needed to be told. I've already expressed concern about your refusing to go to class, and you even refused Lea's offer to meet with her. We have been worried about you."

"With all the wonderful, devoted students Jacques has, why choose me? Why me?"

Sam shook her head. "Don't you understand? You are more advanced than any of them. You have been a teacher many times, and you and I have been teachers together. We both come from strong spiritual pasts in which we vowed always to help each other."

When she said those words, her eyes were focused energy that penetrated him, making him feel a strong pull toward her from his heart. Her words felt true, very true.

"But that's the past, and I don't believe in living in the past," he said. "Even the teaching says to let go of the past."

"Yes, it says not to dwell in the past, but it also says to know it; and knowing it means to understand who you are and what your achievements have been that can be reawakened. If you have been a teacher in the past, you have students waiting for you. In terms of karma, you need to honor that commitment."

"But I didn't know about that commitment."

"But now you do. Being a teacher is extremely difficult; you're not even close to it, and the negative ones are already attacking you. Believe me, they only notice those who can be warriors against them. The fact that they have noticed you is a strong indicator of who you are."

"And if I choose not to do this mission?"

Sam put down her fork, and unhappiness filled her face, her color fading into the candlelight.

"I will believe it's my fault completely. I will feel that I, and only I, have failed Jacques as well as this teaching. I do not think I can do it alone. Without you, the teaching will not continue. I hate saying those words, so I need to add that I want you to do what your heart dictates. If you decide to take on this mission, choose it for yourself, never for me, or even for Jacques. It has to be for you, yourself; otherwise, don't do it."

Anton frowned. "First of all, it's not your fault. Secondly, I can't believe you would ever give up. You may think you would, but I know you well enough to know that it would be impossible for you to not follow your destiny. This teaching has been your life, and that will not change. It seems to me your words are coming from those negative forces that obviously are trying to influence your thinking."

Sam bowed her head. "You're right, of course, and when I think about having said I couldn't do it alone, I can't believe I said it. I was laying a guilt trip on you, so I apologize. But you see, Anton, this is why we need each other. You are my check point, and I am yours."

"No, Jacques is my checkpoint, and he will still be after he's gone. You know that. But it's true we really used to help each other."

"And I want that again." Her eyes looked at him imploringly.

"Right now, I don't know what I want. If I choose to do this mission, I would want us to be friends and help each other." Anton said those words reluctantly, but they were true, and he needed to say them.

She was quiet; only her hand moved holding her fork, playing with the food. Then she said, "I want to say something to you that will be helpful, but I can't. I want to try to persuade you to come to class, to be with all of us, but I can't. I have never gone through what you have gone through. Maybe I was a little rebellious as a teenager, but not for long. This teaching has been my life, while you have been in it for only a few years, and those years have been difficult ones, partly due to me."

Anton interjected, "Don't blame yourself. When I was with you, the teaching took on more importance, not because of my commitment but because of you. I realize tonight that, if I take on this mission, I need to be totally committed to this teaching, to accept it fully in every part of me. If I can't do that, I shouldn't be in it, and I certainly could never be a teacher. If the negative forces can pull me away, then I shouldn't be in it. Don't you see that?"

"Yes, that's true. They whisper through your weaknesses, but the weaknesses are yours to begin with, and only you can change them. Even the teacher can't help. It's always the student's challenge. That's why many don't make it."

She paused and again looked at him, but this time with astute eyes. "But don't you understand how not following your dharma would affect your spirit?"

"Maybe being a teacher *isn't* my dharma; maybe I'm meant to have a reprieve, to bring in the book, be in the teaching, and live a regular life. If I've been a teacher many times, maybe I need a break. In fact, to me, the thought of being a spiritual teacher is—I don't want to say repulsive—but that's a close word for it. Maybe that will change, but right now I can't imagine it."

His tone moderated. "I know you want to help, so excuse me if I sounded harsh just now, but help is the last thing I need."

Anton stood up from the table. "Thank you for dinner. I need to go now but thank you for everything. Tell Jacques that I will be in touch when I have come to a decision. It may take some time. I don't know how long. It could be a long time."

"I will tell him. He has a lot of patience, something I need to learn." She tried to smile as she started to stand up.

"No, finish your coffee. I'll let myself out. Goodbye." And he turned and left without looking back.

CHAPTER 43

Lea called Anton shortly after his dinner with Sam and wanted to see him. He was suspicious that Sam had talked to her about him, so he challenged her right away about whether that was the reason for her call. She said no, it wasn't. They hadn't seen each other for a while, and she simply was missing him. Anton accepted this even though he still had a doubt about it. It was his lower nature kicking up again, he knew; but he wasn't in a place where he wanted to kick it out.

They met for dinner at a restaurant near his condo. It was a small family place with lots of privacy. The first thing Lea said to him was, "Anton, I need to talk to you about Samantha."

"I thought you said you hadn't talked to her about me," Anton interjected.

"I haven't, not about you. But I did talk to her, and what she told me really disturbed me."

He looked at Lea questioningly.

"She is going to find her mother and go to see her."

"What! How can she do that? It would hurt Jacques *and* her. Why would she want to do such a thing?"

"She needs to find out why her mother turned negative. She feels it's important for her spiritually to confront her. Did you know her mother has been contacting her in the subtle world? I think Samantha feels that if she just sees her she can stop her from doing that."

Anton was stunned. "She mentioned it once and then blew it off. But Lea, her mother is very powerful. Sam will not be able to handle her. And I don't know if you know this, but she is working on her fourth initiation, which attracts lots of attacks from negative forces. It's most definitely the wrong time for her to do something like this."

"I know. That's why I'm so worried about her. That initiation, which I do know about, is full of challenges. Very few make it. I told her that she needed to look at this urge to see her mother as coming from her lower nature and not give in to it. I begged her to talk to Jacques, but she refused. She said he would insist she not do it, and then she would have to comply. She didn't want to do that."

"Why did she tell you? Wasn't she afraid you would tell him?"

"She made me promise not to before she informed me about her plans, but she forgot to make me do that concerning you. She only mentioned casually, later, not to tell you; but I never agreed, and she didn't notice. Her concern was mainly that

216

Jacques shouldn't find out."

"Oh, my God! She can't do this. We'll lose her." Only later did Anton realize the importance of his words.

"I know. It's too risky, and she's been acting a little strange lately."

"I think that's because of me." And he told Lea what had transpired between them.

Lea didn't respond at first, and then she said, "I wonder whether her decision to see her mother came after your talk."

"Why would that have prompted it?"

"I don't know. It's just a feeling. Maybe she's worried that you will turn negative, and she wants to find out more about what happened to her mother in order to help you."

"I'm not going to do that. Why would she think it? If that's the reason, it really bothers me."

"I feel you need to talk to her, Anton. She listens to you."

"Not really. If she had listened to me at all, we would still be married."

"Well, maybe she hasn't listened in her personal life, but spiritually she has always admired you."

"She's the advanced one, not I."

"But you have good insight and, from what you just told me, she believes you to be an advanced soul, so she does listen to you in these matters."

"That's true, she feels we need each other spiritually; but, when Sam makes up her mind, it's difficult to change it."

"Then why not convince her you need to go with her?"

That made him shudder. "But Lea, I'm going through my own stuff; contacting her mother and her mother's husband will make me a target, and I don't know if I can withstand them at this time."

"You're much stronger than you know. You're like Jacques. I feel you won't be influenced, but I don't know about Samantha. She is her mother's daughter, and they were very close when she was young."

"Let me meditate on it. I'll let you know."

"Fair enough."

The next morning was Saturday, so Anton had time for a long meditation. He concentrated on whether to go with Sam to find her mother since he was certain he wouldn't be able to persuade her otherwise. Several times he felt his heart say yes, but he wasn't certain whether it was his Higher Self or his lower nature that was answering. He did feel that Sam was in jeopardy, and he decided to talk to her to try to convince her not to go. He called her that afternoon, and when he invited her to dinner at his place she readily accepted.

The evening started off slowly and awkwardly. Anton mainly talked to her about his house and the furnishings he had bought for it. When they were having coffee in the living room, he finally brought up the subject.

"You must be wondering why I asked you to dinner, particularly after our last talk."

"Yes, I was just about to ask you that question."

"I saw Lea last night, and she told me you were planning to find your mother."

She looked surprised. "I am planning to do that, but it really isn't any of her or your business."

"It certainly is our business. We both feel you can be vulnerable when it comes to your mother. She is a high witch, an adept in the negative arts. How can you imagine you will be able to oppose her?"

"I'm not planning to oppose her. I just want to find out why she did what she did."

"Why do you need to do that? You already know she left your father for another man, a man who persuaded her to join the negative forces."

"I need to hear it from her, not from hearsay."

"And what about Jacques? Do you think he would approve?"

"You know he wouldn't, so why ask that?"

"Lea said maybe you were doing this for my sake."

Sam looked startled. "I never said that."

"Is it true?"

"There are a couple of reasons. I need to tell her to stop bothering me in dreams. You remember I told you she was appearing to me once in a while in dreams. Well, it's been happening a lot more often lately. She's even breaking into my meditations."

"Why not tell Jacques to stop her?"

"He can stop her when I call on him, but he can't do it permanently. There's too much karma intertwined. I have to do it."

"If you think he can't do it, how can you? What is the second reason?"

"Lea's right. I am worried about you and want to see how the negative forces operate."

"You think I could become part of that?"

"My mother did, and she was extremely spiritual, yet she succumbed. It can happen."

"Thanks for the trust in me."

"Anton, you know I love you. I have never said otherwise. When Mother was going through her doubts, Jacques tried to help her, but she wouldn't listen. You won't listen to me, either; so, I feel that if I know more about why my mother turned negative, then maybe I can do something to help you if you start to become influenced."

He felt anger but tried to repress it. "First of all, I am not your mother. I spiritually know the difference between working for the positive forces or the negative forces. I assure you I have no intention of leaving this teaching. My doubts are about being a teacher. And maybe I will take a break. I don't know. If I do, I won't go elsewhere."

"I'm glad to hear that, but it sounds as if you don't feel I can handle it. What do you think will happen to me?"

"Just what you fear will happen to me. Your mother could very much influence you to stay with her."

"So, you don't trust me either."

"It's not about trust. From what everyone has said, the fourth initiation is extremely difficult because the negative forces try to stop a person from getting it. Don't you think your mother knows that? Why do you think you are seeing so much of her now?"

"Of course, she does. I know she will try to persuade me to leave Jacques. I want to find out the method she will use. I'm not stupid, and I promise you I will be careful."

Anton could see there was no changing her mind.

"All right, if you are meeting her, I am coming along." He thought, Why did I say that?

She looked at him with astonishment. "Don't be crazy! Of course, you're not going with me."

"Yes, I am. She's going to use me as bait, and I want to be there when she tries it."

"How do you know that?"

"Think about it. Where are you the most vulnerable? She's going to try to convince you that I have already gone over to their side, or that, if you want me back, only they can make that happen."

"I hadn't thought about that, but it does make sense."

"You said that we would help each other spiritually. If that is true, you most certainly need me now to go with you and help you. I insist. It can't be done alone; and, I agree, she needs to know definitely that she can't have you back and that she can't influence me."

"Are you sure? She is very powerful."

"Yes, but her power is not heart power. You have that, and that's why she wants you."

"As do you," Sam commented. "But she might refuse to see you."

"Then you tell her that's your condition. If she wants to talk to you, it has to be with me there; otherwise, you won't come."

"She's in the States, and you're working."

"I'm off in a couple of weeks for spring break." Anton walked into the office and came back with the exact dates and gave them to her.

"Okay, I agree; but we need to plan it, plan how to approach her."

"Let's both meditate on it and come up with some ideas. I'm free next weekend."

They arranged to meet then, and she got up to leave.

At the door she looked at him and said, "Thank you. I'm glad you're coming with me. I was a bit nervous about doing this, to be frank with you."

"That's understandable." And he smiled at her for the first time in a long time.

After Sam left, Anton thought about what she had said, that he also had heart power. Was that true? There were times when he remembered to use his heart, but usually that was when he was teaching a small group of students. And, yes, always with Lea, he tried to be in his heart, but she brought out the best in him. But when he became moody, he knew he was very disconnected, and it was difficult to try then to use his heart to help himself. Meeting Sam's mother and her husband was going to be a big challenge for him. He didn't want to do it, but he felt his heart pushing him into helping her.

Samantha called Anton Tuesday evening to tell him she had contacted her mother. He asked her how she did it; she said her mother appeared to her in a meditation, and she asked her for her phone number. She gave it to her, and Sam called her.

"What did she say?"

"You were right. At first, she seemed upset when I told her I was bringing you with me. She asked me why I couldn't see her alone. I didn't answer but said I preferred having you with me. Then, she tried to dissuade me by implying that I was weak in wanting you or any man to be there. Finally, she did quite a number on me, subtly implying that I may not be brave or strong enough to see her, pushing my ego until I wanted to show her she was wrong. She's so good at what she does that I nearly decided to go it alone, but I stopped myself and realized what she was doing. Finally, she agreed when I gave her an ultimatum: you and I, or nothing. But, I tell you, Anton, she's so smooth, talking with her made me feel enfolded in a sheet of soft, satin silk. We are going to have to take every precaution."

"When's our date with her?"

"Two weeks from today. She insisted that we stay with her, but I said no, we would book our own reservations in a hotel."

"That's good. I can imagine the vibes in her house."

"Oh, I'm certain she cleans them out regularly." There was a pause. "She said very little, but after I hung up, I started thinking about the wonderful times we had together. Isn't that amazing?"

"No, I'm afraid not. They're very good at doing that." And he thought about Orama and how Orama had worked him.

"Anyway, I want to thank you again for insisting you come. I think I can handle her, but it is good to have your help."

She added that she would make the hotel arrangements, confirming that it would be two singles. Anton said that would be fine and he would see her on Saturday.

That week he spent a lot of time thinking about the situation. He called Sam to ask for information about the negative forces. She knew a lot more than he did about how they operated, and she went into detail about some of the ways in which they attack people. Mainly, they would try to work on their individual frailties and the weaknesses in their relationship.

When he heard that, Anton realized he needed to know exactly what those weaknesses were. He wrote down as many of them as he could identify. Then he made a plan that would help him recognize how to counterattack if need be. He left the weaknesses of their relationship last and then decided they needed to do that together.

Saturday was a long day. Anton went to Samantha's house early in the morning, and they sat on the sun porch and went over their lists. Knowing each other enabled them to add to the other's lists those weaknesses that each was unconscious of. Those were the ones needing more work, as they were the most hidden. The effort proved tiring, mainly for the mind. After lunch, they went over their individual ways to counterattack. Sam's were brilliant, and she helped Anton make his more dynamic.

"For example," Sam said, "She might express concern because I had to leave my job and consulting work, which she knows I love, and then offer to give me contacts that would help me find an even better job in Washington."

"How will you answer that?"

"I will tell her I am writing a book; that is far more exciting and rewarding." Sam thought for a minute. "You know, it would be great to write an espionage mystery. I certainly have enough background material to do it."

"How do you know she will even express concern about your job?"

"Because I've been upset about not working, and she'll pick up on that."

"Won't she pick up that the mystery writing isn't true?"

"Maybe, but so what? It's a stopper, and besides, I'll write a couple of pages before we leave and make it true."

The main weakness in Anton was his faulty relationships with women. He would have a difficult time knowing how to act if Sam's mother started on that, particularly regarding his relationship with Sam. Anton told Samantha about this concern, and they thought about it together.

"Well, an unsuccessful relationship will always touch on feelings of failure. I have that one, too," Sam said. "So, she will work on our feelings of failure and make them stronger, hoping that it could cause you to leave early, or for us to have a disagreement in the hotel that would also cause you to back down. This is the area in which we must be the strongest, because it's our most vulnerable one right now."

"But how can we counteract it? It's true."

"By not getting emotional about it. The emotions pull us into our lower natures. The best approach is to be very unidentified with it. In fact, admit the marriage failed, but we are still close friends, and that is true for now. Most importantly, we must avoid any details of why the marriage had failed."

"That's good. Our strength is in our friendship." And Anton thought about how earlier he had felt he never wanted to be her friend again. But now those words no longer rang true to him.

She looked at him. "Remember this: they will try to break us down and make us feel that we aren't friends, that we don't have a relationship. Don't let them separate us. I assure you, it will be their main goal. Once we are separated, they can attack us individually."

"And that's when she will become the loving mother again and appeal to your inner child."

"That's true. I need to work with my inner child before we go. I will try to leave her at home, but that part in me may be strong when I see her. I did love my mother a lot, and her leaving left a big hole in me that Jacques couldn't fill. She brought magic to my life, whereas my father was the stable, strong one on whom I could depend. Her strength was there but very different. She gave me many things. It's difficult to explain. She was a beacon that brought fun and excitement into my life. My father was the anchor that kept me secure."

"She will try to make you feel that loss again."

"Yes, I know. When she left, I felt very vulnerable. After she was gone, Jacques had me work with a therapist, who helped me get through my sadness."

"Why don't you ask your Higher Self to take care of your inner child? Is your Higher Self a woman?"

"Sometimes. That's a good idea. I will keep asking my Higher Self to take care of her. Hopefully, I will remember and catch myself in time. If you see me in that part of myself and getting emotional, do something to pull me away from it. Let's see, what can you do?"

"I can say your nickname, 'Sam,' in some context; otherwise, I will always call you 'Samantha.' 'Sam' will be directed to your inner child. Would that work?"

"No, Mother always called me 'Sam,' never 'Samantha.' Can you reverse it? Call me 'Samantha' when you see my inner child is being affected; otherwise, call me Sam."

"No, that won't work. I usually call you 'Sam,' so I'm certain to slip. Let's think of something else."

"Try to always be close to me; then you can just put your hand on my arm with a little pat. That should do it, as you never have done that with me."

"Okay, that's good; and if for some reason I'm not next to you, I will pat my arm when you look at me."

"But what happens when she asks to talk to me alone? I'm sure she'll manage that or manage to get her husband to take you somewhere, so she can be alone with me."

"True. We will do our best not to let that happen, even if it appears obvious; but it could happen, so we must be prepared."

"When it happens, I will link with my Higher Self even more strongly."

"And you must call on Jacques and your Mahatma to be with you. That's when you really need to do that. Both of us need to have them there from the very beginning."

"But I don't want Jacques to know."

"The minute you meet your mother, he will know."

"You're right, but they won't let him in."

"Maybe they are strong enough to stop him, but they can't stop both our Mahatma and him. We must call on them before we go and ask them to be with us all the time."

"I don't know, Anton. Let's think about this and meditate on it."

Later in the afternoon, they meditated again. They asked their Higher Selves for direction about when to call on Jacques and their Mahatma for help. Both heard: "Do so when you feel their negative energy penetrating your aura."

"What will that feel like?" Anton asked.

"Like tiny pin picks. Before you go, put armor around your bodies to protect yourselves."

Samantha was also told to cover her heart with several layers of metal, for it was mainly the heart that had to be protected. She should do so in the morning before meeting with them and not stay more than three hours. One visit was enough, no more.

"One visit doesn't seem enough, but I got that clearly."

"I would think three hours would be enough for you to accomplish what you wanted to do. More than that may give her a stronger hold on you."

"I guess you're right, but I would like to be flexible with this."

"You can't afford to be flexible. That's letting your armor down. These are high negative adepts. Neither one of us is a match for them. Listen to your guides; if your Higher Self tells you no more than three hours, it knows how long you can withstand their energy."

"Okay, you're right. I can feel my inner child wants to stay longer. I am going to let you handle the time. You will get us out of there and, if I hold back, you insist."

"You need to promise me one thing."

"What is it?"

"That you will not argue with me about anything I decide."

"I can't promise that. You may come under their influence, and I will need to protect myself. That's true for you, also. If I give in, you will need to leave and call our Mahatma for help."

"You're right, but this is very tricky, Sam. They can cast a spell on us that keeps both of us prisoners there, and we wouldn't be able to call for help."

"Let's ask what to do if that happens."

They meditated again. Anton got nothing, but Samantha saw a scene. She and Anton were sitting across from her mother and stepfather, and their negative energy had penetrated both armors, making them look helpless. But Samantha did see Anton and herself calling for help and knew that they would never lose that ability, which was a real relief.

"I hope that scene isn't a real one," she said.

"Me too. Before that happens, we need to be out of there."

"I know. I'm beginning to feel that this may be stupid. Jacques always said it would be extremely dangerous ever to see her again, that she had grown very powerful."

"Well, we can always cancel. Can you forget about it then?"

"The problem is, she keeps invading me. Even when I tell her to leave, she keeps coming back. The last time, she promised me she would stop if I came to see her."

"Have you ever told Jacques this?"

"No; any time he hears about her or sees her, he is deeply affected. He would go after her and then be completely devastated."

"That's not good, and it could affect his health, which also hasn't been good. You're right in not telling him. How about your Mahatma?"

"Oh, I always call on him. That's when she leaves, but then she comes back for another round. No, I need to face her and be strong enough, so she will know she can't control me. Until then, she will keep trying."

Anton's body felt an icy wave of apprehension. He wanted to say that he knew she would never give in but couldn't express it. Instead, he said, "It will be a difficult battle for you. Just remember I'm by your side. You don't have to do it alone."

"I know, but I think you will have your hands full with her husband. Don't forget he conquered her and is really up there in the negative forces' ranks. You'll be his target."

"How do you know that you won't be?" Suddenly, Anton thought his intuition kicked in.

"I hadn't even considered that! It would be a whole different game, but, you know, that could be. He seduced her, so why not try me? And your weakness is certain types of women, and I assure you she's far more seductive and powerful than Orama."

Anton's heart felt constrained, as if a great cold weight had encased it and stopped its warmth. For the first time, he felt afraid. If she was more powerful than Orama, he didn't have a chance.

Samantha must have read his look. "Anton, you're much stronger now. You weren't even a disciple when you knew Orama, and you didn't trust Jacques then, so don't feel frightened. You have a beautiful heart, and that strength will get you through. The main thing is to be prepared."

It was already dinnertime, and they were both exhausted.

"Let's work on this new list tomorrow," Sam suggested. "I'll make some dinner, and if you want to stay over, please feel you can."

"No, I have some things I need to do in the morning, but I can come after lunch. We can always finish it up in one evening if we have to." Their flight was next Saturday, so there weren't any more free days.

Anton added, "You're tired; let's go out to dinner locally."

They ate mainly in silence, both in their thoughts. Anton thought that the reality of their plans was beginning to set in. Worry started to envelop them.

Finally, he said, "Let's not become negative. That will be their first victory. We can do this, and if it fails it was worth the try."

"Yes, I agree, thank you." And she gave him a weak smile.

This day had broken his defensiveness toward her, and he smiled back. It felt good now to have her as a friend.

The next afternoon was even more grueling than the day before. They meditated and talked and found it very difficult to come up with a defense, especially for him. They had never mentioned the names of the negative couple so far. They spoke about her mother only as "her mother" and her husband only as "her husband."

Anton asked, "What are their names? I will need to use them, and you also will have to address him by name."

"Let's keep it this way. I don't want to pull them in, but I will write the names down for you on the plane. I hate the thought of using them. By the way, I plan to call Mother by her given name when I am with her. Mother sounds too intimate."

"I don't think that's a good idea. Names have stronger energy. Unfortunately, we will have to hear his name when I'm introduced, but let's not address him directly after that."

"You're right; that's why Jacques would never mention their names."

"Do you know how he seduced your mother?"

"I'm not sure. She always wanted power, and I think he appealed to that need, and certainly sex was a factor. But she did love my father and had a very close bond with him, so he had to do something at the outset to break that bond."

They looked at each other with the same thought.

Anton said it first, "So, the first tactic will be to break our bond, which probably isn't as strong as your mother's and father's."

"I think it's equally as strong because of our past together. If that happens, let's think about what to do."

"We don't do anything." An idea popped into Anton's head. "In fact, we pretend that he succeeds. That's the answer! We pretend; otherwise, he will keep trying until he prevails. If we pretend convincingly most of the time, they will think they are winning. It will be hard for them to penetrate our thoughts. Only before we leave do we reverse everything."

"That's brilliant! Tactica adversa: you get the enemies to exhaust themselves, thinking they are winning. They talk about it in the teaching as a good method in battle. Of course, that would be much better than trying to fight them at the outset. Only if they start to use energy toward us do we have to defend ourselves."

"But they might not even try that if they feel we are submitting to them."

"Excellent. So, let's look at what may happen. She is going to charm you, and you will be goggle eyed over her. This will upset me, and you won't care. We may even have words over it. Then he will do the same with me. But he won't approach me sexually, as she will you. I don't think he will do that; but then, what *will* he do?"

They both thought about it.

Then Anton said, "Maybe he will try to appeal to your spiritual side, try to impress you with how he can help you develop powers. He may ask you if you are clairvoyant or clairaudient yet and you will say no, and he will act surprised and imply that Jacques could have opened those centers for you."

"But I am clairaudient."

"Of course, but don't tell him that. Go along with what he is offering you. I'm certain that at some time he will imply that I am far beneath you, and you need someone on your own level. He will appeal to your ego."

"I think you're right. We can go along with it and watch them in action. That was one of the things I was interested in knowing: how they seduce people. The question is, When and how do we let them know we have been pretending?"

They meditated a long time and came up with no answer.

It was late afternoon, so they decided to take a break and go for a walk. It was a lovely sunny day, and they walked down a country road that was near the house. It was good to breathe in the fresh air and get some exercise. Spring was approaching, and new buds were sprouting up on the trees. Having concentrated so deeply on the negative forces, the two felt good to be absorbing beauty once more.

Samantha grabbed Anton's arm and said, "Look!"

A fawn ran in front of them. Then it saw them and jumped back into the woods.

They stood quietly, expecting its mother to appear, and when she didn't, they wondered why. The mothers usually stayed close to their young.

"I hope it will be all right. Maybe the mother was already in the woods."

"Most definitely." It suddenly became a symbol for their adventure. They were the fawns, and their mother was Jacques, and he wouldn't be with them. That still bothered Anton. He told Sam how he felt.

"I know, but I can't tell him. Only in an emergency should we call on him. Promise me that."

"I won't make that promise. If I feel he needs to be there, I will call him, emergency or not."

She didn't answer him, so they left it at that. Anton again became worried and tried to brush the feelings away.

After dinner, they again tried to come up with some answer about when they would make a stand against the negative couple. "It needn't be anything major," Samantha said. "Just before leaving, we could tell them we wouldn't see them again. Or, we could not say anything but write them a letter instead."

"I don't know; then they might still be after you on the subtle plane. Whatever happens, your mother needs to know it's over between the two of you. Just to leave wouldn't accomplish that."

"You're right, of course. I need to make a strong statement to them both that I have no intention of following them and joining their order. I came only to tell them so to their faces."

"But Sam, we have to rethink whether or not to pretend to listen to them. Maybe from the very beginning, we need to make it clear that we are only there to demand they stop bothering you." Anton was having a lot of doubts about their strategy now.

"Anton, if we do that, then we will never learn how they use their powers to seduce people, and I really want to see them in action. No, let's keep our plan and only tell the truth when we are about to leave."

"It doesn't feel right to me."

"None of it is right. But what else can we do?"

"I don't know. I think that we just have to follow the plan and 'play it by ear.' When the time comes to oppose them, one of us needs to act, and then we need to pull together."

"How will we know?"

"That's why I said 'play it by ear.' When the time is right, we can look at each other with a nod, and I think you need to make the first statement to your mother."

"Okay, that feels right," she agreed.

"If you want me to make the first move, I can do that."

"No, she's my mother. I need to show her my strength. I can do it."

"Good, but if you lose energy — and she might do that to you — just take my hand and even say it's time to leave, and I'll take over. Promise me you will do that."

"Okay, I promise to let you take over if my strength becomes diminished."

They looked into each other's eyes for a minute without saying anything. The truce was final.

Chapter 44

Anton was busy the last week of school and had no time even to think about the weekend. Friday he packed, and Saturday morning he picked Samantha up to drive to the airport. Their plane was scheduled to leave at 11 a.m., and due to arrive in Washington, DC, in the early evening. The plane was late, so when they arrived in Washington they checked straight into the hotel, ate supper, and went to bed.

The next day it rained in the morning. They slept in and had breakfast together in Anton's room. They tried to go over their various strategies but were too tired, partly from jet lag but mainly from all the work they had done already. They gave up and read the *Washington Post* until lunchtime.

In the afternoon the sky cleared, so they went for a walk on Pennsylvania Avenue and stopped for a late lunch at a small café. They both were lost in thoughts and said very little. Anton broke the silence. "Sam, let's find a place and meditate."

"No, Jacques might pick up on where we are, and he'll know right away the reason we are here."

"But we need to meditate and link with our Higher Selves to prepare."

"I guess you're right, but let's not link with Jacques this time. Okay?"

Anton agreed.

They meditated in the park, where the cherry blossoms were still in bloom and wonderful to sit under, but it was difficult because of the many people walking around to view the blossoms.

The meditation was short, but Sam received something of interest. She looked agitated when she told Anton what she saw: "I was in a very large room with a lot of people I didn't know. Then a woman came in, and I recognized her immediately as my mother. She walked directly to me, and, taking my hand, turned to the people and introduced me as her daughter and successor. I started to protest, but my voice wasn't heard over the applause. Then I came back to my body."

Anton didn't know what to say, so he mumbled, "She's sending you that. Don't let it bother you."

"I know she is, but it was so final. I felt so helpless." She paused and looked at him intently. "Anton, I'm afraid. For the first time, I'm afraid."

He put his arms around her and held her. "She wants you to feel that way. It's your inner child who is afraid now. Try to hold the inner child and get back to the mature you, the part of you that has no fear of her or anyone."

She closed her eyes and, when she opened them, she was back to herself.

"Thank you, Anton. I need to remember this. I'm going to work very hard to calm this part of me before we go tomorrow."

The next day was sunny and beautiful. Samantha's mother and her husband lived in one of the finest neighborhoods, Georgetown, in a charming townhouse. When they walked up the stairs to the door, Anton had a strong urge to grab Sam and run. The urge was still there when the door opened, and Samantha's mother stood waiting for them.

"Beautiful" was an inadequate word to describe her. Her long hair was as dark as Sam's was light. It was black with blue highlights, like a raven's slick wings, and her eyes were blue, like Sam's. The contrast was striking against white skin that had pink overtones and features that were perfect. Anton wondered if the hair was natural or if she dyed it. He looked at Sam and saw she didn't seem surprised at her mother's appearance.

"Darling!" Her mother came out on the porch to greet Sam. When she threw her arms around her in an embrace, Anton could see Sam recoil and break the embrace as best she could.

"Mother, I want you to meet Anton Bauer. Anton, this is my mother."

Anton took her cold hand and looked into eyes that were equally cold. She smiled at him. "Call me Lynn. I am very happy to meet you. Please come in." She led them into a drawing room. "James is on the phone. He'll be with us soon. Please sit down."

The room was tastefully designed, mainly in French baroque furniture. The rug was an Aubusson, exquisite and rare to find those days, woven in a pattern of pastel leaves. A colored mix of cut flowers was on the tables, and there was a large, gray-and-white marble fireplace that conveyed an air of coziness to the whole room. Samantha and Anton sat down together on a couch facing her mother, who was seated in a high-backed, elegant, white-upholstered chair.

Her mother was dressed in a navy pants suit, which was so tightly fitted that when she moved to cross her legs, it undulated with her body, which made Anton think of a snake sliding through grass. A blue lapis locket hung down her chest against a white blouse. It had a lot of gold in the stone that flashed as she shifted in her seat. Anton knew she was in her early fifties, but she looked at least ten years younger, more like Sam's older sister rather than her mother. He was still feeling startled about her blue eyes, duplicates of Sam's, yet with none of the warmth, when James walked into the room.

Anton didn't see him at first but felt his energy. It was a blast that surrounded his aura, and Anton immediately strengthened the protection he had put there. Then Anton looked at him. His appearance also took him aback. James was as blond as Lynn was dark, with sun-bleached, blond hair and dusky hazel eyes. He wore a white casual shirt and jeans. His face was thin with sharp features — handsome, very hand-

229

some. Anton could see right away why Sam's mother, and probably most women, were drawn to him. James was at least six feet tall with a slim, muscular body, and when he walked, he projected an animal magnetism, which made Anton feel he was a predator moving toward his prey. He also looked much younger for his age.

Anton stood up and they shook hands; then James turned to Samantha and unpretentiously leaned over and kissed the top of her head. It came off as being genuine, and he smiled at her and said, "Sam, it's so wonderful to meet you. I'm so happy you came." His tone, too, was sincere.

Anton could feel Sam stiffen next to him, and he grabbed her hand.

"Can I get you both a drink?"

They declined, and James sat down in another chair opposite them.

The talk began casually, just chitchat about their trip and things in general. Her mother asked if they were engaged. Anton said no and told her the truth, that they were no longer married but good friends.

"I can see that." Anton could tell she had already picked up on Sam's love for him and his need for friendship only.

James said very little but sat simply looking at them. Anton protected himself some more as James was trying to read him psychically. James's energy was extremely powerful, and it had the same intensity as Jacques's. Anton knew the negative ones could develop this power, but he had never experienced it before.

James looked at his watch. He mentioned reservations for 1 p.m. at a restaurant nearby, and then he looked at his wife for the first time.

She responded to his look. "Sam, I really had to see you. Besides missing you terribly, I need to tell you something that is very important."

"All right, I will listen to what you want to say, but only on the condition that you stop your visits to me on the subtle plane. I want you to promise no longer to intrude in my dreams and my meditations."

"I did that because I wanted to talk to you. But I need to talk to you alone."

"No, Anton can hear anything you need to say to me."

"This is strictly between you and me." And she looked at Anton with eyes that urged him to stay out of it.

Something in him replied, "It's okay, Sam, you speak to your mother and I will stay here with James." For a minute, he wasn't certain whether those words were his or if James had put them in his mouth. He still wasn't certain when Sam said, "Okay, let's talk," and stood up.

She looked at Anton; he could tell she was strong, and that was a relief.

They went out of the room, and James and Anton sat looking at each other. The battle was on.

"You know you can't win this one." James's words were direct and unexpected.

Anton immediately linked with Jacques before he responded, "What is it that I can't win?"

"Sam belongs with us. You know that but haven't accepted it yet."

"That's not true." But as he spoke a question touched his heart, and he felt a pang of regret.

James smiled. "You came with her to help her, but you aren't able to do that. She always makes up her own mind. You never could change that, so why think you can now?"

Anton realized James had penetrated his protection and knew everything. He hadn't expected this directness. He was laying it all out on the table, so Anton decided to do the same.

"That's true; Sam makes her own decisions, and I am totally confident that she will make the right one now."

"But, if she doesn't make the decision that you consider right and stays with us, what will you do then?"

Here it comes, Anton thought. "I can't consider her going with you. Therefore, that's a moot question."

James laughed. "A warrior always considers every possibility. You know that."

Anton thought, What would Jacques say? Then he answered, "I would fight for her."

"That's more like it. I would expect that from you. But what would you do if you didn't win?"

Anton realized that James was very cunningly trying to weaken him with these questions.

He reversed the tactic. "More importantly, what would you do if you didn't win?"

"You know that's not a possibility." His words were so energetic that they made Anton straighten his back.

Anton concentrated on his heart and tried to blast James with it when he responded, "I know Sam far better than you do, and I know she would never become a negative witch. That is not a possibility."

"You are young in your teaching. You know very little and doubt too much. You claim to know Sam?" And he looked at him quizzically. "Yet you don't know her at all."

If he felt any of Anton's energy, he easily threw it off. James's words for the first time made Anton feel afraid. He stood up. "I'm going to get Sam." And he walked toward the door where she and her mother had exited.

He found them sitting in a sun porch. Sam looked like a zombie, and when he entered, she gave him a blank look. Anton grabbed her arm and said, "I think it's time we left."

She didn't seem to hear what he said to her. "No, I need to stay here with my mother."

"Sam, you are not staying. We are leaving." And he pulled her to her feet.

"Please, Anton, I need to talk to her some more." Her eyes were pleading with him, and he could tell she was lost in her inner child.

Anton called on Jacques seven times and then called on his Mahatma seven times. He could feel the energy change, and Sam collapsed in his arms. He picked her up and carried her out of the room, out of the house.

James was standing by the door. "She will be back," he said, smiling for the first time with the evil that was in his soul.

Sam was limp and listless in Anton's arms.

By the time they reached the hotel, she had composed herself somewhat. Anton took her to her room and ordered some tea and sandwiches from room service. She ate little and did not speak a word, all the time in a semitrance. Just when he was beginning to worry that maybe she had been drugged, she came out of her thoughts and looked at him with clear, sad eyes, the same eyes he had seen in a meditation with Jacques before he married her.

"I need to rest. Would you mind leaving?"

"Yes, I would mind. If you don't feel like talking to me about what happened, that's fine for now, but I'm not leaving you alone. You can go to bed, and I will sit here."

She shrugged and unselfconsciously took off her clothes and crawled into bed. She fell into a deep sleep immediately, and he was concerned that they were reaching her this way. Anton meditated and asked Jacques to protect her. Jacques came into his meditation and asked what had happened, and Anton told him. Jacques looked stern when he said, "Seeing them was wrong to do. Their power is much greater than Samantha's or yours. You should not have allowed her to do this."

"I had no choice. I tried to stop her, but she wouldn't listen. You know how determined she can be! She would not even call on you for help because she didn't want you to know she was seeing them."

"Of course, she didn't. You're right. When she makes up her mind she usually follows through, but this was really dangerous for both of you."

"I know that now. We planned for every possibility and none of them were right. He was extremely direct with me, which took me off guard, and Sam hasn't told me what happened with her mother. All I know is that she is catatonic and in a deep sleep, which I fear they are part of."

"Let her sleep one hour only, then wake her up. Then bring her to me immediately."

"All right." And then Jacques disappeared.

An hour later, Anton woke Sam up. She half smiled at him when she was opening her eyes, but then her face darkened.

"Leave me alone. I need to sleep."

"No, you don't. It's time to get up."

There was still some warm tea in the pot, and he poured her a cup, which she drank down quickly. It made the color return to her pale face.

She sighed, "Okay, okay, I'll get up."

She went into the bathroom. He could hear her splashing water on her face; and, when she returned, some of her hair was dripping water and hanging in wisps on her neck and shoulders. She reminded him of a woeful three-year-old who had just lost her teddy bear.

"Let's sit outside." She walked out onto the balcony.

After they sat down in chairs facing each other, Anton asked, "Okay, what happened?"

"You first."

"No, tell me what happened."

Anton could see her fighting back the tears, and then she blurted out, "She told me that James was my father, not Jacques, that James was my real father!" And the tears came then.

"She's lying. That's not possible." But as Anton said the words, he remembered James's blond hair. When he first met Sam, he wondered where she got her hair color from, as Jacques had dark brown hair when he was younger, and she mentioned her mother had black hair.

"No, when I saw him, I realized I looked like him; so, when she told me that, it felt true. She said he had been a student of their teacher, and she had had a brief affair with him and broke it up when she got pregnant. Jacques didn't know and always felt I was his child. James left the teaching and turned negative, but he came back for her later when I was a teenager."

"Oh, God." Anton wanted to hold her but just reached for her hand.

"Mother wanted to take me with her, but she said Jacques wouldn't let her; nor would I have gone, particularly when I found out she was leaving with someone following the negative forces."

"Why is she telling you this now?"

"She says I belong with them. I have their genes, and I am destined to be their successor." And Samantha choked on the words.

"You know that's not true."

"Yes, I do know that, Anton, but they are extremely powerful. I feel their energy like an octopus tangling me and pulling me toward them."

"Remember, your power lies in the positive, not in the negative. You are still

Jacques' child and his disciple. Remember that. Light will always win over darkness."

"But she said they would never let me go, that the time has come when I needed to take what was rightfully mine, what I had agreed upon before I was born."

"That's nonsense! Don't believe it. You have a beautiful heart. Your destiny is to be Jacques' successor. You know that, and they know that. They are trying to stop you from being a great teacher, from working for humanity instead of trying to destroy it for personal gain, as they have done. You can fight them! You are more powerful than they."

"No, I'm not. I felt their power. It's as strong as Jacques'."

"That's not true. When I called Jacques and our Mahatma to come and help, your mother and James could do nothing. They had to let us go."

"You did that?"

"Yes, of course. When I saw what was happening to you, I called for help."

"Oh God! Now Jacques knows I went to see her." Sam looked at him with stern questioning eyes. "I asked you not to tell him! Why couldn't you honor my request?"

"I never agreed, and even if I had, it was necessary that I call on them to save you. Jacques told me to bring you to him when you woke up."

"I can't go. I can't face him."

"Of course, you can. You need him now more than ever."

"But I can't tell him the truth. I can't tell him he's not my father. How can I do that to him?"

"Maybe he knows already."

"But why wouldn't he tell me if he knows—why?"

"Because it would hurt you too much. Just as it's hurting you now."

"But it makes all the difference in the world. To have a father and mother in the negative forces. Don't you understand what that means?"

"No, what difference does it make? Your heart is pure."

"But they will never leave me alone. She said so. They have a hold over me forever. I could fight one of them but not both. I feel lost." And Samantha bent over, resting her head on her arms, her blond hair spreading across her back, a dismal portrait of despair.

"You are not lost. You have Jacques and your Mahatma. They will protect you always. Don't feel that way. That's what they want. They want you to believe that. I can see she planted that into your head. Stop listening to her."

Anton stood up and pulled her up into his arms, holding her tightly. "I won't let you listen to them. Listen to me. Your destiny is to be with me, remember? We are to be teachers together and help each other. They can't reach us, believe that."

Sam pulled away. "You said you don't know if you want to be a teacher. If you leave the teaching, even for a while, then I will end up alone. Even with my protection, it will be a constant battle, and I don't know if I want to live like that."

Anton knew she was right. He hadn't committed himself yet, but he had to help her, and he couldn't lie about it, so instead he said, "Whether I become a teacher or not, I will help you, I promise."

"That's not good enough."

His heart looked at her and suddenly was filled with the love that he thought was gone, and his heart said, "It is good enough because I will be with you. Sam, I love you. I want you to marry me again." The words came out without him thinking them. They came through the hurt, and the fear, and they felt right.

He pulled her back toward him and kissed her and felt her body tremble against his.

She again pushed him away. "Anton, you know how much I love you, but everything's changed now. You know I want to marry you, but I need to think all this through. Just give me some time."

She gave him a weak smile. "I need to sleep some more. We'll talk this evening."

Anton sat in a chair by her bed watching her breathing, slow and steady. He longed to lie down next to her and hold her in his arms, but it was too soon, so he sat just looking at her and allowed himself to feel all the emotions he had repressed.

The short time they had had together when they first were married had deepened his love for her, which was why the loss had been so hurtful. Now all that was in the past. He desperately wanted her back, wanted to look at her like this, to experience her presence and vitality, to share their lives together, the joys and the pain, and to help each other spiritually.

When he thought about the teaching, he knew it was his path. He had chosen Jacques long before he even knew Sam, but somehow Sam made the teaching more meaningful and alive. That's why he needed to separate her impact on him from his decision-making. He needed to look realistically at his commitment, especially to becoming a teacher, and decide whether that was something he, and not just Sam, really wanted.

Her body began moving around as if she were trying to get away from something or someone. Anton sat on the bed and softly patted her head, letting his hand move down her long hair. Her restlessness ended, and her head relaxed against his hand.

It was getting late, so he decided to go back to his room to shower and change for dinner. He returned to wake her up and saw the door ajar. She was gone. There was no luggage or clothing in the closet.

But there was a note on the bed with his name on it.

"Anton, I love you, and that is why I cannot hurt you again. I cannot marry you unless I am free of them and their influence. I need to see them. I need to be with them. Don't try to stop me. Only I can do this. Tell Jacques I love him, but I need to do this by myself. Just as you have to find yourself, so do I. I need to know who I am. That is why I need to see them again."

Anton sat down, stunned. They had won, after all.

CHAPTER 45

Anton decided not to telephone Jacques to tell him about Sam. He needed to talk to him in person, and so in the morning he took a plane to North Carolina and drove to where Jacques was staying. His student's home was on the outskirts of Durham, and it was easy to find his address, which was listed online. It was a lovely spring day, with plenty of sunlight trying to soften his dark mood. The more Anton thought about what Sam was doing, the more he felt upset and frightened. How was he going to tell Jacques that his only daughter was not his child and that the hold her parents had on her was too strong for her to resist? Anton's heart ached for him. He had already lost so much to the negative force—his wife, whom he adored, and now his child.

It was close to lunchtime when Anton knocked on the door. Fortunately, Jacques was in, and, when he heard Anton's voice, he came running to the vestibule. Jacques saw his face and knew immediately that something had happened, even though Anton tried to hide his feelings.

"Come in, come in. What has happened? Is Samantha all right?"

"No, she's not all right." But he quickly added, "Physically, she's fine. Don't worry about that. But I need to talk to you alone."

John Burke, who was Jacques' host, had opened the door. He was tall, Black, with a warm smile that made Anton feel very welcomed. After greetings, he led them to the living room and politely closed the door behind them.

Jacques sat across from Anton with inquiring eyes. "Anton, where is she?"

"Do you remember speaking with me yesterday in meditation?"

"Yes, I do, and you were to bring her to me. What happened?"

"This is very difficult for me to tell you. She slipped out when I was changing and left me this note." And he handed Jacques her message.

He looked at it for a long time. Anton couldn't tell what Jacques was feeling.

"You asked her to marry you again, and she still went back to them?" His voice was faint.

"Yes." He sadly whispered.

"Tell me everything that happened with them."

Anton explained in detail all that had taken place at the meeting. Then when it was time to relate what Sam's mother had told her, he couldn't do it.

"Did she tell her that she wasn't my child?" Jacques asked.

"Yes, is it true?"

"I believe so. Her coloring wasn't like either one of ours. I knew about the affair, even though they thought I didn't. When he left the teaching and she announced she was pregnant, I picked up that it was his child, and it was verified as Sam grew older and the resemblance was more apparent."

"But why did you stay with her?"

"Love can be strange, as you know, and I did love her very much. I also wanted a child. We had tried with no luck, so I was happy to step in and be Samantha's father. Of course, when my wife finally left me for him, she wanted to take Samantha; but Samantha wouldn't think of leaving me, especially when she realized what her mother would be doing. She never wanted to see her mother again, so I find it strange that now she's reconnected with her."

"The main reason is that her mother was appearing to her on a regular basis in her meditations and dreams. She never told you about it, as she didn't want to worry you. Sam said that when she called on her Mahatma, her mother would leave, but that she wanted to stop it once and for all. Her mother promised to stop if she would come and see her."

Jacques shook his head. "But I could have ended that very quickly if she had only told me."

"She also wanted to observe firsthand how the negative ones operate, but she wasn't prepared to be told that you are not her father. That shocked her deeply and was how they started infiltrating her armor. Why didn't you ever tell Sam the truth?"

"I couldn't. Having him as her father would have distressed her too much, and obviously it has, as she is not thinking correctly. If she spends any time with them, they can put some spells on her and keep her a prisoner."

"I know. She is already under a spell and very vulnerable. Jacques, what can we do? Can you get through to her and try to rescue her?"

"Yes, I can do that, but she will fight me, just as she did you. I can send energy around her to help her, but she needs to use her will to break any ties they are trying to use. I can't do that for her. Besides, she has her own lower nature that is fighting intensely to keep her from her initiation. This is a difficult time for her, and to see them now was a win for her lower nature. If she could only have waited, she would have had more ability to handle them. How did you find out about this? I know that recently you weren't even talking to her."

"She told Lea, and Lea called me for help; finally, Sam agreed that it would be better if I went with her."

"Thank you for that."

"Jacques, I love her. Can I go with you to help?"

He thought for a minute. "Yes, that would be good. She may see you and not me, especially if she feels upset about hurting me."

He looked at his watch. "We need to meditate, and lunch is going to be served soon. Let's eat and then go up to the shrine room here. I will tell John we need to do some work together. I know he has errands to run, so that will give us plenty of time to meditate."

Anton tried to be social at lunch but found it too difficult. It seemed endless — not a simple lunch, but a couple of courses. It turned out that John was a gourmet cook and wanted to entertain Jacques royally. John was in his sixties and had been with Jacques for many years. He talked about all the different cultural things that were happening in Durham and invited Anton to go to a concert with them in the evening. Anton tried to decline, but John wouldn't take no for an answer; nor would he allow Anton to book a hotel room for the night, as he had another guest room. He was very hospitable, and at any other time Anton would have enjoyed being there.

It was two o'clock when Jacques and Anton sat down to meditate. Jacques asked him for Samantha's parents' address and a detailed description of the layout of the rooms. Anton did the best he could, but since his focus had been on the people, he hadn't paid much attention to the townhouse itself except to notice that the decor was tastefully done and obviously expensive.

"She always had a good sense of design," Jacques commented.

Finally, they closed their eyes and linked their hearts, and Anton felt Jacques pull him to the townhouse door. He tried to lead Anton through it, but he couldn't penetrate it. It was a solid wall of atoms that wouldn't accept their movement. Jacques had walked through walls and doors many times, but this was different.

"They have barricaded it with some special energy."

He moved to the wall and tried again, with no luck. He placed his hands on it, and Anton could see him sending energy, but it just seemed to bounce back. Then he took Anton's hand, and they flew up the side of the house and looked through a couple of windows until they saw them. Sam was seated next to her mother, and they were in a deep conversation. Anton saw Jacques staring at Sam's mother, and she turned and looked directly at them. Anton could tell she saw them both, but Sam wasn't aware of what was happening. Her mother smiled and then turned back to continue the conversation. Jacques put his hands against the window but nothing happened, so they returned to the front of the house and sat down.

"We can wait until someone comes out," Anton said, not too convinced that would happen.

"Yes, I plan to leave a subtle body here, but I don't want to wait that long. Time is of the essence. Did you notice how composed Samantha was? She's not afraid. In fact, she seems almost happy."

Anton had noticed, and he had also noticed her smiling once in a while at what her mother said.

Someone walked toward them, and Anton realized it was their Mahatma.

He looked at them both, one at a time, and said, "You must leave her alone. This is her decision; you mustn't try to help her."

Jacques replied, "I can't do that. I have to help her; she's my disciple and my daughter."

"No, you are too close to her and to the situation to be able to help. Only I can help her. I am asking you both to leave."

"Surely, I can stay?" Anton asked. "She leans on me and may listen to me."

"No, you are too attached to know the best way to help her."

"Will she return to us?" Jacques asked.

"I can't answer that. It has to be up to her. This is her challenge, and only she can determine the outcome."

"But you said you would help her?"

"Only if she asks me to. Samantha has to ask; you know that."

Jacques turned toward me. "He's right. We need to leave. All we can do is pray for her." He took Anton's hand, and they opened their eyes in the shrine room.

There was nothing to say. Sam's Mahatma was honoring her request, which they couldn't do. They both sat in silence, remembering the scene of Samantha and her mother.

Finally, Jacques spoke. "Her mother hasn't changed much. It's amazing how someone so evil can be so beautiful."

"What is it that they do that is evil? You have never said."

"They work on the subtle plane to plant negative thinking in people such as you and me. They want to destroy the light forces, and this is part of their method — to approach people subtly, to play on their lower nature. They also consciously try to stop the evolution of the planet, as eventually, when it evolves, they themselves cannot continue. They do this by promoting war, nuclear weapons, and all the atrocities on Earth. They work with the elements to destroy rather than create. They add to the catastrophes of natural disasters. The list is endless."

"Where do they get their money? They look very wealthy."

"They both are brilliant, and I understand they do a lot of corporate and government work as consultants."

"Sam is in the same business. Did she know about their work?"

"No, I tried not to tell her anything that would make her feel the connection. Of course, I realize now that wasn't right. It merely aids them in their strategy to make her feel she is just like them."

"What do you think, Jacques? Will she make it?"

He sat in deep thought. "I can't answer that. I honestly don't know. They are very powerful, especially her husband, and he has trained my ex-wife fully in the negative arts. Samantha also has a lot of power, but she hasn't come into her own yet. Still, she has a loving heart, and that is her main weapon. I can't see her turning negative."

He paused and looked at Anton. "But Anton, I didn't believe my wife would do that, either."

Those words were full of sadness, and Anton realized that Jacques still loved his wife and that seeing her today must have been very difficult for him. He thought about Sam and realized that if she followed her parents in the years ahead, he would become like Jacques, remembering her with lost love in his heart.

In the meantime, Anton needed to do something. His Mahatma had said not to, and he needed to obey him, but he couldn't. He just couldn't sit back and wait. He had promised Sam he would help her, and he had told James he would fight for her, and he needed to do that even if it was too late. If he didn't try, he would never forgive himself.

It was good to attend a concert that night. It took his mind away from the situation.

The next afternoon, Anton returned to Washington, DC. He told Jacques he was returning to Switzerland and to contact him there if he heard from Sam. Anton didn't want Jacques to try to persuade him to stay out of it. He was going to see them one more time, but this time physically.

It was 6:30 the following morning when Anton knocked on their door. Sam was an early riser, so he hoped only she would hear him, but it was her mother who answered the door. She was dressed in exercise tights and a shirt.

"Come in. We were expecting you, but not so early."

Anton said nothing but walked inside and glanced around, looking for Sam.

"She's in the exercise room. We were working out together."

Anton followed her to the back of the house and down the stairs. Sam was on an exercise bike, dressed like her mother, sipping coffee from a mug. When she saw Anton, she stopped. "What are you doing here?"

"I need to talk to you, alone." And he glared at her mother, who smiled and left the room.

"I asked you not to come. Why couldn't you honor that?" She looked annoyed.

"Because you also asked me to help you and not to leave you alone with them. Sam, what are you doing here? You must leave immediately."

She got off the bicycle and came over to him. "I asked you to help me before we came, but afterward I asked you to leave me alone. I need to work this out by myself. I do not want your help."

Anton stepped back. "Then will you promise me that you will call on your Mahatma to guard you and help you?"

"I can't promise you that. There is no reason for me to call on my Mahatma. I need to get to know my parents. That's what I'm doing here. Please leave."

"Sam, they are casting a spell on you, and you aren't defending yourself."

She gave him a piercing look. "I don't need to defend myself against my parents. Now will you leave?"

The force of her words made him step back. She was resolute. There was nothing more that he could do. Anton turned and left the room and the house without looking back.

He didn't want to stay another day in Washington. He couldn't trust himself not to try again to see Sam, so he flew home that evening.

He drove directly to Grindelwald the next day to spend the rest of his vacation there. He prayed for Sam and at the same time tried not to think about what could be happening in Washington. Mainly, he regretted having gone back to see her. It made him feel that it was too late, that she was lost. It was hard to shake that feeling off and have hope.

Anton telephoned Lea and told her what had happened. She was quiet for a long time and finally said, "I can't believe she could turn negative. It's not in her."

"That's what Jacques said. But he also said he believed the same thing about his wife."

"Yes, but others have told me they saw that Jacques' wife had a very strong ego nature, and a couple of people said they weren't surprised."

"But I think they have put a spell over her."

"If that's true, they can't do it for long. She has Jacques' and her Mahatma's protection. Besides, Samantha has a very strong will. Don't be discouraged, Anton. She'll win this, I know she will." She thought for a minute. "You know, Samantha has a deep goodness in her that I feel has to prevail. I can't put my finger on it; but, when she helps someone, it's as if a radiation comes from her that goes beyond the act of kindness. That's it: it's an innate kindness that has no beginning or end because it's so much a part of her essence."

"That's beautifully put, and you're right."

"Is there anything I can do to help?"

"No, this is her battle. Just pray that she wins it."

CHAPTER 46

Anton put the following weekend aside and made no social plans in order to devote that time to his introspection. He needed to decide if his commitment to the teaching was strong enough for him to strive to eventually become a teacher. Now, the decision was more difficult, because he really wasn't certain that Sam would be with him to fulfill their dharma together.

The process Anton went through on the weekend was very deep. He examined himself and looked at all his qualities, the good ones and the negative ones. He tried to gain perspective by writing them down. If he committed himself to this path, then he needed to know who he was now and what would change. Of course, he would become more spiritual; and, if that was true, what would he look like and how would he feel? Anton thought about Jacques and even Sam, who was far more advanced than he was. He considered their qualities and how they conducted themselves in the world. Both were fearless, compassionate, and full of determination to be of service to others. They were committed to that service, and they both had the strong will to go forward and accomplish any task they chose to do. But he also saw that their main focus was the teaching. Could he ever have that kind of desire for God Consciousness?

Anton examined his mundane life: his work, his relationships, his need to have a family and a regular life, his love of the physical, from the desire for sex to the need to hike and climb the mountains. Were those needs stronger than the desire for God Consciousness? He knew he didn't have to give up those things, but he certainly needed to have as strong a desire to achieve God Consciousness. Otherwise, the teaching, and everything required in it, would not be his main priority. Anton guessed that was what it came down to. Could the teaching be his priority in life? When it came to commitment, would there be no question in his heart that the teaching was his main focus?

He seemed to be getting nowhere, and his heart felt pulled in both directions. Should he live a regular life with friends and family, or should he live a dedicated life full of obstacles and change?

He then remembered the joy he had felt when he realized the answer to the question: Who are you and what is your purpose in life? But those spiritual joys were rare and fleeting, and his memories of them lacked the beauty and the intensity of the experience.

Anton's Higher Self gave him a process that helped: He took the first direction of having a regular life and tried to project himself ten years into the future. He saw himself at home in the mountains and in Zürich. He was married with three young children, and he also saw himself at work in the university. He still sometimes attended the Higher Self classes, and he still worked with Jacques, but those things weren't his main priority. They were a part of his life but not the main thing.

After experiencing as much as possible in this process, Anton put all of it into his heart to feel how it felt. Having a regular life really had a lot of joy in it, but a part of him felt sad and empty. He tried the exercise again, but that part wouldn't go away.

Anton took a break and went for a walk.

When he returned home, he mentally projected himself fifteen years into the future when he would be a spiritual teacher. He saw himself in a class with a group of his students, explaining the concept of the higher principles, and he was totally focused on what he was saying.

It was a lively discussion with questions, and, at the end, they all meditated on what had been taught. Anton felt changed; his whole self was accepting and understanding at a different level.

Later, he saw himself with a wife and two teenage children. He loved them very much, but the feeling wasn't the same as in his first vision. The love was as strong, but it wasn't emotional. When he put this experience in his heart, he felt joyful. The sadness was gone. It felt right.

He realized that it would take years for him to reach that understanding, but the goal felt correct: that his life was meant to be dedicated to the teaching. He could be in the world but not be attached to it. He could have love that wasn't full of personal needs, and it would be a love that was so much fuller because of who he was spiritually.

It had been a struggle to arrive at this understanding, but now, finally, he could fully commit himself to the teaching and the spiritual path.

He phoned Jacques in the States, and John answered and said Jacques was en route back to Zürich. That was great news. Anton could see him in person to tell him his decision.

Feeling anxious, Anton called Jacques the next day even knowing that he must be still feeling jet lag. Jacques answered the phone on the second ring. "Anton! It's wonderful to hear from you. How are you?" His voice sounded fresh.

"Fine, how are you? When can I see you? I know you must be tired, but when's the soonest I can see you?"

"I feel fine. How about this evening? Come to dinner."

"Great. I'll be there."

Jacques greeted him at the door, and Anton threw his arms around him and hugged him so tightly that Jacques laughed and said, "Don't crush me. I'm an old man."

They went into his office, and Anton looked around remembering the first time he met him.

"You've made up your mind?" Jacques smiled at Anton.

"Yes, can't you tell? It was very difficult, but I'm so glad I went through it. I am totally committed to you and this teaching. I couldn't live my life without it. I know that now. And I want to thank you for your patience and for letting me go through this on my own."

"It's always that way. The battles have to be yours, not mine. One of my favorite quotes is from the Lakota Code of Ethics: 'Search for yourself, by yourself. Do not allow others to make your path for you. It is your road and yours alone. Others may walk it with you, but no one can walk it for you.'" Jacques smiled. "All I could do is be there if you needed me. I'm so happy for you, Anton. I always believed you could conquer your demons."

They walked down the hall toward the dining room. Anton looked into the living room and remembered seeing his Mahatma there — another beautiful memory. At the table, he and Jacques sat across from each other the same way he and Sam had done the last time he was there, when she had told him they were supposed to teach together. Jacques never mentioned her name, nor did Anton, which he took to mean that it was final, that her name, like her mother's, could no longer be spoken.

Anton could tell that Jacques was tired, so he arranged to see him later in the week and took his leave right after dinner.

It was still early, so instead of going right home he strolled down to the river and sat on his favorite bench. The night sky was clear, with no clouds, and the stars seemed extra large, shining with intense luminosity.

He thought about the future and the vision he had seen of a wife and family. Anton thought it interesting that in both of his visualizations he hadn't seen his wife's face, but he guessed that was for the best; otherwise, he would be searching for her everywhere.

He hoped she would be spiritual, or at least accept that he was on a spiritual journey.

A woman sat down on the bench next to him. He felt her presence but at first couldn't see what she looked like, as it was dark. He could make out that she was tall and thin, and he wondered why she would sit next to a total stranger until she spoke.

"Anton, can you forgive me once more?"

It was Samantha. Anton couldn't speak.

"I stayed until they told me what I wanted to know. Then I told them the truth — that I needed to see how the negative ones worked — and I left."

"But you were under their spell when I saw you."

"No, I wasn't. I was acting. I knew they were listening in. In fact, my response to you made them more open to me. Your coming was perfect timing."

"How could you do that to me?"

"We made an agreement, but you forgot. Remember? I said I was going to pretend to follow them to find out how they operated."

"But that was for the meeting only, not for you to return and stay with them."

"When they told me Jacques wasn't my father, I had to stay on and see how they were going to persuade me to come to their side. It was a terrible shock, but after I finally got over it—I think my Mahatma helped to heal me in my sleep—it didn't surprise me. Jacques is my teacher and that's more important, and he has been my father in every sense of the word. It was a dirty ploy on their part. It made me angry enough to have the energy to want to go back and combat them at the end."

"Why didn't you tell me that, instead of just leaving me at the hotel? Why didn't you talk to me about it?" His heart suddenly felt cold.

"When I woke up, I knew I had to go back because I hadn't done what I needed to do, which, as you know, was to find out how they worked. I also knew you wouldn't understand and that you could leave me again. When I weighed the two in my heart, I still knew I had to go back. It couldn't be our mission. It was always mine and mine alone." She paused and gently laid her hand on his arm, "I did link with my Higher Self and felt it was right to do, even though I also felt the sadness in my heart that I could again lose you."

"But going back without me gave them all the advantage. And they did have power over you. Jacques and I observed you at the window, and we saw you smiling at her. You seemed totally captivated. Even Jacques was worried by it."

"I saw you come, and I tried to distract her so that she wouldn't see you both, but of course she did. Seeing you believing I had turned negative took all my courage to stay."

How could he be sure she was telling the truth? They were sitting in the dark, and he couldn't see her eyes. He needed to see her eyes.

"I need to know everything. Let's go to my place."

They walked in silence back to the condo. He turned on the lights and turned to look at her. As always, her beauty mesmerized him; and, when she looked at him with eyes filled with warmth, he felt her love flow in waves and wrap him in its embrace. It was his Sam, but how could he be certain she wasn't just acting? How could he trust her again? Anton linked with his Higher Self and asked for help in being discerning.

They sat across from each other and he asked, "Tell me everything that happened."

"They of course appeared to be very happy that I returned."

"What did you tell them?"

"The truth is that I hadn't wanted to leave yet, and you forced me to, so I was returning to continue our conversation. Mother took me back to the sun room. She told me that she had wanted to leave Jacques when I was a young child, but taking me to America would have been an impossible thing to do; and, since she didn't want to lose me, she pretended to be happy with him in order to remain with me. She continued to see James when she could, and, finally, when I was a teenager, he convinced her to leave Jacques and marry him. She hoped I would want to go with her, but she knew that Jacques had a strong influence over me, an influence that was very negative."

"You mean she tried to make you feel that he was the negative one?"

"Oh yes! She alluded to it a lot and finally came out and said he was using the teaching for his own gain."

"How did you respond?"

"I had to say I didn't believe it, but I spoke in a way that made her think I was thinking about it. I asked her about her life with James and about their teaching. She said their teaching was very powerful and implied that their knowledge came from the true Source, very different from ours."

"I guess it is different, but was she trying to make you think it was pure?"

"Oh yes, she talked about the importance of owning your power and of using it for good purposes."

"Did she say what those purposes were?"

"To help people in their lives and to give them direction, which they could never find for themselves. In other words, it was all about control, though she didn't use that word. She basically tried to convince me that the work they did was to help those who couldn't or wouldn't help themselves. Instead of guiding students as Jacques does, it's about telling them exactly what they should or should not do. It's total control, and they make a lot of money doing it."

"How so?"

"Later, James talked about that. They both have students in high places, some in the corporate world but mainly in politics. These people have paid them a lot of money to support the work, and in turn the people are shown how to accomplish what they want. It's scary how they help politicians get elected or put through a bill that affects the economy. It's big-time stuff, Anton, and they are right in the middle of it. They use their power to control a lot of what is going on behind the scenes, and, believe me, they know many of the top people in America and in the world."

"I'm not surprised; the negative forces have influenced those areas for a long time. How did you respond?"

"I listened, mainly, and asked questions. This is what I had wanted to find out: how powerful they were and how they used that power. They were stronger than I imagined. At one point, they started to ask me what I wanted. They did it in a way that was very subtle."

"Give me an example."

"They said their Mahatma had told them that I was to succeed them, and it was important that I begin my training now. They knew I had gone far in Jacques' teaching, but they also knew he didn't teach anyone about the way in which to use energy. They said the world is controlled by energy, and I have the leadership skills to learn how to work with it. Wouldn't I want to make a difference, they asked, and help people who are the top leaders? It would give me a profession that was not only lucrative but also very meaningful. I could be the person behind some major political decisions."

"That's not too subtle."

"I'm stating it the way I see it, but the way in which they phrased it was different. They appealed to my love of working with people and to my interest in how energy really works. To begin that work in our teaching, you must be at least a fourth initiate, but they were implying that they know it all and would teach it to me now. There was no reason for me to have to wait. They also kept referring to my power, that I was born with it and needed to develop it, which is something Jacques would never do. For example, they would teach me how to control a thought and send it to others. I asked them in what way they would use this ability, and they said for various causes. If they want to influence a political bill, they send thoughts to the people working on it."

"Did they say how much they were paid for this?"

"No, but it's pretty clear that it's a lot. They kept throwing in how much more I could have with them, and because I was their child, it was my right to have it all. That's another thing they kept referring to, my being their child, implying that's why I have extraordinary gifts, but my gifts have never been fully developed. It was quite amazing how they kept playing on my ego."

"And how did you respond?"

"Always with interest and openness. I wanted them to believe that I was thinking about it and that my being quiet was the quiet of introspection. And I knew that if I was strong enough they couldn't penetrate my mind. I have Jacques' protection there."

"Weren't they at the same time sending you energy to overpower you?"

"I was prepared for that, but they didn't. I think that when they saw my receptivity, they felt they didn't need to. It would have been a bad move on their part. They knew I was advanced in the teaching and would pick up on their doing that. Also, it would make me think they wanted to control me, and they were smart enough to know that would never work with me. If I came over to their teaching, it had to be because I wanted to.

"He worked on me the most. I could understand how my mother fell for him; and, of course, with her, he added sexual energy, and he certainly has a lot of that."

"Did he try to seduce you?"

"No, not then, but I wouldn't put it past him to try if I had stayed."

"How long were you there?"

"A week. At first it was just visiting and getting to know one another. They asked a lot of questions about you."

"What did you tell them?"

"The truth: that I loved you and had left you for work, which was a mistake. I didn't talk about the real work; I said only that I was a consultant, and they seemed to know that. Then they used you in another ploy later."

"What do you mean?"

"When they were talking about power and using the power on someone's unconscious, they hinted that I could certainly get you back. I was much more powerful than you, and I could win you back and even bring you into their teaching.

"I told them you were much more powerful than they knew, and James laughed and said that might be true, but you were a novice still, and your love for me would bring you back. Is that true? Would you have accepted their teaching for me?"

Anton suddenly wondered if this was their game and she was playing it. How could he know what was true? Her story sounded sincere, but it could still be a deception. She could still be with them. "What do you think?"

"I feel you would never turn negative because of me, just as I could never be tempted by them. But they were very convincing. They picked up on your vacillating with the teaching."

"You said you left after a week? What happened?"

"When toward the end they finally started talking about the power and were more outspoken about how they used it, I knew I had found out all I needed to. I felt sorry for my mother. I could see that her weaknesses, especially for James, were what had turned her away from the path. It was sad to understand how she became lost. Her energy was strong but not strong enough to hold me.

"At that point, they tried to build a charm around my aura. It was very subtle, but I felt it and called on my Mahatma for help. He helped me, but even then, it had to be done carefully so that they wouldn't feel him. He told me to pack my bag and leave. I asked if I could confront them, and he agreed and said he would stand next to me so that they couldn't try anything. It was quite a scene."

"Could they see him?"

"Oh yes, and they both were very taken aback. I said I had pretended to go along with them to find out exactly how they used their power, so that in the future I could combat them. I told them they might have given me physical birth, but that my real birth was my spiritual one with Jacques. I said any power I learned would be through initiations because I was ready to use it positively, and I hoped to advance so that I could use my power to battle them and any other negative force that tried to control others.

"I told my mother that I felt sorry for her that she hadn't the strength to turn away from negativity. Jacques would have helped her, but she was too proud and too egotistical to seek help. Basically, I laid it all out to them and told her never to contact me again on the subtle plane. My Mahatma told me to tell them that he will stop them if they ever try it again."

"What did they say?"

"Not much. James was angry, and my mother looked sad. She had loved me as a child, you know, so I think she had a lot more at stake concerning me than he did. He never knew me, and I can't imagine him capable of any kind of love, even for her. I don't want to project regret onto her, but a couple of times, when she spoke against Jacques, it wasn't sincere; at the end, I could feel there was a sense of loss in her heart."

"She could never come back, could she?"

"No, she broke her discipleship with her teacher, and her actions have given her a huge amount of karma that will take her several lifetimes to pay off. By the way, I also told them that I wasn't interested in money or prestige — or their kind of power — that none of what they were offering could buy my soul. I looked at my mother when I said that, and she looked down. When I left, James made some sarcastic remarks and she just said Jacques had taught me well, and again I felt a sadness coming from her."

All the time Sam was telling Anton these things, her face looked serious, and she projected the energy of a warrior. He finally knew in his heart that she wasn't lying. He had planned to check it all out with Jacques and his Mahatma, but he didn't have to. There was such a strong integrity coming from her that he felt she had grown spiritually. She was no longer the same. Her eyes shone.

"Sam, have you received your fourth initiation?"

"How did you know?"

"I just felt it now. This experience took you to the next level."

"Yes, when I left, I went immediately to see Jacques. It was wonderful to see him, but all I wanted to do was meditate. I couldn't do that when I was with them. One day, Jacques and John were running errands, and I spent the whole afternoon meditating. During that time, I received the initiation from my Mahatma. Jacques knew it, too, when he saw me."

"Why didn't you call me and tell me all of this? Why did you wait to see me here in Zürich?"

"You were deep in your own process. I had to wait. I didn't want to interfere with your decision or in any way influence it. Only when you made your decision could I let you know I was here. No matter what that decision was, I planned to be with you, to still marry you if you wanted me. Jacques asked me to join you for dinner when you came with your answer, but I felt our meeting needed to be just between the two of us. I stayed in my room until you left. Then I followed you home. When you weren't in the condo, I felt you might be by the water."

"You would marry me even if I left the teaching?"

"Yes, of course. I love you. I would never leave, but that is your choice, and I would have done nothing to interfere with it. We could have still worked it out, since you have never been against the teaching."

Her smile was full. "But I am very happy you decided to stay."

"You know, I thought I saw you in my future at a class, but I thought it was my desire body. I'm so glad it wasn't!"

"Well, I certainly hope your desire body still wants me."

"It certainly does." Anton pulled her into his arms and kissed her until they were both out of breath. He picked her up and carried her into their bedroom. They made love tenderly, their bodies remembering each other in wonderful anticipation.

Later, they sat on the balcony cuddled in a blanket, again gazing at the late-night sky. The moon was full, with a white light around it and a red circle around the white.

It took Anton back to his childhood. His mother had always said a moon like that meant rain. "I wish Mother could have known we would be together again. She really loved you."

"She did know. The last time I saw her she told me not to worry; you would come around because you were deeply in love with me. I told her that I didn't know if that were true, and she said to trust her, she knew you very well."

Anton grinned. "My mother had great intuition."

"He paused and looked at her thoughtfully. 'You know, my mission was to write the book about Zarathustra, and I have done so as if Zarathustra himself were speaking. Maybe, if I grow spiritually, someday I will become Zarathustra. But, My Darling, you are Zarathustra now.'" "

Samantha tenderly turned toward him and smiled.

PART TWO

Zarathustra's Journey

PROLOGUE

In the beginning, all was energy, and what came out of this energy was form, and that form had life. Throughout the ages, the form changed and became new forms, but the energy within them stayed the same. Whether these forms were rocks, or trees, or animals, or men and women, the energy within them came from the original Source, which was given many names by many religions. Whether it was called God, or Brahman, or Zoroaster, or the sun, or any of the ancient names long forgotten, the Divine Source was within all forms of matter.

We, as individuals, feel this energy in what we term the soul; we feel it in our hearts, we feel it when we experience beauty, and we feel it most of all when we love. Men and women, no matter what their ethnic or religious background, feel this energy the same way.

Zarathustra guides others to recognize this energy within. His mission is to help them use this energy in their daily lives. Men and women at this time hide the energy by pursuing life in a fatalistic way rather than as a journey to return to the Source.

Zarathustra's journey begins with love and ends with love.

Zarathustra's journey comes at a time when all need to understand the difference between life in the physical and life in the subtle.

Zarathustra's journey acknowledges all forms of the Divine, whether it be man and woman, animal, plant, or even the water that surrounds the planet.

Zarathustra's journey encounters all kinds of prejudice, deceit, hatred, malice, and fanaticism.

If you want to make this journey, you need to open your heart, your mind, and your desire for learning more about the different planes of existence.

If you want to make this journey, you need to be willing to face change, obstacles, and being alone.

If you want to make this journey, you must become strong and courageous, loving, and caring, disciplined, and unafraid of any challenge.

Most of all, you must be willing to give up old concepts and open your heart to new ways of seeing.

Zarathustra has come again to teach about the divine energy.

CHAPTER 1

I came down into the valley planning to teach the people living there. I, Zarathus-tra, had been instructed to do so by my teacher on the subtle plane, a place where people go during the night while they are sleeping. She was not dead but very much alive, living in the physical body in a place in southern India, where I studied with her for three years. Later, when I was no longer in her physical presence, she spoke to me in her subtle body when she came to teach me.

After those years of study with her, she instructed me to leave my cottage on the mountain and carry on her work by teaching anyone who would listen. This was my mission, and I needed to try to fulfill it, even though it would be a major struggle for me to have to talk to others who are very uninformed.

How could I teach the knowledge I had been given, when the people I was to instruct lived in the mundane pleasures of distraction? How could I teach them about energy, when they misused it most of the time? How could I teach them about real love, when the love they knew was mainly sexual or based on personal desires and needs? But I couldn't refuse my teacher, knowing that she had given me this mission. Since I had to follow her instruction, I needed to let go of my sadness about leaving my home and my serene life; but I kept the hope that I would return soon.

My life had been a simple one. I lived in a secluded place in the high plains of tall mountains in the Berner Oberland, the heart of Switzerland, where I conversed with nature spirits, who became my true friends.

They were everywhere: in the flowers, the rocks, the trees, and the waters that flowed down the mountainside. Some of their names were *fairies, elves, elementals, gnomes, undines,* and *sylphs*. They were made of etheric matter, and their job was to build and maintain the plant kingdom.

My teacher taught me how to communicate properly with them and with the higher nature spirits, called *devas*, that rule this beautiful area. With sadness, I bade them goodbye for the time being and set out on my journey.

In the valley where I planned to go were several small towns. The main cities of Switzerland I would visit later, but for now, I would concentrate on smaller places until I had built a following. It was early April, and there was still snow around my home, so for the first part of my journey I traveled on snowshoes. When I reached more barren ground, I left the snowshoes and some heavier clothes and spent the night in a mountain hut that I owned and used for food storage.

The town below where I lived is called Wengen. I went there in the summers to stock up on supplies that I couldn't grow in my garden. There was a good path from my hut to town, and I rented an electric luggage cart to carry my supplies. No cars were allowed in town. The only access there from the valley below it was a mountain tram that came from Lauterbrunnen. I never had to spend the night in Wengen on my trip, as I could get there and back.

Wengen is a major tourist town. In summer there are hikers from all over the world, and in winter it is one of the main mountain ski resorts in Switzerland. In April the town isn't crowded, though, so now, when I was hoping to begin teaching people, it was easy for me to find a room at an inn. Most of the people there, at this time, were locals.

After settling my things, I went to a dining place nearby. It was late Saturday afternoon, and some men were drinking beer at a table in the corner. They all looked to be in their late twenties or early thirties. I approached them and asked if they knew of a place I could use to give some talks.

"What kind of talks?" a tall, heavyset man asked.

"My talks will center around a spiritual teaching."

"What's the teaching about?" asked another man.

"It's difficult to give a brief explanation of it. Basically, it helps people find wisdom within themselves and guides them to explore hidden planes of existence. It is an ancient teaching that has been given to initiates throughout the ages, and now it is time for people to learn more about it."

"This sounds religious. Are you a minister?" A fair-haired man leaned forward with penetrating blue eyes.

"No, it is not a religion, but all the esoteric branches of all religions understand it. I don't call myself a minister, but I am a guide. In the East, I would be called a guru; in the West, a teacher whose mission it is to give out this most sacred knowledge."

A short, stocky man laughed. "Well, it sounds very weird to me. I'm a good Protestant. That's all I need, and the only hidden plane I care about is going to heaven."

"Keep drinking this and maybe you'll find yourself heading in the opposite direction." The blond man raised his beer to his friend. He then asked me, "All right, Sir, you say you want to teach us, but I want to know, Why here? Surely you can find people in the big cities who would be more interested in your strange notions than in this small town. If they are Catholics, people here will laugh at your words and think listening to them would be a sin. Catholics aren't supposed to attend religious talks unless they're given by priests. And the Protestants here are also very religious and would find your ideas unbelievable."

"There are others here who are not that religious." I looked at the blond man. "Karl, you say you are Catholic, but when was the last time you went to church? I think it was two months ago, for your sister's baby's christening."

Karl was startled. "How did you know that? And how do you know my name? Who told you?"

"I came into this town an hour ago from my home in the mountain, but I know all about you."

I looked at the stocky man. "Your name is Gus, and you have been in love with Karl's sister most of your life. It broke your heart when she married someone else." Gus's face turned into a white cloud of moving emotions.

"And you, Lucas," I said, addressing the tall man, who suddenly looked frightened. "You will finish college next year. It's taken you a long time because you support your mother and young siblings. You have the heart to learn my teaching."

"I don't want to learn your teaching. You're too strange. How did you know those things about me?"

"My teaching develops these skills."

Karl said, "That's cool."

"Can you help me find a hall? Not a big one. Just big enough for twenty to thirty people?"

"How much can you spend?"

"Very little. I don't have much money."

"Well, maybe we can arrange that people pay after your talk. Then you will have some money."

"I don't charge for my talks."

"What do you mean, you don't charge? That's nuts. You have to live," Lucas said.

"I can't charge for wisdom coming from above. That is the law."

"Crazy law. Can you take donations? That leaves it open," Gus suggested.

I thought for a minute. "Yes, it's okay to have a donation box. That could maybe cover a rental cost and help toward my room expenses."

The next couple of days were spent preparing for my lecture. Karl knew all the hotels in town because he delivered food to their kitchens. He found me a meeting room in a hotel called the Silberhorn. The hotel was large and very elegant, built in the Victorian style, and was a few stories high. It had several restaurants and bars and other facilities, as well as a conference room. The room would hold thirty to forty people, which was perfect. I had hoped to find a room in a smaller hotel, but the only smaller one available was a very Christian hotel, which wouldn't consider my lecturing there. The Silberhorn was much too expensive, but fortunately, because Karl knew the owner, he persuaded him to reduce the fee for me because we were in the off-season.

The first talk was to be in a week's time, so there was much to do. I dined with Gus, Karl, and Lucas several times, and they kindly offered to help. They made posters, called friends, sent out emails, and promoted my talk around town. When they told people how we had met and what I had said to them, many were interested. Most were curious, and since there was no fee, some decided to come and check it out.

After most of the work was done, I spent the rest of the week meditating and going for long walks along the Lauterbrunnen rift, which had spectacular views of the Jungfrau summit in the Bernese Alps, with its steep wall of snow that dominated the valleys and towns below. There were several well-maintained paths that brought me to panoramic views of the majestic mountain ranges, reminiscent of the views I had at home. At dusk, I would sit on a bench and watch the moving clouds blanket the sleeping mountains and think about the coming lecture.

Experiencing the beauty of these mountains calmed my nervousness about my talk. This was to be the first one I had ever given, and even though I was prepared and knew my teacher would overshadow me, it still felt very stressful.

The plan to start small was a good one. If I could only stay in these mountain villages, I wouldn't feel such a loss. It was the large cities I dreaded the most. I had lived as a hermit for seven years. At times, I found conversing even with the few men who helped me difficult to do.

I had prepared my teaching plan previously, and I would follow the outline unless something happened to make me change it.

My wardrobe was limited and consisted mainly of rustic clothing, but in Zürich the year before, I had bought one nice suit and tie in anticipation of my journey. I didn't want to give the impression that I was a hippy or some mad prophet, so I chose the clothing with care, finally buying a navy-blue suit with a white shirt and light blue tie that matched my eyes. At home, I hadn't bothered to shave but had a full brown beard and long, wavy hair. I knew that would look too preachy now, so I shaved it off and had my hair cut short.

When I was in my twenties, my friends thought I was a dashing, handsome man; now that I am thirty-eight, my face has settled into a maturity born from my lifestyle these past years that has added an inner depth to my character. In my youth, I was a carefree cub, but now I am a solemn lion.

I would still be considered a good-looking man, as I am six feet tall, muscular, and trim. Living on the mountain, having to fend for myself, has kept me fit through the years. In Wengen, I noticed some flattering attention by women I passed on the streets. Having enjoyed dating extensively in my younger years, I knew I would need to be careful not to be tempted now. I had chosen to be celibate in recent years — not because my teacher instructed me to do so, but rather because I'd discovered that in the past, sex had distracted me from my spiritual path.

The night of the lecture was a clear one, making the walk to the hotel easy because the moon was nearly full. I stopped for a minute before going in, closed my eyes, took some deep breaths, and linked with my teacher, asking her to be there to guide me.

I arrived at the hall early to observe the auras of the people as they entered. The aura is an energy field that surrounds the body. Of the people arriving, some had auras that were colorful and pure. Others had dark and muddy-colored auras, and I saw that a couple of the older people were ill, as indicated by the black spots in their auras next to the physical area where the sickness dwelled. Auras are also a good indicator of thoughts and feelings. If the thoughts and feelings of a person were good ones, then the aura color was clear and brilliant, but if a person was negative, the aura was dark. If a person was spiritually advanced, the aura was multicolored, lovely to see.

I have been clairvoyant most of my life, beginning in childhood. That was the first time I saw nature spirits and tried talking to them. I never told anyone because I instinctively knew others would think there was something mentally wrong with me.

The room filled up quickly. I estimated that there were around thirty-five people present; more than I expected. It was in a back section of the hotel and was well decorated with good, cloth folding chairs, a lectern, and, fortunately, some original paintings on the walls, done by a talented local artist. They were mostly scenes of the mountains, and seeing them made me feel at ease.

I stood in front of the lectern and just looked at the people who had come. I must have stood there for a while because they started getting restless, but I continued to look at them, and as I did so I felt strong love in my heart for all of them. Only then did I leave the lectern and take a chair to sit down closer to them. I spoke about inner wisdom.

Finding God Within

"My mission is to teach you how to find the vast sources of wisdom that are available to you. You are men and women mostly living what I would call a mundane existence, having no awareness of who you really are. You are born, you live, get married, have children, work, love, and die without knowing who you really are.

"Some of you believe in God, a celestial being who watches over you, but how many of you know anything at all about this Divine Force? Jesus taught that the spirit of God is in each person. He died, and appeared to his disciples after death, to prove that everyone has the same potential. The church has made him into a God, when actually he was a man who discovered that he was simply part of the Divine, as is each of us.

"You . . ." and I pointed gently to a woman in front, "You are God, and you . . ." as I pointed to a man next to her, "You are God. We all have the Divine Spirit within, but how many of you believe this enough to find it? You may say you pray to God, particularly when you seek help for something, but when you pray to God, you see the Divine up in the heavens and forget that God is much closer. God's spirit is within every one of you. You may ask, 'But how can I pray to myself?' And I would say: you don't pray; you listen and find God's wisdom is there."

A man in the rear of the room raised his hand, and I asked, "Otto, what is your question?"

The audience stirred when I called him by name.

"Sir, you say God is within each of us, but if that is true why don't I feel it? I am a sinful man, and if God were in me I wouldn't be this way."

"We all have goodness and evil within us. The battle between these two forces has taken place throughout our many lives. The more you seek the God within, the stronger will be your earthly desires. The path of awakening is a long and difficult one. We all must walk in Jesus's footsteps. We all must face our true selves and transform our lower nature into the light. All the great prophets have done this. They are our guides on the path: whether it be Buddha, Moses, Jesus, or Mohammad, their mission was to tell all of us that we, too, would follow someday, whether it is in this life or another."

I paused to look at my audience and saw that most were astounded and bewildered by what I was saying, but a few looked engaged in their interest.

I continued, "When you begin the spiritual journey, you will be embarking on a difficult path, a path that leads you to the Source but also makes you look at every aspect of yourself. You will need to recognize your inner demons and face them. You will have to learn the true meaning of love and compassion. You will have to struggle with earthly desires and earthly demands. You will need to find the God within, and when you touch upon it there will be no turning back. Once you have made the choice to walk the path, you will find yourself alone. Your family, your friends — all those you love — may surround you and share your days, but you will feel alone, and in this feeling you will want either to give up or try harder. Giving up releases the tension but leaves you feeling full of sorrow."

Another man raised his hand. "Sir, why would I want to start this path in the first place? I'm content with my life. Why make waves when I don't have to?" Others nodded their heads.

"Why do you eat? Why do you sleep?" I asked kindly. "You have to eat to live; you have to sleep to rest your body. It is the same on the spiritual path. How many lives can you live without needing the God within? How many times can you feel the call to find your true Self? Some of you will find that your mundane life is enough. Others may study these wisdoms and even be a little interested, while still others— only a handful—will feel in their hearts that I speak the truth and will experience a longing to seek more. That is the way for all humankind. My mission is simply to teach the truth. Each person can decide for themselves into which category they fit. It is always an individual quest. No teacher can do it for you. You must walk this path alone — with guidance, but still alone."

I stood up and strode up and down in the front of the room.

"The higher wisdom does not seek you out. The God within you does not seek you out. No higher force seeks you out. It is always up to you to do the seeking, and in that striving energy you will be helped. This is the law. You must take the first step. You must desire wisdom. You must seek guidance from a teacher."

A red-headed woman spoke up, "Are you such a teacher?"

I smiled at her in recognition. "Yes, Dorina, I am a teacher, and there are many teachers. There is an old saying: 'When you are ready, the teacher will appear.' Again, if your heart longs for a teacher, the teacher with whom you are meant to study will appear; you will find him or her. It is destined.

"I want to speak more about God and the concept of God. The God that you envision, a being that sits in heaven, does not exist. There is no God that resembles humankind. Human beings want to anthropomorphize God, make God into a Divine Being. So, I tell you: there is no such God. All esoteric teachings think of this God concept as a force of energy. It is beyond explaining, beyond human understanding. It is energy that is neither masculine nor feminine but pure energy. Your seed of the spirit is pure energy. So, let us forget God the man and talk about the source of wisdom within."

When I said this, I could hear some mumbles of discontent and saw a couple get up and leave. Others soon followed. One of them called out, "This is blasphemous."

Dorina raised her hand. "Where did you learn this, and how do we know if what you say is true or false?"

"My knowledge comes from my teacher." I thought for a moment. "You do not have to believe me. All I ask is for you to listen to me, and then take what I have said and put it into your heart. Your heart will tell you if it is true or not: it will respond warmly, or it will feel withdrawn."

I continued, "My lesson for today is about the God within. The God I speak of is pure energy, not a man sitting on a throne in heaven judging us. The God I speak of has no name, even though we put names on it. The Judeo-Christian image of God does not exist. There are higher beings who are mistaken for God. There are also vast storehouses of wisdom to which we have access. Are there any more questions?"

I answered questions and spoke for an hour, and when I returned to my room at the inn, I laid down to rest. I was exhausted. After having lived in the mountains for so many years, the energy of the group felt very disturbing to me. I decided I needed to protect my aura better. For the next session, I would remember to use a method taught to me by my teacher. I would put an imaginary glass bell around me with an open "window" over my heart area. This is a method to protect the aura from experiencing the various vibrations of others, and the open window over the heart allows one to send heart energy to people in the audience.

I linked with my teacher, thanked her, and went to sleep.

CHAPTER 2

The next morning, I felt tired and somewhat agonized. Had I done a good job last night? Did they understand me? Could I reach them better? I was a man of the mountains; how could I know what they would accept or reject? How could I reach them in their lives when I had never lived as they did?

When I meditated, my teacher appeared to me. She was dressed in a blue sari that fell lightly over her head and reflected highlights in her long black hair. Her dark eyes looked at me with love and seriousness. I felt enormous relief when I saw her.

She said, "Stop listening to them. Don't you know that they want to dissuade you from doing the teaching?" Then she disappeared, and I recognized my weakness in having listened to the negative forces in the first place.

I ate my breakfast slowly in the inn dining room, trying to decide what I needed to do next. Was it worthwhile to stay here and try to do another lecture tonight? I had meant to ask the audience if they would like me to stay, but I had forgotten, and now it probably was too late to set it up. I pondered the oversight and realized that my concentration had been too involved with their reactions rather than with the follow up and follow through. In future lectures, I would plan that part more carefully.

There was an elderly couple sitting next to me, and I noticed they took turns staring at me. Finally, the man said, "You are the preacher from last night."

"Yes."

"What are you going to speak about tonight?"

"I hadn't planned anything. What do you mean?"

"Well, your friends who organized the event told us all to come back tonight at the same time. You will be there, won't you?"

I felt relieved. "Of course, I'll be there."

The door opened, and Gus and Lucas came in. They sat down at the table and ordered coffee.

"Father," Gus said, "we hope you will stay a while and continue your lessons."

"I will be glad to, but maybe it would be all right to do an afternoon session out in a meadow. The hall is expensive, and what we collected last night in donations just paid for that and a couple of nights for me to stay here at the inn."

"Don't worry. It's taken care of. The owner has donated the hall for your use as long as you want it. It took a little twisting, but he agreed." Gus winked at his companion.

"What do you mean, 'twisting'?"

"Never you mind, Father, it's okay."

"First of all, please don't call me 'Father.' I am not a priest, and secondly, I don't want you to do things that are in any way wrong. So, what do you mean, 'twisting'?"

Gus looked downward. "Well, we kind of reminded him of his sins. You see, Father, he got a girl pregnant and wouldn't marry her, so we told him this would be a good deed that would help him to get to heaven."

"Well, it may not take him to heaven, but it *will* be considered a good deed according to the law of karma. You need to tell him that. And if he still agrees to offer the conference room, then I certainly will accept his offer."

"I'm sure he'll agree," Lucas answered. "He did say that he wanted to hear you talk again."

"Good, then let's plan for another teaching this evening, and possibly more after that if the group wants."

That evening the hall was full. Word had gotten around, and now many were coming out of curiosity. I noticed two priests sitting in the back and thought that maybe they would challenge me. I was right about that.

The Source of Wisdom

"All of you believe in the Divine unless you are an atheist. Even an atheist must believe in something or someone, even if it's simply in his or her own self. Yesterday, I talked about everyone having God — or the Divine, or what is called the Higher Self — within. This Self is connected to Divine Wisdom and can access this treasure at any time. Let's be clear about what I mean by 'Divine Wisdom.' "

I held up a stone in my hand. "This stone is made of millions of particles, and each particle is unique unto itself; yet together they form a solid piece of matter. This solid piece of matter called *stone* is part of a larger rock formation and has broken away from it into this smaller piece. You can equate Divine Wisdom to the mountain. The mountain contains many rock formations and plant life. It holds the knowledge of its origins in its formations. It is ancient and has had many stories attached to its passage of time. You are like the stone. The knowledge you contain comes from a Higher Source, and even though you are now a separate piece, like this small stone, you can relate back and understand all that is contained in the Source, which I call 'God Consciousness' and most of you call 'God.'

"The passage of time through the ages that the stone went through, from being part of a rock formation on the mountain to this individual rock, correlates to your passage from the smallest particles of matter to being a human being, to the evolution of your individuality, to where you are today.

"Because you have this divine spark within you, you can reach up to the Source and bring down wisdom that you have not accessed since you separated from it."

Dorina raised her hand and asked, "How can I do that?"

"A good question, one that requires a deeper understanding of who you are and what your personal passage has been. Always, the conduit to Higher Wisdom comes through your Higher Self, that part of the Divine within you. To access it takes time and concentration and, most of all, the desire to do that. That's why it is different for each person.

"For example," I said, pointing to a young woman seated in the last seat in the back holding a small child. "Louise, you have little time to concentrate on your inner Self or to meditate, even though you desire to know more about the Divine. Your children take up all your time.

"But you, Dorina" — and I turned toward her — "Your children are grown, and you have more time to devote to meditation practices and to experiment with contacting the Divine within. That doesn't mean, Louise, you can't begin the process now, and when you have extra time, devote that time to developing your ability.

"But let's return to what I mean about Divine Wisdom. When I use the word *wisdom*, what does it mean to you?" And with this question, I pointed to the younger priest.

He stood up. "It means God. Only God has wisdom and is all-knowing and omnipotent."

"But if you have God within, how do you think that manifests?"

"I don't claim to have God within me, but I do his work by practicing my devotions and helping those people who come to me to do the same. What you are saying has no humility in it. Your claims are not based on any known doctrines."

"What I claim is based on my inner experience. No doctrine can change or enhance that. No doctrine can give me wisdom; no doctrine can help anyone find the beauty of his or her Divine Spirit. Only the individual can claim that for him- or herself."

The elderly priest stood up and addressed the audience. "I see this man is an unbeliever. Those of you who are good Christians — why are you listening to him?"

I responded, "A good Christian needs to have an open heart and listen to every individual. I have not spoken against Jesus. He found the wisdom I am speaking about and is a good example of what I am saying. The esoteric priests in your faith would understand me, but what I am stating is not part of the exoteric doctrine, which is very limited, that is provided to the public more broadly. I am asking you to listen to me, put what I say in your hearts, and feel if it is true."

I stared at the young priest and saw him nod his head and sit down. "Each person's wisdom is defined by their culture, their family, and, most of all, by what their religion teaches them. All these influences can be helpful for living daily life and being a good person, but I am asking you to want more than that. It is your right to have wisdom. It is your right to demand higher knowledge; to go beyond what you are taught and tap into the higher realms where beauty and wisdom abide."

I could see some eyes questioning me. "Erik, your wisdom is to take care of your wife and family, and to be there for a neighbor who needs help, and that is good. Your wisdom is to say your prayers, and to go to church, and to live a good, worthwhile life."

I turned to another man. "Adler, your wisdom is to work but spend your free time having fun. No marriage for you. You like to spend time with lots of women and drink lots of beer."

Some people laughed at this.

I looked at a woman in a wheelchair. "Lois, your wisdom is to deal with your pain, and try not to complain too much, and wait to die."

I again held up the stone. "This stone's wisdom is to stay solid. That flower's wisdom is to bloom, and be beautiful, and to die. But each person's wisdom goes far beyond all that has been said. It is infinite. How many of you have looked within to find out about the universe? How many of you have looked within to discover hidden realms that are not visible to your eyes? How many of you have looked within to see Higher Beings? How many of you have looked within and heard music coming from the other planets? How many of you have looked within and had visions of beautiful places? How many of you have looked within and seen the future?"

I stopped, as there were rumblings in the room.

The older priest stood up again. "Don't you see, people, he is telling you false things. Do not listen to him. He is evil."

Some people stood up to leave.

"What have I said that was evil? What have I said that can harm you? I only ask that you seek more and desire more knowledge. That's what Jesus did. He came to teach from the heart about love — divine love — and knowledge; and he came to tell all of you that life is everlasting and that the Divine Spirit is within each and every person."

"No, only Jesus was the son of God," an older lady protested.

"That's what the church teaches, but what Jesus really said was that God was within him, and you, and every living creature."

"That's blasphemy!" And a man stood up and shook a fist at me.

Everyone started to talk. I held my hands up and prayed that calming energy would flow through them to the crowd. It took a few minutes, but the room fell silent. Many had left, but the priests remained.

"Those of you who have felt in your hearts that something I've said could be true, please listen. Those of you who feel that all I have said is lies, please feel free to leave." And I looked at the priests to respond.

Several more people rose from their seats and left, leaving around seventeen people still seated. The priests also remained, and I addressed them.

"Fathers, since you have stayed, then you also must have felt I speak the truth?"

"No, Sir, you do not speak the truth. We remain to protect these naïve people." And the priest pointed to the other people around him.

"They need no protection from me or anyone," I said. "They have minds and hearts of their own and can judge the truth accordingly."

The priest said, "No, they are the unbelievers and need protection from slanderers."

This caused a stir among the people. One man spoke up. "Father, I will not stand for your insults. We have a right to listen to all beliefs and question them. He's right, you don't belong here if you don't have open minds."

A woman agreed. "I'm a good Catholic, but the church can sometimes be limiting. I go to church not because of what you dictate but because I love Jesus. This man loves him, too; I feel that coming from him, and so I will listen."

The old priest stood up. "So be it. Come, Heinz." And he grabbed the younger priest's arm, pulling him up. The younger priest whispered to him and sat back down as the older priest, mumbling all kinds of things, left the room.

I looked at Heinz and knew he had advised the other priest that he would remain to find out more of what I was preaching, and I also knew his heart had responded to me and needed to know more.

I held up the stone again. "Just as you see this stone in its solid form, there are many other forms within it that you can't see. For example, you know your body contains bones and nerves and organs, which you can't see because they are hidden under your skin. The same is true of the finite world we are in. We see the physical dimensions of this world, and, because we are physical, it feels good to be here. But there are other worlds, or what are called *planes*, around us that we cannot see in this physical body. If you look at the air under a microscope, you will see particles floating in it. The air itself is full of objects invisible to the eye, but if you used your inner eye, you could easily see those objects without needing a microscope."

"Are you talking about someone who is clairvoyant?" someone in the back asked.

"Yes, I am. How many of you have heard the terms *clairvoyant* or *clairaudient*?"

A few people raised their hands.

I started to explain the terms, but a woman interrupted me and said, "I have a friend who is psychic and talks to a guide from those planes you are talking about."

"Before I talk about psychics, let me explain more about these other worlds I have mentioned. There are seven other realms of existence in what is called the subtle world. At this time, we can only access two of these worlds. One is called the *astral plane*, and the other the *mental plane*. Each one of these planes has seven parts, starting at the bottom or lower and ascending to the higher. People can travel to these planes during sleep or during meditation. Most people travel to the lower plane in its various levels, but some have the ability to travel to the higher astral levels and the mental plane; those people are called the adepts or higher initiates. When someone is psychic, that person is only seeing or hearing those beings on the lower astral plane, and those beings deceive and are harmful. They do not come from the higher levels."

"But my friend has told me things that are true and have been helpful," the woman protested.

"Yes, they can do that. They sound wonderful and slowly beguile people into believing them. Once a person is caught in their web, they can then express untruths that distort the universal truths and laws. They want to convince as many people as possible that they are the Higher Beings and in so doing can eventually insert untruths in what seems true."

I sighed. "It's sad for these psychics or mediums, as their ability to ascend to the higher levels is inhibited."

"But how do you know the psychic isn't on the higher levels?" another woman asked.

"Only an initiate, with a teacher who is guiding him or her, can develop clairaudience and listen to those beings from the higher planes, or develop clairvoyance and see those beings. Someone who hasn't the guidance, or the initiation and protection of the teacher, will channel these lower beings. Channeling always comes from those lower realms, and I advise anyone that does so to stop, because it will close down the higher chakras, or centers."

"I for one don't understand what you are talking about," a man spoke up.
Other people agreed.

"All right, let me draw it for you." I had a big pad ready and drew a chart.
"The first, at the bottom, is the world we live in: the physical plane.
"The others are in what is called the *subtle world*, and they are the following:
"The second is the lower astral plane, where these impersonators dwell.
"The third is the higher astral plane, which is where most people go.
"The fourth is the mental plane, and you have to be a High Being, or what is called a Higher Initiate, to go there.
"The fifth is the Buddhic plane.
"The sixth is the nirvanic plane.
"And the seventh is an unknown plane.
"The last three are planes we cannot enter yet.
"The physical plane you know. It is what we as human beings live in daily. All

these other planes are unseen to our physical self or body. But just as there are other worlds and planes that we can't see, we also can develop another body that can travel into them. We will simply call this our subtle body, and an initiate who is studying with a teacher can develop the subtle body so that it can go to these higher levels. It is the right of all human beings to do this someday, because it is part of the evolutionary plan on Earth."

"How do you know this?" Heinz asked.

"The knowledge comes down through the line of teachers in the esoteric tradition, and I myself have traveled to some of these planes and have experienced what they are like."

Dorina then offered, "I had a dream that I will never forget. It was incredible. I was in a different country, and I was walking through a garden with flowers that were huge, almost double the size of ours, and the colors were so vivid it was like looking through stained-glass windows. There was a man there." She stopped abruptly and looked at me with an awareness that seemed to have suddenly dawned on her. "I think it might have been you," she said softly and slowly, and covered her mouth with her hand for a moment before continuing. "The man talked to me about the flowers there. I couldn't remember all that he said, but it was beautiful. Was that on one of the planes you are talking about?"

"Yes, when you dream in full color you are on the higher astral plane. If a dream is in black and white, it is a psychological dream, in which you are working through some psychological things, and not on another plane but mainly in your mind. The colored dreams one tends to remember because they are so beautiful; and, yes, all objects seen in these dreams look double in size, especially the plant life."

"I've seen a ghost," Gus then blurted out. "I know that was real. Where would they live?"

"A ghost is someone who has died suddenly and often doesn't know she or he is dead. Or a person might die and stay close to Earth to wait for a loved one to pass over to the other side. They are in the lower astral plane.

"I met a ghost myself years ago when I was staying at an old inn by a lake. It was a woman who came into my bedroom and walked out. I spoke to the owner, who said that the ghost had been there for a long time and that several guests had seen it. The next night, I contacted her and asked why she was there. She said there had been a fire, and she was looking for her baby. She was desperate to find her baby. When I explained that she was dead and so was her baby, she didn't believe me; so, I took her out of the inn and showed her the automobiles parked there. She didn't know what they were because she had been driven there in a horse and buggy. I told her the year and that these were new ways to travel. Only when she saw a car drive up did she believe me, and then I helped her to go on to a higher plane."

A few more people in the audience told similar stories of ghost encounters. As it was getting late, I ended the meeting, inviting everyone to come back for another lecture in two evenings.

Heinz, the priest, stayed on and waited to talk to me. "Sir, I believe in some of what you are saying; but these people are not ready to hear esoteric material. Don't you realize that?"

"Yes," I replied, "that is why more than half of them have left. Those who stayed are ready, if only for a little knowledge. There is an old saying: 'Some touch the hem of the robe to stay a while and not continue, but then they return in the next life to stay a little while longer.' Now is the age when more people need to touch the hem."

He nodded his head and left.

CHAPTER 3

The next day I had breakfast with Lucas before his classes started. I had found a charming café down the street from the hotel that had tables far enough apart for privacy. The food was good and inexpensive. Enough money had been collected for me to stay a few more days, so I planned to have two more lectures, one the next evening and the second one two days later. The hall was still available for our use, free of charge, so that reduced expenses. I was hoping to leave in a week to go to Meiringen, a town similar in size.

Lucas asked, "Teacher, when you leave what will happen to us?"

"What do you mean?"

"Well, you come and teach things that no one has ever heard before. The philosophers I've read don't talk about these things. I want to know more, but I can't leave my family and school right now; otherwise, I would go with you. You've awakened our curiosity, and now you say you are leaving. That's not the right thing to do."

His words stunned my heart, and I realized he was correct. I had planned this trip badly, not even thinking about the outcome. What about those people who wanted to learn more, some of whom I had already recognized as my students? How could I desert them when they had just become interested? Lucas was one of them, and I knew that if he could leave his family, he would; but that wouldn't be responsible and would cause difficult karma. And Dorina was married and also had children. These students could not follow me on my trip.

"Your point is well taken, Lucas. I need to meditate on this."

"If it's about money, we can find you a place to stay, and we can feed you." Lucas looked eager now.

"That would be good, but let me tell you my answer tomorrow."

That afternoon I took a walk in the countryside surrounding the town. It was a lovely day: the sun was shining, and the mountains stood like sentinels watching the silent awakening of the grasses and budding of its trees. The farms outside of town had open fields for grazing and rows of newly plowed dirt being prepared for spring planting. I found few people around, just a couple of young children playing in a yard and a woman hanging up laundry on a line.

A dog came bounding out of a field, wanting to be patted, and, after I performed this loving task, he accompanied me down the road. I told him to go home, but he ignored my command and looked at me dolefully, asking to come just for a while.

I found a hiking trail that climbed slowly into the hills, and as the two of us walked together I thought about making a plan. A student wanted to be near me but couldn't. A dog wanted to walk with me even if just for a little while. A student wanted to hear more than four lectures and was genuinely interested in the teaching. The dog's sole purpose in life was to protect and love; the student didn't know what to do next and needed direction from me. The dog knew he had to go home eventually. These were the realities of my situation. To come and lecture and leave and expect followers was not realistic. To come and lecture and *not* expect followers had no purpose. The teaching would be lost because there was no plan to give it a foundation.

I sat down against a tree, and the dog curled up by my side. When I meditated, I saw students, at least three: Lucas, Dorina, and Karl. They looked frightened, and they were hugging each other. I saw that I was leaving the dog, and then he sat down and watched me continue out of town.

I shook my head and prayed to my teacher. What should I do? My intention was to go to as many towns and cities as possible and to bring this teaching to many, not just a few. These were modern times. I couldn't be a wandering monk with followers leaving their lives and families to be with me. This teaching wasn't for ascetics. It was for people living in the world, having to face the challenges of everyday life and still find the God within. This was the teaching of today, not yesterday. It also wasn't for monks living in ashrams who spent all their time meditating. To reach God, one had to be in the world. One had to face the temptations of the world, the relationships that caused karma, and the work in the world that needed to be accomplished. This teaching didn't take people away from the responsibilities they need to encounter. That's why it was a difficult teaching.

The followers needed to live and be in the world but not part of it. They needed to love and have families but not be attached to them. They needed to work, and play, and feel compassion, but not in a convent or monastery. Yet I had planned this trip as if I were living in older times, expecting my students to come with me. What a paradox! I was not following my own teaching.

I had a strong urge to give up then, to return to the mountains and live my secluded life and ask my teacher to give this task to another disciple. It was too hard for me to relate to these people, to know how to teach them correctly when I, myself, had left the world all these past years.

My meditation continued to take a negative turn. I really wanted to get my belongings and leave. The urge was so strong that I even began walking back to my hotel to carry it through. Halfway back on the road I saw Dorina. She ran toward me and threw her arms around me in a big hug and said, "I'm so happy you're my teacher!" Then, obviously embarrassed, she continued running and was soon out of sight.

That stopped me, and I felt once again the beauty of my mission. I can make this work, I determined, but I will just have to change my plans a little.

Back at the hotel, I took out my notebook and the schedule I had so carefully planned before leaving home. Instead of going from town to town to spend only a few days in each, I changed the route and adjusted the time to spend at least two weeks in every town and more in the cities. Then I would return to all those places I had been and again teach and work with students for another two or three weeks. I could see that this would be an involved process and that I would need rest along the way. I saw that I could return to my home for the summer and then set out again to the same places, maybe adding a town or a city with each trip.

I had hoped to complete my mission to disseminate the teaching in just a year or two, but now I realized that it would be ongoing. When I meditated on this, I saw my home in the mountains and other buildings surrounding it. Students lived there when they came to visit me in the summer. They would stay for short vacations or even long ones.

Okay, I sighed, I will be such a teacher. But will I ever have alone time again, I wondered? Those years of solitude felt far away now, and even though the ascetic in me longed to have them back, I knew I had to follow my own teaching and surround myself with people.

At the next lecture, there were fewer people, only twenty, but I could see that those twenty were truly interested in what I was teaching. Soon it would be just a handful, and then we could meet in someone's home. I saw some familiar faces in the group and some new ones. The young priest was there, maybe to check on me, or maybe not.

The Spiritual Journey

"Those of you who want to learn more, who are willing to strive and are able to study this teaching, will be what is called a neophyte on the path. The path or road is one that every student must travel. It is a path that takes you directly to God. But it is a journey that will be the most difficult one you have ever made.

"First, let's look at what this journey is about. To find the God within, you must throw away a lot of baggage that you have collected throughout your life and even throughout many lives. It is difficult to observe yourself without attachments, without emotions, and without desires. To achieve this, you must first know yourself. I have spoken about finding the inner state of Being, but when I say you must first know yourself, I am referring to all your characteristics, both negative and positive. Psychologically, you must delve into the subconscious and investigate those areas that resist your moving forward.

"Some of you may have to do this inner work with the help of a professional therapist. Fortunately, in our modern world we have people with these skills who can help you. Some of the baggage you need to drop relates to the core beliefs and conditioning you learned in your childhood, and often this baggage is the heaviest to carry and the hardest to let go.

"Much of this baggage contains what I call core beliefs, which are ingrained in your psyche and cause you to do things and think about things in ways that prevent you from being successful, whether it is in your vocation, in your relationships, or in your spiritual life. These beliefs come from childhood and sometimes have been carried over from past lives. For example, if you have a core belief that you will never be successful in life because you aren't good enough, then this belief will block your progress on the path until you can let go of it. A student cannot achieve God Consciousness with such feelings.

"You may think that you understand yourself. But there is no one here who truly does. When you walk the path, you will encounter aspects of yourself that have been hidden, and they will surprise you when they are revealed."

Heinz raised his hand. "If you know so much, why can't you just tell me and the others what those aspects are?"

A couple of the others mumbled in agreement.

"I can do that, but it would not be right. Each person walks the path with his or her own baggage. Learning what is in that baggage is part of the journey. The student must be ready to look at the baggage. If I should instead tell the student what is there, then the student would not have the experience of probing deep within for that information, which is where true learning and inner transformation occurs. Once the baggage is seen, though, I can guide the student in how to handle it. A teacher's role is to guide, not to control or command. A teacher's job is to encourage students to reach their own Higher Selves and, in so doing, go through an inner transformation."

"When you say, 'inner transformation,' what do you mean?" Dorina asked.

"When you start to discover your own baggage, some of it will be from your lower nature. It will try to block you on the path, and many times a student will turn back and stop the journey as a result. It is up to you to look at the negative qualities that suddenly arise within you and to see them in an objective manner, or what I call a dis-identified manner — not with judgment or emotion, but with understanding — and then actively use your will to transform them. To achieve God Consciousness, the lower nature has to be transmuted into the higher nature or the Higher Self."

"That must take a long time. If I look at my lower nature, I suspect it will take years just to conquer one bad habit. And you say it's difficult. It sounds more like it's impossible!" Gus remarked.

Some laughed, but others looked concerned.

"My teacher used to say, 'Nothing is impossible. The impossible only takes a little longer.' And that's true. You may think it's impossible, and such thoughts will certainly be sent to you by your lower nature, but it can be done. It's step by step. The key is to observe yourself and to do so without self-criticism. No one is perfect; even the high initiates say they are not perfect. Transformation is about developing the ability to be in the Higher Self so that it is stronger in you than your lower nature is. Everyone in this room can do that. For some it may be easier because they have had recent spiritual lives, but even they can become stuck on the path if they become caught in the desire body and make difficult karma for themselves."

"But it seems there is so much to learn and to do on your path. I'm a busy man, I don't have that kind of time," said a man in his thirties.

Again, there were sounds of agreement from the group.

"Fredrick, everyone is busy, that is true in our modern world, yet everyone has an hour or two a day that can be used for this work. Even one hour of time begins the journey. Once you start the process you will find the time, because it will bring you moments of joy. Some of you have more time and others less, but in the end, each person's journey will bring them to the same goal. It's how you spend the time that is important. A person can read and study for several hours a day and go out with friends and not practice any of what she or he has read. Another person may spend only an hour but put all that was learned into practice and therefore move faster on the path."

"That makes sense. It's like going to church and confession and then the next day doing the same thing you confessed about again. I always felt that was hypocritical," an elegant older woman said.

"Exactly. No amount of reading and meditating will help people who cannot see how their lower nature controls them. This is what makes the path difficult.

"When a person starts a spiritual journey, the person has to have an open heart and mind as to what will be revealed. The barriers and obstacles can stop the student from progressing on the path. These obstacles, or what I prefer to call 'challenges,' can even cause someone to leave the teaching, when in reality the challenge can easily be overcome. I'm going to tell you a true story that illustrates this:

"Alfred and Maria lived together in the suburbs of Zürich. They were not married. Alfred was in a spiritual teaching, but Maria was not in the least bit interested in his beliefs. Consequently, Alfred never spoke to her about any of his practices. Everything else in their relationship was going well; and, in fact, they were even talking about getting married and having children.

"One day, Alfred asked his teacher if he approved of his marrying Maria, and his teacher said only if Maria would let him be in charge of their children's religious upbringing. When Alfred asked Maria about this, she became very angry and said that she didn't care what he believed in, but she did care about her children's beliefs. She would never allow them to follow their father's odd religious practices. He was shocked that she was so adamant about it, because she wasn't religious and even considered herself an agnostic. Arguments ensued, and they could not come to any resolution and finally parted ways.

"Alfred was very upset at the outcome, as he truly loved Maria and felt a lot of anguish over losing her. He again went to his teacher and asked him if in any way it would be possible that his children not be taught his beliefs. When they grew up, he certainly could talk to them, and they could decide for themselves. That way, perhaps he could convince Maria to come back to him. The teacher replied that no, there would still be problems. Once they were married, Maria would start to object to him being in the teaching.

"Alfred accepted this conclusion for a while, but then Maria approached him and pretty much said the same thing he'd said: let the children decide when they were older if they wanted to be religious and follow their father or be agnostic and follow her. Despite his teacher's warnings, Alfred married Maria, and they settled down to start a family. In two or three years, she began to question the time he spent with the teaching; and, after the children were born, she resented the time he spent with his teacher more and more. Slowly, he listened to her and began not attending regular meetings, and within five years he had left the teaching.

"Several years later, Alfred bumped into his teacher on the street and almost cried when he saw him. Even after Alfred had given in to her, Maria kept controlling all aspects of their marriage until he could no longer stand it. He'd left her a couple of years earlier and was too ashamed to go back to his teacher, as he felt he had lost all possibility of returning. The teacher assured him that wasn't true, and so Alfred once again pursued his spiritual practice. He had lost seven years of time in the teaching as a result of this interlude, and he'd also lost the opportunity to meet a woman in the teaching who would have been a perfect partner for him. She'd recently married someone else."

I looked around the room to see the reaction to the story.

"This story is about a challenge not considered properly. Even though his teacher warned him not to marry Maria, Alfred's love for her caused him not to listen to his teacher's advice. He had karma to pay off as a result of the marriage, along with the many responsibilities of raising his children in a divorced family. You may say this can happen to anyone, and that's true, but in this case, he had the good fortune to have a teacher who could foresee the future. His challenge was about listening to his teacher. If Alfred had followed his teacher's advice, he would have broken up with Maria and found the woman he was destined to be with."

"I wouldn't want anyone to tell me who I can marry or not," a young man in his twenties called out.

"Me too," a woman agreed.

"I can understand why you would think that. A teacher usually doesn't interfere, but Alfred's teacher saw that he would be pulled away from the teaching and lose many years of his spiritual journey. Alfred was also destined to be a teacher, but the karma and the loss of time would keep him from making that initiation in this lifetime.

"Listening to the teacher is always one of the major challenges on the path. The lower nature, which connects to the ego, always tries to keep an individual locked into believing in the rightness of decisions such as the one that Alfred made. The ego has a hard time taking advice of any kind. The teacher never has to set up the challenges, because the ego and the lower nature put them into place. Alfred lost his chance for God Consciousness in this life, and his heart feels sad at that loss. I know, because Alfred is a friend of mine."

"Did his children come into the teaching?" Uli asked.

"No, his children never came into his teaching because his ex-wife moved back to Italy, where she came from, and took them with her. He saw very little of them, not enough to really explain the teaching to them.

"But what about karma? Could it have been his karma to marry this woman? And, if so, how could he change that?"

"No, his karma wasn't to marry her, but he was meant to be with her for a while. If she hadn't wanted children, they would have stayed together for a year or a little longer and then broken up as friends. Having the children was an act of free will, not karma, at least for him."

"What's the difference?" asked Dorina.

"That will be another lesson. For now, let's talk more about the journey. When I say 'journey,' I am referring to a long period of time. This journey, once it is started, will continue from lifetime to lifetime. In the quest for God Consciousness, the individual will have to go through many lives, some spent in spiritual teachings, and others spent in worldly matters. This is the evolutionary path that the soul has to travel. When we look at this journey, it will have many paths and roads on it. Some will take you away from the main road and keep you away for a long time, as in Alfred's case; others will be minor diversions from which you will come back more quickly.

"Each path is a learning experience that can be difficult or easy, depending on how you look at it. If you remain objective and see the challenge as just a challenge, then it can be easy; but if you see it as an obstacle that is too difficult to surmount, then of course it will be difficult. The key is in not letting your emotions take over and keep you blinded from the right direction. No obstacle or challenge needs to be difficult if you look at it as a learning experience. The worst hardship always carries learning experiences, and in the learning, one can move through it more quickly."

An older woman sitting in front said, "I have a friend who is a physically challenged. That's an obstacle that she can't get through, and all she's had to learn is how to handle the pain."

"Your friend is paying off karma by having a physical disability. If she can accept that and look at ways in which to offset it, then she has learned something. If instead she is bitter about her illness and has an unpleasant personality because of her bitterness, then she hasn't learned anything from her situation and is making more karma for herself. I know people with disabilities who lead rewarding, productive, and fulfilling lives. Her challenge is to remain positive in her illness."

"She tries, but it is hard."

"Pain is never easy, but in suffering one can leave the body and find great peace in meditation. I would be glad to teach her how to meditate and give her some healing energy."

"Thank you, I will ask her."

"My friends, it is getting late. I will answer a few more questions, and then we must end for this evening."

I spoke for another half hour, and most people stayed. Only a few, this time, left before I had finished. Heinz again stayed and asked me, "Zarathustra, why do you take the name of a prophet of olden times?"

"As you probably know, *Zarathustra* is another name for *Zoroaster*. My teacher gave it to me when I was initiated. The spiritual name is to help the initiate in the work he or she is meant to do.

"It is an honor to carry such a name, as Zoroaster brought in the religion of Zoroastrianism. It is a religion of preaching about the fiery energy and the God within. Since this is my mission, I think that is why I was given this name."

"Yes, I have read about it."

We talked some more, and finally I returned to my room, tired but feeling good. I had scheduled two more lectures and told the people I would be returning later in the year. The response was positive.

CHAPTER 4

The next couple of days passed rapidly. Several of the people who attended my lectures wanted to see me privately. They were mainly those who needed advice and help. Some even wanted me to heal them of illnesses, and two people became upset when I said their illness was karma and I couldn't help them. But there were others who genuinely wanted to know more about the teaching.

Dorina at this time asked me to be her teacher, and I accepted her as my first student. It was a strange feeling to have a student, a feeling that would take a little while to get used to. I still wasn't certain about when it would be right to leave this group and city. Each lecture seemed to attract still more people, so I decided it would be best to leave only when the attendance grew smaller because my students felt secure enough to continue to work without my being physically present. I hoped to have some private, small talks with them before I left.

The next lecture occurred on a dismal evening. It had rained all day, and the dampness had penetrated the hall, making it feel like an ancient castle whose stone walls had suffered years of moisture and mold. Most people kept their coats on, and I felt their discomfort.

I was careful not to look too disappointed when only ten people arrived. That was half the number who had attended the previous lecture. I reminded myself that there was only a handful of people who were ready for this teaching.

I asked those in attendance to bring their chairs into a circle, and I sat in the circle with them. The priest was there and greeted me kindly. I still couldn't decide if he was spying or was genuinely interested.

The Law of Reincarnation and Karma

"My friends, we live many lives, and even though we do not remember them, they are all inside us. As you grow spiritually, some of these lives will be revealed in order for you to understand yourself better. It is because of these lives that you exist today. It is because of these lives that you experience hardships and, in contrast, also wonderful rewards. It is because of these lives that you draw to yourself others whom you have known before. This is the law of reincarnation and karma. You may ask, 'Why am I ill, or why do I have to suffer when others are free of suffering?' I would answer that you suffer for those wrong acts you have done before. Your church proclaims that God says, 'Mine is the right to punish.'

"That punishment comes through the law of karma. It is a just law. What you sow you reap ten times more, and in that reaping you learn not to do the same wrong acts again.

"All of us in previous lives have been murderers, and thieves, and wealthy, and poor. There is an old saying in the East: 'Many beggars walk the streets for things done and not done.' We have all been beggars, and we all have had to learn many lessons to know the difference between right and wrong action. If you go to a church and confess your sins for forgiveness, it will help clear your consciousness, but you still need to pay the karmic consequences of your actions."

"So, you don't believe in redemption?" asked Heinz.

"What is redemption? Is it God saying you are forgiven? Or is it a feeling of forgiveness from within? A man may be forgiven but still feel the guilt of his actions. Only through giving back to others can the man feel less guilty of his sins.

"I will tell you a story. A very wealthy man came to a guru and asked to be his student. He told the guru that he was a sinful man and had done a lot of harm to others to accumulate his wealth. He asked, 'Guru, can I be forgiven for all those deeds I have done which injured others?'

"The Teacher said, 'Take this bag of feathers and go to the top of the mountain and spill them all out, then come back to me.'

"The man did this and returned to his teacher. 'I have followed your orders.'

"'Now,' the guru said, 'Go and pick up each one of those feathers.'

"'But teacher, that would be impossible!' exclaimed the student.

"'Of course it is impossible, and it is just as impossible for you to be forgiven for all your harmful actions. The only thing you can do is ask forgiveness from those people you can find, and from now on, do acts of kindness.'"

"So, you are saying confession and prayers mean nothing?" called an elderly woman.

"If it keeps you from again doing the same act you have confessed, then of course it helps; but the original act still will have incurred karma that needs to be repaid."

"But human beings are weak and often have to repent again and again for doing the same wrong thing. This law you talk about is unfair," Gus stated flatly.

"Just the opposite. There is nothing fairer. If a man steals, and repents, but steals again, the man has not learned the lesson not to steal; but if instead the man steals and then someone steals from him, then he feels what it's like to be the victim of a theft. He learns that stealing brings pain to the victim and, in that learning, does not steal again.

"My friends, look around you; look at your neighbors and realize that no two of you are alike. Even children in a family differ from one another. Why did you get cancer and you are cured, while your friend who also had cancer died?"

I gestured to a man in work clothes sitting across the circle from me who had been listening quietly. "It was your karma not to die and his to be taken. When you understand that all relationships are karma, then you will experience the first step toward freedom. And when I say *freedom*, I mean forming relationships that will bring about good karma and offset the bad karma. As I said before, the pull one experiences in some relationships is always karma, and we don't know at first whether that pull is because of good karma or bad karma with that person. Only when the net of karma has entwined you with that person does the real karma start to develop. How many of you have thought you were in love and become involved or even married to find out later, in a year or two, that the relationship was terrible? How many of you thought you had a wonderful friendship and had the friend turn against you?"

There were a few mumbles in response.

Dorina said, "That happened to me. Nora, my best friend for five years, suddenly started to talk negatively about me behind my back, and it became very nasty. I tried to talk to her about it, and she just attacked me more, so I ended the friendship and frankly never understood why it happened. I hadn't done anything she could name."

"Dorina, your friend was someone you had killed in a previous life. It was a duel over a woman you had both loved."

"Oh. Wow. Well, that makes sense. One of the things she claimed was that I flirted with and propositioned her husband, which wasn't true at all."

"That's a good point. If you have negative karma with someone, it brings up feelings that often don't have any reality in this life. For example, you meet someone for the first time and have a strong feeling of distrust toward the person and don't know why; or, after talking to a stranger for five minutes, you feel as if you have known the person for years. There are many signs to inform you whether there is a past connection with a new acquaintance."

"If I make karma continuously, how do I stop making it? It sounds almost impossible," Lucas asked.

"It's about finding balance. It's like the man with the feathers. He can offset his negative karma by doing acts of kindness. All acts can produce either good or bad karma. If you understand the law of karma and try to abide by it, then you will be careful in your work and relationships and try to make only positive karma. In so doing, you will develop a reservoir of good karma that will help you grow spiritually. Obviously, everyone will still have negative karma to pay off, but it will be easier for those who are consciously trying to live a life that is positive.

"For example, if you find yourself in a difficult karmic relationship and have tried to make it a good one and it hasn't worked, then it is best to leave the relationship rather than continue to produce more negative karma. But if you both can understand the karma, then you can agree either to be friends and continue the relationship or to end it on a friendly basis."

"I wish my parents had done that. They have never stopped fighting. I just hope I'm not with them again," a young woman said.

"As long as you don't interfere or take sides, you can free yourself from them but if you are emotionally attached to what they fight about, then you can be caught in having to repeat it again."

"How can I do that? I definitely side with my mother against my father. He's very cruel to her."

"You need to understand your karma with him and clear it out. Be the observer. Free yourself of your karmic attachment to him. Fight your own battles, not hers; that's her karma, and she has to deal with it. And love their positive qualities; that breaks the karma."

"It's hard to love him as I don't see any good qualities, just meanness."

"I understand. Then love his spirit within. Even though he is out of touch with it, if you send him love it will reach his spirit and make a difference. And it will free you from your negative attachment to him."

"Only saints can do that."

"The only difference between you and a saint is that a saint has learned to use the heart correctly and has no attachments. You can do the same and find freedom."

"Will you help me?"

I looked at the woman's young, intense face and saw the beauty of her inquiring blue eyes. When I had observed her earlier, she had seemed too frivolous — young, maybe in her early twenties — and I had felt she didn't belong among the others. A pain came into my heart knowing I had prejudged her, and I wondered how often I was doing this.

"Yes, I will be happy to help you, Gertraud. We can speak later."

The priest raised his hand. "How do you know this law of karma is true?" he asked, not aggressively.

"How do you know there is a just God?" I replied, equally gently. "When I was a teenager, I questioned what a priest told me about God being just. I questioned it because I saw inequities all around me. Why is one person wealthy and someone else poor? Why was my close friend killed in an accident while I was unharmed? Why were children in lesser developed countries starving to death when we had abundant food? Life is full of injustices, yet we are all God's children.

Only when I read about reincarnation and karma did any of it make sense to me. I was in my family because I had karma with them, and the child in Africa starving from lack of food was there because of his karma. That child may have been a crusader who burned the food of Muslim villages, starving the people there. It's about lessons to learn to understand experientially good from wrong, love from hate. I have seen some of my lives as well as the lives of others, and I know the patterns that pull us into learning situations.

"In your family, your father victimized your mother and you. If you are victims now, in this life, it means that in some past life you both were perpetrators of harm — the victimizers — and maybe your mother did the same to your father at that time.

"Karma is a just law. As you sow, so do you reap; and, instead of it being punishment and damnation, which the church preaches, it is a learning process and an evolutionary journey."

"So, you don't believe in a heaven and a hell?" Heinz the priest again inquired.

"I believe in subtle planes of existence. One of these planes is a *plane of illusion*, where most people go to play out all their desires before they are reborn. For some it will be like a heaven. Then, when the soul has fulfilled those desires, a part of it returns to God, and that is true bliss. I also know there are lower planes of existence where there are many types of ugly creatures. Someone with no spirit consciousness, or what you call soul consciousness, will dissolve back into that pool of energy. Others, who have awakened a little of their spirit but have lived addictive or truly evil lives, will linger in those lower levels, and you might call this a hell because its inhabitants resemble those creatures often depicted in paintings of hell."

"A friend of mine committed suicide; where would he be?" another woman asked.

"Suicides also will be in those lower levels, having to live a painful existence there until the destined life span has been spent; and only then do they go on. In terms of everyone else — those who have harmed others, those who murder or steal, those who commit all the known sins — they will have to pay off the karma of their wrongs in their following lives. As a result, some will have lives of suffering, but there is no hell where they will go when they die. They go with the others to the plane where they play out their desires. If, for instance, someone was a thief, he would go to that plane and have a lot of money, so much money that he would never have to steal again, or he would imagine committing grand burglary and evading the police. Someone who loved sex would continue to have affair after affair until the urge had been saturated. Whatever the desire, it will take place on this plane of illusion."

A man who was at the lecture for the first time asked, "I am here because Lucas is my friend and he persuaded me to come. I am a bit confused about what you are preaching, and I want to understand your teaching better. What do you call this teaching, and what are you planning to do with it?"

"That's a good question. This is an esoteric teaching based on all the esoteric teachings that have been given to us from the beginning of humankind. This particular teaching has no name *per se*, but it contains yoga principles, Buddhist principles, and Christian principles. It holds the essence of all that is taught in all the religions, much of which was given to human beings throughout time by various enlightened Beings who have achieved union with God. I teach the love and wisdom of the heart and mind, the striving for God Consciousness, the true meaning of the evolutionary path, the concept of karma and reincarnation, the laws of nature and how to communicate with that world, and, most of all, how to work consciously to achieve oneness with the Higher Self. This is all information that comes from all esoteric teachings. And there is much more."

I paused to listen to my teacher, whose voice I suddenly heard. "I think I will call it *Higher Self Yoga*."

"I would like to learn about communicating with nature," Dorina said.

"That will be another lesson later." I smiled at her warmly.

"Returning to the subject, understanding the law of karma is an important step on a spiritual path. People who are not in an esoteric teaching are under the law of karma tenfold, meaning that, if you do a wrong act, then a similar wrong will be done to you ten times. If you understand the law, then the penalty becomes higher, to one-hundredfold, and it continues to climb higher the more you grow spiritually."

"That's a lot. If I understand the law, that means it's one-hundredfold for me, what is it for you?" a man asked.

"It's one thousandfold. But remember, you are also making good karma, which offsets the negative karma. For example, if you yell at a friend and become very angry, that doesn't mean that a hundred people will in turn yell at you. How it may work is that the friend may in turn act negatively toward you, which would offset some of your karma toward the friend. Then, if you apologize to the friend and in turn do some good things for that person, those good acts are also one hundredfold and will negate the initial negative karma. It's true, though, that continuing any kind of negative behavior toward the person will eventually lose you the friendship."

I could tell that people were thinking about their relationships, so I waited and let them reflect. I heard Lucas whisper to his friend, "I'm glad I didn't know about this when I dated Anna. It was only tenfold then."

The lecture lasted another hour, with many examples and questions about reincarnation. Some already believed it was true, but one or two of the others still questioned it. I explained that it is all right to question, because it leaves a door open. Saying absolutely no, it's not true, shuts the door. A married couple, Uli and Sara, had even seen a life they had together, and it helped to have them talk about it with others.

Many asked to know how they could experience a past life, and I answered, "Past lives usually are given to people in dreams or meditation. When you see one, you will know it's true for several reasons. First, you will be wearing strange clothing, or you may be the opposite sex but know the person is you. The other main clue is the feelings. You will experience the feelings all over again, but be careful. If you start to experience feelings that are too painful, such as about a murder or being tortured, then ask your Higher Self to let you observe what is happening and not feel any of the pain."

I also stressed, "Do not ever force yourself to see a past life. It should come to you for a reason, with a learning that is important for you to know at the time. Forcing it can cause psychological damage. That's why it's better not to delve into the past unless it comes to you naturally. There are people now doing past-life regression. It's a fad in some countries, such as the United States, and it can be dangerous."

"But," Gertraud protested, "how am I to believe in past lives without seeing one?"

"Your heart will tell you it's true. Otherwise, read some of the many books that have been written about reincarnation. There are doctors who cite case histories of people who remember past lives that have been researched and proven correct. Don't accept it because I say it's true; study it for yourself and have an open mind. And maybe one day you will experience it for yourself."

I looked at the group around me and saw that everyone was attentive and thinking. "I ask you, is there anyone here who has not experienced a feeling of having known someone before? You meet a stranger and simply know in your heart that this person is so familiar to you that you could swear you have met him or her at another time. Or you go out on a first date, and you both feel an immediate closeness and hit it off right away. You have friends whom you liked right away and felt comfortable with and others whom you still feel you don't know. Sometimes it's about personality, but usually it's about having been with the person before.

"When people reincarnate, they come back in the same groups of people over and over again. It can be within the same families or, often, in friendships and romances. Definitely, in spiritual esoteric teachings, you will be drawn together again and again."

"That's amazing; how does God do that?" asked Gus.

"It's not God; it's the karmic pull. It's a magnetic energy that attracts people to one another. You may call this energy made by God if you want, but it's really still a mystery as to how these energies work."

I finally brought the lecture to a close. I had been talking for nearly three hours with only a short break, and I was beginning to tire rapidly. Back in my room, I meditated in bed and fell asleep to wake up in the middle of the night chilled from the night air. I got up and stood by the window and looked out at the evening sky. Low clouds hung around the moon, which was almost full. The mountains stood as imposing silhouettes in mysterious darkness. My weariness lifted, and I felt a longing to go home. When I went to sleep, I asked my subtle body to go there, and during the night, in my dreams, I did.

CHAPTER 5

When I woke the next morning, I felt a deep sadness in my heart, a sadness that stemmed from the night before. I realized that most of the people couldn't understand what I was teaching and that it was now time to move on. Instead of planning another lecture, I called Dorina and asked her if she could have a few people, those who were sincerely interested, to meet at her home that night. If they couldn't make it that night, then to try for the next night. She agreed, and I gave her the names of the people who might want to continue. For some reason, at the end of the conversation I added Heinz, the priest, to the list. I told her to ask each one if they wanted to continue the work and if not to say so now. That way I would know who my true followers were.

Dorina called back and said that most of the ones I had named could come and that two were no longer interested. The two were Lucas and Gus. I had felt that Gus wouldn't come, but I was very surprised about Lucas. He had seemed eager to learn more and was very attentive at the lectures. Heinz, the priest, was coming, and again I didn't know if it was out of curiosity or true interest. They all preferred the next night, which gave me the day to spend in meditation. Fortunately, it was a sunny, warm day, so I decided to hike up the mountain and be alone in nature, with which I was so aligned.

I found the mountain trail fairly steep, so I didn't travel too far. The rocks were gray and cut in long, sharp formations as if a pharaonic sword had cut through the layers in a fit of rage. Even in the sunlight they seemed cold and remote, very different from the blue-purple of the higher terrains where my home was. I found a spot off the trail in a little, cozy cove that was sheltered from the wind, and I spread a blanket down to sit on.

As soon as I started my meditation, I knew something was wrong. It was difficult to grasp at first, but then it became clearer. It concerned Lucas. He was interested in being my student, but something had happened to dissuade him. That something was what I was trying to see. I saw the shape of a woman and thought it was his mother. Then I realized it was someone much younger, someone his age. I kept trying to see her face, but it evaded me; only later in the meditation did I realize it was one of the attendees, whose name was Lona. Somehow, she was connected to Lucas, and, since she was not included in the names to ask, he had decided not to come.

What a pity, to lose one's spiritual path for a jealous girlfriend. I knew she would have loved to come, but I felt this teaching was not her path; and I had planned to write her a note to explain that she had a teacher waiting for her in India and that she should go there someday to find him. Probably if I had told her this before, she wouldn't have talked Lucas into not coming. But it was a test for him, and besides, he could still meet up with me another time, since I would be coming back. All of this gave me the material for my talk the next day.

I stayed until nearly sunset, then hiked back to my hotel just as the evening sky put on its dark clothing. In the lobby I found Karl waiting for me. He was very emotional as he greeted me.

"Teacher, I've been waiting for you. I need your help: My brother was in an accident and is suffering from a serious concussion. He's in a coma and they don't know whether he will come out of it. Please help him." Karl's voice cracked, and there were tears in his eyes.

"Where is he?"

"He's in the local infirmary, but they were talking of transporting him to Interlocken or Bern, where there are better equipment and doctors."

"Let's go right away. Hopefully, they haven't moved him yet."

The infirmary was a couple of blocks away, and we ran almost all the way. Fortunately, Karl's brother was still there. I sat next to his bed and looked at his face. His subtle body was hovering around him and looked ethereal in the light of the lamp. I asked him silently, "Were you told to return, that it wasn't your time to go?"

Soundlessly he answered, "Yes, they sent me back, but I can't get my conscious self to wake up."

"I will help that happen, but promise me that you will be more careful in the future and that you will try to remember your experience on the other side."

"Yes, I want to remember. It was beautiful, and I didn't want to come back. It was so very peaceful there." And he added, "I will be more careful. Thank you."

I then laid my hands on his physical head and sent him healing energy. It flowed from my hands for fifteen minutes and then stopped abruptly, and I knew that was enough. At the end of it, Karl's brother stirred and slowly, very slowly, opened his eyes and stared at me.

Karl cried, "Erik, Erik you're back, you're back!"

His cries were so loud that the nurse came running in and also exclaimed at seeing Erik awake. Soon the doctors came, and Karl and I departed so that Erik could be examined.

When I left, he raised his hand and whispered, "Thank you." And I knew he remembered.

Outside the room, Karl said to me, "Teacher, I had my doubts about you and your teaching, but now they have left. What you did was a miracle, and I want you to be my teacher."

"Don't ask me that because of your brother; ask me that because your own spirit wants wisdom."

"I do want wisdom, but most of all I want to learn from you."

I accepted Karl as a student. After Dorina, he was the second person to ask me to be his teacher, and I knew his brother would follow.

That evening I spent alone, first having dinner in the tavern and then sitting in my room reading. Dorina had asked me to dinner, but I declined, seeking solitude more than company. I still found it difficult to be with people all the time. Those many years I spent alone on the mountain had turned me into a recluse, and it took a lot of energy for me to reach out to others, something that was most important for me to learn if I was to be a teacher.

The gathering at Dorina's house the next evening was small. Only five people from Wengen remained. They were Dorina, Karl; the couple, Uli and Sara; and Heinz, the priest. We sat in the living room and sipped cups of tea, and I asked them to talk a little about themselves.

The energy was very different from that in the lecture hall. Here, there was more harmony and even some shyness on the part of the couple and Dorina. This was the first time they had spent time with me in a small group setting, and I could feel they didn't know what to expect. I watched their auras and saw all kinds of mental activity. I could have read their thoughts, but I would never do that because it would be an infringement of their privacy.

You may wonder how I could do this mind reading. When the higher chakras or centers are opened, one has these abilities and many more, but they must be carefully guarded and used with caution. They are important to have when working with students and disciples, as they give the teacher the ability to help on a much deeper level, but they cannot be abused in any way. I can pick up names and some biographical material, but the rest I don't pursue.

In that intimate gathering, I felt it was the right time to tell them about my ideas concerning the classes and how I planned to continue teaching them. I also told them I would be seeing them on my way back from my lecture tour.

Dorina asked, "While you are traveling can we talk to you or email you?"

"Yes, of course. Right now, I don't have a cell phone because there was no service in my mountain home. I plan to buy one in Interlaken as there's probably a telephone service store there. I also need to buy a computer and take some lessons, since I haven't used one for over ten years." I paused to look at everyone and asked, "Who would be the best person for me to contact later with all my information?"

Karl immediately raised his hand. "I would love to do that, and on your return, I can give you some more lessons on the computer."

"Thank you so much." I felt Karl would be the one to volunteer. "Speaking of lessons, when I get my computer, I will write some more teaching lessons and exercises for the classes and email them to you."

"That's wonderful," Dorina's face glowed with a sunny smile that warmed the room, and the others also happily responded.

It was time then to teach the following lesson, which I felt was an appropriate one to do before I left.

How to Remain Steadfast on the Spiritual Path

"We all have people around us who have no interest in finding the God within. These people are very one-dimensional and see anything spiritual, other than the church, as being dangerous." I looked at Heinz for a reaction but saw none.

"When someone enters a spiritual path, it is very important to keep that knowledge to oneself, particularly at the beginning of the journey when everything is new and there is no firm foundation to stand on. Too often a student wants everyone to know about the teaching in the hope that his or her friends will also want to become part of it. Usually, this is not the case; instead, those whom they tell will put doubts into the student's head and cause the student to question whether the path is correct or not. So, I ask all of you to say nothing to others and to keep your experiences to yourselves. Even sharing them with another student can cause difficulty if that student is jealous of your experiences."

"You mean I can't tell my sister about you?" Dorina asked.

"Not yet. Learn more and feel if the teaching is what you truly want; only then, when you have built a better foundation, can you talk about it to others. Even then, be careful not to say very much. Just mention that you are studying a spiritual teaching; if the person wants to know more, then the person will ask questions. Never give out too much, as it may be more than can be accepted at any given time. Usually, a person will ask questions and keep asking, and those questions you can answer. But, obviously, to answer questions you first need to understand the teaching. So, all I am asking is for you to wait and learn more before attempting to explain a teaching that, while simple and open in some ways, is very complex in others."

"I've not noticed anything simple about what you have been teaching," Heinz said with a smile.

I laughed. "You're right, but it is simple when you put the information in your heart. The heart takes all knowledge and contains it, and in that process it responds in a clear, focused way. For instance, if you put in your heart all that I said about reincarnation, your heart will respond positively, and you will know that what you heard is correct. Understanding the whole death and rebirth process is more complicated and can be learned later, but knowing that reincarnation is true is simply a felt experience. It is the same for any theory or revelation. The heart will know instantly if it is true or false, so my first lesson to all of you is to learn how to develop your heart and accept that it understands and has deeper knowledge."

"That sounds very abstract to me," Karl said in a low voice.

"Yes, it does sound abstract, because you haven't developed the ability yet. Let's try to experience it. I want all of you to close your eyes and focus your mind on your heart chakra, which is right in the middle of your chest. As you focus on that place, ask your Higher Self to help you experience it. The feeling may be warmth, or a movement, or even a light. When you feel you are sensing it at all, place a question in your heart. It can be any kind of question. For example, if you are planning to go on a trip, ask if it is all right for you to go. Or, put a name of someone you know in your heart and ask if this person is really a good friend; or even ask if you should study this teaching. Ask anything you want, and notice how your heart responds."

I waited and noticed that some people were smiling and that Heinz's face was upset.

I then asked the people to open their eyes and talk about their experiences.

Dorina said, "It was wonderful. I felt real warmth in my heart. I asked if I was doing the right thing by asking you to be my teacher, and it felt as though my heart expanded. I could feel the warmth move across my chest, and I knew it was right."

I smiled at her. "That's correct. Anyone else have an experience like that?"

Karl said, "Mine was a little different. I saw a light, and when I asked if my brother would be 100 percent okay, the light got bigger, and I also felt it was right on."

"And you, Heinz, what was your experience?"

"I'd rather not talk about it."

"That's okay. In fact, I'm glad you said that, as I meant to tell all of you that you don't have to share your experiences if you don't feel comfortable doing so."

Sara raised her hand. "I'm not certain about mine. I felt a little movement, but when I asked my question there was no movement at all."

"That means the answer is "no". Now take a moment and put the no in your heart and ask if no was the answer to your question."

She did and then opened her eyes. "When I did that, I got the movement again. I guess I didn't want no for the answer, but it must be the right one."

Uli patted her arm and said, "I think we asked the same question, and my answer was no also."

Sara explained, "We want to have a baby, and it's been difficult for me to conceive, so I asked if I would be able to get pregnant in the next year."

"Don't worry; you will have a baby, not next year but the following year," I reassured them. "In fact, you will end up with two children."

"You can see that?"

"Yes. Now let's talk some more about staying steadfast and focused on the path. When you start to study this teaching and work more consciously with the Higher Self, the Wise Being within, you will learn to whom you can mention the teaching and to whom not to mention it. Your heart can help you be discerning.

"When you work with the heart, you are linking with the Higher Self, which contains wisdom and knows what is right for you. The more you work with it, the more you will develop this ability—just as the more you work with your heart, the more you will feel it and know when something is true.

"The Higher Self is your guide and the part that will keep you focused on the goal, which is to become one with God, or one with the spirit within. Being steadfast is being in your heart and working with your Higher Self. It holds the knowledge on how you personally can best walk the path."

"This Higher Self you talk about, is it the same as what Jung calls the Wise Being?" Heinz asked.

"Yes and no. The Wise Being that Jung talks about is part of the collective unconscious and is accessible to everyone. The Higher Self is part of your own unconscious and your individuality and is different from everyone else's. Yet all the Higher Selves are one in essence and are part of what is called the Over Self, just like the seed of your spirit is one with all of humankind's spirit or what is called the God within."

"This is where it gets complicated and you lose me," Karl remarked.

"All right, I'll simplify it. The seed of your spirit is one and the same as everyone else's. What is different is your individuality, which has lived many lives and has gone through many experiences. That individuality goes with you from lifetime to lifetime, as does the seed of your spirit.

"Your Higher Self contains both your individuality and the seed of your spirit and therefore differs from Dorina's Higher Self, which contains her individuality and the seed of her spirit. The seed of the spirit is the same. The individuality is different. Is that clearer?"

"Yes, we differ because our lives have been different, but our essence is the same," Heinz added.

"That's it exactly."

Seeing him write down some words, I said, "Please, take notes on what I say. Truth can be spoken but disappear quickly, so it's always best to take notes to bring it back. The same is true with your dreams. Always have a notebook or some paper by your bed to write down significant dreams as soon as you wake up; otherwise, you may forget them."

Dorina raised her hand. "Can you tell me more about the Higher Self?"

"Rather than tell you more about it, I will give you an exercise that will help you experience it. First, think of a question you may want to ask your Higher Self. It can be any kind of question; remember, the Higher Self is part of you and knows everything about you."

They all thought for a few minutes and wrote down one or two questions.

"Before we start the exercise, let me explain a few things. I am going to take you up a mountain, and at the top you will meet your Higher Self. The energy of the Higher Self is often personified in a form, which can appear as a woman or man. The gender does not have to relate to your gender. The Higher Self can also take the form of an angel, a mystical animal, a light, or a color, or it can even be experienced more as energy in your body. The most common form is human, which is why I will mention seeing the Higher Self as a figure; but for you the figure may just be a shaft of bright light, and that is perfectly fine."

Karl said, "I for one can never see anything. I don't think I'm going to get anywhere with this."

"In doing the exercise, be aware that everyone is unique and experiences visualization differently. Some people can see the scenes in their mind's eye, whereas others will just feel or sense what's happening. That may be you, Karl. There are also people who are auditory, they hear sounds and voices. Some will experience a combination of sensory impressions. Therefore, when you communicate with the Higher Self, it may send you impressions that appear as thoughts in your mind, or you may hear its voice. It can also send body sensations that relay messages.

"Sometimes personal desires can interfere with the message. Therefore, after receiving an answer to your question, I recommend checking the answer by using signals. For instance, if you see the Higher Self, ask it to show you a visual signal for yes, no, and maybe. Yes and no signals may be conveyed simply by the nodding or shaking of its head. If you have more body awareness, you may feel a twitch in your left leg for a yes answer and a twitch in your right leg for a no. Then ask questions accordingly to verify your previous answers. The Higher Self will always reach you in some manner. If you haven't received actual answers to your questions, the signal method is another way of communicating.

"Since the Higher Self is your wise Self and is part of you, it knows everything about you and everything about your personal evolution. It therefore can help you in all your life's problems, from the most mundane to the most profound. Utilizing it to help you makes it stronger, until you will totally begin to bring the Higher Self into your consciousness in your everyday life. Eventually, you will not even see a form; you will simply feel it in your body as being one with you. Remember, its role is not only to help you with problems but also to guide you spiritually, so that you become a wise being in all your thoughts and actions.

"Working with the Higher Self is a process. There will be times when you experience it fully in the meditation and other times when nothing happens. When you first contact the Higher Self, it can be very evasive. It may appear and then quickly disappear. The more you persist in contacting it, the stronger it will become. If it should disappear when you are communicating with it, just link with your heart chakra, repeat the end of the meditation, and literally demand that it return."

"Ok, but how I can trust what I get?" Dorina asked, looking perturbed.

"Good question. If you have a strong desire around something, you should question whether the information you have received is correct. You then need to ask several times and put the answer in your heart and try to experience if it feels right.

"I also will mention in the exercise that you need to shine light on the Higher Self when you first experience it. Sometimes desires coming from your personality will impersonate the Higher Self. Shining light on it will verify that it is your Higher Self. If it is truly the Higher Self, when rays of light shine on it, it will either stay the same or get brighter. If it is something else, it will disappear or turn dark. If this happens, and it usually happens to everyone at some time or other, simply tell it to leave and repeat the end of the exercise. If during the exercise you experience blocks, resistance, or fears, see these as a black ball, and then give the ball to your Higher Self, saying, 'Please take these away from me temporarily, so that I can receive clear answers from you.'

"After doing this, again shine light down on the Higher Self to be certain it is still the true Higher Self. I recommend doing this at least once during the communication, just in case some inner desire or fear has replaced the Higher Self."

"But what if I don't see the Higher Self? How can I check the answers?" Karl inquired.

"If you can experience body signals for 'yes, it's correct,' or 'no, it's not,' that should be a good indicator. You can verify that answer by putting it into your heart chakra. The Higher Self should convey a warm, expansive feeling if it is verifying something. Its energy is never cold, so, if you are experiencing a sudden cold feeling in the chest, it could be another part coming in. In that case, again reconnect with the heart chakra and ask the Higher Self to come back. If you receive a no response when you put the answer into your heart chakra, that would indicate the answer you picked up isn't correct. As you work with it, you will intuitively know what feels right or what doesn't.

"Working with the Higher Self is always a wonderful experience. Its wisdom and humor create a magical combination. Sometimes it will take on other forms to indicate something you need to do. For example, it may appear as a frolicking child or elf, indicating you need to have more fun or play. It will even take on other nationalities and appear in different genders. If it suddenly changes from what you are used to seeing, ask it why it has taken on this new form.

"It will sometimes appear as you were in a past life, usually one that was deeply spiritual, such as a monk or lama."

"If that happens, should I try to find out more about the past life?" Uli asked.

"Not necessarily, but you can ask the Higher Self if it is important for you to do a past-life regression to find out more about it. The Higher Self can be showing you how you looked in that life in order to experience the energy, but you may not be ready to know about it.

"Sometimes the Higher Self may also show you something you don't understand. An example would be a symbol. It's important, then, to take the symbol, visualize it in your heart chakra, and ask to see or receive more information about it.

"Always the Higher Self works with your whole being. It will never reveal information to you that you are not ready to receive. It will never hurt you or scare you. It is gentle and loving at all times. It always knows what's best for you, and it will never deceive you. If any of those negative things occur, be aware that they are coming from something other than your Higher Self."

"That feels scary to me," Dorina said.

"You need never be frightened. If it is not your Higher Self, just tell the impostor to leave and stop the exercise. Usually it comes from your desire body or your lower nature or the spiritual part of you that is distorted. It can never harm you."

"That's good to know." Dorina seemed relieved.

"There are other signs to look for. If you can hear the Higher Self, it will always speak in short, direct sentences. If it starts to ramble on with a lot of spiritual content, then you are probably listening to what I call a *spiritual subpersonality*.

"The exercise we are going to do will introduce you to your Higher Self. The more you work with it, the easier it becomes to contact it. You may eventually eliminate most of the exercise and start from a point toward the end. The Higher Self will appear to some people just by their linking with the heart chakra. Remember, it operates through the heart.

"As I lead you through the exercise, I will pause after each step so that you will have time to do it. Let's do the exercise now:

Higher Self Exercise

"Get comfortable, close your eyes, and feel your whole body relaxing from the tips of your toes all the way up to the top of your head.

"Each part of your body is feeling relaxed.

"Take some deep breaths and center yourself by linking with your heart chakra.

"Now imagine that you are in a meadow and in front of you is a mountain. You will climb the mountain, and at the top you will meet your Higher Self. The path is in front of you. You will walk on it, and immediately you will be entering a forest. It is a forest of evergreen trees and pine trees. You gradually climb upward through the forest, and as you walk you can feel the crunch of pine needles under your feet, and you can hear or sense the sound of birds singing. Once in a while, rays of sunlight will break through the branches, lighting your way.

"You are now leaving the forest, and you will find yourself on the side of the mountain. All around you are trees and rocks, and as you walk on the path you can feel the warmth of the sun on your body, and there is a nice breeze blowing. You continue to climb upward on the path, and it is an easy climb.

"Now you suddenly hear water, so you leave the path and go to the edge of the cliff and look up and see a stream of water flowing down from a waterfall. As it hits the rocks near you, you can feel the spray on your face and hear the roar of the water hitting the rocks below.

"You turn and walk back to the path and continue to climb upward. Now there are no more trees, just scrub brush and boulders or rocks. If you stop and look around, you can see that there are other mountain ranges on either side of you. And if you look downward, you can see the meadow from where you first started.

"Next, you will turn and continue to walk upward. You are nearing the top of the mountain, and, as you round a bend, you can see at the very top is a flat plateau of land. On that plateau is a bench, and you go and sit on it. Take time now to look at the beautiful vista of mountain ranges all around you.

"You can feel the sun on the top of your head, so you turn and look up at the sun, which is directly above you. As you look, you see a figure emerge and slide down on a sunbeam and stand in front of you. The figure is your Higher Self. It may be a figure or just a light or warmth in your heart. When you are experiencing any of these sensations, then imagine the sun shining down on the Higher Self. Notice if the Higher Self stays the same or disappears. If it turns dark, simply tell it to go away, and again look up at the sun and ask your Higher Self to come down.

"When you feel the Higher Self is there, link your heart with it and ask your Higher Self to give you a signal that will represent a yes, a no, or a maybe answer. When you have the signals, ask your Higher Self your question; and, after you receive the answer by way of signals, then ask to know more and try to receive words or impressions.

"Thank your Higher Self and say you will return to be with it again."

People took notes, and, when they appeared to be finished, I asked, "How many of you experienced the Higher Self?"

Everyone but Uli raised a hand.

"Remember what I said: it is often difficult to contact the Higher Self at first, but the more you work at it the easier it becomes. I suggest you do this exercise every day and also ask the Higher Self to be with you during the day. Contact it by linking with your heart and ask that it guide you in your work.

"Anyone want to talk about their experience?"

I looked at Dorina. She said, "At first I saw a figure; then it disappeared, and I called it back as you suggested. That happened a couple of times until it finally appeared clearer, and it looked very white. I think it was a woman, and she was wearing a long, white robe. I couldn't see her features, but her hands were visible, and she raised them in the signals. The question I asked is very private, but I received a direct answer and, even though it wasn't the answer I wanted, I knew it was the correct one."

Karl raised his hand. "Mine was also a figure, which surprised me. He was very tall and also white, with a long, white beard, and he gave me the most wonderful smile and then disappeared, and I couldn't get him back."

"It sounds as if he startled you so much that you may have become fearful."

"I guess so, but I will keep trying. It was a wonderful experience."

"Anyone else?"

"I don't know if what happened was real or my imagination," Sara said. "I couldn't see anything, but I did feel a lot of warmth in my heart, so I asked for signals, and I felt the weirdest movement in one arm for a yes, and the same in the other arm for a no, and then nothing for a maybe. When I asked my question, the answer was a maybe, so I checked and asked if that was correct, and I got a movement that indicated a yes. It was really strange, but I think it worked."

"Yes, that's a good example of what I was saying before."

"But I have a question. If it's just a feeling like that, how do I shine the sun on it?"

"Imagine the sun is shining on it anyway. If it is the Higher Self, you will still feel the warmth in your heart; and if it's not the Higher Self, the warmth won't be there."

"Okay, thank you."

I looked at Heinz to see if he would participate, but he remained silent.

I continued talking. "Everyone is capable of opening his or her heart and becoming one with the Higher Self, but it requires discipline and practice. It is an ongoing process that develops one's spiritual nature. When blocks and fears arise, as they surely will, look at them as obstacles you need to work through. Break down the fears and see the root of them. Ask for a process from your Higher Self that will help you go through the blocks, starting with a first step. Work with that step and ask for another one.

"Once you begin working with the Higher Self on a regular basis, you will find that connection will help you be steadfast. It most definitely wants you to develop and grow spiritually, and having that connection firmly established will keep you focused on what you need to do to make that happen. It will help you to find God Consciousness."

Heinz raised his hand. "I teach that God is separate and that only Jesus had access to Him, and you teach that we all have access to God and that Jesus wasn't any different from any of us. I could never accept that."

"Yes, I teach that we all have God's spirit within us, but I have never said that Jesus wasn't different. He was very different in that he had developed and opened his chakras; and, when he died, he became a Mahatma. While most of us have those possibilities, we also have a long journey to reach what he achieved. He showed us the way and was, indeed, a very High Being, as was Buddha and others who have achieved that initiation. But that is another lesson. I will teach you more about Hierarchy and the Mahatmas at another time."

It was getting late. We arranged to meet again the following evening.

CHAPTER 6

I awoke early the next morning to a cloudy day. It looked as if it would rain, the kind of rain that felt as if the mountains were crying for humankind. These were downpours that were so strong you couldn't see where to walk, and if there were an accompanying wind, which was most of the time, then no matter how many layers of waterproof parkas you wore you were soaked to the skin. To get caught in such rain was difficult, to say the least. It was best to find a crevice in the mountain to hide in until it stopped.

My room felt hot and stuffy, and, even though I was tempted to go on a hike, I knew it best not to go with such a sky. I tried to meditate but couldn't, so I decided at least to go downstairs and have breakfast and then reassess what to do. As I was eating, the rains started with such a force that the windows shook, and a little girl who was playing near them went running to her mother, who was still eating. The girl was very frightened, and I didn't blame her. No one ever got used to these downpours. It made all of us feel very small in comparison, and there was a sense of the real power of nature in its ultimate force. Thunder and lightning gave force to the storm, and soon there was a flickering of lights and finally an outage. In places like this, not having electricity can last for hours and sometimes days.

I went into the lounge, which still had lights. It was spacious and nicely decorated in warm tones of red, yellow, ochre, and brown. It had a large, stone fireplace with a couch and a couple of armchairs in front of it. Even though it wasn't cold outside, there was a fire burning, and some people were sitting around it. The rest of the lounge had separate armchairs and groupings of chairs, and there were a few tables with cut flowers giving touches of beauty. More people were there than usual, probably because of the storm.

Settling into a wing chair, I picked up a magazine from a table and was starting to read an article about the bad economy when I felt a sudden surge of energy so strong it almost lifted me out of the chair. Startled, I looked around at all the people who were sitting there. I was certain that the energy was coming from one of them. In the corner sat an older woman who was busy crocheting. No, it wasn't from her. Across the room sitting on a big sofa was a middle-aged man who seemed intent on a jigsaw puzzle laid out on the coffee table in front of him. His energy seemed low, so I didn't think it came from him. There was a family with several children playing a game. At the end of the room was a young couple engaged in a deep conversation. They glanced at me once and then continued to talk in very low voices so that no one could hear them. My immediate sense was that they had both zapped me at the same time, taking me off guard. The energy was too powerful to have come from just one of them, unless the person was a high adept, and, looking at their auras, I could see that wasn't true.

I thought for a few minutes, trying to decide what to do. It's best not to try to fool with energy when there is a storm in process. But why were they zapping me? Finally, I walked over and sat down in a chair facing them. They looked up and smiled at me, and I saw right away who they were. Both were practicing black magic and were using the power of the storm in a negative manner.

"Good morning, why are you targeting me?" I inquired.

A look of surprise came across their faces. "I don't know what you mean," the man answered.

"Of course, you do. You just infiltrated my aura and sent me a shock in the heart, and I want to know why."

"My dear sir, you must be mistaken. I have no idea what you are talking about."

His mouth turned downcast into a soft grin. He was fair haired and seemed a bit naïve, in contrast to the woman, who was his exact opposite.

Her beauty was stark with no warmth to embellish it. Long, black hair flowed in snake-like twirls around an oval face. Heavy makeup accented her black, piercing eyes, which had a hint of malicious glee in them.

The woman then spoke. Her voice was deep and throaty. "Whatever you are talking about sounds very interesting. Tell us what you are experiencing."

"You know what I experienced. Don't tell me otherwise. If either one of you try it again, I will respond in like manner, and you will be sorry you attacked me." I stood up and walked away and saw the woman give a subtle sign to her friend. She was stronger than he. Probably he was a student, even though they were the same age— possibly in their late thirties, or early forties.

When I sat down again, I watched them carefully. Again, they were in a deep conversation, glancing over at me from time to time. In the meantime, through visualization I fashioned some armor around my body to protect myself. What were they doing here? Who sent them? This was the first time I had seen them. I realized now that I was being watched not only by my teacher but also by the negative ones. That awareness made me feel good. If I were being watched, that meant the work was going well.

Shortly after I sat down again, the couple got up and left. Since the storm was still in full force, I assumed they returned to their room to wait it out. Once they were gone, I sent positive energy around the room to clear up the pollution they had left behind.

Fortunately, they had arrived too late to infiltrate my lectures, but I now needed to be careful when I taught the smaller group. Later, I went to the desk and asked about them. The clerk said they had just arrived and had asked if there were someone here who was giving lectures, and he had told them my name.

"Did you give them my room number?"

"No, that would be against rules. We never give personal information to a stranger."

"That's good. Please keep it that way." I went back to my room and tried to meditate. It was difficult to do, so I took a nap instead. I had an interesting dream. I was standing in the mountains in front of my house, and the man from the lounge came and stood in front of me. I asked him what he was doing there.

He replied, "I want to be just like you."

This surprised me, so I asked, "Then why are you studying with that woman? Don't you know she is a negative being?"

He looked genuinely surprised: "No that's not true. She's a good witch."

"There is no doubt about who she is. If you continue to study with her, you will also become a negative force. Do you want that?"

"No, she told me she was good and that she would help me grow spiritually, but when I saw you, I felt you to be more powerful, and I now want to study with you."

I looked at him and thought about it. "If you leave her, she will attack you."

"That's okay. Won't you protect me?"

"Yes, but I need to know if you are sincere or not. You may be lying to me. If you really want to change and work with positive energy, then this afternoon after the storm, you are to walk by yourself, and I will meet you at the edge of town just before you hike into the mountains. If you come, we will talk; but be careful, as she will want to destroy you."

When I awoke it was early afternoon and the heavy rains were gone, leaving a scattering of showers. I waited for another hour until the sun was finally shining and walked through the town to the trail. I waited for half an hour, sitting on a large rock and enjoying the smell of the earth after recently fallen rain, relaxing my mind to absorb the beauty of the sun hitting the rain-clustered leaves of the bushes and trees around me. It always amazed me to see the aftermath of a storm — as soon as nature's strong masculine energy had made its voice heard — it then reclined back, resting in the arms of the feminine. I, too, was reclining more and more into her soft splendor when I heard steps coming toward me. It was the man.

He sat down in front of me in yoga fashion and simply said, "I have come." He paused and added, "My name is Alex Kunz."

I looked at him again, this time more carefully. He was tall with a strong, healthy body that showed he did a lot of exercise. Brown eyes that had flecks of gold when the sun hit them caused his ordinary face to light up in an animated manner. His intensity was serious and was focused on me, trying to pick up what I felt about him.

"Well, Alex, do you know why you have come?"

"You said if I came I could study with you."

"Good, you remembered the dream. But I need to know more about you and the woman."

"We are lovers, even though she is my teacher. I didn't want to be her lover, but she insisted so I complied. You know how powerful she is, so I will need your protection. I have not told her I have left her for you yet, but I think by now she knows, and I must say she frightens me. We met two years ago at a party, and she immediately went after me and told me she could make me powerful. At the time I had a job that wasn't a good one, and almost right away my boss offered to promote me to a really good position, one that I had always wanted to have. That made me think she was truly a goddess, and I followed her then with no thought as to how she did this magic."

"Why did you attack me today?"

"One day last week she told me we had to spend the weekend here. She said there was a great teacher staying here, and she wanted to challenge him and prove she was greater. It sounded very interesting to me until I saw you this morning. I saw the colors around your body, which I believe is a person's aura, and it was very beautiful. It was the first time I have seen one, and then I looked at her and saw her aura, which had a lot of blackness in it."

"Yes, it does, and yours also is starting to grow dark."

"I know. But when I saw your aura, I wanted to bathe in its radiance, and just when I was feeling that way, she commanded me to work with her energy and zap you. I said no, but she insisted, so I complied as I always do when I am with her. Then you came over and I felt your energy — felt how powerful it was and so very different from hers."

"Then what happened?"

"We went upstairs, and I said I wanted to go back down and read. She went to meditate, and I also meditated but not with her. I went back to the lounge to find you, but you had left, so I sat in your chair and meditated and saw you right away. That's why I'm here. May I please be your student?"

"I see she did not initiate you."

"No, she said I needed more training and that I wasn't ready. I'm so glad; otherwise, I couldn't study with you, could I?"

"You could study but not be an initiate. You can only have one teacher who initiates you in a lifetime. Fortunately, you are free still to change teachers. If she had initiated you, it would be far more difficult to leave her, as she would have a stronger hold over you. Do you sincerely want to be my student?" I looked into his eyes.

"Yes, I do."

I could see he was telling the truth.

"Then you may come with me tonight, but first you must tell her about your decision to leave her."

"Would you come with me when I do that?" His voice sounded anxious.

"No, you must do it alone, but I will be protecting you, so do not worry. She cannot harm you." This would be a major test for him, as she would do everything in her power to get him back.

"Go back now and do this, and when you are finished return here to me."

I watched him as he walked down the road to his hotel. When he was out of sight, I closed my eyes and sent my subtle body to accompany him. I touched him lightly on his arm so that he knew I was there, and I could see him smile when I did that.

She was sitting in a chair in their room looking out the window.

"Where did you go?" Her voice was shrill.

"I went to the teacher and asked him if I could study with him."

"You did what?" Her eyes turned into burning coals of anger.

"I asked him to be my teacher."

"You can't do that. I am your teacher. You can only have one teacher, and you belong to me."

"I'm sorry, but I don't want to study with you anymore. What you teach is negative and his teaching is positive. That is why I want to be with him now."

"You can't change your nature. It is already negative, and it can't change. He will destroy you."

"That's not true. I'm not an initiate, so I can change."

"But you've already done things that can't be changed. You attended some of the ceremonies. You've seen too much to be allowed to leave." Her threats became waves of black energy moving toward him. I quickly sent them back to her, and they hit her with full force. I could see she knew what I was doing, but she wouldn't acknowledge it, as she didn't want him to know about my protection. But I sensed he knew.

Her voice purred with persuasiveness. "Darling, we have been wonderful together, and together we have enormous power. I will teach you everything I know, I promise, whereas he will teach you very little. It will take you a long time to realize even a small part of what I can give you." I could feel him taking her enticing words in, and so could she.

She continued, "Look what I did for you and your job. Do you think this man would do that? No, he would tell you to work harder. His magic doesn't give gifts like mine does. If you go with him, you will lose your job—that I promise."

I could feel his fear around the issue of his job, and I tried to take his fear away from him so that she wouldn't sense it, but she did.

"You wanted that job for so long, and now it will be lost, just because you are enamored momentarily by his power. I have the same and even stronger power, but you are accustomed to it and don't realize how it has affected you. Be wise—stay with me. Not only will you keep your job, but you will be given more and higher positions. His teaching doesn't use the power for personal advantages like ours does."

Those words hit him very strongly, and I felt he would weaken, but something else happened and he responded, "Yes, you're right, his power isn't for self-interest; it's used to help others instead of for personal gain. I'm good at my job and my boss knows that. If you cast a spell over him and I lose the job, I will find another one, because I'm good at what I do. But I won't use magic selfishly anymore, like you do."

I felt his inner strength and was happy for him, as that was an important test to pass. He would go far, this student.

The woman's voice became stronger and more intense. Her anger turned from being burning to becoming a cold dagger. "Do you really think you can leave me? How stupid you are! Knowing some of our secrets, do you really think you will live?"

"I will never reveal those secrets unless my teacher asks me to. But I don't believe he will ask me to do so; he doesn't need to know your secrets because his are more powerful. I will never tell anyone about you, and I can only pray that someday you will understand that what you are doing is wrong. It is not too late for you to change. Please consider it. Now I must leave." And before she could respond, he turned and left her in her fiery fury.

I never left his side until he approached me by the mountain, and only then did I return to my body and open my arms to embrace him.

CHAPTER 7

I was tired after the previous day's challenge. The woman was trying to blast me with negative energy all night, so I had had little sleep. Her energy was a whirling wind that hit against my body. I put a shield around myself so that it couldn't penetrate my aura, but the impact still jarred me awake. I was also protecting Alex on the subtle plane from being burned by her. Finally, I sent her a very strong burst of energy, stronger than I like to use, but it worked. When I went down to breakfast, I asked the man at the hotel reception about her, and he said she had left in a hurry first thing in the morning.

I expected her to continue her attacks. She was very likely going to get help from some of her friends in the negative teaching. It didn't matter; I had some helpers, too.

I ate alone in the dining room. Since it was a little late, others must have come and gone. It was good not to have to talk to anyone. I could just sit and think about my journey. I needed to move on to the next town, something I was reluctant to do. It was nice to be with my students here and not have to start over again, but I knew it was time to go. I would return, but not for several months. That would give the students time to decide if this teaching meant anything to them. I had some written lessons I would leave with them, and I would start working on some more to send them later, so they could continue to meet and work together. These were all new students and my first ones, so my desire to stay and help them felt greater than my need to go. But in my morning meditation, my teacher appeared and told me it was time to move on, and I needed to follow her instructions.

I made arrangements to leave the next day, but that night I would have a last class at Dorina's house. Sitting, drinking coffee, I thought about the subject and didn't notice that someone had come into the dining room. When the person moved toward my table, I looked up to see a young blonde woman. She was naturally tall but still wore high-heeled shoes that made her blue silk dress flow around her as she walked. Standing before me, she looked attentively at me with deep, solemn blue eyes.

"May I sit down?" she asked.

"Certainly. Do I know you?"

"Not in this life, but I know you. My name is Maria Schwamle."

She pulled out the chair and sat down across from me.

"May I offer you some coffee or breakfast?"

"Coffee would be fine."

There was an extra cup on the table, so I filled her cup from the coffee decanter, which was always set at each breakfast table.

"What can I do for you?"

"I'm here to ask you," and her voice stammered a little, "to ask you to be my teacher."

I was taken aback because she was a complete stranger. I know I would have remembered her from my lectures, as her type of magnetism was very rare.

I didn't answer her at first but linked my heart with hers to feel if she was truly serious about becoming my student. I needed to be certain this wasn't a trick of Alex's former lover. Maria's heart felt pure, and her aura was also a very clear blue.

"I haven't seen you before. How did you find me and know that I was your destined teacher?"

"I work the night shift in the infirmary. I'm a nurse, and I saw you at a distance when you came to see a patient, Erick Messerli. People have been talking about you, and I knew who you were right away."

"How did you know that this was your teaching and I, your teacher?"

"I felt it in my heart. I don't know very much about your teaching, but it doesn't matter what I will learn, since I do know you're my teacher." And she smiled a sweet smile that made my heart respond.

Should I accept her? I didn't know what to do because I was starting to feel attracted to her, which was something that hadn't happened to me in years. I thought all that sort of desire had left me, and for a moment I felt as if my teacher were laughing at me. I remembered what she had said to me: "Sexual desire is one of the last things that leaves you on the spiritual path. This is why so many gurus go off spiritually, even though they keep teaching." But I had thought it would never happen to me.

I looked into Maria's lovely, soulful eyes and sighed inwardly. This was going to be a major challenge for me. "Yes, I will accept you as my student."

"Oh, thank you!" She jumped up and threw her arms around my neck and hugged me, something I didn't need to have happen.

"Please, sit down and tell me about yourself."

Maria spent the next hour talking, and I gave her a brief overview of the teaching. She was divorced, now single, twenty-six, and full of enthusiasm. This was her day off, so she could attend the evening class. I gave her the directions to Dorina's house and was getting ready to leave when she said, "Please, may I ask you a personal question?"

"Yes, of course."

"Are you married?"

When I didn't answer right away, she said, "I'm sorry, it's none of my business, but is this a teaching of celibacy?"

I laughed. "No, it's not. I believe in marriage, but not for myself. I'm too busy being a teacher to have a family, but it certainly is permitted for you to be married."

I could see she was relieved, and I couldn't wait to leave her; she radiated irresistible charm.

That evening, we all gathered at Dorina's house. Maria and Alex came early, and I introduced them to the others. I could see the men responding to her, especially Karl. They would make a good couple, I thought.

I explained that I would be leaving in the morning to travel to Meiringen, and there were a lot of protests from everyone.

"My students, you know I need to continue my journey to bring this teaching to others. This is my first town, and I have many to visit. I am leaving reading material and hope you all will continue to work together until I return, which I promise to do within six months. Then I will spend some time with you all again. Also, as I said before, I will be sending you additional lessons during my travels. But now, here is another lesson for you."

Love, Unconditional Love

"All of you understand love, personal love. Love of your mother and father, your siblings, your friends, and, most of all, romantic love.

"But what is love, and where does it come from? It is energy, warmth, yes, and it is a deep feeling in the heart. But answer these questions:

"Heinz, are you born with this love?"

"I don't know. It depends on how much your parents love you."

"So, you say it's conditional. You have it if you are given it. Does this mean that someone who doesn't have loving parents will never know love?"

"No, a person can learn to love," he answered.

"All right, then, love can be learned. Does everyone agree with that?"

"I don't think I do. If you don't have an open heart, how can you learn to love?" Uli asked.

"So, you are saying learning to love is impossible for someone with a closed heart. Does anyone agree with that?"

A couple of hands went up.

"Do you think someone can be born with a closed heart?"

A few students said "no".

"Does everyone agree that a baby is born with love in its heart, but, depending on how much the parents love the baby, the baby's heart will either open or close?"

This time there were many "yes" responses among the class, but one "no" came from Maria.

"Maria, why do you say no?"

"I think it depends on past lives. If I had lacked love in past lives, I would come into this life with either a strong need to have love or the opposite: a fear around loving and being hurt, particularly if that had happened before."

"Yes, that's correct, an open heart is preconditioned by past lives and karma. Parents are karma, and you may have a parent in this life who is unloving toward you even though you are his or her child, because of a previous difficult relationship together. But, in general, if one has unloving parents, there is always someone else — a grandmother or even a close friend — who really loves you; and that love will help you open your heart to others.

"How many people here came from a loving family?"

Only two raised their hands.

I looked at them, one by one. "Only two, yet all of you have beautiful hearts, which is why you are sitting here. Those hearts are part of who you really are. They have been developed over many lifetimes, not just one, and they are your hidden treasure. When someone is hurt by love many times, that person will close his or her heart to protect it from more hurt. Protecting the heart doesn't mean it has no love. It just means that there is fear around it. And fear is a strong force that can make a person become unloving."

Heinz raised his hand. "What if the fear cannot be removed or the hurt is too deep?"

"Fear can always be removed, but sometimes it just takes more time to uncover it. Fear is always based on something; once you discover what that something is, then you can slowly work to release it. Even hurt can become healed by love, and, in this instance, I mean self-love. If you can really love yourself, then when someone hurts you the effect won't last, because you know you are lovable and that others will come along who will really love you, too. But if you feel that no one could ever love you, it means that you cannot love yourself. Then you will project that feeling onto others so that, indeed, you will not attract love to yourself."

"But isn't it egotistical to love ourselves?" Alex asked.

"No, self-love is very different from being egotistical. Loving oneself means that you can accept yourself and believe in yourself. It doesn't mean that you have an inflated ego and believe you are better than anyone else. Loving oneself helps you to face life in a positive manner. When there are difficulties, you can confront them without complaint. When there is joy, you can experience it wholly, whereas egoists feel that life should give them everything because they deserve everything. They generally look at life pessimistically, and under their inflated self-worth are deep feelings of unworthiness. People who truly love themselves are not conscious of needing a lot of attention. They feel worthy so, therefore, don't in any way try to take from others. There is a big difference."

"Thank you, that makes sense. But how do you love yourself when you do have deep fears and feelings of unworthiness?" asked Uli.

"It takes time and positive thinking. I believe in psychotherapy and feel that if any of you have deep wounds from childhood, then it is important to go to a therapist who can help you heal them. If you carry the wounds with you on a spiritual path, in time they will reappear and stop your progress. Loving and accepting yourself is very important for spiritual growth. It helps you to become open to others, and it gives you the ability to develop unconditional love. If you love yourself, you have no need for others to love you. It frees you and allows you simply to love others without needing them to return your love."

"I understand what you are saying, but to do that seems way beyond my grasp. May I ask how you learned to love unconditionally?" Dorina asked in a weak voice.

"It took me many years and difficult work to find out who I really am. It goes back to what I was saying about finding the inner being within, which I call *Be-ness*. When I found Be-ness, I could love myself and love others because I could see that everyone, no matter who it was, had this same state of Be-ness within her or him. The heart holds the key to it all. When you use it constantly, it operates like a musical instrument. It becomes more and more refined and responsive; but if it is left unattended and not used, not only will it not play well, but it will need an overhaul and tuning to be able to be used correctly again. In order to love unconditionally, the heart needs to be utilized and given a lot of positive attention."

Looking at each one there, I saw several things I hadn't seen before. Heinz was nervous about this subject. He had become a priest because he was afraid of love relationships. He was gay and had kept it a secret from his family. Uli and Sara were having conflicts in their marriage and maybe would separate. Dorina's aura changed rapidly with her thoughts. There was fear there, fear of being vulnerable. Karl and Maria understood the most and already had developed warm and loving hearts. Alex was trying, really trying, to understand every word I said. He was very much in his mind and needed a lot of work on the heart. I felt love toward all of them and knew that they had been my students before in a previous life.

"Let's do an exercise now," I continued. "I will take you through the Higher Self exercise once more, and when you feel connected ask the Higher Self the following question: What do I need to do to open my heart more? Give me a process and a first step."

They wrote down the question, and, when they were ready, I took them through the exercise, first going over the information about the Higher Self for the new students.

When they were finished, I asked if anyone wanted to share what they had received.

Uli sat next to me and spoke first: "Last time I didn't get much, but this time I felt my Higher Self as a warm feeling in my heart, and I sensed that I needed to do some volunteer work with people who were ill and maybe also with children, because they are the easiest for me to love."

Sara exclaimed, "Oh! I was told something similar, but it was to help the elderly."

"Well, I wasn't told anything," Dorina said next. "My Higher Self came for a minute and then disappeared and wouldn't come back, which surprised me."

"Maybe you need to look at your fears around this issue and possibly do some therapy," I said to her, "since I think the fears come from your childhood."

She nodded, and I looked at Maria. She said, "It was a wonderful exercise, but I also didn't get anything yet, though I do think I felt my Higher Self for a minute."

"It takes time, so keep working on it."

Karl looked troubled, and I asked what he had received.

"I don't think it was my Higher Self. When I shined light on it, the shape turned dark, so I tried again, and the next time it turned dark again, so I didn't get anything.

"It shows you have some fear around this."

"But I don't feel afraid. I've always thought of myself as being warm-hearted, and I've been told so by my friends."

"That's true. But you are a pleaser, and that's because a part of you needs love from others. You can open your heart very easily, but you will block it at a certain point unless you work on your unworthiness issues."

Heinz again declined to share.

Alex, who was last, said, "I was surprised to see my Higher Self; I thought it would take me a long time to begin working with it, particularly because of my past. But I saw it, and it was a woman, and she was luminous."

Tears came to his eyes. "And she told me to send love to everyone I know, especially to those whom I may have injured. That was my first step."

I was pleased. "A good step. Keep working with it. You have a real connection."

Then I said, "I am going to give you another exercise to do. After it, you will do a sharing process. One person will tell the others what he or she received from the exercise. Everyone else will take that information into his or her heart, connect with the Higher Self, and meditate on it for a few minutes. Then each person will give the feedback they received to the person who had shared which can help that person. If you receive feedback that you don't feel is right, you need to tell the person who is giving it how you feel. Maybe it could be a projection of what that person is feeling. Then the next person will talk, and all of the rest of you will give feedback, and so on until everyone in the class has had an opportunity to share what they received and to receive feedback from the others on it."

I knew this process would not only bring them closer to each other but would also deepen their experience of using their hearts.

The exercise I gave them to do was to ask their Higher Self, "Do I have any resistance to opening my heart?"

Following that, I had them do the sharing process.

Dorina was the first person to talk: "What you told me before about doing therapy was right. My Higher Self said I did have a fear about using my heart that came from my childhood. I guess I need to do some therapy about that."

In the feedback, the first couple of people were hesitant and just agreed with Dorina. When it was Alex's turn, he said he saw her as a child hiding in the corner and her parents in another room screaming at each other. And he added, "I think they were screaming about you, but I don't know what about."

Dorina nodded her head. "That sounds right. They were always arguing, and often it was about me and how to raise me. I never felt much love from them."

The rest of the evening was mostly spent doing this process.

I wanted them to continue this type of class work together after I left, so I gave Dorina a series of other exercises for them to do over several weeks until I returned.

It was a long class. When I hugged each person goodbye, I felt sad to leave them.

Alex and Heinz stayed behind and asked if they could walk me home and speak to me privately. I sat with each one separately in the hotel lounge. Heinz was first. "Zarathustra, I know you must be wondering if I have been coming to your classes as a spy for the church here. Initially that was true, but now I no longer want to be a priest and would like to study with you instead."

I was surprised. "You can certainly be my student, but I strongly advise you to take your time and think about it more if you are considering leaving the priesthood. You can be of service in that role, and it doesn't conflict with the teaching. In fact, you will be able to work even better with people when you develop your heart and Higher Self connection more."

"But won't I be a hypocrite if I stay?"

"No, this teaching believes in Jesus and his teaching. He is a high Mahatma, and his message to love one another is exactly the same in this teaching. In 553 AD, during the Second Council of Constantinople, the church added many things as well as removed many things from Jesus's teaching, such as the law of reincarnation. Reread just the words of Jesus, and you will know his true teaching. You can find these most clearly and authentically in the Thomas Jefferson Bible. Jefferson took the indisputable sayings of Jesus and put them in his version of the Bible.

"But think about it, Heinz, and, if you still decide to leave, when I come back we can talk about what your future work should be."

Alex was a little nervous when his turn came. He asked me, "Teacher, can I go with you and help you on this journey? I have some money saved, so I can afford to leave my job and accompany you."

I intuited that he would ask and felt good about it. "Alex, yes, you can come with me. Thank you, I can use your help, but I will allow it for no more than six months. Then it will be important for you to return to your true vocation, and we will talk about that soon. We leave right after breakfast in the morning."

CHAPTER 8

The next morning, we took the tram down from Wengen. Alex picked up his car in the parking lot in Lauterbrunnen, and we headed for Meiringen, which was a few hours away. Having a car made the journey a lot easier. I had planned to take trains, but this way was much more direct. He assured me he had enough money to cover his expenses, so that also was a gift.

Alex called his supervisor at work and told him he had to quit, due to personal reasons, and could not work for at least six months. His boss told him he wouldn't accept his resignation but would give him a leave of absence, as he would like to have him back. This reaffirmed for me that I made a good choice in having him come with me. My worldly experience isn't the best, and I'm often uncertain about what to do in certain situations. All I knew was that I had to make this journey down from the mountain. Having Alex to handle the details in Meiringen, as Lucas had done in Wengen, was a relief to me.

On the way, we stopped to admire the beauty of the Staubbach Falls in Lauter-brunnen. The falls plunge nearly a thousand feet from the crest of the hanging valley that looms high over the town. In spring, the force of the water launches clear over the precipice of the rock wall and descends into a wide mist of spray and cloud that, as Lord Byron once put it, looks like the "tail of the pale horse ridden by Death in the Apocalypse." I prefer to think of it as the inspiration of Goethe's 1779 poem *Gesang der Geister über den Wassern*, or "Song of the Spirits over the Waters". Goethe's poem describes the repeated ascent and descent of water over a high cliff which flows through grassy meadows to a lake where the stars see their reflection. Some have interpreted this flow of water between Heaven and Earth as representative of human-kind's effort to comprehend both the mundane and the eternal.

After enjoying the view and energy of the place, we drove north to Interlaken and then east to Meiringen.

Meiringen is larger than Wengen, with a population of over four thousand, but it is still a country village, similar to Wengen in terrain and in the types of people who live and work there.

Alex and I found a nice inn and settled down. The next day or two were spent looking for a room large enough for my lectures. We finally found it in one of the larger hotels.

Alex made signs and posters to put up on bulletin boards in stores and hotels. He even made an announcement to be put in the local paper, while I went to various coffee shops and restaurants and met a few people who passed the word around to come. My clairvoyant ability to know people's names and stories always proved helpful.

The evening of the lecture, almost fifty people attended. This was the largest audience I'd ever had. It felt very joyous to me to see so many interested people. There were even some teenagers among them. I recognized one or two faces from past lives, and several others also seemed familiar. In this lecture, I started with a history of esoteric religion and ended by talking briefly about karma and reincarnation. Again, there were several ministers and priests attending, and one of them challenged me by asking, "In your experience as a teacher, have you ever found a student who questioned your knowledge and background?"

It was his way of doing that without asking me directly.

"In answer to your question, of course I have, just as I'm certain some of the people in your parish have questioned some of the rules and principles of your religion. I welcome it when someone questions what they hear. It means they have minds of their own and don't just accept everything that is told them."

A young Asian man raised his hand. "Are you saying it is always better to question rather than simply accept what someone is saying?"

"No, that's not quite what I'm saying. If your heart feels that what is being taught is true, then follow your heart and accept it; but if doubts arise, whether they be in your heart or head, then put a question mark next to the thought, instead of saying that it definitely is not true. One's truth is very changeable; what is not true for you today may be true for you tomorrow. Keeping a question open can sometimes lead to acceptance later."

After some more discussion, I continued with a talk about nature. It was a good time to speak about it, as spring was blossoming everywhere.

Nature — How it Functions

"How many of you have outdoor gardens?" I began. Almost everyone raised a hand.

"And when you work in your gardens, are any of you aware of the energy the flowers emit?"

Only a few raised their hands.

"Every flower, and plant, and tree has what is called a *nature spirit* attached to it. We can't see these spirits, but we can feel them if we try to communicate with them. They are what some cultures call *elves* and *fairies*. They are the life force of the flower and help the flower grow buds and open its petals."

I heard someone murmur, "That's nonsense."

"Something only seems to be nonsense because you can't see or experience it," I said. "Once you can, you will enter a world that is very different from this one, a world that functions in a very balanced manner. Let me show you something."

There was a vase of cut flowers on the table in front of the room. I walked over and took a tall, light pink mum from the vase and brought it back. I silently connected to the nature spirit of the flower, and when it responded, I asked it to help me show these people what it looked like. It was reluctant at first, but I convinced it that it would help them understand its kingdom more. Suddenly from the mum floated a small, white, cloud-like shape that began to move around the room. After a moment, just as suddenly, the shape returned to the flower in my hand and blended itself back into the flower.

During this demonstration the room fell completely silent, and then a man exclaimed, "You're doing magic! That's just magic."

"No, it's not magic. I asked the nature spirit to take its form and show itself to all of you."

A distinguished woman in her early forties raised her hand and said, "I saw the same thing once when I was working in my garden. It was around a rose bush, and it moved in and around some other flowers, too. Then it disappeared. I just thought I was seeing some optical illusion. Oh, that's wonderful!"

A few people started talking among themselves, and another woman raised her hand. "Can you please do that again?"

"I will try, but let me take another flower." I chose a red tulip that was just a bud. But it said no, so I put it back and tried a daffodil. It emitted a light yellow shape, somewhat smaller than the mum's but much faster moving. Everyone watched it move quickly around the room and back into its petals.

"I am showing you this to illustrate that there is life in everything. Even this pencil has life forms in it — not as advanced as the flowers', but, still, it has life. We can't see these things because our world separates us from seeing into these other realms."

I then talked more about how nature spirits work. "Each object and thing has such nature spirits—also known as *elementals*—that form its functioning energy. They are what you might call the workers, and they perform various jobs to keep the object vital and alive. The flower, for example, has some elementals in charge of its budding period and others in charge of its leaves and roots, and so on.

"There is always one nature spirit that is in charge of a flower, and another, more advanced nature spirit in charge of the whole garden. In turn, an even higher nature spirit is in charge of a broader area of several acres, and so on, up a hierarchal chain. Some of these higher nature spirits are called *devas* and can be in charge of whole areas, such as the mountains here," I said, motioning my arm toward the ridge of darkened mountains outside the window of the hotel.

"How do you know this?" asked someone in the audience.

"I know because I can see and hear them. I have lived for many years high in the mountains alone, and they are my friends."

"That's why you are a little nuts," a stocky man called out, and everyone laughed.

Alex jumped up and answered him, "My teacher is not nuts. He has deep wisdom, a word that you probably can't even spell." More laughs.

I raised my hand. "My friends, remember: you can question anything I say, just try not to close your mind through doubt. You live here in the valley with the majesty of the mountains around you. Surely, if you think about it, you also can come up with unusual stories about nature. You may not have the ability to see or hear the spirits, but certainly you must have felt them."

A teenager raised her hand. "I saw them a lot when I was very young, but they didn't look like these little clouds. They looked more like fairies, and I talked to them, too, but I never told my parents because they would have thought I was making it up."

"These nature spirits take on other forms to please the specific person, and certainly with humans they enjoy appearing as fairies or gnomes or elves. Many children have the ability to see them," I replied.

There were more stories. A man in his thirties, tall and lanky, with skin already browned from the sun and a mop of hair just a shade darker, talked about something that had happened when he was ten years old. He had been walking home at night and a snowstorm was coming. He got turned around and lost sight of the right direction, as the snow became a whiteout.

"Suddenly there was a light in front of me," he recounted. "Holding it was a little man only about two feet tall, and he said to follow him. I was afraid to do so. I didn't know where he would take me, so I just stood there. He turned and came up to me and told me he wanted to help me; otherwise, I would die in the storm. His wee eyes were so sincere that I followed him, and he led me directly to my house where my parents were already calling friends to be part of a search party to find me."

After a few more shared their stories, I ended the evening and arranged to have three more lectures in the next couple of weeks. Once most people had left, I spoke to the woman, whose name was Sophie Helfenstein, who had spoken about her garden.

I liked her immediately. When she spoke to me, her face bubbled with enthusiasm, making her even more appealing. Underneath was a good sense of humor. I knew she was one of my old students from a past life. The last man, the one who'd spoken about having been led home during a storm, was Bruno Dobler, who thanked me for helping him remember that rescue in his childhood. He was very outgoing, so I wasn't surprised to find out that he was in sales and marketing.

Alex was a wonderful help. He took charge of all the arrangements and details, and I didn't have to worry about a thing. He handled all the expenses and the donations in a discreet manner. The basket was full, which surprised me. I thought this community would be more challenging, but so far the reception was more open than in Wengen. Someone said that they had heard I was coming here, so my journey was already beginning to be noticed. That was good.

The next two lectures brought fewer people, as was expected. At the end of the third lecture, I again asked those I felt were interested if they wanted to attend some private sessions. There were only five people who were: Sophie; Bruno; a young teenager named Ernst; his friend Leonie; and, lastly, Dominik Bandi, an older man in his sixties, stocky, with gray hair that made him look much older than he was. We met in Dominik's house. He was retired, and his wife worked during the day, so the classes were held in the afternoon. All of the others were free at that time. Ernst and Leonie were out of school by three; Sophie's engagements permitted her flexibility in her calendar; and Bruno, working in sales, could adjust his time to be able to come in the afternoons.

During the first two meetings, I introduced them to the Higher Self and gave them some of the same exercises I had given to my first group of students in Wengen.

Leonie decided this wasn't for her and didn't continue after the first session, but Ernst hung in there, which made me happy. He was a very bright young man, only sixteen and already six feet tall. When he filled out he would be a handsome man, with dark-brown, curly hair and brown soulful eyes — beacons that had already attracted girlfriends. I felt he had a lot of spiritual potential. I could see that he had some doubts, but that was all right.

The last session was a long one. I talked more about karma and reincarnation and introduced them to the Mahatmas and Taras. Then I added some lessons on meditation.

Meditation Lesson

"Meditation is a spiritual practice that all of you need to do. It is the only way you can directly connect to the higher planes and the Higher Beings that dwell there. It is also a way of connecting with me when I am not with you physically. How many of you have tried to meditate?"

There was no response. "All right, then we will start with some basics. To truly meditate, it is necessary to clear the mind of any thoughts. This is very difficult for all beginners and even difficult for those who meditate on a regular basis. I urge you not to be discouraged and instead be persistent. It will come.

"First, it is important to find a place where you can set up a personal space that is or will become sacred space for you to meditate in regularly. Create the sanctity of the space. Set up a small personal shrine. The shrine should include a sacred object, such as a Buddha or a statue of Jesus or a Jewish star or a cross — any sacred object that you feel will represent the highest. You will need some pictures of those you feel are High Beings and also a picture of your teacher."

Dominik raised his hand. "Zarathustra, do you have a photograph of you that you'd like us to use specifically? Or could I take a picture of you with my cell phone before you leave? I would like a photo of you for my shrine."

"I don't have one specifically, so we can certainly take a photo at the end of class this evening," I replied. Dominik smiled in gratitude.

"Back to the shrine. It is important to have candles and incense lit during meditation. Seeing the flames and smelling the incense is a way of telling your body that this is the time to meditate. They signal the body to go into a calm state, and the mind to control its thoughts. In front of the shrine, you should have a chair or a cushion on which you sit. When you sit there, try to keep your back as straight as possible; and, if you can sit on a pillow and fold your legs in yogi fashion, that is best. Your chair or meditation cushion should be used only by you. No other person should sit on that seat, as that would change the vibration. The purpose is to set up a vibration that is strictly yours and to use that vibration to help you condition the mind not to have any thoughts."

"How can you stop thinking? I can't imagine not having my mind going on all the time," Sophie said.

"It takes time and patience, but learning to do that will strengthen you spiritually and help you explore the beauty of the subtle world.

"You need to start your meditation with a simple prayer and include in that prayer a dedication to your teacher, even if you don't know who that person is yet, and also to the Mahatmas and Taras." I took out some pictures I had brought with me of the different Mahatmas. Jesus and Buddha were there. I also had a picture of my Mahatma, and when Dominik saw it, I could see that he resonated with it. He asked if he could make a copy of it.

"No, not at this time. The pictures of the Mahatmas and Taras can only be given to a student when when the student becomes a disciple. You can find your own picture of Jesus, and, if you want, a statue of Buddha. The following is a simple prayer that you can use in the beginning of your meditation:

"May I grow closer to my teacher, my Mahatma or Tara, and bring into my everyday life the ability to use my heart in everything I do. May I be one with my spiritual brothers and sisters and use my heart in all my relationships and deepen my striving for God Consciousness. I ask to be of service and help others when help is needed. I pray for the sick, and that there be an end to war and suffering, so that the planet someday will

be a place of peaceful coexistence among all peoples. May my heart be open; may my mind be full of wisdom; may my body be renewed with energy; and, most of all, may my Higher Self be fully in my consciousness. I dedicate this prayer and meditation to my teacher, to my Mahatma or Tara, and to all the Mahatmas, Taras, and Higher Beings, to all who are helping the evolution of this planet."

People started to write down the prayer and I told them they needn't do that since I had copies for each of them.

"You can add to the prayer or change it, but it is important to start your meditation with some prayer and dedication. At the end of the prayer, try to focus on your third eye, which is in the center of your forehead. Visualize a lotus; see the lotus rise and go out the top of your head and try to follow it. Then let everything go and keep your mind blank.

"There are several things you can do when a thought enters your mind while you are meditating. When you are sitting, have your hands cupped in front of you with palms upward. The hands can be folded under each other, or just the fingers tips can be touching, or the fingers can be entwined. When a thought comes in, focus your attention on your hands; then go back to meditating. This keeps the thought from moving into another thought. You can also envision a blackboard and see the thought written on the board, then erase it. Or envision a piece of black velvet with the thought on it and shake the velvet so that the thought falls off. Some people like to draw a symbol in the mind's eye; when they do that, it stops them from going to the next thought."

Several hands were up. I pointed to Bruno.

"Teacher, can you tell me which method I should use?"

"I suggest trying all of them at different times, and you will then know which works best for you."

Ernst asked, "How long should we meditate?"

"It depends on the person. The average time is a half an hour, but some people can only meditate for fifteen minutes, and others prefer an hour. It is important that you choose a time early in the morning or late at night when most people are still sleeping — the atmosphere is purest then — and try always to meditate daily at that time. Consistency in your meditation schedule is another way of conditioning your body to know it's time to meditate. If you can, meditate two or three times a day, even if they are short meditations. The more you meditate, the more you will improve your concentration. Even if you are not at home, go to a park or a church that is open, and meditate."

Sophie's hand was up. "I feel a little uneasy about meditating. What if I see something I don't want to see?"

"If that happens, just open your eyes. Nothing can harm you. If you link with me in your meditation, you are protected. But if someone is on heroin, cocaine, LSD, or other psychotropic drugs, and goes into those planes and has a bad experience, they cannot control it because they are under the influence of the drug. Also, you are never to meditate after you have had a drink. You must wait at least six or seven hours for the alcohol to leave your system. Any drinking should be in moderation. Unless you are ill, taking hard drugs such as opioids are forbidden in this teaching. Never meditate if you are doing that. If you smoke or ingest marijuana in any form, you should not meditate for three days. It takes that long for your body to be completely free of its influence."

I noticed that Ernst looked nervous.

"Cigarette smoking can also interfere with meditation. Not only does it harm you physically, but it also affects you spiritually. Those of you who smoke need to stop. If you are a heavy smoker, you cannot become a disciple."

"Why is that?" Bruno asked.

"Nicotine is a drug and very addictive. That's why it is one of the hardest things to give up."

"I know. I've tried, but I will try again," Bruno answered.

"Good, now let's have a meditation together. Ernst, you sit this one out."

I set up a small shrine with my pictures and a candle and incense and took them through the stages of meditating. I kept it short, about fifteen minutes, and when it was over asked for sharing of the experience.

"I tried the blackboard and it worked. It stopped my thoughts, but then they came back!" Sophie exclaimed.

"I tried the blackboard, too, but it didn't work for me. Focusing on the hands was better, but it'll take a lot of practice to do," Dominik shared.

Bruno was quiet, and when I asked him about his experience he reluctantly said, "Not so good. I saw some colors, and then everything went black, which bothered me."

"You did very well. Seeing colors means you were on a higher plane. If it turns dark, just keep concentrating on the darkness, and the colors may come again, or a light. If you see a light, try to go into it and enlarge it. It can then open up into a scene."

"Oh, that's cool!" he replied, feeling better.

Alex didn't share his meditation. He was very good at it and experienced many things that were best not to share with this group of beginners.

The discussion continued until almost six o'clock, the time when Dominik's wife was due home.

We planned to meet briefly the following morning at my inn to take the picture and say goodbye.

The next day I awoke with a ringing in my ears. When I closed my eyes, I saw my teacher, and she told me I needed to stay with this group longer.

"But why?" I asked.

"There is someone you will meet, and there is also a student here who needs your help. Stay five more days and speak with everyone privately. Find out more about them before leaving."

I got up early, went downstairs, and booked our rooms for another five days. I decided to go for a walk and think about what she told me. It was a brisk, cool morning. The sun was only beginning to rise and there was still some fog floating through the valley. Only a few people were on the streets—mainly pet owners walking their dogs. I headed for a small park I knew of nearby, sat on a bench, and thought about each student, one at a time. Who would need my help, I wondered?

When I reflected on Sophie, I saw a woman of many potentials who hadn't developed any of them, mainly because of low self-esteem. She needed to believe in herself more, and that was something I could help with. But her issues certainly weren't so significant that they'd preclude me from leaving.

Bruno and Ernst both seemed self-confident and secure. That left Dominik. Somehow, as he became the focus, I felt something wrong or missing and realized he was the one to whom my teacher was referring.

Previously, when I met with Dominik, I had felt that he was quite lost. He had retired at sixty-five from a highly-skilled, executive role in a large, multi-national corporation headquartered in Zürich. After he left his career, he and his wife moved permanently to their weekend home in Meiringen. His wife, who was fifty-eight, took a job in a local tourist shop. This left Dominik alone at home much of the days. They had been here three years. He thought it would be wonderful to have free time, but now he was becoming very bored and generally unhappy. Dominik had devoted most of his life to his career and had never learned truly to relax, develop other interests, or enjoy other activities. Even though he now wanted to do many different things, he hadn't the understanding of how to begin, and as a result, was losing enthusiasm for the pursuit.

I set up my private visit with him immediately, and later that day Dominik and I met up. We spent most of the rest of the day together and I realized that he was contending with depression and likely heading for a breakdown. His eyes were sad, and he spoke in a low voice that had little life in it. I suggested he consider some volunteer work, but he said he had inquired around town but found nothing that really interested him. I came to understand that, as many men of his generation, he had worked hard his entire career, rarely socializing or developing many true friendships throughout the years. I proposed a few ideas which might offer him connection to others, a sense of renewed purpose, or an opportunity to be of service. I felt at a loss myself, as every time I suggested an activity or idea, he declined, saying, "No, that's not for me," or, "I tried it and didn't like it." I even took him through the Higher Self exercise, and he was in such a state of resistance that he couldn't connect with it.

At the end of the day and before I took my leave, I asked him to meditate with me. My teacher appeared to me and simply said, "Ask him what he wanted to do when he was a child."

When I asked Dominik the question, he replied almost immediately. "Oh, some stupid kid thing. I wanted to grow up and be an actor. I even did some acting in high school and college, but my father wouldn't hear of my pursuing such a career."

"Are there any theater groups around here?" I asked.

"I think so. There is the William Tell theatre in Interlaken that runs from June to September, and also some summer stock companies that often come through some of the towns in the region. Oh, and the Bern Theatre is about an hour's drive and its production schedule is all year."

"Well, I think you should look into volunteering for one of the theatre groups that are operating permanently. They always need backstage help and business advice, and you can even try out for some senior roles."

"I'm too old for something like that," Dominik protested, but I could feel it was halfhearted and his resistance was lifting.

"You're never too old, and it may be a fun thing for you to do."

His face started to light up. "Do you think so? Really?"

"Yes, really. Look into it."

I felt a smile in his heart and warmth that hadn't been there before.

The fifth day came, and there had not been a new person to arrive as my teacher had mentioned, so I again meditated and asked my teacher what was happening. I received no answer, so I assumed it was not meant to be after all. Alex was out doing some shopping and, since it was a lovely, sunny day, I decided to take a last walk around town and enjoy some of the sights Meiringen had to offer. The *Hauptstrasse*, or "Main Street" was lined with low-rise buildings of different Swiss styles along either side, many with retail stores or cafés on the ground floor. Some were cream-colored with red tile roofs, and others had black tile roofs that were arched or square flat. Most had shutters that were closed to keep out the bugs at night, but they varied in color from bright red to green or even black. Each was a unique building.

Walking along, the main street became *Bahnhofstrasse*, or "Railroad Street," the main shopping street, and every two or three houses there was a colorful banner that hung between the buildings on either side of the street. Trees lined the street, and there were hills and mountains surrounding the town that could be viewed from anywhere as I made my way along.

I meandered off these main streets to the smaller side streets. These were lined with wood, chalet-style residences that had behind them blooming gardens. I stopped to look at the flowers and sensed they wanted to escape their enclosures so that their beauty could be fully enjoyed and seen. As I came to the upper part of the village, I saw a church with an imposing Romanesque tower and a wooden spire. I decided to go inside for a short meditation.

A pamphlet on its history said it had been rebuilt five times due to flooding from the Alpback, a torrent that formed a waterfall behind the building. It also said that there were a series of fourteenth-century interior Romanesque frescoes with scenes from the Old Testament. The frescos were in the niche at the front sanctuary. I found them a bit disappointing because they were poorly lit and much of the detail was lost. The only light came through small, higher windows.

I was just turning to leave when I felt a tap on my shoulder. A short young man stood there. Holding what looked like a large flashlight lantern, he whispered, "There's no one around, so I'll use this."

The light was a strong floodlight, and, as he moved its beam across the frescos, we could see the beauty of the paintings for the first time.

"This is the area I liked the most." And he pointed the light at a corner where the artist had painted in some landscape with interesting-looking animals grazing in meadows and exotic birds perching in the trees.

He turned the light off quickly when we heard footsteps, and he tucked it into a bag he was carrying. The footsteps belonged to another visitor, but having seen most of the frescos by that point, we turned to go.

"Thank you so much for sharing your light with me," I told him.

"Oh, I'm glad I had it. I usually carry one when I am traveling because so often I find churches such as this are in darkness and do little to light some of their beautiful paintings. It's a shame. Even the sculptures aren't lit, so it's not just about protecting the paintings. In some churches I've visited, I've seen that they use mechanized lighting equipment, which are usually not maintained, and they charge a lot for just a minute or two of illumination. It makes me angry."

I invited him for coffee, and we went to a nearby café. The man's name was Pierre Bouton, and he was from Marseille. He had two weeks' vacation and was traveling through some of the smaller towns in Switzerland, exploring their art and architecture. Pierre was in his late twenties with a strong, square face that had a mature and determined look, resembling a warrior ready to take on any mission. Pierre was not married and was enjoying the freedom of just going anywhere he felt inclined to go. He explained he was an accountant, but art was his hobby and he even liked to paint landscapes. His blond hair framed greenish blue eyes that flickered with enjoyment when he talked and made me feel an instant connection to him.

I mentioned what I was doing, and he asked me questions. Before we realized it, the sun had set, and it was becoming dark.

When I told him where I was going he said, "I have no definite plans. If you don't mind, I will go there next. Then I can have the opportunity to attend your lectures."

I told him where we would be staying in Interlaken and that I looked forward to continuing our conversation there. I returned to the inn to find Alex patiently waiting.

CHAPTER 9

When we arrived at Interlaken, I introduced Pierre to Alex. He had arrived before us and was able to book a room in the same hotel. It was lunchtime, so we all dined together. I said very little and listened as Alex and Pierre talked about themselves in the process of getting to know each other.

Both were single and both really wanted to get married and have a family. I found out that Alex was also very interested in art, and they both loved medieval art and the Impressionists. I could tell that these two would be good friends, as I saw immediately that they had been brothers in a past life and had had an excellent relationship. It was always good to see how connections can mature right away into something lasting. Pierre offered to help Alex look for a hall for my lectures and find a place to make copies of the event notices.

After lunch, they left to do these tasks and I went to my room for a nap. I suddenly felt tired from the drive and the many people in the city. Even though the local population isn't large, Interlaken is the tourist center of the Bernese Oberland region. Grand hotels line the broad avenues, and the busy casino attracts many visitors, so the streets were full of people. Their various vibrations affected me immediately.

When I lay down, I fell asleep right away and had a very noteworthy dream. I was standing in a market where there were many stalls and carts of food and various meats for sale. On one side of the aisle was a long line of people waiting for their turn to buy an item from what looked like slabs of red meat hanging from a line tied to the ceiling and dripping blood on the ground underneath. On the other side were some stalls of produce, where only a few people were buying what looked like huge bunches of green, leafy vegetables. I watched as the red meat was wrapped in brown paper and stuffed into shopping bags for the buyers. It looked like an assembly line, with one man cutting the meat, another man wrapping it, and still another man at the end who weighed and priced it. I stopped a woman who had just bought a piece and asked, "Madam, can you tell me what kind of meat that is and why there are so many people wanting to buy it?"

She looked at me as if I were crazy and said, "Don't you know? It's the finest lamb in the country, and it's available only once a week here at this market."

I then turned to one of the vegetable sellers and asked, "Your vegetables are huge and delicious looking. Why aren't there more customers?"

She also looked surprised and commented, "Something this good is never sought after. It's too healthy for most people."

I woke up knowing that this city would be a difficult place for my lectures, and I wondered if we should move on and not even try to do something here. The lamb meant that the churches here were very strong and had large congregations that would not be interested in my teaching. That there were so few at the vegetable stands meant I would have very little attendance. I was thinking about what to do when there was a knock at my door. It was Pierre.

"Zarathustra, forgive me for disturbing you, but Alex and I could find only a few places that might be suitable for the lectures. One should be booked right away, so we need for you to take a look at the options first."

I checked the places they had located, and they were all too big; it would be best to have a smaller space as the attendance would not be large. Both men were surprised, and Alex said, "But, Teacher, you've had large audiences in the other places. Why would it be less here?"

After hearing about my dream, they understood, and we continued to seek a smaller venue. They eventually found a smaller room adjacent to one of the larger spaces we had already seen. The owner agreed that if the audience was larger than expected, we could move over to the larger hall, which wasn't booked for the night we were holding our first event.

I was feeling uneasy about booking even the smaller room, as it was expensive, but Alex said everything was expensive here. There was some money to cover expenses but not a lot. Each event so far had given us just enough to continue, and, even though Alex offered to pay for some things, I preferred not to take any of his money. I worried now that the lectures here wouldn't produce enough for us to carry on.

Maybe it was wrong to go to larger places; the smaller towns were more intimate and cordial, but my teacher had told me to go this route and stop at all the towns, cities, and villages, no matter the size. I needed to consult her again, so I went to my room to meditate. She appeared immediately and said, "It is never quantity but quality that you need to find. Even one person should not be lost. You will find at least one here who will follow you."

"Can't that one find me elsewhere, in the next town, for instance?"

"No, she is here. Trust that if you do the work you will be taken care of."

I trusted, but I still worried. Worrying was something I had developed, now that I was back in the world. I longed to be in the mountains, planting my own food and living in nature. In a couple of months, I would go home to regain my center and renew my spirit; but, until then, I had to follow the route my teacher had given me.

The lectures would begin in five days, but this time I kept it to three talks instead of my usual four or five.

During that time Alex and Pierre did a good job of posting flyers, placing ads, and using social media to get the word out. Both Alex and Pierre knew how to do all of that. They also helped me get a cell phone and a computer. Alex insisted that I have my own website and said that during his spare time he would design one for me and set it up.

Pierre had heard a great deal about the teaching and me from Alex, so even before the lecture, he asked me to be his teacher. It was nice to have him back with me, as he was an old disciple of many lifetimes. If I could only find more students like him and Alex, I would feel content.

I was right about the turnout. Only twenty people came, and half of them walked out when I started talking about God being within each and every person. That left eleven people, so I asked them to move the chairs closer into a circle. Then I talked about the journey to finding God within. It was the same first lecture that I'd given previously, but the questions here were different. One elegantly dressed woman in a navy designer suit asked, "I can understand the part that God is energy, not a big man on a throne, but I don't understand what you mean by God being just an energy. If He's energy, how does He direct the universe?"

"I would say to you, if God is a being, how could a mere being direct the universe? Energy is fast and has no boundaries. It flows in all directions, and when it contains wisdom, it knows how to make the universe run correctly. There are many beings that help in this process of using God's energy correctly, and even though these beings are pure energy, they can take on a form for those people who need to see form.

"Our universe is complex, just as your body is complex," I continued. "You are made of millions of atoms that make your body function, and the universe is made of zillions of atoms that form the nucleus of its life. All that energy comes from the Source, or what you call God. Science someday will understand it better. The big bang is essentially the energy which is called God, expanding."

"But how can I relate to this energy? It is too abstract for me. I feel God is around me, and I feel I can pray to Him because of that," said a young man.

"Gustav, it is around you because everything comes from energy, which comes from the Source. The Higher Beings that I mentioned are the Gods that you know. These are the planetary rulers called *Kumaras*, who run the solar system, and there are lesser Gods. You can pray to them and they will hear your prayers. The Jewish God, Jehovah, is one of these Higher Beings but not the Supreme God that I am talking about."

"If there is a Jehovah, then why talk about something higher? Let's just keep praying to Jehovah, that's a big enough God for me," Gustav replied.

"But that limits you from finding the God within. Jehovah is not that God. Your Divine Spirit belongs to the highest, and that spirit longs to return to the Source. The lesser gods can't fulfill that need. They can only help you find it. Christ on the cross became one with the Divine Spirit and was helped in his journey by the Higher

Beings. He now is with them helping all of humankind achieve becoming one with the Source His vibration is much higher than mine."

"You're saying I can become another Jesus?" an older woman blurted out.

"You cannot become Jesus. He was an individual. But you can achieve God Consciousness just as he did. In fact, that is the destiny for all of humanity."

"Have you achieved God Consciousness?" a somber-looking man asked disbelievingly.

"I have achieved moments of it, just enough to help me yearn for more."

"What does it feel like?" another man asked.

"I can't describe it in words. But let's do an exercise that may help you experience a touch of your spirit."

I then took them through the Higher Self exercise, and, when they were connected, I told them to ask their Higher Self to give them a touch of what it would feel like to have God Consciousness. As I waited to see what the reaction would be, I wondered if I had made a mistake in trying this exercise with new people. I was certain that several would achieve nothing, and that would make them turn away. But maybe there would be one or two who would stay. I looked around the room and saw one woman begin to smile. She looked radiant in that moment, like a dazzling star shining in the sky.

When I asked if anyone had experienced anything, she immediately raised her hand and said, "It was incredible! I felt a calmness come over me, and you're right, it's much too difficult to describe it in words. Thank you."

"Anyone else experience anything?"

The man who had asked the original question said, "For me, it wasn't the way she described it, but I did feel an inner longing to continue the exercise, so I will try it again when I go home."

"Yes, I would encourage all of you to keep trying, and, more importantly, if you didn't see or feel the Higher Self, continue to try. The more you try to connect to it, the more you will experience it in your consciousness. The Higher Self can help you in your daily life, psychologically and spiritually."

It was getting late, so I ended the meeting with the short prayer.

Before they left, I asked how many would be coming back to the next meeting. Surprisingly, everyone except two people raised a hand.

Pierre and Alex remained behind with me, and the three of us returned to the hotel for some tea. I felt exhausted, more so than usual after a lecture.

Alex picked up on this and asked me what was the matter.

"There was an energy in the room that was difficult to bear; that's why I'm so tired."

"Zarathustra, you mean a negative energy?" Alex's voice sounded worried, and I knew he feared that his former teacher was around.

"No, not negative. The opposite. When we did the God Consciousness exercise, I felt my Mahatma come in to help people there experience God Consciousness. His energy is very powerful, and even though most people didn't feel it, because I am very sensitive, I felt it immediately."

"But why would it make you tired?" Pierre wondered.

"His vibration is much higher than mine, and although he reduces it a lot in order to be there and not adversely affect those present, I still had to make a strong effort to withstand that energy level. It's wonderful that he came. Because he was there, some people experienced something. That 'something' awakens the spirit and causes the person to seek more."

I looked at them. "How was the exercise for the two of you?"

Alex said, "Wonderful. I felt the energy just for a second, and it was wonderful."

"Me, too," said Pierre. "Thank you. I'm so happy to have met you and grateful that you are my teacher." His sincerity warmed my heart, and then it suddenly grew cold with the unexpected knowledge that he would someday leave me. Later, I tried to keep the sadness out of my eyes when I embraced him and said goodnight.

Interlaken was full of interesting sights. Alex and I enjoyed the next three days touring with Pierre, who had thoroughly researched the best places to go. The town sat between two lakes, Lake Thun and Lake Brienz, which is how it got its Latin name, *Interlaken*, meaning "between two lakes." It was founded in the twelfth century around an Augustinian monastery, the remains of which are only the cloisters. We walked down the main street, Bahnhofstrasse, which turned into Hoheweg, a promenade that links the center of the town, Interlaken West, with Interlaken East, where the town was more scattered and less clustered with large hotels. It offered spectacular views of the majestic Jungfrau peak across the valley. There were gardens and the Hohematte Park on one side, where we stopped for a brief meditation and then refreshments at a small café. On the other side were the grand hotels, presided over by the Victoria-Jungfrau Grand Hotel and Spa. Built in 1865 and designed in heavily decorated Victorian style, with a tower in the middle and wrought-iron balconies for every room, it housed celebrities from around the world.

We also took a leisurely stroll along the Aare River, which connects the two lakes and is lined with elegant residences. This area was busy with tourists as it was a favorite district for them to explore. Interlaken had always been a big tourist center but now was even more so.

Our last day of touring we spent taking a boat ride on Lake Brienz to the resort of Brienz. In Brienz we took a boat across the lake and then a funicular up to Giessbach Falls. The falls rumbled from a height of four hundred meters as they cascaded down the mountainside, forming waterfall after waterfall until they landed in the lake at the bottom. It was as if one of the ancient gods had cut a staircase on the mountain and then asked the water goddess to drop a torrent of water down it to create a splendid scenic view for their heavenly abode.

I loved water and didn't have much of it where I lived on the mountain. Watching the falls was breathtaking and somehow made me feel how important it was to leave my home and experience the other beauties in nature. It made me feel for the first time that my journey was not just a thing I had to do but would also be something that would prove meaningful and essential for me.

I felt like a different person during those three days. Switzerland was my home, but even though I had basked in its bountiful beauty, I had never participated in the usual touristy things. The same was true for Alex. It was very interesting to see our country through the eyes of a stranger. Pierre marveled at all the sights, especially the mountains. I realized that I needed to be more open to what surrounded me, instead of sometimes taking it for granted.

My next lecture took place on a rainy, stormy evening, and I thought some people would not return. Surprisingly, the nine people did still come, and they brought friends with them, so again we were back to around twenty attendees. This time I did my lecture on karma and reincarnation. It went well mainly because most of the people knew the concept, and again there were interesting questions.

"Zarathustra, I think that people who believe in reincarnation are coming from wishful thinking. They can't accept that when you are dead you are dead. Reincarnation is an easy way out," a friend of Gustav's said.

I laughed. "I don't see reincarnation as being easy. It's just the opposite. You may have done some nasty things in your life. When you die, you may feel you got away with them, but the reality is that you will have a lot of negative karma to pay back when you are reborn. Living lifetime after lifetime is never easy; but knowing about karma and reincarnation helps people to be more careful about how they live their lives."

"Can I come back as an animal? I wouldn't mind being a dog."

"No, that is involution, not evolution. It is a cosmic law that all things evolve. The mineral kingdom evolves into the plant kingdom, and the plant kingdom evolves into the animal kingdom, which then evolves into the human kingdom. Man and woman are the highest animal form on this planet. A dog's next life would be as a human being, but not here; at this time, dogs and horses evolve into the human form that exists on Mars."

That brought a lot of questions, so I talked about the seven bodies of every planet and said that Mars had life forms on one of those bodies that we cannot see.

Then I explained the life cycle of our planet, which is called the *Manvantara* in the East. On a large pad, I drew a circle and divided it into seven parts, like pieces of a pie. "These are the seven rounds," I said, explaining that each piece of the "pie" represents one round of the Manvantara. "We start off as pure spirit at the top, or twelve o'clock, "and descend counterclockwise into pure matter in the fourth round at the bottom, or "six o'clock," which is where humankind is at this time.

"Then we ascend," I continued, tracing my finger up from six o'clock to nine o'clock and back above the twelve o'clock, "and become pure spirit again at a higher level from where we began; and at that level we have full knowledge of all the experiences we have gone through by that time. The Manvantara cycle lasts for 4,320,000,000 solar years."

"You mean we have to live that long? No wonder you said reincarnation isn't an easy way out!" a man exclaimed.

"No," I laughed. "That would be too long. Humankind as we know it didn't come into being until the end of the third round in this cycle. In the previous, longer rounds, other kindgoms were developed. The later rounds will be shorter."

This conversation continued for the rest of the lecture.

At the end of the lecture, I again asked who would be attending the next time, and fifteen people raised their hands. By this point in a lecture series, I usually had a good indication of how many people would want to continue the work after I left, but somehow with this group, I couldn't readily identify the future students. The only one of whom I was certain was Winifred, the woman who had the beautiful experience during the God Consciousness exercise. The others felt nebulous to me when I concentrated on them. I could feel their interest move in and out. My last lecture would occur in three days. At that time, I would do another Higher Self exercise and observe them more closely.

The weather on the day of my last lecture was terrible, and there was a gloominess over the entire town. It poured rain all day, the kind of rain that makes even the ducks hide for shelter. The dark clouds were menacing, and I felt it was an ominous forecast for the evening's lecture.

I was correct; the turnout was quite small. Only eight people came, and they were all in a pessimistic mood. I thought I had lost Winifred, but she arrived a couple of minutes late, soaked to the skin. I could tell it had been an enormous effort for her to be there. I was glad that Johann, one of the men at the last lecture, was able to come. The other seven came from either the first or the second lecture, and there were no newcomers this evening at all. No surprise, I suppose, given the prohibitive weather conditions.

We settled into a circle, and I started with a short meditation. Reflecting on the evening later, I wondered what had happened at that point. It started during the meditation, when a man named Leonhard suddenly jumped up and exclaimed with some fear, "The devil is here! I can feel him. The devil is here!"

"That's not true," I assured him. "There are no negative spirits here. But if you feel it is true, please feel free to leave."

He promptly did and another woman got up and left with him. After they were gone, I turned to the six remaining people and could see that a couple of them seemed frightened. I again assured them that there were no negative spirits in the room. I pointed to the bouquet of roses and the burning incense. "Roses and incense keep a room pure."

"But Leonhard is a very spiritual man. I don't understand why he would make up something like that," a woman who had been sitting next to him said.

"Delusions happen even to the most spiritual. It is important to develop discernment, so you can determine what is real and what is not real."

"But how does one know that?" Winifred asked sincerely. "I may think I can discern and believe something but be totally wrong."

"You know by working with a teacher," I explained to her. "That is one of the main reasons it is important to have a teacher when one pursues a spiritual path. A teacher is there for you, not only to protect you but also to advise and help you."

"But I don't want a teacher to tell me what to do," a man mumbled to a woman sitting next to him.

"A true teacher doesn't tell a student what to do. He or she guides the student on the path."

"That's not true! I've read enough about Indian gurus to know they are very controlling; the students have to obey them or they can't stay in their ashrams," he said.

"That's true of some teachings but not this one. This is a teaching for this age that we live in. It's about everyone having the opportunity to work with her or his Higher Self and to do this spiritual work in the world, dealing with all the mundane issues that arise in everyday life. It is not about a select few who live in isolation in ashrams. It is easy to live in ashrams or monasteries and devote your life to prayer and meditation, not having to deal with the stresses of a family and having to work. This teaching is more difficult because it requires you to be a part of the world but not of it."

"What do you mean by that?" the same man asked.

"I mean that students in this teaching participate in all aspects of everyday life but are striving to not be attached to, or identified with, the desires, emotions, and attachments that can accompany living in the world. You can evolve and grow spiritually, following your spiritual path, without having to live an ascetic life of seclusion. Rather, you can be a delivery driver, investment banker, or politician, have a spouse and children, or neither—so long as you are able to approach, consider, and address everything in your life in an unattached manner."

People laughed when I said "politician," so I added, "Yes, there are spiritual politicians, and I, for one, welcome anyone who is spiritual to take on that kind of work.

We need more men and women who are spiritual, compassionate, and ethical running the countries of the world."

"That's for sure," Winifred said, nodding.

Energy and How to Use It

It was time to start the lecture. I got up and walked around the outside of the circle. Everyone watched me, wondering what was going on. When I returned to my seat, I stood in front of it and explained, "I want to talk about energy. When I walked around the circle a moment ago, how many of you felt my energy as I passed your chair?"

Only one person raised her hand.

"All right, I will do it again; and this time try to feel my energy as I walk by you."

I again slowly walked behind all of the chairs in the circle. This time when I asked who had felt my energy as I passed, several people raised their hands.

"What did you experience?" I queried.

Wolfgang spoke without hesitation, stating, "It was like air moving across my back."

"Yes, I thought it felt very light, but I also felt a warmth," Wilhelm added.

"I felt it more like a light that came across my vision and then left," Pierre said.

"Good. That is an indicator of how you may experience energy. I deliberately sent the same energy to each one of you as I passed you. Yet each of you experienced it differently, not because the energy is different, but because the way in which you individually pick it up is different. For example," and I looked at Pierre, who had experienced the energy as light, "you pick up on energy in a visual manner. Others may feel it in the body, as Wilhelm and Wolfgang did."

"I experienced both," Alex said. "I felt it in my body and saw a light."

"That means you have those two senses awakened."

"Oh, I like that. Would you do it again please?"

I agreed and walked around them again, but this time at the end, when I stopped, I pulled in my aura. I heard a gasp and Pierre exclaimed, "You disappeared!"

Everyone started talking at once.

"How many of you saw me disappear?"

Three people raised their hands.

"What I did was pull in the energy field around me, and doing so causes that phenomenon to happen. Again, it's about being in control of your personal energy. Disappearing is not necessarily a good thing to do, but historically, adepts used it when they journeyed across dangerous regions where there were marauding tribes of bandits. In Switzerland, you won't need to use it, but I wanted to show you that energy is very flexible. As you grow spiritually, you start to understand how best to use it."

"How would we use it?"

"You are already using energy when you send love to someone or when you help someone. Love is a very powerful energy that can be used consciously." I paused to let that register. "I once attended a lecture by the Dalai Lama, where someone asked him about how she could help the multitudes of homeless and hungry people in India. He said that, obviously, she wouldn't be able to feed or give money to all of them, but she could send them love, as that feeds their souls. Being in your heart, listening to your heart, and giving with your heart are part of every spiritual path. Loving others, even your adversaries, is the proper use of energy. Most of you are Christian. I know you know that Jesus taught us to love one another. That was his teaching and his mission. Follow that teaching in your lives, and you will be working with the highest energy, and it will change you spiritually."

"What do you mean, 'change me spiritually'?"

"If someone yells at you or verbally attacks you, what is your reaction?" I was looking at Winifred.

She replied, "I guess I might get angry and defensive, and maybe yell back."

"Yes, and I'm sure you've experienced that the fight then becomes worse. If instead, you can remain calm, be in your heart, and respond in a loving way, or a quiet way, the energy of the attack doesn't get fueled and therefore will subside. Obviously, if the person yelling at you is more than verbally insensitive or unkind, and his or her emotions seem out of control, it can be best not to respond at all and to leave the scene. If it is someone you care about, you can later address the situation when the person becomes calmer."

"But how can someone be loving and calm if offensive things are being said to them? That's not possible," Wolfgang said.

"Yes, it is very difficult not to be emotionally affected by what the person is saying, which is why it might be best to wait until you both are in a calmer place. Then you can connect to your heart and, in so doing, listen to your Higher Self. This will help you to know the proper words to say in return. Those words may be kind ones, or they may be words that are strict but said in a kind manner. If the person was too offensive, then you need words firmly to address that behavior. In no way should anyone accept any kind of verbal mistreatment without doing something about it. If you are being mistreated in this manner and don't assert a healthy boundary with the aggressor, then you may select to end that kind of relationship. But I'm not referring to that level of unhealthy relationship. What I am talking about here is when something occasionally difficult happens with a friend or loved one and hurtful words are spoken. I am not talking about repeated ill treatment."

Again, I looked at Winifred; I knew she was in an emotionally abusive marriage.

"What happens if you can't get out of the relationship, as with a close relative?"

"Even with a relative, you can end the relationship if the relative doesn't try to change their attitude and behavior toward you. Karma is always the key factor with relatives, but you can choose not to participate in perpetuating bad karma."

We talked more about relationships of all kinds and how to approach various types of situations, and then I returned to the subject of energy.

"Other than love energy, what other kinds of energy do you use on a regular basis?" I asked them.

"Well, I guess the negative energy that you just talked about — yelling and using unkind words," Gustav observed.

"Absolutely. Energy comes from all your words. You can say words in a kind voice and the same words in an angry voice, and the words themselves then take on different meanings. For example, I can say to you, Alex, 'Would you please do the dishes tonight?' I can say it with some frustration and rebuke if I've been doing the dishes every night, and you'll hear it that way. Or, I can say those words with a loving voice, because we always take turns doing dishes, then it's more like making a request, and you won't hear any edge when the words are spoken."

I looked around the circle. "Any other kind of energy?"

Wolfgang offered, "Well, we use energy to exercise, to have sex, to do sports — really to do everything."

"You're right. Every action requires energy, or what is called *prana*, to undertake, but the kind of energy I'm referring to is subtler and comes from your inner resources. Words are a good example, as is using the heart. Think in those directions and give me other examples."

"What about our thoughts? They take on a certain kind of energy."

"Good! Thoughts are definitely full of energy that is deep within. Sometimes you can tell what a person is thinking because of the intense expression on the person's face. And you can definitely tell when one's thoughts are full of emotion—positive or negative. When the thoughts are full of energy, that energy gets expressed in the body either through action or expression. Keeping thoughts neutral is important to a yogi. When thoughts are charged, it can cause wrong actions to happen."

"But how can we keep thoughts neutral?" Winifred asked.

"If you look at your thoughts through the eyes of an observer, then your thoughts will have little energy connected to them. You can then choose to keep them or discard them. It puts you in control of your thinking and helps you learn to keep them focused."

"But how do you do that?"

"Practice, practice, practice. It's about training your mind to watch a thought instead of getting immersed in it. It's about learning self-discipline."

"I hate that word. It's so rigid," Pierre said.

"*Discipline* has become a bad word for those people who hate order and self-control. It's also a word associated with the military, and some people dislike anything to do with the military. But in actuality, it has been part of every teaching throughout history. To achieve God Consciousness, you must have self-discipline. Try to see the word and the concept in a different light. Being disciplined gives you the power to control your thinking, to complete any task, to meditate, and to study the ancient teachings. It takes concentration and hard work, but, in the end, discipline gives you freedom."

"How can it give me freedom?"

"If you are in control of your thoughts and actions, you are free to choose what you want to do. Instead of the thoughts or actions governing you, you govern yourself. It gives you the ability to grow spirituality and to establish the right relationships that will help you in life rather than hinder you. Is there anyone here who has a relationship with someone in which you feel completely free — no shackles, just freedom?"

The only person to raise his hand was Johann. "Almost free, not completely, but almost."

Some laughed.

"What you say sounds enticing, but it certainly must be an exceptional person who can achieve this." Wolfgang's voice sounded doubtful.

"Yes, that's true. But everyone here is an exceptional person and has the ability to find such freedom. What's most important is to have the desire to achieve it, and that desire comes from the heart. The more you use the energy of the heart, the more you will desire to find the God within. That takes us back to the beginning of this class."

Although it was beginning to get late, they stayed on for another hour, during which I took them through a Higher Self exercise. Five of the eight present that evening decided they wished to continue in this teaching, so I arranged to meet with each one privately over the next couple of days. After the meetings, I arranged to have one more group class at Winifred's house. And then my third-city visit came to an end.

It was also time for Pierre to end his trip and return to his home, so I said a fond farewell and we made arrangements to keep in touch. He and I would part many times in the future before our final farewell.

CHAPTER 10

We arrived in Luzern late in the afternoon and found rooms in an inn on the outskirts of town in a suburb called Tribschen. Alex knew the area. On a prior visit he had toured the former home of the famous composer Richard Wagner, where he lived in the mid-1800s, and which was now a museum. The suburb was only two miles from the heart of the city and less expensive than anything closer to the city center.

Luzern is a city with ten times the population of Interlaken. It is a large, bustling metropolis and very different from the small towns in which we had spent time until now. This would be a real test as to whether I could attract followers from a more cosmopolitan setting. I knew that getting the word out would be a challenge where there is so much competition for everyone's attention and time, but when it came to attendees, I knew in my heart that those who were meant to be with me would come. But how to let them know I was here was the question.

The next day, when Alex and I meditated, we each asked our Higher Selves what the best approach would be to advertising our lectures here. I received no guidance, but Alex came up with a new plan. He felt it was best to start with a small lecture in Tribschen, where we were staying. We would advertise it locally in Tribschen and try to draw even a handful of people. Then, after the first lecture, we could ask those in attendance if they knew others who would be interested in the subject and were located in the heart of the city. He believed it was important to continue that gradual outreach process by word of mouth and then ask people to mention the lectures on their social media posts until we had a larger audience, and only then seek a hall in the city and increase the advertising.

It sounded like a good plan to me and we followed it. The first session drew about ten people, but then it escalated, and after the third lecture we had nearly a hundred people in the room. It was at that third lecture that a newspaper reporter attended, and afterward he wrote a positive, supportive article about me and the teaching. Alex rented the auditorium at the local school for the next lecture. It could hold two hundred people, and, quite unexpectedly, it was almost full when I appeared to give my fourth talk. I had never had that many people gather to listen to me, and it was very disconcerting at first. My style is an intimate one, but with this many people, that kind of atmosphere was impossible.

There was a stage and a lectern and many bright lights, so I couldn't see people's faces. I felt a little unnerved and almost a bit frightened. I knew the feeling was due not to stage fright but rather to not having a clear view of those in the audience. I also knew that there were some negative souls in the audience, casting negative energy. What to do? For a fleeting moment I felt paralyzed, but then an inner voice said, "Be calm, you are the teacher; act like one."

I asked that the lights be turned on in the auditorium and the spotlights focused on the stage turned down. When I believed the lighting adjustment was the best it could be, I scanned the audience and spotted the intruders. I imagined them covered with a thick, glass bell, intended to prohibit their negative energy from leaving them and permeating the room. This helped the energy lift right away.

I started my introduction standing in the front of the audience, not on the stage. I even walked down the aisles so I could get a better view of the faces. This helped me, and it also enabled people to feel my presence better. I cast my aura as far as possible so that people could better experience my vibrations. Then I returned to the front and began my lecture on the meaning of right action.

The Meaning of Right Action

"Most of you come from a Christian or Jewish religious upbringing and believe in acting ethically. Is that not so? But sometimes what *you* believe is ethical action may differ from what your neighbor believes is right. Such beliefs are as individual as the shapes of snowflakes on a winter evening. Sometimes a group of people will agree about what the correct course of right action is, but the manner in which that right action is carried out may reflect a variety of individual desires, some of which are correct and others that aren't.

"You may say, what does it matter, as long as the right action is achieved? And you are correct to a certain extent. But that attitude becomes questionable when you are dealing with time and energy. Say for example, you as a group collect used clothing for a worthy cause and there are various ways to distribute that clothing. The outcome could be chaotic without a coherent plan. Time and energy are what make the plan happen, but both can be wasted. It is therefore important to give sufficient forethought to these two factors.

"I will give you another example: When I go into towns and cities, I usually choose an area that is small so that it is easier to meet people and have small, intimate talks. Tonight, though, I have switched to a large gathering, much larger than my usual audience. Is this right action on my part, or would it have been better to stay with smaller groups where I could talk with people on more of a one-to-one basis?" I waited for a reply.

338

"I would think smaller is better," a woman near me said.

"Ok. Now, among all of you who live in this large city, if I had advertised small-group talks on the Higher Self, how many of you would have come?"

Only about half raised their hands.

"How many of you feel safer coming to a big gathering where you have the option of staying or leaving without being noticed?"

Ninety percent raised their hands.

"Right. I prefer small groups, but I knew intuitively that people who live in large cities feel more comfortable in larger group settings. Because I felt more comfortable in smaller group settings, I started in smaller villages and towns and suburbs, where people were comfortable with smaller gatherings, and I expanded to a larger group in the city. That is called knowing what the right action is for a given situation." I paused, then asked them, "How many of you think you always perform right action?"

No one raised a hand.

"How many of you feel you sometimes do right action and other times fail to do the right thing?"

Just about everyone raised a hand.

"Now let's take this to another dimension. How many of you think you perform right action spiritually?"

A man in the first row asked, "What do you mean by that? Do you mean do I go to church every Sunday?"

"No, I mean much more than that. I mean that you follow your spirit in doing the actions it guides you to do. For example, you suddenly have a longing to go watch the sunset on top of the mountain, or you feel love for a friend and need to tell the friend how you feel, or you listen to a child laugh and stop to appreciate the joy in that sound as it resonates in your heart. Listening to your spirit is listening to the God within. How many of you take the time to listen to your spirit?"

"That's very abstract," a young man said.

"It sounds abstract, but it really isn't. It's just that most of you, first of all, haven't acknowledged that the spirit exists within you; and secondly, even if you do believe that it does, you don't believe you can hear it or follow its directions."

A few people murmured among themselves, and I waited until it was quiet again.

"If you follow your spirit's direction, you will always be doing right action, so let's begin with a process of understanding what I mean by *spirit*. Within each one of you is what is called the Higher Self. This part of you contains all the right actions, the beautiful gifts of the heart, and the knowledge of God. Within the Higher Self is the seed of the spirit. Once the seed is awakened, it activates the Higher Self, and you then can develop the ability to access the Higher Self at all times.

"This teaching I am giving to you is called Higher Self Yoga. It is a teaching that helps you to work more consciously with this part of yourself. Every time you help others or love others, you are in your Higher Self. It is the real you, but often it is not heard because the temptations of the everyday world obscure it. The more you acknowledge it and try to follow its direction, the stronger it will become and the clearer will be your understanding of right action."

A man at the back raised his hand. "Can you give an example of this Higher Self?"

"Yes, I'll be glad to give you a couple of examples. A disciple of a guru in India was seeking wisdom, so he asked his teacher where he needed to go to find it. The guru sent him to his own guru, who lived in a cave in the mountains. There the disciple asked the same question: 'I want wisdom, where do I go to find it?' This guru told the disciple to go back to his guru and ask him the question again. When the disciple did, his guru sent him back to the mountains with the same question.

"This pattern kept repeating until the disciple couldn't stand it anymore and asked his guru, 'Why do you keep sending me to your guru and he to you when I ask that question?'

"'Think about it. I am telling you that you will find wisdom within him, and he is telling you that you will find wisdom within me. You don't have to go anywhere, it is right here.'

"The disciple finally understood and then asked, 'Teacher, will you then teach me the wisdom that you have?'

"'No, I cannot teach you my wisdom, but I can help you find the wisdom within yourself, which every being possesses. It is the wisdom of your Higher Self. I will help you find the Higher Self, which has access to higher wisdom.'

"That story illustrates that the Higher Self contains spiritual knowledge, but the Higher Self also has practical knowledge that can help you in your everyday life. The story I'm going to tell you next illustrates this as well as illustrating right action.

"A friend of mine told me this story. He was traveling for his company to the Far East and found himself in a precarious situation. The man with whom he was to have a meeting was late, and, as he sat waiting for him, he saw a young woman sitting at another table. She was alone and looked a little distraught. He tried not to stare at her, but he couldn't help it. He had a strong feeling that he needed to do something, but his business contact would be arriving very shortly. The feeling became stronger, so he followed it and got up and went to her table, sat down, and said to her, 'I apologize for this interruption, but I could tell that you were having trouble, and I just wanted to offer my help if you need it.'

"When he said this, she burst into tears. 'Thank you, I just don't know what to do. My father was to meet me here an hour ago. He's never late, and I phoned him and was told by his secretary that he left in plenty of time to meet me. I'm very worried about him. He would have called if he was going to be late.'

" 'Could he have gotten stuck in traffic?'

" 'No, his office is near here and he was walking.'

" 'All right, let's walk the route he would have taken.'

"The two of them got up, and she took my friend to her father's office; then they slowly walked several of the streets that her father could have taken. On the second route they pursued, they passed an alleyway, and my friend instinctively went into it and found a man unconscious on the ground. It was her father. He had been hit over the head but was still alive. It turned out that a mugger had threatened him with a knife and forced him into the alleyway, where he hit him and took his wallet."

I added, "The father had lost a great deal of blood, so he could have died if my friend hadn't followed his feelings. The feelings he had about the young woman were coming from his Higher Self, and even though his business contact came and left while this was happening, it became secondary to his inner knowing that he had to help her. He saved a man's life by listening to his Higher Self and taking the right action."

"Wouldn't that be called the intuition rather than the Higher Self?" an elderly woman asked.

"No, but I'm glad you brought that up. The intuition works with the Higher Self, but it is still very different from it. For example, in the story, when the man noticed the woman looking distraught, his intuition told him something was wrong, but the intuition didn't tell him that he had to do something about it and that it was important for him to follow through. That additional information to do something and follow through and the strong feeling he had came from the Higher Self. Listening to the intuition, he would have known something was wrong, but he wouldn't have known that he needed to do something to help her. That's the difference. In fact, if he merely had intuition, he would have been more focused on his business meeting."

I was still standing next to the stage, but now I went up the stairs and pulled a chair over to the edge and sat down. I could still see their faces, though not quite as clearly, but there were people in the back of the room who undoubtedly were having difficulty seeing me from where I had been standing, so I moved up onto the stage instead. This decision came from my Higher Self, and I told the audience what had just happened.

A man in the rear of the auditorium verified what I said. "That's amazing. I was just thinking that it would be nice to see you better, because it is hard for us back here to get a good look at you when you're in front of the first row."

"I apologize for not having picked up on that before." I looked around. "But this is another example of how your Higher Self works. It always knows the right action, and you can count on it being correct."

A woman raised her hand. "That may be true for you, but how do I know I'm listening to my Higher Self and not to my desires?"

"You're right. Desires can certainly interfere with receiving the correct message. I always suggest that you write down all your desires and really be honest with yourself. If you get a message that in some way connects to a desire you can identify, then question the source of the message, because it may not be from your Higher Self but rather one of your desires. Obviously, it's not going to be clear if you have an attachment around it. In that case, I would ask a friend to ask his or her Higher Self for an answer for you. A friend can ask his or her Higher Self to connect with your Higher Self and should receive a clearer answer because the friend will not have any of your desires around the outcome. For example, you may have a yearning to travel to a particular foreign country, but you aren't certain whether the country is safe for you to travel to. Your desire could cloud the correct answer for you. A friend could meditate on this question and give you a correct answer."

"That is if you can trust the friend to get it right," I heard a man mutter, and those around him laughed.

"I want to talk a little more about right action. As I said before, what is right action for you can be wrong action for someone else and vice versa. How many people follow what their friends do and get into dire circumstances as a result?"

Several people nodded. "So how do you know you are following what is the right action for you?" a young woman asked.

"I follow my gut feeling," a middle-aged man called out. "It's always right."

I responded, "Yes, now you're again talking about intuition. You follow your intuition and it is always right, but sometimes people negate or dismiss their intuition. So, what do these people do?"

"I guess they make mistakes," another man said, and everyone laughed.

"Yes, that's true, and you always learn by mistakes, so that's not terrible; but before taking an action, is there some way you can be certain that the action is correct?"

I heard some more mumbles, but no one gave a solution.

"Okay, let's try an experiment. How many of you have to take a physical action this week? It can be any kind of action, from going to a doctor's appointment to talking to your boss about a project."

Just about everyone raised a hand.

"Take a moment to think about the action you're going to take. Go over it in detail." I paused to give time for this process.

"Now close your eyes and live the action. See yourself doing it from start to finish." Again, a pause.

"After you are finished doing the action, picture putting the whole experience in your heart and ask, 'Is this the best way for me to do this action?'

"If you feel it is the best way, then open your eyes. But if you feel there is another way to do the action that could be better, then ask to know what that is and see yourself doing the new action."

I waited for all to be finished and noticed that several people had repeated the exercise. I asked, "For those of you who received a new action, how was the experience of doing it differently?"

A woman raised her hand. "I needed to confront my daughter about something, and the new way was much gentler and didn't put her on the defensive. The way I was planning to do it would have made her very upset with me."

"That's a good example. Anyone else?"

An older man raised his hand. "It was a very strange experience for me. I plan to take a trip later in the month, so I originally saw myself taking the transit bus to the airport. When I asked for a better way, I saw myself hiring a taxi to the airport, which would not have been my first choice because it is more expensive and I live on a small pension. I visualized the first scenario of taking the bus to the airport and asked what was wrong with that. This time I saw that the bus got stuck in traffic because there was an accident and I came close to missing my plane, whereas the taxi was able to get off the highway and take some back streets to avoid the traffic jam. A bus is required to follow its route."

"That's wonderful. It shows that sometimes what you think is best isn't, and only the Higher Self knows what the outcome could have been. This is also a good example of why it is important to check things out with your Higher Self."

The audience became enthused hearing these two stories, and others freely began to share their stories.

I ended the evening by telling them another story.

"There were two siblings who lived together, Andrin and Rico. Andrin was the older one and worked as a lawyer in a well-known law firm. Rico was eight years younger and had finished college but wasn't certain what career he wanted to be in. His main interest was science, but he needed a higher degree to pursue it. At the time, he was tired of school so instead found a job doing filing work in a big corporation. He stayed there a short time and then quit, next finding a job in another corporation doing sales work. Hating that, he quit again. This became a pattern. The longest job he kept was for six months.

At that point, Andrin was exasperated with him. He was paying for all the expenses. He also was dating a woman with whom he was falling in love, and he wanted her to come and live with him.

Finally, one day Andrin told Rico he had to leave. He bought him a small condo and said he would pay all the maintenance fees, but Rico had to cover the rest of the expenses. The job Rico had at the time was being a receptionist in a small dentist office. He had again planned to leave because it was so boring, but realized then he could no longer do that as Andrin would no longer take care of him.

For several unhappy years Rico stayed at the dentist's office, until one day a friend tried to convince him to get career help. Fortunately, he followed his friend's advice and worked with a career therapist, discovering that science was still his main interest and that he should be pursuing a career in research. He started taking courses at night and then got a scholarship, quit his job, sold his condo, and went full-time, ending up with a doctoral degree in biology. He was in his late thirties when he got his degree.

The right action in this case would have been that instead of buying Rico a condo, Andrin should have persuaded him to get help and go back to school, and assisted him financially. Rico would have finished many years earlier and been so much happier."

I added, "Right action takes time and discernment to develop. Try not to feel disappointed if you find out that you didn't follow the action that would have been best. There will be times when right action can't happen, even if you try, because of unforeseen circumstances."

At the end of the talk, several people asked if I was planning another lecture. I decided to do one more and asked how many people would be interested in coming the following week. I was surprised to see more than half raise their hands. I had already reserved the auditorium for two more days in case there was interest in more lectures. And, since the people were already coming here from Luzern Center, we decided it wasn't necessary to find a larger hall there.

I spent the following couple of days preparing for the new talk, after which I wasn't certain what I needed to do. Since the crowd was so big, it was difficult to determine whether some would want to continue the work in a small group. I felt there were one or two, but even those were questionable. It is difficult for me to read someone when he or she is surrounded by a lot of people. The vibrations get intermingled and confused.

Finally, on a beautiful, sunny day, I went into the old town center of Luzern and walked along Lake Luzern. A concert was taking place in the park there. I stopped to listen to an overture by Offenbach. It was lovely and uplifting. I continued my walk along the shoreline into a less busy area of town, where I found a serene place by the water to meditate. Almost immediately, I saw my teacher and asked her for guidance.

She told me, "Zarathustra, you believed that in each town you would have a handful of students who would want to continue to study this teaching and that, after going to about six or seven towns, your work would be finished and you could go back to your home in the mountains. You thought you would guide the groups of students from there, and after a year or two, you would return to the groups and teach. And afterward, you would return to your home again."

"Yes, I did think that. Isn't that true?"

I saw her face, which is usually serious, break into a smile, "No, it is not true. You are now in a city and have many people attending your talks, and you are trying to predict how few of them will become students from this large group. Maybe there will be more than a few. Have you ever thought about that?"

"No, because all esoteric teachings have only a few followers."

"That was true in earlier periods of history, but we are going into a new age in which many more people are ready to learn the esoteric knowledge."

"But surely here, in Luzern, most people are just curious, and many will drop away at the end?"

"Not as many as you think."

"Really? How many will be left here?"

"At least twenty people will want to learn more from you."

"Twenty?" I found that difficult to believe.

"Yes, in all the larger cities there will be more than in the small towns."

"But that would mean I would end up with" — I made a quick calculation — "close to a hundred people. That's too many! How can I work with so many people?"

"Not all of them will become disciples. Many will stay for a year or two and leave, but at least half will have that potential for discipleship. Then, of course, you will eventually be traveling to other places, and maybe other countries, so that number will increase."

"Teacher, I am not ready for this! I thought I would have maybe thirty students at the most and maybe even fewer. And, certainly, I thought they would all be local!"

"There are many teachers who have even more disciples, but always there are only a few students who are able to work with the higher energies. You also will have only a handful of these close disciples who will continue the work and become teachers in the future."

That, at least, made me feel better. "But how do I manage so many people, and can I still go home for some time between teaching engagements?"

"You can go home, but not for long periods of time, contrary to what you expected. You are now teaching in the world, and in the world you must stay."

I felt a deep sadness at these words, as my heart was already longing to be home, surrounded by the majesty of nature and in the serenity of my solitude, with only my nature friends for companionship.

My teacher said, "It is a sacrifice, I know. But what is more important — guiding others to God, or living as a hermit?"

"Both are important. I need to do both, but I guess I won't have the long times I had planned on to be home in the mountains." Then I asked, "Teacher, what do I do about this large audience? How will I know the twenty?"

"Teach two more times to the large group and then ask to meet with those who want to continue the work. You will know then."

I followed her advice. The next talk had as many people as the last one because people brought friends to hear me. I gave my talk about the spiritual journey.

The third week brought, again, more than I had anticipated—at least a hundred people. That talk was on karma and reincarnation. At the end I announced that if anyone was interested in continuing to study the teaching, I would meet with him or her over the following three days. Alex had sign-up sheets; and, when the last person had left, there were not twenty but thirty-five names on the sheets. When Alex saw how many were waiting to meet with me, he added a fourth and fifth day so I wouldn't be so burdened. Even then I had to meet with people for seven hours a day. In the meantime, Alex looked for a place to rent where we could have a couple of meetings with the new group before we left for Bern.

All went well. After the private meetings with individuals, several decided the teaching was too much for them at that time, but they asked to know when I was returning so they could attend my next talks. I ended up with twenty-six people who were willing to continue the studies. I was pleased to see that there were several people from different cultures in the group. We met, and I took them through the Higher Self exercises and gave them instructions in meditation. It was a larger group than I liked to work with, but I found that the diversity was helpful in explaining the teaching. I provided each with a copy of the exercises that I had given to the other groups. Fortunately, one of the twenty-six was an unmarried, middle-aged man with a large home that would accommodate most of the group. His name was Boris Feuz, and I immediately felt a heart connection with him. I added another meeting to be held at his house to establish the energy there and to see where it was, so I could visit sometimes in my subtle body and listen to how the class was doing.

Boris's house was centrally located and in a very good neighborhood, with ample parking nearby. It turned out that he was a lawyer and quite well known, which accounted for the luxury of his home.

Boris invited Alex and me to dinner before the meeting, and he greeted us with such warmth that I felt at ease right away. Boris was tall with blond, curly hair and dark blue eyes that emanated a deep intelligence. Before, when we had met privately, he had confided to me that he was gay.

A person's sexual orientation or gender expression has no bearing on that person's spiritual growth potential. During our discussion, I asked him if he was in a relationship and he said he was, but it was fairly new so they were still living separately. He explained that his partner had also attended my lectures but had decided not to continue, which disappointed him. I explained that it was better for his partner not to continue unless he could be committed to the work.

The class met in the living room, which was large and very comfortable. Boris

346

had plenty of folding chairs that accommodated everyone. I carried with me some shrine pieces, and, beforehand, Boris and I set up the shrine with a picture of my teacher on it. I also gave him a photograph of me to frame and have on the altar after I left. I explained the need for candles and incense; and I gave a blessing to the shrine and to the whole room and, in so doing, purified the energy. I asked Boris to do the same each week before the class began and gave him a prayer to use. I could tell he felt honored to be able to have the classes in his home. I knew he was meant to be one of the close disciples my teacher had mentioned. He already had the steadfastness and commitment that was needed.

After everyone was there, I talked about the path and the Higher Self. Then I gave them a lesson on the meaning of one-pointedness.

One-Pointedness

"When you strive to develop spiritually, it is important to learn how to discipline your mind and be in a place of one-pointedness. What I mean by "one-pointedness" is the ability to focus your mind on one thing at a time and keep that focus for as long as you need to. Without that ability, you will have scattered thinking and a lack of focus that will inhibit your ability to transmute your lower nature into the higher. Having one-pointedness keeps you centered and enables you to start a project and complete it in a shorter period of time."

I looked around the room. "How many of you here start to do something and then do something else before you complete the first task?"

Many raised their hands, and I noticed the hands were mainly from women.

"Women tend to do many things at the same time. Taking care of work inside and outside of the home seems to require that. Let me ask some of you: what would happen if you concentrated on one thing at a time?"

A woman raised her hand. "I don't think it's possible. I have three young children, and they are always diverting my attention."

"Rosemarie, everything is possible. Are your children in school?"

"Two are in school and the youngest is still home."

"Obviously, when they are all at home you would find it difficult always to focus on one thing at a time, but surely when two are in school it should be easier. In any case, even with children, you can focus your attention on them, and, when you leave them, focus your attention on something else. The idea is not to have a million thoughts come into your head but to keep your mind clear except for the object of your concentration."

"I don't have children, but I always have a lot of thoughts running through my mind. How do I stop that?" Miriam asked.

"The mind is like a sieve. It collects and dispenses all types of information, much of which is extraneous. To discipline the mind takes time and patience, but it's worth the effort. A disciplined mind learns more quickly and retains that knowledge. I am going to give you some exercises to do that will help in this process. The first exercise is a simple one. Draw a circle on a piece of paper."

"Shall we fill it in?"

"No, just a simple circle. It doesn't have to be perfect."

Once that was done, I said, "Now, look at the circle and focus all your attention on it. Try not to think any thoughts when you do this; just keep looking at the circle and notice anything about it."

I had them do this for about five minutes. "Now, close your eyes and again see the circle, but this time with your mind's eye. Try to notice if it is different or the same as the one you have drawn. If you lose the image, open your eyes and look at it again."

After another five minutes, I asked, "How many of you could keep the image in your mind's eye?"

Half the group raised their hands. "That's good, very good. This takes time to learn, so if you didn't succeed now keep trying."

I then had them draw a triangle and a square, and we went through the same procedure with those shapes.

"You may find as you continue to work with these simple shapes that they will sometimes change and become three dimensional. Just go with that, and then see if you can make the shapes turn into color. This is harder to do, so don't force it."

"My triangle turned into a yellow line," Boris said.

"That's very good." I wasn't surprised, as I knew he was an old yogi.

"Focusing on an object, any object, really helps you learn to concentrate. Try looking at a flame: if you have a fireplace, that's a good way to start. If not, just light a candle and look at the flame. Since it moves and changes shape, a flame is easier to look at than a stationary object. Another object that is used by yogis is a crystal. Hold the crystal in the light and turn it and notice the colors and shapes that take place in it. Any questions?"

Several hands were raised. "Yes, Kurt." I pointed to a man seated in the back.

"My eyes are very poor, so it's difficult for me, to see the drawing."

"Have someone draw a very dark one for you or draw the circle and fill it in with a black marker. That should help; and I think that, if you really work with it, it will be easier for you to open up your inner vision."

A young woman named Gretchen raised her hand. "When I look at the symbol with my eyes open, I think about how imperfect it is, and that makes me lose my concentration."

I laughed. "If that is occurring, you need to look at everything else in your life, as it sounds as if you are a perfectionist. I do have a couple of sets of perfectly drawn shapes. I will leave a set with Boris to make copies for those of you who need them be perfect. I personally think the imperfections make the shapes easier to concentrate on.""I can see that learning concentration is good discipline, but isn't there more to being one-pointed?" a young man named Mies asked.

"That's a very good question. Yes, there is more. The first step is to develop concentration, and all these exercises will help you do that. It is also important to have strong meditation skills. You will find these exercises will help you let go of thoughts. The next step is to use this skill in simple tasks. For example, making dinner: As you fix the food, concentrate on each step and try not to think about anything else. If you have dinner guests, do not think about them. Literally keep your mind going one step at a time until everything is cooked and the table is set. Or, if you are in a gym doing a series of exercises, instead of thinking of the next one to do, stay with that one until you are finished and only then think of the next one.

Even at work, if you have a simple project to do, concentrate on one step at a time until you complete it. Start with a task that is simple; then you can build up to something more complicated."

Another woman, Frieda, spoke up. "But how do I stop my mind from wandering? I know it will."

"Every time your mind wanders, bring it back to the task you are doing. Being focused isn't easy, and no one here will be able to do it right away. Notice the kind of thoughts that come in. If, for example, you constantly are thinking about someone, then set a time deliberately to direct your concentration only on that person. Think about the person and clear the mind, so that when you go back to doing your task, you have dispelled those thoughts and can focus better."

After some more discussion, I ended the lesson by taking them through the Higher Self exercise again. During the exercise I had them ask their Higher Self to show them a symbol that they could personally work with in the concentration exercise. Some of the symbols they saw were very interesting shapes. There was also a mixture of abstraction and realism among them.

There were several people who didn't receive a symbol. I told them, "Try asking your Higher Self again after you have worked with the simple shapes of the circle, the square, and the triangle. The symbol is something you will work with later. For now, all of you should keep working with these simple shapes until you feel you can hold them in your mind's eye for five minutes without any thoughts coming in. Then, and only then, begin working with the symbol the Higher Self has given you. At the same time, try to keep your mind focused on each task you do. Hopefully, when I return all of you will have developed more one-pointedness."

I said my goodbyes to each student, and by the time I returned to the inn, it was almost midnight. Tomorrow we would leave for Bern, but I was tired, very tired, and thought about home with a longing in my heart.

CHAPTER 11

We were to leave early in the morning, but I awoke with overwhelming fatigue. I told Alex I needed to sleep more and that we might have to wait another day until I felt better. He was concerned and wanted to buy me some medication, which I refused. I didn't need medicine. I needed rest. The crowds here had depleted my energy, and I simply needed to restore it.

I slept all morning and had some vivid dreams. One was full of surprises. My Mahatma came and took me to a beautiful place in India. He wanted to show me some shrines there, and when I awoke I recalled them all in detail. Toward the end of the dream, he asked me, "How do you feel about the classes?"

Much to my surprise, I replied, "For some of the people I have a deep love, and for others I don't. I would rather have only those few as students and not the others. I know this is wrong of me to say, but you asked how I felt and I am being honest about it."

"Some people you have known many times and have had close relationships with them, and some you haven't, but that doesn't mean you can't love them as much as the others. When you begin your inner work with them, you will understand what I mean by that."

"I hope so, as they turn to me for advice and love; but sometimes I have the urge to tell a student to find another teacher."

"But you don't do that, which is wise. They are attracted to you because this is their teaching."

"I know, and that's what matters the most to me, to give out this teaching and then move on."

"Are you becoming used to the moving on?"

"No, I really want to return home and not do any of this, but I have no choice. My teacher has asked me to do this work."

"You always have a choice. If you don't want to do the work, your teacher will find someone else who will take over."

I thought about this in the dream. I was now half-awake, watching myself in the dream make this decision. I tried to tell my dream self no, don't say no to this mission, but I couldn't. At the same time, I felt all the inner conflict and even felt my dream self wavering. Again, I cried no, to no avail, but maybe I did get through, as my dream self finally shook his head and said, "No, this is my mission. I will not turn back, but I do need to rest in the mountains once in a while."

I woke up fully and rested there for some time, worried that there was such a strong part of me that wanted to give up. I also felt, for the first time, what it meant not to want some of the students. Was this really true? I had always seen myself as being loving to everyone. With some, I had immediate recognition, but that didn't mean I loved them more than the others — or did it?

This dream showed me my lower nature and how, in subtle ways, it was still trying to influence me. I thought that while I had been in my mountain abode, I had overcome that part of me, that I was completely one with my Higher Self, yet now I could see that wasn't true. It was easy to be spiritual on a mountaintop, but here in the world, the mundane could still influence me. I'm certain my Mahatma asked me those questions so that I would see my true feelings. On the subtle plane, one always speaks the truth. I work with my students that way, too. There, I hear from them their true feelings, most of which they would never reveal to me consciously. That is how I came to know who was sincere and who wasn't, and that had governed, up until now, whom I asked to attend the smaller classes.

I got up and wrote down this last dream in order not to forget it. It was ten in the morning, but I still felt tired, so I lay down again. I thought I was awake when I heard a knock at the door. I called for the person to come in, but when the door opened, it was my teacher standing there.

"How are you feeling?"

"Not so good. I'm still exhausted."

"You need to take a break after each place you go to now. The crowds take a lot out of you, and even though you try to protect yourself, you are still taking on some of their energy. You must take a trip up the mountains, even if it's only for a day or two. Then you can continue."

"You mean I can go home?"

"No, your home is too far away. Just a short trip in the hills will help."

Disappointed, I agreed.

When I got up for lunch, I met Alex in the lodge, waiting for me. I told him what my teacher had said, and he agreed that I surely needed a break. We looked at a map and saw that instead of taking the northern route to Weissenstein and from there south to Bern, we could retrace our steps and return to Interlaken and south to the mountains and from there north to Bern. That route was a little longer, but Alex didn't seem to mind, and he was the driver. He suggested I go to Mürren, a charming town similar to Wengen that was also in the mountains and only reachable by cable car or mountain train. I had been to it years ago and indeed remembered how beautiful it was. I still longed to return to Wengen, which was only a short distance from there, but the temptation to do the day climb to my home would have been too great. The only other place on the way was Interlaken, and I didn't want to go back there because then I would have to see the students, and I needed to rest.

After lunch, we drove to the parking lot in Satechelberg, where we left the car and took the cable car up to Mürren. Much as in Wengen, the only vehicles allowed there were owned by the locals to carry supplies from the valley. Mürren is a small village perched on a green pasture shelf overlooking cliffs that steeply fall into the Lauterbrunnen Valley. It also is a ski and hiking resort with inns, hotels, and restaurants, but not quite as touristy as Wengen. Fortunately, we were able to find rooms in a Swiss chalet-styled inn that had balconies facing the Jungfrau. It was a charming place, and very quiet.

Everywhere there were panoramic views of the mountains that were breathtaking. Moss-green foliage at the bottom blended into creviced, dark-gray rock, which in turn carried upward veins of snow that thickened and became denser at the top. Their presence made the town feel minuscule, holding humankind there subject to their grandeur. The mountains always made me feel closer to the Source. They gave me an inner peace that connected me back to my spirit. I had missed them in Luzern. They were there, but at a distance, whereas here, I was held inside the mountains, and they were my supreme sentinels.

I planned to stay for two days and told Alex that I needed to be alone to meditate and even wanted to eat alone. He understood and decided he would rather go back to Luzern and spend his time with some of the new students there. There had been a mutual attraction between him and Gretchen, and he wanted to know her better. He would return the morning of the third day to pick me up.

It was late afternoon when Alex left, so I just strolled down the streets of the town and looked at some of the interesting alpine architecture. Most of the houses were old, with weathered, darkened wood. The windows had colored shutters and window boxes with flowers. I loved the woodsheds, which were in the alpine style and open on the sides. They had different-sized shelves holding a particular type and cut of wood, from big fireplace pieces to small kindling, all carefully stacked on their given shelf. One place had a built-in box in which stood a pot of red flowers, and around the box were stacks of round wood. The wood was all different colors, making the final impression look like an abstract painting.

The next day I walked up the mountainside, taking small trails off the main ones, where there were fewer hikers. I was able to find quiet places to sit and meditate, particularly when a trail went through a thick pine forest. I even took a path by a creek that flowed down from the mountain, creating baby waterfalls along the way as it surged over rock formations and boulders. There were small pink, lavender, and yellow flowers growing on the banks with patches of elephant-ear leaves. It reminded me of the creek by my house where I had spent many hours of contemplation. Somehow the sound of gushing water brought an inner tranquility into my being.

either, so, with the continuous conversation between the two of them, I'd developed a bad headache.

Our destination was Bern, a few hours' drive from Mürren. Usually, I enjoyed the drives, as they gave me an opportunity to see some lovely mountain terrain, but because I needed to nap I missed some beautiful scenery. We stopped for a late lunch at a pleasant inn, and again Gretchen went into a soliloquy, this time about her family. Never once did she inquire about the teaching or ask me a question. Alex, who always had some good questions, remained silent, as did I. I finally said to her, "Gretchen, I am a quiet man, and I would appreciate you not talking so much. I am used to silence time, so I can think about my work."

She looked at me with astonishment and said, "Are you saying I talk too much?"

"Yes, I am."

"Well . . ." and then she began to pout.

Alex looked embarrassed. I could see he wanted to say something but didn't, which was a good thing, because I knew he was about to defend her. We ate the rest of the meal in silence, a silence full of negative energy. I decided it would be best for all of us if I ate separately from them in the future, as it is very important to digest food properly, which needs peaceful surroundings.

The rest of the journey went better, except for the tension in the car. Gretchen had to stop frequently to go to the restroom, which delayed us even more. We had previously decided to spend the night in the small town of Murten, about a half-hour drive from Bern, to determine whether it would be less expensive to stay on the outskirts of the city. By the time we got there, I was utterly exhausted. Alex had booked us rooms at an inn. It was past dinnertime by the time we arrived, so our only recourse was to dine in the local bar, something I never liked to do because of the entities that hung around alcohol. Ghosts who had been alcoholics during their lives sometimes stayed in bars trying to possess the alcoholics that go there. I explained to Alex that I felt he and Gretchen needed to be alone, so I would get a quick bite and go to bed. Gretchen immediately agreed, and I knew she would complain about me to Alex as soon as I left. This would be a major test for him, and I could only hope that he would pass it.

The room was small and damp. I thought I would fall asleep right away, but, instead, I lay awake thinking about how to draw people to the lectures. Alex did all the search and legwork in terms of finding a suitable place, and he was also good at doing all that was needed to advertise and promote the lectures. But I wasn't certain he would be as dedicated as he had been now that he and Gretchen were in a relationship.

I was right. The next morning, he came down to breakfast late, and he looked tired. Gretchen was still in bed, so I gathered they had had a late night.

He apologized, and I said, "Alex, this was a mistake. I know you are fond of

Gretchen, but it is clear to me that she is not at all interested in this teaching. During the whole trip yesterday, she talked only about herself and never even inquired or asked a single question about my work."

"I thought she was interested, but you're right. I talked to her last night and she admitted she just wanted to be with me; in fact, she asked me to leave you and spend the week with her."

"Are you going to do that?"

"No, you're my teacher, and I'm committed to being with you; but I wanted to ask you if, after I set everything up, I could go with her for a few days."

"That would be fine."

He looked relieved, and I was happy not to have her energy around me.

We talked about changing inns, and definitely finding something in the old town of Bern. When Alex left, I wouldn't have a car for transportation, and at least in Bern I would be able to walk everywhere or ride the trams. We sat down at Alex's computer and looked for an inn or small hotel that was in a better location. It took us a while to find a few places that weren't too expensive and were centrally located. Then we had to go into town to check them out and didn't return until early in the afternoon. Gretchen was waiting in the lobby, looking very miffed.

Alex went to talk to her, and I paid the bill and got my luggage to leave. Alex joined me quickly, but we had to wait another hour for Gretchen to finish packing. She was really testing my patience — a quality that I obviously needed to work on more; but Alex had expressed a desire to continue to be of service, and in all honesty, I'm useless at finding hotels and doing the advertising that is needed.

We left Gretchen at the new hotel and spent the rest of the afternoon checking out a couple of venues the hotel manager had suggested. The hall we chose was within walking distance from our hotel, which was important for me. The only problem was that it might not be big enough. It held maybe fifty to sixty people, but to accommodate more, the back wall of the room, which was a movable partition, could be removed, allowing the room behind it, which held another thirty people, to be joined to the original hall. For the first lecture, though, this extra room wouldn't be available, because it was already rented to another group for a week. But since there wasn't anything else close by, we took the space. We booked just the original hall for the first lecture and then both the hall and the additional room for the other lectures.

When we came back late in the afternoon, Gretchen was out. She had left a note for Alex saying she was shopping and would see him later for dinner. We had tea and talked. I asked him directly, "Are you in love with Gretchen?"

He replied, "I don't know. I certainly like being with her, and the sex is great. But I don't like the way she's been with you, and, I must say, I've been less interested in her since she said she had no desire to be in this teaching."

"Well, you don't have to marry someone in the teaching, but you do need to have someone who is sympathetic and supports your spiritual path. Do you think she could do that?"

"I don't know, but I my guess is that she wouldn't be supportive. She's made some nasty digs about you, and I had to stop her from continuing." He looked downcast, and I felt sorry for him.

"I think it's too soon, anyway. Maybe you will meet a woman along the way who truly loves the teaching and would be a better companion."

We talked about the advertising of the lectures. It cost substantially more to do anything in the larger cities than in the smaller towns we'd been in to this point, but we still had a significant amount of money from our collections in Luzern, which covered advertising in the weekend paper. Alex already had posters and other advertising materials set up on his computer. All he needed to do was to change the dates and the place where the lectures would be held. We had them printed up and we both went around to local businesses, coffee shops, stores, and any place that would allow us to post them. It took us a couple of full days to do this. Gretchen never offered to help, which didn't bother me but did bother Alex, especially because she knew the sooner the work was done, the sooner they could leave.

When they left, Alex promised to return after Gretchen's vacation was over, which would be in another week and a half.

My first lecture was to take place in four days, so I had plenty of time to prepare and to meditate. After a day or two of doing this, I started to miss Alex. He had been so much a part of my journey that I hadn't realized how much I depended on him and mainly how much I enjoyed talking to him. I felt lonely for the first time in my life.

Strange, isn't it? I lived alone for seven years in the mountains without anyone to talk to other than the devas, yet I never felt lonely. Only now in a city, with hundreds of people around me, did I feel the loss of someone who had been with me for a couple of months.

Attachment, that's what it was. I was experiencing attachment, another quality that I thought I had rid myself of a long time ago. To see the characteristics that I had transmuted come back so easily really disturbed me. I should be an example to my students, yet here I was feeling attachment, when letting go of attachments is the first lesson a student needs to learn.

I had not been in Bern for many years. It is the Swiss capital, and a close uncle of mine, who was no longer alive, had had a government post there. When I was younger, I used to visit him. I enjoyed exploring the old town, which is one of the oldest in Europe, with its lovely medieval architecture. I particularly loved the arcades that lined the streets with shops of every kind. At that time, I was really into clothes and did a lot of my shopping there.

For the next couple of days, I sat in outdoor cafés in the market squares, drank coffee to pass the time, and watched the people walk by, wondering if any of them would be at the lectures. I even went to the famous clock tower, the *Zytgloggeturm*, to see the clock perform. At four minutes to the hour, it starts: the jester comes to life, Father Time turns his hourglass, the rooster crows, and the man on top hammers the bell.

I walked the streets admiring the historic architecture. The gray buildings that contained the arcades had been built in the seventeenth and eighteenth centuries, with different facades of decorated motifs. In the middle of the wide main streets were attractive fountains. Each was decked with flowers at the bottom of a long shaft that sat in the middle of the water. The shafts were sculpted with colorfully painted and gilded animals or mythical heroes, uniquely Swiss in style.

One day I went down by the river Aare to watch the swimmers as they floated by. The current was so strong that people jumped in the water higher up the river and drifted down to a place where they could swim to a post to where they could hang on to help get out. I remembered how difficult that was to do when I had done it years ago; I had missed the first post and nearly hadn't made the second one.

I spent some time making a list of all the tasks that Alex did at the lecture. When people arrived, he greeted them, helped to seat them, and talked to them about me, answering questions that they were afraid to ask me directly. He set up meetings and appointments and took care of our entire schedule. I realized, almost too late, that there was no one else except me to do the things he usually did, and there were still many things to prepare. It was two days until the lecture, and I had no idea how many people would show up. The ads came out and they looked good. What if more than sixty people came? What would I say to them? For some reason, I became more and more anxious.

My photograph was included in the ads, and a couple of people came up to me during my walks in town to say they looked forward to my talk. It was advertised as a talk about Higher Self Yoga, with a description of the Higher Self and a general description of the topics I would cover. It also included a list of the talks and topics I would be giving in the future lectures. Many were ones I had given in other cities, but I always added a new one in each place I went to, and, of course, questions that were raised in each city always expanded the subject and became the impetus for new topics.

I accomplished all the things on the list. When the day for the first lecture arrived, I meditated and asked for guidance, which I always did, but this time I was nervous, very nervous, almost scared.

I tried a method I'd used many times in past: giving these feelings to my teacher. That helped. But as I walked to the hall, the fears came back. I arrived early to the hall, as I always did to cleanse the air and send out positive vibrations.

I did all of that but still felt something was wrong. What could be wrong? What had I forgotten? Then I remembered the charts. Alex had made a powerpoint presentation of all the charts I had done. The chart that I needed tonight had the Higher Self exercise on it and described the various ways a person could experience the Higher Self. The charts really were helpful, and now I realized they were on his computer because he always ran the presentation. I had no idea how to make them on my computer. I could rearrange the lectures so the ones needing the charts would be at the end, when Alex would be back, but tonight I had to let that go. Again, I felt what it was like to be dependent on someone, and I didn't like the feeling.

The collection box and the sign that went with it were also missing. I looked around the hall, and in the kitchen I found a box that would do and a piece of paper to tape on it, asking for donations to help cover expenses. Alex always asked for donations at the end of the lecture, but I felt it would be wrong for me to say anything. I put the box on a table by the door and hoped it would be noticed. Just as I was doing so, the door opened and Alex walked in.

He grinned at me. "Take that away; I have the proper one. And I have all the charts. I noticed them on my computer this morning and naturally drove here as fast as I could."

I embraced him. "Thank you so much, Alex. I just realized they were missing. What a blessing to have you return! How long a drive was it?"

"Gretchen wanted to see Lugano, so we went there. Took about five hours to drive from there to Bern, maybe more, because of the mountain passes."

"Wow. That's on the Italian border and a long distance from here. How wonderful of you to come all the way back just to bring the materials to me. Is Gretchen with you?"

"No, she stayed there. I'll go back in the morning."

"Are you sure? You could go now and stop along the way; that will give you some more time."

"No, I'm pretty tired. I'd rather get a good night's sleep and leave early tomorrow.

That night ended up being quite special. The hall was full but not overflowing, and I felt the people who came were very positive and interested in learning. Even the questions were astute and insightful. I felt relaxed and could focus on the various people without hesitation.

My nervousness was gone. I didn't know whether that would have happened naturally or whether having Alex there made the difference. We talked in depth about the Higher Self, and at one point a woman asked me, "Sir, is my Higher Self different from his, or hers, or even yours?"

"Individually, each one is different because it contains aspects of the particular person, but collectively they are the same. What I mean is that, after death, the Higher Self separates from the individual and returns and becomes one with God."

"You lose it?"

"No, when you are ready to be reborn, it will separate back into the new fetus to go through the life process once more."

"When it's back with God, what does it do?"

"It merges with all the other Higher Selves, and they become one with God."

"Do we ever experience that?"

"Yes, the part of you that is within the Higher Self goes with it and experiences bliss. Also, if you grow spiritually you can experience moments of it in the physical. The great yogis have experienced what is called *samadhi*, which is a pure state of bliss."

"Have you ever experienced that?" a man asked.

"Yes, but not for long. Yogis have died when they've been in that state for too long. The energy is too difficult for them to handle physically."

"I've read about Ramakrishna. He was in that state a lot until the Mother told him to stop," the man continued.

"Yes, he was a great yogi, and the Mother this man is talking about is what Ramakrishna called the Feminine Principle. She would manifest into a beautiful woman, and he worshiped her with great devotion. She is sometimes called the Mother of the World, Kali, or the Divine Feminine. In Christianity, she is called Mary and also the Black Virgin."

"I've seen the statue of the Black Virgin in Einsiedeln."

"Yes, isn't that a beautiful one? There are also several statues and images of the Black Mary in Poland and in Mexico, where she is often depicted that way."

Another man raised his hand. "I think it's interesting that in some statues she is depicted as a Black woman. Since she is usually depicted as white, do you know why?"

"I think the one in Einsiedeln was the result of a natural coloration of the wood as it aged. Some people believe this is the case, mainly because the material used was dark wood or ebony, and candle soot over time aged the figurine. But some people believe that such Madonnas were intentionally made of dark wood or granite because the historical Virgin Mary was dark skinned."

When the evening was over, I asked how many people would be coming to the next lecture, and almost everyone raised a hand. I told them to bring friends, and to mention the lectures on their social media channels as the room would be much larger when the partition was opened to the additional room.

It was late when Alex and I returned to our hotel, and, even though we were tired, I wanted to talk to him. He put the charts on my computer and said he would ask the hotel manager if there was someone there who knew how to do a PowerPoint presentation for me. He said he would teach me how to do it when he returned. I asked about Gretchen, but he said very little, and I could tell he was reluctant to talk about her. This worried me, but I held back any comments. He did mention that he might have to go back to work sooner than he thought.

I reminded him that he had promised to travel with me for six months, and it hadn't yet been three. If he was concerned about money, I told him there was enough for the two of us, and that he didn't have to pay his own way now. He knew that but said we needed to talk more about this when we both weren't so tired. On that note, I said goodbye to him and wished him a good remaining vacation.

After he left, I felt the loss again. Something had happened with Gretchen, and I feared the worst.

It was summer and hot in Bern. My room was not air-conditioned, and staying so cloistered made me depressed. I tried to go for long walks every day toward early evening when the heat was less oppressive. I disliked being in the city where there was no place to find a reprieve in nature. The bigger the cities, the less possibility to be close enough to the mountains. At least if I had a car, I could drive to a more remote area. I even considered renting one for a couple of days, but I hadn't driven in years and would want to brush up on my skills first. Starting out in congested city traffic wasn't a good plan, and it would be worse here because there were dozens of trolley cars, which ran on overhead wires, and intersecting tracks along the streets going in a plethora of different directions. When Alex returned, I would help drive on the country roads and get back into shape. Fortunately, my license was valid, since I always kept it updated.

One evening as I started a long walk back to my hotel, a woman passed me and then turned around and caught up with me. She introduced herself as Ita Bahn and said she had attended my lecture and would like to speak with me privately. She invited me to have a cup of tea, and I said yes. We found a place nearby and sat outdoors, even though it was still very hot. I watched her closely as she ordered and wondered who she was. Her appearance was unusual. She wore jeans but obviously designer ones, and she had a long, black scarf entwined around her hair, which was also long and black. Her blouse was an open-collared, cream-colored silk, simple yet elegant. I guessed her to be in her early thirties or late twenties, yet there was an air about her that made her seem much older. Her eyes were gray, with long, black lashes that made an otherwise plain face seem exotic.

Ita didn't say much at first, other than a few remarks about how much she loved my talk, and of course, planned to come again. After the tea and some scones arrived, I asked her about herself.

Her mouth, which had been smiling, suddenly became serious. "I don't know where to begin, but I need to tell you that I had an Indian guru, whom I met when

I was traveling in India with some friends. I was eighteen at the time and looking for something spiritual. When I went to a lecture by him, I felt a longing to be his disciple, and I asked him to be my teacher. He said yes but that I needed to be on probation, and he suggested that I come and live at his ashram. It was early summer. My plan had been to continue traveling in India and return home in September to start college here. Instead, I told my friends that I was going to spend the rest of the vacation in the guru's ashram, instead. They felt I was foolish, but they couldn't convince me otherwise."

She paused, and I could tell it was difficult for her to continue. So, I asked her, "What was it like for you to live in the ashram?"

"It was horrible, just horrible," she said quietly but deliberately. "At first, I was thrilled to be there, because I was the only Westerner. I felt a little out of place, but the women and men were very kind and taught me a lot about living in an ashram. The guru would teach every day before dinner and then ask one of the students to remain and dine with him. This I was told was considered an honor. I was there for a week when he asked me to stay." Tears came to her eyes.

"His quarters were very luxurious. There was a beautiful shrine with flowers and pictures of holy men. Tables and couches were placed in small groupings, and a large bed in the corner was covered with silks and Indian scarves. It was also air-conditioned, which the rest of the ashram wasn't. The table was set for two, and the guru rang for the dinner to be brought in. It was the best food I had eaten there, with several courses: mainly vegetables, but there were also some small birds and a piece of fish."

"He sounds like a fairly wealthy teacher."

"Yes, he had some wealthy disciples who were householders, and they supported the whole ashram. During the dinner, he talked about the teaching, and I, of course, was awestruck to be given this private lesson."

"What did he talk about?"

"Mainly how precious the relationship with the guru was and how important it was to feel the energy of the teacher. His talking was hypnotic, and his English wasn't good, but I managed to understand most of it. I was completely mesmerized by his power, so when he took me by the hand and led me to the bed I went without thinking about what was happening. He told me how special I was and how what he was going to do would give me a very special gift . . ." Her voice faltered and she paused. Quietly she said, "And then he raped me."

Her eyes were looking down at the table. After a moment, she continued. "I was too scared to resist. I didn't know what to do, and he kept telling me what an honor it was to have intercourse with a guru. It was horrible. I had never been with a man before, and it was horrible, and he didn't stop. Over and over again . . ." She was crying with the memory and couldn't go on.

My heart filled with love and compassion for her and the terrible trauma she had had to endure. I sent her warm, calming energy to help her. After a moment she composed herself. I softly said, "I'm so sorry that you had to experience this. What was done to you was a horrendous violation of who you are — your body, your heart, your spirit, and the trust you had in a spiritual teaching."

"Yes. I was in shock and felt overwhelmed with shame that I had let it happen. And I felt trapped at the ashram as well. The next day I asked another woman disciple with whom I had become friends if he had had sex with her, and she said he had — that it was a requirement of the women disciples. When I asked how she could do it, she only said that it was considered an honor, so they all went through it, and she said it was wrong to talk disrespectfully of him."

"I'm afraid I have heard of this happening to women disciples at some ashrams, and sometimes to the men, also. It is absolutely wrong, and I believe that such a teacher is not a true teacher in the esoteric tradition and deserves to be expelled from his ashram."

"Yes, well, I fled that night. I packed my bags and left. I still had my original itinerary with my friends, so I was able to catch up with them and they helped me. It's been many years, but you don't forget something that traumatic, and it's kept me away from any spiritual teaching. I thought I needed to tell you all this because I am very attracted to your teaching. It has awakened me spiritually, but it also has brought back these awful memories."

"Of course. I can understand why. That would be a normal response. I can assure you that I'm not that kind of teacher. But giving you assurances isn't going to change your distrust. I think it's important for you to keep your guard up, to question, to listen, and to use your discernment, whether it is with this teaching or any other you come across. There will always be those teachers who misuse their power. To abuse a student, whether it be physically, sexually, emotionally or mentally, is absolutely wrong, and it causes that student to distrust anything related to a spiritual path."

"I know, and I don't know what to do. My heart longs to find God and to work with my Higher Self. This other guru spoke about the Higher Self, too, and I felt that what he said was true, but because of what happened I am afraid again."

"The Higher Self is part of many yoga traditions. Negative influences, unfortunately, influence some teachers to misuse their power and responsibility. This is their battle of the lower nature versus the higher nature. I encourage you to be cautious with every guru and teaching. If you are able, try to attend these lectures and even attend the classes I will be setting up before I leave. This teaching is different because I do not have an ashram; nor will I ever have one. My students live their lives in the world, as do I. They live at home, do their work, have families, and study the teaching on their own and in a class."

"So, you do not stay here?"

"No, I go from city to city and stay for three or four weeks and teach, and those who are interested can continue in classes that I set up. I leave the class materials to study, and, when I return, it will be to those classes to answer questions and give out more of the teaching. When I go home, which will be in a year, it will be to my cabin in the mountains, where I live alone with nature. That is my mission and my life, which is very different from having an ashram with students around me."

She was smiling once again. "I like that. That makes me feel safer." Then she said, "I'm sorry, I don't mean to imply that you are someone who is not safe to be with."

"I understand, and it's good to be careful. I would expect that from you or anyone else who has experienced what you have. I would hope that you would never be a victim to violation again, whether it is in a love relationship of any kind, or mentally or emotionally in a friendship relationship."

"Thank you. I spent a while in that kind of pattern after I came home from India, but thankfully I was able to get some therapy and it helped me a lot. Before that, I had several boyfriends who treated me badly, but now it's different. I'm with someone who also came with me to the lecture. In fact, he's the one who suggested that I meet with you privately to have this talk. We're going to be married next month."

"I'm very happy for you. I look forward to meeting him. My plans are to have individual meetings with each person who is interested in continuing."

"Where are you going to meet?"

"My hotel has a comfortable lounge where two people can find a private corner."

It was getting late, so we left the café, and she walked with me part of the way back to the inn and said goodbye.

Ita's story upset me. It was quite common for Indian gurus to have sex with their students. I had even heard of a guru, who lived in the United States, who was a gay man and had AIDS. He infected all his male students, including his married ones, who in turn infected their wives. This teacher thought his spiritual energy would keep the disease from affecting either him or them and was very surprised when he died of it. What difficult karma! I felt compassion for all the abused students and even for the abusers who would have to suffer some very hard karma because of their behavior.

I thought about Maria, how beautiful she was and how attracted I was to her and how tempted I was to be romantically involved with her when I met her for the first time in Wengen. I also knew that it was one temptation I would never give in to with Maria or any other student. I felt that I must have done so in a previous life because my heart strongly understood the karmic consequences.

Later that night, I meditated, and sent healing energy to all those who needed it.

CHAPTER 12

The next couple of days I spent walking the streets of Bern. I needed a couple of new shirts and a pair of pants that were lighter weight. It was much hotter here than in the mountains, so I didn't have appropriate clothing. Somehow shopping put me in a better mood. I rarely bought things for myself, so when I did it was a special occasion. In my earlier years, I had had quite a wardrobe. Shopping was like a sport to me. I was always aware of the latest fashions, and I dressed stylishly to impress the women in my life. In fact, that was one of the hardest things I had to give up, and of course it was a necessity when I became an ascetic.

I get a modest monthly income from a family trust, so I could afford to shop a little bit, but I was mindful not to fall into my old ways of thinking about attire. Temptation after temptation was constantly being thrown at me now that I was back among people and engaged in day-to-day activities. I could see how easy it was to succumb and understood why the life of a hermit couldn't bring you God Consciousness. The teaching says you have to be in the world with all its temptations in order to achieve that goal. It's easy to give things up when they aren't around you.

My shopping took me into some of the best stores in town, and it was there one day that I bumped into a man named Brian. Brian had attended my previous lectures, and I recognized him as being very distant, aloof, and a bit of a snob. He was also shopping and, after greeting me, invited me to lunch with him.

He took me to a nearby restaurant and, after ordering, said, "Zarathustra, tell me about yourself. How did you become a teacher?"

His black eyes were full of inquiry. Brian was maybe in his late thirties, tall, trim, and well dressed in a dark blue suit and red tie. His black hair had been carefully cut and combed, and there wasn't even a touch of a beard on his square chin, which was a firm anchor holding his face steady and unexpressive.

I thought about whether to answer his question and decided it was best to be completely open. "It's a long process, which took many years. I met my teacher when I was in my late twenties. I was vacationing in India and met her through various circumstances. I spent the rest of my vacation and the next couple of years with her.

"You have a woman teacher?" he asked in surprise.

"Yes, women can be teachers, too. It's not restricted just to men."

I continued my story. "At her suggestion, I went to the mountains. I had enough money to buy land, a small cabin, and seeds to plant in my garden. From then on until recently I stayed there to study, meditate, and commune with nature. During this time I received the higher initiations, which gave me the ability to be a teacher and work with students on the subtle plane. Only when I received those initiations did my teacher tell me that someday I would also be a teacher."

"Didn't you miss people? You must have had family, friends, or lovers?"

"Yes, I did miss my family and friends at first, but that soon left me. In terms of girlfriends, I was quite a playboy in my younger years, and I did miss those relationships the most. Fortunately, I wasn't married or in a special relationship when I met my teacher. I had just broken up with a woman I had been living with for a couple of years."

"Wow! That would certainly be too difficult for me to do."

I noticed he wasn't wearing a wedding ring, but I still asked, "Are you married?"

"No, I was married for several years, but we were both too young and it didn't work out. Now I enjoy being single. Maybe someday later I'll settle down, as I would like to have children."

We sat for a few minutes in silence. Then our food arrived, and we concentrated on eating it, engaging only in small talk. Finally, he put his fork down and looked at me.

"I have a problem I want to ask you about. Would it be okay to do that?"

"Of course."

"This may sound strange, but my ex-wife has been seeing a man who was one of our good friends when we were married. In fact, he was mostly my friend, and a close friend. But after our divorce he began to date her."

"Is that a problem?"

"No, I'm fine with it. Beth can date anyone she likes. Hell, there's no reason for me to interfere with that. My problem is Alix. I feel betrayed by him. We were very close, and I feel he's been disloyal. He never told me he was dating her. She's the one who told me."

"But again, why would that bother you if you're divorced and dating other women?"

"I guess it's pride. Even though we split up, to have my best friend date my ex-wife really seemed like a betrayal. He's tried to continue to be friends with me, but I'm having a difficult time forgiving him."

"Do you think he was seeing her secretly before you split up?"

"No, I don't think so. My wife wouldn't have done that. But shortly after we separated they started seeing each other, and I didn't know about it for a while."

"This sounds to me like jealousy. Are you certain you no longer want to be with her?"

He thought for a minute. "No, I don't. I was the one who wanted to break up. I love my life now, and I was beginning to feel like I was trapped in my marriage."

I could see he was struggling to see what was quite clear to me. He was beginning to irritate me a bit. "Do you want her to be happy?"

"Yes, of course."

"Well, to me, it sounds as if you are still holding on to her. You may think that's not true, but I think a part of you still wants her not to be available to anyone else. If you didn't have those feelings, you would be happy for them both."

"Beth said the same thing. She told me I was jealous, and I got very angry with her. But I swear to you, I never want her back."

"Of course you don't. It is like a child who has a lot of toys, most of which he never plays with anymore. But if another child takes one of the discarded toys, the child takes it back, not because he wants or needs it, but because he's not willing to give away anything he has possessed. That's called selfishness and control. It comes from greed, not love."

Maybe my words were too harsh. I was losing my patience with Brian, whom I judged to be selfish.

He threw his napkin on the table, along with some money, and without speaking got up and left.

I sat there thinking about what I had said and how I could have expressed my words in a more gentle and loving manner. I thought about my teacher. What would she have said in this situation? Probably she would have asked more questions — probing, gentle questions, causing Brian to go deeper into his feelings and motivations. I had lost my patience, which was a big mistake.

In that realization, I felt all my energy drain from me. Why was this my mission? Why couldn't it be someone else's mission? Someone who had more experience working with people? Even when I was out now in the world, my universe centered on me. Maybe I saw myself in Brian, and that's why I lost patience with him. My teacher was so patient with me! I had spent two years traveling with her and saw her love and patience, but obviously I hadn't learned how to behave that way myself.

By the time I left the restaurant, the afternoon had turned cloudy, and it began to rain. It was a long walk back to my hotel. I could have gotten a taxi but decided to walk instead. I didn't mind the rain. It felt refreshing.

My head was bowed, so I didn't see him in the alleyway, but I felt him just before the attack. I turned and ducked my head just in time. The baseball bat landed on the pavement with a crack. It was a teenage boy, who started to run when the bat didn't land me. I grabbed him by the arm and felt him push against me with all his weight, but I held fast. He was shorter and thinner than I, so I could easily hold him in my grip. People were running up. One man said, "I saw what happened; let me help you." And he grabbed the boy's other arm.

I heard the sound of a siren, and the police arrived. I could tell the boy was very scared when they handcuffed him.

Before they took him off, I asked him, "How old are you?"

He sneered at me. "Fifteen."

I heard one of the policemen say, "Yeah, and he'll be on the streets again tomorrow, too young to prosecute."

I looked at the boy. "Do you know you could have killed me with that bat?"

"So, what if I did?"

His lack of heart was so appalling that I felt sick. I tried to send love to him but found I couldn't. Someone took me by the arm, and I heard a voice say, "Come, sit down, you look as if you're going to faint." I felt an arm around me guiding me to an outside bench. I closed my eyes and turned my face up to the rain. Taking deep breaths, I tried to center myself again. I felt the person who helped sit down next to me, still holding me by the arm in case I should faint.

"I'm all right now, thank you." I opened my eyes and saw it was a Black man whom I recognized from my lectures.

He inquired, "Zarathustra, are you sure you're not going to faint?"

"Yes, I'm fine. Thank you for your concern. Your name is Rudy, isn't it?"

"Yes, I'm Rudy Bancroft. I was on my way to the bookstore to buy some of the books you suggested."

"It was fortunate that you were here to help me."

Just then one of the policemen came up to me. "Is everything okay?"

"Yes, thank you."

He then asked me some questions and wrote down my name and hotel to file the report.

"Is there a lot of crime here?"

"Yes, particularly this area has a lot of gangs. They love to go after tourists. You're fortunate that he was by himself. If it had been the whole gang, you could have fared far worse."

"Can't something be done about it?"

"Oh, we've tried, but the drug problem is bad, and they need money. There's so much of it that it's hard to keep up."

"What will happen to him?"

"Unfortunately, not much. They'll give him a couple of therapy sessions, and he'll be back on the streets again. He'll either get killed in a fight or die of an overdose. Happens all the time."

"Sad, very sad," I heard Rudy say.

The officer offered me a lift back to my place, and I accepted it. Rudy wanted to accompany me, but I declined, saying I just wanted to rest.

Back at my hotel, I went to my room and sat down to meditate. I saw the young boy clearly and sent him love, praying that he could change his life. Then I slept a few hours, a deep sleep with no dreams. It was eight in the evening when I woke up. I went down to the dining room to have supper and found Brian waiting for me in the lobby. He came up to me and took my hands and said, "I want to apologize for leaving you the way I did. If I hadn't reacted that way, I would have taken you home, and you wouldn't have been attacked."

I was astonished. "How did you know about the attack?"

"It was on the news this evening. They said you could have been killed."

"But I'm just a nobody. This must happen a lot; why have a news story on me?"

"Well, a reporter at the scene questioned Rudy Bancroft later, and he told the reporter all about you. He said you were a spiritual teacher doing lectures here. When I saw what happened, I felt terrible. So will you forgive me?"

"I'm the one that needs your forgiveness, Brian. I was much too harsh with you, and I think what happened to me was what I call instant karma for not having been nicer."

"No, what you said was correct. It was direct and true, and that's the way I like to hear things. Otherwise, I don't get it. If you had said what you did in a nice way, I wouldn't have heard you. At the time it was tough, but when I thought about it, I knew you were exactly right. I was planning to thank you later, then I heard the news."

Again, I was surprised. We talked some more and then said goodnight. As I ate my dinner, I thought about the day and all that had happened. I remembered linking with my Higher Self when I had lunch with Brian; nevertheless, when I had spoken those harsh words, I had assumed I was in my lower nature. Now I realized that each person needs to be treated individually. It's always "by *their* God," not mine or someone else's. Here was a case of a man needing a candid and direct observation. I recalled reading something by the Dalai Lama in which he said that compassion is not just about being loving; sometimes, compassion means confronting someone on an injustice.

The next day I was inundated with messages from people, mainly those who had attended my lectures but even from others who were concerned. All expressed wishes for my welfare.

At the next lecture, I was glad we had the additional room as almost double the number of people attended. Many came almost an hour early and helped me set up. It was the largest crowd I had ever addressed, and it felt a bit daunting. I prayed a lot that day as I was going to speak about reincarnation and the law of karma, which is a difficult subject for people with a Judeo-Christian upbringing to accept.

I brought some printouts of real-life stories that I had collected about people who had full memory of their previous lives, which, when investigated, were verified. After I gave my lecture, I shared with the audience one of the stories:

"One of my favorite stories is about a young boy in America who at the age of three told his mother that he had been her father and had hidden some money in the fireplace behind a loose stone. Her father had died suddenly of a heart attack and hadn't left any notes about the money. The boy showed her where the stone was, and, when it was removed, she found a box with several thousand dollars in it.

"The boy then reprimanded her about the way in which she took care of his desk, saying that it wasn't neat enough and that when he grew up he wanted it back. The desk, by the way, was the only piece of furniture of her father's that she had kept. The boy continued to remember little things until he was around six; then the memories faded, and he forgot what he had told her. A spiritual brother of mine told me this story. The mother was a close friend of his. Some of the other stories have been published in articles and books on reincarnation. I will leave those on the back table for you to look at during the break."

During the question-and-answer period, a woman asked me, "What part of us goes on? Can you talk more about that?"

"I will try to, but it's very complex." I pointed to a flowering plant on the table. "You see this plant? It has flowers and leaves and stems and roots. When the plant dies, first the flowers will die and fall off, and then the leaves will wither and die. Finally, the stems will dry out and the roots will follow soon after. Each one of those parts has a function, and each goes through its individual death. It is the same with humans. Each person is made up of what are called *principles*. There are seven principles. The first principle is what is called *prana*, or "life force." Prana is your breath and keeps your body functioning. The second principle is what is called the *etheric double*. This body is attached to your physical body and stays close to it.

"As soon as the physical body dies and stops functioning, then the first two principles also die. When your breathing stops, there is no more prana, and the etheric body disintegrates. Those are the two principles that die.

"The third principle is what is called the *kamas* or 'desire body.' It is the part of you that has desires, some of which come from the lower nature, such as the desire for money, fame, etc., and some of which come from the higher nature, such as the desire for wisdom or the desire for spiritual knowledge.

The fourth principle is called *manas*, or 'mind,' and is the thinking, rational mind. The fifth principle is also called *manas* or what is called the 'The Higher Mind' and has the ability to bring down wisdom from the higher sources to which it is connected. The sixth principle is called *buddhi* and is connected to the heart. It is sometimes called the 'chalice' or 'divine soul.' The seventh principle is called the *atman*, or the 'seed of the spirit.' These top principles — the fifth, the sixth, and the seventh — form the divine triad and are the highest principles. These three are the Higher Self and when fully awakened bring the Higher Self fully into consciousness."

"So, you mean these three are still alive after we die?" Brian asked.

"Yes, these three, along with the desire body and the mind. What happens is that your top five principles go into a place called *kama loka*, where you play out all your desires."

"That sounds like heaven."

"For some it may feel like heaven, except that if you have some lower desires, you will play those out, also. For example, if you want to have sex, you will have a lot of sex there, or, if you want to be powerful, you will play out that role there."

"I like that," someone in the audience said. And a few laughed.

"You will be in this place as long as you have those desires. Once you have played out the desires, you leave, and the three higher principles will separate and go into what is called *devachan*. There you will be in a place of bliss."

"That's really heaven, then."

"If you think of heaven as being that, yes. So, your higher principles are in what is called *devachan,* and your human soul waits until your time of rebirth, at which time it reconnects with the higher principles and through the law of karma is attracted to the fetus it is meant to be in."

"That's mind-blowing. How can all that happen to each person who dies?"

"It is very complex and even more so than what I have told you. It is the great mystery and miracle of life and death."

Of course, then came the questions about ghosts, which I answered with some stories. Most people just listened and didn't ask questions. I feared that this lecture went over many people's heads, yet I hadn't said nearly as much as I could have said.

I only had one more lecture to do; and, when I asked how many would be coming to that final one, the response was much less than I expected. I needed to refigure whether this material was right for these large audiences. Then I remembered that my teacher had said, "Teach the truth but realize that only a handful will understand you." This made me feel better. Just a handful when I left this city was my goal.

CHAPTER 13

Before the last lecture in Bern, some people called me for individual appointments, and I met with them before breakfast and after dinner, as most of them worked. Out of the dozen or so, only three seemed to want to continue the work. Ruby and Brian, surprisingly, were still interested, and a woman named Jana Keufen, whom I liked very much; it felt like a good heart connection. She was in her late twenties and single. She said she was interested, but both she and her fiancé had so much to do when they got married that they felt it best to wait until I returned the following year.

It was strange that so far only three wanted to continue studying. This city was more difficult than the others. The last lecture would give me a clearer idea of what would be happening later here. Maybe it would be better to go only to the smaller cities and towns such as Luzern, where I had been very successful and which has half the population of Bern. Maybe because Bern was the seat of the government, the people were less spiritual and more political. I didn't know, but I planned the last lecture to take that into account.

When the night of the lecture arrived, there was a heat wave, which made it difficult because the hotel wasn't air-conditioned—as is common in most of Switzerland. This of course reduced the turnout even more. Instead of seventy to one hundred people, there were only thirty-five. We set up fans and had the people sit in a circle. I could tell that some felt uncomfortable with this arrangement and preferred rows of seats in order to remain inconspicuous.

After we were seated, I suggested that there be a short meditation and guided it. The woman who sat next to me kept her eyes open all the time and continuously looked at me in a way that was unsettling. She was young and attractive, with a subtle sexiness. I felt she was demanding something of me that I couldn't give her, and later I found that to be true. She was infatuated with me and wanted a romantic relationship, not a spiritual one. I found her energy disturbing, and it affected my concentration.

Then I began the following talk:

Truth: What Does It Really Mean for You?

"What is truth? Some of you may wonder why I am asking this question. You may say that obviously if something is true then it can't be false and vice versa; but when you analyze it, then it becomes much more complex. What is true for you may turn out to be false for someone else.

"For example, you"—and I pointed to a young woman—"may know that it is important for your health to do strong physical exercises, and you may even overdo it in that area in order to have a trim and muscular body, whereas this woman" — and I gestured to the lady next to me—"has an injured knee that has to be gently exercised. So, what is true for you is not true for her.

"Another example is John here, who works for himself and works long hours to make enough money to care for his family, whereas Stephen works for a corporation and has a job that doesn't require overtime. The amount of time worked in both cases establishes what is true for each of them. These are a couple of mundane examples, but when the matter becomes more spiritual, then what is true becomes less defined.

"If, for example, you were my student, I would know exactly what you needed to do to grow spiritually. I may tell you to meditate three times a day, as that is most important, while I may tell another student just the opposite—not to meditate at all."

An elderly Asian man raised his hand. "Why would you do that? I thought meditation is important for everyone."

"For most people, yes. But in the case I am referring to, the student was clearing his system from having smoked marijuana for years, and meditation wasn't possible until that was done.

"The same is true with the teaching itself. I can teach general truths that impact students the same way, but when I work with someone individually, what I say to one student may be the complete opposite of what I say to another, which is why I suggest never comparing personal notes. Everyone's soul or individuality is different, and what can help one person may not have any impact on another."

"I thought everyone's soul was the same," a woman said.

"Everyone's *spirit* is the same, but each person's soul or individuality is unique. Every lifetime makes an impression on a person, and that impression is part of the person's soul and is carried with the individual into future lifetimes.

"For instance, if you have been a soldier many times and carry that essence into new lives, you would have the inclination to join your new country's military. You would believe in war and think it a good way of resolving problems. Or, if you have been a soldier many times and have been killed in battle, your soul might do the opposite. You would resist joining any army and even go to another country to dodge the draft. The person in the first example will eventually tire of war also and become like the second person. Those are two different truths coming from similar backgrounds.

"Obviously, karma plays a very important role in all of this. It is important to know exactly what is personally true for you. Often people will follow a leader or a spouse and not even consider what they themselves might want.

"Childhood conditioning determines those patterns. For instance, you are Swiss, and the models you had in your childhood have helped you feel either strongly about your nationality or not so strongly, depending on how your parents raised you. Being Swiss can be a truth for you that means a lot, or a truth that means very little, in which case it loses any vitality.

"If you are a man, you may feel a woman should be a housewife and raise your children, or you may feel a woman is your equal and should work. These are individual truths. I can go on and on about various truths, but the lesson here is much deeper than those examples. It concerns knowing who you are and what truths you base your life on.

"When you look at yourself, do you really know what the truths are that form who you are—the truths that you unconsciously follow?"

I next displayed a chart on the screen with questions for them to answer.

"These questions will take you deeper within yourself. You may have trouble doing them, so I suggest you first link with your heart, and then with your Higher Self, and ask yourself the questions."

These were the questions on the chart:

What is True for You
- *When you look at your life, do you feel you are living the kind of life that you are meant to live?*
- *Are you really happy, or do you pretend you are happy?*
- *Are you fulfilled in the work you are doing?*
- *Are you fulfilled in the nationality and culture you were born into?*
- *And when you look at your relationships, do you feel they are good, or is there something missing?*

I read the list out loud and then said, "Try to look at these questions in terms of your soul. What does your soul need? Link with your Higher Self. Try to feel what your Higher Self is saying."

I watched them do the exercise and saw that a couple of people were very uncomfortable with it. These were two young people who had come more out of curiosity than interest. At the break that followed, they left.

I asked people how they felt doing the exercise. "Did anyone find out something that was very different from what they would have thought?"

A woman raised her hand. "I feel I'm a happy person. I love my work and family, so I was surprised to have a definite response of no to the question about being happy. When I looked at it more deeply, I felt a profound sadness come over me. When I asked myself why I was feeling sad, I realized that it was because I had stopped painting. I painted a lot when I was younger, but with a family and work, that disappeared out of my life. I always say to myself that when I am retired I will paint again, but now I know I miss it too much to wait until then. I need it in my life."

"Good, that's the kind of truth that is important to discover. Anyone else have a similar realization?"

"Different and very shocking to me," an older man said. "I looked at my marriage and realized I have been bored for many years. I felt it was normal when you've been married as long as I have, to feel this way. But I realized that my boredom was because my wife and I have nothing in common. She does her thing and I do my thing, and we don't even share what we do because neither one of us is interested. We don't even share a bed together anymore.

"I knew I wasn't happy, but I didn't realize that my unhappiness centered around my marriage." He looked very disturbed.

"Now that you know the truth, it's important to find out if you want to keep that truth or change it. You can stay in your marriage knowing the truth, or you can leave your marriage because that truth is not what you want for the rest of your life."

I looked around the room.

"These questions are hard to absorb. Out of them come realizations that are difficult. The main thing now is to look at what is really true in your life and whether that truth is your soul's desire. Change can happen over time. This is just the beginning, but if your soul longs for happiness, then your soul will help you find it."

More people shared, and then after the break I continued, "Now we need to look at what is true for your spirit." I put up another chart of questions:

What is True for You Spiritually
- *Does your spirit long for God?*
- *Do you have any desire at all to learn more in an esoteric teaching?*
- *How do you see yourself in terms of your individual spiritual needs?*
- *How does your heart respond when it hears truth?*
- *How does it respond when it hears falsehood?*
- *When I spoke about the Higher Self last week, did you have any longing to know more or to do the Higher Self exercise?*
- *A few of you came back, so ask yourself why: do I want to learn more, or did I come back because my friend was coming, or out of curiosity? Ask yourself: why am I here?*

I asked the people to think about these questions—to put them, one at a time, in their hearts, and try to come up with answers.

When everyone was finished, I asked for comments.

A few raised their hands, and one woman said, "I'm an agnostic and I question everything. When I put the question in my heart, 'Does my spirit long for God?' I was shocked when I heard an inner voice scream, 'Yes, Yes!' I'm still surprised, and I don't know what to make of it."

"Just stay with the feeling for a while. Try not to analyze it. The mind often takes a person away from the truth; the heart never does."

Another man said, "I felt I came back because I wanted to hear more and was also surprised suddenly to feel that wasn't true. I came because my wife insisted we come, not because I wanted to. I realized I often do what she wants and pretend I it too"

"That's good to know. Now you are getting at a deeper level of what is true for you. You may do something because your wife wants you to, but at least now you know you are doing it for her and not pretending to do it for yourself."

A blond woman said, "I had a very difficult time answering how I see myself in terms of my spiritual needs. I don't have a clue what those needs are."

"When you are at home, try doing the Higher Self exercise and ask your Higher Self that question. Do the same for all the questions. Ask the Higher Self if the answers you received were correct. The Higher Self always understands what is true for you."

There was more discussion and sharing.

It was late, and I asked if anyone wanted to continue these studies. I still didn't know who would stay and expected no one new at this point.

Five people raised their hands. There were the three—Ruby, Brian, and Jana—who were already interested. The two new ones were Ottilia Mullar and Gilbert Ernst. I arranged to meet with the new class at the end of the week in the home of Ottilia, a woman in her forties who was recently divorced.

The meeting went well, but it was more social than instructive, as Ottilia cooked a delicious dinner for everyone. I set up the class with all the lessons and promised to return in a few months. I tried to leave enough lessons for them to work on until then. After Alex had left, I'd had more time, so I'd prepared some new lessons to give to the classes. I intuitively knew that Alex might not return to Bern, so I also took lessons from the man who did my PowerPoint presentations for me and had him show me how to set up new charts.

Finally, I did receive an email from Alex saying that he had to go back to work. He wasn't able to return to Bern and would be in contact soon. He also sent me bookings that he had made for hotels and places to hold the lectures in Basil and Zürich. A part of me knew that this would happen, and I didn't know if I would ever see him again.

Now it was time to move on. My next destination was Basel. With all the materials that I had accumulated by now, I decided not to take the train, so I rented a car and drove for the first time in many years. I still missed Alex.

CHAPTER 14

Arriving in Basel, I settled in my hotel, which was close to the Rhine River in the old part of town. I took a walk as the sun rose in the morning, reflecting its radiant, fiery self in the river, christening the day. In some places on the road there were steps that went directly down to the water, and I had my morning meditation sitting on those steps.

I also enjoyed just standing and looking at the panoramic view below from a bridge called the *Mittlere Brücke,* or Middle Bridge. The oldest bridge in Basel, it resembled a medieval bridge that would have lain across a moat and ended up at castle walls. It was gray, held up by round columns, with arched passageways in between for the boats to go through. Flags of the cantons were displayed along the bridge, and and in the middle was a small tower with a pyramidal roof, with maroon, green, yellow and white tiles laid into a beautiful pattern.

The hotel turned out to be just right for my needs. It even had a conference room, which Alex had booked for me to have in a week— perfect timing. With those arrangements made, my main task was advertising. Everything seemed more difficult without having a student accompanying me. I had sent an email to the leaders of the classes with my itinerary, but most people thought Alex was with me, and I didn't feel comfortable asking someone to come and help me. Instead, I asked the hotel's front-desk clerk if he knew anyone who could assist me in promoting my lectures. He gave me the name of two teenagers who often ran errands for the hotel. I hired them both, and they were very helpful and knowledgeable about preparing advertisements and getting them out to the public in local papers and social media.

That first week in Basel I made all the arrangements for the upcoming lectures. This left me with time before the lectures and full days in between. Previously, I had taken advantage of the extra time to explore the towns and fine-tune my talks, but Basel was different. Now, I felt I needed to spend the time making some kind of strategy about how I would continue this teaching.

I also wanted to start looking into buying a house. The city of Thun seemed like a probable choice, but I wanted to look into that more and search for places on the internet. I also wanted to decide if buying a house was the best way to proceed.

When I meditated, I contacted my teacher and asked her for advice.

"It is very expensive to buy a home in any of the resort areas, and my spirit needs to live near the mountains," I said. "Maybe I could live in my cabin in the summer and then spend the rest of the time traveling, as I am doing now, but I don't know if it will be too physically and spiritually hard for me to travel all that time."

"You have money in your trust to buy a house, and I think Thun would be a good choice as it is in an area that is not a ski resort, so it wouldn't be crowded with skiers in the wintertime," she responded. "And besides the beautiful mountains, it has Lake Thun, which I know you will enjoy. You can then break up your class visits so you can go home at times to rest and revitalize yourself."

"I've lived on very little because I don't like using that money."

"This teaching doesn't say a student needs to be impoverished. It's your good karma to have money."

"But I planned to give most of it away."

"That was when you believed your permanent home was your mountain cabin, but now that has changed, and you need a house and money to live."

"All right, I will start looking. It's going to be difficult, but I will try. Thank you." And I ended my meditation.

The evening of the lecture it rained heavily. Weather would make a difference in attendance, so I expected only a handful of people, but, instead, there were at least fifty. Alex had designed an ad campaign for the bigger cities, and it seemed to be working. I hired a woman who worked at the hotel to help me, and she took charge of the seating and setting up the PowerPoint presentation.

When I meditated before my lecture, I saw my teacher. She smiled at me and said, "Remember to speak from the heart."

The audience was a mixed one. There were more women, which usually happened. Women generally were interested in spiritual talks, but there seemed to be a wide diversity of age from what looked like teenagers to the elderly. I liked having both ends of the age range. There were also people of diverse cultural backgrounds, which I was happy to see. Several people looked very well-dressed, and others were dressed in jeans. I looked around the room in silence, trying to send harmonious energy to bring it all together. Then I began my talk.

Allow Change in Your Life

"When I started this tour of cities in Switzerland, I wasn't certain who would come to hear me; nor was I even certain about what I would say. I have spent many years in the mountains living as a hermit surrounded by nature. When my teacher appeared to me in a meditation and said I needed to leave my home and begin my teaching, I became very upset. My lifestyle was to be totally changed. It was like beginning a new life, and, frankly, it also was frightening to me. Change is a positive thing but difficult for most people because it takes them into the unknown."

I looked around the room and asked, "How many of you here have had major changes happen to you, changes that caused you to live differently?"

At least twenty people raised their hands.

"Looking back at those changes, can you say you learned from them?" Many people again raised their hands.

"That's good, because change can be a catalyst for personal growth, and it certainly needs to be seen as positive even when it may appear negative. In my case, having to teach brought me into contact with some very nice people and forced me into having relationships, which were absent in my life. You can never achieve spiritual attainment living in a cave — or a cabin, in my case — so this challenge, even though it has been difficult, has been beneficial for me.

"Would someone like to share what their change was and how it has affected them?"

A woman raised her hand. "Mine is fairly common. My husband left me for another woman."

"And how did it benefit you?"

"Not at all at first. I was devastated, as we had been married for twenty years; but now I am far more independent, doing things I never would have done before. I also have met a man whom I'm dating and who treats me with a lot more respect than my ex did. Even though it was hard at first, when I look back I realize I'm much happier now."

"That's a good example of turning something that seems negative into something positive. Anyone else?"

A man raised his hand. "My business partner said he wanted out of our company and demanded the money he had invested in it. That was a shock since we'd been partners for over ten years, and he'd never said anything about being unhappy. I didn't want to sell the company, so I took out a big loan to pay him. I thought I would never be able to pay it back, but I ended up doing better without him. I found another partner who is very creative, and the business has blossomed. But those first years were horrendous. If I hadn't loved my business, I would have folded it up."

"Yes, thank you both. Those are two good examples of how change can be beneficial."

I looked at the woman and then the man and said, "Hedy, you may have stayed at home and lived a bitter existence; or Graf, you may have sold the company and worked for someone else. That could have happened, too, and would have made the change feel not so good. But it didn't happen because you both had an inner desire to learn and continue with your lives. That inner desire comes from the spirit's need to evolve, to learn from the past and try new things. Hedy, in your case, you were too dependent on your husband and were stifled by him, and your new independence has helped you make better choices in life." Hedy was nodding her head. "And Graf, your love of the business you've created helped you through the hard times, and now it is prospering. Giving up wasn't an option for you because of that love. It gave you the strength to carry on.

"Most people in times of conflict, when facing major change in their lives, find an inner strength that naturally comes out. You see it in times of war and natural disasters, as well as when personal hardship happens to you. This strength comes from the spirit and enhances all the resources a person has developed.

"Change of any kind causes this to happen. Even when change is initially positive, it still evokes an inner fear because of its nature. Humankind settles into patterns that are familiar. These patterns are part of your childhood conditioning and make you feel secure. Even a positive change, such as moving to a better community, or receiving a promotion in your job, can cause feelings of insecurity. That is why some people live in the same house all their lives and never think about trying something new. If their house burns down, change is inevitable, but even then they will build the same house."

A few people laughed at this, and I heard a man say, "I know someone who did that."

I remained silent for a while. "Why do you think change is so important in a spiritual teaching? Why do you think I am talking about this in my first lecture, instead of telling you about the Higher Self Yoga teaching?"

"Are you going to say that your teaching is going to make us feel insecure?" It was an older woman who spoke out.

"You are a wise person. That is exactly what I am going to talk about. No matter how religious or spiritual you are, when you learn esoteric things that are new to you, insecurities will come up, particularly if those things differ from what you were taught as a child. In every lecture I give, people walk out when I talk about certain subjects, subjects they won't even consider, such as reincarnation, karma, the subtle plane, the God within. Some listen and become fearful as their belief systems are challenged. So, when I designed these lectures for Basel, I decided to talk about change and spiritual change in my first lecture to help you understand some of the feelings that may arise in my later lectures."

I paused and looked at one of the teenagers, who was whispering to a friend. "When you are a teenager, such as Margarita there, change can be exciting or scary."

She looked down at her shirt. She wasn't wearing a nametag, which I now use in my lectures, and she put her hand over her mouth in astonishment.

"But when you settle down in marriage or a job, then change is undesirable. Why do you think change is so necessary — indeed, inevitable — in a spiritual teaching?"

No one wanted to answer that.

"If you enter an esoteric teaching, each step requires courage, determination, discernment, and an inner desire to find God. Each step will bring you face to face with who you are, both your negative characteristics and the positive ones. Each step requires change to happen.

The negative aspects need to be transformed, and the positive ones need to become utilized and strengthened. Each step brings challenges that require you to make changes in your thinking and your perception of life. Each one requires you to see your patterns and to have the willingness to understand and change the unhelpful ones. If you are unwilling to make the necessary changes, then you will be stuck and cannot grow spiritually."

"When you say, 'grow spiritually,' what do you mean?" a young man asked.

"I mean just that. It's about growing your spirit, freeing it so that it can be part of who you are consciously, in order that you walk with your spirit, talk using your spirit, and act always with your spirit. And in this teaching, the spirit I speak of is your Higher Self, that part of you that is one with God and has that consciousness. After the break, I will speak more about this teaching and about the Higher Self, which each one of you has within.

"Are there any more questions before I continue?"

A priest in the back of the room raised his hand. "If you believe in Jesus and follow his teaching and covenants, there is no need for the kind of changes you are talking about. You will follow the Ten Commandments and free yourself from sin."

"I believe in Jesus and know he is one of the Mahatmas, and I also believe he taught the teaching I teach, which is esoteric, to some of his chosen disciples. He faced change every day of his life and preached it to many. He threw out the moneylenders from the temple and demanded change in his religion. There was no security in his life, and he didn't need it; nor do you. Security can stifle you and keep you a prisoner. Change keeps you in motion and allows you to expand your horizon."

"But I have a family. They need security," a woman dressed in jeans and a T-shirt protested.

"Yes, but they mainly need love. That is the major security a child needs. Riches won't make a child secure; only love will. Of course, it's important to provide for your family. I'm just saying to put the need for security in its proper place and to be open to new possibilities."

More hands were raised, but I waved them off. "Let me continue, and then I will hear more questions.

"When I speak about spiritual change, I speak about listening to your Higher Self and following its directions. To do this, you have to be open to all possibilities. You may not realize the importance of expanding your consciousness because you have never tried to do it. For example, if I asked you to draw a square it would be four connecting lines, but if I asked you to expand that square into a cube you would have to add an additional eight lines.

"What I am asking of you tonight is to expand your literal thinking into many dimensions and stay open during the process. If during that time you realize you need to change your old views, then try to do that. If during that time you realize you are stuck in some old patterns, then have the courage to see the patterns and plan how to transform them into new healthy patterns. Open your minds and hearts to hear my teaching. Let your heart tell you whether what I say is true. Don't listen to the old beliefs from your parents or even your church. Listen only to your heart."

I had my PowerPoint program turned on and opened to my first chart. "This chart has listed some of the old beliefs that give you spiritual security."

Everyone began to read the list on the chart, which was as follows:

Beliefs that Give You Spiritual Security
- *When I die, I will go to heaven and be with my family there.*
- *Jesus is the Son of God, but I am not.*
- *Someday I will devote more time to my religious practice, maybe when I retire.*
- *If I help others and am a good person, I will be rewarded in heaven.*
- *I need to go to church on a regular basis to be saved.*
- *Marriage should be with someone of the same religious background.*
- *If I have children, they need to be baptized right away; otherwise, if something happened to them, they could be damned.*
- *I need to follow the religion of my father and grandparents.*

When I saw that people were finished reading, I continued, "These are just some of the beliefs that keep you from growing spiritually. They keep you stuck, disconnected from the truth." I looked at my audience and asked, "Do these beliefs seem familiar to you?"

Some people nodded their heads. I am going to go over them one at a time and give you this teaching's concepts around them:
- *"When I die, I will go to heaven and be with my family there.*

"There is no heaven or hell but rather planes of existence on the other side. After you die, you will go to the first of these planes, and there you will play out all your desires. This plane is a plane of illusion.

If you want to paint, you will paint. If you want sex or food, you will be saturated with those. If you desire to see your family, they will all be there. You may believe this is heaven, but it is just an illusion, and when you get tired of the activities there, you will leave that plane and then be reborn. The other planes you may go to before rebirth offer lessons that will help you in your next life.

• *"Jesus is the son of God, but I am not.*

"Jesus's spirit was fully awakened, and his spirit is God or Brahman or any higher force you may call it. Every one of you has the same spirit. God is in every one of you, and everyone here can awaken that spirit and become it. Every one of you has the possibility to grow into a Mahatma. Jesus is a Mahatma, and every one of you can follow in his footsteps."

There was a lot of mumbling from the audience when I said this.

• *"Someday I will devote more time to my religious practice, maybe when I retire.*

"If you are to grow spiritually, you need to devote time today to your spiritual practice, not when you retire; you may die before you retire. Every day should have time for contemplation, meditation, and spiritual striving. Every day should have those three things in it so that you will take another step on the path to God.

• *"If I help others and am a good person, I will be rewarded in heaven.*

"If you help others, you will be rewarded by making good karma. Karma determines everything in your life. Good karma begets good rewards, and bad karma begets bad rewards. As you sow, so shall you reap: not in heaven but here on Earth, now and in your future lives.

• *"I need to go to church on a regular basis to be saved.*

"Church is a building and a religious structure. It represents security. God is everywhere, in you, in nature, in all creatures. Finding God is an inner quest that needs to happen all the time, not just on Sundays. What do you need to be saved from? God is within; you need to seek the Divine within.

• *"Marriage should be with someone of the same religious background.*

"Marriage should be with someone with whom you have good karma. It makes it easier to be with someone from the same religious background, but that doesn't necessarily make a good marriage. Marriage is about love and sharing. Marriage is about learning from each other. Going to the same church on Sunday doesn't mean the marriage is a good one. How many couples do you know who stay in a terrible marriage because the church won't let them divorce, so they are miserable, and they make their children miserable?"

More whispers at this.

• *"If I have children, they need to be baptized right away; otherwise, if something happened to them, they could be damned.*

"If you believe that God made humankind and is a benevolent being, how could you believe that God in any way would harm an innocent child? The church made this pronouncement about baptism to frighten people into becoming good Christians. It also implies that, in other religions that do not have baptism, all those people are damned and will go to hell. The insinuation is that Christianity is the only true religion and all others are false.

• *"I need to follow the religion of my father and grandparents.*

"You are born alone, and you die alone. If your parents don't believe in a God, does that mean you shouldn't believe in one? Or, if your parents don't believe in monogamy and have affairs, does that mean you should do the same? Your parents and grandparents are individuals with their individual likes and dislikes. Let them do what they feel is right for them, and you do what is right for you. The same holds true for your children. Let them decide what their hearts respond to, and what path they need to take. Do not make them follow in your footsteps."

Many hands were raised, and I could see some disapproving faces. I continued, "I won't answer questions about these eight statements at this time. Each one will be a lesson about which I will go into detail. I will discuss the process of death and the subtle world and what is there, and I will go into length about the law of reincarnation and karma. I will teach you the meaning of God Consciousness, and I will talk about marriage and children, and psychology and its impact on your spiritual striving. Mainly, I will teach about the Higher Self and how you can access it. This will be my lesson after the break tonight. For now, I ask that you be open to changing some of your established viewpoints. Hear what I have to say and then decide for yourself. Everyone's path is different, and everyone has to choose it for him or herself. Are there any questions about anything other than the subjects I just mentioned?"

A woman in the front raised her hand. "I just want to know more about you. How do you know about these things?"

I picked up a paper that Alex had insisted I prepare. "My background is explained in this handout, and copies are available in the back. After you have read it, if you still have questions, I will be happy to answer them."

"I came early, and I did read it," she answered. "It explains a lot, but how do I know whether I can trust you or not? How do I know you are speaking the truth?"

I looked more carefully at the woman. She was well dressed, and she sat tall with a straight spine and gazed at me with keen, piercing eyes. I liked that she was questioning me. "Erna, it is good to question everything. Do not believe in anything just because I say it is true. Put it in your heart, and if it feels true to you, then believe it. When you connect with your Higher Self later, check what I say with it; verify everything with your Higher Self. I will explain how to do that."

"She's right," a man in the back said. "Your teaching is new to all of us. How do we even know whether our Higher Self is advising us correctly?"

"When you connect with it, you will know. In the beginning, question everything; but don't doubt, as doubt closes the door to knowledge. There are many people here." I looked around the room. "Many of you won't come to my next lectures; just a handful will be curious enough to want to understand. I will challenge beliefs that you have held for years. All I ask is that you save judgment and be open to change, that you question, but not doubt, and work consciously with your heart, which links you to the Higher Self. Now I think it best to have a fifteen-minute break."

During the break, I went up to my room and meditated, just for a few minutes, but it restored my energy. When I returned to the conference room, I noticed that only a few people had left. I then talked about the Higher Self and went through the exercise with them. Several people had good responses, and that helped the others to realize that what I was teaching was positive. There were many questions, but I had to end the lecture by ten o'clock.

After the hall had emptied, a few people remained to speak with me. One of them was Erna. She said, "Thank you for your teaching. I can't make the lectures for the next two weeks, as I will be away, but can I come to the last week?"

"Of course. I look forward to seeing you then."

"Is there anything written that I could read in the meantime?"

"No, I'm afraid not. I do have class exercises for those who want to continue."

"That's good. Thank you again."

I was glad that she had told me this, as she was the only person here that I recognized as an old soul and a student of mine from previous lives. Sometimes I pick that up right away and other times not. A couple of other people asked if they could see me before the next lecture, and I set up times to meet with them. I was exhausted and exhilarated at the same time when I finally went to bed.

In the morning, I went for a long walk and arrived back at the hotel just before lunch. The desk clerk said there was a man waiting for me in the lounge. I looked at my watch. My first appointment was for 3:00 p.m., so I was wondering who it was as I walked into the room. I recognized the priest from last night. Father Joseph was his name. He struck me as being very stern and harsh, so I wasn't pleased to see him. I linked with my Higher Self and tried to act pleasant.

"Father, what can I do for you?"

His face scowled. "What you are teaching is very wrong. I am here to warn you. Leave town or I will have the church authorities condemn you and your teaching publicly."

There was so much anger in his tone that I felt it blast against my heart, and it made me step back. I had to get my breath and calm down before I could answer him. "I have no intention of leaving town. This is not the Inquisition. It is Switzerland, where freedom of speech belongs to all who live here. I have just as much right to teach spiritual lessons as you do."

"We'll see about that." And he stood up and walked past me, leaving a heavy odor of tobacco that clung to his suit. It made me feel sick, so I decided not to have lunch but to rest instead.

Later in the afternoon I had an appointment with Margarita Lehmann and her friend, Matteo Haari, who had been with her at the lecture the night before. It was a breath of fresh air to see the two of them. Both were dressed in jeans and T-shirts and obviously were very nervous. Margarita wore her long dark hair in a ponytail that swung around her shoulders if she turned her head, which she did frequently as she clung to the back of Matteo's arm for moral support. He was stocky and tall, very blond, and seemed solid, like an unmovable stake in the ground. When they had asked to see me the night before, I had had no idea what about and I still didn't. We sat down in the corner of the sitting room. No one was there at the time, so it was very private.

Margarita spoke first. "I needed to know how you knew my name last night. I didn't have a name tag on."

I had forgotten about that. "I can see those things clairvoyantly. I like to address people directly, but now I have people wear nametags so as not to upset them. I hadn't realized you weren't wearing one. I'm sorry if it disturbed you."

"When you say you see it clairvoyantly, what do you mean?"

"I see it as if I'm looking at a tickertape, over your head. It tells me your name and how old you are."

"That's amazing," Matteo said.

"I want to learn how to do that," Margarita blurted out.

"Why?" I asked.

"I guess because I think it's cool, real cool."

I smiled. "I have that ability only because it helps me in my spiritual work. It's a spiritual accomplishment that a person achieves through striving and hard work. It's not used for fun or games."

She looked downcast. "I know I sound silly, but I would like to help people, too. I want to study psychology and be a therapist someday. Wouldn't being clairvoyant help me in my work?"

"Yes, it would; but are you willing to devote time to studying this teaching?"

"I think so." And she looked straight into my eyes, and I saw the beauty of her spirit.

"Come to all the lectures, and if you still are interested in learning more you can be a part of the class that I will be starting here."

"Thank you. I would like that."

Matteo, I could see, wasn't too certain as to what was happening, but he gave me a broad, thoughtful look as they were leaving.

I sighed: youth, open to change and open to learning. As we age we lose that desire to learn, to long for more. If only all my students could feel that. If only they could experience longing for God Consciousness. That longing keeps them moving forward on the path. It gives them the courage to face the challenges and obstacles and strive to learn more. Without that, a student can become stuck and give up. It is the key to spiritual growth—a key that many forget about in studying an esoteric teaching.

I went to bed that night and dreamed about my home in the mountains.

CHAPTER 15

I did four lectures in the next couple of weeks on some of the questions I had addressed in the first lecture. Margarita and Matteo volunteered to help me. School was out, and they had plenty of free time. It was nice to have their company. Matteo was able to borrow his parents' car, and they drove me around the outer city and even to the mountains for a picnic. I enjoyed their questions and their conversation. It made me feel young again and somehow not so serious.

Erna came back and also wanted to spend time with me. I found her to be very stable. She thought about each topic we discussed and asked me some very profound questions.

By the second week the attendance had gone down, as I expected, but there was a steady return of around twenty people, and some new ones often came with them. Four more people asked to see me privately: a middle-aged Black couple, Gottfried and Dora Ackermann; a young man in his twenties named Rubin Wyler; and Anna Roth, a woman in her late thirties. They all seemed interested in continuing the work and having a private class. Erna immediately volunteered her home. She was married to Olivier and it was fine with him that she host the class in their home. He had no interest in anything spiritual but didn't object to her doing it. He watched TV in his office during class time. Later, I found out that he joined the group for refreshments afterward and eventually became a good friend of Gottfried. It was Gottfried who explained the teaching in such a way that Olivier became interested and surprisingly started attending class.

Father Joseph continued to be a problem. Two days after his visit there was an article in the local newspaper blasting my teaching and me. I thought about calling the editor and asking for equal space to reply but decided against it. His language was so outrageous that if people believed him then they were not meant to study with me anyway.

At the next lecture, a man said, "Zarathustra, that was a terrible article in the newspaper. How do you feel about it?"

"Truth always attracts enemies and fanatical people who can never be open to it."

Then I talked a little about fanaticism in any spiritual teaching. "Fanatics are so rigid that they cannot hear anything other than what conforms to their viewpoint. It is the cause of prejudice, lack of understanding, and obsessiveness, and mainly it leads to conflict. All the religious wars are caused by fanaticism. I do not insist that any of you believe what I say. In fact, I ask you to question everything and only let your heart decide what is true for you. When someone preaches that his or her way is the only way, and that you must follow that way or burn in hell, then that is not God's way — not the God I know. It is the way of the fanatic. The priest who wrote this article is a fanatic. Fortunately, there are many others who are not and who understand Jesus's teaching."

Another article appeared the following week asking for people to protest my lectures; and, sure enough, there were several people in front of the hotel with signs warning that I was a heretic sent by the devil and that people who attended my lectures would be in league with him. It was disturbing and amusing at the same time. The disturbing part was that the hotel manager didn't like this kind of attention. Fortunately, he was liberal and believed in freedom of speech, and he protested to the news reporters who were beginning to gather. The amusing part was seeing the attendance temporarily grow as a result of the negative publicity—people are always attracted to something sensational. But by the third week the attendance was down by more than half.

The news media wanted to interview me, but I declined. They did interview several of my lecture attendees who were very positive about my teaching, which helped to produce an article that supported what I was doing. The main newspaper stopped publishing Father Joseph's articles, and soon the matter died down. Only a few protestors continued to show up, but even those numbers declined.

But Father Joseph wasn't deterred. Just prior to the commencement of my last lecture, he appeared at the door to the hall and tried to enter the lecture. Matteo was there, recognized him, and refused him entry.

Matteo told me later that the priest became irate and even tried to push past him, but he blocked his way, which was easy to do since Matteo was at least six feet tall and a strong athlete.

The people at the scene didn't seem to know what was happening and tried to stop Matteo, but he stood his ground until Father Joseph left. Then Matteo explained why he refused him entry. I was glad I'd asked him to stand by the door this evening. It was a sudden thought, as I hadn't done this before. I silently thanked my teacher for that guidance.

There were about thirty people at the last lecture, so I arranged the chairs in a circle and sat down at the center. The topic was as follows:

Relationships That Produce Positive Karma

I asked the group, "How many of you are married?" Half raised their hands.

"How many of you are in a relationship but are not married?" A quarter raised their hands.

Then I asked, "How many of you are single and not in a relationship at this time?"

Another quarter raised their hands.

"How many of you are not happy in the situation you are in and would like to change it? For example, the single ones want a relationship, or those in a relationship would prefer to end it."

Another set of people, about a third, raised their hands.

"That's a high percentage of you who aren't happy. Why do you think that is?"

A man raised his hand. "Boredom. I'm just plain bored with my wife, but I have two kids I love, so I won't leave her."

"Another reason?"

"My husband comes home from work, eats his dinner in front of the TV, and that's where he spends the evening," one woman said. "That's our life. If I want to do anything at all, I do it with my friends."

Anna raised her hand. "I've been in a relationship for ten years. We aren't married, and, because we're not married, we keep good boundaries. We both agreed that marriage could hurt our relationship, which is why we prefer to keep it this way. Often, I wonder what it would be like to be married, but I don't tell him that."

A woman seated on the right protested, "That's not a good reason. I'm married, and the relationship's good because we also work at it. Having a ring on your finger shouldn't change that."

There were some more stories, and then I spoke. "It's true. Being married or not married shouldn't change the relationship, but often it does. There is a finality in marriage that a couple doesn't have if it's only an affair, but sometimes that finality can go wrong and cause a relationship to turn sour. Since by now you know I see everything as karma, what is the karma that causes this problem? Sometimes it's simply the marriage vows that cause old memories to arise from another lifetime, and sometimes those memories aren't good ones. Amazingly, patterns from past lives are repeated time and time again in our relationship with the same person, and those patterns can come up at any time in the present life.

"You may be in what you think is a good karmic relationship and everything goes well for several years, and then suddenly the old karmic pattern will emerge and everything will go wrong. I'm sure you know some couples who broke up without warning, whom you felt were the perfect example of marriage bliss."

A few heads nodded.

"It's important to understand the karma involved before going into a relationship, no matter how much you are attracted to each other. Karma will bring real enemies together in what seems like a loving relationship. This karma will lie dormant until the relationship is solid, and then it will arise and destroy it. This is because the negative karmic energy has a stronger impact than the positive karma has and can cause more hurt, especially if the karma is to inflict pain on someone in retribution."

"That's awful," someone remarked.

"Awful but just. Karma is never paid back unjustly, so if you know someone who has had a very hurtful and difficult relationship, then know it is the person's karma to experience that. Obviously, that person caused someone else to suffer the same way in another life.

"A loving relationship is what most people long for," I went on.

Again, people mumbled in agreement.

"Yet how many people find it? They instead get caught in the net of someone who unconsciously is acting out a karmic pattern."

"But what can one do to avoid it?" Erna asked.

"You don't have to be caught in it if, at the beginning, you are careful about getting involved. Always check out whether your karma with the other person is more positive or more negative."

"But how does one do that?"

"Good question, and an important one. You need to check it out with your Higher Self, when you are feeling very objective and not at all emotional. Otherwise, your emotions will keep you from connecting. Mainly, take your time before getting involved with anyone. Stay in your Higher Self when you are with someone, and ask your Higher Self to give you a sign. If it's a no, then it is easier to break the relationship before it becomes too intimate."

"What happens if it's a member of your family? My sister and I never get along. She always bullies me."

"It's more difficult with families because you usually can't end the relationship, though some people still do. When you recognize that there is difficult karma between you and a relative, try to do your best to change it. Part of the pattern is to act a certain way with each other; so, when you start to fall into the pattern, change it. If your emotions become aroused, give them to your Higher Self, and try to speak to the person from the heart. It's best to avoid any conflict, even if the avoidance means not speaking what you believe to be true. 'Silence is golden' is an old saying and a good one. Someone can't argue with you if you don't argue back."

"That's so hard to do. I get accused so many times of doing something that I haven't done. My brother is the culprit, and I get blamed for it. If I don't speak up, my dad will think I'm the one at fault." Matteo said.

"Does your dad believe you?"

"No, my brother is his favorite."

"Well, obviously there is negative karma between you and your father and not between him and your brother. If you are being accused of something that's not true, it's important to say something, but do it in a calm manner without blaming your brother. Just say you didn't do it and then drop it."

"Even when I get punished?"

"Yes, that's not going to change anyway, is it? Just realize it's some karma you are paying off and try not to hold on to any resentment or the need for revenge. That just pulls you back into more karma later. If it's a very bad relationship, it's best to let it go with love in your heart, so as not to have to return another time with the person."

"I hope I don't have to come back with him," Matteo mumbled, and I saw Margarita squeeze his hand.

"Getting back to having a loving relationship: even if you have good karma with someone, you still need to work at the relationship. No one is perfect, and I've talked about that a lot. Perfectionism can really damage a good partnership. A perfectionist will always expect more from others as well as from himself or herself. Living with someone like that is a constant struggle because usually there is nothing you can do that is right. It's important that anyone with this characteristic receive counseling to keep the relationship a good one and not make negative karma, instead."

"I know a perfectionist who prides himself in being that way, and you're correct — I can do nothing right in his eyes," Dora spoke out.

"So, he's an egotistical perfectionist?"

"At a certain point, you have to decide whether the friendship is worthwhile or you're best giving it up. If it's the former, you need to find an attitude of not listening to him when he starts being perfectionistic. Don't respond, and don't get upset by any of his behavior, and that will help. He expects you to respond a certain way to his criticism. If you don't do that, it will break the pattern.

"Building a loving relationship takes time, patience, understanding, and the ability to confront any difficulties that arise. It's not easy, because everyone is a different type of individual. What matters the most is the desire to develop a good relationship and not to be afraid to explore ways to make that happen. Love is the basis, but it takes more than love to grow it into something very solid.

"Most couples are sexually attracted to each other. They have an affair or get married, and when the sexual attraction dies down, they start to realize that the other person is someone they don't know very well. Then they have children to compensate and to give the relationship an energy boost, and that takes up much of their time and gives them a common ground of relating. If they get through those years without separating, then they settle into old age and maybe travel and do other activities together. Couples can go through life in this manner, and everyone thinks of them as being very happy because they are still married. Yet they may never have been fulfilled or happy with each other."

"If they don't get divorced, they must be happy," a woman said.

"Not necessarily. Don't you know anyone who has been married for years who has settled for his or her life?"

"That's not so bad. It's better than divorce and having to raise children by your-self." "Maybe it is and maybe it's not. At least the single parent has a chance to start over with someone new. In any case, what I am saying is that all relationships take work and need to have a strong base of love and respect. Then the chances of making it an ongoing positive experience are good. Just settling doesn't achieve this. It just adds to the negative karmic consequences.

"Karma is a strong attraction. Sometimes the best relationships are with people you have no karma with at all. Initially, you will meet someone who seems very nice, but to whom you have no attraction. Instead of dismissing the relationship, realize that this may be someone with no karmic past with you, but the person could be a far better partner and someone you can build good karma with."

"But if you're not attracted to someone, how can you have a relationship with him? I couldn't do that," an woman in her thirties said.

"You don't have to jump into intimacy. Just take your time. At the beginning, even though the attraction isn't there, it could happen in the course of getting to know the person, particularly if the person turns out to be very nice. Your heart will pick that up and become more interested.

"People feel they need to fall in love immediately. That's part of our romantic con-ditioning put out by movies, media, and other socio-cultural messaging. True love, though, comes from understanding each other on a heart level, and that usually takes time and a serious commitment to the process. If there isn't a deep friendship that governs the relationship, then it usually can't last unless the karmic hold is so great that all of that is overlooked.

"Strive to have a partner who will be a support and who also has a good heart. Remember, no one is perfect. There will always be disputes and disagreements; but, if the love is strong, it will override any negative consequences. The main thing to remember is that, if you are in a negative karmic relationship, try to make it positive; and, if that is impossible, try to agree on dissolving the relationship in an amiable manner so that no new negative karma can be incurred."

There were more questions and answers after the break, and, finally, the lecture ended at ten. Since it was my last lecture there, I talked about my schedule and possi-ble return and asked if anyone was interested in attending the classes. A man named Edwin Schneider and a woman, Olga Bachmann, raised their hands and I talked to them briefly after the lecture and introduced them to the others who were committed.

I had already packed my bags to leave in the morning. Matteo had offered to drive me to Zürich, so I didn't have to rent a car. Zürich is the largest city in Switzerland, and the last one on my tour. After that, I would restart my journey by returning to the first city, Wengen. But before that, I would have a short vacation in my home in the mountains.

CHAPTER 16

My hotel in Zürich was a small one, near the river and centrally located. It didn't have a conference room, but it was across from a larger hotel that did. Since I was going to be there a few weeks, staying in the larger hotel would have been too expensive. The small one was comfortable but not air-conditioned, and it was now August, and we were having a heat wave. At least the large hotel had air-conditioning in the conference room.

My main task the first week was to do the promotional plan for the lectures that Alex had also prepared for me for Zürich. It was very comprehensive in detail as to where to put posters and what social media to place ads in. I again got help from the hotel and even though it was a lot of ground to cover we were able to complete it before my first lecture.

I walked everywhere or took the trolleys. Nearby was a small section of town with narrow streets lined with restaurants and bars with live music. It was alive active with young people and tourists. Even though I was alone, I didn't feel lonely, as people were friendly and talked to me.

This was Alex's hometown and where he currently worked and lived. He had said to call him when I arrived, but I felt reluctant to do so. He'd sent me an email when I was in Basel but hadn't called me there. He knew my schedule and could have been in touch. By now, I felt Alex had decided not to pursue the teaching, and I sensed his relationship with Gretchen was the cause. I was disappointed, but realized that students will always be tested and that some of them wouldn't pass. I needed not to be attached to any of them but simply to be there for those who needed my help. My teacher had prepared me well, but I hadn't realized that I would experience love and loss and that I needed to learn not to be attached to the outcome.

One morning a couple days before my first lecture, the hotel clerk stopped me as I was heading for breakfast.

"Good morning Sir, did you see the article about you in this morning's paper?"

Bewildered, I took the paper and read the headline on the third page, "Spiritual Teacher to Do a Series of Lectures." The article went on to describe some of the subject matter of the series with some very positive comments coming from my previous stops. There was an excerpt from the Basel newspaper, which I hadn't seen, describing my last lecture on love and relationships. I was flabbergasted. Who had written this article? I looked at the author's name and didn't know who he was. I decided to call him and thank him for the article: it would certainly make a difference in attendance.

His name was Alfred Bühler. I called his office and was told he was out of town for a few days. It would have to wait until he returned.

The night of the first lecture arrived, and, as always, I had no idea how many people would come. I would be giving the introductory lecture on the Higher Self and talk about the teaching in general and the subjects that would be covered in the next three weeks. I had concluded that two lectures every week was appropriate for the big cities, which gave time in between to meet with anyone privately. There were around a hundred chairs, which surely would be more than enough. In my experience, I discovered that the larger the city, the smaller the attendance. There were so many activities and things to do that spiritual lectures would be at the bottom of the list. Basel had brought in more people because of the news article, and maybe that would happen here, too, who knows? I had tried again to reach Alfred Bühler, but again he was unavailable, but he was back in town according to his executive assistant. I was hoping he would attend that evening, so I could thank him in person.

People arrived early, and I tried to greet them at the door, but there were too many coming in at once, so I retreated to the front of the hall. There was a raised platform, which I now liked because I could see across the entire audience right to the back rows, taking in all the faces. In my youth, I had acted in a lot of the school plays and even had a desire for a while to be an actor. Maybe this was why I wasn't afraid to speak to an audience. In fact, it exhilarated me.

At a certain point I realized there weren't enough chairs, so I hurried to the desk and asked for more to be provided. When the chairs arrived, there was a fair bit of shuffling to squeeze in more seating, and I apologized for the disruption. Then still more people came, and I was shocked. I had never anticipated such a turnout. Some started to sit down in the aisles; the manager came in and announced that they couldn't do that, but if they wanted to wait outside, he offered to provide a larger room down the hall for the event. While the transfer of so many people took a bit of time, it was worth it. The new room was almost double in size, and it was stately with high ceilings and elegant decor. I looked out at the largest audience I had ever had. There were probably more than two hundred people there. For the first time in my journey I needed a microphone, and there was even a floating one for questions. I took a moment to look at the people and my heart blossomed to again see an audience that was multiracial. Besides the usual Caucasians, which dominated my main audiences, particularly in the smaller towns, I was happy to see Blacks, Asians, and multicultural couples — people of all ages and ethnicities.

I had just started to speak when something terrible happened. A woman standing in the back stood up suddenly and began screamed obscenities at me. Fortunately, the manager had some hotel staff in the room, and they quickly escorted her out. But the outburst and the emotion around it released very bad energy into the atmosphere of the room. I had to do something, so I sat down in a chair that was on the stage and closed my eyes and cleared the energy out. When I opened my eyes and stood up, the audience was very quiet. Some looked at me questioningly.

"What I did just now was remove the negative energy the woman had just put into the room. So, I will start by talking about energy. Everything has energy: your thoughts, your actions, and your words. Everything around you is full of energy. When you walk into a room where someone has been fighting, you will feel that energy; or, in the reverse, if you walk into a room where there are people who love each other, you can pick up the positive energy. How many of you have ever felt that?"

Quite a few raised their hands.

"Each one of us is responsible for the energy we produce. Everyone here can build a home with beautiful energy just by being conscious of your words and your emotions, and by bringing into your home beauty such as paintings, flowers, and playing melodious music. By doing so, you create an atmosphere that helps you spiritually and mentally. If your office or place of work contains beauty, you will have an easier time working because you will be surrounded by that energy. If instead your office is untidy and chaotic, you will find it more difficult to complete tasks or to do them with full concentration."

A few people nodded their heads, and I heard one of them say, "I wish my husband were here to hear this."

"But what is energy? A physicist may say it is measured in wavelengths, the frequency of which varies according to its function. A physician may describe energy in terms of the body. A person may have low energy, and that can signify a variety of ailments. *Prana* is the life force or energy in the body that keeps everything functioning. If a minister talks about energy, he may say that God's energy created all things. All of these explanations are correct, but energy is even more than this. It is the prevailing force of the universe, and it transforms all nature — of which we are a part — and governs all things.

"If energy did not exist here, Earth would be a dead planet with no life forms, but even then there could be energy of a different nature. The moon, for instance, has energy that affects the tides and gives a certain type of people a lot of energy. There were ancient sects that worshiped it for its energy, and some current ones still exist. This teaching is not one of them," I quickly added.

"The Higher Self that I will be speaking about tonight is also energy, the highest energy that a human being has. Its energy can transport a person into the higher realms of the subtle world, which I will speak about later. But mainly, it helps a person develop spiritually. It contains the highest qualities of an individual. Without the Higher Self, a human being would be a lower species of animal with no soul or spirit."

I then talked at length about the Higher Self. There were many questions, all dealing with what the Higher Self really is.

One woman said, "You say it is the 'wise being within.' What do you mean by that?"

"I mean wise in the context of wisdom. Your Higher Self has access to all knowledge and has a full understanding of the process of evolution and your personal process; it also understands God Consciousness in the real sense of what that means."

"Will it tell me all of that?"

"It will tell you what you can understand and what you are ready to hear and strive for. The more you work with it, the more you will grow spiritually, until at some point you will be ready for the higher knowledge."

"But if it is part of me, why can't I know anything I want to know?" a man sitting next to her asked.

"God is part of you, but are you ready to become one with God?"

"Christ did."

"Yes, but Christ went through his personal evolution and many initiations to reach that point. You can also do that if you so choose."

"But how?"

"When you start to work with your Higher Self, you will know how. The first step is to find a teacher who will also help you."

"But Christ did it on his own. Why can't I?"

"No, that's not true. Christ's teacher was John the Baptist. When he baptized Him, he initiated Him as his disciple. No one can walk the path to God alone. Every great Mahatma has had a teacher who has guided him or her. John the Baptist said that Christ would surpass him, and that also can happen, the student can go beyond the teacher, but initially every student in an esoteric teaching needs a teacher to guide him or her."

"Are you such a teacher?" a young woman asked.

Before I could answer a man way at the back stood up and said, "Yes he is, and I personally can tell you he is a truly wonderful teacher."

It was Alex.

I was deeply moved to see him, and all I was able to say in that moment was, "Thank you, Alex." It was truly wonderful to see him again.

I turned back to the woman and talked about the many teachers who have devoted their lives to helping others grow spiritually.

It was time for a break.

I stayed at the front and waited for Alex. He hugged me tightly and whispered, "Please forgive me."

There were people all around wanting to ask questions. I told them I would be happy to answer questions after the lecture, but now I needed to talk to my student. I led him to a room next to the stage, to which I planned to retreat during break times.

When we finally were seated across from each other, Alex said, "I think the witch that was my teacher came back to get me through Gretchen. She was so lovely at first, and as you know I was falling in love with her; but then slowly she started talking against you in small, deliberate ways, trying to point out your imperfections and make them larger than what they may be. Then when I said I needed to call you and be with you here in Zürich, she said I had to pick either you or her."

Alex smiled a wry smile. "That was the mistake on her part. The idea of losing you was far more terrible than that of losing her." He added, "I almost succumbed, though, but I meditated yesterday for the first time in a long while, and I saw you in a distance. I knew then that I needed to be here tonight. When I told Gretchen I was coming tonight, she gave me that ultimatum."

I looked at Alex and love filled my heart. "Alex, I thought I had lost you, as I haven't been able to reach you in meditation for several weeks. That was an incredible test you passed, and I'm so happy to have you back. I've missed you."

"And I've missed you! I'm looking forward to being with you again and being part of this teaching. Now, what can I do to help tonight? This is a huge crowd."

"I think it's because of the article written about me in the Zürich paper this week."

"Yes, I know about it. Alfred is a friend of mine."

"So, you're responsible for the article?"

"Yes, and I asked him not to tell you."

"Now I know why I haven't been able to get through to him to thank him."

"You can do that later. He's with me tonight."

"But why not let me know?"

"I still wasn't certain whether I would stay with Gretchen. I was torn between you and her, but I always felt a great love for you and this teaching, and I wanted to help you anonymously. Her ultimatum made me realize how stupid I've been."

"Thank you for your help, but now I have a problem that I could use your help with."

"I'm here now for good. How can I help?"

"I thought I would have my usual turnout of thirty to fifty people, and I had planned to give them the Higher Self exercise after the break tonight. But with this large an audience, there are too many people to do the exercise. It wouldn't work with such a variety of energy, yet I've found lately that it's very important to give the exercise at the beginning of my lectures. If people have a positive response, it helps them to stay through the rest, and, even if they don't stay, they have the exercise to work with."

"Why not have around forty people who can't come back later this week stay at the end to do the exercise tonight? Then rent a smaller room and have the rest of the people come back in smaller groups for the next three or four evenings."

"That may work. Can you find the manager while I'm talking and ask if there is anything available? But how will we sign them up?"

"Let me handle that. I'll find out what nights are available and have some sign-up sheets on the tables outside. But it will take some time, so you will need to keep the second half of your talk shorter than usual to allow for that time."

It worked out fine. There were four nights available in a smaller room, and most people didn't seem disturbed about coming back. Those who didn't want to do so weren't meant to continue, anyway. The people who wanted to do the exercise, but couldn't come back, stayed at the end of the lecture to learn it.

Afterward, Alex and I had a drink at the restaurant in my hotel. I didn't know if I was pleased that so many people had come or if I was worried about the numbers. Also, the donation basket was overflowing. Alex had started to empty it early on, and at the end it was still full. I needed more money because of the additional expenses, but too much made me uncomfortable. I mentioned that to Alex, and he brushed it aside saying, "This will help pay for the computer and cell phone you bought in Interlaken."

"I guess you are right. But my main problem is I don't want to attract lots of people. This is an esoteric teaching, which means it's only for the few."

"Teacher, this is a new age; maybe the teaching is for more than you think. You can't turn them down if they want to learn from you."

"No, but please, no more articles about me in the newspaper."

"Why not? If people are meant to come, why not? You've said some will come once or twice, or linger for a while, and then leave, and will come back, if not this lifetime, then the next or the next."

"True, but the classes need to be small and handpicked. Otherwise, negative people can come in and disturb the energy."

"You can still have small classes. Not all these people will want private time with you, and they will still go away having learned some of this beautiful teaching."

"What happened to your friend, Alfred, who wrote the article?"

"Alfred signed up for the exercise later in the week and didn't stay to meet you. When he comes next time, I will introduce you."

"Can you call him and make certain he won't write another article about me?"

"No, I can't do that. He's a reporter, and that's his job. Don't worry, it will be all right."

But I was worried; and, sure enough, the next day the paper had another article about the previous night's lecture. Again, it was positive. If new people came, hopefully others would drop out, though when I asked who was returning at the end of the first lecture, it seemed that everyone raised a hand. The room was the largest one available — so be it. If more came, the last to arrive wouldn't be able to get in.

I suddenly heard my teacher's voice say, "Then do two sessions on the same topic."

I started to protest but stopped. Surely none of this was happening. I thought of the little towns and wished I were back in those places. Even Basel now seemed small next to Zürich. I picked up the phone to call Alfred Bühler and then put it down. Maybe in the crowd there were one or two who were destined to be my students. They would be harder for me to find, but they would find their way to me. I tried to think about how I could make that happen.

At the end of the first lecture, after doing the Higher Self exercise with the smaller group, I offered individual meetings with me, and ten of the fifty people were interested. At that rate, after the other smaller meetings, there would be another thirty. If new people came to the additional lectures, how could I handle all of them? Surely there would be those who didn't continue. In the previous towns, almost 60 to 70 percent of the audience had left before the last lecture. But, when I thought about it, I realized that some of those places, such as Basel and Bern, had half the population of Zürich and were more religious. I hadn't seen a single priest or minister at my lecture here. I felt at a loss in terms of what to expect.

I met Alex near his office for lunch, and again I expressed my reservations about what was happening.

"How can I set up a class if it gets too large?"

"Have several classes. Your other classes have been very small; maybe have a larger group here, up to fifteen people. It's a big city. You can have two or three classes in various locations."

"But Alex, it's not just about the classes. I work with each student individually on the subtle plane at night. At the rate this is happening, I could have a hundred students. That's too much.

He just smiled at me. "Surely you can divide yourself enough to handle that?"

He was right, of course, but I had hoped to have just a handful of students to carry on the work. I expressed this to him.

"I didn't think it was up to you. You always say, 'The student finds the teacher when the student is ready.' "

I sighed. "Maybe there will be a lot fewer when the next weeks are over." But my heart said that wasn't true. Out of the ten that asked to see me privately, I already recognized five or six who had been with me before.

"Look at some of the other teachers, such as those in India. A couple I know about have thousands of students."

"Yes, but what they are teaching is exoteric not esoteric material."

"Not completely. They do have an inner group that is esoteric, but even those groups can be larger than a hundred people."

I decided not to discuss it anymore. Alex was right; if my teacher wanted me to have larger classes, then I would, but I would have to get used to it.

The next three evenings were spent teaching the Higher Self exercise to the remaining participants. In addition, I had appointments with individuals privately throughout the day and evenings after the smaller Higher Self lessons were done. Alex set up all of these appointments for me.

One of the people asking to study with me, a woman named Rosina Stoller, volunteered to help at the lectures. I liked her immediately. She was in her forties, warm-hearted, with dark brown eyes whose inner depths penetrated me with feelings of acceptance. At our private meeting, she told me she was gay. She was a little apologetic about it, and I reassured her that sexual preference had no bearing on one's involvement in this teaching. The God within belonged to everyone, no matter what his or her ethnicity, nationality or sexual orientation or preference.

She sighed and said, "I wish all religions believed that."

I introduced Rosina to Alex and suggested she work with him. A couple of other people were already helping out under his guidance. Unfortunately, his reaction to Rosina was quite negative, and he told me later that he didn't want to have anything to do with her.

"I know you are going to say it's because of something that happened in a past life; but, even so, there is something about her now that I don't trust."

"Can you tell me what it is?"

He thought for a minute. "She is controlling. In my meeting with her, she immediately made suggestions as to what should be done to make the meetings run more smoothly. Then when I said we had already made some changes that were better, she got very insistent and stubbornly wouldn't let go of what she felt we still needed to do.

"Were they good suggestions?"

"Yes, but that's not the point. She should have asked what the plans were before making her suggestions. Some of them we had already come up with. She's very impudent."

"Did you say something to her?"

"No, I know what you are going to say. I need to talk to her."

"Yes, and I think it good to do the exercise of looking into each other's eyes and trying to find out what the past is. If you don't come up with anything, I'll explain it."

"Why not just tell me now? Then I won't have to look at her."

I laughed. "That's the easy way out, and you need training to be a yogi."

When I saw Alex later, he looked very serious. "I spoke to her and explained what your advice was. She was taken aback at first, but to her credit, she listened to me and even apologized. Her explanation was that she had been victimized a lot in the past and now was trying to be strong and maybe sometimes came off as too strong. She even thanked me for telling her and asked me to point it out to her if she does it again."

"Did you do the exercise?"

"Yes, we sat a long time looking into each other's eyes, and then I suddenly felt great love for her. It was almost overwhelming. I think that in the past I was a woman and she was my lover or my husband who left me for another woman. It was strange: right after I felt the love, I felt enormous anger and feelings of abandonment."

"What did she feel?"

"Not very much, just that she had known me before and that we had been very close. In fact, she was surprised when I told her my feelings, as she didn't feel any animosity toward me at all."

"That's because she didn't have any."

"I guess not. He left me."

"Yes, but not for someone else. He died in a so he forced a duel with over you."

"What!"

"So he forced a duel with the man, who turned out to be a famous dueler. When you insisted he not go, his pride kept him from canceling out, and as a result he died, leaving you with his child and no means of support. The rest of that life was extremely difficult and lonely for you."

"That's interesting. When I've read about the dueling that took place during the seventeenth and eighteenth centuries, I've always felt disgusted with the innocent deaths that occurred because of that sport. It was barbaric. So, my feeling of anger was because he wouldn't listen to me and ended up abandoning me."

"Yes, that's why when Rosina suggested how to do things you got upset."

"Yeah, she didn't listen to me then, and I felt the same way now. Man, these lives can be really difficult."

"Let's hope you get more in touch with your love for her and let go of the hurt."

"Thanks a lot. Shall I tell her what you said?"

"Yes, it might help her understand her stubbornness. Tell her to come to see me if she needs to talk to me about it."

Rosina did come to see me to thank me. "Stubbornness is one of my main problems in relationships. That past life really explains it, but I would think that now I would be the opposite."

"It depends on how strongly you have the characteristic and also on how you interpreted what happened. For instance, while you died in the duel, you could still have felt justified in demanding it, and your stubbornness would have made you never want to back out. You would have thought backing out dishonorable; yet you knew your chances of dying were very high and that, in doing so, you would leave your wife and child helpless. It really wasn't worth it. But if you didn't learn that lesson, you would have come into this life still having those strong tendencies, which will always hurt your relationships."

"So, how can I change this stubbornness?"

"You need to look at all the areas of your life in which you play it out. Are you more stubborn with certain people in your life? How does it play out in your work? Then, when you have identified those areas, ask your Higher Self for a process and a first step in overcoming this characteristic. Asking Alex to point out to you when you get stubborn about something is a good step. Also, every night look back on the day and notice if you were stubborn about something. It's hard work to change a negative characteristic, so don't be discouraged if it doesn't happen overnight."

"Thank you, I will try all of those things, and please tell me when I act that way." Then she reached up and hugged me.

The next few days went quickly, with appointments taking up most of my time. I took a day off to prepare a new lecture, one that was different and somewhat stronger than the others. I think unconsciously I was trying to reduce the attendance this way.

I meditated regularly with Alex and, during those meditations, felt my teacher's presence. One early morning she said to me, "Being a teacher is never easy, but it's always rewarding when you have a student like Alex. He will not desert you again. There is great potential in him, but don't let him know that at this time."

The last Higher Self lesson was that evening, and I met Alfred Bühler for the first time. I liked him very much. He was intensely intelligent, articulate, and curious; someone with whom I wanted to spend more time. That would happen soon, as he invited me to his home for dinner later in the week.

Chapter 17

My days were filled with appointments and preparing for my next lecture. It would mainly be about karma and reincarnation, but I also wanted to talk about the meaning of evolution on this planet. This was a sophisticated audience, so I felt I could introduce some of the esoteric knowledge concerning this subject. Preachers speak to the lowest level of their congregation, keeping everything simple so everyone can understand. That may be best for a certain kind of audience, but I prefer to address those who want to be challenged intellectually. Every esoteric teaching has many interpretations. The same book can be read many times, and each time the reader will see something new or understand something he or she didn't understand before. As a person's mind and heart open, new perceptions take place. This constant movement and growth make life very exciting. When the mind and heart become stagnant, the person no longer feels the need to strive for more. Life itself, with all its mundane demands, can make that happen.

Dinner with Alfred Bühler was a nice break in the work. It was a small party: Alfred, his wife, Klara, Alex, and I. They lived in a very wealthy suburb on the Right Bank section of Zürich in a large house with views overlooking the river. Their wealth came from Klara's family, who were all bankers and ran one of the largest banks in Switzerland.

Klara was attractive, not so much in her looks, but in the way in which she carried and conducted herself. She was warm, open, and very charming. Within minutes I felt at ease with both her and Alfred. They were dressed casually in slacks and shirts. She wore a touch of makeup to emphasize her pretty greenish, blue eyes. When she looked at her husband, it was with genuine love, and the same was true for him. They had been married ten years and had two small children, and I could tell they still deeply loved each other, a rare thing, indeed.

The evening was warm but not too hot, so we dined on the patio. Our conversation centered on the teaching, and Alfred seemed to be very knowledgeable about Eastern philosophy. He finally admitted that he had minored in religion at the university and had even considered becoming a professor in that field.

Halfway through the dinner Alfred asked me, "Zarathustra, would you tell me something about your background? How did you ever become a teacher, and why did you choose that path?"

"I will tell you if you promise not to put it in print."

"No more articles, I promise."

"Basically I'm from Zürich. I was born here and grew up in what is now called District 10, a nice neighborhood, which, of course, has changed a lot since I lived there. I went to Zürich's United International Business School and got my Bachelor's and Master's degrees there.

"Really!" Alex looked very surprised. I had never gone into any detail about my past with him. Somehow, I was feeling very talkative.

"When I finished my degree, I took a position in my father's corporation where he was a manager. Basically after that I did nothing but play in my free time. You know, lots of women, lots of alcohol and running around with friends. When I could, I spent long weekends in Italy and France and made excuses to my father, who was my boss at the firm, about why I wasn't at work some of the time."

"Wasn't he concerned about that?"

"Not really. He figured I was young and sowing my oats, and I would soon settle down when I got married and had a family. I think he was considered the rebel in his family, so I came by it naturally."

"Were you interested in religion at all?" Alex asked.

"Heaven's no! Not in the least."

"When I was twenty-eight my grandfather died and left me some money. This motivated me into taking a leave of absence from my job and travel to the East. I had always been interested in Asia. I also was an avid lover of Eastern art of any kind. My girlfriend at the time decided to go with me but at the last minute dropped out, particularly when the trip we were planning seemed to become longer and longer. I was somewhat tired of her anyway, so that was fine with me. I was looking forward to meeting other women on my journey."

Klara laughed, "I can see where women would be attracted to you."

Alfred nodded, agreeing with her.

"Yes," I smiled in reflection. "Anyway, I started out in Greece and planned to travel to India, Thailand, maybe China, and end up in Japan."

"How long were you planning to travel?" Alfred asked.

"It was meant to be for four months, but I it ended up being much longer."

"Was that because you met your teacher?" Alex asked.

"Yes. In fact, I found her in India and never continued on to the other countries."

"How did you meet her?"

"It's an interesting story. First, I must say I was never looking for a teacher. I truly had no religious interests and only went into the temples to see the sculptures of the different deities in the Hindu religion. I found them fascinating and quite beautiful. I was spending the night in Mumbai, as I planned to fly to Aurangabad the next morning to see the Ajanta Caves. It was very warm in my room, so I took a late-night walk down by the water where a cold breeze was stirring up. I walked past what looked like an old man seated on one of the docks and noticed he was meditating. Just as I moved past him, he opened his eyes and called me by name.

"Naturally, I stopped and was very surprised.

"He beckoned to me and said, 'Your teacher is waiting for you. She has asked me to tell you to come to her ashram,' and he handed me a piece of paper with an address written on it.

" 'But I don't have a teacher. What is this about?' I was beginning to believe that this was some kind of con situation. The man could have followed me and found out my name from one of the hotel staff.

" 'She said you wouldn't believe me, so she asked me to give you this,' and he reached into his pocket and pulled out a picture of a woman seated in a yoga position. I looked at the picture and went immediately into a state of ecstasy. Later, I found out that this was called *samadhi*. I can't explain how incredibly beautiful it was. I've only experienced it a very few times in my life, and all I can say is it is joy that can't be explained in words."

"They say it is touching the Divine," Alfred added.

"Yes, it is being in the presence of God. I sat down for a while, and then the man took me by the arm and helped me back to my hotel room, where I remained for nearly three days still experiencing this state. When it finally left me, I knew I had to find this woman who claimed to be my teacher. I had her photo and the address of the ashram, which turned out to be in a remote area in northwest India."

"What was your teacher's name?" Alfred asked.

"I'm not allowed to tell you that or the name of the town where her ashram is. She has just a few disciples, around thirty, and if someone is meant to be with her, the person will find her, or she will find the disciple, as she did me."

"But how did she know where you would be?"

"She was shown that by her Mahatma."

"The '*Mahatma*,' what do you mean by that? Is that her teacher?" Klara inquired.

"Yes, it is. Come to my next lecture, as I plan to mention the Mahatmas and how they help the planet."

"So, go on. What happened when you met her?" Alex interrupted.

"It took me almost two weeks of traveling to find her, since it was across India and I had to take trains and buses to get there. In the end, I hired a car to drive me part of the way until the roads became barely passable. At that point, I had to hire a guide with horses to get to my final destination. All I can tell you is that the town is in the foothills of the Himalayan Mountains."

"That's amazing." Everyone started making comments and asking questions all at once.

"The rest of my story is very personal. All I can say is that the time I spent with her was the happiest I have ever experienced. I had contacted my family on a visit to a nearby village, so they would know where I was, and to quit my job. Three years later I got a letter from them saying my father had just died and the family needed me to return to settle some legal business. I didn't want to return, but my teacher said, "Yes, you need to do that, and then you need to be alone for a few years to prepare yourself to teach someday."

"Alex told me you were living like a hermit in the mountains. Is that why you did that?" Alfred asked.

"Yes, I resolved the business I needed to do for the family, and then I found my place in the mountains and settled there. I came down from my home last spring to fulfill my teacher's request that I take her teaching out into the world. That is the only reason I am here."

"How long did you live in the mountains?"

"Seven years. It was an incredible, wonderful experience."

"Didn't you miss your friends and family?"

"No, I was a different person and no longer had anything in common with my friends; I was close only to my father and not to the rest of my family."

Alex asked, "Is your family still here in Zürich?" I could tell he was wondering if I saw them.

"My mother remarried and now lives in Italy, and I have a younger brother who lives here. Both he and my mother believe I have gone mad and have little to do with me."

"How sad," Alex commented, and there was a pause in the conversation.

Then Klara bluntly asked, "Do you ever miss women? It sounded like you really enjoyed them."

"Sometimes I'm lonely. My teacher said I could marry and even have children if I wanted to. That would not change my mission. But I haven't met anyone I feel enough love for to give up living in solitude. My years alone have made me a recluse, so I doubt if that will change."

Alex looked disturbed. "But I thought to be a teacher you had to be celibate."

"That's true of some teachings, not mine. In the old days being celibate supposedly kept you from attachments and temptations. Some gurus tried that and failed because of strong repressed sexual desires. My teacher believes it is better to live those desires out; that way they will leave you naturally at a certain stage in your development. Otherwise, your lower nature can make them erupt and cause negative karma to be made. I'm glad I was promiscuous in my youth."

"I thought that if you were married you could never spiritually achieve what a celibate, unmarried disciple could achieve," Alfred said.

"Again, that is part of the Indian yogic tradition, not my teaching. Love and relationships are major ways of learning. To achieve the higher initiations, you have to be living in the world. To overcome your lower nature, you need to have it fully awakened, and that can only happen by living in the world."

Alfred smiled. "My life is full of temptations, challenges, and choices to make. If I were meditating all day it would be nice, but certainly, it would not put me in the situations that I find myself in at my job." He paused, then added, "But you've been a recluse for many years and now you're a teacher, so how does that relate to what you've just said about living in the world?"

"Good point. It's true I have been isolated and not in the world, but now as a teacher I must again be in the world. I will not be returning to my home in the mountains except for an occasional period of retreat, which I recommend for every student."

"You're not returning home?" Alex asked.

"No, I will buy a house, probably in a town in the mountains, so I will still not be in a big city. There I can communicate with my students by phone and electronically, and I plan to return to the classes that are set up in the different towns and cities. My new life will be very different from before."

"Are you happy about that?" Klara asked.

"Yes and no. I admit I enjoyed being alone in the mountains and I will miss it, but I am beginning to feel happy to have the interaction with my students and people like you."

"Well, I, for one, will be happy that you will be returning and hope you will be our guest when you come back," Alfred answered.

I felt pleased at this response. The rest of the evening was spent talking about the world I would be returning to. I was out of touch with so many of the political developments; it was good to hear other people's viewpoints.

Later in the week, I saw Alfred privately and he asked to study with me. He even offered to have the Zürich classes at his home. This would be good, as he was centrally located, and people could easily come there from both sides of the river. I still hoped to be able to fit them all into one class, not several.

In the meantime, I continued to meet with people on a regular basis. I never mentioned the classes unless someone asked how to continue studying the teaching. There were a few people who wanted to continue, but mostly, people wanted personal and not spiritual guidance. I explained that I wasn't a therapist, but if I could give spiritual insight I would do so. I realized I needed to explain this to the larger audience, as well, and maybe that would limit my individual interviews.

One of the people who came to see me was a woman named Martha Bondon. She was Black, in her fifties, married with grown children, and at first, was very shy and afraid to talk to me. I tried to put her at ease by discussing Zürich and asking her what attractions would be interesting for me to see. Finally, she said, "Zarathustra, I mainly needed to talk to you about my daughter. She is twenty-eight years old and has a strange illness that none of the doctors can diagnose."

"What are her symptoms?"

"She has constant pain in her stomach, but none of the X-rays show anything that could be causing it. She doesn't have ulcers, no tumor — nothing. They had her swallow a camera that is the size of a pill, and it scoped the whole area. There was nothing there, yet she swears the pain is located in that area. They even checked her lungs and chest and found nothing."

"Is she very emotional?"

"Not really. She also went to a therapist to determine whether the pain was psychosomatic, and the therapist felt it wasn't. She's engaged to be married to a wonderful man whom she adores, so there doesn't seem to be anything psychologically wrong with her. I was wondering if you could see her and help her?"

"I would be glad to help her. Have her call me in the morning for an appointment."

I met her daughter, Catrin, the next day. She looked like a younger version of her mother except for her brown eyes, which were larger and reflected an inner thoughtfulness that suggested a deep intelligence. After she explained her symptoms, I suggested to her that I might be able to do an energetic healing process with her. She was enthused by the prospect of resolving her pain. We found an unused meeting room where there would be some privacy. The moment I began the process, I felt the pain in my stomach and knew that her ailment wasn't physical. I asked her about her fiancé and whether she had any fears at all about getting married.

She replied, "No, I love Erik very much. We've been together for three years now, so we know each other very well."

I didn't think this was true. "Tell me about him."

"Well, he's white and a lawyer and has an excellent practice. His home is in the wealthy section of Zürich and certainly big enough for a family, which he wants right away."

I thought for a minute and asked, "Are there any concerns about being a bi-racial couple?"

"No, absolutely not! We have discussed this and it has never been a problem for him. We do love each other very much. And his family has really been wonderful. I have a great relationship with them."

"You mentioned he wanted a family right away. How about you? Do you want a family right away?"

"Well, I would like to wait a couple of years, but I'm willing to start earlier if it's so important to him."

"Why did you want to wait?"

"My job is very exciting, and I was just promoted to a management position. If I left now, I would be losing a huge opportunity that I wouldn't have again. If I wait four or five years, it would be easier to take a maternity leave and return to the same job."

"You're still young; four or five years isn't long to wait to start a family."

"I know, but Erik is insistent about having a child now."

"That explains the pain."

"What do you mean?"

"The pain is psychosomatic. It's right in the region where you would be carrying a child. You are the bearer of the child; you have every right to say no, that you need to wait. Do that, and your pain will leave you.

"But I might lose Erik then."

"If he leaves you because of that, then it's better to know that now. If he loves you, he will understand. Otherwise, you will have a child you will resent, and that certainly is not right for the child. Follow your heart. Your heart and body say no, this isn't right for you now."

"You know, just hearing those words has lessened my pain." And she patted her abdomen. "Thank you, I will follow your advice."

After she left, I thought about how we humans cause ourselves to suffer unnecessarily. With more honest communication, Catrin and Erik can hopefully come to understand each other's needs better, and hopefully he will be able to hear and respect her choices. If not, then she would be better off not marrying him..

My second lecture was the following evening. Again, there were many people attending. The hotel added folding chairs at the back of the ballroom, but it still overflowed, and some people were turned away. The room felt unusually quiet when I walked in. I wasn't certain about the vibration I was picking up. Something was wrong. When I turned and looked at the audience, I sensed there were some negative forces there. I needed to spot them right away before they made a disruption. I spotted three couples with dark auras. One couple was seated on the left aisle about two-thirds of the way down the room and the other couple was at the end of the same row on the right aisle. The third couple was a few rows from the front, in the middle. This formed an upside-down triangle. Changing the direction of a symbol, particularly a triangle, makes the energy negative. All the people within that triangle would be affected by their energy.

I had to break up the triangle. I saw two women enter the room. They were both elderly. I called Alex and told him to escort the two to where the left-aisle people sat and give them those seats. He should tell the couple that the seats were reserved but the sign hadn't been placed correctly. Fortunately, there were two seats together farther down. They protested, of course. Alex was polite but insisted on the change, saying the elderly women needed to have aisle seats. Since the couple's new seats were better ones, they couldn't refuse. This move placed them close to the third negative couple, breaking the triangle. But I knew I would be receiving some strong, angry vibrations from the couples throughout the lecture, so I immediately put a shield between them and me.

The lecture began with the talk on God and nature. The questions were the usual ones until one of the negative people raised his hand and asked, "If God prevails in nature, then He is very unjust. Look at the floods we have experienced in recent years. Do we need another ark to live on this planet?"

I laughed, "With our population now, we would need thousands of arks! God is most certainly just. The negative thinking of humankind causes natural disasters. They take place as a purifying way to cleanse the atmosphere. In Noah's day, the continent sank because of the negativity. I spoke about energy in my first lecture. Those of you who attended will remember that I said everything is energy and all energy has a vibratory force within it. When there is too strong an accumulation of negative energy, then nature has storms and earthquakes to purify the planet again. These will always take place as long as people create negative energy. It may seem terrible for those who suffer the losses in these major catastrophes, but those who perish will be reborn, and life will continue."

"If God is so almighty, then He could do the purifying without using nature to cause destruction," the man answered.

"God is nature, and nature in the wilderness lives in perfect cycles of birth, death, and rebirth. Only humanity has destroyed nature with pollution and negativity. But let's go to another question."

That man and the others tried a couple times more to throw a negative curve, and each time I sent positive vibrations at them to break their intent. It worked, because at the break they left and didn't return. Obviously, their work was intentional, and I wondered what group they belonged to. I asked a few people, but no one seemed to know.

I was glad they weren't there when I spoke about Hierarchy and the Mahatmas. It is always a difficult concept to talk about, particularly the concept of any structure or organization where there is a hierarchy in today's world. I started simply.

The Hierarchy of Light

"When I first met my teacher, I understood immediately that she was very advanced and had much greater wisdom than I. It's like taking a course in a subject you know nothing about. She explained concepts that were all new to me. I was a novice in every way, and it was only through her guidance that I could begin to grow spiritually.

She explained that there were advanced souls who led the way. These advanced souls were men and women who had had to walk the same path I was on, but they had done so centuries before me. These advanced souls are called *Mahatmas*, or *Taras*— the name for women Mahatmas. Jesus became a Mahatma on the cross."

A few people started whispering to one another.

"These Mahatmas and Taras have even Higher Beings who are their teachers. It goes all the way up the ladder to God. All these Higher Beings are part of what is called the Hierarchy of Light, and they basically are in charge of the evolution of this planet."

"You mean it's not just God and Jesus? That's a ridiculous concept. Why would God need anyone to help Him? He is almighty." I saw that one of the negative ones hadn't left.

"God is the energy that is running the whole universe. You tell me why He wouldn't have helpers."

I went on. "The Hierarchy of Light is in charge of the Earth. It works with nature and humankind in helping the planet go through its many cycles."

"What do you mean by 'cycles'?" a man asked.

I then went on to explain the Manvantara and projected on the screen a chart Alex made to illustrate it. "How do you know this?" someone in the front asked.

"The system comes from the Hindus and was given to them by the Mahatmas, thousands of years ago."

"How do you know it's true?" the same person asked.

"Personally, I don't know, but I do know the Mahatmas exist. I have seen and spoken to them, and they tell me it's true. There is an enormous amount of knowledge and wisdom about the universe that only They know and we can strive to know ourselves someday."

An elderly woman asked, "How can we do that?"

"Follow in the footsteps of Jesus, and you too can become a Tara or Mahatma. Everyone is destined to grow spiritually and have that knowledge. The teaching of the Higher Self is one of the ways to obtain that knowledge, as are other esoteric teachings. They all reach the same goal."

"You are saying everyone can be like Jesus?" someone asked in the back of the room.

"Yes, that's what He taught."

"But He was the Son of God."

"And so is each and every one of you. The spirit of God exists in everyone."

The rest of the lecture was on the God within.

I had expected that this talk would bother many of the people, and I was right. When I asked how many were coming to my next lecture, fewer than half raised their hands, and I must say I was relieved.

Afterward, Alex and I went for some tea, and he was very silent at first.

"I know you have talked about Hierarchy in the small classes, but I'm surprised that you did so in the large group. May I ask why?"

"I decided to include it because it is a major part of this teaching."

"But wouldn't it be better to give some of the other lectures first, ones that people could more easily accept? Then they would have a stronger belief in you, so that when you presented this far-out concept, they would accept your words more easily. Otherwise, you will be losing people who were meant to stay."

"If they are meant to stay, they still will." But I knew he had a point, and maybe I had done it because I wanted the numbers to decrease.

Later, when we said good night, I told him, "I plan to think some more about what you said concerning Hierarchy. Maybe it was too soon to mention it tonight, and my motivations for doing so weren't good ones. Thank you for pointing it out to me."

"How can you have wrong motivations?"

"It concerns the number of people attending the lectures. Talking about Hierarchy will cut the number of attendees and that's what I had hoped would happen, ultimately. That's why I think my reasons for doing so could have been incorrect. I need to meditate on it some more."

"But I still don't understand why the numbers bother you."

"It relates to my beliefs that an esoteric teaching is only for a handful of people. That has been the tradition, but this is the time in which more and more people will open their spirit and seek more knowledge. I know that's true, but the traditionalist in me still believes in the small numbers. That was my teaching plan, and now, when the crowds keep coming, I am having to rethink everything."

"I couldn't understand why the crowds were bothering you, but now it's clear to me. If you expect to have a handful, and then suddenly there are a hundred people, that is a big change."

"Yes, but to be open to change is one of my core lessons. I need to look at that in myself. Again, thank you, Alex for causing me to look at this."

When I went to my room, I meditated and tried to connect to my teacher to ask her advice, but she wouldn't come. For the first time on my journey, I felt uncertain of the future.

CHAPTER 18

The next week passed quickly, and I met with the people who would be in the newly formed class. There were three additions now made up of friends of Alfred. There were already eighteen people in this class. I hadn't mentioned a class to the larger audience yet, and I still wasn't certain that I would. I thought about what Alex said about the classes being larger, but a part of me still wasn't ready, or wasn't able to envision anything other than small classes. I kept asking in my meditations for clarification and strangely received nothing. Finally, I realized that it was up to me to determine how to handle this.

I could select students for the classes through interviews, but I also felt that maybe someone who hadn't asked for an interview could be a potential student. Some people have a difficult time speaking to an authority figure, which I certainly was. I decided to address the issue at the next lecture, and I even arranged to stay another week and have one more lecture at the end.

I also tried to have some free time to spend in the city. Sometimes Alex or Klara accompanied me, and they even drove me to some of the outer towns along the lake. Since I had lived in Zürich in my youth, it was nice to walk the streets of the town once again and visit some of the places I had enjoyed back then. One was the Kunsthaus Fine Arts Museum with its excellent European collection; and another — a new place for me that I chanced upon — was the Fraumunster Church, with its colorful Chagall stained-glass windows depicting biblical scenes.

I devoted my mornings to meditation and various excursions and the afternoons and evenings to interviews.

One morning, I took a boat ride that ran around the lower part of the Limmat River, which flowed through the city. It was a beautiful day, and I wanted to be alone. Alex and the others were busy making final arrangements for the lecture the following day.

The boat was full of tourists, but I was early and found a chair on deck rather than inside. As soon as I sat down, a thought came in that was totally foreign to me. It said to be brave and stop being afraid of boats or water. Since I loved the water and had even owned a boat, I knew such a thought was not coming from me. I had to be picking it up from someone else.

I looked around and saw a teenage girl holding onto the hand of her father, and I could tell she was trying to conceal her fears. I knew immediately that she had drowned in a boat accident in her previous life and her fear was coming from that experience. I wanted to talk to her, but her father did not seem the right type of person for me to address. He would probably think my wanting to help came from ulterior motives.

The girl had dancing freckles across her nose and light blond hair that curled up at the ends, corkscrews holding on tightly in fear of losing the straight hair above. She wore dark purple jeans and a blouse with a splattering of lavender flowers. Someday she would be famous, maybe in the movies, or art — I couldn't tell — but I could see fame in her aura.

They sat down next to me, and I said, "Isn't it a beautiful day? There isn't a breeze, so the water is very calm."

He just said, "Yes, it is."

"Are you from here?" I inquired.

"No." And he turned away from me, indicating that he wasn't interested in any more conversation.

The girl, who sat closer to me, asked me, "Are you from here?"

"No, I'm here on business."

"You look familiar to me."

"My picture was in the paper, maybe that's why."

"Yes, you're doing religious lectures."

"Well, I guess you could call it that, but not really."

Her father turned back, "Luise, look at the water, that's why we are here. You know you shouldn't talk to strangers."

She gave a look that said, "He's nuts," and looked at the water, again with some fear coming up.

I decided to address the issue. "This boat is very safe; nothing will happen."

"I know, but I can't stop worrying. I've had dreams about drowning. Daddy insisted I come on this boat and get over it," she whispered.

I whispered back, "That was in the past. It won't happen again in this lifetime. Don't be afraid."

The father glared at me. "What are you whispering about? Leave my daughter alone, or I will call a guard."

"He's not done anything wrong. He's trying to help me," Luise protested.

"Help! I know what kind of help an older man wants to give a young girl." His voice was so loud that people were beginning to stare at us.

A guard came over and asked, "Is something wrong here?"

The father said, "This man is bothering my daughter."

I protested, "That's not true. We were simply talking."

Luise supported me. "This man has not been bothering me. He's done nothing wrong. My father is overprotective."

"I've seen men like this before." The father was getting angry.

I stood up. "I will gladly move if that will make you feel better." As I went inside, I could hear him still making remarks, and some people were whispering about me. I thought I heard one woman say, "Isn't that the preacher? I went to his lecture last week."

I was right. The next morning there was a short article in the newspaper reporting that I had been seen trying to pick up a teenage girl. The account was greatly exaggerated. I told Alex what had happened, and he said, "Well, that story needs to be revoked immediately. I'll call Alfred to tell him to put in the paper what really happened."

"He needs to say that it was just an innocent conversation to talk about her fear of the boat and my interpretation of it."

"True. He'll make it right, but this should make your wish come true."

"What do you mean?"

"That you have a smaller attendance."

He had to be right about that, and I wondered if I had somehow sabotaged myself so that this would happen.

That evening, around fifty people came, a lot fewer than had been anticipated. I noticed that Rosina wasn't there, and I wondered why.

When I asked Alex where she was, he said the article upset her. He told her the true story, but she still had doubts. I felt disappointed that she hadn't passed that test. The other class members felt bad for me that my trying to help had ended in my being falsely accused.

When everyone was seated, I immediately addressed what had happened, concluding, "Whatever happened to this man in his past he projected onto a friendly conversation. Of course, it is part of human nature to exaggerate the truth, but I'm surprised the reporter who wrote the article didn't get my side of the story."

Alfred raised his hand. "I spoke to him and the editor about this. I found it very upsetting that they didn't get all of the facts and engage in proper, unbiased reporting. The reporter is new on the paper and doesn't know the right procedures. What you don't know is that a man called and said he would be a witness for you, as he heard what was really said in the conversation.

"And you'll be glad to know that the girl also called and said the story was untrue, that you were trying to help her because she was afraid to be in the boat, and that she was grateful to you for your help. I quoted them both in my article, which will be published online this evening and appear in the morning paper."

"Thank you, Alfred, for standing up for me. Some people are so suspicious of others! I guess today's world with all its crime makes that happen. I'm glad the girl had the courage to call."

I started the night's lecture with a talk about karma and reincarnation. After the break, I began a new topic.

The Art of Giving

The other night, I spoke about the Mahatmas and how they serve humanity. Tonight, I want to speak about service that you can each do. Service of any kind helps you grow spiritually and in the course of that action you are changed. What do I mean by *service* or the *art of giving*? Basically, it's anything you do that helps another person, whether it's helping a blind person cross the street or volunteering in a hospital or homeless shelter on a regular basis. Any act of kindness and compassion opens the heart and changes you.

When I speak about service, I am referring to work that affects others. I do not mean giving money to a charity. That is a different kind of service and certainly will help you accumulate good karma, but I am referring to labor that takes your time and can even strain you mentally and physically. This type of service not only benefits others but also will set in motion a series of changes within you."

I then used the PowerPoint slide I'd prepared with Alex's help to explain this further. I went through the list:

* Service expands your understanding of people because you will be working with others who are not necessarily people with whom you would choose to have friendships.

* In the process of giving to others, you lose a sense of the ego self and are mainly connected to your Higher Self.

* When you help someone, you are literally sending the person your vibration. If those vibrations are pure, it will give the person a sense of well-being and even heal the person emotionally.

* Service extends your range of knowledge, particularly if you are required to learn and study something new in order to provide the service.

* In doing service of any kind, you fine tune your intuition and sense of knowing the right thing to do.

* When you deal with people, you open your heart more, and that process helps develop love and compassion.

* Finally, the art of giving requires dedication and lots of patience. These are both required qualities that will help you grow spiritually.

"Are there any questions?"

"Yes." A man in the back raised his hand. "I work long hours and have a family to be with when I go home. I literally have no time for anything else."

"I'm not talking about a lot of time. You eat lunch every day. Instead of going to a restaurant, take a sandwich and spend the time doing something of service."

"But what can be done in an hour?"

"Find out if there is a hospital or other charities around your workplace. Hospitals need volunteers, as do senior-citizen homes, and charities can always use an extra hand. There are many charitable organizations on the web. Research them and ask one that interests you if you can do some computer work for them. You also have time on the weekends to do some volunteer work. It doesn't have to be every weekend. Even once a month for a few hours is sufficient."

"If I volunteered to help you with your next lecture, would that be considered service?" a woman asked.

"Yes, of course, any act of giving help is service, and it extends to helping the people around you. Volunteering to take a friend to the doctor or making a sick relative a hot meal is also part of the art of giving."

"If I did that in my family, they would never stop calling me."

Some people laughed and nodded their heads.

"If that's the case, then you need to say no. People who are pleasers will tend to overdo, particularly with friends and family. Again, I suggest moderation."

An elderly woman raised her hand. "I have been caretaking my husband for twenty years. Isn't that enough?"

"Yes and no. Caretaking like that is part of your karma with your husband. Doing the extra work outside the home is strictly free of karma, although certainly you will incur good karma that way."

"You said that giving in the form of service is necessary for a yogi, but there are many yogis who live in ashrams and never go out into the world, and they don't do any service other than meditating. Why is your teaching saying that service is so important to do?"

"Good question. The yogis in ashrams serve by praying for peace in the world. They grow spiritually but not to the level of yogis who live in the world and face all the worldly challenges. They also make less karma, because they have very little interaction with others. The yogis in the world are constantly making karma, and some of it can be negative. Doing service counteracts negative karma and keeps yogis still focused on their spiritual development."

I then talked about the differences between being in the world and living in an ashram.

When I finished, a young dark-skinned man in front raised his hand. "How would I know what is best for me? Should I go to India and live in an ashram, or should I follow someone who teaches to be in the world, such as you?"

"Follow your heart and ask your Higher Self who your teacher is. If the teacher is in an ashram, you will find him or her; or, if the teacher is in the world, you will also find him or her. Simply ask what your dharma is in this life. The word *dharma* covers several things. The right vocation, right spiritual path, right relationships, and right action are all part of your dharma, which you bring in with you when you are born. Living in an ashram means you will not have a vocation that is worldly. If your vocation is in the world, you know your dharma is to find a teacher who lives actively in the world. Much has changed in India. More and more teachers are asking their students to be in the world. I am one of those."

"Could you tell us how it feels to make that change, particularly in your case, since you lived in an ashram, and alone in the mountains, and now you have to be in the world?" Klara asked.

"At first it was very difficult. I felt the differences in the vibrations of the mountains and the towns and cities. In time, I became used to it. Also in time, I began to enjoy the companionship of some of my students. I never was lonely in the mountains, as I had many nature spirits to talk with. Now I have my students with whom to communicate. This is different but still equally interesting. I also didn't know I would enjoy doing this work. Teaching is new to me, and now I really feel it's much more important than sitting in my mountain retreat. It's the service I can give to others."

"Well, I for one am very happy you are doing it," Irma said.

"Thank you. Any more questions?"

A young boy who was with his mother raised his hand. "Sir, can you tell me what kind of service I can do? I'm only twelve years old."

"It's never too early or too late to do service. I'm sure you do acts of service already. Do you help your friends with their homework when you understand something they don't? Or perhaps you help a neighbor carry in groceries? In the future, if you see a fellow student in trouble or doing something dangerous such as taking drugs, you can try to help by talking to the student. You can start a school program, as a lifeline that will help students in trouble. Some schools have such programs, so join them and try to help in any way you can. Students have collected money when there are natural disasters and have done some remarkable work. There are also ecology programs that students are involved in. Go online and try to see some of those programs started by youths who are your age."

I ended the lecture with a short talk on beliefs that keep one from growing spiritually and then again took the people through a Higher Self exercise.

Afterward, I asked how many wanted to come to the last lecture the next week. I also talked about a class being formed in Zürich and mentioned that anyone interested needed to see me privately in the coming week. Over a dozen or so stayed and signed up for interviews. I noticed two of them were the young boy and his mother.

The next morning Alfred's article was in the paper. I wondered if it would make any difference. People tended to believe the worst, and, even when the worst was proven false, they still had doubts.

Luise from the boat telephoned me shortly after I had read the story, saying, "My name is Luise Rutschmann. I am very sorry about all of this. I think now my father is a bit ashamed of what he said and did, though he would never admit it to me. My mother died last year and, since then, he's become very protective of me, too much so. I wish I could come to your lecture, but he won't let me. Maybe someday when I'm older."

"That would be good. Where do you live?"

"In Basel."

I told her about the class there and gave her Erna's phone number. "She can tell you when I return to teach, and maybe in a couple of years you will have more freedom."

"I hope so, and I will certainly call her. Thank you again. Next time I see you, I hope to take another boat ride with you and be perfectly calm."

When I hung up I felt a burst of joy in my heart, a feeling I often had when I met someone I knew was destined to be my student. Unless free will took her elsewhere, that would happen. Maybe I hadn't sabotaged myself after all.

CHAPTER 19

My last week in Zürich was again full of appointments. The weather was still hot and humid, but the lounge where I met with people was surprisingly cool. The interviews went well, and almost everyone asked to come to the class. There was only one person who I knew wasn't intended for this teaching, and I told her to study another teaching, and suggested Buddhism.

The boy and his mother came toward the end of the week. Her name was Mina Meyer and his was Jon. Mina was petite with a radiate charm that showed in her eyes and manifested in the way she spoke and moved her hands. Jon was almost her height with the same small body frame. He would end up being tall and lanky. The eagerness and anticipation that flowed in warm waves from his young face made me feel for a moment the pleasure of what it would be like to have a child, a feeling that was completely foreign to me.

After they greeted me, Jon said, "I really want to study with you. Is it possible?"

"Yes, of course. You will be my youngest student, but hopefully there will be more young people your age coming in to this teaching."

I told them about the class and said I would be returning next year.

Mina said, "I know what you are teaching is good, and I want to study it, too, but I'm not very religious. I can't promise you that I will be a good student or that this is a teaching for me. Jon really has the enthusiasm, so I will be happy to take him to the classes."

"That is fine, and it is also all right to question everything. I have a computer, so I can answer questions from my different classes via email, and I hope you will be part of that group."

"Yes, I would like that. I have taken a lot of courses over the years. It's part of who I am. Jon, I think, takes after me in that way.

"What about your husband?"

"I don't have one. I got pregnant when I was very young and decided to keep Jon instead of giving him up for adoption. You talk about joy in your teaching — he's been my joy."

"Oh, Mom." Jon was a little embarrassed but pleased, I could tell.

I really liked them both. She was honest and direct, a quality I always admire; and, as we both observed, Jon was full of enthusiasm.

Rosina wrote me a note apologizing for not being at the meeting. She never mentioned the article but gave a weak excuse for not attending. This bothered me, but I realized that reading the article for some reason had to be scary for her. When I saw her, I asked her about it. "I know you were disturbed by the article and that's the real reason you didn't come to my last lecture. But why didn't you call and discuss it with me?"

"I know I should have. But it was embarrassing for me."

"How do you think it was for me?"

"It must have been awful."

"Yes, it was, to have those lies published about me." I paused for a minute and linked my heart to her heart, "Can you tell me why you reacted this way?"

"I didn't tell you this, but when I was a child my uncle sexually abused me, and the article did make me scared."

"Oh, I am so sorry. That's certainly understandable. It must have been very difficult for you to read that about me." I looked into her eyes with love in my heart, "I just want to be clear with you that any time you believe I may have done something wrong, or if you question what I am saying, I hope you will be honest and tell me directly how you feel. I believe in transparency."

"I just didn't know I could do that."

"Yes, I recognize that now, and I expect it will take time for you to really trust me."

"I'm sorry about that. Also, don't forget, I just met you."

I smiled at her, "No, you've been with me many times. If you listened to your heart, you would have known, and at least you would have known to ask me about it, like the others did."

"I'm happy that I've been with you before. I had that feeling when I first saw you."

"I'm also happy to have you back with me."

In retrospect, when I thought about what happened with Rosina, I realized that I had felt disappointed at her reactions to the false article. I favored her and had high expectations about her spirituality because of her past life accomplishments with me as her teacher. I wasn't considering that there might be wounds she experienced in this lifetime. It was a lesson for me to never do that again and to see each student with potential instead of selecting ones whom I believed or thought had more.

I stopped wondering about the future and focused on the here and now, a lesson I always taught but wasn't following myself. Every teacher looks for the students who will be the ones to carry on their teaching; but it's not good to do this, and, inwardly, I thanked Rosina for this lesson.

My stay in Zürich was coming to an end. The last lecture would cover some of the subjects in my previous lectures, and I would add one more that concerned the future of my teaching and how it would continue. Again, on the evening of the lecture I wasn't certain how many people would come; and, again, it was more than I had anticipated—over a hundred. Some had returned after reading the second article, and some were new. How to handle the new people? That was a question I still had to answer. There was still so much to do and so much to decide, but it would have to wait until I was home.

After a couple of short lectures and before the break, I spoke about the teaching in the future.

The Teaching and Its Future

"Many of you have been coming to all these lectures, and some of you have wanted to continue studying this teaching. There are also some of you who don't want to continue but are curious and would still come to the occasional lecture when I'm in town. And there are some new people tonight who have missed the previous lectures and haven't even participated in the Higher Self exercise, which is essential in this teaching.

"I have started a class here in Zürich that now has around thirty-five people in it. This is much larger than any of my other classes. I will be teaching the first class in this hotel, in a smaller room, tomorrow evening before I leave, and at that time I will decide whether it is better to divide the class into smaller groups that will meet in people's homes.

"You may be wondering why I am speaking about this as part of my lecture rather than as an announcement."

A few people nodded their heads.

"It is because you should know the general plan for the future. I need to develop more lectures and return to teach those people who are in the classes. When I began this teaching, I never thought about my mission and where it would take me; and, mainly, I never thought about having students with whom I would continue to work. For me to decide how to carry this teaching forward, I need some input from all of you — those who are already my students as well as those who haven't made any commitment to me or this teaching.

"I want you to take a few minutes and think about what I have just said. My questions to you are the following:

"If you are a student at this time, ask yourself what you need from me and from this teaching. How do you envision the future, and what are your wishes?

"If you aren't a student and aren't interested in continuing, I would appreciate it if you would tell me what you liked about me and the lectures and what didn't you like.

"If you are new tonight and have no background in any of this, please tell me what you need to happen in your life spiritually.

"Please take time now and set your thoughts down on paper."

I turned on the PowerPoint presentation deck and put up the slide with these questions for everyone's reference.

"You have fifteen minutes to do this writing, and then we'll take a break. You don't have to put your name on your answers; just give your page to Alex who is in the back." Alex raised his hand so everyone could identify him. "During the break I will look at them. Head your paragraph with "student," "non-student," or "new" so that I can group them accordingly."

When the time came to review the submissions briefly while the others were on their break, I focused on the students wishes. Most of them said they needed to stay in contact with me and even visit me at my home. One said she felt intimidated by me and wanted to get over that feeling. Generally, the consensus was that they needed more. They wanted some written material, preferably a book they could study.

The students mainly expressed what they needed now; only a few envisioned the future. Those who did saw this teaching as becoming a strong influence on society. They felt it would grow quickly, mostly by word of mouth, and due to technology and social media, once I had a website and social media accounts. One felt there needed to be more structure in order to handle the teaching better. That sounded like Alex to me. Someone else saw the teaching as a spiritual journey that would help others along the way.

The non-students basically felt the teaching was too unbelievable for them. Some liked me, and others felt I was too much an authoritarian figure. They enjoyed coming to find out what I would say but generally doubted me.

The new students were very diverse. Some liked me a lot and wanted to see me again, whereas others weren't certain about any of it until they heard more.

When the people came back after the break, I saw that some had left.

I again talked about the teaching and mentioned some of the results of the survey.

One man said, "People want written material. Do you have any?"

"No, this teaching has been an oral tradition, but I will consider writing some of it down. I have left lessons for the classes to work on, and they can be put into book form. I basically would like to know if any of you feel you understand the concept of working with your Higher Self. Since this teaching is built around doing this, are there any of you who need to know more about the Higher Self?"

A few hands were raised, and a man said, "I think I'm starting to connect to it, but I'm not certain, and sometimes it feels weird to see a figure there. How can I be certain what I'm getting is correct?"

"You can't be 100 percent certain until you know yourself. What I mean is that you need to know what all your desires are; then you can recognize whether those desires are clouding what you are receiving from your Higher Self. For example, you may hear from your Higher Self that you will meet someone with whom you will have a loving relationship. If you recognize that having love is a strong desire of yours, you should question this answer. It may be truly from your Higher Self, or it may be your desire body talking instead. Question it, and don't feel disappointed if it doesn't come true. Remember, the Higher Self is very practical and succinct. It says things directly and simply, with no embellishments. A good way of checking is to imagine the sun shining down on it. If it is your desire body and not your Higher Self, it will disappear or turn dark."

"But we all have strong desires, and if they cloud the Higher Self, how can we ever trust what we receive?" the same man asked.

"The answer is: Practice! Learn to recognize what information is true and what isn't, and see how the misinformation is part of who you are. Certainly, it is important to have a teacher who can check your answers and verify whether they are true or false."

Jon raised his hand. "You're my teacher; how do I check with you?"

"I will be discussing that in class tomorrow night."

"What about those of us who don't want a teacher but would like to work more with their Higher Selves?" someone else asked.

"You will have to be very careful to keep shining light on the figure to be certain the Higher Self hasn't been replaced by your desire body, your lower nature, or a spiritual subpersonality. Read about the Higher Self. There is a lot written about it. Research it on the web and see what's available. You need to know your ego self and your lower nature and to be aware of how they try to influence you. Another way to check is to take the information you were given by the Higher Self and put it in your heart. The heart will respond with warmth or a movement if it is true. If is not true, there will be no response."

A woman raised her hand. "I don't see a figure, I just feel a warmth in my heart. How can I know what's true or false?"

"Like I said, if you are feeling the warmth in your heart, then you are connected; but if the warmth disappears, you are listening to something else. The same is true when you feel movements in your body that represent the yes, no, and maybe answers. If your Higher Self disappears, you won't receive those vibrations."

"Can't your ego interfere with that?"

"Sometimes, but again question any answer around which you know you have a strong desire. Write it down, but don't believe it unless it comes true. And then another time check it out again. If the answers are different, then you know there is interference."

"It seems like a lot to do if all of what you are saying can happen," a woman said.

"Yes, in the beginning it is going to be more difficult, particularly because you haven't worked with the Higher Self before. As I previously explained, it could be very illusive at first, so you should question everything you receive until the connection becomes more solid. The more you practice, the stronger the connection will be, until you can simply link with your heart and be connected to the Higher Self without doing the exercise. You also will start to develop more discernment in understanding what is correct or not."

"Is it really necessary to connect at all? My intuition is good, why not just keep working with that?"

"That's up to you. Realize that your intuition is coming from the Higher Self, and if you work directly with your intuition, you can receive wisdom to which the Higher Self has access. For example, your intuition may tell you to stay home and not go out, and you may follow that advice but not know why you need to stay home. But if you have been working with the Higher Self and have a strong connection to it, then you could ask the Higher Self why you need to stay home and receive an answer. It may be that there will be some kind of accident you could be in, or it may be that something could happen at home and you need to be there to take care of it. In other words, the full knowledge is there for you to receive."

"But is it necessary to know that?" she asked.

"Not always, but there are certain things that you really need to know. For instance, you apply to a number of universities and are accepted to several, but you have no idea which university would be best for you to attend. You can read about the courses and the teachers, but still you're not sure about which university to pick. You aren't even certain what profession to pursue. Your Higher Self can direct you to the right school and the right major. It knows what is destined for you and can help you fulfill that. It also knows what you need to work on psychologically, and it can give you the right process to do that work."

"Can you give us an example?"

"Yes. You want to change some of your negative characteristics. Let's say you are very stubborn."

I saw the woman's face become startled when I said "stubborn" and looked at her directly.

"Your friends have mentioned it to you, and you really have tried to change this trait, but you still have it. You can ask your Higher Self how to change it and to give you a process and a first step. You can also check with the Higher Self on how you developed this trait in the first place. Was it from your childhood or from a past life? Knowing the origin can help you let it go. Remember, I said the Higher Self is very practical. It wants to help you change and grow spiritually. Negative characteristics need to be transformed on the spiritual path. Even if you choose not to walk this path in this lifetime, it still is good to change those characteristics that you feel prevent you from having good and loving relationships."

"Is my Higher Self different from someone else's?"

"Yes and no. Yes, in the sense that it contains your highest achievements spiritually, which differ from someone else's. No, in the sense that it can access higher wisdom and be connected to the Higher Beings, and, at that level, everything is one."

A young girl around twelve asked, "When I am your age, will I be wise like you?"

Everyone laughed.

"When you are my age, you will be even wiser because you are starting to learn now. I started much later than you." And I spoke the truth, as I could see in her aura signs of her past achievements.

Another youth asked, "When you come back, would you do a special class for those of us in our teens? I don't feel comfortable attending a class of adults."

I looked at him and suddenly knew that his father was very abusive and he was afraid of any type of authority. "I think that's a great idea. Give me your name and phone number and I will try to arrange it, maybe even before I leave." And I looked at Jon who smiled at that remark.

"Let's look at this teaching from a different viewpoint. You have been coming to several lectures and have learned a lot. How many of you have taken the time really to look within yourselves and focus on what a spiritual path means to you? How many of you who are continuing in the classes are doing so because you long to find the God within? I can teach you a lot. I can show you another reality, worlds you have never explored. But do you want this out of curiosity, or do you want it because your heart longs to know more and longs to find the God within?

"There is a fine line between wanting knowledge and wanting wisdom. The former you can find in books, but the latter comes from within: striving to be the Higher Self, striving to open the heart and mind to the higher worlds; striving to find wisdom that comes from the Divine Source. If you want the former, then read everything written on the Higher Self, learn everything about the different religions and delve deep into the ancient teachings of the East. If you want the latter, then find a teacher and ask him or her to guide you on the path to God Consciousness. It can only be found that way. If you truly want this, you will find it just as I did. Then you will know there is no turning back. Once you have entered an esoteric teaching, be prepared to find your real Self and in so doing go through many changes, some difficult and others full of joy.

"Both paths take much work and dedication. Both can be full of happiness and full of challenges. One develops the mind. The other develops the higher mind and heart. The path of wisdom contains the path of knowledge and therefore will require more work, more commitment, and more sacrifice.

"You may choose the path of knowledge for now, and that would be fine, but keep an open heart to moving from that path to the path of wisdom. Some of you I will see again and others I will not. For those of you who won't come back, I wish you a happy life. I hope you will continue to work with your Higher Self. To touch the spirit within is a blessed beginning.

"For those of you I will see again: I look forward to the next time and to working with you individually. I will be back next year at the same time. Sign the mailing list and you will be informed as to when.

"And for the students who will continue, the last class is tomorrow evening, and I will speak to you then."

It was late, so I did not ask for questions. It was my last lecture on my tour. It was enough.

CHAPTER 20

The morning after the lecture I spent going through all the people's comments from the night before. Then I looked at my lecture notes. Most of the time I spoke without looking at notes, but I realized that I needed to have my lectures more structured in terms of subject matter. I still could go off the subject according to what the questions were, but I didn't want to repeat myself. I needed to write a record of each talk afterward and describe the main themes. This work took me all morning and kept me from my morning walk around town.

My first appointment was just after lunch, so I decided to pick up a couple of pieces of fruit and spend my lunchtime down by the river. It was a day full of shimmering light that broke through the clouds. I found a bench and sat down to eat my lunch.

Before I knew what was happening, I was surrounded by a group of teenage boys and girls. They looked to be fourteen or fifteen years old, dressed in jeans and colorful t-shirts. There were around six or seven of them, and they stood back from the bench waiting for one boy to talk to me. He was Peter Keufen, the boy who had asked me for the special class for teenagers.

Peter stepped forward, greeting me with a lot of warmth and a bit of shyness. He was a nice looking boy who had the potential of becoming a very handsome man. His short chopped, sandy hair had a stray falling lock, which longed to touch his deep blue eyes but fell short in a dissatisfied curl. Peter told his friends, "This is my teacher, the one I was telling you about." Then he began introducing me to each one there.

I was in a semi-meditative state, so it took me a couple of minutes to adjust to what was happening. One of the girls said, "Peter said you would come back and start a class just with us. Is that true?"

"Yes, and if some of you are free tomorrow afternoon, we could meet for a couple of hours for a lesson." I was supposed to leave in the morning but just then decided to stay to start this class.

"That would be great," Peter said. "I've been trying to explain about the Higher Self, but all I know is from your lectures. I did take lots of notes, though."

I looked at him and saw an old soul in his eyes. "That is very good. Why don't you find a place we can meet tomorrow from two to four? Maybe, Peter, we could meet in your parents' home?"

A dark look came across his face. "No, my father would never allow that, even though Mother would love it."

Another boy said, "It's going to be another sunny day tomorrow. Why not meet in the Zürichhorn Gardens?"

"Fine, let's do that."

I opened a map on my phone and they showed me the spot they thought would work and how I should get there. On the way back to my hotel, I thought about how to arrange this new class. I would ask Alex if he would take charge of it. He also was a novice but knew more than the others, and I would give him some lessons to work with. I knew he was busy and worked full time — it would have to be up to him. It felt good to be attracting young people. But I also thought about the parents of these teenagers; they needed to know about the class. What would they say? If any were like Peter's father, they would never allow it.

It turned out that one of my interviews in the afternoon was with Peter and his mother. Her name was Emma Keufen. I told her about the new class, and she was delighted we were starting it. She asked to attend the main class and I agreed. I guessed she was in her early thirties, much too young to have a child as old as Peter. Emma wore a pastel, flowered dress whose warm colors were mirrored in her sunny expression and attitude. Peter didn't look at all like her, and I kept thinking she might be his stepmother. Finally, I asked her if Peter was her son. She said no, that his mother had left his father when Peter was very young and hadn't wanted custody of Peter.

"I've never seen her since," Peter added.

"How does that make you feel?" I asked him.

"It's okay because I have my real mother here," and he smiled at Emma.

Emma smiled affectionately back at Peter. "Yes," she said, "he was only three when I married his father. I have raised him since and certainly love him as my own son."

"Do you have other children?"

"No, and I'm fine with just having Peter."

"I believe that in cases like this, and also in adoption, that the adoptive parents are the karmic ones with whom the child needs to be. The birth mother is just a vehicle to make that happen. There are no accidents. Peter was meant to be your son, and I can tell it was good karma on both your parts. I'm not sure the karma is good for Peter and his father."

"No, it's not," Peter responded. "He is terrible to me and never trusts me. He's also overly demanding and cruel to me."

"Is that true?" I asked Emma.

"Yes, it is true. I've tried to change it and have even left his father and taken Peter with me, but then we got back together. He's always been good to me, but somehow, even when things are calm, he always manages to say nasty things to Peter. Maybe it's because Peter looks like his mother."

"Well, obviously you have very bad karma with your father, Peter."

"Yes, I guess I must have killed him or something in a past life." And he tried to laugh as he said it.

"Karma can be very difficult, and usually it's paid off in childhood. Fortunately, you have good karma with Emma."

"Yeah, I lucked out on that one."

I told him about Jon and asked if he knew him. He didn't, but he remembered seeing him at the meetings. Earlier I had spoken to Jon and told him about the new class. He was going to attend to see if he liked it, but he still wanted to come to the adult class this evening and make up his mind later. He didn't mind being with older people.

Peter and Emma were my last interviews that day. I had only an hour before dinner and then the class in the evening. I told Alex I needed to stay another day. He had planned to drive me home to Wengen, but now that I was having another class I needed to leave on Monday, and he had to work that day. There were several people coming to class who didn't work full-time, and he hoped that one of them would offer to take me instead. Otherwise, I would have to take the train, which would be difficult with all the supplies I had accumulated along the way.

I invited Alex to have dinner with me to talk to him about taking over the new class. He was very receptive to doing the work, and we planned to spend the morning together going over some of the lesson plans. I felt suddenly overwhelmed with all that I needed to do to keep up the pace of all these new classes. "Alex, as I mentioned before, I have been thinking that I need to be in a town where people can come to see me, where I can have Wi-Fi for my devices so people can reach me."

He responded, "Zarathustra, you came to teach and then go back to your home in the mountains. Are you certain you want to change your plans? Your place there sounds incredibly beautiful and fulfilling for you. Why do you need to sacrifice it? How many of these students do you think will follow this teaching? How many do you think are deserving of your sacrifice?"

I was surprised by his questions. "This is not about me, Alex. Even if there is only one person to carry on the work after I am gone, that is worth any sacrifice. Of course, there will only be a handful. That is the way it is in any esoteric teaching, but the others will still have gained something that will have changed them. I agree, I need my home in the mountains and I will not give it up. I will use it for retreats in the summer and do my traveling more in the fall and winter. I may buy a home in Thun, for example. It is not a skiing resort, so it has fewer tourists, but it has beautiful views of the mountains, so I can still enjoy my mountains and return to my home outside of Wengen when the weather is good. It is also on the River Aare, which flows into Lake Thun, a beautiful, large lake like Lake Zürich. I really do enjoy being by water, so maybe I can buy a house on the lakeshore there."

"Can you afford that?"

"I have some inheritance from my grandfather that I haven't used. Also, from Thun, I can easily go to the mountain towns to conduct classes, and it's even close to Interlaken and Bern. In the summer I will return to my mountain home and students can visit me there."

"No, don't do that. Let the students visit your new home but keep your mountain retreat for you alone. Promise me that you will always keep that place isolated."

"Wouldn't you want to see it?"

"Of course. I've heard you talk about it and your connection to the devic kingdom there. But outside energy will change the vibrations that you have built for years. Don't sacrifice that."

We fell silent, and I thought about what he said and knew he was right. I had been in the world so long now that I couldn't remember what it was like to be alone, to live in solitude with the nature spirits around me. A part of me said, don't be alone anymore, share everything, and I knew that part was new and dangerous to listen to.

"Alex, you are a wise man. Thank you for your advice; I will take it."

Later that night after the class, I remembered our conversation and knew that part of my loneliness now would be because I had to say goodbye to him.

The class was very large. Around forty people came, and I was glad I'd changed the location from Klara and Alfred's home back to the hotel. Right away I knew this wouldn't have worked at their place, and there needed to be two classes now instead of one large one. I naturally went back to the idea of the classes being divided according to those who lived east of the river and those that lived west of it. When I asked who lived where, it worked out to be around twenty-three people on the eastern side and sixteen on the western side.

Alfred could handle twenty-three in his house, so that would work; and when I asked who could hold the classes in the west, there were two couples who volunteered to give it a try. One home seemed to be more convenient than the other, so the other couple agreed to be a standby in case the first place didn't work out. The names of the hosting couple were Felix and Martha Avener. Since I was now staying over, I arranged to meet with Alfred and the Aveners in the morning to go over the class structure and lesson plans.

The lesson that night was on community. Since this was such a large group, I felt it was an appropriate topic.

Being Part of a Spiritual Community

"Most of you do not know each other, yet you now have formed a spiritual community, and in this community, you will soon find that you do know each other. This is not the first time you have been with one another, and right away there will be a familiarity that comes from having been together before in past lives. Some of those lives could have been in spiritual communities with me, and some of the times you could have been in personal relationships such as physical family members or even lovers. There will also be some of you who feel an immediate dislike for someone here, and that dislike is coming from a negative past life together. Unless those feelings are understood and resolved, they can cause discord in the group."

People started to look around at the people near them.

"Naturally, I do not want this to happen, so I am asking that each one of you be responsible in clearing out those kinds of feelings. You can do this by being aware of what feelings come up when you talk to someone here. If you immediately feel an aversion and an urge not to be near someone, address it to the person right away. Then the two of you need to sit down together, look into each other's eyes, and ask yourselves, 'What is my past history with this person?' In most cases, you will know right away about the relationship. If you can't find out what it was, please contact me and I will tell you what I see."

Someone asked, "Should we do the same with those people we have an instant liking for?"

"Yes, but first work with the ones you feel aversion toward. It's important to clear out any negative feelings, and, of course, it is also good to connect with the positive relationships."

"What happens if I still don't want to be around someone?"

"You don't need to be good friends with everyone here. But you do need to be cordial and open, even with someone you don't like. Hopefully, understanding the past will help you let go of the dislike enough to feel all right in that person's company, especially when you will be sharing the class together. Remember, the past is the past. You are not the same now as you were in those distant lives. Don't carry a grudge over something that happened centuries ago. Someone you hated in the past could be someone you will like now. And, if you still don't like the person, at least you know why; and, hopefully, it won't interfere with the atmosphere in the class.

"Let's do this now so I can help you understand the process. Turn to the person next to you and face each other."

People shifted around and got into position in pairs.

"Close your eyes and link your hearts together and ask your Higher Self to help you understand your past relationship with this person, if there is one. Now open your eyes and look into each other's eyes, and, as you do this, try to see your connection."

I watched as the group did this, and after a few minutes I told them to take notes and then compare what each had received.

When everyone was finished, I said, "How many were able to pick up a past connection?"

There was a show of hands from over half the group.

"That's wonderful for a first try. How many found they had a positive connection?"

Again, there was a show of hands.

"How many found a negative connection?"

Again, several hands were raised.

"Does anyone want to share their experience?"

"I'll share." A woman raised her hand.

"It was really quite something. As soon as I looked into her eyes I felt that I was a man and that she was my wife. Then I felt that something happened between us, something really bad. Then when we shared, my partner felt that I left her and never returned, and she was pregnant at the time. That's all we got."

"That's very good. So, you know your partner will never trust you, and you will feel guilty toward her. So now that you both know this, you both will need to be kind to each other and let the past go. Are there any other stories?"

"My experience was a good one," Klara said, "My partner right away said she felt a lot of love in her heart when she looked at me, and I felt the same. I think we were siblings, maybe sisters, and were very close. She feels we were good friends."

"Both could be true. There is a basis there to develop a good relationship in this life."

"Yes, we are already talking about getting together."

Another woman raised her hand. "Our experience was very strange. Neither one of us felt anything. It was blank, and we were wondering if we were blocking feelings and didn't want to go more deeply."

"That can be true, or it could be difficult as it's the first time you've done an exercise like this. Or it may simply be that you never knew each other in a past life. I think the latter is the case. In other words, this would be the first time you've been together. It's like starting out with a clean slate, which can be very beneficial."

We continued to look at the various couples' experiences. Some received nothing because it was too new, and sometimes just one person would pick up something and the other person didn't; but, in general, it was a good exercise to start a new class with. Next, I asked them to find a new partner, and we did this exercise for another hour.

When we were finished, I said, "This is an exercise to do when a new person comes to class. Anyone feeling any emotion toward someone needs to clear it out. Otherwise, it can interfere with the energy of the class."

A man named Alan raised his hand. "If you have a very negative reaction toward someone, and even after you both do this exercise together, the energy still remains very negative. What do you do then?"

"You try to give your feelings to me in the opening meditation of the class. Just ask me to take them away and try to be in your heart. Again, remember that the past is the past, and it's important not to dwell there. Everyone here has a new start."

"Wouldn't it be better to switch to the other class?"

"That's a solution, but one I don't like. It's avoidance. Besides, when I return, all of you will be together again, and if the negative feelings aren't resolved, they will come up again. It's always better to let those kinds of feelings go. All of you are in one community, and I hope that, even though there are separate classes, you will plan events when you all can meet and be together, even when I am not here."

It was getting late, so I said goodbye and arranged to see the class leaders the next morning.

Alex drove me back to the hotel, and we sat in the lounge and talked a few minutes. He asked me, "Have you developed a plan yet on when you will be returning?"

"No, I haven't. I've been traveling now for over five months, and it's already September. I need a rest. Originally, I thought I would first go back to see how all the classes are doing, but I'm really thinking it best to go home. During that time, I will set up a new schedule; but, even before that, I have to find a winter home where I can have a telephone, and internet, and be accessible for any questions from the classes. That's primary when I do my planning. If I'm not in my mountain home, maybe I can even travel more in the winter."

"You mean you want to buy your new house right away?"

"Yes, I need to have a home that has modern conveniences."

"That's great! Can I come to see you there?"

"Yes, you can, and I know I will need your help to become more computer savvy. Writing out my lectures would be helpful, and maybe they will end up as a book. I don't know. But I do feel it's easier to write on a computer."

"Yes, it is. And answering student's questions by email will be very helpful to you, also. Why don't you come back here for the winter? I have an extra room and would love to have you with me. Then you can look for a place in the spring."

"No, but thank you. I appreciate your generous offer, but I need to be alone. As you know, others have offered to have me stay with them when I am here, but I really need my alone time."

"I understand, but why not buy a condo here? It's centrally located and near all the major cities. You can then stay in your mountain home in the summer."

"I've thought about that but prefer the energy of the mountains. If I have a place in Thun, I'll have the beautiful mountains and lake to look at every day. It won't be the same as living in the mountains, but it still will be better than living here."

"I understand. It must be difficult for you to pick up all the vibrations of many types of people. You certainly seem to need a rest from all of this. If I can help you in any way, please let me know."

"You can help me the most by doing what you've already been doing. Taking charge of the arrangements for the lectures and my hotels has been such a great help, and I thank you again for everything."

"I have a surprise for you. I took the phone numbers and email addresses of your students in the different classes and put them on my computer in a file. I will send you the file and, when you are settled in your new home, I will send them your address, email address, and home phone number if you have one, so they can contact you, if they need to. When you decide to return, I will gladly write them all, so they have your new schedule."

"Thank you so much. I've been thinking I need to be in greater contact with them."

We talked a little while longer and then Alex left.

Before going to sleep, I meditated and saw my teacher for the first time in several weeks. She smiled at me and disappeared. I felt her love and fell asleep in the luxury of its warmth.

CHAPTER 21

Alex picked me up in the morning, and we drove to Felix and Martha Avener's home. They had invited the Bühlers and us to brunch to discuss the structure of the new classes. Their condo was large and on a high floor with nice vistas overlooking the city and a clear view of the river. Felix owned a jewelry store downtown, and Martha was a writer of children's books. It was a wonderful location, with easy transportation.

After brunch I took out some of the lessons and went over the form they should take and the general structure of the class. I had also made up some rules that I felt were important to keep the class harmonious. I had mentioned them briefly at the class the night before but went into more detail now. For example, if someone was in a foul mood or felt angry or irritated about something, that person should stay home and not attend class.

Martha asked, "Wouldn't it help the person to attend class? It could be soothing."

"No, just the opposite; strong negativity can overpower a calm atmosphere."

I also suggested, "If someone is disruptive in any way, the leader of the class needs to speak with the person privately and then send that information to me."

"It's hard to believe that people would be disruptive when they are attending a Higher Self Yoga class," Felix commented.

"Many times, when people start working with the Higher Self, it brings up their lower nature. There are some people in the group with strong egos who could try to take over the class. Be careful never to let that happen. I will be available by phone and email." And I told them about my plans to buy another house.

I felt a camaraderie developing between the Bühlers and the Aveners, but Alex seemed distant and didn't take an active part in the discussion. Later, when I asked him about it, he told me, "When couples get together, I often feel left out because their lifestyle is so different from mine."

When we left, the four of them were in a deep political discussion that probably would go on for a while. We were off to the class of teenagers, which Alex had agreed to lead.

It turned out to be a beautiful day, as Peter had predicted, and we arrived in the park to find ten teenagers, male and female, sitting under a shady tree. They became quiet when we approached, and Peter stood up and greeted me with a kiss on each cheek. Jon was also there, and he stood up but didn't come over, which surprised me. A couple of others started to stand up, but I indicated for them to remain seated.

After introducing Alex, I sat down, and we formed a circle. I began the class by asking, "How many of you feel the urge to explore the unknown?"

Amazingly, almost everyone raised a hand.

"Good, because it's important to have the desire to understand everything, to want to know how our universe runs itself, to discover how energy flows and works, and to investigate nature and communicate with other forms of life. All of this is available to the inquiring mind and heart. If you want to study with me, you need to have this inner desire to learn."

A young girl raised her hand. "I want to learn, but I'm carrying a heavy load of school work this semester. Can you tell us how much work this will require?"

A couple of kids agreed.

"It will require learning to meditate and doing this practice every morning before going to school. Some of you will have to get up earlier to do this. It will also require some reading, not a lot, and doing some exercises, also not a lot. Class can be held every two weeks on a weekend, and that will only be for two or three hours. The main thing is the meditation, as that will help you learn concentration and focus. Not only does it bring you joyful experiences, but it also helps you get in touch with your Higher Self and with me. It will be difficult for some of you to do at first, but once you have developed the ability to meditate you will find it will help you in your school-work and be a positive influence in your life."

I then gave them different methods to use to help them meditate, and we tried a fifteen-minute meditation. Afterward, Jon asked, "When I meditate, I don't feel my body at all. Is that normal?"

"Yes. In fact, you want to reach that state where you don't feel your body and don't hear outside sounds. Otherwise, those sensations will keep you from going out into the subtle world."

Another boy said, "It's really hard to keep still. I have a million thoughts coming in, and I tried a couple of the things you suggested, but I keep getting distracted."

"That always happens at first. It shows how little control most people have over their thoughts. Just imagine what it would be like for you to control your mind. It would free you to concentrate on those things that are important to you. I will give Alex some exercises for you to do in class that will help you discipline your mind."

I then talked more about reincarnation and the Higher Self. It would have been too much for them now to take them through a Higher Self exercise. They could do that later with Alex. Next time they met it would be at Alex's place, which was in the part of town where most of them lived, so that wouldn't be a problem.

When I said goodbye, Peter hugged me, and the rest followed suit. I told them they could write me, and they were thrilled about that. It was a fond farewell.

Later that evening I again meditated and put each of them in my heart. The response was very strong, especially with Peter. One or two of the others would also continue the work. I wasn't too certain about Jon, but he and Peter seemed to connect, so that could also work out.

Looking back at my journey, I wondered how the earlier classes were doing. I thought about whether I should travel backward and spend a day at each place to see what was happening. I was in the midst of trying to decide when the phone rang. It was Alex.

"Teacher, I just got an email from Erna in the Basel class, asking if you could pay them a visit soon. I think something has happened, which she wouldn't explain to me. She only said, 'Would you ask Zarathustra, when he is finished in Zürich, if he could possibly come back to Basel on his way home? Something has come up and we need him to advise us.'"

"She has my number. I'm surprised she didn't call or email me directly."

"I don't know. Maybe she feels she shouldn't bother you. In any case, can you do that?"

"My original plan was to go back to Wengen, have a rest, and revisit all the classes for a day or two, but then I decided not to because I need to look for a house. Now it seems I must go back to my original plan to visit the classes, but in reverse. My problem is that I have all the charts and materials to carry if I don't go home first."

"That's no problem. Leave all those things with me, and I will bring them to you when you are settled in your new home. Just take a suitcase with you to revisit all the classes. Before you leave I will give you some more computer lessons.

"Thank you so much. That will be very helpful.

Alex emailed Erna that I would be there in three days, and he spent his lunch hour and evenings with me giving me some more lessons on my computer and cell phone.

All of it seemed very complicated. When I was young, I had learned how to type, so that was a help, but the rest was so foreign to me. The cell phone was also a bit convoluted, but he patiently programmed it for me, and uploaded apps and all the contact details of the students with whom I had worked more closely, especially those whose homes were the location of a class. Modern technology really made things easier and more accessible.

I took the train to Basel. It was just a short, one-hour ride, and Erna was at the station to greet me. I could see she was very nervous, and I tried to calm her by sending her thoughts of love.

She asked me about Zürich, and we chitchatted during the ride to my hotel. Once there we went into the dining room for some lunch. Finally, after we ordered, I asked her to tell me what was wrong.

A worried look came across her face. "I don't know where to begin. I guess the best way is to start at the first class meeting after you left. Everyone came, and we followed the instructions you gave us. But just before we started the Higher Self exercise, Edwin said he felt it should be changed."

"Changed? What did he mean?"

"Just that. He explained that, in reading it over, he felt it was too literal and that it would be easier to do if we left out going up the mountain and simply visualized the Higher Self seated on the bench waiting for us. Some people protested, but he insisted and said he would lead the exercise using his method; if people didn't like it, then we could go back to yours."

I shook my head. "And you agreed?"

"Yes, he insisted that he was right. So, we did the exercise, and some people were okay with it, and the others didn't protest and just went along with it. That was the first class. At the next class, he changed another one of your exercises also and added something that was strange."

"What did he add?"

"The exercise was the one in which you have us look at our childhood and identify any characteristics or beliefs that came from our parents. He added a part to identify the beliefs of our siblings as well and then think about how they interacted with our parents."

"That makes it very complicated and takes the focus away from the process."

"Yes, and I made a point of saying this; but he said he was experienced in these matters and I wasn't."

"What is his experience?"

"His background was in corporate training, and he said he had a ton of experience working with people in this manner. In fact, at this point he suggested that he should lead the class."

"What did you say?"

"I told him you had put me in charge, and I couldn't change that."

"That's good."

"Yes, but from then on, he started to pull people over to his side. Matteo and then Margarita were very impressed by him, and then Olga gave in to anything he suggested. Dora and Gottfried sided with me more, but I could see that he also had them questioning some of your exercises."

I could see where this was going. "I wish you would have telephoned me."

"I know. But you were busy in Zürich, and I felt I should be able to handle it myself. I didn't realize how powerful and manipulative he was — it was so underhanded. Before I knew it, he had taken charge of the class. I led the meditation, but after that he simply took over, and when I tried to intervene he stepped in and overrode me."

I tried to remember what Edwin looked like. I had met him only briefly at the end of my stay in Basel and hadn't had a real interview with him. He seemed genuine, and I was in a hurry to leave. A lesson learned: it is not good ever to do that. If I had spent time with him, I would have gotten a better read on him. I remembered there were about eight or nine people who wanted to continue.

"Tell me about the rest of the class. Is everyone still coming on a regular basis?"

"No, after the third or fourth class several people dropped out. They didn't do well with the revised exercises, and Edwin told them they needed to practice more, and he said it in a demanding voice. He even told everyone they needed to study more and suggested some books I have never heard of. One was a book on Buddhism that was very strict. I said this wasn't the way you set the class up, and he said you would want people to learn more. Classes became more and more academic and my husband, who had become interested at first, decided this teaching wasn't for him."

I remembered she had called me when I first was in Zürich to ask if her husband could attend and that he and Gottfried had become friends. "What about Gottfried, is he still in the class?"

"No, he apologized to me but said he and his wife just couldn't tolerate Edwin anymore."

I felt upset at this point, as they were both old students of mine. "But why did you wait so long to tell me?" I tried to keep my voice kind.

"I know I should have told you right away. It's entirely my fault. I was so embarrassed in not being able to handle the situation, partially because you entrusted me with the task, and I didn't want to fail you." She started to cry.

"No, it's not your fault. It's mine; I told him he could come without really checking on him, and I didn't have a private meeting with him. So, it's definitely my error and a major one; don't feel upset."

"But you could have told him to leave. I couldn't."

"Neither could I. Once someone is in class I cannot tell the person to leave, but I can make it clear to him that the class is run a certain way and that he is not in charge. Who is still in the class at this point?"

"Olga, Margarita and Matteo. The rest have disappeared. When Dora and Gottfried left, that upset me the most, along with of course my husband, who was so enthused at first."

"So, about half are gone."

"Yes, that's right

"When is your next meeting?"

"Tomorrow evening."

"All right. Please call the ones who have left and tell them I am back, and will be conducting the class. Also tell them that I hope they will want to come. Give me Edwin's phone number; I will try to see him before the meeting."

Later, I called Edwin and arranged to have lunch with him the next day. That evening I went to Erna's house for dinner. It was the first time I had met her husband, Karl, and I liked him immediately. I could tell he felt a little awkward around me, which was due mainly to his feelings about attending class and then leaving. While Erna was in the kitchen, I broached the subject directly with him.

"I understand from Erna that you and Gottfried are friends and that he spoke to you about the teaching."

"Yes, that's true. He's a very nice man, and I learned some of the basic things from him."

"Do you still see him?"

"Yes, we sometimes have dinner together, but it's strictly social."

"You mean you don't talk about the teaching anymore?"

"Yes, neither one of us is interested anymore. I'm sorry, but that's the truth."

"You mean you're not interested because of what happened with Edwin in the classes, or you're not interested because you don't believe in the basic concepts given originally?"

"I guess both. Edwin really was a turn off, and it made both of us question everything you set up."

"That's understandable. I didn't know this was happening; otherwise, I would have done something right away. I hope to set it straight tomorrow night so that the teaching will resume correctly. Please consider coming to my class here, particularly since you have never seen me teach."

He paused before answering. "I will consider it, but, honestly, I wasn't into spiritual things from the beginning, and now that I have had a taste of it, I feel even more opposed. Erna can do her own thing. I won't interfere, but to be frank it isn't for me."

"I like your honesty. I leave it up to you, but from what Erna has said, Edwin took over the class and misinterpreted the lessons I left."

"I don't know if that's true since I never saw the lessons, but he certainly is bossy, and any time Erna tried to do or say something he would take over and push her aside. That bothered me a lot and, quite frankly, Erna should have done more, and I told her so. She became a wimp, a characteristic I hadn't seen before."

Erna walked into the room at that time. "He's right; something about Edwin's personality made me feel like a little child. It was a horrible feeling."

"Was your father like that?"

"No, but my mother was. I guess that's it. He reminds me of my mother. Wouldn't you say that's true, Karl? She still has to rule everything, and it drives us both crazy when she comes for a visit."

"You're right. Edwin's the male version of her." Karl agreed

"So, Erna, maybe the lesson here is to learn how to deal with your mother more directly; then you won't let others like her victimize you."

"That feels impossible. You have no idea how difficult she is."

"What's difficult sometimes takes longer, but it still needs to be done. We'll talk about it later."

Karl added, "I find Erna's mom impossible. I generally stay away when she's here."

"Well, it sounds like you did the same with Edwin. You left."

"Yeah, you're right."

"He always disappears when there is any kind of problem or confrontation," Erna said.

"It's much easier that way, but nothing gets resolved. These are usually behavior patterns you developed in childhood or even from previous lives. After dinner, I'll be glad to give you both some exercises to do to try to change those patterns."

It was a long evening, and, when I returned to my hotel, I went to bed immediately without meditating. That night I had a dream. In the dream I saw Edwin, and I tried to talk to him, but he turned his back on me. This was a bad indication for the meeting I was to have with him. It showed me that he was angry with me for something, probably in a past lifetime, as I had barely had anything to do with him in this one.

The next morning, I meditated and asked my teacher for help in understanding my past with Edwin. I saw a scene from a previous life when I was a teacher in India. Edwin was a woman and came to me for advice concerning a lover. I told her to let her lover go, that he would take her away from the teaching, which wasn't good. Since she was my disciple, she had to obey me; and in so doing she was devastated by the loss and eventually died an early death. I now understood why he was still angry with me and was unconsciously trying to destroy the class here.

I had hoped to persuade him to leave by helping him see that this teaching wasn't right for him, but now I realized I couldn't do that. Karmically, he was meant to be with me and be given the chance to make it a better relationship. I felt stuck. Keeping him in the class would cause the others to stay away; yet making him leave would be going against the karma we had established. It was equally impossible to immediately change his domineering manner, which was the result of his meek lifetime in India. That would take time, and it would work only if he was willing to do it.

I meditated on what to do but didn't come up with a good solution. It was a beautiful day, so I took a long walk by the river. I wasn't meeting Edwin until one o'clock, so there was plenty of time. I had to confront him in a way that he would hear me.

A chilling wind suddenly enveloped me so I quickly went into a nearby café and ordered a coffee. My table was in a corner next to the window, and I watched the people walking outside. They moved against the wind holding their coat collars up around their faces to protect themselves from the sudden gusts that rose off the water. It reminded me of Edwin. His attitude would make him push fiercely against the wind, not realizing that maybe he could get to his destination by moving with the wind in another direction. That direction might take longer and be roundabout, but it certainly would be easier and less enervating.

I sipped my coffee and formulated a plan.

We met at a restaurant near his office. It was a good choice because it was large and spacious, which made the noise level low enough that we could talk in privacy. Edwin looked much older than his years. When I had first met him, I thought he might be retired, but he still worked as a corporate executive for a large financial institution. I thought he was in his mid-sixties, but it turned out he was fifty-five. His hair was pure white and his leathery, wrinkled face either was a result of too much sun, or more appropriately, came from years of working in a stressful executive job. In either case, it made him look unapproachable, and I could understand why Erna had difficulty dealing with him.

There was no attempt to greet me affectionately. Instead, he gave me a strong handshake and was very formal. I immediately felt his strong ego self. This man was used to being in charge. I knew his background also included conducting training sessions, but it turned out that now he was in charge of a large department and had advanced to being a Vice President in his company.

We ordered lunch and spoke in general. He asked me about Zürich and my plans, and that took a short while to explain. His mannerisms were confident and direct, which I liked, but I could sense an edge there, as if he were waiting for me to say something to throw him off guard. Surely, he knew I would ask him about class.

"I understand you have taken over leading the class?"

"Yes, I have. I know you put Erna in charge, but she was losing the people. She's a nice lady but doesn't have good leadership skills."

"And you think you do?"

This surprised him. "Well, of course I do. I've been working with people and have been an accomplished manager for years. That's why I'm in the position I have now."

"Running a corporation is different from guiding a spiritual group of people." I emphasized the word *guiding*.

"People are people. If you work well with one group, you can work well with other groups."

"If you look at it in terms of the masses that might be true, but I have found everyone is different, and every class I have is different because of the makeup of the people. Because of this, the guidance they are given is also different from person to person and class to class."

"Well, I can see that being true between a class of farmers up in the mountains and a class of professionals in a city. Here in Basel everyone in the class is a professional and is used to working professionally."

"This class started out that way, but all your professionals, except for Erna, have left the class. The ones who have remained are college students or ones starting out in the world. Have you ever wondered why all the professionals have departed?"

"I think this teaching is too simplistic for them. They need to read and study more, and I planned to talk to you about that."

"But you brought in a reading list for them, and they still left."

"That's their business, not mine. They all had their reasons, and it's just possible that the teaching isn't for them. It's not for everybody. You've said that."

"Do you think it's for you?"

A frown came over his face. "Yes, of course, that's why I'm still attending class every week."

"But you're not following my lessons or the structure I had set up, so how do you know if this is your teaching?"

The frown deepened. "Are you questioning if I should be in this teaching?"

"Yes, I question every student's motivation."

"But I've been the most faithful of anyone here, except for Erna, because the class is in her house, which is another thing I want to speak to you about."

"I'm not asking about your attending classes faithfully; I'm asking you what your heart says about being in this teaching."

"I don't know what my heart says, but my mind likes this teaching."

"Then maybe that's what you have to learn: to listen to your heart, because only the heart will give you the right answers. If you listened to your heart, you would have known that to change the teacher's instructions shows a lack of devotion. If you listened to your heart, you would have known that the people who left did so because of you, not because they weren't interested in the teaching. If you listened to your heart, you would have understood the best way to guide people rather than control them. If you listened to your heart, you would have let me overshadow you when you tried to lead the class."

Edwin remained silent. I could see he was struggling to answer me. Finally, he said, "I've been told I lack heart quality, but the mind is equally as important. I think you need more of that in this teaching."

I quietly looked at him and sent him love. "This teaching is about balance, and for you to find balance, you need to focus on opening your heart; otherwise, you will become stuck on this path."

He sat for a few minutes in silent contemplation, then said, "To be honest with you, I find trying to work with the heart very scary. Using my mind is much more comfortable."

"Of course it's scary for you. I don't know your childhood conditioning, but I would guess your parents weren't warm and loving but were instead more intellectual."

"You're right. They were, and they emphasized that feelings of any kind were destructive to one's career. Particularly my mother was that way. She was a professor in the university here." He was deep in thought. "You know, I think one of the reasons I was attracted to you and to this teaching is because it is heart-based. Something in me felt I needed it."

"Yes, it's good that you recognized that." I looked into his eyes and kindly asked, "Why didn't you remember that developing your heart is what you needed to learn? Erna has a beautiful heart, and she could have helped you."

"I only saw that heart quality in you, so when you left I just reverted to what I knew best. But you're right; Erna is warmhearted, and so were a couple of the other people who left." He looked downward and quietly said. "I apologize for what I did and how it affected the class. That wasn't my intention. How can I help now?"

"Tonight, I hope that some of the people who left will return to the class. I've spoken to a couple of them who said they would try to come. Erna said some of the others have said no, they were no longer interested, but those people obviously weren't meant to stay. For the others who will be there, it would be good for you to apologize to them."

"All right, I will be glad to do that."

"In terms of your learning to listen to your heart and using it more, that will require a lot of daily practice. After you speak with someone, look back on the conversation and notice if you were in your heart. When you go into any meeting, first connect with your heart and the Higher Self. My question is, why are you afraid to use your heart? Are you afraid of being vulnerable? Look at all your relationships. Are they mainly mind-oriented? If so, try to find someone who is open-hearted and cultivate a friendship with that person. Look at your need to control. Where does that come from? These are all the questions you need to ask yourself and take one at a time to work on."

"Will you help me to see this?"

"Absolutely. I will be here tomorrow. If you are free, I can meet with you tomorrow evening."

We made those arrangements, but before we left, I said to him, "I have talked to you about the things you need to change to grow spiritually. You also have some wonderful qualities that you need to acknowledge. When I told you what you needed to work on, you never protested or made excuses, so you can take criticism very well, which many people can't. That means I can be direct with you and you will listen. In addition, you have been faithful to this teaching, and I feel you have a deep desire to learn more. If you feel you can make the lessons better, I will be happy to go through them with you and add your suggestions if I feel they are appropriate. You are right in believing there should be a reading list. I have already been thinking about developing one, and again your suggestions will be helpful. But I request that you speak to me about it and not try to implement it on your own. Much of this we can do on the phone or by email."

I told Edwin about my future plans, and he seemed happy that I would be more accessible. Afterward, I was relieved that he hadn't responded negatively. He could have easily done so and left. When I looked into his eyes, I felt the strong bond between us and knew that being direct was the best way to handle him. As a teacher, it was always good when I could do this. Many people are too sensitive to handle the truth, so it has to be given out in small doses. Edwin had a lot of personality problems, but he had great potential.

That night's class went well. Several people came back to it. Unfortunately, Dora and Gottfried said they were busy, but Karl came and after class said he was willing to try again. That left me with the hope that he would be able to talk to Gottfried and persuade him to do the same. Edwin was very quiet and at the end of the class apologized to everyone there. He asked their help and told them to directly stop him if he tried to take over the class again, saying that being controlling was so much a part of his background and personality that he might not be aware he was doing it.

I suggested that the class meet socially once a month and talk about the dynamics that were happening in class. I also reminded them that if there were any problems among any members they should meet privately and try to resolve them.

After class, Edwin apologized to Erna for having interrupted her and taken over the class. He said he would like to become her friend so that this wouldn't happen again.

She said it was also her fault for not confronting him directly and she would try to do so in the future.

I thought about the way I had structured my classes. In the past, I had chosen one person to lead the class, and that person's home was always the one where the classes were held. Now, I decided instead to try rotating the people. Each person who attended class on a regular basis would take a turn in leading the class, unless someone really felt too uncomfortable to do so. Questions and answers should be a team effort. The only exception would be Alex's class of teenagers. I felt it better that he continue to lead it.

The next day, I had several private meetings. Olga was very eager to talk to me. We hadn't had an individual meeting before. She turned out to be very charismatic, with a good sense of humor. She was finishing her last year at the university and planned to go on to medical school and become a doctor. In our meeting, she talked about the class and Edwin. She said, "I know I must have had a past life with him. I just adore him, and so I guess I didn't mind when he took charge the way he did. But I can see how damaging it was to the others and particularly to Erna, who really tried to keep the class directed along the lines you had indicated. We all got a little carried away, so I need to apologize for my part in that."

"Thank you. You also are very intellectual, so it is easier for you to relate to Edwin instead of Erna. I will give you the same advice I gave Edwin, which is to start consciously to work with your heart more."

"That's going to be difficult, since all my school work is very mental and next year in medical school it will be even more so."

"That's even more reason to work with your heart in all your relationships."

We talked some more about the importance of using both the mind and the heart and how to balance them.

Then she said, "I'm dating a man who is much older than I. I know he's somewhat of a father figure, but I really love him. I've tried to break it off, but I just can't. It has to be karmic, and I need to know if it's okay to continue or whether I should really end it."

I immediately wondered if it was Edwin she was talking about but didn't say so.

"I need to know more about him. What's his name and age and how did you get involved with him?"

"He's forty-eight, and his name is Hermann Steiner. He was my dentist, but I changed dentists when we became involved. I guess the main thing you should know is that he's married — not happily, but still married. He wants to leave his wife and marry me, and I don't know what to do."

It was a relief to know it wasn't Edwin, but Hermann was still a big problem. She didn't want me to say to leave him. I picked that up right away. I couldn't be direct, as she wouldn't hear me then, so instead I said, "What do you think your karma is with him?"

"It has to be good. Our love is very strong, so it has to be good."

"Not necessarily. You can have a huge attraction for someone who in the end turns out to be very difficult karma for you. The love attraction works both ways. My sense is that, if he leaves his wife and you marry him, there may be some negative karma coming up. But let me ask you, does he have any children?"

"Yes, two boys, both young. One is ten and the other one is seven."

"How does he feel about them?"

"He is very close to both and wants joint custody."

"So, you would have to take care of his children when you are in medical school?"

"I guess."

"Think about it then. From what I understand, medical school is very demanding and consuming to a medical student. It requires 100% of a person's time, and med students have little time for themselves and relationships like marriage and children. My concern as your spiritual guide is about you incurring karma with Hermann's wife and children, which would happen if you were the cause of his breakup. If you say no to marrying him, and he still breaks up with his wife because he really wants to and not because of you, then the karma would only be his karma. Later, if you change your mind and decide to marry him, then you wouldn't have that karma."

"In other words, I can stay in the relationship and not promise to marry him?"

"Definitely don't promise to marry him. Whether you stay in the relationship or not is up to you. My suggestion is to concentrate on finishing med school before you consider a deeper involvement with him. Maybe see less of him, which you will have to do anyway. If in four years he's a free man, then decide if you still want to be with him."

I knew that if she followed my advice she would meet a med student with whom she would fall in love.

"That sounds reasonable to me. I really don't want to make karma with his wife and kids, and, it's true, school is going to be much too demanding to have any outside pressures. In the meantime, it would be nice to see him once in a while. By the way, I'm not the first woman he's been with while married. He's pretty much played around since the beginning of his marriage. His marriage was the result of a lot of family pressure, but I don't need to go into that or justify his unfaithfulness."

"No, you don't. That's his karma; just don't make it yours."

I would have preferred to say to Olga that she stop the relationship. Being involved with a married person always produces negative karma, but she would have rebelled against that suggestion. In her case, it was better to suggest a way out that she could accept. In time, the relationship with Herman would fizzle out. If she did marry him, he would have been unfaithful to her. He needed reassurance from younger women.

I also suggested that, since she was attracted to older men, maybe she needed to look at her relationship with her father. That had occurred to me when she said her father had died when she was very young. She claimed to have done therapy around it, but I told her to consider doing more, particularly at this time.

After Olga left I thought about her. It was difficult to remain totally non-attached when I had to give advice and spiritual guidance to beautiful women. I could feel sexual feelings come up that I had to repress. There were several women students now who fell into that category. Strangely, I thought I had managed to work through all such desires and move past them, so to have even some of them come back disturbed me. It was so much easier to be in my mountain home, meditating and connecting with nature. I couldn't wait to go back there and refocus my energies. It would be another ten days of visiting the classes before I could make that happen.

CHAPTER 22

The next city I revisited was Bern. From there I would return to Luzern, then Interlaken and Meiringen, and finally to where I had started the journey, in Wengen.

Each class I visited had changed completely. Many of the people had dropped out. Some new ones had come in and, in general, the work seemed very incomplete and no longer focused. Even the lesson plans I had given them hadn't been as useful as I thought they would be. Some people got stuck on a lesson or an exercise and repeated it several times in class, whereas others got bored and wanted more.

In Bern, where the class had begun with six people, only four were left. Ottilia was still having class in her house but indicated right away that she would like for someone else to host the class. I picked up that she also wanted to leave the teaching. It had been more of a social adventure for her. The only three left were Brian, Rudy, and a new person named Anna, a friend of Brian's. I liked her right away, and when she volunteered her apartment I accepted.

Bern had been a problem from the beginning, so I wasn't surprised at the outcome; but it still seemed strange to me that I had so many students in Zürich and Luzern and just a handful elsewhere.

I brought new lesson plans for the students in Bern and changed the structure of the class. I even gave them a partial reading list to start working with. These I then carried forward to the other classes.

My next stop was Luzern. I expected better results there but was again disappointed. Boris was still very devoted and committed to the teaching. Even though the class had dropped down to fifteen people, he felt it was very solid; but when I met with them, I could see there were some people who were having difficulties with the lessons. I spent three days there holding classes and meeting with individuals to make the class run more smoothly.

There were also three new people and a couple more wanting to attend class with whom I met privately. One of them I directed elsewhere; another one was already in the class, so I couldn't ask her to leave. Boris had forgotten that any new people had to be checked with me before attending class. The new woman would be a problem for them, as she was very demanding, with a lot of negative masculine characteristics. When I met with her I tried gently dissuade her from coming and suggested another teaching; but, in response, she became a permanently installed concrete statue that was set on staying in the class.

I gave Boris a list of those in the class who were ready to take turns in leading. She was not on the list, and I hoped that fact would discourage her enough to leave. It took some time, but eventually that did happen.

Interlaken proved even more discouraging. The six people were still coming most of the time to class at Winifred's, but they had stopped doing the opening meditation and didn't seem to understand how to do the Higher Self exercise correctly. I spent three days with them to correct some of the mistakes and give them more lessons to work on.

It became clear that the longer the span of time from my original visit and my return, the less the classes retained its quality. Lack of communication was the key reason and I was very disturbed at my not having had enough insight at the outset to know this could happen. I was going by my experience with my teacher, which wasn't comparable. I had spent those years at the ashram developing an inner communication with her, and somehow I had felt this could happen with my students instantaneously. My lack of foresight depressed me. I dreaded going to the last two places; I hadn't spoken to them for several months.

Meiringen was cold and damp when I arrived, setting the stage for another disaster. Sophie met me at the station and took me to my hotel. The class with the four of them was still ongoing, but only twice a month, and usually even then only one or two people came. They would all be there tomorrow night and wanted to have dinner with me beforehand. Again, the lack of follow-through bothered me, and when I met with them I saw that none of them had that deep an interest in the teaching. Even Sophie, whom I felt had a lot of potential, seemed caught up in a new relationship. The dinner and the class were more social than anything else, and I left the next day for Wengen with a heavy heart.

It was late September, and I needed to have a couple of weeks in my mountain home before the deep snows came. Then I needed to concentrate on buying a house. Because of that, my stay in Wengen was just for one day, and in that day, I managed to see each of the students. There had been six in the class, and those six were still there. It was wonderful seeing these first students, and they were the same—devoted, interested in the teaching, and eager for new lessons. Maybe it was the energy of the mountains or that Wengen was close to my home, but somehow nothing had happened to the quality of this particular class. In fact, they had really grown close, and my premonition about Maria and Karl turned out to be correct. They were now a couple living together.

Telling the class I would be back in two weeks, I gathered a few food supplies and early the next morning started my journey home. It had been a long time since I had been hiking, and I found myself tiring and having to rest every hour. It took me six hours to get to my hut at the halfway point, whereas before it would have been around four. After spending the night, I filled my electric cart, which I had left there, with more staples and continued my trip home.

When I'd started my journey the air was crisp, turning cold, and autumn leaves were falling heavily, covering the ground with colors that ranged from wine reds, burnt orange, and rust browns to golden yellows — a beautiful blanket warming and protecting the terrain from the snows that would be coming. As I climbed the mountain, I entered the area where the pines stood glorious in their deep greens that reigned supreme because they never changed; it felt like they knew they were the majestic managers of the mountains. When I reached the forests of pine, I stopped to inhale their fragrance and felt awed once more by their grandeur embracing the sky. It was the pines that sheltered me from the sun and wind and welcomed me once again.

My cabin looked lonely and forsaken when I arrived. I wanted to become a giant so that I could put my arms around all of it and say, "I'm back. I will always come back. I haven't forgotten you."

The wood was still stacked high, ready to burn, and I lit a fire immediately, then spent the late hours of the afternoon cleaning the dust from shelves and tabletops.

That night the sky was clear with brilliant stars to bring me back to the glory of the heavens so lost in the cities below. I sat and meditated outside and breathed in the freshness of the air. My lungs couldn't get enough of its purity. I had forgotten that breath sustains life and mountain air is like an elixir that rejuvenates every cell in the body.

The next few days that's all I did: I meditated and linked my heart to my Mahatma, my guru, and my new students. I also contacted my nature spirit friends. My heart felt full of love for them all.

My journey was complete; it was finished, and it had just begun. Each journey would take me to new cities, new students, and new learnings. Each journey would give me new material to teach and new material to discard or change. It all was so new yet so old. It had been written before in ancient texts or scriptures. It needed new words to have meaning for the new generations, yet it was nothing new. Zarathustra's journey had started centuries ago with other names and other places, and in all those journeys only a few could understand, only a few comprehended the quest.

In those two weeks, I renewed my commitment to my spiritual journey and myself, as well as my commitment to others, to guide them into the mountains of their souls. In those two weeks, I envisioned many things that inspired me to write a book about my journey. I saw that the future would change, that the world even in its worst moments of war and destruction still would survive, and that Zarathustra's journey would be many people's journey.

Something happened during that time, something very remarkable. It was the end of my stay, and I was meditating outside in the early evening, when I heard a noise and saw a figure approaching. The figure was a young woman who cried out,

"Help me!" when she saw me. She was totally disheveled, her pants and jacket covered with leaves and pine needles; and, when she came close to me, she collapsed on her knees and started crying.

"Thank God I found you. I've been lost for two days and haven't seen anyone on the trails. I have no idea where I am."

I helped her to her feet and took her inside the house. There was hot water on the stove, so I poured her a cup of tea and found some cheese and crackers to give her. Even though the cabin was warm, I got a blanket for her to wrap around herself, as I could see her body was still shaking.

"Thank you so much!" She gave me a weak smile. "Even though my jacket is very warm, I think I'm still chilled from being out all night. I went into the woods, which kept the wind away, but it was still pretty cold. I don't think I could have survived another night."

"How did you get lost?" I asked. "The trails are very well marked."

"I was stupid. I love photography and wandered into a field to take pictures thinking I knew the way back, but I didn't. Then I found a path and followed it to a mountain shed, where it ended. When I turned back I got onto another small path, which just kept going. I hoped it would come out to the main trail, but it didn't, and after a while I realized I was slowly climbing up the mountain. I took another path, and it became a huge maze."

"Those paths are for the locals who move their cows around the pastures. None of them are part of the main tourist trails. You're very lucky to have taken one of them to here. But are you traveling alone?"

"No, I came with a couple of friends. We are staying in Murren, but I wanted to explore other places and they were content to just be there. I took the train up to Wengen two days ago. They must be frantic because I didn't come back."

"Did they know you were going to Wengen?"

"Not really. I wasn't sure when I left. Our car was parked below Murren, and I said I was going to several places; but when the train arrived in the station I saw there was a train to Wengen, so I decided to come here first."

"So, there's probably not a search party for this place here yet. Anyway, it's a good eight hours back to town, and I'm afraid it's too late for us to go now. You need to rest first anyway. We'll start in the morning, but now you must rest."

I took her to my bedroom, and she curled up in a ball with the blanket around her and fell asleep immediately. A wisp of black hair fell down her cheek, and she looked like a ten-year-old who was exhausted because she played all day.

I went outside again to watch the sunset over the mountains and to finish my meditation. I felt glad that I could rescue her, but I also felt disturbed that my solitude had been interrupted. It meant I would lose two of my days here, as I would have to spend the night in Wengen. Thoughts started to invade my mind. How could I be so selfish that I was disturbed about this? This woman could have died on the mountain. The temperature dropped drastically at night. Fortunately, it had been a warm day yesterday or she could have gotten frostbite last night. Was I so insensitive to others? My whole journey was about helping new students, yet I was still acting like a recluse who wanted nothing to do with others. My inner critic kept knocking me over the head until I finally ended the meditation and went back inside.

I decided to make a hearty soup for dinner and was simmering it on the stove when she stumbled into the room.

"That smells delicious. By the way, my name is Evelyn Andrews."

I told her mine and looked at her more closely. Her hair was still disheveled and her face drawn and tired, but her eyes seemed bright and alert. For the first time, I realized how she looked. She was young, probably in her early twenties, with hair so dark that the cabin light dusted it in blue highlights. When she looked at me, her electric blue eyes had movement and depth, making her face breathtakingly lovely. Now that she was no longer wrapped in the blanket, I could tell her body was tall and thin and most definitely shapely.

"I hope you like soup. It's my mainstay when I'm here, and I have a freezer, so it's easy to make up a big batch and store it."

"Yes, soup is a favorite of mine. How come you have electricity, and you even have plumbing?"

"At first, I didn't, but then I found out that it wouldn't be too difficult to tie into a transmitter that carries electricity up to the ski areas. In the winter months, refrigeration wasn't a problem, as I put food in containers outside; but the summer months can get very hot, even here, and then it's more difficult to keep food fresh. It was almost impossible to stay here for more than three or four days at a time, so it was worth paying the initial cost to have a line put in."

"Do people know you are here?"

"Oh yes, some people do but not many. You're the first person to stumble onto my home. Others who have come here needed a detailed map, but they are mainly workers whom I have hired for various projects."

"I know it's none of my business, but is there a reason why you live in such a remote place away from town?"

"Yes, I'm a yogi. This is my spiritual retreat."

"That makes sense. I noticed your shrine in the bedroom, and I gather that the Indian woman is your teacher."

I had forgotten about covering my shrine, and I felt immediately upset about having a stranger look at it.

She must have noticed my reaction because she said, "I'm sorry. I didn't disturb it;

on the contrary, I felt really drawn to your teacher. Her face seems very familiar. Can you tell me her name?"

"No, I'm not allowed to." But, as I said the words, I felt my teacher's presence and she said, "Tell her my name." So, I did.

During dinner, she asked me questions about the teaching, and I told her everything. She wanted to know where my teacher lived, and I told her that also. I was being used to guide her to my guru, and I knew that was the reason she had found me in the first place. She knew it also because she said, "I've been looking for a teacher for a couple of years, and I think it's your teacher, which is why I am here."

She told me she was an American, living in Boston, and had just finished her senior year at the University in Zürich. She and her friends from school were taking an extended vacation. The more we talked, the more I felt drawn to her — not as my student, but as my spiritual sister. When she spoke, her face was animated with an inner energy that was very compelling. It changed her into Aphrodite, the Goddess whose beauty enchanted men. I had to strongly resist that happening to me.

Reluctantly, I insisted on her going to bed early, as she needed to rest. I slept in the living room on the couch. Rather, I tried to sleep but kept seeing her face. We had some past together, but it evaded me.

The next morning after a hearty breakfast, we set out. She looked rested and happy. But she wasn't a hiker, so we stopped more than I would have. I packed us some food for snacks, and we again talked a lot, so we didn't arrive in Wengen until just before sunset. We went directly to the police station and found that there had been a report of her missing filed that morning. They believed she had to be in this area, as her car was still in the garage below. Already there were some search parties out looking for her.

Her friends were there also, and we found them. They cried and hugged her and also hugged me for rescuing her.

When we parted, she gave me her phone number and email address and said she wanted to see me again to continue our talk about the teaching. Then she reached up and kissed me on the cheek.

PART THREE

Jacques: Journey's End

Jacques Ulrich was sitting in his study waiting for his son-in-law, Anton, to arrive from the mountains. It was summer, and they were vacationing there. Jacques thought about the last six years and ruminated about his role in all that had happened. Without a doubt, he was relieved that a favorable end had occurred. There had been many challenges, challenges that he at times felt would end his relationship with Anton. Some of these challenges he had made himself, fully knowing that they were extremely difficult for any student to overcome, but he had always had a deep faith in Anton's spirituality and in his eventual success in coming to a deeper realization of who he was.

Jacques got up from his chair, opened a drawer, and took out the small painting of his wife. He rarely did this, but tonight he felt he had to look at her one more time. It always made him feel sad to remember their early years together. Her spirit was soaring then, and their love was strong and vital.

He should have known that they were in the full stages of good karma, but that there was some negative karma also that he had neglected to look at. His teacher had mentioned it but still felt positive about them marrying. He had also realized later that his wife had a narcissistic ego; but, again, he had ignored it because of his love for her.

Tonight, he sat looking at her face and knew that, before he died, he needed to forgive her and pray for her. In the past, he had tried to do this, but each time it wasn't sincere. He also knew that if he didn't let her go, they would return again together in another life and play out more karma, which he didn't want to do.

Jacques held the picture to his heart and sent heart energy to her, and, finally, he felt all his feelings of sorrow and loss leave him. Only then could the forgiveness happen. He closed his eyes and saw his teacher smile at him. He also felt that his wife knew about his closure and felt relieved.

He took scissors from the desk and slowly cut the portrait up in very small pieces and put them in a paper bag. Later, he would go out and throw them in the forest that lined his property. He had planned to burn the picture, but he realized that, if he did, it would go back to her, and he didn't want that to happen.

Returning to his study, he sat down and thought about the classes and his disciples. Several of his teachers now had students of their own. Lea had her own class, with four disciples. There were others in Switzerland and America; they connected with him frequently by phone, email and video. Before, he had visited them every year, but now it was too difficult for him to travel. His daughter, Samantha, had recently met two of her own students and had started working with them. Anton still had a way to go before he would be a teacher. But they were both young, and there were many years ahead of them before they started their real mission.

Looking back on his life, Jacques breathed a long sigh. There were students he'd lost and still missed and others, to whom he'd never felt close, who remained and continued to grow spiritually. There had been heartbreak and joy, and hope and disillusionment, but none of it affected his journey in a way that ever made him want to turn back. When he had first married, it broke his life of solitude, but that was easy to give up because of his love for her. And when they had Samantha, she had added a new dimension to his life, one that was even more fulfilling. No, he had no regrets, and now he could leave feeling he had completed his dharma in this life.

Anton drove down to Zürich early, as he wanted to go to their condo to change clothes. He was wearing jeans and a t-shirt, and he wanted to put on nice clothes for dinner. He and Sam had been fortunate to find a larger unit in his current building, with the same lovely view of the Limmat. Their two children needed to have their own rooms. Julien had just turned three, and Sophia was a year old. Both were very active kids and were a handful for Sam. She had decided she preferred to be at home with the children when they were small, and was enjoying being with them in those early years. They'd planned that she would return to her consulting work when the kids were a little older. But never for the government again.".

They still had their problems, mainly around communication, but they had a good couples therapist who helped them resolve them. He also had continued his therapy with Karen and only recently was at a point where he could end it.

It was nice to have the two homes, because sometimes they both needed to get away and have some alone time. In the summer when they lived in the mountains, they took turns taking care of the kids and sometimes one of them would come back to the condo simply to meditate and to see friends and, of course, Jacques. It was a good solution for them both. In the winter, if the weather was good, they did the opposite and again took turns going up to their home in the mountains.

Anton also wanted some time today to meditate. Jacques had made a point of asking to see him alone, and he was wondering what the meeting was about. He had just received an initiation, so he knew it wasn't about that. He wondered how Jacques' health was. He and Sam were concerned, because her father had become more and more frail in the past couple of years. Jacques had talked a couple of times about leaving, so maybe tonight's discussion was about that.

Anton had planned to also see Lea. The last time he had seen her, she said she had met a man whom she liked a great deal. He was a Buddhist, so he was open to her teaching and the fact that she was a teacher. Anton had been hoping that she would find love in her life, maybe because in some ways he felt he had let her down.

He made himself a sandwich for lunch and sat on the balcony to enjoy the view. It was a hot day, but he didn't mind the heat. There was a swimming pool on the river below him, and he enjoyed the specks of people moving across the water like dots on ticker tape. It was a public pool, and when the kids were older he would take them down there to learn how to swim.

Being a father was something he had always wanted, but he'd never realized how difficult it could be, probably because his parents had servants helping to take care of them. He and Sam decided to not do that. Once in a while, they hired babysitters when they wanted to go out in the evening, but during the day they were there for the children. Julien was talking fast, a turkey that never stopped gobbling, and Sophia was crawling and getting into everything.

Anton smiled when he thought about them and wondered what everyone's karma was in the family. Neither he nor Sam could pick up anything about it, nor would Jacques tell them. He basically said it was best not to know and just to treat the children with unconditional love. Knowing there was negative karma made for favoritism, he said. When they were older, he and Sam would probably pick up on it. They already knew that the children had good karma with Jacques, because every time they saw him both laughed in delight and wanted to be held.

Finally, Anton went inside, meditated, took a shower, and left for Jacques'.

They had drinks and hors d'oeuvres on the screened-in porch overlooking the gardens. It was a lovely evening, with a clear sky that allowed the stars to cluster in close companionship.

Jacques asked, "How are the children and Samantha?"

"The kids are making her and me on constant alert. They both have a lot of energy. We took them on a walk to the meadow, and Julien jumped for joy when he saw the flowers. He wanted to pick them and bring them home. That was one of Mother's favorite places to take us as children. I wish Mother could see them. Which reminds me: how and what is she doing?"

Jacque smiled. "You know I can't tell you, but she is getting ready to be reborn."

"Is there a possibility . . .?"

"No, you would favor her too much over the others."

"Sorry, but I hope it's to a good family that has a house in the mountains."

"There will be mountains, but not here in Switzerland. I can tell you she will be American in her next life, and she will be born into a nice family with good karma."

"That makes me happy."

They talked some more about the family and the children.

Finally, Jacques looked serious. "I need to talk to you about something important."

"Is something wrong?"

"No, but I know you are about to have your book reprinted. I am going to ask you to wait. You need to add an additional part to the book."

"What do you mean?"

"Right now, the book is about the spiritual teaching of Higher Self Yoga — our teaching — but your journey is a very important part of it. Your story needs to be added."

"Why?"

"Because it is the student's story. Now, the book is about a teacher's teaching and his story. What is missing is your story — all you went through, all your doubts and fears, all your struggles, including what happened with Sam."

"But why now? Why wasn't I told to add it before?"

"You couldn't write it then. You hadn't gone through the difficult part of your journey, and I didn't know if you would stay with me or in this teaching. It was your test, and I couldn't help you because it was something you had to experience and decide by yourself."

Jacques paused in thought. "My heart has always loved you, so when Samantha fell in love with you and it was mutual, I really was so happy. Maybe I was a little too attached to that outcome; and, when Samantha decided to do what she needed to do and I nearly lost you, I realized I had to step back and honor both of your decisions, whether it was what I had hoped for or not."

"Thank you. I felt you doing that. But to add my story will take a long time, and I don't know if my publisher would hold up the reprint."

"It won't take too long; you have already written it."

"Of course, I somehow knew you were going to say that." Then Anton laughed, "You really want my family and friends to disown me again?"

"I want them to know who you are, and I think anyone who loves you will be awed by your story."

"But my relationship with my family and mother would be in it."

"It doesn't have to be. Just tell your family and friends that it is a work of fiction to describe a spiritual person's journey and that not all of it is true. You can make up things about the family and even put in another brother."

"But my family knows about the valley, and all of that is true. And what about Sam? I don't want her to be in any danger."

"Remember, this is fiction. Make what she did fictional."

"But she did get mixed up in some danger, and she did leave me for a while, and we both did therapy to work out our problems. That is real, and the rest is quite real."

"Yes, but you can add to it to make it sound supernatural."

"Even if I do that, you know a lot of what happened to me was real."

"Oh yes," and Jacque smiled. "I need to give you something."

461

He left and came back with some papers. "There needs to be an addition to the Zarathustra book. It needs to end this way." He handed the papers to Anton. Then he handed him another page saying, "I also have written you an epilogue to the whole book. Here it is."

Anton started to read it and, startled, looked up at Jacques.

Jacques responded, "Yes, this is the true ending."

EPILOGUE

I came down from the mountain to teach for many years. My teacher was correct, as I ended up with over a hundred disciples from all parts of the world. My first home was in Thun, but then I ended up in Zürich, where I continued to have many students.

Since my wife was American, I took the teaching to the United States and developed classes in some of the major cities. People came and went and always just a few remained. The teaching of the Higher Self became popular with some well-known lecturers. I was not the only one to bring this knowledge to humanity. Over the years I stayed more and more in the background, and after the classes were established, I no longer did lectures for the public. The teaching then went back to the traditional way of reaching people through word of mouth.

I am old now, and it's nearly time for me to leave my body and join my teacher. A few of my disciples have become teachers, but my daughter, Samantha and her husband, Anton, are the ones destined to take this teaching out into the world, to many people.

My name is Zarathustra. It is a name of teachers, and it carries the vibration of the fire of the heart. There were many before me and many will follow, until all of humanity will seek the God within. That day is thousands of years away, but I will be there to welcome the age of spirit.

Zarathustra is my spiritual name, but my birth name is Jacques Ulrich. This is my story and yours. Feel your heart, link with your Higher Self, and know that wisdom is there for you to seek. It's everyone's right to find it.

I came down from the mountain to live in life, but I return for a month or two to my cabin there. I always go there alone, and no one else knows where it is. After I am gone, it will be left to nature and to anyone who discovers it will look abandoned. I'm not leaving it to my child, as she needs her own cabin. My advice to all of you is to find your mountain, your cabin, your joy, even if it's only for a short while. Live in solitude during that time and ask yourself, "Who am I? Why am I here?"

When you come down from the mountain and live in the world, try to see everything around you through your mountain eyes. Try to remain calm in times of challenges and, most of all, look at others in a nonattached manner. Only then can you truly love and feel compassion.

Zarathustra's journey is a long one. Each one of you will someday walk in his shoes. Wear them well, and remember where the journey ends.

About the Author

Nanette V. Hucknall has spent a lifetime studying spirituality and psychology, using what she has learned to help others on their personal journey. She has been a teacher, writer, psychotherapist, career counselor, and painter.

Forty-five years ago, she combined the wisdom and insights of her own spiritual path to develop the teaching of Higher Self Yoga. The concept of the Higher Self—the inner wise being that connects with the Source, or God within—is a spiritual tradition that dates back thousands of years. Higher Self Yoga adds a psychological approach to help people overcome the inner obstacles that keep them from their higher nature and from growing spiritually.

Nanette has developed many Higher Self Yoga classes and retreats in the United States and Canada, and has written a series of books on related topics that include compelling stories and exercises to make the teaching come alive. Along with Dr. Judith Bach, Nanette designed and facilitated spiritual and psychological workshops in the U.S., Canada, and Europe.

Before introducing Higher Self Yoga, Nanette studied Agni Yoga for many years and is trained in Psychosynthesis. She maintained a psychotherapy practice for twenty years. She is the Founder of the Center for Peace Through Culture, and the Founder and President Emeritus of Higher Self Yoga, Inc. She holds a Bachelor's Degree from Cooper Union and was for many years an Art Director in New York City.

Nanette's books have received 9 national writer's awards.

Also by the Author

- *Karma, Destiny and Your Career:*
  A New Age Guide to Finding Your Work and Loving Your Life
- *Higher Self Yoga, Book One*
- *Higher Self Yoga, Book Two*
- *Higher Self Yoga, Book Three*
- *How to Live from Your Heart:*
  Deepen Relationships, Develop Creativity, and Discover Inner Wisdom
- *The Spiritual Teaching of Higher Self Yoga*
- *Higher Self Yoga: A Practical Teaching*
- *The Rose and the Sword,* with co-author Dr. Judith Bach

Follow Nanette

www.NanetteVHucknall.com
www.facebook.com/nanettevhucknall
www.twitter.com/nvhucknall
www.instagram.com/nanettevhucknall

ACKNOWLEDGEMENTS

The main person who has my gratitude is Kathy Crowe, the Co-President of Inner Journey Publishing. She was an early reader, designed the book, and made the changes needed, keeping everything in order and coordinated all the work that was done. She has been more than instrumental in making this book become a reality.

I want to thank our main editor, Sharron Dorr, for her excellent work. I also acknowledge and thank my additional editors who were of wonderful help along the way. First, Edward Claflin, the editor who worked with me at the beginning in establishing the right storyline and much more. Olga Denisko, Ariana Attie, and Sharon Magruder gave it a first edit. Then Renee van Kessel, Kathleen Frome and Susan Lord did some edits that were very helpful after my final rewrite. Mark Solomon and Stephen Ringold gave me good feedback on some of the content.

I also want to acknowledge the other Co-President of Inner Journey Publishing, Laraine Lippe, who handled the finances, did some editing, and added help needed to publish this book.

Additional thanks to our media people: Georgia Pettit, Hannah Stember, Tom Faddegon, and Amy Davenport, for their promotion of this book.

Made in the USA
Middletown, DE
06 December 2023

44805276R00265